"COLE . . . DON'T . . . PLEASE . . ."

She managed to get out the strangled words but only barely as his mouth slid demandingly over hers, parting her lips hungrily in an endless kiss that left her weak-kneed and breathless.

This isn't the way it's supposed to be, she screamed silently. She felt betrayed by her body, by the way her heart pounded at the touch of his mouth. It had been so long for her . . . so many years of denial that a long-forgotten need to be held and touched and caressed seized her in a vicious, traitorous grip. God help me, she thought as the pressure of Cole's mouth increased and her starved body began to respond. With a low moan, she gave in, wrapping her slender arms around his strong neck and pulling his hard, lean, aroused body against the full length of hers.

Suddenly, he drew away, and she gazed at him with such intense desire that a triumphant laugh ripped from his throat and with one sweep he lifted her effortlessly into his arms, and carried her to the bed.

Unfair Advantage

Jessica Summers

ST. MARTIN'S PRESS/NEW YORK

UNFAIR ADVANTAGE

Library of Congress Catalog Card Number: 87-60622

ISBN: 0-312-90847-4 Can. ISBN: 0-312-90848-2

Printed in the United States of America

First St. Martin's Press mass market edition/November 1987

10 9 8 7 6 5 4 3 2 1

To Gayle who said I could

To Phil, Jennifer and Judd who held my hand while I tried

To Bert who made sure that I did

ACKNOWLEDGMENTS

A special word of thanks to all those wonderful people who laughed and cried in all the right places; Andrea, Melissa and David, Claire and Ronnie and especially Robin.

Prologue

At ten A.M. on a May morning, Reggie Gates stood facing Cole Weston. Appearing calm outwardly, a seething rage simmered within her slim, five-foot-six frame as she stared angrily at the famous financier who had just made her the most outrageous overture she had ever heard during her short career. She glared at him with restrained fury, while he, a hint of satisfaction in his black eyes, merely waited for a reply.

So confident was he in his ability to succeed with this carefully orchestrated plan, that to him this meeting was a mere formality; the culmination of six months of meticulous planning. He had devised a scheme, done the research and now waited for the inevitable climax.

She tried to reason with him once more. "You won't reconsider?"

"No."

"You will live to regret this, Cole," she warned.

"Quite possibly. But I'll take my chances."

Defeated, she sank into a chair. "Exactly what do I have to do?"

Part One

Chapter 1

"You're a fool, Reggie Gates!" she declared angrily to her reflection in the bathroom mirror as she began to towel off her body. Blazing green eyes, set deeply in a high-cheekboned, finely chiseled face stared back at her, uncommenting. She stamped her foot in frustration, sending Coco, her violet-eyed, chocolate point Siamese cat scurrying for the safety of the bedroom. "That's right, traitor!" she yelled after her. "Disappear! Hide under the bed. You're never around when I need you, either!" She settled wearily on the edge of the bathtub and took several long breaths. Calm down, she told herself sternly. Calm down? How could she possibly calm down? She had gotten herself into an impossible situation, a horrendous, catastrophic mess. And despite all her careful planning and maneuvering, she saw absolutely no way to get herself out. She slammed down her fist on the sink. "It's just not fair!"

"Fair?" came the familiar berating voice of her mother, and suddenly Reggie was transported back a dozen years or so to her parents' Early American kitchen in Boston. She was twelve again, awkward and ungainly with a mouth filled with metal braces, about to get dressed for her first important boy-girl party, and once more, she and her mother were at loggerheads. But this time, Reggie vowed she wouldn't back down.

"I've told you before," Norma Gates began, "life's not fair. A fair is a place where children go to ride on carousels and eat cotton candy."

Reggie stood pouting behind a shiny, stenciled black Hitchcock chair, her hands placed defiantly on her slim, undeveloped hips. She was stubbornly determined to outstare the smartly dressed woman who was holding up a beribboned, ruffled, pink organdy party dress.

"Mother, I *can't* wear that dress!" she stated with all the conviction of a twelve-year-old on the brink of puberty. No, she wouldn't, couldn't possibly walk into Laurie Travis's Newton mansion looking like "Barbie goes to the prom."

"I don't see why not. Do you have any idea what this dress cost? Amy wore it last year and she looked like a princess. It's perfect for this party." Norma sat down, unperturbed, smoothed her taupe cashmere skirt and waited for her youngest child to come to her senses in their latest battle.

Of course it was perfect for Amy, thought Reggie. With her sister's golden curls, delicate rosy complexion and wide cornflower-blue eyes, the party dress would have made her look like a porcelain Madame Alexander doll. But Reggie instinctively knew that it just wouldn't work on her. The begonia-colored froufrou would be hideous, clashing horribly with her russet hair, causing her unusual translucent skin to appear sickly white and drawing immediate attention to the disappointing truth that, at twelve, she still showed no signs of developing the inviting curves that she so envied in her older sister.

Norma's mouth formed a thin, tight line. "Either you wear this dress or you don't go. It's as simple as that. I know what's right and you don't!"

In the end, Reggie had given in and had left the house in the bubble-gum confection, her overnight case tucked firmly under her arm. No sooner did she arrive at Laurie's house then she scooted, unobserved, into the guest bathroom where she rid herself of the hated garment. She emerged, glorious, in a vibrantly hued striped caftan, which she had smuggled in her tote bag. I'm going to get killed for this, she thought. But as she twirled this way and that in front of the foyer mirror, tilting her head to study the way the kelly-green and royal-blue satin shimmered, enhancing and heightening her distinctive coloring, she felt any punishment would be worth looking like this. She was almost pretty. As she entered Laurie's living room, the six silver bells that she had tied to her left ankle jingled merrily.

No, she reflected, life certainly wasn't fair. Not hers, anyway. She'd always fought an uphill battle, trying hard to figure out where she fit in this perfect family of blue-eyed, flaxen-haired strangers. And the sad truth was . . . she didn't. She would always be different—a little eccentric, certainly nonconforming, but most importantly, from the point of view of her very proper Bostonian parents, an imperfect addition to what should have been the perfect all-American family.

Even her birth had been unconventional, and Reggie suspected that had someone warned her parents what lay in store for them, it might have saved the family much anguish later on. On the night she was born, a devastating fire in a Boston shoe factory kept the emergency room in turmoil. Every available attendant, resident, intern and nurse had been called down from his or her regular floor to care for the scorched, tortured burn victims. An unexpected severe summer electrical storm hit the city of Boston, dumping a record four inches of torrential rain on streets that were already dangerously snarled with traffic of ambulances and rescue vehicles.

In the labor and delivery room, critically understaffed at the time, a set of twins and a totally unexpected set of very premature triplets with multiple medical problems were delivered within minutes of each other. It was hardly surprising, therefore, that when Norma Gates walked calmly and serenely into Mass General to deliver her fourth child, no one paid her much attention. Norma left Admitting, entered the elevator and, as the doors closed, she turned to her husband Ned, opened her mouth, suddenly shouted, panted and unceremoniously squatted on the floor and delivered a normal, healthy, carrot-topped baby girl. The baby lay on Ned's sport jacket, screaming her head off, and when the doors opened again, Norma wanted to die, mortified that someone of her stature should have given birth in such an ignominious fashion. Like a field hand, she thought! A peasant! She could never forgive her daughter.

At thirteen, Reggie's burgeoning hormones were starting to play havoc with Norma's sanity. One cold December day, Norma stormed into the house after a harrowing parent-teacher conference. She was cold and wet and furious. She stood in the foyer of her perfectly appointed, almost authentic New England colonial and completely lost her cool.

"Regina Anne Gates, get down here this minute!" she screamed from the bottom of the curved maple staircase.

"In a minute, Mom. I'm just finishing the sequins on the dungaree jacket."

"Get-down-here-this-instant-or-I'm-coming-up-to-get-you!"

What now? Reggie wondered. She was sitting in the middle of her room, cross-legged on the floor so completely covered with sequins, appliqués, rhinestones and swatches of fabric that it was impossible to determine the carpet color. In the corner of the crowded room stood an old pipe rack which held faded, yellowed evening gowns, satin bed jackets, maribou boas and an assortment of clothing memorabilia that Reggie had accrued in her many forages through Aunt Hattie's attic. Recognizing her mother's staccato tone, she quickly stuffed everything into a shopping bag and ran to the landing, racking her brain for what she could possibly have done now to so enrage her mother.

"Don't think you can hide up there," yelled Norma. "Get down here!"

Reggie walked down the steps with exaggerated slowness. What had she done? She knew she hadn't taken apart any of her father's silk ties or cut up her mother's fox jacket . . . although the idea had entered her mind because it *would* make a smashing trim for that little black-beaded sweater that Aunt Hattie had given her two days earlier. But she *hadn't* done it, and she didn't think that her mother had read her mind.

Norma stood at the foot of the steps. She hadn't even bothered to remove her beaver coat, which was shedding water all over the floral needlepoint rug that had been a wedding gift from her sister Hattie. This must be serious stuff, realized Reggie. Nobody was even allowed to walk on that rug with shoes, and now her mother was standing in a veritable lake.

"Who-is-Desdemona?" asked Norma, through clenched teeth as a rivulet of water fell into her right eye.

Reggie flushed. So, that was it . . . her new name. Desdemona Bianchini. Anyone with half a brain would see that it was a more appropriate name for her than Regina Gates. What was the big deal? They couldn't send you to prison for changing your name to something that better fit your personality, your *image*. Geez! Her friend Gail had changed her name to *Gayle* and Lucy was now *Lucee*, and nobody had made a federal case out of their actions. Besides, she tried but there wasn't any other way to spell Regina and, furthermore, it was the name of a *vacuum cleaner*. She might as well call herself

Hoover or Electrolux. *Electrolux Gates*—swell! No, ma'am! If she was ever going to be *someone*, Regina Gates just wouldn't work as a name.

Reggie sat down on the bottom step, hoping against hope that if she tried very patiently to explain how important this name change was, her mother would understand. "Don't get mad until I explain to you, okay, Mom? Regina is a boring name. B-O-R-I-N-G! There are no fashion designers in the world with a name like that. Wait!" she cried as her mother advanced on her waving a sheath of school papers. "Just listen," she pleaded. "Balenciaga . . . Chanel . . . de la Renta . . . Cardin! Not Joan Brown or Sally Miller. Can't you hear the difference?" But when she saw the grim expression on her mother's face and the way Norma was digging her nails into the palms of her hands, Reggie knew with a sinking feeling that her mother would never, never understand Desdemona Bianchini.

"Listen very carefully to what I'm about to tell you, and don't you dare utter one word until I've finished," warned Norma. "Your name is Regina Anne Gates. Period! Finished! And for as long as you make your home with us, that is your only name. I've put up with nonsense from you for as long as I can remember, but I will not tolerate being summoned to school to listen to the principal admonish *me* about *your* misbehavior! Do you understand?" She didn't even pause to take a breath. "Do you know that I was seen by Dina St. James? How am I ever going to explain that at the Garden Club luncheon? You don't care, do you, young lady?" Reggie opened her mouth to answer, but Norma ignored her. "Well, let me tell you one more thing. I don't ever want to hear the word Desdemona again. Not ever! Have I made myself perfectly clear?" Norma was shaking with rage.

"Mother, it's only a name. What difference does it make?"

"The topic is closed. Irrevocably, totally closed, and don't you dare speak to me about it again. Get up to your room and stay there until I call you for dinner!"

Reggie jumped up, tears threatening. She ran into her room, slammed the door as hard as she could and threw herself facedown on the bed, hugging her pillow and sobbing. Just wait! she thought. Just wait until she was famous and everyone was begging for a Desdemona creation. She'd show them all!

She'd have a glamorous atelier with crystal chandeliers and two afghan hounds guarding the door, and there would be runways and models and everything. Then they'd be sorry! They'd all be sorry they didn't listen to her when they wanted to buy an original Desdemona, and she would be too busy to even talk to them. Just wait! She buried her face in the pillow. As the last rays of daylight began to fade and Reggie slipped into an exhausted sleep, Desdemona Bianchini was quietly put to rest. But not her dreams . . . never her dreams.

By the time she was fifteen, Reggie had calmed down considerably. She had learned that it was easier to go along with her parents than to fight them since she usually had to give in anyway. But once in a while, her indomitable, restive spirit slipped from its semiharcoleptic state and stubbornly reasserted itself.

Thanksgiving morning dawned gray and overcast with the unmistakable smell of snow in the air. Norma awoke early, slipped into her beige velour bathrobe, pulled her hair into a bun and made her way downstairs to put up coffee. It didn't feel like Thanksgiving. She had nothing to do. No turkey to put up, no pumpkin pie . . . she shook her head angrily; she never should have accepted this invitation from her sister Hattie. But the idea of missing an opportunity to mingle with judges, senators, writers and the crème de la crème of Boston society at Hattie's Swampscott mansion was more abhorrent than putting up with her sister for the afternoon. And then, of course, one never knew who one would meet . . . and she *did* have the children's future to think about. She sighed heavily. She would just have to go for their sake.

Ned scuffled into the kitchen in his oldest plaid bathrobe and worn, cracked leather slippers. He kissed his wife's cheek. "Where's the *Herald?*"

"On the driveway like it is every morning!" she snapped.

"What's the matter with you?"

"Nothing. Everything! I hate going to these theatrical productions of Hattie's. There's no tradition at all. She's as likely to serve fried octopus with raspberry aspic as anything else."

"If you don't want to go, why did you accept? We could have had a perfectly lovely dinner here."

"Because," she said with infinite patience, as if she was explaining to a child, "once in a while it's good for the children to be exposed to the kind of people who Hattie invites. I don't know why they accept her invitations . . . but they do." She flapped her hands in Ned's direction. "What do they see in her?"

"She's fun, attractive in a flamboyant way and rich. Positively loaded. I suppose—"

"What do you know!" But when Ned started to tell her, she shut him up. "Don't talk to me now. I have to get breakfast ready and lay out the children's clothes."

"Aren't they old enough to do that for themselves?" Matthew was seventeen, Robert, eighteen, and Amy, almost twenty. Laying out clothes for them seemed ridiculous . . . though of course Reggie was a different matter altogether.

"Where is Reggie? Her room's empty," he asked.

"She slept at Lucy's. Don Brooks is bringing her to Hattie's at two o'clock." She glanced at the kitchen clock. "Go into the den. I'll call you when breakfast is ready."

When they all arrived at Hattie's, white-gloved waiters were already passing platters of unrecognizable hors d'oeuvres to the other twenty-four guests. Norma looked around at the decorations that Hattie had used to create a festive atmosphere. Sneering, she whispered to Ned, "Do you have any idea what those things cost?" She pointed to the four-foot-wide baskets of fresh giant chrysanthemums that stood at the entrance to each room. "Disgusting waste of money!"

"Shh!" ordered her husband as Hattie flew by, waving merrily to Norma and her family and pouring mulled wine into everyone's etched amber goblets. Norma gave Ned a scathing look then turned her back on him to check out the guests. She heaved a sigh of relief. Her children were dressed perfectly for the occasion. Amy was magnificent, as usual, in a high-necked hunter-green dress with a froth of antique lace at her cuffs and hem. The boys were spiffily attired in navy blazers with shiny brass buttons, and Ned's muted heather tweed jacket and knit tie were adequate. Her own floor-length plaid wool skirt, silk blouse and black velvet blazer were certainly proper. Only Hattie, in a silver lamé minidress looked ridiculous. But that was always the case. Hattie thought just because she had money she could get away with anything. Even those inch-long false eyelashes, for heaven's sake!

At three o'clock, a bell sounded signaling dinner, and Hattie began to steer her guests to the dining room, which, though Norma was loath to admit it, looked splendid. The massive oak dining table was set with a sunny yellow and rust hand-embroidered Belgian linen cloth. In the center of the table stood a huge crystal vase filled to overflowing with acorns, pine cones, walnuts and dried, crystallized fruit. From the center of the vase exploded enormous sprays of forest-green eucalyptus branches, whose pungent perfume permeated the whole room. Hattie's famous collection of twenty-four carat Minton china added to the overwhelming aura of opulence. As the guests entered the dining room, they were each discreetly handed a small, bronze-edged porcelain place card with a picture of a botanical flower that corresponded to a like drawing at his or her seat.

Norma swelled with obvious pride as her children took their seats, displaying the proper etiquette that she had so painstakingly instilled. She was just turning to talk to the charming, silver-haired judge on her left when she heard a loud gasp from Ned. One look at his pain-stricken face and she jumped from her seat, fearing the onset of a heart attack or stroke. But even her wildest nightmares, her most lurid fantasies, couldn't have prepared her for the sight she saw when she followed Ned's shaking finger. Poised nonchalantly in the doorway of the dining room, a purposeful smile on her impish face, her green eyes glinting mischievously, stood Reggie, outfitted in an authentic, well-worn and bemedaled World War I uniform, complete with puttees and helmet.

"Hi, everyone," she said with a grin, then suddenly remembered her manners and turned apologetically to Hattie. "I'm sorry I'm late Aunt Hattie but Mr. Brooks's car broke down."

There was total silence in the room as everyone turned to stare at Norma, who made an odd, little gurgling sound in her throat, rolled her eyes into the back of her head and slid, unconscious, under the table, but not before she heard Hattie's enthusiastic accolade—"Bravo, darling!"

After that, Norma gave up. "There's just no point in trying anymore," she told her husband. "Look at me! I'm a wreck!"

The gray hairs on her head had increased in direct proportion to her daughter's outrageous antics. Now when she looked at this unconventionally attractive teenager with her full, upthrusting breasts, long curve from waist to hip, flat stomach and slender, coltish legs, Norma felt as if she were looking at a stranger. Who was this girl whose hair changed from russet to cinnabar to carmine with the seasons? And why wasn't her senior year over so she could go away to college and leave Norma in peace?

One particularly dreary February day, mother and daughter were glaring at each other as they sat in the kitchen reviewing two letters of rejection that had arrived from Wellesley and Vassar. Norma was shaking her head.

"That's it, then. If you don't get accepted by Smith it looks like you'll be going to Boston University." She still couldn't resign herself to the mediocre level of academic achievement that Reggie had attained. "B.U.!" she cried with unconcealed contempt. "Regina, anyone from Boston can get into B.U."

"By the way, Mother, you can forget about Smith."

"I most certainly will not! Smith is a fine school with a wonderful—"

"Mother, I said forget it. I got rejected two days ago."

Norma picked up her head, and Reggie could have sworn she saw tears in the corner of her mother's eyes. "You didn't tell me," she whispered.

"I know. I didn't have the heart to disappoint you again."

Norma's sigh was one of weary resignation. "All right. It's not the end of the world. You'll attend B.U. for a semester, bring up your grades and with a little pull, I bet we can get you into Penn or Cornell. If I have to, I'll call your Aunt Hattie and she can ask that judge—"

"Stop it!" commanded Reggie.

Norma stared at her in surprise. "All right! You can stay at B.U. for four years. It's not the end of the world."

Very quietly, Reggie said, "I'm not going to B.U., either."

"Then where are you going?"

"I've had an interview and been accepted by Parsons."

"What kind of university is Parsons?"

Reggie cleared her throat nervously. "It's not a university. It's a design school in New York. I'm going to study fashion design. I've already discussed it with my guidance counselor, and she agrees that it's the right move for me."

"Is that so? Is that so! Then let *her* daughter go because you're not! No daughter of mine is going to go gallivanting around New York City with *those* kind of people. It's out of the question, and don't bother to look at me like that. We'll settle this once and for all as soon as your father comes home!"

Much later that night, Reggie heard the conversation between her mother and father through the air-conditioning ducts that connected the entire house. In fact, everyone who lived on the block could have listened if their windows were open.

Ned raged. Norma ranted. Reggie planned.

On August 22, Reggie caught the Eastern shuttle and arrived at New York's La Guardia Airport fifty minutes later. Only Aunt Hattie had come to Logan Airport to see her off, but she didn't mind much. She took one huge gulp of New York's polluted air, smiled, crossed her fingers and thought—I'm finally where I belong.

Chapter 2

Reggie trudged into the student union of Parsons, lugging her heavy black leather portfolio containing her entire semester's sketches. The handle on the case had long since broken and been discarded, and the piece of twine that she had improvised cut painfully into her hand. It had been a long, horrible day, beginning with an argument with a fat, sweaty lady on the bus who insisted that Reggie had taken her "permanent" seat, and ending with a heated discussion with her textile professor on the need to improve the quality of synthetic fabrics. Dick Tolley insisted that industry had already taken rayon and acetate as far as possible and Reggie bitterly contended that it wasn't far enough. Not when wash-and-wear fabric had the distinctive look of plastic or rubber.

"And *you're* going to improve this industry, Miss Gates?" he had asked, clearly skeptical.

Reggie had nodded. "Someday. Isn't that what we're here for? To learn and to change things?"

"If the fabrics that are now on the market are the most advanced that are chemically feasible, and the *experts* haven't been able to improve them, what makes you think you can invent something better?"

Reggie shrugged. "Because I *want* to. Because there's a need for it, and because I think we're on the brink of a textile revolution."

"Is that so? And I assume you're going to start this revolution, Miss Gates?" Now the whole class was paying attention. Some students were snickering behind her back, but other, more enlightened students were quietly cheering her on. She felt a heady rush and plunged ahead.

"Mr. Tolley, every new inventor or designer has been told that what he wanted to do was impossible . . . until he *did* it. Willie and Orville *did* fly, despite what everyone thought." There was a small smattering of applause and Tolley's face turned bright red. Reggie was on one of her rolls, and if the bell hadn't sounded at that precise moment, Lord knows what would have happened next.

"We'll continue this conversation another time, Miss Gates. Preferably when you have more knowledge of textiles under your belt. Good day." And he had turned to concentrate on some papers on his desk, clearly dismissing her.

He was a small man with small ideas, she decided, and as Reggie took a seat at one of the round tables in the union, she wondered if she was accomplishing anything at all at Parsons. She unzipped her portfolio and took out her sketch pad, rapidly flipping through the pages. She frowned. There was something wrong with her work, something disturbing that had been irritating her for weeks. She chewed thoughtfully on the back of her ball-point pen and sat back in contemplation. Suddenly, she reached into the depths of her portfolio and withdrew the latest issue of *L'Officiel*, checking the date—May 1972. She compared her sketches to the glamorous haute couture clothing that was pictured on each page of the slick, glossy French fashion magazine. It hit her immediately. Every time she tried to emulate the fashions depicted on those pages, she came up empty and now she knew why. She didn't believe in the clothes! No one she knew or would probably ever know could afford to wear dresses that cost thousands of dollars. This wasn't reality and it certainly wasn't what she had come all the way to New York to do. Not at all.

Slowly, she put the magazine down and began to study her fellow students. Denim was the order of the day. In fact, Reggie realized with a start, the whole union seemed to be bathed in a haze of blue. Rather than being an expression of individuality and self-expression, it now appeared that jeans were the uniform of the masses. Faded, torn, ripped, studded, rhinestoned, overalled, shorts, jackets, shirts—it didn't matter. Her peers were all dressed like clones in various versions of the same thing. The utter sameness of it all was ludicrous! And these were the up-and-coming designers? Where was their initiative, their creativity, their individualism and courage? Certainly not in their own costumes, which reflected nothing more than a negative reaction to fashion as it existed today.

Reggie looked down at her own outfit and grimaced. Even she, who had always been considered avant-garde, had fallen into the trap. Comfort had taken precedence over style, safety over setting a trend, and she was as guilty as everyone else. Denim shirt, tight, faded jeans and sneakers. If she closed her eyes and imagined numbers over the pockets of everyone's shirts, they all could have fit beautifully into a prison photograph. All that was needed were bars on the window.

It struck her with such ridiculous clarity that she laughed out loud. This was going to be her niche! Designing clothing that, like denim, was adaptable to mass production, that was comfortable, affordable and stylish. Clothing that called for no costly craftsmanship, that wasn't trendy and that would fundamentally change everyday dressing forever. All she had to do now was to figure out how to accomplish all that. But a seed of an idea was germinating, in part due to her conversation with her textile professor, and in part as a result of her own innate fashion sense. She *could* liberate American women from suits and brocade cocktail dresses. She could provide an alternative to blue jeans, hot pants and the revolting midi. Yes, she would! And all at prices that housewives, students, young marrieds and working girls could afford. Professor Tolley be damned!

The answer lay in synthetics. There were still limits within which she'd have to work . . . but cutting, stitching and a novel approach to design were going to revolutionize daytime sports clothes, and Reggie Gates was beginning to understand how she was going to do it! With clothing that would give everyone room to laugh. Screw firmly structured clothes and stiff, constricting fabrics! Her mind spun with ideas, and it was such a simple concept she couldn't understand why no one had ever thought of it before.

With an enthusiasm that Edison surely felt when he was close to inventing the light bulb, Reggie jumped from her seat and raced out of the union, dropping her portfolio into a litter basket that stood outside. She hurried to the House of Fabrics on Twelfth Street, where, once inside, she made a beeline toward the racks of rayon and dacron jerseys and a newly introduced silky fabric called Nyesta. She completely ignored the expensive silks, satins and velvets, leaving those opulent fabrics for the students who still dreamed of being the next Norman Norell. Her glittering green eyes lit up as she fondled and caressed the inexpensive piece goods, discarding all of the prints which looked garish. She chose an odd assortment of colors. Some were clear and springlike, others were totally unexpected—mauve, puce, rose, off-gray and rusty brown. As she touched the fabrics, she was starting to get a feel for how they draped and fell and what such fabrics would or wouldn't be able to do. What she learned in the hour and a half on Twelfth Street would forever inspire her fashion designing.

The goods cut and paid for, Reggie juggled the four huge brown bags through the streets, down to Sheridan Square. Tired but exhilarated, she arrived at her apartment, a fifth-floor walk-up where she lived, worked and studied. Coco, her violet-eyed, chocolate point Siamese kitten—Aunt Hattie, again: "No one should live alone, darling"—jumped from the oak mantel into her arms. She dropped the bundles and cradled the cat as, cross-legged on the ancient rag rug, she snuggled into Coco's creamy fur. "We're about to become very rich," she whispered. "But you can't tell anyone yet because they will think we're crazy."

Coco purred contentedly in the back of her throat. Reggie understood this to mean approval and agreement with the proposed project. The kitten, bored of the conversation, disengaged herself from Reggie's arms to delve into the cache of treasure she was certain she'd find in the brown bags.

Making a hasty dash to retrieve the bags, Reggie shook her finger at the cat.

"Don't touch these. Just sit here and be a good cat. When I'm all finished, you can tell me what a genius I am. Then we'll open a can of Bumblebee for you, a bottle of champagne for me, and celebrate. Oh, and we have to call David to help us celebrate. Don't you think?"

The cat hissed at the mention of Reggie's boyfriend. "Stop it, Coco. I told you that David didn't intentionally kick you." Coco arched her back and walked away.

All night long, Reggie sat up working with scissors, needles and pins. Coco alternately slept or nudged her while she worked. By four in the morning, her eyes gritty from lack of sleep, she had exactly what she wanted. A "Collection." Her first. She stood up, working the cricks from her back and critically studied her work. It was good. It was damn good! The entire collection of clothing made her smile—it was so right! Tolley had scoffed at her when he'd asked her if she was going to start a revolution, but as she looked at the clothes on the floor, she knew that because of what she had done tonight, a new, innovative kind of American fashion had been born.

The whole concept of her line began with the mental picture of the female body and the ability of the fabrics she had chosen, when unlined and unfaced, to move and drape with fluid grace. Her shapes were soft, unconstructed and informal. Honest clothes that didn't look like big T-shirts or flour sacks. Reggie's clothes would flatter most women, especially those who weren't afraid of pulling things over their heads because not one article in the line had a button, snap or zipper. It wasn't necessary. The very fabrics she had used, all machine washable, would give enough to make such findings a thing of the past. There were soft, sexy dresses with highly visible zigzag stitching at the hems and seams; long, reedlike gowns with plunging backs; off-the-shoulder, long T-shirts with matching ankle-length elastic waisted skirts; bias-cut day dresses with matching unlined stoles or cardigan jackets—all of which weighed next to nothing. And the beauty of the whole line was in its agelessness. Not only could a secretary afford each piece, but she would look as good in it as the President's wife! Women could accessorize these clothes with wild plastic or wooden jewelry or diamonds and sapphires. It wouldn't matter—they were both functional and elegant—and *new*. The most remarkable thing to Reggie, as she sat staring at her work, was that nobody had ever done this before. She grabbed Coco, hugging her close as she waltzed around the tiny apartment.

"We've done it, Coco. This collection of sportswear is going to make us very famous and very, very rich!" Exhausted but exhilarated, Reggie dragged herself up to her sleeping loft. Coco curled up in a tiny ball by her side. "The whole country is going to be running around in these rags," she whispered as she fell into a deep, dreamless sleep.

In her zeal to complete her line, she had forgotten to call David.

On the floor below, David Astin had been asleep for hours. He had seen Reggie stumbling up the front steps with her enormous packages but had been so absorbed in his studies for the upcoming bar exam that he hadn't bothered to go to her aid. Somehow or another, he knew she would manage. That was one of the things he liked about their relationship. There were no strings . . . he'd made that perfectly clear from the beginning.

She was an unexpected bonus to his life in Manhattan. She was cute, sexy, intelligent and compliant—he couldn't ask for more. Actually, he didn't want more. As far as he was concerned, the relationship was perfect.

He had hoped to finish studying by ten o'clock, at which time he thought he'd pop into her apartment for a snack and whatever else she might offer. But by nine, he'd been tired, so he had opened a can of ravioli, eaten it cold and had fallen asleep in front of the TV.

Chapter 3

Early the next morning, Reggie awoke with a feeling of nebulous contentment. Coco lay curled in a beige ball between her neck and shoulder, mewing softly as Reggie's hand reached up to stroke her sleek, silken fur. They both stretched simultaneously and, with a reluctant yawn, Reggie sat up. Coco arched her back in irritation.

"Sorry, love, but we have things to do today. You can sleep while I'm gone later," she explained to the disgruntled cat, but Coco wasn't in the mood for explanations and jumped off the bed, regally making her way down the loft's stairs to the kitchenette in search of her breakfast. "And see if you can figure out how to put the coffee up," Reggie called after the cat.

As she straightened the bed, pulling the patchwork quilt tightly around the mattress that barely fit into the tiny sleeping loft, Reggie suddenly remembered Parsons. She had to call and make an appointment to see her advisor. Today was the day, the beginning of a new life . . . success and money, real financial security were right around the corner. She could taste it! The line was smashing—so exciting and novel that it surprised even her. Oh, she knew she had talent, but she'd always assumed that it would take her a good four years of work before she learned how to put it to use. Not anymore! She'd done it. In one long, crazy night she'd accomplished everything she'd hoped for when she left Boston. All the fighting with her parents would be forgotten, and when they heard about her success, they'd come around, realize that she'd been right all along. She even pictured her mother in one of her outfits, shopping the Chestnut Hill Mall, telling all her friends proudly, "Of course—it's a Regina! Didn't you see it on the cover of *Bazaar* last month?" Or over lunch with hoity-toity Dina St. James—"Reggie?" her mother would say, her eyebrows raised ever so slightly. "Why, she's in Paris now . . . something about a photo session with Avedon for *Elle*."

Still cooking up scenarios, she showered quickly, brushing her hair into a long, shiny ponytail and donning an oversized New England Patriots jersey over her scant bikini panties. Fifteen minutes later, she was in the kitchen preparing breakfast for herself and Coco—no mean feat in a room that was little more than a small closet with a pullman stove, teacup-sized sink and wicked refrigerator that belched and roared whenever she opened it. She called Parsons and was told that her advisor, Alvin Kitteridge, would see her at four that afternoon. While she was spooning a half can of Friskies Buffet into Coco's chipped Wedgewood dish and suppressing a gag at the noxious sight and smell of the grayish-brown glutinous cat food, she heard the doorbell.

"Eat it quickly, Coco. I can't bear to look at that stuff this early." The cat ignored her and sat licking one paw delicately while Reggie went to answer the door.

Her heart gave a familiar leap when she saw David leaning casually against the door frame. Barefoot, as usual, dressed in his standard uniform of faded, wrinkled corduroys, David Astin was the most magnificent man Reggie had ever known. Even now, after eight months, he still had the ability to startle her with his incredible handsomeness.

"No school today?" she asked hopefully. She wanted him to stay awhile, at least until she had shown him her new line and gotten his opinion. But she never could tell with David—one minute he acted as if he never wanted to leave her side, the next minute he was off and running . . . to the library, the cleaners, the bookstore for a forgotten notebook or just downstairs to his own apartment when he needed "his own space." His behavior was never predictable, keeping Reggie constantly off balance. But when he was with her, when he did stay, nothing else mattered. She could forgive him almost anything for those precious moments when they were together. Unfortunately, they were never enough for her and she suspected that he knew. She tried to hide her disappointment whenever he told her he couldn't stay, but every emotion she had ever felt was reflected in her eyes.

He bent down and planted a kiss on her nose. "Classes are

canceled until two, but I want to spend most of the morning studying for the bar." He walked past her into the kitchen, where Coco gave him a perfunctory sniff and stalked out. David and Coco were sworn enemies, having taken an instant dislike to each other from the moment they first met. It didn't shock Reggie that David didn't like cats—a lot of other, perfectly-normal-in-other-respects people didn't understand them—but Coco . . . that was a different story. She was usually such a good judge of character, hating the people that Reggie hated and approving of the ones that Reggie liked. Except David. In her heart of hearts, Reggie suspected that Coco was probably jealous of the attention she lavished on David.

"Got anything to eat?" David asked, poking around in the cabinets. "I meant to call you last night. I thought maybe we'd grab a bite to eat, but I fell asleep early." She looked annoyed. "Forgive me?" he asked, playfully grabbing her around the waist and nuzzling her neck. He began to nibble on her earlobe.

She wrenched out of his arms. "Stop it!"

He stared at her in surprise and mild vexation. "Why?"

She shrugged. She didn't know. All she knew was that at that particular moment she didn't want David to kiss her. She *was* annoyed, but she didn't know why. "I'm just cranky. Maybe I'm getting my period. Help yourself to breakfast," she said, then to lighten the mood, added, "You have your choice of Wheaties or Raisin Bran today." Coco stuck her nose into the room again, but Reggie managed to shoo her out before David noticed. "Oh, there might be a corn muffin."

He padded over to the bread box, opened the lid and peered in. Yawning, he picked up a muffin and unwrapped the cellophane. "Banana nut," he said, disappointed. "Who ate the corn?"

"You, probably. You're the only one who eats muffins around here." Taking the muffin from him, she cut and placed it in the new toaster oven. The expensive appliance had been her latest gift from Aunt Hattie before Hattie embarked on a five-month around-the-world cruise.

"Why do you spend so much money on these home-baked things?" David asked, wetting his finger and picking up the crumbs.

"Why do you always come up here in the morning to eat them?" she countered.

He smiled. "Because they're always here." He opened the refrigerator and took out the carton of orange juice, giving it a few vigorous shakes. "Don't tell me you buy them just for me, babe." He looked around the kitchen. "Any coffee?"

"Not yet, but I'll make some in a minute."

"Make the one with the cinnamon. The one you picked up at Zabar's last week."

"Oh," she smiled sarcastically. "The one you said was so expensive that I had no business buying? That one?"

"Yeah."

"And do you have any idea why I bought it?"

He shrugged. "I guess you like it."

Reggie shook her head. "No, I bought it because *you* like it."

He threw her a puzzled frown. "Thank you." Then something registered. "Wait just a minute. I get the feeling I'm supposed to feel guilty about this. Is that it? Am I supposed to feel some sort of responsibility because you buy expensive coffee? Is it the money?"

"No, it has nothing to do with money."

"Then what is it?"

She couldn't speak, couldn't explain what was bothering her. It had nothing to do with muffins or coffee or money. She would have bought all those things for David if she had to go into hock. Didn't he understand that? For God's sake, she loved him! All she wanted was for him to tell her how he felt about her. But he never did. He was considerate and attentive when they were together, but uncommunicative. She still felt they had a very tenuous relationship. He never spoke of plans for a future with her. In fact, other than a few brief words about the Midwest, he never spoke of his past, either. When she had asked him once in an offhand manner what he intended to do once law school was over, his face had assumed a faraway expression, and he had murmured something vague about a job. But she didn't know if he meant New York or Chicago or Timbuktu. She couldn't pin him down and was too afraid to try, sensing that she would push him right out of the relationship. If she did that, she'd die.

Just yesterday she'd heard that her childhood friend, Lucy,

was becoming engaged. The heavy white card with the formal black announcement really did a number on her. Not that she was ready to settle down. She still had so much to accomplish for her career and certainly David wasn't nearly ready . . . he still had to graduate, pass the bar and set up a practice somewhere. Still, it would be nice if he gave her some indication that marriage was on his list of priorities, no matter how low down on that list it was, or how far down the road.

"You're a million miles away." His voice brought her back to the present and the pungent odor of burning banana muffin. He grimaced at the sight of his charred breakfast. "It's a good thing you're studying designing, because a chef you'll never be."

Smoke was pouring out of the back of the toaster oven. She yanked the cord from the socket, opened the door and stared. David was leaning against the counter, watching her and shaking his head. He made her so nervous. Whenever he was around she was all thumbs, couldn't do anything right. She couldn't understand it . . . it was so unlike her to be intimidated by anyone, but she wanted to please him so much, make everything perfect, be perfect! And it wasn't as if he demanded anything from her. He didn't, although sometimes she wished he would. No, it was all her.

Lighten up, she warned herself, mindful of how David's mood changed whenever she tried to explain how she felt. "Heavy, heavy, heavy," he would say. "Life's short, babe. Too short to spend all of it being serious." Okay, David. No heavy stuff today. She picked up the muffin, took a plate from the cabinet and presented his breakfast to him.

"Well done," she explained with her most dazzling smile. "That is how you like your muffins, isn't it?"

He held the plate in his hand and stared at the incendiarized bun. He blew out a long sigh. "Why don't you put up the coffee. I'll just pick around the burned part."

He patted her head and walked into the living room, grabbing the most recent issue of *Time* on the way. It was the only decent piece of reading material that Reggie kept in her apartment, and he knew she subscribed to it only for him. Once he had commented that *Glamour*, *Vogue* and *Women's Wear* made lousy reading and next thing he knew, *Time* began appearing on her coffee table. She was great that way, anticipating his likes and dislikes, always thinking of him first. A nice kid, pretty, sexy, terrific body, great in bed . . . he couldn't ask for anything more. If only she'd stop with "the future" crap! It drove him crazy. He wasn't ready to make those kinds of plans with her. Christ! He liked things the way they were between them . . . easy, uncomplicated, no strings. Why was it every time he got comfortable in a relationship, there had to be talk about the future . . . commitment. Why couldn't his girlfriends just enjoy what they had together and let the future resolve itself?

Reggie heaved herself onto the countertop, letting her long slender legs dangle. While the coffee slowly dripped, she picked up a soapy Brillo pad and started to work on the damage she'd done to the toaster. Sunlight slanted through the tiny kitchen window. May, already. Eight months since she'd met David. Glorious, delirious months . . . most of the time.

It had been October when she first met him, late in the afternoon. Dark clouds and a cold, bone-chilling cold had followed her all the way home from school. Wherever she looked, small whirlpools of leaves, old newspapers, empty brown grocery bags and shattered liquor bottles littered the streets. As she turned the corner of West Fourth Street, juggling her huge portfolio, oversized handbag and the night's dinner, she frowned at the old, delapidated buildings with their iron fire escapes, rusty barred windows and filthy red brick facades. How naive she had been to think there would be anything remotely glamorous or romantic about living in Greenwich Village. It wasn't even charming . . . smelly, dirty winos in ripped clothing living in doorways; hippies, leftover relics of the sixties with their gold earrings and their long, greasy ponytails; pairs of young, handsome men, totally absorbed in each other's whispered intimacies . . . no, it wasn't charming at all. It was lonely, depressing and more than a little frightening. Always looking over her shoulder to make certain that she wasn't being followed, checking doorways and vestibules for lurking strangers, double- and triple-locking your doors.

She paused in front of her building, rummaged for her keys, rearranged her packages so she had a free hand to unlock the front door, which probably wasn't even locked anyway, and was so intent on getting herself organized that she never saw him until, both heads down, they collided on the steps, sending her sprawling on her behind, her bags and packages flying.

"Would you look the hell where you're go—"

"God, I'm sorry. I never saw—"

She pushed her hair out of her eyes at the sound of the rich, husky voice and looked up into the face of her accoster. The breath caught in her throat at the sight of the Adonis who stood in front her. Deep sapphire eyes gazed down at her with grave concern.

"Let me help you," he said apologetically.

Even in the rapidly oncoming dusk, with just the light of the streetlamp for illumination, the sharply etched lines of his strong square chin and incredible cleft were clearly visible. But it was more than his face that kept her eyes locked on his. It was the stark masculinity of the man, his lean, muscular frame, his height. From her vantage point on the sidewalk, he loomed over her like a colossus, and when he leaned down to offer his hand to help her up, she instinctively pulled back, awed by the sheer size of him.

"I'm sorry I knocked you down. At least give me a chance to put you on your feet." The smile he gave her was movie-star quality. "You're Gates, right?"

Suspicion clouded her eyes. How the hell did he know her name?

He laughed at the veil of doubt. "I swear I'm not a peeping Tom. I live on the floor below you and always see you coming and going, so I checked out your name on the mailbox . . . 'R.' How do you do? I'm 'D.'"

He'd been watching her since she moved in in August and the more he saw, the more he liked. Her tight jeans and T-shirts, the saucy way her backside wiggled, the full, firm young breasts, the wide-eyed innocence . . . yes, he liked the package a lot. He admired her closely as she gracefully untangled her long legs and stood. He bent down to retrieve her packages.

She half smiled, tentative, unsure . . . as if she wanted to trust him but wasn't quite sure she should. "D?" she asked when he had handed her all her parcels. "Donald?" She shook her head and wrinkled her pert, freckled nose. No, no one who looked this good could possible have a plebian name like

Donald. "Daniel? Maybe. No! I have it! Devlin. It has to be Devlin!"

"As in *Notorious?* With Cary Grant and Ingrid Bergman?"

She flushed becomingly. "You like old movies, too?"

"Carole Lombard in satin pajamas is my fantasy woman. Dorothy Lamour's sarongs aren't half bad either . . . oh, by the way, I'm sorry to disappoint you, but my name is David. David Astin."

"David?" She tried out the name and nodded. "David's okay. It's not Devlin, but it'll do."

They both laughed and somehow it was decided that he was safe. He helped her into the building and up the four flights with her bundles and she boldly invited him in for a glass of wine. It was precisely what her mother had warned her not to do. Looking back now, she wondered if that was why she had done it. She didn't care at the time. She was lonely and starved for companionship, for someone to talk to, to laugh with, to spend time with in this cold city with its millions of strangers.

In the two lonely months since she'd lived in New York, she'd met only a few kids at school and Alison Granger, the divorced, part-time model who lived upstairs. But Alison was twenty-six, busy working or dating and, although she was always friendly enough—chatting on the staircase, borrowing an occasional egg or an emergency pair of pantyhose—Reggie sensed that she really wasn't interested in forming an intimate friendship with an aspiring eighteen-year-old fashion designer.

But David was. There was a remarkable untouched quality about Reggie Gates that he found intriguing. She was fresh, wholesome. She wore no makeup and, as far as he could tell, had no artifices whatsoever. He didn't understand what she was doing in New York, living alone with only a cat to keep her company. It was obvious that she came from a comfortable home . . . the six little gold rings that gilded her hands; the Cartier tank watch, which she told him was her high school graduation present; the studio apartment, that although small, was relatively well furnished, unlike his own, which boasted only a bed, an old maple dresser, two bridge chairs and a scarred folding table.

She had instructed him to wait in the living room while she unloaded her parcels, then returned five minutes later bearing a tray with a bottle of wine and two glasses. "Chateau

Woolworth," she said as she set the tray on the bamboo trunk that served as her coffee table. "It's better than it sounds."

He uncorked the bottle, sniffed the cork and poured. "I feel a little guilty about drinking this. I knocked the wind out of you and here you're the one providing the wine. I should run out and get a bottle of champagne or something to make it up to you."

"Don't be ridiculous." She grinned; showing perfect white teeth. "I've been saving this bottle since I moved here, and if it takes being knocked on my ass to open it, it's fine with me." Shut up, she told herself sternly. You're babbling like a baby. That wasn't the impression she wanted to make on David Astin. She wanted him to think that she was sophisticated and worldly, experienced. She reckoned him to be about twenty-three, maybe older. He wouldn't bother with a baby.

David leaned back and slowly sipped the wine, studying her through thoughtful, curious eyes as she finished her glass in four gulps. God, she was young. It wouldn't have surprised him at all to discover he was the first man she'd ever invited to her apartment. That was fine with him. In fact, the idea of her inexperience was exciting, challenging. He scanned her ripe body under the guise of pouring more wine. The thin cotton T-shirt she wore accentuated high, full breasts with tiny pointed nipples. Her stomach was flat, her waist incredibly small. Her jeans looked like they had been painted onto her long, long legs. The wine was loosening her tongue, relaxing her. As she spoke animatedly about her plans for the future, all David could think about was touching her soft flesh.

Reggie's eyes were glowing when David reached down and casually curled one arm around her neck, caressing the column, sliding his tanned hand beneath her thick lustrous hair, wrapping his fingers in it and imagining the auburn waves fanned out on a pillow, her full lips slightly parted, the tip of his tongue—he stopped abruptly, suddenly aware of the tightening between his legs. He shifted uncomfortably.

"What's the matter?" Reggie asked, a nervous fluttering in her stomach. Had she talked too much? Bored him? He had taken his hand from her neck and now sat ramrod stiff. It must have been something she'd said to make him react so oddly, but for the life of her, she couldn't imagine what it was. All she had been doing was speaking of her parents and . . . had she stuck her foot in her mouth? Maybe he had no parents. That would account for his sudden mood change.

David cleared his throat. "I'd better be going. I have a lot of studying to do." Even to him, the excuse, popping out of the blue like that, sounded lame. "What time is it, anyway?" He had to get out of there before he did something he'd be sorry about.

Reggie tried to focus on her watch, but the wine had gone to her head and she could barely read the tiny numbers. "It's a quarter past something."

He took her wrist and studied the face of the watch. "Seven! It's a quarter past seven. I really have to leave." Beneath his fingers, her pulse was pounding.

"I could make dinner," she volunteered hopefully. Anything to make him stay.

He shook his head. "Another time. I'll take a rain check." He stood up, grateful that the telltale bulge in his pants had subsided enough not to be noticeable. "I had a great time. I'll call you tomorrow or see you or something." He leaned over and pecked her cheek. He would have liked to do more, much more, but tonight wasn't the night. He would frighten her and that would ruin everything. "Come," he said, pulling her to her feet. "Walk me to the door."

She rose on unsteady legs, still hoping that he would change his mind and stay for dinner. She almost asked him again then bit back the invitation. It occurred to her that he must have plans for the evening already. Otherwise he would have stayed. She might be young and inexperienced but she wasn't blind, and it had been more than obvious that David was attracted to her. She giggled just thinking about his arousal and how he hadn't even thought she'd noticed.

"Uh-oh," he remarked as he watched her sway precariously. "You'd better go lie down for a while. Looks like you've had a little too much to drink."

"I most certainly have not!" she denied emphatically. The room was spinning wildly, and she had to lean against the doorjamb to maintain her balance. She blinked rapidly, trying to focus on his face. He was laughing at her! Those unbelievable blue eyes were positively twinkling! "It just so happens that I didn't eat lunch today, so the wine went to my head. But for heaven's sake, I'm not drunk."

"I never said you were."

"But that's what you meant, isn't it?"

"No. I wasn't suggesting anything of the kind. In fact, I think it's cute."

"What is?"

"Your reaction to two glasses of wine."

She purposely took a step away from the wall to prove that she was able to maintain an upright position without the aid of the doorjamb. "There!" she stated proudly then burst into a fit of giggling. "As you can see, I'm perfectly sober." There was no reason at all for Reggie to tell him that her studio apartment had suddenly taken on a forty-five degree tilt. Another giggle escaped her lips and her hand flew to her mouth.

He couldn't leave her like this. "Come on," he sighed, taking her hand and leading her back into the room.

"Where are we going?" She crossed her fingers behind her back.

"You're going to bed. If I leave, you're liable to pass out with dinner cooking or something."

She grinned crookedly. "You don't have a thing to worry about. I can't cook. Not even water. And, for your information, I am *not* going to bed because I have a very important date in half an hour." If she couldn't get him to stay, she would be damned if she'd let him know she was sitting home alone.

"Is that so?" he asked skeptically.

She nodded then put both hands on the sides of her head to keep the room from spinning so crazily. It didn't help.

"If you already had plans, why did you ask me to stay for dinner?"

"Did I do that?"

He nodded.

"Silly of me, wasn't it?" Then, in a conspiratorial whisper she added, "Richard's a jerk. Shh!" She put a finger to her lips. "Don't tell him I said that."

"I'll go to my grave with the secret." He was at the foot of the little staircase that led to her sleeping loft. "Gates," he said as he half dragged, half pushed her up the steps, "you're a silly drunk, and in the future I'd be mighty careful who I share a bottle of wine with. One day, someone may try to take advantage of you."

She cocked her head. "How?" she asked, plopping down on the edge of the bed and kicking off her shoes. She covered her mouth to hide a yawn, but the bed looked so inviting and suddenly she was so sleepy. Without thinking, she lay back on the pillows, completely unaware of the provocative picture she made. Her T-shirt had gotten caught up behind her back, stretching the thin cotton knit tight against her chest, outlining and defining her firm, rounded breasts. She closed her eyes and, for a moment, David was sure she had fallen asleep.

Come on, baby, he groaned inwardly. How much self-control do you think I have? His hands itched to touch her, to feel the ripe fullness of those inviting mounds. Even her nipples, erect under her shirt, seemed to be screaming for his lips. Could anyone be that trusting, that naive? Or was she teasing, daring him. He stood frozen . . . torn between the intense need that was building in his body and the knowledge that leaving her alone was the right thing to do. His organ was throbbing, and when he saw her open her mouth slightly and begin to run her tongue over her lips, he gave up. What the hell! She was goddamned asking for it.

He leaned down and pressed his mouth to hers, parting her lips and tasting the sweetness of her breath. When she didn't respond immediately, he was convinced that she really was asleep. Then, ever so slowly, her lips answered his, and she drew his tongue into her mouth. Her hands reached up and snaked around his neck to pull him closer so that their bodies met and the upper part of him was pressed against her breasts. Desire engulfed him. He deepened his kiss, probing her mouth, nipping gently at her lips with his teeth. He could feel her answering response as she arched toward him. With his mouth still pressed to hers, he gently separated from her so that his hand could reach between them to touch her. But when he cupped her breast in his hand, she gasped in surprise, pushed him away and sat up angrily.

"Just what the hell do you think you're doing?" she spat out angrily.

Baffled, he stared at her. "Me? What the hell do you *think*

I'm doing?" Christ! Just what he needed, a goddamned cock-tease! "Listen lady, I was the one who wanted to leave a half hour ago, remember? You asked me to stay!" If this wasn't what she wanted, why had she let him lead her upstairs to bed?

She swung around and put her feet on the floor of the loft. It made her feel safer, more in control. She cringed when she saw the cold, angry look in his eyes. "I think you'd better leave."

He took her by the shoulders. "Why don't you make up your mind what you want?" he asked, blue eyes blazing.

It was the wine and loneliness and the scent of his cologne and the need to share with another human being . . . but how did she explain that to someone she'd only just met? She *hadn't* been leading him on. When he had touched her, when her hungry body had responded to him, she thought she could go through with it . . . let him make love to her. Then she chickened out. He had every right to be furious. "I changed my mind," she said in a very small voice, almost a whisper.

"Terrific!" he snapped and turned his back to her so he could readjust his clothing.

"I'm sorry." There was nothing else for her to say. She'd screwed up everything, and if he never wanted to have anything to do with her again she had no one to blame but herself.

David still had his back to her, but when he heard the little-girl voice begging for his forgiveness, a peculiar tremor passed through him, something he had never felt before. He couldn't put a name to it . . . it was too new a sensation. He savored it for a moment. Curiosity? Protectiveness? No. It was different. It had something to do with the odd combination of Reggie's genuine artlessness, her trusting, and the hunger and passion that he knew lay beneath her fear. A sly smile spread over his face. He remembered the feel of her breast against his hand, and he imagined much, much more. She was young, way too young for him, yet that was part of the allure, part of the excitement. Though she didn't know it yet, he sensed that she was on the brink of awakening womanhood . . . poised precariously on a fence, needing only the slightest spark to ignite her. Still a child, really. But a child who, with the right instructor, could develop into an extraordinarily passionate lover. He knew it as surely as he knew his name. And he intended to be the force behind the explosion when it came.

He turned, ready to forgive. "There's nothing to be sorry about. We just got carried away."

Her heart gave an exuberant leap. "You mean it? You're not angry?"

"I was," he admitted, "but I'm not anymore. What do you say we start all over with dinner tomorrow night?"

She couldn't believe it. He wanted to see her again even though she'd made a complete fool out of herself. He was giving her a second chance. "I'd love to have dinner with you."

He chucked her under the chin. "Great! Oh, and one more thing."

"What?"

"No more wine until I see you."

She laughed with relief. "Promise."

David ran his fingers through his hair, then leaned down to kiss her gently on the lips. "Stay here and take a nap. I'll let myself out. I'll pick you up tomorrow at eight."

"I'll be ready."

He arrived at her door, dressed beautifully in a tan and black tweed sport jacket, putty button-down shirt and black gabardine trousers. From behind his back, he whipped out a four-inch round, orange plastic pumpkin filled with candy corn, which he presented to her with a flourish. "In honor of the upcoming holiday."

Her eyes lit up like a child who had just been given a puppy for Christmas. "Halloween? Don't tell me you celebrate Halloween?" It shocked her that anyone as worldly as David Astin would even think about such a babyish holiday. But she liked that he did. It made him more human, less godlike. She stood back to let him enter, but he shook his head.

"Maybe we'll come back later," he said. "Right now we have to leave because I made an eight-fifteen reservation at La Groceria." Reggie nodded as if she knew the restaurant intimately. Actually, the only eating establishment with which she was familiar was Rikers, the German deli across the street, where she bought her tuna on rye for dinner every night.

"Do you have a coat?" he asked. "It's cold out." Damn right, he thought. It was cold out and she'd freeze in her scanty navy satin hot pants, silk blouse and calf-hugging vinyl boots. She really was a peculiar little thing . . . her outfit, though sexy and very chic, was different from what David was accustomed to. He had a mental picture of another girl who dressed only in cashmere skirts, matching sweaters, pearls and pumps—nice and proper but not nearly as intriguing as this sassy outfit that hugged Reggie's impudent behind so provocatively. Was she aware, he wondered, what the gripping dichotomy of little-girl innocence and sultry woman did to him? She was totally unlike any woman he had ever met and she fascinated him. Memories of the night before flashed through him . . . Reggie in bed, tight jeans, straining breasts, sensuous, teasing lips . . . then wide-eyed outrage when he'd fondled her. He still couldn't decide if it was all an act.

She returned to the door, having dispensed with the pumpkin, and was carrying a floor-length sweater coat of navy, red, beige and teal stripes. "My coat of many colors," she explained as she allowed him to help her into it. The coat would have been atrocious on anyone else, but, inexplicably, it looked right on Reggie Gates.

Reggie was excruciatingly aware of David's eyes on her. It made her nervous. Was she dressed wrong? Had she chosen something too far out? When she'd dressed, she thought the shorts and shirt were cute and stylish; now she wasn't so sure. Finally, she couldn't stand the uncertainty any longer. "Am I dressed okay for this restaurant?" She desperately needed his approval.

"You're dynamite . . . for La Groceria or any other place." He took her hand and began to walk downstairs.

La Groceria turned out to be a lively Italian restaurant on the corner of West Fourth Street and Sixth Avenue, unpretentious and comfortable. They were seated immediately and a carafe of Chianti was placed between them. David frowned.

"What's the matter?" asked Reggie.

"Wine," he commented. "Did you eat today?"

"Breakfast, lunch and two snacks. I wasn't taking any chances," she answered brightly.

"Good girl. That being the case, I think it's safe to pour." He filled two glasses and handed her one. "Just so we understand the ground rules, if anything happens, you take full responsibility."

"Agreed."

"Then . . . to a lovely evening." He raised his glass.

"To a lovely evening."

They were well into their third glass when the waiter arrived to take their orders. Despite her assurances that she was prepared to imbibe, Reggie's tolerance for any kind of spirits was woefully low. The fancy script on the menu swam before her eyes. She blinked, but the letters were still undecipherable.

"What would you like?" asked David.

Reggie tapped her delicate finger on the menu as if she couldn't decide. Both David and the waiter waited patiently for her to choose, neither one aware that she couldn't even see the menu, much less read it. After what seemed like an eternity, Reggie looked up into the waiter's face. "Are there any specials tonight?" That would take care of reading the menu.

"Certainly. Osso buco and rigatoni de pomadoro."

"Really?" She thought for a moment. "I think . . . I think I'll have the first one."

David grimaced. "You like that?"

She bit her lower lip. "You don't?" She'd made a mistake. She knew it by the look on David's face.

He shook his head. "Not especially, but it doesn't matter—it's your dinner." He gave the waiter his order of veal limone and, when the waiter had gone, refilled Reggie's glass, acutely conscious of how she nervously finished it in a few quick swallows. "Reggie?"

"Hmm?"

"Watch the wine."

She giggled. "Where's it going?"

"Right to your head."

"No, I'm fine. I swear." She did feel fine. In fact, she felt terrific, warm, mellow, relaxed. She wanted to keep the feeling, hold on to it, not minding in the least if it was the wine that was responsible. She reached for her glass then frowned when she saw it was empty. "Is there any more?"

"Not for you, there isn't. In one minute you're going to slip under the table." Tipsy was all right, but passed out would end the evening.

Dinner arrived, and Reggie stared in horror at the dish set

before her. A cylindrical bone with some sort of meat clinging to it, swimming in a thin brown sauce, surrounded by nasty pale green peas and carrots, challenged her. Gingerly, she picked up her fork and made a half-hearted stab at the specialty. She pushed the food around her plate. What the hell was it? she wondered. Whatever it was, she knew she couldn't possibly eat it.

"What's wrong?" He had picked up his head and noticed that she wasn't eating.

"Hmm?" She looked at him, startled. "Nothing."

"You're not eating."

"I did. I mean I already ate as much as I could. I have a very small appetite."

There was one small medallion of veal left on David's plate. With a sigh he pushed it over to her. "Try this."

"I really couldn't."

"Force yourself."

She ate it in three bites. "Delicious," she commented, daintily wiping the corner of her mouth with the napkin. "To be honest, I didn't particularly care for my dish."

"I gathered as much. Why didn't you send it back?"

She hesitated then plunged ahead. "I was embarrassed," she admitted. "For one thing, I can't read Italian. And even if I could, my head was swimming from all the wine and I couldn't even make out the words on the menu." In her tiny voice, she added, "I really wanted to make a good impression on you after last night."

"Let's set some ground rules right now. I like you a lot. I think we can have fun together, but it's got to be on the up and up. No bullshit. Don't do things because you think it's going to please me, and I won't play games like that, either. What do you say?"

She wasn't exactly sure she understood what he meant, but she would have readily agreed to being planted on Saturn if he thought it was a good idea. "Sounds reasonable."

"Good. You be you and I'll just be me."

"Okay." She began to relax, comfortable that there would be some sort of future with David if she complied with his rules. By the time they were drinking their final cups of espresso with sambucca, she let her hair down at last, telling him about her childhood, her zany antics and a little bit about her parents. She even mentioned Aunt Hattie. "She probably was my savior. If it weren't for her, I'd be certifiable by now. They hated each other."

"Who?" asked David, somehow having lost track of the story.

"My mother and her sister Hattie. Mother always thought Aunt Hattie was crazy, wacko! She once told me that she was sure I was meant to be Hattie's daughter, but some ironic twist of fate put me in the hospital when my mother was giving birth. I wish Hattie *had* been my mother," sighed Reggie. "Wait till you meet her. She's a cross between Auntie Mame, Mary Poppins and Peter Pan."

"And your mother?"

Reggie thought. "Mrs. Danvers."

"The housekeeper from *Rebecca?*"

"Only worse!" laughed Reggie. "What are your parents like?"

A shadow passed over David's face. "They're dead."

"Oh, David. I'm so sorry. I never meant—"

"Don't worry about it. It was a long, long time ago."

"It must be very hard for you." What else could she say? No matter how awful she thought her own parents were, at least they were alive. David had no one. "David?"

"Mmm?" He had been thinking about Chicago, his past and his future.

"Shouldn't we leave? I think they're trying to close."

He and Reggie were the only people left in the restaurant. "I guess so. I really hate to end this evening. It's been one of the nicest I've had since I've been in New York."

Me too, Reggie thought silently. "It doesn't have to end yet. Do you want to come back to my apartment for a while?" She looked at her watch. "It's early. Only eleven. Do you have classes tomorrow?"

"Not until twelve. You?"

"I have to go to the Met to study some costume designs from the twenties, but I can do that any time." She thought about the mountain of work waiting for her at home and pushed it to the back of her mind. It would just have to wait.

The night air was crisp and cold, but neither Reggie nor David seemed to mind as hand in hand they strolled home. She sneaked a look at David's face in the moonlight. He caught her looking and smiled. "What are you thinking about?" he asked.

"Nothing in particular. Why?"

He pulled her close and wrapped his arm around her shoulders. "Because I was thinking how nice this is, how nice you are, and I was just wondering where your thoughts were."

"Pretty much in the same place, I guess," she admitted shyly.

He kissed the top of her head. "I'm glad."

When they reached their building, David took out his key and opened the front door, allowing Reggie to enter first. The hallway was barely lit, dirty and unattractive, with peeling wallpaper in a sickly green print, and a floor of worn-out black and white linoleum. Stale odors of overcooked food, mildew and age permeated the air. Reggie wrinkled her nose in distaste. "If you didn't live here, I'd be too embarrassed to bring you home."

He nodded. "I know exactly what you mean. But I won't always live like this. Someday, I'll have money, lots of it, and it won't be too long, either."

"You'll be successful. I can feel it."

"You have no idea how I hate being poor. Having to count every penny. I go to bed wondering how next month's rent is going to get paid." They had climbed to her floor and David took her key. "Being poor sucks!"

Somehow, the struggle to make ends meet didn't affect Reggie that way. She was a natural optimist and she viewed this particular time in her life as just another hurdle to jump over on her way to her goal. Being short of cash didn't especially bother her, not the way it did David. If she had money left at the end of the month, she treated herself and Coco to a special dinner. If she didn't . . . she didn't. It was as simple as that. She didn't dwell on her lack of funds, nor did it make her miserable.

As she closed the door behind her, making sure to turn all the locks, she tried to explain how she felt. "I know I'll make it big someday. I've always known it. So whatever I have to go through to get there, I'll go through. Don't you feel that way?"

"No, not at all," David answered as he sat down on the newly slip-covered couch and put his feet up on the coffee table. "Whatever short cuts I can take to get where I'm going, I'll take. Nothing will stand in my way."

"You mean the end justifies the means?" David nodded but Reggie shook her head vehemently. "That's a lousy attitude, David. You're going to hurt people along your route to success, and in the end it's going to come back to hurt you."

"I doubt it." He leaned his head back against the cushions and closed his eyes. "When I think of what I've had to do to get where I am now, anything in the future pales in comparison."

She sat down next to him. "Do you want to talk about it?"

"No." Then, seeing the disappointment in her face, he added, "I don't mean to shut you out, but there are things I'd rather not talk about to anyone." And certainly not to an eighteen-year-old, still-wet-behind-the-ears kid with stars in her eyes. What the hell did she know about real life, with her monthly allowance and a wacky aunt who sent surprise presents when the going got rough? This kid's conception of poor was not being able to order filet mignon and having to settle for shell steak. He'd known kids like this all his life. For David, poor wasn't a temporary condition, it was a state of mind that he knew intimately. How he'd gotten this far—having his college and law school tuition paid, a monthly stipend for living expenses, the three good sport jackets in his closet—wasn't an accident. He'd earned it, the hardest way possible, and somewhere down the line, someone was going to make up to him for all he'd sacrificed. He'd never discussed his past with anyone and he wouldn't start now. It had nothing to do with her.

"Come closer to me," he said, changing the subject. "I need someone soft to hold."

Reggie gladly complied, moving into his arms and laying her head on his broad shoulder. She sighed contentedly as he began to stroke her wavy, auburn hair. Her eyes closed and David studied her face: the long, dark lashes that fluttered against her peach-tinted cheeks; the full mouth, her lower lip trembling ever so slightly as he began to run the back of his hand down the soft contour of her cheek to her neck. She was so unbearably young, so trusting. A shiver of excitement rippled through him as he imagined her naked, her flesh pliant against his muscular frame. She might be frightened at first, but he would lead her so slowly that her wariness would fade under his skillful tutelage. He felt the pulse in her neck pounding. His lips traced the delicate outline of her earlobe, stirring new feelings, sending waves of pleasure to the tips of her toes. When he moved his mouth over hers and parted her lips so that his tongue could slip easily into her mouth, he felt the beginnings of her response. Hesitantly at first, then with greater confidence, her tongue darted into his mouth, and David held her to him, refusing to allow her to break away.

Reggie didn't want to move. Her pulse was roaring in her ears as his mouth became more demanding, more insistent. She gasped in surprise when his hand cupped the soft swell of her breast, but she didn't pull away this time. His thumb began to caress the tip of her breast, and he smiled to himself as he felt her nipple harden with excitement. When he slipped his other hand inside her blouse to touch her more intimately, she instinctively drew back, but David, fully aroused, held her firmly with one hand behind her neck.

He whispered huskily, "No. Don't be afraid. This is so right, baby. Don't you feel it? I know you do." The ache between his legs was extraordinary, his rock-hard organ pushing painfully against the restrictions of his clothes. He took her hand and forced it between his legs to feel his need, but she jerked away as if she had been burned. Urgently, he tried again, this time firmly holding her hand against him, whispering words of love to her. "Oh, baby. Touch it. I want you so much. I never wanted anyone the way I want you. Don't you know how much I need you?"

She'd never touched a man there before, and the fear that she would do something wrong almost overcame the terror of doing nothing at all. Last night she'd behaved like the worst kind of tease, and tonight she knew was her last chance. Awkwardly, she fumbled against the length of his turgid organ.

David unfastened his belt and unzipped his trousers. His hard, excited organ suddenly sprang free, and he moved Reggie's hand to it, showing her how to surround it, stroke it. He flung back his head in ecstasy, panting, "Don't stop, don't stop, don't stop."

She wouldn't have dared. Drops of moisture appeared, making it easier to move her hand along his shaft. The lower half of his body was arching, gyrating. A sheen of perspiration broke out on his face as he encouraged her with unintelligible words of passion. Suddenly, he pulled her hand from him. "Stop!" he cried. One more stroke, one more movement and he would have been over the edge. "Wait," he panted, trying to regain his breath.

Reggie's eyes flew to his face in alarm, frightened by the violence in his voicc. "Did I do something wrong?"

"No." He stood up, towering over her. "Come with me." He took her hand and led her to the loft, where he placed her on the bed then rapidly undressed her. He took off his pants and lay down next to her, gazing with rampant desire at her fully developed breasts, the small waist and reddish-gold triangle that half hid between her long legs. He wrapped his arms around her, kissing her lips, her eyes, her cheeks, then nipping at her neck and the edges of her breast, finally taking the whole of her taut nipple into his mouth, running his tongue around it. He pressed himself against her and, when the lower half of her body began to arch, his hand reached between her slightly parted legs to feel her, soft and wet.

With a groan, he moved over her and parted her thighs with his knee, placing the tip of him against her, rubbing his hard, slippery shaft over the engorged bud of her sex. He tried to be gentle but his need was so great that he couldn't wait any longer. With a last groan he plunged into her, mindless of the thin barrier between them. She wrenched away in pain as he pierced her, then she buried her face as he thrust rapidly toward completion. With a thunderous roar, he collapsed on top of her.

"Sweet, sweet baby," he crooned, caressing her hair. "Lovely baby . . . so beautiful. Perfect."

Reggie lay beneath him, sore and uncomfortable, feeling oddly flat, baffled by the sudden sense of emptiness. Something had gone wrong. There had been no firecrackers, no explosions, yet David had said it had been perfect. Maybe this was all there was . . . maybe all the books she'd read had only been romanticizing this act. Or maybe it was because it was her first time. She didn't know, and she didn't know how to find out or whom to ask. Maybe, she rationalized, she would get better with practice and she would float off into space. She fell asleep dreaming of the next time.

* * *

She was right and she was wrong. Over the next eight months their lovemaking *did* improve. There was never pain again, but neither did she ever experience the violent explosions she expected. Once or twice, when they had spent a great deal of time fondling and caressing, she almost felt as if she were about to reach some peak. Then he would stop, enter her and whatever she thought was about to happen didn't. Not that she was unhappy. She loved the feel of David's hands and mouth on her body, reveled in the fullness of him inside her . . . and for her it was enough. Just having him near was enough.

"Hey!" he called from the living room. "Did you go to Colombia for the coffee?" His voice brought her abruptly back to the present.

The coffee had long since finished dripping, and Coco had sneaked back into the kitchen and was now perched on the windowsill, sunning herself. "If David sees you in here we're all in big trouble—shoo!" The cat ignored her. Reggie sighed. She took down two mugs and poured the coffee, then walked into the living room.

David whistled as she approached. "You have great tits."

She winced. "I hate that word."

"Stop being so sensitive. You're beginning to be a drag." Things were starting to irritate him about Reggie, little inconsequential things—a raised eyebrow when he told her he had to spend the night studying in the library; veiled questions about his plans for the future; not so veiled demands for Saturday evening dates, three and four weeks in advance. Or her latest . . . "should we live together this summer instead of paying two rents?" He wasn't interested in making those kinds of commitments.

She sat down on the edge of the sofa and handed him his coffee. She needed to talk to him about the summer, but from his last comment she knew the timing was wrong. She understood the pressures he was under—finals, the upcoming bar exam, looking for a job. But where did she fit in? She'd vowed not to mention anything about the future until he'd completed the bar exam, but the landlord was pressuring her daily about signing a new lease, which meant leaving a two-month deposit. If they were going to live together, she had to make some plans. David was so difficult to pin down.

She put her coffee cup down and turned to him, her mind made up. It was now or never. "How's the job-hunting going?" she began.

"Mezzo-mezzo. I may have something lined up, but it's still too premature to tell."

"Really? Where?" she asked, trying to sound casual.

"Chicago."

Ugh, she thought. "What about New York?"

"Maybe. A lot of firms are starting to interview. It's only May, Reg. I really don't have any idea yet. Why?" Now he had turned to face her, a challenging look in his eye.

She took a deep breath. "Because . . . because . . . I have . . . " She couldn't get the words past her lips.

"What?" he asked, annoyance obvious in his voice. Here it comes, he thought . . . fish or cut bait. "What is it you have to do?"

"Copeland is bugging me about the lease for next year, and I don't know what to do about it."

David played dumb. "What's the problem?"

You! Us! she screamed inwardly. Tell me, for God's sake, that I shouldn't sign a new lease to live in New York if you're going to be living in Chicago. "Do you think I should sign it?"

"If it's what you want to do," he answered. "Look, Reg," he said, pulling her closer to him and speaking softly into her hair. "I understand that you still have three more years of school. How can I put pressure on you now?" He was turning it around. "Besides, everything is still so up in the air for me, it wouldn't be fair for me to tell you what to do." There! Now he'd laid it in her lap.

"I could always finish school somewhere else," she suggested.

He moved his hand around her shoulder, caressing her slender white neck, thinking about the possibility of a quickie before he went to the library. "Whenever you're near me, I can't even think straight. Feel," he said, drawing her hand between his legs. He was hard as steel, swollen, throbbing, pulsating with anticipation. It was true, what he'd said about being near her. Something possessed him, a fever burned in him, a thirst that could only be quenched by having her helpless under him, her legs spread, her back arched, waiting anxiously, still nervously, for him to plunge into her. He wanted her now . . . on the couch, on the floor . . . it didn't matter, as long as he could dig his fingers into her soft, innocent flesh and crush her beneath him.

His hand moved, fanning out to touch the voluptuous curve of her breast. He squeezed her nipples lightly until he felt them begin to swell, growing hard beneath his hand. He could do this to her, arouse her desire even when he knew she didn't want it. It was a lever he held over her, and it fired his blood to know he had such power. "Move over. Lie down, baby. Lie down and let me touch you," he said, his voice thick with passion. He eased her into a prone position, slipping his hands under her shirt, reaching up to cup her breasts. His hand curled around each mound, squeezing the soft flesh.

"Ow!" she cried suddenly, pushing his hands away and sitting up with a start. Her breasts were unusually sensitive from her expected period.

"What's the matter now?" he asked, scowling.

"That hurt, dammit!"

He stood up, his handsome face now dark and foreboding. "Oh, Christ, Reggie. I didn't do anything to you. You're in one helluva mood today."

Now it was her turn to be angry. "I was in a terrific mood before you walked in. I designed a super line last night, and I was really on a high. I hoped you'd share it with me, but it seems the only thing you want to share with me is getting laid!" Her chest was heaving; sparks flew from her green eyes. "I'm not an idiot, David. I want to know about next year, and you keep avoiding the issue." Her legs were parted and her hands were planted firmly on her hips as she waited. "Well?"

"Well, what?"

"I want an answer!"

"I told you before, don't push me!" He felt as if the walls were closing in on him. He had to get out of there fast.

For a moment, she just stared at him, torn between telling him to get out of her life and terrified that he would do just that. "Forget it!" she said finally. "Just forget it. I am in a rotten mood, and if you stay we're just going to have a big blowout. Maybe I should be alone."

"Maybe you should," he agreed. "Call me when you've cooled down. I'll be at the library all day and probably tonight, too. I'll be home by twelve." He walked to the door then turned. "You ought to go take a long walk or something."

She nodded her head. "Or something," she whispered, then burst into tears as the door closed.

Chapter 4

She sat on the couch for a very long time after he left. Her eyes were red and swollen, but, mercifully, the two-hour crying jag had stopped. Whoever said that weeping was cathartic? She felt anything but cleansed and relieved. Rather, she was exhausted, frustrated and depressed. She'd accomplished nothing by cornering David and putting him on the spot. She was further from an answer now than she had been before she'd brought up the whole subject of their future.

The rest of the morning was a waste. Reggie moped around the apartment, cursing herself for forcing a confrontation. She'd lose him for sure that way. It was just that he made things so damned difficult. She was forever walking on eggs, trying not to say or do anything that would set him off. And then there was his temper. In recent weeks it had reared its ugly head with increasing frequency, and it was becoming harder and harder for her to get through to him. She knew he loved her . . . but knowing was not enough. She still didn't know whether to sign a new lease or not.

She hadn't moved from the couch until, an hour later, her doorbell rang. David! He'd finally come to his senses! But when she opened the door, Alison Granger stood there, white-faced and shaking, clutching an ice-filled red and white dishrag to the side of her face.

"Reggie, could I please come in for a minute?" she pleaded. Her eyes darted to the hallway then back again.

"For God's sake, Alison! What happened to you? Should I call the police? Is there someone out there?" Reggie grabbed

Alison and pulled her inside by the collar of her terry-cloth robe. She felt the frightened woman tremble.

"Close the door, Reg, quickly!" She stumbled to the couch and sat down, still gripping the makeshift ice bag. Alison drew several deep breaths then, seeing the alarm in Reggie's eyes, said, "I wasn't mugged or attacked or anything like that."

"Then what *did* happen to you?"

Alison's blue eyes blinked rapidly. "You have anything to drink?"

"Only coffee or soda," answered Reggie, apologetically.

"Nothing stronger?"

"Stay here," she said. "There might be some wine left in the fridge." She ran into the kitchen and returned a moment later with a filled glass and watched in amazement as Alison swallowed it in four gulps. "Alison, what the hell happened to you?"

"I'll tell you, but it's just between us, okay?"

Reggie looked at her curiously. "I don't even know anyone you know. Who would I tell?"

"No one, I guess. I'm not exactly thinking straight." She took another couple of deep breaths. "I met a guy a few months ago and we started seeing each other. He's always been a perfect gentleman—well, pretty much, anyway—but this morning he came by and he was in a really lousy mood. I thought I could cheer him up—you know. We were fooling around and I got . . . playful. He really got into it, then out of nowhere—he frigging slugged me!"

Reggie's eyes flew open. "He *hit* you?"

Alison pulled the rag from her face to reveal an angry red bruise. Reggie gasped in horror. "He didn't mean it!" Alison said then realized how peculiar that sounded. She touched Reggie's hand and added, "He's not dangerous or anything like that . . . he was just out of control."

And I think *I* have problems! thought Reggie. "You're not going to see him again, are you?" asked Reggie. "Hell, if I were you, I'd call the police!" Alison must be crazy. This guy could kill her. What was the matter with her?

"It wasn't like that!" she insisted. "He started to bawl and apologize, but I ran out. I know it sounds sick, but I really think it was an accident."

"Alison," she said gently, "tell me something. Did your ex

ever do this kind of stuff?" Maybe Alison was into S&M. You never knew. Her own predicament paled in comparison to this story. Hell, she was lucky that the only problem she had with David was getting him to make a commitment. He'd never so much as layed a finger on her. If he ever did, he'd be out on his ass!

Alison shook her head. "Don't be ridiculous! He drank some, but he never got nasty. That's not why I dumped him. I walked out on him because he was sleeping with my stepmother." She laughed at Reggie's double take. Poor sweet kid . . . still believing in happily ever after. Well, it wasn't up to her to open Reggie's eyes. "I hope you never wake up to the real world, honey. It stinks. Stay up there in your ivory tower. It's safer." And with that, she stood up. "I'm okay now. I'm sorry I barged in here like this. I usually handle stuff pretty well by myself." She thanked Reggie for everything and, at the door, stopped to give the younger girl a hug. "You've been great. Thanks. If I can ever do anything for you, just knock."

Reggie stood shaking her head after the door closed. It had been quite a morning. First David, then Alison. Maybe the whole world was crazy. It certainly seemed that way.

By that afternoon Reggie's mood had improved considerably. She'd shaken off her depression by deciding to take a completely new tack with David. She'd made a mistake by pushing . . . now she had a better idea. But before she put it into action, she had to concentrate on her new line and her appointment with her advisor. She could hardly wait to see the expression on his face. Kitteridge was a professional, always on the lookout for new, fresh talent. When he saw her innovative approach to sportswear, she knew he would help her get started.

She showered, dressed and quickly tidied up the apartment. By three o'clock, she was busily packing each new garment in tissue before placing it in her huge orange and yellow plaid sample case. Before leaving, she opened all the windows to air out the stuffy apartment. It was the kind of day that New Yorkers wait seven gray months to see . . . warm, sunny, breezy and bright. No one could be in a lousy mood in this kind of weather.

She lugged the heavy suitcase down the five flights of stairs and, for once, the long climb down didn't bother her. When she passed David's door she almost stopped, then reconsidered —he owed her an apology, not the other way around. *She* didn't have anything to sort out! Besides, once she'd seen Kitteridge and gotten some pointers on how to market her line, she could tell David that money wasn't going to be their problem anymore. He was so terrified of being poor . . . but by the end of this summer, if things went the way she hoped, she'd be able to support them while he got started with his practice. That, she decided as she stepped outside into the glorious sunshine, would be her new approach!

Her spirits continued to soar, dollar signs and wedding invitations dancing before her eyes as she hummed her way through Sheridan Square to Sixth Avenue. Spring in New York! The metamorphosis was incredible! Overnight, the city had gone from dirty gray-brown to vivid celestial-blue. Brilliant, unexpected pockets of color sprang from window boxes and small curbside gardens. Golden daffodils, fuchsia tulips and a wild profusion of geranium, crocus and royal-purple iris spilled from corner sidewalk vendors' baskets wherever she looked. A hawker noticed her smile and handed her a posy of violets, shaking his head as she delved into her pocket for money. She thanked him and continued on her way uptown, whistling cheerfully. Even her favorite doorway wino looked cleaner and happier today, tipping his ragged baseball cap and waving as she passed. Hopefulness must be contagious, she thought. During the long walk to Parsons, whenever the scene with David played through her mind, she shoved it away. She was finished with depression and unhappiness! Now, on the brink of success, she wanted hurrahs and accolades. She had earned them.

At exactly ten to four, Reggie pushed open the doors of Parsons and walked upstairs to Kitteridge's office, which was really nothing more than a closet, a dirty little room which reeked from mold and the faint odor of dirty socks. It hadn't been dusted or straightened for years. Reggie walked in, cautiously avoiding the sketches, shoes, bags, sweaters and dresses that lay on the floor like remnants from a Columbus Day sale at Gimbel's. It was a pitiful way to dispense with other people's hopes and aspirations, she thought as she sidestepped into the room. Kitteridge nodded for her to take a seat while he continued to speak on the telephone.

Short, balding and pudgy, Alvin Kitteridge was laughingly referred to by his students as the Pillsbury Dough Boy. His dreams of fame had long since faded when he had given up the hand-to-mouth existence of designing for the steadier, more secure field of teaching. After seven years of teaching sample-making and grading, he had been pushed up the ladder to become an advisor. It left him with more time to dwell on the disappointment of his lost youth. It also gave him the opportunity to hone a latent streak of jealousy which, on an especially depressing day, he would use on his more talented students. As she entered his office, Reggie had no way of knowing that Al Kitteridge had just been told that his live-in boyfriend was leaving him.

Kitteridge's face registered none of the fathomless despair he felt as he returned the telephone to its cradle. He gestured to Reggie to begin her presentation. Proudly, she unpacked her suitcase on his cluttered desk. He stared silently at the oddly colored clothing. Reggie held her breath. Kitteridge carefully fingered each garment, making no comment. After what seemed like an eternity, he looked up at Reggie with a puzzled frown. "What is this mess?" he asked cruelly.

Reggie felt a cloud of doom settling over her as he spoke. "I beg your pardon?" she asked, hoping she had misunderstood.

He grabbed the clothes in his fat, piglike fingers and flung them from his desk. "Is this a joke?" he barked. Paying no attention to her anguished face, he threw piece after piece on the floor. "This is awful! Gaudy, pretentious, ostentatious! It's an . . . an abomination!" He jumped from his seat and strode around to her side of the desk. "What on earth have you been doing at this school all year?" he asked. "Are you serious about this vulgar display of garbage? Do you honestly think anyone in their right mind would wear these?" With ferretlike eyes he demanded, "Show me your portfolio, your sketches!"

With as much pride as she was able to muster, she returned his stare. "This," she said quietly, gesturing to the clothing on the floor, "is my portfolio." She began to pick the garments from the filthy floor, lovingly dusting them off. "These are the examples of my very best work." For one hideous moment,

Reggie thought she would cry, but she blinked back the tears and looked up at her advisor. "You will never know how helpful you have been to me today, Mr. Kitteridge." She finished repacking her suitcase. "Please remember what happened here because this 'abomination' is going to make a fortune for me. Every last one of these garments is going to appear in the pages of *Women's Wear.*"

Kitteridge called to her to stop, but Reggie never turned as she walked through his door, down the corridor and out the doorway of the school.

She would never step foot into Parsons again.

As she wandered aimlessly through the New York streets, the warm May breeze blowing her copper ponytail, she pondered her future. When her parents found out that she had dropped out of school, they would cut off her funds. That meant she would either have to go back to Boston and face the smug satisfaction and "I-told-you-so's" of everyone in her family, or she could remain in Manhattan and look for work. Whatever her decision, it would have to be made soon, she thought as she mentally calculated the small balance in her checkbook. Right now, if she lived frugally, she would have enough money left for one, possibly two, months of rent and food.

Then there was David. What would become of their relationship if she returned to Boston? He would be taking the bar exam soon. After that . . . the future was cloudy.

If only Kitteridge had liked her line. He had the ins to the right people, to the buyers. Despite his caustic response to her presentation, Reggie still believed in her collection. She knew it was good and knew it would sell. She just didn't know where to begin. One could hardly stroll into Bloomingdale's unannounced and expect to see the head buyer. It just wasn't done. It was a Catch-22 situation. She couldn't sell her line because she didn't know the buyers, and she didn't know the buyers because she had never sold a line.

She walked aimlessly for a long time, desperately searching for an answer until, exhausted, she paused in front of Godet, one of the many Madison Avenue boutiques. The four mannequins in the store window stared at her with unblinking eyes and expressions of utter boredom; two brunettes, a blonde and a redhead. The scene that held Reggie's attention was a mock-up of an ocean liner dining salon. The captain held his champagne glass high, in a toast to the four women at his table who were all dressed in some of the most poorly designed and executed evening dresses that Reggie had ever seen. One brunette, whose Dynel wig had slipped precariously over one ear, was attired in a manly black silk tuxedo with silver lapels and bow tie. Her twin wore a white panne sheath trimmed in white fox. The brunettes, thought Reggie critically, were atrociously dressed, but their attire didn't compare to the blonde's Forty-second Street gold lamé hot pants and halter, or the redhead's flowing Hawaiian-printed chiffon evening pajamas.

She shrugged her shoulders in absolute exasperation and moved on to the next store window, dragging her heavy sample case behind her. Her confidence in her newly designed collection was rapidly but inexorably slipping away as she studied the window of Deidre Belliot's. Long touted as one of the most trend-setting and prestigious boutiques on Madison Avenue, Deidre's display was just a replica of every other window along the avenue. The only noticeable departure was in Deidre's use of Oriental and black models. But to Reggie's discerning eye, the clothes were still old hat—slight modifications on overused themes that had earmarked evening clothes for the past five years.

If this was what American women really wanted to wear, and Kitteridge's reaction to her own line seemed to underscore that it was, then Reggie was truly on the wrong track. And yet, it didn't make sense. The time was ripe for a major fashion change . . . she felt it. But it was beginning to look like Reggie Gates wasn't going to be the designer to make it happen.

Quietly, she wiped away an unexpected tear as she walked on, stopping every so often to check another window in the slim hope that she was wrong. But she wasn't. And with each step, each block, she became more and more disheartened. She was about to turn around when, at Eighty-third Street, she stopped short. The aroma of fresh pastry wafting from Greenberg's bakery hit her with such force that her mouth watered. She gazed with unabashed longing at the lush confectionary display of sacher tortes, almond crescents, Mexican wedding cookies and double-fudge brownies. Yesterday, she wouldn't have thought twice about spending the five dollars it would cost to satisfy her sweet tooth. Today, with the specter of an almost empty bank account staring her in the face, she reluctantly held back. She would need every penny she had to stay in New York. And she *was* staying. No matter what!

The abhorrent possibility of calling her parents for a loan to tie her over occurred to her, but she dismissed it immediately. To do that would mean begging and crying and admitting that her year in New York had been folly. She wouldn't do that. Even if they were to offer, which she knew in her heart that they wouldn't, accepting their help was impossible—out of the question. Money from her parents would come with too many strings and obligations. The emotional price Reggie would have to pay would be far too great. The only one she could possibly turn to was Aunt Hattie . . . then she remembered that that, too, was impossible. Hattie was bouncing around somewhere on the high seas on one of her Auntie Mame excursions. For the first time in her life, Reggie was furious at Hattie's fanciful, irresponsible life. Once she eliminated her aunt, there really was no one else she could turn to.

She hitched up her jeans and bypassed Greenberg's with a heavy sigh, settling for a salted pretzel from a sidewalk vendor, then crossed Madison Avenue and began the long trek home. The plaid suitcase, coupled with her despondency, was dragging her down like a ten-ton weight. After walking twenty blocks she almost gave in to the overwhelming desire to hail a cab then, mentally calculating the fare to Sheridan Square, she shook her head and continued walking. By the time she reached Sixty-second Street, she was exhausted. Her sneakered feet burned, and the strap from the sample case had raised an ugly blister on her palm. She stopped in front of Nikki's and sat down on the marble ledge that abutted the window of one of New York's fanciest boutiques. If only she had the guts to march right into the cool, luxurious, imposing store and demand to see the buyer. For another five minutes, she sat, resting her aching legs, watching chic Manhattanites enter the store.

Suddenly, something snapped inside her. Screw Kitteridge! Screw Parsons, and screw fancy, uptight Madison Avenue! Somewhere, someone had to make changes. Why shouldn't it be Reggie Gates? Wasn't that what she came to New York for? From an untapped source, she summoned new courage and boldly opened the heavy green-tinted glass doors.

Once inside, she gaped at the lushly furnished establishment. Hunter-green marble, so highly polished that Reggie could see her reflection, echoed the sounds of the squeaking wheels of her suitcase. She strode purposefully toward the mirrored counter, behind which stood a beautifully dressed Oriental woman. Huge chrome bird cages filled with exotic parrots and cockatoos towered overhead. In the rear of the store, the sounds of a waterfall, carved out of granite, played out the fantasy that one had entered the garden of a palatial, tropical estate.

An uneasy quiet fell over the store as the well-dressed women who were doing last-minute summer shopping turned to stare in surprise at the unsophisticated redheaded teenager who was dragging a dilapidated suitcase behind her. Reggie's face flushed. Ill at ease among the smartly dressed shoppers, she wanted nothing more than to disappear into the huge rubber plants that flanked the main counter. What could she have been thinking when she entered the store? She broke out in nervous perspiration. Turning her head, Reggie looked longingly at the exit when she heard a voice.

"May I help you?" A woman in her mid-thirties, plantinum hair held tightly off her face by an elaborate rhinestone barrette, stood next to her. Reggie stared at the striking apparition. She had never seen anyone as arrestingly beautiful. The woman was dressed simply in a white linen long skirt that ended at her ankles. Sexy, slender, perfectly pedicured toes, encased in strips of black snakeskin, peeked out from under the skirt. She wore a simple, black crew neck sweater, belted low at the waist.

"I . . . uh . . . I would like to see the buyer, please," Reggie answered in a small voice. She wiped her upper lip surreptitiously.

"I'm Nikki Broad. I'm the buyer as well as the owner. May I help you with something?" She disdainfully glanced at the young girl's faded jeans, T-shirt and sneakers. It reminded Reggie of the way her mother had always looked at her. She could almost hear the well-remembered "tsk-tsk."

Taking a deep breath, Reggie introduced herself. "I'm Reggie Gates. I was hoping I could show you my line of sportswear and evening clothes."

There! She'd said it!

"Whom did you say you were representing?" queried the blonde.

"Regina Designs." Without giving Nikki a chance to make the obvious connection, Reggie unzipped the pitiful case, pulling all of her hopes and dreams out and spilling them on the floor. The unexpected sight of a dungareed teenager, sitting in the middle of the quiet, elegant store, caused the few shoppers to stare open-mouthed. Reggie heard whispers and titters.

Nikki Broad, owner of Nikki's and an extremely astute retailer for ten years, did not laugh. Instead, she eased her graceful frame onto the floor next to Reggie and sorted through the clothes. In an offhand manner, she asked, "Have you shown these to anyone else?"

"No," answered Reggie.

"Wonderful!"

Reggie looked bewildered. "Wonderful?"

Nikki ignored the question and motioned to the Oriental woman. "Koo, pick these up and bring them upstairs to my office. She turned to Reggie. "Come with me."

Reggie followed her up a Lucite and chrome spiral staircase to the owner's private office. Decorated entirely in black, it was a perfect foil for Nikki's blond beauty. Reggie watched silently as Nikki slipped behind her black lacquered desk. "Sit down, Reggie," she said. "How old are you?"

"Eighteen," Reggie answered. "Why?"

"I'm thirty-five and I've rarely been wrong since I've been in retailing. I'm not being vain, just honest. I think your 'collection,' and I use the word cautiously, is one of the most innovative I've seen in a long, long time. But"—she paused to light a cigarette—"you're not going to get anywhere with it if you continue to show it the way you just did."

Reggie's spirits sank. "What do you mean?" she asked dully.

"You can't walk into a store, any store, and spill a suitcase on the floor and expect to be taken seriously. You will get nothing but rejection after rejection."

"Then why are you bothering with me?" Reggie asked in a flat voice.

"Because I told you that I'm rarely wrong and, from what little I've seen, I'm interested. Your things are good—creative, exciting. Even the fabrics are novel. I've never seen Nyesta used like this. I think that if they're marketed well, they'll sell."

A quiver of excitement shot through Reggie as she realized that Nikki was taking her clothes seriously.

"Do you think," Nikki continued, "that if Anne Klein put her clothes in Filene's Basement or sold them to K-Mart, she could command three hundred dollars for a simple silk blouse? Could Ralph Lauren get five hundred dollars for a plaid wool skirt if he didn't have his own department in every important store? Fashion doesn't work the way you think. Most of the time, young designers like yourself don't make it simply because they don't know how to promote their designs."

Cautiously, Reggie asked, "Why are you interested in this young designer?"

"Believe me," she laughed, "it's not personal. I'm a businesswoman first. I think I can make a great deal of money with your clothing—provided you are willing to listen to everything I say."

"And if I'm not?" Reggie asked.

"The chances are that you will still be a success, but it will take a long, long time. Look, I can save you a lot of time and energy because I already believe in what you've shown me." Nikki pointed a finger at Reggie. "What kind of production can you guarantee?"

Reggie had no idea, but she knew she had to give Nikki an answer. "I can do whatever I have to do." She assured her with far more bravado than confidence.

"Here's what I would like to do," Nikki said. She reached into her desk drawer for her checkbook. "I will give you . . . four thousand dollars now, against as many different pieces of this line as you can produce in the next two weeks. You are not, and I repeat emphatically, *not* to show one piece, one single design, to any other buyer until you have cleared it with me. The only way I will buy this line is if I can have it exclusively. Do you understand?" Reggie nodded her head. Nikki wrote a four thousand dollar check and handed it to

Reggie. "The line must be in the store within two weeks. You are already very late for the Spring-Summer season."

Reggie stared in disbelief at the check. Then a horrible thought occurred to her. "What happens if I can only produce a limited amount?"

Nikki laughed. "You won't. You will want to produce as many of these garments as you can. You're too eager to see your clothes sell, not to. Whatever you produce, whether it's five pieces or five dozen, you get to keep the whole amount. I'm banking on your ego."

For the first time since Reggie had entered Nikki's a smile played at the corners of her mouth. She had to bite back the urge to shout. "Do you want to write down the name of my company?" Reggie asked.

"It's not important. For now the clothes are going to be sold under my label. They will sell much better that way. I already have a well-known name and reputation. You don't." Nikki stepped from behind her desk. She had finished with the interview. "That's the deal. What do you say?"

"What do I say?" Reggie repeated incredulously. "I'll be back in two weeks with the most exciting clothes you have ever seen." With great care, she folded the check and put it in her jeans pocket. "I don't know how to thank you."

Nikki walked to the door, opened it and allowed Reggie to precede her. She motioned to the suitcase which was standing outside the office. "There are your things. I'll see you in two weeks."

Reggie flew through the streets of New York. The weight of her sample case was forgotten in the excitement of what she had accomplished and what she was about to attempt. She still couldn't believe her good luck at choosing Nikki's. Reggie knew Nikki had been right. She would work nonstop and well. She could hardly wait to show David the check.

She ran up the stairs to his apartment, her spirits soaring. But her excitement and exuberance were short-lived. David's response was lukewarm. For the three years he'd been in law school, he had been struggling for passing grades; now Reggie, with barely one year of design school behind her, had earned four thousand dollars for one night's work.

"Where's the written order? The contract?" he asked, trying to contain his rancor.

"Nikki and I have a verbal agreement. She trusts me and I trust her," Reggie said defensively. "Why else would she have given me this check?" she added, waving it in his face.

"Why not?" David shrugged. "You'll produce four thousand dollars worth of clothing and she'll probably triple the price." It was what he would have done if an inexperienced girl like Reggie had walked into a store that he owned.

"I don't care how much she sells them for," Reggie insisted. "I know she's smart, but I also think she's fair. She wouldn't have handed me four thousand dollars if she wasn't investing in my future. And she wants me to be exclusive with Nikki's," she argued hotly.

David laughed. "So what?" he asked sarcastically.

"So . . . I'm going ahead with the order just the way she offered it to me," she said stubbornly. "I'd be an idiot if I didn't."

"You'd be worse than an idiot if you did."

Reggie scowled. "Stop trying to play corporate attorney. You're just jealous because I've made money and you haven't."

Swearing savagely beneath his breath, he said, "Have it your way, Reggie, but don't expect me to hold your hand and wipe your eyes when your pretty little bubble bursts. I'm not going to do it!" he concluded emphatically. He picked up his business law textbook and buried his nose in it as she slammed the door behind her.

The next ten days passed in a blur of activity. Reggie spent every waking moment at her cutting table or sewing machine. The floor of her apartment was covered with scraps of old rose and dusty gray fabric. Days and nights ran together as she struggled to meet Nikki's deadline. She was so hyped up that she couldn't sleep anyway, often waking at two or three in the morning to finish a piece she had been dreaming about. Her days and nights got confused. She ate breakfast food at midnight and found herself emptying a carton of egg foo young at six o'clock one morning. For two whole days she didn't even shower or dress because she was too busy working out a sample for a three-piece outfit that could change from a working girl's day dress to an evening gown by simply turning the pieces upside down. Her face broke out and she completely skipped her period for the month of May—two things that had happened only once before, when she was cramming for her College Aptitude tests. She ignored them, knowing that as soon as the pressure was off, things would return to normal.

David stayed away, his method of punishing her for not heeding his advice. That was something else to be worked out when her line had been delivered. She would ultimately have to seek him out and apologize . . . just what for, she wasn't certain.

On the morning of the fourteenth day, Reggie placed each finished garment in a plastic bag, then carefully packed her hideous suitcase. She left her apartment and walked crosstown to take the subway to Nikki's. The day was clear and not too warm, an uncommonly pleasant June day. Today she wouldn't dwell on her anger with David. She had never been more excited.

Madison Avenue was unusually quiet for Friday when, at 10:30, she approached the entrance to Nikki's. It occurred to Reggie that most people who made their homes on Manhattan's Upper East Side left the city on the weekends for the beaches of New Jersey or the Hamptons. Reggie had lost all sense of time while she had mindlessly worked on Nikki's order. Now she realized what a pity it was that she hadn't met Nikki earlier in the season when the wealthy New Yorkers were doing most of their summer shopping. Still, she mused wishfully, there were others, like herself, who didn't leave the city for the summer.

Nikki was in the back of the boutique as Reggie entered. She could just make out the platinum head amid the towering palms and trees. The woman was arranging a display of bathing suits on the tropical plants. With an artist's eye, Reggie admired Nikki's flair. Customers had to peek around huge fronds of the palms to discover what was hanging. Each bathing suit looked like a tropical flower about to burst through the greenery with its bright color and pattern.

"Nikki?" Reggie asked as she reached the area that the store owner was decorating. For a moment, Nikki stared at her blankly.

"Reggie . . . Reggie Gates. The designer. Remember?" She prodded the woman's memory.

Nikki recalled Reggie Gates but a far different Reggie Gates. This one had slimmed down considerably in the two weeks since she had seen her. At their first meeting, there had been nothing remarkable about Reggie's looks. Now, with the loss of weight and her reddish-brown hair pulled severely off her face in a knot at the back of her neck, Nikki's educated eye saw the promise of great beauty in the high cheekbones, almond-shaped emerald eyes and tiny nose. A familiar flash of jealousy pierced her. She gave Reggie a curt good-morning. Reggie looked surprised and hurt. Nikki immediately recovered, realizing she had made an error. "Sorry, I didn't recognize you."

Reggie regained some of her confidence. "Wait till you see the line," she said excitedly. "It's even better than the original."

"I knew it would be," Nikki said. She stared at Reggie. "Are you feeling all right? You've lost a tremendous amount of weight. Haven't you been eating?"

"No," Reggie admitted honestly. "Food was the last thing on my mind these past two weeks. Even when I thought of it, my appetite was gone. I guess I was too excited to eat." Reggie didn't think that her fight with David or its effect on her appetite would interest Nikki.

"Let's bring everything up to my office." She led the way and Reggie followed with quaking knees. Her whole future depended on the reception she would get from Nikki. Nikki settled herself behind her desk, smoking a cigarette as Reggie unpacked each garment. Occasionally, Nikki would murmur her approval. When each piece lay like a jewel against the black desktop, Reggie stood back and held her breath.

Nikki examined each piece. Never overly generous with compliments, the owner was hard-pressed to keep the praise from her voice. "Well done!" she said finally.

Slowly, Reggie expelled her breath. Nikki reached over and picked up the phone. She pushed a series of numbers. "Koo, upstairs. Koo, please," she repeated.

Koo appeared moments later. "Take this merchandise into the back and tell Grace to sew our labels on them. When she's done that, have Lauren ticket them and bring them to the front desk. I'll do the display as soon as both of you finish." Koo collected the clothes and left the office. When Reggie coughed discreetly, Nikki turned around. "Oh, I'm sorry," she said. "Did you want to speak with me?"

Reggie looked uncertain. "What comes next?"

"Next?" asked Nikki, impatiently.

"I mean, have we finished?" Reggie clenched her fists nervously in her lap. "I thought you would tell me something, some sort of advice on how to proceed." She responded cautiously, lest she annoy her benefactress. As much as she hated to admit it, Reggie was awed and a little frightened by Nikki's aloofness.

"Honey, the line is terrific. It has great potential but it *is* very late in the season. I have to see if I can sell it. That will take some time," Nikki explained, trying to keep the impatience out of her voice. "Do you have anything left from the check I gave you?" Reggie nodded, not trusting her voice. "Good. Take the summer off or work on a fall line. If we do well with this line, I'll call you for fall. Leave your phone number with Koo at the desk. As soon as I have an indication of how it's going, I'll call you. Okay?"

Reggie had been dismissed. Nikki had nothing more to discuss with her. She picked up her suitcase and left the office, feeling a vague disquiet in the pit of her stomach.

As soon as Reggie had walked down the spiral staircase, and Nikki was certain that she had gone, she picked up the phone to page Koo. "Koo, get Lou Parisi on the line. His number is in my book under the counter."

Lou Parisi was a pattern maker. He had worked with Nikki many times. Whenever she found an interesting line in Europe that she was unable to buy, Lou copied it for her. With her astute eye and innate fashion sense, Nikki called upon Lou's expertise many times. She had an unmistakable eye for spotting a hot item. Lou would copy it to the last minute detail, often making the garment in nine or ten different fabrications. Nikki then put her own labels on the garments. She had made a fortune copying other designers.

The moment that she saw Reggie's line, she knew it would work. She felt no guilt whatsoever about what she was about to do. She had paid the little designer handsomely for only two weeks' work. Nikki thought nothing of stealing Reggie's designs —it was done all the time. She knew it would be a painful lesson for Reggie to learn . . . but an inevitable one. To Nikki's way of thinking, it was far better that Nikki Broad benefitted.

Within a month, Nikki's new sportswear and evening line was on the cover of *Women's Wear*. Nikki, herself, was interviewed on TV. Reggie watched in utter disbelief as Nikki explained how she had thought up the concept of using synthetics more creatively. The moderator of the program applauded her foresight and ingenuity and wished her good luck on the upcoming opening of Nikki's on Los Angeles' Rodeo Drive.

Reggie sat in her hot apartment, staring at the walls and wondering dully how to tell David about Nikki's treachery. He'd been right all along. She'd only seen him once in the last month and on that occasion, he had barely inclined his head in passing. He was still furious with her.

And then there was the other news she had to tell him . . . the last few weeks she had been trying hard to deny it, but the evidence was overwhelming—she was pregnant. She had all the signs. Her period hadn't appeared, her breasts were engorged and painful, and she awoke each morning with vertigo and the vague need to vomit. She desperately needed David, yet when she thought about the way he had been acting, the thought of telling him her news scared her to death. She had no idea if he would be happy and understanding or fly into a towering rage at her carelessness. Unfortunately, she'd have to roll with whatever his reaction was. She had no choice. As soon as she could, she'd tell him, and together they would do what had to be done.

Chapter 5

The minute studio was stifling. Behind closed, shuttered windows, the oppressive July air barely moved. For well over a week, Reggie had huddled miserably in the fetid room that had once been her refuge. Now, with the knowledge of Nikki's coldhearted betrayal and her own rising hysteria, the very room she had loved threatened to close in on her. She hadn't seen anyone, seeking solace in solitude. Her obsession to succeed had been replaced by an aching despair that promised to destroy her. As she sat staring blankly into space, she twisted a strand of unwashed, tangled hair, waiting for something, anything to shake her from the overwhelming melancholy that enveloped her. Whether it was due to what she was now all too certain was her pregnancy, or the relentless sense of failure, Reggie had lost the strength to shake her lethargy. She had been defeated.

She still hadn't been able to cry. Sick with grief, she had simply hidden behind the triple-locked steel door, desperately hoping that both David, then Nikki would call to rectify the mistakes. When ten days passed without the longed-for calls, Reggie plunged still deeper into a pit of wretched self-pity.

On the eleventh day, she broke down. Starved for comfort, she tried to reach David, but the phone in his apartment went unanswered. On the thirteenth day, the first glimmer of real fear grasped her when she heard a taped voice inform her that his line had been disconnected at his request. Her blood froze. David—gone? It didn't make sense. Her mind could not comprehend the meaning of the message even though she understood the cold words with bitter clarity. With trembling fingers, she dialed again only to hear the same mocking recording.

The still air in the room was suddenly shattered by a choking sound that ripped from Reggie's throat. "No . . . oh,

God . . . please, no!" she cried brokenly. Mindlessly, she ran from the room, her legs giving out as she reached the stairwell. She sank to her knees when she suddenly realized how profoundly alone she was. With David gone, there was nothing, no one. A bottomless pit. An unfillable void. His leaving was the ultimate betrayal, the final blow to her fragile ego.

Tears welled up in her eyes, and this time she could do nothing to blink them back, as silently they slipped from under her tightly closed eyelids and rolled down her cheeks. Her cry began as a whimper, building in volume until great racking sobs rent the air, echoing down the five flights. With her arms wrapped tightly around her body, Reggie rocked back and forth, giving in to the pain that had been accumulating for two weeks. She wept for all the injustices that had been heaped upon her. She swore at her family, at Nikki and finally at David, who had deserted her without a word. They had lied to her, cheated her, ultimately betrayed her. In one blinding moment of despair, everything crystallized; she couldn't even depend on her own instincts.

After forty minutes, Reggie wearily picked herself up and was about to re-enter the apartment when she heard footsteps on the stairs. Quickly, she looked around, but there was no place to hide. A moment later, she came face to face with Alison Granger. She hadn't seen or heard from Alison since that day she had come running into Reggie's apartment with the huge welt on her cheek. This time, with her eyes red and swollen from crying all morning, it was Reggie's turn to play true confessions.

"Good God, Reggie!" exclaimed Alison. "You look horrible. What in the world happened?" Reggie must have lost ten pounds since they had last seen each other. There was an almost ghoulish look to her now, too, with those deep purple rings under her eyes and the skin of her face mottled and yet very, very pale.

For the merest fraction of a second, Reggie almost told her that everything was fine, but the lie died on her lips when she saw a faint black and blue mark, which Alison's heavier-than-usual makeup had failed to cover, on her face. Certainly Alison was in no position to judge her . . . and although they weren't great friends, it was *someone*, another human being, to talk to. She had no one else. She needed Alison.

Reggie swiped at an unbidden tear. "I need someone to talk to. Could I come in for a few minutes?"

Alison put her arm around Reggie's painfully thin shoulders. "Of course you can, honey. I told you that day I barged in on you to come to me if you ever needed anything." She pointed to her bruised face. "I can't seem to get out of my own way, but I'm a marvelous listener and I do have a way of solving other people's problems. Come on."

Alison saw Reggie sneak a peek at her face and its ugly bruise. Two goddamn weeks and the thing hadn't gone away. She hadn't been able to answer any of the modeling calls, and her agent was becoming increasingly suspicious of the "flu" that was taking Alison so long to recover from. Thank God she was finally finished with that rotten bastard . . . a sicko, it had turned out. Hell, she ought to have known better. Not like this poor kid who knew nothing and was sitting alone on the stairwell crying her heart out. It had to be a man. It was always a man, thought Alison as she unlocked her door and led Reggie into the living room. Four months! Four lousy, wasted months it had taken until Alison finally woke up to acknowledge that the man she was seeing was a total creep.

"All right, what gives?" asked Alison. No sense beating around the bush. The sooner Reggie told someone and got it out of her system the better she would feel. It always worked that way.

Reggie burst out crying again. Alison sat down next to her and held her like a baby while, in between sobs, Reggie poured out the whole story of her stolen line, her long, tumultuous relationship with her boyfriend, his abrupt disappearance and finally her pregnancy.

"Are you certain? About the pregnancy, I mean?" asked Alison.

Reggie nodded. She'd heard enough to know the signs. There was no doubt in her mind. "I thought when I told David—"

"Who?" Alison sat bolt upright.

"My boyfriend. David. The one I told you disappeared."

"Nine months, you said?"

Reggie nodded. "I met him in October. He's a law student at NYU."

"I know."

Reggie didn't hear her and went on to explain how she thought they were going to get married after he took the bar.

Suddenly, Alison stood up, angrier than she could remember being in a long, long time. "You stupid fool!" she shouted, and Reggie stared at her with frightened eyes. Seeing the shock on Reggie's face, Alison recovered. "Not you. I didn't mean you. I meant me . . . and you, too, I guess. Both of us!" She pointed to the bruise on her face. "David Astin," she said bitterly. "The love of *your* life. The guy *I* ran away from that morning."

"No," Reggie whispered.

"Yes! Yes!" exclaimed Alison. "Four months, Reggie! *Four* months! Oh, shit! I should have known. The 'library,'" she mimicked. "The library! Where were my brains?"

Reggie couldn't speak. She couldn't even think. All at once she seemed to shrink into the corner of the couch, her arms wrapped around her body protectively. Something deep within her was shattering, something warm and vital. The essence of Reggie Gates, with all her joyful anticipation of the future, was dying, seeping out of her and leaving nothing but an empty shell. Alison watched in horror as the once lively designer, with her ready smile and sparkling green eyes shriveled before her. Reggie's face was like a death mask, her eyes expressionless as she stared off into space, no longer aware that Alison was even in the room. A soft noise began to escape her lips, not a cry exactly, more like a keening . . . a sound that a wounded animal might make.

In two quick steps Alison was beside her. She reared back and slapped Reggie across the face in a blinding blow. It worked immediately. Reggie screamed and jumped off the couch to go after Alison, but the older woman was quicker and stronger. She grabbed Reggie's hands, then enveloped her in her arms while Reggie's cries tore from her heart.

"No more, no more, no more" were the words that ripped from Reggie's lips and echoed in the living room. "I can't take any more pain."

"Shh, shh. It's over, Reggie," crooned Alison, suddenly

maternal, her own problems paling in comparison to Reggie's complete devastation. "This will pass. You'll get over him." Empty words of reassurance, words that were spoken simply because words *had* to be spoken.

"What am I going to do?" asked Reggie like a lost child. "What am I going to do?"

Alison led her back to the couch. She held Reggie's hands in hers and stared hard into the young girl's face. "You are going to pull yourself together, decide what you want to do with your life and go on and do it! You're not the first woman who's been deserted and, God knows, you won't be the last. You've cried over that bastard enough. He's not worth another tear. Do you understand? Not one more lousy tear!"

"Alison?" Reggie asked.

"Yes?"

"Why are you doing this? For me, I mean? You ought to hate me."

Alison gave a bitter laugh. "Why? Because you were taken in? So was I. You didn't do me dirty, Reggie. David did. David used both of us. You weren't sneaking around, sleeping with my boyfriend behind my back. Hell, if anything, *you* should be mad at *me*."

"But you didn't know, either."

"Stupid of us, wasn't it?" Alison remarked. "Two bright women taken in by a worm. That's what he is, you know. A worm. And I'll tell you something else, honey. You'll never let this happen to you again. It'll be a long, long time until you trust anyone again. I should know."

Reggie nodded. She wouldn't trust again for a long, long time. Maybe never. The tears were gone but in their place came a new resolve. Reggie Gates would go on. She would survive, and somehow she would learn to use people the way she had been used. Silently, she vowed she would never, ever give her heart again.

"You don't have much time to decide," Alison said, clearing up the remnants of the tea cups and English muffins that she had prepared for both of them once Reggie had calmed down. "If you want to keep the baby, that's one thing . . . but if you do decide to go ahead with an abortion, you have to make plans."

Abortion. Just the word was repellent. People from Boston, her family's kind of people, didn't even speak the word out loud, much less contemplate the act. "I don't know if I could go through with it," Reggie said dully. "I'm just not sure."

"What would you do with a baby if you kept it? Or are you thinking of adoption?" She was doing her best to be nonjudgmental, to keep her opinion to herself so that whatever decision Reggie reached would be her own. But it was hard. One look at the pathetic kid and Alison wanted to shake her. She *should* have the abortion—a lousy half hour and it would be over, and Reggie could go on with her life. But keeping a kid? What kind of life would that be? Alison had been through this decision-making process . . . twice. She was only waiting for Reggie to give her the go ahead before making the phone call.

"Adoption would be worse," said Reggie. "Giving away my baby to strangers?" She shook her head. "I couldn't." The words came out in a whisper.

"You'd be very surprised to discover what you can do when your back's to the wall," Alison told her sagely. "Look, go home and get some sleep, even a couple of hours will do. Think about it . . . I'll be home when you decide." She walked Reggie to the door and leaned over to give her a peck on the cheek. "I know it seems like you've reached the bottom, but I swear you will live through this."

As Reggie walked down the flight to her apartment, she thought about Alison's words and wondered whether she was speaking philosophically or medically. Abortions killed more than just babies.

Sleep eluded her. Reggie tossed and turned for over an hour before she finally kicked the covers off and gave up. Coco stared at her indignantly from the end of the bed, angered at the disruption of her nap. Reggie reached for her, but Coco sprang off the bed with her tail held high. "You were right all along about him," mumbled Reggie, hating to admit that an animal had sharper instincts than she did when it came to judging David Astin. She almost wished she could get Coco's opinion about what she should do now.

Reggie sat with her feet dangling over the edge of the bed for about fifteen minutes then, suddenly, knew what she had to do. She jumped off the bed, ran downstairs and into the kitchen and began rummaging through drawers. She finally found the extra key to David's apartment—a key she had never used because David had warned her that he hated surprise visitors. Now, of course, she knew why. She had only been given it so that if he ever locked himself out *he* would be able to get in. Now she would use it. She would collect the few things he had borrowed over the months and, in so doing, finally convince herself that he had gone.

As she fitted the key in the lock, she smelled fresh paint. Fighting the nausea that suddenly rose within her, she pushed open the door. The apartment was completely empty. There was no trace that David Astin had ever lived there. Without a word, with no attempt to see her, to explain, to say good-bye . . . he had gone. She stood staring in disbelief at the empty rooms until, at last, the acrid odor of turpentine and paint forced her to flee to the bathroom to give up the contents of her heaving stomach. She dropped to the floor, faint with perspiration. Wave after violent wave of nausea hit her. Death would have been preferable to the gut-wrenching spasms that assaulted her body. It was over. Every dream she had dared to hope for had ended in this tiny six-foot-square bathroom. She rested her head on the cold tiled wall.

From the hallway came footsteps and the muffled sounds of voices. David! He was back! He can't see me like this, she thought in a panic. Hurriedly, she slammed the bathroom door, leaning heavily against it. She was trapped. There was no way she could leave without being seen.

"I insist that the locks be changed before Monday," demanded a male voice. Crouching behind the door, she strained to recognize the voice. It wasn't David's. The doorknob jiggled above her head. "What's the matter with this door?" inquired the unfamiliar voice. "Did your crew paint it shut?"

"No, sir," answered another voice, this time a more familiar one. "I was in here this morning with the plumber."

"Why is it locked?"

"I don't know, Mr. Taggett. Maybe the plumber did it when he left here. Wait here. I'll get the extra set of keys and open it right up."

Caught between alarm at being discovered and a sudden

urge to laugh at the picture she would make, Reggie pondered her escape. How the hell could she get out of there? She looked up, hopelessly, at the tiny window. But before she had time to think, the door burst open, hitting her on the head and knocking her to the ground.

"What the hell?" exclaimed the startled tenant. "Who are you? What are you doing here?"

Reggie looked up into a pair of the bluest eyes she had ever seen, vainly trying to formulate an answer when a big black man loomed up behind the stranger.

"What are you doing in this bathroom?" the superintendent asked angrily. "This apartment belongs to Mr. Taggett now. Astin's gone and you can't come and go in here anymore."

Reggie blushed scarlet. Had everyone in the building but Alison known about her affair with David? The new tenant was watching her curiously as she tried to wriggle out of the bathroom, which was blocked by the two massive bodies.

"Excuse me," she said, drawing herself up proudly. "I came to pick up some things that belonged to me, and the wind must have slammed the door behind me."

Mr. Taggett looked skeptically at the apartment's sealed windows. "Wind?" he repeated.

Reggie ignored him, pushing past the two men and running out of the apartment. She didn't hear the new neighbor call after her. She was so embarrassed that she wouldn't have stopped if she had heard.

Once back in the safety of her own apartment, Reggie's breathing slowed. She leaned her back against the door, taking a good look at the filthy room. Had she really lived like this for two weeks? Her eyes caught on the overflowing wastebaskets, the dirty clothes, the kitchen sink filled with half-eaten meals and crusted plates. The corners of her mouth turned down in disgust. A sudden burst of energy hit her, and an insane need to clean, disinfect and sterilize the room drove her to the kitchen. Armed with Lysol, Ajax, mops, rags and sponges, she set upon the apartment with a vengeance, as if by cleaning her room, she could begin to regain some order in her life. Obsessively, she scrubbed, scoured and polished every inch of the tiny apartment, until exhausted, she sank onto her freshly made bed three hours later.

"Damn them all!" she said out loud. "Damn every last one

of them!" Reggie squared her delicate shoulders, stood up and headed toward the bathroom to wash off two weeks of despair. There were things that she *had* to do . . . important things with her life. And no one—not David Astin, not Nikki Broad, not Alvin Kitteridge—could stop her. Only the baby . . . her baby with David would have stopped her. But she knew she wasn't having this baby. Not now and not alone. She just wasn't that courageous.

There would be time in her life when marriage and children and perhaps love would once again take priority but not now. It couldn't be—so she made her decision. She was going ahead with the abortion, and somehow she would learn to live with what she had done. Maybe with time, she could forgive herself and start over.

Chapter 6

Abortion! She couldn't believe she was going through with it, but here she was at seven thirty in the morning, in the backseat of a Checker cab, trying to gag down a pint of Bacardi, while Alison clutched her hand and urged her on. Bile continued to rise in her throat, making it almost impossible to swallow the searing liquor, but every time she turned to Alison with tears in her eyes, her friend nudged her.

"Those were the instructions. At least a pint. It's supposed to relax you, make everything happen quicker. Please, Reggie. You've come this far. Do what Dolores said."

Dolores Williams was a registered nurse at Mt. Sinai hospital, who happened to have a very lucrative little sideline. No knitting needles or wire hangers. She'd been in ob-gyn long enough to have picked up the tricks of the trade from the "big boys." Fifteen hundred dollars—but her clients never bitched because they knew they wouldn't end up hacked to pieces in a back alley somewhere. She was scrupulously clean, too. After all, she did have a reputation to maintain.

Meticulously, the businesslike woman in the crisply starched uniform layed out the disposable needles, the vials of Pitocin—a uterine contracting drug—the spoon-shaped curettes, douche bag, vinegar and mustard powder. She snapped on a pair of sterile surgical gloves and sat back to wait.

At seven forty, the doorbell rang. "You're late," she told the two girls who stood in the darkened hallway. She had seen the blonde before, but the other one—shit! She was a baby! "Hurry up and get her inside before my neighbors get nosy, and put the money on the table before we start."

Alison had to hold Reggie up. As Dolores had prophesied, the rum had gone right to Reggie's head and she was mumbling incoherently. "Where should I put her?" asked Alison.

"Get her into the bathroom, undress her from the waist down and get out. I'll call for you when I'm finished."

Alison shook her head. "I can't leave her alone."

Dolores put her hands on her hips. "You've been here before?"

"With a friend."

"Then you know the rules. Nobody stays."

Reggie was sagging against her shoulder. Her eyes were half-closed, and Alison knew it was only a matter of seconds before she passed out. "Look, this is my sister. I'll give you an extra hundred to stay. I can't leave her." For some unclear reason, Alison felt responsible for Reggie. In her head she believed that if she hadn't gotten involved with David Astin, he might have married Reggie. It probably wasn't true and it didn't make sense, but it created enough guilt in Alison to keep her by Reggie's side. At least until the abortion was over.

"All right," agreed Dolores, "but hurry it up. We don't have all day!" When Alison made a move to follow her down the hallway to the bathroom, Dolores stopped her. "I changed my mind. You stay here," she said, pointing to the kitchen. "I'll do what I have to do in the bathroom—without observers." Her technique was a well-guarded secret, which was why she didn't allow anyone to stay. She walked over to Alison, scooped Reggie's thin body under her arm, picked up her paraphernalia from the kitchen table and strode off toward the bathroom.

An hour later, Dolores emerged from the tiny bathroom and

walked into the kitchen where Alison had been pacing nervously.

"Go get her. She's out cold."

Alison blanched. "What happened? Is she all right?"

"I said she's out cold. Hasn't she ever been drunk before?" she asked angrily. A real pain in the ass, this one . . . crying, vomiting, then, when she saw the needle, passing out. Dolores wanted her out of there quickly before the next client saw her.

"Did it work?" Alison asked.

"Hard to tell," shrugged Dolores. "You sure she was pregnant? Did she have a pregnancy test?"

Alison tried to think. "I don't know. No, I don't think so but she was so sure."

"Well, I'm not. She's staining a little, but I didn't see evidence of a pregnancy. If she was . . . she's not anymore, but I have my doubts. Should've seen something for six weeks. Now get her out of here."

Alison ran to the bathroom where she found Reggie leaning against the wall, weeping silently. As quickly as possible she dressed her and half dragged her out of the apartment, down the one flight of stairs and into the sunshine. She hailed a cab and, all the way down to Sheridan Square, Alison held Reggie while she sobbed. It had been the worst kind of nightmare, one that she would carry with her in the dark recesses of her mind forever. The acute pain would fade, but not the memories. They would haunt her forever.

Looking at her, Alison made a decision. She would never tell Reggie that what she had gone through might have been a needless abortion. What difference would it ever make?

Chapter 7

At the moment that Reggie was undergoing the abortion, David Astin was just awakening in his parents' home in Evanston, Illinois. He vaguely remembered that he and five of his best buddies had gone out drinking and whoring the night before in his formal "rite of passage" from bachelorhood into the unwanted but totally necessary state of matrimony. He would be getting married that afternoon.

His mouth tasted rancid as he ran his tongue over his perfect white teeth. He could hardly wait to wash the stench of too much scotch and sex from his body. He would have showered when he had gotten home the night before, but he didn't even remember getting home. At best, it was a foggy memory. He had left the elaborate prenuptial dinner early, telling his fiancée, Patrice, that he needed his sleep for the rigors of their honeymoon. She had blushed in embarrassment. In her ignorance, she had believed him and had kissed him goodnight before returning to her guests. It never occurred to her that David was not going home.

Patrice Munsey was an anachronism in the 1970s. Shielded and protected by her father in their Lake Shore Drive mansion, she had never had to face reality. She was a virgin when it was no longer fashionable or even desirable. She wanted nothing more from life than to be David Astin's wife, to stand by his side as he rose through the legal ranks of Chicago's courtrooms and later, with her father's help, the Illinois Legislature. Her aspirations were neither idle wishes nor fantasy. It was what she had been bred for. Her father was one of the most important attorneys in Chicago, with powerful connections in the political arena. He had promised his only daughter that she would be the wife of an important politician, and he would make it happen. In nineteen years, he had never failed her. There was no reason to believe that he was wrong.

The only error he had ever made was to marry a woman who died in childbirth.

Patrice met David at Pinebrook Country Club when he was caddying for her father. On a sunny, beautiful day, Patrice had succumbed to her father's urgings and had agreed to walk the course with him. She was sixteen that summer, old enough to decide that the eighteen-year-old boy with the sapphire eyes would be her husband one day. She fell in love with him the moment he turned to her, a knowing grin on his face, and asked her if she approved of his choice of irons. Knowing nothing whatsoever about golf, she nonetheless agreed with whatever he said. For the remainder of that summer, Patrice followed David around like an adoring puppy. Initially, it annoyed him, but he soon realized how advantageous a relationship with her could be.

A novice with men, Patrice was hypnotized by David's attention, revelling in the jealous glances of her friends as she danced her way through the summer evenings with him by her side. With Patrice's father, Francis, as his benefactor, David was invited to every club function. He slyly insinuated himself into their lives and, before long, David held Patrice in the palm of his hand.

Francis watched as his daughter fell under the magnetic spell of David Astin, marveling at how well the young man handled himself in the heady atmosphere of Chicago's super-rich. He felt certain that he could control David and, in doing so, could assure Patrice's future. When David went off to the University of Illinois—Francis made sure he was accepted—Francis promised that they could soon become engaged.

In the summer of his junior year, David gave Patrice a three-carat diamond. He obtained the money for the extravagant engagement ring from Francis Munsey. Patrice was never told. It wasn't important. David's foot was poised on the first rung of his ladder to success. Francis was advised by his powerful friends to send David to an out-of-state law school where his poor grades would go unnoticed by Chicago's legal community. It was a sound decision; David almost failed his final year of law school. On his second attempt, David passed the Illinois bar exam. Now he could marry his fiancée and become a full partner in his father-in-law's law firm.

His affair with Reggie Gates in New York had been exactly

what he had needed to fill up his time in New York. Smart, sexy and sassy, Reggie's untarnished innocence and youth had piqued his interest and surprisingly enough, had held it for nine months. Except of course for his brief fling with the Granger broad, but, hell, that didn't even count. Now, on the eve of his wedding, the memory of Reggie's slim, boyish hips and upthrusting, full breasts rubbing against him, made him hard. Too bad she'd gotten so serious, he lamented. He wouldn't have minded having her in Chicago—setting her up in a little studio, seeing her a couple of nights a week . . . maybe sometime after he was married, once he got control of Patrice's checkbook . . . the idea began to take shape in his imagination and between his legs. A year, maybe less. He would like that. He lowered his hand and began to stroke himself as he thought of all the possibilities that life had in store for him. His hand moved with increasing speed and pressure. He smiled.

On a lovely July day in Chicago, David Astin married the radiant Patrice Munsey in an opulent wedding for six hundred of Chicago's most influential people. Patrice knew they would live happily ever after. Daddy had promised her that they would.

Chapter 8

Her first year in New York robbed Reggie of much more than her innocence, her designer collection and her baby. Her verve, enthusiasm and spontaneous laughter ebbed as she was forced to face the realities of making a living on Seventh Avenue With no marketable skills with which to secure a well-paying job, she was forced to seek employment wherever it was available. After several fruitless interviews, Alison pulled through for her again, prevailing on an old friend to get Reggie a job at Macy's. It wasn't much of a job, but it paid the rent and fed her and, for the time being, it would suffice. She felt indebted to Alison, a virtual stranger who had befriended her when she most needed an ally. It was a shock when Alison suddenly announced she was returning to Kansas to be near her family. Reggie spent two weeks making her an entire new wardrobe in appreciation for all she'd done. Since her departure, Reggie had spent most of her time alone. She preferred it that way.

There were countless days during the first year after David disappeared when Reggie would drag herself home from an eight-hour day at Macy's, her feet swollen from standing. It was in the evenings, when she sat at her sewing machine creating fantastic costumes that no one would ever see, that she relived the pain. There was an aura of bleakness, a despondency that surrounded her whenever she permitted herself to think about the lousy deal life had dealt her. That first autumn was filled with sorrow, regret and grief.

It was Lee Taggett who drew her out of her self-imposed shell of remorse. From the day he moved into David's apartment, he had been determined to befriend the unhappy girl he had discovered hiding in his bathroom. It hadn't been easy. For the first few months, whenever he saw Reggie, she avoided him. The abortion had left her with a stubborn pelvic infection and a low-grade fever. That illness, coupled with her melancholy, robbed her of her energy and her desire to go on. She had only to pass David's apartment on her way to her own, to start weeping. If she happened to pass Lee on the stairs, Reggie turned her face. He, on the other hand, was obstinate. No matter how many times she rebuffed him, he continued to try to speak to her in the hallway. Finally, in desperation, he grabbed hold of her arm as she walked by his door. He noticed the tears once again gathering in the corners of her brilliant jade eyes.

"Hey! What's with you?" he asked, spinning her around to face him.

"Me? Nothing!" she said, angrily shaking off his hand.

"The tears," he said, pointing to her face. "Every time I see you, you're crying. Life can't possibly be that bad. You're beginning to give me a complex." He gave her a smile. "Is it me?" he asked. He looked down at her face, detecting a slight glint of interest. So far, so good, he told himself. "Why is it that every time we meet I send you into a frenzy of hysterics?"

Reggie wiped the tears, giving the handsome, older man a tentative smile. "It's not you personally. It's the apartment. I can't seem to walk by it without crying." She shrugged. "That's just how it is."

Lee was moved. She was too young to be so unhappy all of the time. "Why is it that way?" he asked, gently.

She glanced up at him, seeing him for the first time. Suddenly, she was embarrassed. He was . . . beautiful. She thought how peculiar it was that she should choose that word to describe him, but with his thick, blond hair, blue eyes under a fringe of dark heavy lashes, high prominent cheekbones and strong jawline, it was the first word that came to mind. Dressed immaculately in white jeans, blue V-neck sweater and loafers, he leaned against the banister with the warmest, friendliest smile she had ever seen. She reddened under his gaze.

Immediately, he was sorry. The last thing he wanted was to frighten her away. "You don't have to answer," he said. "I had no business asking."

Reggie continued to stare at him. He was a good deal older than she. Thirty-ish, she guessed, judging from the tiny lines that radiated from the corners of his eyes, lines that were probably caused by repeatedly squinting into the sun. Those lines were the only spots of white which disturbed an otherwise perfect tan. Her eyes moved down his body.

"Do I pass inspection?" he inquired, chuckling.

Her cheeks flamed, and he grinned in amusement. "Was I that obvious?" she asked.

"Well . . ." He sought vainly for a way not to add to her furious blush but could find none. "Yes," he said honestly, "I suppose you were. I had the feeling I was being auditioned." He leaned a little closer to her. "Tell me, do you always look at people that way?"

"Please . . . I didn't think," she sputtered, "it's just that I . . . you were standing there and I . . ."

"Would you prefer we converse in another language?" He laughed. "This one seems to be giving you a great deal of difficulty."

She smiled so brilliantly that it lit up the dark hallway. Lee was startled at how lovely she was. Somewhere, under the stammering, gauche little girl, was a beautiful woman. With her copper hair, the deep glinting emerald eyes, the finely sculpted bones of her face, there lurked a beauty. But she was a beautiful woman whose pride and heart had been badly bruised. He wondered what had caused her such pain. Boldly, he stuck out his hand to her, determined this time to make her his friend. "I'm Lee Taggett, harmless, nice, wholesome. You look like you could use a friend, among other things."

Instantly her smile was gone. Reggie was on guard. "What other things?" she challenged.

He threw back his head and laughed. "A couple of good meals, a walk in the park, a movie, someone to talk to," he finished quietly. "Nothing sinister, I promise. Are you interested?"

"Maybe," she answered cautiously. Should she accept friendship from a perfect stranger? She thought fleetingly about the last time she had formed a relationship with a man. Her track record with the opposite sex was dismal. But this man seemed . . . nice. He had warmth, an openness that David had never possessed. She suddenly decided they would be friends, but only that . . . nothing more. "Okay!" she said putting out her hand to meet his. "But I think I'd better warn you about something first."

"Go ahead," he said seriously.

"I'm very skeptical about friendship."

"So I gathered," he said dryly. "May I ask why?"

"No, you may not!" she answered emphatically.

"I see," Lee responded. "However, I can assure you that I am very trustworthy. I was even a Boy Scout." He put up his left hand. "Scout's honor."

"That happens to be the wrong hand," she accused.

He looked at it. "So it is," he agreed, lowering his hand. "But I can still be trusted to be a good friend, if you'll let me. And as I said before," he repeated in a conspiratorial whisper, "you look like you can use one."

"Yes, I can," she admitted finally.

Lee was smiling. He had won the first round.

"You should know two things before we begin this friendship," Reggie said. "I can be the best friend that you ever had but I can also be a formidable enemy. If you ever hurt me in any way—"

"Whoa! Why would I want to be your friend if I were

planning on hurting you?" He didn't give her a chance to explain. "Is that your experience with all of your friends?"

Reggie nodded.

"No wonder you're so careful." Then Lee did the oddest thing. He took her small hands in his and solemnly whispered, "I, Lee Taggett, take thee, Reggie Gates, to be my trusted and valued friend from this day forward; in sickness and in health; for richer or—I hope, never—poorer; till death—or one of us meets someone special—do us part." Then, with reverence of a suitor from another century, he bent down and kissed her hand.

Reggie giggled irreverently. "Does this mean I get lunch now?"

"Is that all this friendship is based on? Meals?"

She nodded again.

"Good!" he replied. "In that case, my 'friend,' you can have lunch now or dinner later. What's your pleasure?"

Faced with the choice, Reggie was at a loss. She struggled to decide. Though she was hungry now, the prospect of a long, lonely evening stretched out before her if she chose lunch. If she skipped lunch, she could look forward to a pleasant evening. "Dinner," she decided.

"Wonderful. I'm looking forward to it. Friend," he added.

"Me, too. Friend."

Friendship was usually something that developed slowly with time and nurturing. Not so with the relationship between Lee and Reggie. It took seed immediately, flourishing as the Indian summer days grew shorter and the first chill of the year hit Manhattan. They were constantly together. Lee bolstered Reggie's ego. He tended her and she thrived on his tenderness, his gentle good humor. One day she realized that a week had gone by without a thought of David. Lee had succeeded. He had earned the right to call himself her friend. He had convinced her to bury the past, though she would carry the scar forever.

One evening as Reggie was relaxing in Lee's apartment, waiting for him, the telephone rang. Although she often came downstairs to prepare a light supper for them, she never answered his phone. His answering machine was always on taking his messages. Tonight, however, the phone continued to ring, and Reggie realized that the machine wasn't connected. She debated whether to pick up. In the months they had been friends, Lee had told her little about his private life. She knew only that he had been married, divorced and was the father of a three-year-old daughter. He had told her that after the divorce, his wife and daughter had moved to California. The pain in Lee's eyes was clearly apparent whenever he discussed his family.

The insistent ringing of the phone was driving her crazy. Whoever was calling had no intention of hanging up. Reggie wondered nervously whether it might be his ex-wife calling. Perhaps something had happened to Lee's daughter. On the fifteenth ring, she picked up the receiver. "Hello, Tagget residence," she said.

"Hey, I like that. Could I hang up and call again?" Lee asked.

"Lee!" She was totally taken aback.

"I called your apartment and when no one answered, I figured you were at my place. What took you so long to pick up?" he asked.

She settled back into the cushions of the sofa, relieved. "I didn't know if it was a good idea for a strange woman to answer your phone. What if it had been your daughter?"

"How many three-year-olds do you know who can make long-distance phone calls?"

She laughed. "Then it might have been your ex-wife or your girlfriend or your partner. I didn't know how they would feel if they heard a female voice."

"Neither do I," Lee admitted. "Nor do I particularly care. Anyway, I'm glad you finally summoned the courage to answer the phone."

"What's up?" Reggie asked, tucking her feet under her.

"I have to cancel our dinner plans for tonight. I have to entertain an out-of-town client. I'm stuck with him. Do you want to join us for dinner at La Grenouille?"

"God, no!" After a hard day at Macy's, the last thing she felt like doing was getting all dressed up to sit in a fancy restaurant. "Bring me home a doggy bag, okay?"

"Try to stay up. It may be very late. I don't know where else I'm going to have to take him."

She promised to try to stay awake.

It was true that Lee was entertaining an out-of-town client, but his plans for the rest of the evening were off the beaten business track. After dinner, the two men were going to a small, little known bar on the West Side, the Command—a gay bar that Lee frequented. Many times he had tried to tell Reggie that he was a homosexual; he wanted her to know but could never find the right words. Now the charade had gone on for so long, it was impossible to tell her the truth. It would appear as if their whole relationship was a sham.

He didn't have the courage to subject himself to the kind of accusations his ex-wife, Liza, had hurled at him the night he had tried to explain his sexual proclivities. He had been fighting them since he was a teenager. Two years of psychotherapy had convinced him that he could marry Liza and live a healthy normal life. He had tried. They had had five relatively normal years, years when he had worked such long hours that, when he pleaded he was too tired to make love, Liza understood.

When Liza became pregnant, Lee was overjoyed. It was such a huge step for him, an event that symbolized genuine progress in overcoming this problem that plagued him so. But during the pregnancy, Lee found himself back in his old haunts, actively looking. He made a million excuses for himself for his lack of control, but one night Liza woke to find him staring out the bedroom window, tears streaming down his face. So torn was he between his love for his wife and the perverse longings of his body that he poured out the whole sordid story to his wife, swearing to re-enter therapy to preserve their marriage. Liza wouldn't listen. Their marriage was finished.

That had been three years ago. Since then, he had more or less accepted his sexual orientation. He was gay, or at least bisexual. It was a fact that he doubted Reggie would understand. Was it another betrayal, another lie? He couldn't bring himself to hurt her.

Had Lee made the attempt to tell Reggie, he would have saved himself a great deal of soul-searching. He would have been startled to know that she had already arrived at the truth by herself. They had been very good friends for months when it suddenly occurred to her that there were no other women in his life besides her, and she knew conclusively that theirs was strictly a platonic relationship. If he was out for the evening, the invariable excuse was work, and Reggie never pressed for more information. She didn't have to. On a few occasions when they had gone out together, Reggie had seen Lee make eye contact with good-looking men. She chose to ignore the whole subject, truly believing that his private life was his own. It only saddened her because she felt in her heart that he was as lonely as she. Someday she hoped he would confide in her. She had told him about her past because she trusted him implicitly, and she wanted him to feel the same way about her. Perhaps with time, he would.

Chapter 9

"My poor baby," Lee said as he massaged Reggie's aching feet. She looked so exhausted that his heart broke for her. "When are you going to quit this job? You're too talented to waste your time in a dead-end position."

Reggie leaned her tired head into the deep cushions of Lee's corduroy sofa while she let him try to ease the soreness from her ankles. His strong hands continued their blissful kneading, stopping to work on a knot halfway up her calf. "Don't stop," she pleaded. "Don't ever stop. This is better than sex."

"How would you know?" he teased. "You haven't been out on a real date in two years."

"That's not true!" she denied hotly. "Arthur was a date."

"Arthur was an animal," he corrected, remembering the bull-necked part-time actor with whom Reggie had been fixed up. She had called Lee at two in the morning, hysterically begging him to come upstairs and throw the offensive actor out of her apartment. After that experience, Reggie had decided not to bring her dates home. "Come on, Reg. You can do better than Arthur. You don't even try to meet men. Admit it."

Reggie stretched out on the couch, her feet in Lee's lap, and yawned. "I don't have time," she insisted for the hundredth time. "And I won't go to singles bars. Since I don't go to bars and I work eight hours a day, how would you like me to meet men?"

Lee was at a loss. How did single women meet normal men in Manhattan? It seemed unjust that this vital, sensual woman should have no social life at all. Yet every time he brought up the subject, Reggie shrugged her shoulders, insisting that she wasn't eager to get involved. She was happy with her life the way it was. Lee suspected it wasn't the truth. She deserved some happiness. He just didn't know how he was going to make it happen. "Would you consider a vacation? A cruise, maybe, or Acapulco? Something like that?"

She sat bolt upright. "Are you crazy? Where would I get that kind of money?"

"I would lend it to you," he said gently.

"No, thank you. I would have to work for a year just to pay you back."

"No, you wouldn't," he assured her with a knowing smile. "You could pay me back as soon as you begin designing again." They had been through it many times before. Lee knew all about her first designs and their theft. But no matter how he poked and prodded her, she refused to start again. Her stubborn refusal infuriated him. "You are wasting your life, selling cosmetics all day." He took her small face and held it between his hands, forcing her to look at him. "You have a gift—for heaven's sake, use it!"

She took one of his hands and turned it palm up, planting a tiny kiss in the center. Everytime they had a discussion about her work, it ended with Lee insisting she go back to designing. But she wasn't ready. For the time being she was content with the mindless job she held. It was uncomplicated. She didn't have to make presentations, risk rejections. The only problem was that her job at Macy's gave her sore feet. That, she could contend with.

"Are you still with me?"

Reggie continued to muse, this time out loud. "I'm not unhappy at Macy's. If I were, I would do something about it, wouldn't I?" She pushed a strand of hair out of her eyes. "I would change jobs if I had a reason. But I don't. You do believe me, don't you?"

"Not for a second, my friend. I think you're hiding behind that ridiculous job because you are still frightened of failure.

The world should be shouting about your talent. Face it, my dear child, you are a coward."

"I am not!" Reggie laughed.

Lee watched her intently. "I say you are," he challenged.

"You would!" Reggie answered meaningfully. "That's a little like the pot calling the kettle black, wouldn't you say?"

He stared hard at her, his eyebrows raised. "What is that supposed to mean?" He had sobered considerably.

She flinched at her gaffe. "I'm so sorry. I didn't mean to say that. You are not a coward, I take it back."

"Don't take it back. You were right. I am a coward." A touch of irony was in his voice. "How long have you known?"

"That you were a coward?" Reggie asked, intentionally misunderstanding.

"Reggie . . ." he warned.

"Oh, *that*?" she said blithely. "I've known *that* almost from the first day we met." Then she corrected herself. "No, that's a lie. On the first day we met, I fantasized that I would be having a mad, passionate romance with you. Then I realized that . . . I was not your type." She paused to study Lee's face, which was registering a mixture of shock and amusement. "Anyway," she said, pointing to her feet which Lee had unconsciously begun to massage again, "I much prefer this."

"I see." Lee's arm slid gently around her seeking comfort, which she readily gave to him. Sliding her feet under her, she rested her head on his shoulder. "I wouldn't trade what I have with you for all the passionate love affairs in the world," she said with aching tenderness.

"Thank you, my friend," he said and gently kissed the top of her head. "Nor would I."

Glancing up, she saw the emotion in his eyes. "Lee, may I ask you something seriously?"

"Anything."

"Would you mind terribly getting up? My foot has fallen asleep."

Reggie adroitly jumped from the sofa in time to avoid the intended swat. Laughing gaily, she leaned toward Lee, offering her hand. "Truce?"

Lee grabbed her around the waist, pulling her down on his knee. "I ought to . . ." He stopped when he saw the merriment in her eyes. "No, I won't. That would give you another reason to continue your silly games." He stood up suddenly, sending Reggie falling to the floor. He helped her up. "Come on, child, let's go get some dinner. I have some important calls to make afterward." An idea had struck him and he was eager to see if he could put his thoughts into action. He took Reggie's elbow and guided her to the door.

Later that evening, Lee made the first of a series of phone calls designed to get Reggie out of Macy's and into a position that would offer the possibility of better hours and more money. He was searching for a job with a future, somewhere where she could use her talents even if she was not ready to step out on her own. After four lengthy phone conversations, he had lined up three interviews for her. She would balk, he knew, but he was convinced that with a little prodding, she could be persuaded to go on the interviews. The rest would be up to her.

Three weeks later, Reggie started her new job as assistant accessory buyer at Galaxy Department Stores. The chain had a fine reputation, if not a steady one, but rumor had it that the president was in the process of revamping Galaxy's image. Reggie liked the idea of being in on the ground floor of such a major overhaul. When it was explained to her Galaxy now wanted to compete with Bloomingdale's and Neiman-Marcus, she began to feel the first stirrings of interest. The job wasn't prestigious, but, she rationalized, it was better than standing on her feet all day selling cosmetics at Macy's. And the salary was almost double what she had been making for the past year.

Reggie fell in love that year. She positively glowed with it. In the tiny bathroom mirror of her apartment, her face reflected her radiant happiness. Often she found herself hugging herself with the pure joy of it. Alive again, after two years of standing in place and marking time, life had resumed and it was marvelous.

Strangely, it wasn't a new man in her life. It was her job that was responsible for her new-found happiness. Her spirits soared each day as she entered her office; it wasn't precisely an office, rather a part of a room, a desk to be exact. But it belonged to her and, as she slowly began to prove to her superiors that she had a flair for buying, more and more hopeful designers were directed to that tiny desk.

When Pinkie D'Angelo first walked into Reggie's tiny office with her beat-up gray leather duffel bag slung over her shoulder, Reggie barely acknowledged the chubby, fidgety belt designer. It was four thirty on a wet Friday afternoon, the end of a long, hectic week of inventory taking, and Reggie's mind was on a hot bubble bath, two aspirin and the last hundred pages of *Gone With the Wind*, which she was rereading for the fourth time. She had no appointments that day—nobody made any during the week of inventory, so Pinkie's arrival was not only unexpected—it was unwelcome. There were still mounds of papers stacked high on Reggie's small, cluttered desk that had to be reviewed before she could even think about going home that night.

"Excuse me," said Pinkie, nervously from the doorway. "Are you the accessory buyer?"

Reggie looked up, irritated at being disturbed. She had no idea who this person was, nor did she particularly care. Her head was throbbing, and all she wanted was to be left alone to finish her paper work. "No," she said curtly. "I'm the assistant buyer. Barbara DeVine is the buyer and she's gone for the day." Go away, she added to herself as she lowered her eyes to her papers again. Every bone in her body hurt from bending and lifting all week.

Pinkie cleared her throat. "Uh . . . mmm . . . do you think . . . would you mind looking at a line of belts?"

"You have to make an appointment to see the buyer. Her name is Barbara DeVine."

"I know. I've tried. I've been trying to get an appointment with her for three months but you see . . . I've never sold anything before and she won't see me."

The plea in Pinkie's voice was so reminiscent of Reggie's own voice the day she first met Nikki Broad that all the anguish of that experience came rushing back in one gigantic wave. Now it was Reggie who was sitting on the other side of the table, and it was she who had the power to make or break a designer. As tired as she was, she didn't have it in her to throw Pinkie D'Angelo out the door.

She got up and walked over to Pinkie, who was nervously chewing on her thumbnail. "I don't actually have much clout around here," she told the belt designer. "As I told you, I'm only the assistant buyer, but I *can* look at your stuff and make some recommendations to Barbara tomorrow or Monday."

That wasn't precisely true. As an assistant Galaxy buyer, she was given a small budget for buying. But, minuscule as it was, she hadn't spent it—she was waiting for the perfect item.

As Pinkie began to unpack her duffel, Reggie knew she had found it.

The strips of leather, heavily tooled untreated cowhide, were regulation cowboy fare, and Reggie had seen them in every pseudo-Western Greenwich Village head shop, paired with Harley-Davidson heavy brass buckles. But Pinkie had taken the two- and three-inch raw belts and, with an artist's eye, had handpainted simple flowers, birds and geometric patterns in luscious, novel colorations. She had dispensed with the expected browns, tans and rusts and had employed pale pastels, vibrant primaries and pearlized metallics, all complimented by buckles that were hand set with twenty-millimeter rhinestones in complimentary colors. The excruciating attention to detail was not lost on Reggie, who had designed her clothing line with the same painstaking patience.

". . . so after my trip to New Mexico, I thought I could translate the concept into a more contemporary, upbeat accessory," explained Pinkie.

"I'm sorry?" asked Reggie who hadn't been listening to one word of Pinkie's presentation. She didn't have to. She knew this was her chance. Hers and Pinkie's.

"I was saying that I saw some girls at a rodeo wearing them, you know—the cowboy belts—and I liked them. With jeans and calico blouses—"

"How about with mink coats and silk shirts?" Reggie was beginning to think out loud.

"What?" asked Pinkie.

"Anyone can wear them with jeans . . . in fact, I suspect they will. But it's the unexpected—pairing the belts with dressier sportswear . . ." The wheels were in motion as Reggie thought about how she would display this original accessory. "I'll take two dozen."

Pinkie's hands began to shake. "Two dozen? Two?" She couldn't believe her ears. "But I didn't even tell you the prices. They're expensive."

"How expensive?" asked Reggie, although it wouldn't have made any difference to her. The belts had no price to them since there wasn't anything on the market to compare them to. For the first time since she had been at Galaxy, *she* had discovered something she knew would be hot. As Reggie fingered the leather strips, the adrenaline started pumping. The whole accessory market—bags, belts and costume jewelry —needed a stiff shot in the arm, and Pinkie's line might just do it.

She felt an incredible surge of excitement, not unlike the feeling she had had when she first designed her own line. But she was going to share the glory with Pinkie. Not steal it, as Nikki Broad had done to her.

Two weeks after delivery, Pinkie's belts sold out. Reggie reordered, this time doubling the original order. A week later, the showcase was empty. Reggie called Pinkie again.

"Six dozen—we're going to the branch stores with it," Reggie told the pudgy designer. "And I need them in a week."

"I don't think I can paint that fast."

"Use your toes . . . or hire someone, Pinkie. You're hot now, not three weeks from now." Reggie knew the importance of timing. "Will you do it?"

"Yes. I just have to scrape together some money to buy the stones. They're expensive."

"How much do you need?" asked Reggie. When Pinkie told her, Reggie did something unheard of in retailing. She lent Pinkie the money.

"Why are you doing this?" asked Pinkie.

"It's in my best interest to sell as many of your belts as I can and . . ." She thought about Nikki. "Sometimes a young designer needs a hand."

Five dozen belts were sold in ten days. Suddenly, Barbara DeVine's star started to dim as Reggie's gained ascendency. Someone in the executive office whispered that the little assistant accessory buyer had "the eye." Reggie thought it was just plain dumb luck. She happened to have been in the office when Pinkie had walked in—Barbara DeVine hadn't.

But it kept happening. Lucite jewelry turned Reggie on. It left Barbara DeVine cold. So, once again, Reggie took a chance with her tiny budget and purchased six pieces of Caro Lama's line. Three art deco frosted Lucite pins, a choker of angular chunks of Lucite embedded with pearls and colored glass, a four-inch wide crystal cuff sprinkled liberally with gold and silver leaf, and an outrageous black Lucite and sterling silver belt that retailed for over two thousand dollars. Nobody in the department thought it would sell. It did. Not only did it sell, but there was a heated argument over the costly piece, which sent Reggie running to the phone to call Caro Lama.

"I need another black and silver belt," Reggie said, fully expecting the piece to arrive the next day.

To her surprise, Caro refused. "I never duplicate anything. Each piece is a signed original . . . one of a kind. I'm awfully sorry."

Reggie couldn't believe that she was going to lose the sale, but the designer remained adamant. When she hung up the phone, she was furious, especially when Barbara DeVine began to needle her.

"That's precisely why I don't deal with these 'artsy' types, Reggie. You get one good consignment and then"—she snapped her fingers—"they disappear. You'll do much better if you stick to tried and true resources."

"But," Reggie argued, "everything on the market is so boring!"

"It may be boring, but we get delivery. This is a department store, Reggie. Not an art gallery." So much for the "innovative" assistant buyer.

If Barbara had thought she had put Reggie in her place, she was sadly mistaken. The words *art gallery* stuck firmly in her mind, and that night Reggie went home with a broad smile on her face and her sketch pad tucked firmly under her arm. Late into the night she worked on a new retailing concept. In the morning, she marched into the executive offices to present her plan.

"Galerie Galaxy" was Reggie Gates's baby. Four display cases and a wall. That was all she needed, and they gave it to her when they saw her presentation and reviewed her outstanding buying record. As the mirror men, lighting contractors and display people went busily to work, Galaxy was buzzing with the news of the exciting new department that would carry only original, one-of-a-kind accessories—"art-to-wear" signed and numbered by the artists and craftsmen who were beating a furious path to her desk as word got out.

As Reggie's reputation and buying budget soared, Barbara DeVine became more and more furious. For fifteen years she had been successfully handling the accessory department in Galaxy. Suddenly, with the appearance of this Reggie Gates, she was becoming a nonentity. But it was the decision to give "Galerie Galaxy" the Christmas window that finally pushed Barbara over the edge. In a fit of pique, she quit, and it took exactly two hours for the powers that be to name Reggie Gates as her successor. She raced home to tell Lee the remarkable news.

"Phenomenal!" he said, giving her a congratulatory hug. "Reg, I couldn't be happier for you." That wasn't exactly true. He was thrilled that her new career was taking off, but he knew that designing was still her first love and that she continued to push it to the background. Every time he spoke to her, he asked if she was designing, and each time she successfully changed the subject. He tried again. "You're going to be busier than ever now. What about your own line? Your designing? Are you doing anything with it?" he asked wishfully.

"A little," she admitted.

"And?"

"First let me accumulate some money. Then I'll be able to think about it more seriously. I'm beginning to understand how nice it is to be able to eat out once in a while or buy a sweater now and then. I don't think I'm ready to starve again." In the last year, money hadn't been much of a problem. She was comfortable. She knew that giving up her job at Galaxy for designing would mean no money coming in for a while, and the idea terrified her.

"Would you let me lend you the money you need to get started again?" He already knew that she would refuse. She was so damned proud.

As he suspected, she said no. "When I'm really ready, when the time is right—I'll let you know."

"Okay, brat, but remember that I'm always here for you if you need me," he reminded her.

"You don't have to tell me that. That's the one constant I have: our friendship and your faith in me."

They chatted for a few more minutes then Lee asked, "What about dating? Are you seeing anyone?"

"Who has time?" she laughed. Since David, men were lowest on her list of priorities. The few dates she had accepted had bored her, and she had opted happily for evenings at home, reading or sewing. She simply wasn't interested in inane conversation or casual sex. Reggie tried to explain that to Lee who was forever pushing her to meet men.

"I do understand," he said. "But are you certain that you're not hiding behind this facade of indifference because you're still afraid of being hurt? Not all men are like your former boyfriend. If you stay home every night, you'll never meet anyone," he warned.

"I don't care. I swear I don't. Right now, I'm perfectly content running 'Galerie.'"

"Right now is not forever! For heaven's sake, Reg, you're only twenty years old. Don't you think that's too young to give up on men?"

She laughed. "I haven't taken any vows yet. When I'm ready to enter the convent, you'll be the first to know. There is no one around who holds my interest as much as my job," she told him.

"There will be, someday," he assured her with certainty.

Reggie changed the subject, unwilling to pursue the line of conversation any longer.

They spoke for a few more minutes, gossiping about mutual friends, and then made a dinner date for a week later. Since Reggie had started at Galaxy, they hadn't been able to spend much time together, and both missed each other's company.

"Don't cancel again," Lee warned.

"I won't," she promised and showered him with friendly kisses to apologize for the three broken dinner dates of the past two months.

She was able to keep that one date with Lee, but after that, her time was completely taken up by her job. Her career exploded as she was asked to open more and more "Galeries" in Galaxy's branch stores. The workload was enormous but so were the benefits. Little by little her bank balance grew—and so did her prestige.

After four quick and exciting years with Galaxy, she was

promoted to executive buyer and moved from accessories to sportswear with the hope that she could do to the ailing sportswear department what she had accomplished in accessories. She had climbed as high as she could within the Galaxy hierarchy. Now she was twenty-four, very successful and very, very bored. She knew without a doubt that she could increase sales in sportswear by finding the right resources, but somehow the prospect had ceased to excite her. Suddenly she knew why. Galaxy didn't belong to her. She was tired of working for somebody else.

In May, a month before her twenty-fifth birthday, she handed in her resignation. She had made her decision to go back to designing.

Reggie spent three weeks trudging through SoHo, TriBeCa and Chelsea looking for a small loft. If it hadn't been for Lee's connections, she never would have found the sunny, large space on Broome Street. It was perfect. Lee was horrified when Reggie informed him that she intended to live and work there. On Houston Street, browsing through the used equipment stores, Reggie located all the machinery she needed. When everything was in place, and the first bolts of fabric arrived, Rag's Raggs, the name she had chosen for her new company, was born.

The first pieces of her line were cut and sewn without help. She was bursting with design ideas that had lain dormant during the Galaxy years, and she worked quickly, as if waking from a deep, nourishing sleep. With trepidation, she contacted the new sportswear designer at Galaxy, her replacement. An order was placed, and two weeks later she was called for a reorder.

Her capacity for work astounded her. Slowly, as word got out, her business grew to the point where she could no longer handle designing, sewing, cutting and her books alone. Inundated by orders that were beginning to frighten her, she thought about hiring someone to take some of the load off her shoulders; someone who understood fashion, who was trustworthy and, most importantly, who she could depend on. It hit her immediately. Alison Granger! The two women had stayed in touch over the years. Reggie knew that Alison's life in Kansas, although safe and secure, was boring her friend to death. She yearned to return to New York but hadn't come up with a job or the money to make the move.

Reggie called Alison that night and made her an offer.

"I can't pay much to start," explained Reggie, "but I know in two or three months things are going to take off like crazy around here when I become a little more liquid. What do you say?"

"Are you kidding?" Alison answered without any hesitation. "If I can eat and pay the rent, you've got me!"

She was on the plane two weeks later.

Shortly thereafter, Reggie hired two sewers, a pattern maker and a cutter. Her overhead increased four-fold. Suddenly, she realized with dismay that her flourishing company had depleted her finances. Reluctantly turning to Lee, she asked for advice.

Lee spent an entire evening reviewing her orders, accounts receivable and accounts payable. When he had finished scrutinizing her books, his face was grim. "Reggie," he said, "what you need is a great deal of capital, fast. You don't have enough money to carry you through this month."

Reggie looked at him in alarm. "Can you get me a bank loan?" she asked wishfully.

He shook his head. "Your company is too new. No bank that I work with will go along with you." He chewed on the back of his pencil, deep in thought. Suddenly, an enigmatic smile softened his stern expression. "I have another idea. It's a long shot, but it may work." He was thinking about his friend and partner, Cole Weston. "I'm taking these papers with me." He gestured to the dining room table. "I'll speak to you in a day or two. We may be able to get you a loan after all."

Chapter 10

Cole's head ached dully. He sat at his desk, frowning slightly as he tried to erase the memory of last evening's bitter argument with his mistress. Yes, he conceded silently, he was all the things that Evyan had charged him with: indifferent, aloof, uninvolved. But, he rationalized, he had never pretended otherwise. Why now, after a year, had she suddenly awakened to the realization with such anger? He closed his eyes, trying to blot out the look of undisguised hatred on her face when he told her that he wasn't planning to marry her. He flinched, feeling again the sting of her hand against his cheek. What right did she have to be so enraged?

Women! he thought bitterly, stretching his long legs in front of him and running his hand through his thick black hair in frustration. Every damn time he thought he had found a woman who understood, who wanted the same things from a relationship that he did, he was sorely disappointed. It always boiled down to the same thing. Commitment and love. Neither emotion had any place in his life. He was far too busy.

At forty-two, Cole Weston controlled an empire that included oil wells, real estate and major holdings in thirty-five public companies. He had his hand in everything from computer manufacturing to a chain of Midwest pizza parlors. But to describe him merely as the sum of his balance sheets would be a gross injustice. He was much, much more.

In an age which boasted few self-made men, the breed having died out with the advent of income taxes, Cole was often compared to Andrew Carnegie and J. P. Morgan. True, he had had the advantage of a first-rate financial education, but that was possible only because he waited tables and tended bar at Philadelphia's finest restaurants to pay his tuition. Starting as a novice in an environment of purebred moneyed contemporaries, Cole had to overcome the closed doors and tight-knit prep-school clannishness of the financial world.

Though he graduated with honors from the Wharton School of Finance and held the same degree as his classmates, the business world still viewed him as an interloper in their sphere. He didn't belong, and he knew it.

With the front doors locked to him because he hadn't competed on the playing fields of Andover or Choate, Cole became a wildcatter. With his last few hundred dollars, he worked with a chemist classmate from NYU who was trying to develop a process to separate the "slops"—the oil and water emulsion that was found in the bowels of the huge supertankers after they unloaded. In a world that demanded more and more oil, there was a fortune to be made for the man who had the foresight and the knowledge to discover and develop a way to cheaply and efficiently utilize this sludge. Dumping, soon to be illegal, whether it was in the harbor or far out at sea, was the only method employed for discharging this mixture. Cole and his associate found an alternative. The fuel-hungry world would soon pay them handsomely for the process.

Above all else, Cole loved the action of the financial world. He screened every friend, every acquaintance and every partner as a new source of contact with other industries. He thrived on difficult, challenging projects but was astute enough to hire experts in unfamiliar fields. It was the job of these men to study the industries and to advise him.

People who dealt with Cole Weston praised him for being unfailingly honest, straightforward and aboveboard. His greatest strength lay in his integrity. There were times when his candor and outspokenness squashed a deal, but that merely developed his reputation as a man of his word.

His projects were varied, and he often took stock or a percentage of a venture, rather than cash, constantly building his portfolio. He always followed his own instincts. When silver and gold were soaring, he bought modestly, selling when the market was still on the upswing, but not at the peak. He didn't make a killing, nor did he get wiped out when the bottom fell out.

Slowly, quietly, he began to build his barony. In the field of finance his name wasn't shouted, it was whispered. He preferred it that way. His privacy was jealously and fiercely protected.

Only two men knew the true breadth of his holdings. One

was Francis Munsey, the sharp-witted, brilliant Chicago attorney who had befriended Cole many years before and who had served as combination mentor and surrogate father to the youthful financial wizard. The other man privy to Cole's life, both on a personal and financial level, was his best friend and business associate, Lee Taggett.

A year ahead of Cole at Wharton, Lee had watched Cole very carefully, noting his brilliance. Even at school, where Cole had begun to dabble in the stock market, he had the uncanny ability to choose stocks that skyrocketed. The two young men admired each other, forming a friendship based on mutual respect and approval. While Lee spent the three years after graduation attending Harvard Law School, Cole began to build his empire. When Lee graduated, Cole asked him to join WestCo as legal counsel. The thought appealed to Lee. He didn't want to waste his talents in the back room of a Wall Street law firm. Cole offered Lee a starting salary ten times that which he would have received as a legal associate. Cole also gave him a handsome percentage of WestCo.

Lee's attention to detail and fastidiousness became Cole's lifeline. It was Lee who sorted through the desks, pockets and wastebaskets every day, trying to retrieve and make sense of Cole's scribbles on the backs of envelopes and crumbled pieces of paper. Lee soon became an indispensable part of WestCo and, with his increasing bank account, a fierce loyalty to his partner developed. Both men benefited monetarily from the partnership, but more importantly, each was rewarded with the other's friendship, a commodity they cherished as much as their business arrangement.

On a cold, stormy day, Lee knocked on Cole's office door. "Come in," boomed Cole's deep voice from the other side of the door. Lee stepped into the quiet gray flannel office. Cole was sitting with his long legs up on his desk, studying a financial report.

"Something interesting?" Lee asked, joining him on the other side of the desk.

Cole whipped his head around. "Stop looking over my shoulder," he growled. His dark eyes scanned Lee's smiling face. "To what do I owe the pleasure of your company on this dreadful day?" he asked dryly.

"Are you interested in making some money today?" Lee asked enigmatically as he strolled over to the well-stocked bar that Cole kept concealed behind a set of leather-bound books. He poured himself a scotch and soda in a Steuben highball glass. Casually, he leaned his hip on the bar, sipping the drink.

Cole stifled a yawn. He had not recovered from the all-night fiasco with Evyan. "What have you got?" he asked.

"Am I boring you?" Lee asked good-naturedly, sinking into an overstuffed leather armchair. Kicking off his shoes, he put his blue-and-gray-argyled feet up on Cole's enormous desk. With his toe, he pushed aside a pile of papers.

"Comfortable?" inquired Cole, the merest hint of a twinkle in his eye.

"Almost." Lee pulled a pipe from his blazer pocket and filled it from a Dunhill tobacco pouch. Cole chuckled as he watched Lee try unsuccessfully to light the pipe with a gold lighter. After several attempts, Cole leaned over and handed him a match. "Try this," he suggested derisively. Lee lit the pipe. "Ready, now?" Cole asked.

Lee nodded. "Now I'm comfortable."

"You're sure you don't want a pillow or an afghan?" Cole paused. "How about a snack?" He grinned with amusement.

"No, thanks, I'm fine."

"Good. Now what's this about making money today?" Cole queried.

Lee raised his head. "Did you ever hear of Rag's Raggs?"

"No . . . should I have?" Cole asked.

"Yes and no."

Cole pursed his lips in concentration. "Good answer, Lee. Fine answer, as a matter of fact. Yes and no. Says it all, doesn't it?" He started to get out of his chair.

"Sit down," Lee said exasperatedly, then went on to explain. "Rag's Raggs is a small sportswear manufacturer that happens to be very hot right now. It's getting a lot of press from the high-fashion magazines and all the trade papers. Its owner, Regina Anne Gates, hence the acronym, Rag's—"

"Clever," Cole interjected caustically.

Lee ignored him and continued. "—has hit upon a very interesting garment phenomena. She discovered that suburban women and teenagers want to be comfortable as well as fashionable. More and more of them have started parading around in sweat pants."

"The things I throw on after tennis?" inquired Cole.

"Exactly!"

"Oh, that must be very attractive!" Cole said distastefully.

"That was the problem," Lee pointed out. "In an effort to make them more attractive, women decorated them. The garments were cut, appliquéd, painted, shortened, even turned upside down, and although they were improved, sweat clothes were still better suited to health clubs than the street." He paused in his explanation to see if Cole was paying attention. Cole's eyes were half-closed slits. Lee wasn't sure he was awake.

"Go on, I'm listening," Cole assured him.

"Reggie—"

"Who?" asked Cole.

"Regina Anne Gates—Reggie," Lee explained.

"I thought her name was Raggy."

"No, the company's name is . . . will you please shut up!" Lee implored.

"Certainly." Cole yawned again.

"Reggie, who also prefers comfort—"

"She probably weighs three hundred pounds and can't fit into anything else except sweat suits."

Lee chuckled, thinking of Reggie's hard, slim body with her tight little derrière and high jaunty breasts. He smiled. "Not quite three hundred pounds, yet." He sipped his scotch. "Anyway, Reggie took a long hard look at the phenomena and developed a fabulous concept for leisure clothes. She used the basic lines and styles of sweat-shirting and transferred them into attractive sportswear. Working with an engineer and a textile expert, she developed a computerized loom that can weave a totally new fabric which she uses for these clothes." He paused to see if he still had Cole's interest, ambivalent though it was.

"I'm still listening, dammit! Get on with it," sighed Cole.

"After she patented the machine, and that's very important to the story"—Lee saw Cole's ears perk up—"she designed a line of sportswear that was flattering to large women—"

"I knew it!" interrupted Cole with a look of sorely strained patience.

Lee barged ahead. "—as well as young girls. Her colors are crisp and clean, the lines of the clothing are easy to wear and, best of all, the stuff washes like a dream and wears like iron."

Cole couldn't control himself any longer. He burst out laughing. "That sounds like a commercial. Where's the jingle?" he asked when he had caught his breath.

"Listen, you pompous ass. Laugh all you want but this fabric has the entire garment industry sitting up. *Vogue* did an eight-page spread on it. They featured Brooke Shields wearing these clothes at an al fresco breakfast, at a garden party for two hundred guests and at a dinner at the Palace. Brooke wore a sexier version of it in a little scene in front of her fireplace. *Teen* magazine photographed ingenues in it on the way to college, and *Good Housekeeping* had six mother-daughter combinations cooking Thanksgiving dinner in Rag's Raggs."

Cole sat up lazily. "It sounds like the company is doing very nicely without us."

Lee shook his head. "It should be. But Reggie's new at business and has made a very costly error. She needs help to bail her out."

"What kind of error?" Cole asked, although he was rapidly losing interest in the whole subject. He had no desire to get involved in a penny-ante business. He was too involved with a half-billion dollar sports complex, an apartment development and a mall in Chicago.

"Cole, am I boring you?" Lee asked, annoyed at Cole's lack of enthusiasm.

"Frankly, yes. But finish the story. What kind of error did she make?"

"You're familiar with Galaxy, aren't you?" asked Lee.

"I don't want to appear uninformed," said Cole, "but don't we own Galaxy?"

"Now we do," Lee answered. "The bulk of shares were originally held by Simon Hastings who started the company. He took it public, made a fortune, then decided he wanted to buy back all the outstanding shares. He was able to buy back some, but we maintain a majority stock position."

"Go on, but for God's sake, Lee, hurry it up. I have a haircut in twenty minutes."

"About a year and a half ago, Claire Connors, one of the assistants to the president of Henri Bendel left her job and approached Simon about copying Bendel's 'street of shops' idea. They are really tiny little boutiques that line the ground floor of the store. Apparently she and Simon hit it off, he liked her idea and gave her carte blanche. The rest is history. She's been very successful. Galaxy's name is on every other page of the important trade news. Women are lining up waiting to get in."

"Women are fools," Cole concluded simply. Briefly his thoughts returned to the way he and Evyan had parted. He'd send her a trinket from Buccelati. That ought to soothe her bruised vanity. "Where does Raggedy Raggs come in?"

Lee winced at Cole's intentional mistake. "Cole, please!"

"Sorry, I couldn't help myself."

"Three months ago," Lee continued, "Claire Connors came to Reggie with orders for each of the five Galaxy stores. She also offered Reggie the opportunity that every designer dreams of, her own boutique in each store. Reggie leaped at the chance. The catch was—"

"Don't tell me," Cole interrupted. "The catch was . . . 'I'll order X dollars of merchandise with a written order and you match it on consignment, of course.'" He looked at Lee smugly. "Am I close?"

Lee nodded, startled once again at Cole's perspectiveness. "That's exactly what happened."

Cole looked disgusted. "How could any businesswoman be so stupid? Where was her legal counsel?"

Lee muttered something unintelligible.

"Speak up! Didn't she have legal advice?" Cole repeated.

"Yes!" Lee admitted finally. "But her lawyer happened to be busy at the time. She went ahead on her own and wrote orders for five hundred thousand dollars and promised the same amount of clothing on consignment."

Cole couldn't believe the woman's stupidity. "She doesn't belong in business," he said scathingly. "How does she expect to finance this fiasco? He sat upright, suddenly suspicious. "Lee?"

Lee was quick to come to Reggie's defense. "The whole deal would have worked if Galaxy had paid for the first shipment on time. That would have given Reggie enough working capital. However, Galaxy's payment is sixty days late. The second order is half cut, but Reggie has run out of money. She needs two million dollars."

"I'm not surprised," Cole said dryly. "She sounds like a very poor businesswoman."

"God dammit, Cole, she's not. She's just inexperienced," he finished lamely. It was difficult to admit that Reggie's strong suit was not finance. When she had told Lee of the commitment she had made, he had been horrified.

Patiently, though clearly trying very hard to remain so, Cole asked once again, "And where was her legal counsel while all this was happening?"

"Sitting here in front of you with egg on his face," Lee admitted finally. "She is a very dear friend—"

"I don't care if she's the President's mistress. How could you mix business and—"

"It's not anything like that!" Lee countered angrily. "Reggie and I have been friends for years. She's like a sister to me. You'll be very surprised when you meet her."

"Who says I have any intention of meeting her?" Cole asked.

"Can it, Cole! Since when have you ever turned down the opportunity to meet an interesting woman?" Lee asked, a slight smile on his face.

Thoughtfully, Cole drummed his fingers on his desk. "Interesting? You mean 'not beautiful,' I presume? No, thank you, my dear friend. Find a benefactor for your friend elsewhere. Better yet, send her to a bank or a factor."

"You know a bank won't give her that large a sum. She needs a private investor," Lee insisted.

"Does she have a decent credit rating? Collateral? Anything that would give me a chance to recoup if she goes under?" Cole snapped impatiently.

"She's got her factory, a co-op loft, and she also holds the only patent for the computer loom," Lee answered.

"And you want me to lend her two million dollars with *that* as collateral. Why?" Cole asked.

Because you are perfect for each other, and I can't think of any other way to bring you together, were the words that suddenly were on the tip of Lee's tongue. Instead, he said, "Because she is red-hot now, and you stand to make a great deal of money if you back her."

Cole sat back in his chair and took a small black cigar from the box on his desk. He smoked in silence for a few moments. Abruptly, he straightened in his chair. "Lee, I'll meet with her, although I have a healthy dislike for the garment industry and especially designers. More than a preliminary meeting, I won't promise. Get her in here in the next two weeks with all her financial statements, her accountant and her lawyer."

Lee grinned contritely. "I am her lawyer."

Cole stubbed out his cigar and leaned over his desk, his black eyes glinting like steel. "That's not possible, Lee," he said in a deadly serious tone. "You have a serious conflict of interests, here. You can't represent both Raggedy Rags and WestCo, and you know it."

"All right, all right. I'll get her another attorney. Does John Moran meet with your approval?"

Cole stood up. "I don't care who it is as long as it isn't you." He started to walk away from his desk. "I'll be leaving this afternoon for my cabin in Old Forge. As soon as those papers are ready I'll review them. Can I interest you in any ice fishing or skiing? The lake had two feet of solid ice, and it's supposed to snow tomorrow."

"No, thanks," Lee said, shaking his head. "Do you know that Old Forge is the coldest spot on the map today? How can you stand it up there?"

"Frankly, the question should be turned around to 'how can I stand it here?'" Cole gestured to the view of Manhattan from the fiftieth-floor window. "In the Adirondacks, I am simply Cole Weston, fisherman and hunter."

"Okay, sportsman," Lee said with a wicked smile. "In that case, you go fishing and I'll get to work on the papers."

Chapter 11

Two weeks later, on a Monday morning, Reggie dressed with extreme care in a simply cut black turtleneck dress from her new holiday line. She loved the feel of the slim tube dress against her lean body and the thick cables that molded to her curves. The dress was a masterpiece in simplicity; understated, yet elegant. She added a strand of chunky fresh-water pearls, large black Lucite earrings and a pair of black lizard boots. When she had finished dressing, she examined herself critically in the full-length mirror and nodded to her reflection. No one meeting this calm, implacable, self-assured businesswoman would detect the hammering of her heart. She had successfully hidden her nervousness.

A slow, secret smile worked its way across her face. Today was the most important day of her life, and she was more than ready to face its challenge. Cole Weston was about to lend her two million dollars. With that one check tucked firmly in her grasp, her future was virtually unlimited. One last look in the mirror and Reggie was ready. She picked up a black alligator attaché case, which completed the desired look of affluence. Then, with her black wool coat swinging jauntily from her shoulders, she left the apartment.

When Reggie arrived at WestCo, she was ushered into a private conference room where her cousin and accountant, Sam Kroy, and her new attorney, John Moran, were already waiting. Reggie didn't care for Moran. She found him pompous, showy and immensely impressed with himself.

A large silver coffee urn had been set out on one of the side tables with plates of freshly baked muffins and buttery croissants. Sam stepped forward to greet her. "Good morning, Reggie. Did you finish going over all the papers?"

She shrugged out of her coat, nodding, then turned to pour herself a much-needed cup of coffee. Her eyes roved appreciatively over the sideboard that was laden with large white china coffee cups, heavy Georgian silverware and crisp linen napkins. She compared this to the business meetings that she held, sitting crosslegged on the floor of her loft, surrounded by plastic foam cups, greasy brown bags and paper napkins. Her hands trembled slightly as she poured cream into the cup, sloshing the coffee over the rim. Surreptitiously, she glanced over her shoulder before she mopped the spill with a napkin. She rolled the linen in a ball and tucked it behind the urn.

Steady, she warned herself as she took the first tentative sip of the scalding brew. Balancing the cup carefully, she eased herself into a chair facing Sam. "I reviewed the papers, Sam, but I can't honestly tell you that I completely understood everything I read. By the time I reached the fourteenth page, I gave up." She turned her wide green eyes to Moran. "Are you and Mr. Kroy satisfied with this deal?"

Sam looked at Moran who merely lifted his eyebrows. Neither man understood why Cole Weston would want to invest anything in such a small, unknown company. They had been over it many times in the past two weeks and it still remained a mystery. The mere fact that Cole had scheduled this meeting surprised them.

Reggie noticed the perplexity on their faces, and her heart began that dreadful thudding again. "What is it, Sam? Did I miss something?" she asked impatiently. Her eyes flicked over to John Moran. "Mr. Moran, have you reviewed the papers?"

"Yes, Miss Gates. Several times."

"Did you find anything wrong?" she asked, apprehensively.

Moran cleared his throat and straightened his tie. "I think Mr. Weston's requests are quite reasonable given the amount of financing involved. You realize you could never get that much money if you applied to a bank for a more conventional loan."

Lee had informed her of the same thing. "So I've been told."

"No bank will lend you the amount of money you need without a credit rating. Since this is the first time you've borrowed money, you haven't established a rating yet. You *do* understand this, don't you?" asked Moran, as if he were speaking to a small child.

Eyes blazing, Reggie turned to the attorney. "Listen," she

said through clenched teeth, "I may be inexperienced with the banking world, but I'm not an idiot, and I resent your treating me like one. If there's something you want to explain to me, then please do so."

Moran looked at her icily. "Quite frankly, Miss Gates, neither Mr. Kroy nor I understand why an astute businessman like Mr. Weston would even entertain the idea of lending you two million dollars. It doesn't make sense to either one of us."

Reggie's head whipped around to face Sam. "Why is that?"

Sam stared at the glinting green eyes. "If you can get this money, Reggie, it will be miraculous even with Weston's demand of interest at the rate of two percent over prime. Everything in this deal, the entire way it has been structured, works to your advantage. Even if you were to default on the loan, I can't see how Mr. Weston could recover his losses." He concluded, "I would like you to go over the contract one more time. Perhaps you will see something that John or I missed." He handed Reggie the thick stack of papers.

"If you insist." The room was silent except for the occasional clink of a coffee cup. Reggie was too embarrassed to admit to these men that the whole contract was a mass of legal mumbo-jumbo. The whereas and therefores baffled her. All she wanted to do was sign the damned thing and get her money. When she neared the end of the contract, in the very last paragraph before the space where the "party of the first part" and "party of the second part" were to sign their names, Reggie realized with sudden clarity exactly how Cole Weston intended to secure his loan. Her tenuous hold on her temper snapped and she turned angrily to her accountant and attorney. "How the hell do you explain that neither one of you mentioned this clause about the patent?"

"What about the patent, Miss Gates?" Moran asked coldly.

Raking him with a furious look, she said, "Do you realize that you offered ownership of my loom patent should I fail to repay this loan in six months?"

"Of course, I realize that!" Moran said irritably. "Did you think Weston would walk away with your car and a few sewing machines? Grow up, young lady!"

"Let me tell you something, Mr. Moran," she said so quietly that the attorney had to strain to hear, "you have no idea what this patent is worth. Within five years, this country is going to put a quota on the amount of imported textiles. It *has* to in order to protect domestic manufacturers. When that happens, my computerized loom and its prototypes will provide the fabric to replace the banned imports. You don't believe me, do you?" she asked, noticing the skeptical look on Moran's face.

Reggie opened her attaché case and withdrew two letters, waving them in the air. "Take these, Mr. Moran. These are letters of inquiry from Burlington Mills and DuPont about the possible purchase of my patent rights." She waited until Moran looked at the papers. "There is nothing else like it on the market. Don't you understand that the patent is my insurance policy in this business? I may have a good year or two as a designer and never come up with a line again. But the loom . . . the loom is going to be used for decades." She carefully folded the letters and put them back in her case before she stared, steely-eyed, at Moran. "Do you honestly think I would part with this for a loan of two million dollars? I may look naive, but I've learned something since I've been in this business."

Moran looked at Sam Kroy helplessly. "You talk to her, Sam. Maybe she'll listen to you."

Sam smiled. Since he had known Reggie as a child, she had never taken advice from anyone, but he would try. He put a fatherly arm around her shoulders. "Reggie, are you prepared to blow this deal and tell Mr. Weston you won't give him the patent as collateral? Without it, he'll never go ahead." He recognized the determined look in Reggie's eye, the firm set of her chin, all familiar signs that she had no intention of listening. He tried again. "Do you know how much interest he is going to lose by lending you this money at the ridiculous rate that Mr. Taggett worked out?"

Reggie shrugged her shoulders. "That's his problem, isn't it?" she asked, raising her graceful eyebrows. When neither man answered, Reggie stood up impatiently. "Are you two coming into this meeting with me, or am I going to do my own negotiating?"

Against his better judgment, Sam agreed to sit in on the meeting, but as much as Reggie tried, Moran refused to be convinced. He didn't like this brazen girl-woman who thought she could outsmart one of the country's foremost financial wizards. And he didn't want his name associated with her failure. "I'm sorry, Miss Gates, but when Mr. Taggett asked me to attend this meeting it was with the understanding that it was to be a mere formality. Everything was supposed to be in order before today. Now I see that this is not so. I don't have time today for lengthy negotiations. If you want to postpone for a month or two, perhaps I will be able to find time to accommodate you. Today, however, is out of the question. I have to be in court." He gathered his papers, placed them methodically in his briefcase and waited impatiently for Reggie's answer.

"Mr. Moran," Reggie said, trying to hold her temper in check, "my company just might fold long before you have time to 'accommodate' me." Caustically, she added, "Please send me a bill for your 'valuable' time." She turned her back on him as he walked to the door.

A moment later there was a knock on the door. It swung open to reveal a well dressed, older woman. "Miss Gates, Mr. Kroy"—she gestured to a door across the hall—"Mr. Weston is ready to see you."

Reggie picked up her attaché case and casually looped her arm through Sam's. "Are you with me?" she asked hopefully.

Sam Kroy wished he were anywhere else on the face of the earth. Dreading the debacle to follow, he picked up his briefcase and followed her through the open door. "I'm with you, Reggie. I'm not happy, but I'm with you."

"I knew I could count on you," she said. "I just wish Lee were here, too."

Reggie had just echoed Sam Kroy's thoughts.

Cole stood looking out the window. Dark storm clouds were gathering in the sky over Manhattan, sending a shadow of gloom over his office. He wondered what drove him back to this pollution every Monday after the beauty and pristine silence of the Adirondacks. It certainly wasn't money. He had more than he could ever hope to spend in two lifetimes. That left the challenge, the quest, the desire to outwit his opponents. He sighed. He wasn't entirely certain that he enjoyed doing that anymore. Lately, no matter how exciting the business deal, he found that it was becoming more and more difficult to return from the mountains every week. He turned away from the window in disgust. Now, he had to meet with Lee's little fat friend. He was sorry he had been talked into it. It was an annoyance.

He heard the soft knock on his door. "Come in!" he barked.

"Don't you roar at me," his secretary warned. Now it was her turn to glare at him. After working for Cole Weston for eighteen years, Marjory was no longer afraid of him.

Cole smiled. "Okay, okay. Are they ready?"

"Yes, sir. Shall I have them come in?" she asked.

"Unless you think I can conduct this meeting through the intercom system."

Moments later, Marjory returned. "Mr. Weston, Miss Gates and Mr. Kroy are here to see you."

He looked past his secretary at the young woman standing in the doorway, inspecting her with unconcealed admiration. A slow, disbelieving smile swept over his face as he regarded her. How very like Lee, he thought, to lead him to believe that he was meeting an overweight, aggressive female. Instead, a woman of vivid beauty faced him. Smoky umber eyelashes framed unusually eloquent eyes that alternated between aquamarine and emerald. Her body was slim, with graceful curves. Glossy auburn hair accentuated the finely chiseled features, high cheekbones and a sensual mouth.

Standing just inside the door, with her imperturbable green eyes fixed on him in an icy stare, she betrayed none of the uneasiness she felt. For a moment their eyes met and held. Reggie raised her chin, conscious of the sudden thudding of her heart. Insolently, his dark eyes left her face and made their way slowly down her body, missing nothing. He smiled in surprise. She was utterly magnificent. Under the guise of offering her a seat, he continued to study her as her agile form moved across the room. Lithe body and impossibly long legs melted into the chair. The morning's grayness had vanished; this meeting had suddenly become more than interesting.

Reggie suppressed the urge to flee and the perverse desire to shatter Cole's complacency. She casually crossed her legs as she took the proffered seat. She lifted her head, deeply disquieted by the glint in his eyes, to find him still staring at her. With the merest hint of movement, he signaled his approval.

Embarrassed, she quickly turned her head away, the task of trying to concentrate now was formidable. Suddenly it dawned on Reggie that this was what he had intended. A frown marred her smooth forehead as she realized he had succeeded in making her uncomfortable. Mentally, she shook herself and boldly returned his stare. She asked in an icy voice, "Can we begin?"

"I rather thought we had," he said softly as if they were the only people in the room.

She tried to ignore him. Sitting as solemnly as possible, with her hands now folded decorously in her lap, she appeared calm and unruffled. She waited patiently for him to get down to business.

But it was not business that Cole was thinking of at that moment. The faintest glimmer of an idea was taking shape inside his head, an idea, so bizarre, so outrageous, that had Reggie suspected what it was, she would have fled from the office.

"E-hem," Sam Kroy broke in. "Mr. Weston, we have reviewed the contract."

"Miss Gates," Cole asked pointedly, "have you studied the proposal?"

"Yes, I have," Reggie answered coolly.

"I assume you understand everything."

She inclined her head. "I understand everything—perfectly!"

"If everything is in order, shall we proceed?"

Reggie's eyes narrowed. "Mr. Weston, I understand everything in the contract, but there is one clause that I insist be deleted."

He arched his eyebrows in surprise. "Which clause would that be?" His scorching black eyes never left her face, but she sat determined and unflinching.

"I don't care to pledge my rights to the patent as part of the collateral," she said emphatically.

He scowled. Nervously, Reggie waited. "You don't care to pledge your patent rights . . . is that correct?" he asked.

"That's correct. I informed Mr. Taggett that I would like to secure this loan with my co-op, car, fixtures, factory, inventory, etc., but not the patent."

Turning to the accountant, Cole asked, "Kroy, did you know about this?"

"I just found out, Mr. Weston," Sam said apologetically.

"Well, Miss Gates," Cole admitted ruefully, after a long pause, "if nothing else, I admire your audacity."

Reggie opened her mouth to retort. Quickly, Sam coughed behind his hand in an effort to stop her.

Cole whipped around and gave him a menacing look. He turned back to Reggie. "Somehow, you have managed to make some kind of name for yourself in the fashion industry." He noticed Reggie bristle at the implied slur. "But frankly," he continued, unconcerned, "women are fickle. Fashions change. A designer is only as good as her last successful line. I could not, in good conscience, lend you two million dollars unless you include the patent rights. Your business doesn't warrant—"

"Then, why—?" Reggie was trying to contain her mounting alarm.

"The patent," he stated simply. "You have developed a highly marketable piece of machinery that you were bright enough to protect with a patent. The rights to that patent are the only valuable assets that you have."

Enraged, Reggie pushed herself out of the chair. "Mr. Weston, I am not interested in discussing the patent—period! I believe that we have reached the end of our negotiations." She picked up her attaché case and headed for the door.

"You know, Miss Gates," he drawled casually to her back, "you would make a poor poker player."

She whirled around to face him, but before she could say anything, he said emphatically, "Never try to manipulate me, Miss Gates. We both know that you are out of aces. The moment you walk through that door without my money, Rag's Raggs will fold."

"Things are not quite that serious, Mr. Weston," she replied with an assurance she was far from feeling.

He sighed. "I see that you are determined to play this hand out." He strolled back to his desk and sat down. "All right, Miss Gates, let's play," he suggested, a touch of amusement in his voice.

"This isn't a game!" she replied hotly.

He laughed knowingly. "I could assure you that it is, but

you wouldn't believe me, so I will dispense with that part of your education for now." Seeing the barely concealed fury on her face, Cole continued, smiling. "How do you expect to borrow two million dollars without putting up the patent as collateral?"

She regarded him coldly. "Since you aren't interested in this deal any longer, I think it's a waste of time to pursue it," she said.

"Excuse me," Sam interrupted. "Miss Gates, can I speak to you privately?" He had to tell her that this was no way to negotiate with Cole Weston. She was simply irritating the financier.

"Keep quiet, Kroy," Cole commanded. "She's doing splendidly without your advice."

Wearily, Sam sat back, waiting for Reggie's complete destruction. He couldn't even motion to her because Cole's eyes were riveted to his face in silent warning.

Aren't I doing splendidly? thought Reggie sarcastically. As far as she was able to determine, she was singlehandedly destroying her chances for future success. She needed this loan but she wanted it on her own terms. Weston was right, of course. She would be finished without the money and he was her only hope. Somehow, she had to convince him. She had not missed his frank appraisal of her body. Could she use his interest to her advantage? Did she have the nerve?

From under half-closed eyes, Cole watched carefully as Reggie fought with her emotions. She was a study in contradictions and, to his astonishment, he found that he was beginning to enjoy himself. He could not help but admire her stubborn determination, especially when they both knew her back was to the wall. There was an unspoiled charm that radiated from her face even as she glared at him with contempt. As yet, he didn't completely understand what drew him to her. However, at the very least, she amused him. If she insisted on fencing with him, it would be his pleasure to comply. After all, he mused, the result would be the same; she would ultimately agree to his conditions. He wanted that patent.

"It's a pity to see a talented person fail, and you will fail, you know," he said with certainty. "Your situation will go from critical to hopeless. Your reputation will be irreparably damaged when your orders go unfilled. There isn't a buyer in the country who will commit money to your firm when you don't meet due dates. That kind of reputation will stay with you forever." He paused to look into her eyes. "Miss Gates, your orders may represent a great deal of money, but you haven't enough petty cash to buy a cup of coffee," he told her bluntly.

"I'll find the money elsewhere," she insisted, uneasy beneath his frank stare.

"Where?" he shot back.

"It is no longer your concern," she said haughtily.

"Miss Gates, we are rapidly going nowhere," Cole said lightly.

Reggie looked directly into his smiling black eyes and was overcome with an irrepressible desire to scratch the laugh from his face. "I am not a financier—" she began.

A chuckle escaped his lips. "That much is obvious."

She ignored him. "I came here with the understanding that you were interested in providing financial backing for a healthy business."

"I am," he stated simply.

"I won't pay your price," she countered, standing up and readying herself to leave.

"Will you please sit down!" he barked. "You are wasting everyone's time."

"My own included!" she said furiously. "I'm sorry to have taken up so much of your valuable time." She began to walk toward the door.

"Don't be an idiot!" he snapped impatiently.

"I beg your pardon?" she said, drawing herself up to her full height.

"Miss Gates," Cole said with as much patience as he could muster, "no one is trying to *steal* anything from you. If you have that much faith in your company then you should be able to repay this loan within six months, and the rights to the patent will revert back to you. I am simply trying to protect a two million dollar investment." His white teeth flashed, and he enunciated, "Do you or don't you want this money?"

"Of course I do, but only under my conditions," she insisted.

"And those are?" Cole waited for her answer.

Suddenly, Reggie was stunned by a Machiavellian idea. She

gave him a wicked grin that caused him to raise his eyebrows in surprise. She carefully considered her next move. If she were clever, she could feed his vanity and capitalize on his obvious interest in her. Conspicuously checking her watch, she exclaimed, "Oops, I'm late for an appointment with the president of the Olympic Committee." She lowered her thickly fringed eyelashes and leaned toward him provocatively. "Do you think we could continue this conversation over dinner? Perhaps tomorrow evening?" she asked huskily, playing her last card.

Cole was not deceived by her pretense of an appointment. Miss Gates, he thought to himself, you're in well over your head. Out loud he simply said, "It would be my pleasure."

Chapter 12

Reggie was as nervous as a cat as she dressed with exceptional care for her dinner date the next evening. In an uncharacteristic move, she left work earlier than usual, stopping at Bloomingdale's to purchase a simple, but elegant "little black dress." The matte jersey dress draped provocatively over her slender body. It fastened at one shoulder with a single rhinestone button, leaving the other graceful shoulder deceptively uncovered. Beneath the clinging fabric, she wore only a pair of shimmering black pantyhose with three tiny rhinestones at each ankle. Black silk pumps completed the ensemble.

She critically surveyed the finished product. It was very important to her plan that she portray the "right" mixture of elegance balanced against the promise of restrained sensuality. She wanted to tempt rather than flaunt. Her burnished hair cascaded down her back in wild abandon. No, she thought critically, that wasn't the look she wanted. Returning to the dressing table, she brushed her hair severely from her face and into a tight knot at the nape of her neck. As an afterthought, she added two sparkling rhinestone hairpins. Better, she thought. The severe hairstyle counteracted the revealing dress.

Promptly at eight o'clock she heard the buzzer. She hesitated, uncertain. Should she invite him upstairs or meet him in the lobby? With a quick glance at her unimpressive loft, she decided to go downstairs.

"I'll be right down," she said into the intercom. She suddenly wished she owned a fur coat. Then she remembered an antique opera cloak she had acquired in her travels. Quickly, she rummaged through her closet, found it and swept it over her shoulders. The old-fashioned velvet cape, with its ermine-lined hood, gave Reggie the added boost of confidence she sorely needed.

As the creaking elevator descended, Reggie reviewed the plan she had devised. The doors opened and she stole a quick appraising look at the dark-haired man upon whom her entire future depended. Well over six feet and startlingly handsome, Cole Weston's body, leaning against the wall in the lobby, emanated a vigorous forcefulness. Even relaxed, there was a sense of unleashed power about him. For a moment, her courage deserted her, and Reggie hung back in the elevator.

It was too late . . . Cole had seen her. Now it was his turn to level a cool gaze at her, examining her jewellike green eyes and translucent skin, which shone like alabaster against the backdrop of the dramatic velvet cloak. As she moved toward him, her cloak fell away, revealing her nearly naked body within the gently clinging fabric. His burning eyes paused momentarily on her breasts. Quickly, she drew the cape around her body.

"Why did you wear that dress if it makes you uncomfortable?" he asked with the merest hint of a smile.

Her face flushed hotly and her throat constricted. Was she so obvious? From the way Cole was staring at her, she felt he could see right through her and read her mind. Don't be ridiculous, she chided herself angrily. There was absolutely no way he could know what she was planning. It was just his haughty, insolent manner that was so disconcerting, as if he were toying with her, letting her know from the outset that she was no match for him. It was the very same feeling she had had in his office the day before. He likes to play with people, she realized with a start. Well, she could play, too. If he expected a nervous ninny, he was going to be very disappointed indeed.

She found her voice at last. "On the contrary, Mr. Weston. The dress happens to be very comfortable. It's the way you look at me that makes me uneasy."

He raised his eyebrows a fraction of an inch. "How do I look at you, Miss Gates?" he asked innocently, beginning to enjoy himself.

"As if I were a strange specimen that had just landed from a different planet. And, as you can see," she said as she slowly twirled around, "I have two legs, two arms, a head and a torso. Not unlike yourself."

He took a few seconds to absorb her statement then amended it. "There are *some* subtle differences between us," he said with great seriousness.

She walked toward him, nodding amicably. "You're right. I have longer hair and you shave your face. Shall we go?"

He laughed, a low, throaty sound that echoed in the empty lobby. "Touché," he said and took her arm.

Cole helped her inside the waiting limousine and slipped in beside her. As casually as possible, Reggie edged closer to him so that their thighs brushed. He glanced at her in surprise but her face revealed nothing and he had no way of knowing whether it was accidental or not. When he had agreed to dinner tonight, he was fairly certain he understood her game plan. Women were women. The faces and the hair coloring might change but their basic nature was consistent. They had one thing to sell and if the object they desired was dear enough, it had been his experience that every one of them would eventually offer themselves up for sale. It was a game, as he had tried to explain to Reggie yesterday. A game at which he was a master. He had never, never lost.

In the darkened limousine, Reggie's mind was revolving a million times a minute. Would sleeping with Cole Weston get her the money she needed? And even if she was assured that it would, could she go through with it? Women often slept their way to the top, but could she? For two million dollars? Possibly. Without having to pledge her patent rights? Probably. For a handshake deal with no written agreement? Absolutely! It wasn't as if he was repulsive, she rationalized silently. He was quite possibly the most virile man she had ever met. If she was a different person, going to bed with him could be a fabulous experience. She looked down at the seat where his hands rested and imagined them touching her. She reddened in the darkness.

"A penny for your thoughts," Cole said, jolting her back to reality.

She bit back a chuckle. "Not even close," she answered.

"A dollar?"

Two million, she thought. "We haven't even reached a point where we can begin negotiations," she said cryptically, then looked up into his face with an impish grin.

"Somehow," he said with a boldness that chilled her, "by the time this evening is over, I suspect we will. Any time you're ready to bargain I'll be happy to listen."

"Bargain for my thoughts?"

He shrugged nonchalantly. "Or anything else."

"Like what?" she challenged.

"We're still playing games, I see."

Reggie sat up straight. The man absolutely *could* read minds. She was certain of it! "Mr. Weston, I have no idea what you're talking about."

"Miss Gates," he said with infinite patience, "I have tried to be honest and aboveboard with you. I've warned you that you can't outmaneuver or outsmart me. You still don't believe me, but I assure you that it's true. You're an extremely attractive, intelligent young woman, and I think we can probably have a lovely evening together, but please," he implored, "drop the Scarlett O'Hara routine."

"What—"

"Why-yy-yy, Mistah Butlah, Ah don't know what yo'all is talkin' about," he mimicked. "*I* know what *you're* talking about, and *you* know what *I'm* talking about." He placed his hand under her chin and tilted her face up so that he could look into her eyes. "Don't you, Reggie?" he asked.

She wrenched her face away from his hand. "No, I don't!" she said firmly.

"I can't convince you, can I?" asked Cole as the car began to pull over to the curb in front of Lutèce. He saw her blank expression and threw up his hands in frustration. She just wouldn't budge. "All right, my dear," he said as he helped her from the car, "but remember you have been amply warned and rewarned."

"Yessuh, Mistah Butlah, suh. Ah certainly have," she said

sarcastically and walked into the restaurant followed by a smiling Cole Weston. He was much better at this game than she was, she began to realize with dismay. But the night was barely beginning . . . she could get better.

Once inside, Cole was greeted familiarly by the maître d'. "Good evening, Mr. Weston. It's nice to see you again. Your table is ready or would you prefer a drink at the bar first?"

"Reggie?" Cole asked, but her head was turned in the direction of a tall potted palm, and she didn't hear the question. He tapped her on the shoulder. "Reggie?"

She whipped around with a puzzled look on her face. "I'm sorry, I didn't hear you."

"Would you like to sit down or would you prefer a drink at the bar first," he asked.

"Whatever you like," she said, then turned her head back.

"Is something wrong?" asked Cole, trying to follow her line of sight, but he was unable to see anything behind the tall tree.

"What? Oh, no. Everything's fine. For a moment I thought I saw someone I knew. The table will be fine." She recovered quickly, but as they followed the maître d' to the table, Reggie kept turning her head to try to see behind the palm. Finally realizing the impossibility from the angle of their table, she gave up and allowed herself to be seated. She felt vaguely uncomfortable and an unexpected shiver passed through her.

"Cold?" asked Cole as he took the seat next to her.

She looked up, startled. Warm dark eyes smiled at her. For a moment, Cole Weston looked almost human. Beware, she warned herself. Beware of falling into his web. Remember that he's an adversary, and you're here for one reason and one reason only. But when he smiled and flashed his perfect white teeth that contrasted so beautifully against the rugged tan of his handsome face, it was hard not to think of him as the most exciting man she'd met in a long, long time.

"Reggie, are you cold?" he repeated.

"No. Not at all."

"Good. Victor's waiting to take your cape."

The maître d' was standing like a statue next to her chair. Reggie remembered the way Cole's eyes had positively bored through her when her cape had opened in the lobby. She wasn't one hundred percent certain how she wanted to handle him yet. She didn't know him well enough to gauge which kind of tack would be most effective and, until she did, she wanted to hold on to all her options. Getting rid of the cape meant exposing herself to him, and for some reason she felt it would be more than just her body that would be on view.

"Maybe I am a little chilly," she decided. "I think I'll keep this with me."

When Victor walked away, Cole leaned back in his chair with a huge grin on his face. "Coward," he accused.

Reggie bristled. "Me? Why do you think I'm a coward?"

"Because," he drawled, "you don't have the courage to remove your cape. You obviously dressed tonight to be sensual and seductive, and you haven't the guts to see it through. Do you?"

She was stunned by his insight, but she managed to keep an implacable expression on her face. "You really are an egotist, aren't you?"

His lips twitched at their name-calling. "Very, very astute of you. However, my being an egotist has little to do with the matter of the cape, does it?"

She leaned forward, green eyes glinting dangerously. "If you want this cape removed so badly, do it yourself. And furthermore—don't try to goad me, Cole Weston. I can stand up to you any day."

He burst out laughing. "Feisty, too," he observed. "Beautiful, witty, intelligent and a fighter. What a unique combination. I think I like it."

"I don't really—" she stopped herself in mid-sentence. It wouldn't do at all to start fighting with him. That would be the worst possible thing she could do. It wouldn't get him into her bed, and it wouldn't get her his money. He'd hardly feel passionate and loving to someone who acted as if she wanted to scratch his eyes out . . . which, she thought with a grin, was exactly what was going to happen if he didn't stop teasing her.

He had gotten up and was now standing directly behind her chair. He lowered his hands to her shoulders as if he were going to lift the cape off, then allowed his fingers to wander up the soft, silken column of her neck. Despite herself, she found his touch pleasing, and she made no move to dislodge his hand when he began to play with a tendril of hair that had escaped its pins.

He leaned down to whisper in her ear, "If we weren't in a restaurant . . ."

She turned and gave him her most dazzling smile. "Then I'd probably be working. Now, if you don't mind, decide what you want done with this stupid cape and do it. Everyone is starting to stare at us."

"Do you care?" he asked huskily.

"Yes, as a matter of fact, I do." With that remark, she pushed his hands away and removed the cape herself. "Now do something with it."

He gave it to a passing busboy with instructions to put it in the coat room. "Much, much better," he murmured appreciatively as he sat down and studied her.

"Mr. Weston—"

"Cole," he corrected.

She ignored him. "Mr. Weston, could we please stop this silly sparring and get down to the purpose of this dinner?"

"You mean sparring isn't the purpose?"

"No. The fact of the matter is . . . is that I rarely get to eat in such an elegant restaurant and, as long as I'm here, I really would love to enjoy the ambiance."

"And the company?"

She sighed heavily. "Yes. And the company."

He shook his head in disbelief. "Your heart wasn't in that. It really wasn't said with conviction."

She picked up the tulip-shaped glass of champagne that Victor had quietly placed on their table. "Must you comment on every one of my comments?"

"I'm just trying to get to know you better. I would hardly lend money to a stranger."

She was just about to respond when she heard a voice behind her. "Cole? I just knew it was you! How are you? How are you, darling?" The voice was husky and honeyed and slightly familiar to Reggie.

Reggie willed herself not to turn around. Suddenly she knew exactly who was standing behind her. She'd only caught a glimpse of the woman through the fronds of the palm, but she hadn't needed more than that to recognize her. Her heart beat uncomfortably. Under the table, Reggie's nails dug into her palms as she waited for Cole to introduce her.

Cole's eyes lit up with interest as he spoke to the statuesque blonde behind Reggie's chair. "Well, well, well. Look who's back in town," he drawled. The corners of his mouth turned up in a smile.

"It's been three long years, darling. I was beginning to get positively lonely. You know," she said in a breathy voice, "you ought to have called."

Reggie felt as if she were an eavesdropper at an intimate party for two, and a slow rage was beginning to simmer inside her. What the hell did the two of them think she was? A potted plant? "More champagne, please," she said deliberately and held out her empty glass to Cole.

Cole recovered his manners and refilled her glass. "I'm sorry, Reggie," he said pleasantly. I'd like you to meet a very old friend of mine, Nikki—"

"Broad," finished Reggie as she turned with a glittering smile to stare into Nikki's ice-blue eyes. She noted with smug satisfaction that the years had not been kind to her enemy. Oh, Nikki was still a beautiful woman, but there were unmistakable signs that time was creeping up on her. Reggie calculated that Nikki must be about forty; tiny lines radiating from the corners of her eyes, a slight softening of the skin on her high cheekbones and the brittleness of her once lustrous hair were dead giveaways. Good! thought Reggie.

"Do you two know each other?" asked Cole in surprise.

"Have we met?" Nikki inquired at the same time. Nikki didn't recognize Reggie at all. Enough years had passed to change the skinny, immature teenager into an alluring, attractive woman. There wasn't the slightest resemblance to the unsure, eager-to-please child that Reggie Gates had been so many, many lifetimes ago. Both Cole and Nikki were staring at her, waiting for an answer.

Reggie formulated her response with great care. She'd waited years for this moment, sitting up nights trying to decide what kind of retribution she would deliver if she were ever given the chance. Now that it was upon her, she held back, the time wasn't quite right yet. "Years ago," Reggie began blithely, "I was in your Madison Avenue store. I was much younger then; there would be no reason for you to remember me." She smiled sweetly. But, oh lady, I sure remember you! There were two scores to be settled in Reggie's life and Nikki Broad was one of them. Reggie continued to smile, her jaw muscles aching with the attempt as she lied. "The years haven't changed you a bit."

The line was delivered with such biting sarcasm that Cole's eyebrows drew together in surprise, expecting some kind of explanation for the tone of her voice. But Reggie averted her eyes and toyed with her champagne glass. After several more minutes of listening to the cloying sound of Nikki's voice as she attempted to rekindle Cole's interest, Reggie had had it.

She set down her glass with great care and stared coldly at Cole. "If the two of you would like to spend the evening reminiscing, I'd be happy to leave." She stood up. "Nikki, why don't you sit here," she said and motioned to her seat. Cole began to stand, but Reggie stopped him. "No," she said, "don't bother. I'm sure Victor can get me a cab." And she turned on her heel and started for the exit.

By the time Reggie had reached the coat room, Cole was beside her, having made some vague excuse to Nikki. He grasped Reggie's wrist in a painful hold. "What the hell do you think you're doing?" he hissed angrily.

"Why, I'm going home. I thought I had made that obvious."

"Do you mind telling me why your nose is so out of joint?"

"I don't like threesomes," she said cheerfully. "Now would you be kind enough to release my wrist? Do go back to Nikki, why don't you? She's simply *dying* to continue your 'friendship.'"

"I already excused myself."

"How unfortunate for you. Dining alone can be such a drag."

Cole looked at her curiously and then did something he couldn't remember having done since he was a child. He apologized. "Please come back to the table and have dinner. I'm sorry I was so rude." He looked at her with such puppy-dog eyes that Reggie was momentarily taken aback. "I mean it," he said softly. "Please come back."

Part of her wanted to have the satisfaction of laughing in his face and destroying his complacency, but another part knew what it had taken for Cole to apologize to her. Just the way he said it made her realize that it wasn't something he did often. He didn't have to—with his money and his power, people would flock to him whether he was rude or not. This man, the one asking her to return to the table, wasn't the caustic, insolent man of the day before. Just the few lines he had uttered had shown her another side of him and it touched her. Business aside, she was absurdly pleased that he had let down his guard long enough for her to catch the briefest glimpse of another Cole Weston. She wondered which one was real.

When they were seated at the table once again, Cole asked her what she would like for dinner, and she picked up her menu. Under the guise of choosing his own dinner, he studied her carefully. He had been furious when she left the table, but, grudgingly, he admired her for it. She didn't dissemble. . . didn't plead a headache or fatigue. She told it the way it was—she didn't like the attention he was showing Nikki when he was supposed to be concentrating on her. Christ, he thought! Didn't she know that Nikki Broad couldn't hold a candle to her? Never, not even in Nikki's heyday did the blonde come close to Reggie Gates. But most of all, he thought ruefully, he liked Reggie's courage. Anyone who could actually plan to try to beat him at his own game was courageous indeed. He looked forward to the rest of the evening with an odd mixture of delightful anticipation and reserve. She would lose the battle—that was a foregone conclusion—but playing the game would no doubt be an unexpected source of pleasure.

"Have you decided what you'd like for dinner?" he asked.

She smiled shyly. "This is going to sound a little ridiculous, but I don't speak French. From experience I've learned not to pretend I can read menus that aren't in English. So, if you'd care to make a suggestion or two, I'd appreciate it."

Cole made some suggestions, and Reggie settled happily for the chateaubriand. She sat back, sipping her wine, and told Cole the story of her experience ordering ossa buca. "I've done that several times since then," she continued with a lilt in her voice. "I have been served dishes that would probably make better pets than food. Finally," she admitted wryly, "I gave up any pretense at sophistication."

He looked at her with frank admiration. "I wouldn't think it would be necessary for you to make a pretense about anything."

"Is that a compliment?" she asked. Sometimes, with Cole's exquisite use of the double entendre, it was hard to tell.

"By all means."

She cocked her head prettily. "Well then, thank you."

"You're very welcome. And if we're going to dispense with pretense, how about telling me how you know Nikki and why you dislike her so much." Not for one minute did he delude himself into thinking that it had anything to do with him. Her overreaction to his conversation with Nikki made him extremely curious.

"It's a long, boring story," she warned. "You wouldn't be interested."

"Let me make that decision myself. I would very much like to hear the story," he told her truthfully. The more he knew about her, the more he understood her, the better able he would be to put his plan into action. He had every intention of getting his hands on her patent. Even though she knew it was valuable, she had no way of knowing its true worth. He *did* and, if his plan worked, he would get two things he wanted. One was the patent right.

While they ate dinner, Reggie told Cole the entire story of Nikki's treachery, the crushing incident that destroyed her confidence and had stifled her creativity for so long. Sometime during the recounting, Cole had reached out to take her hand in an uncharacteristic effort to comfort her. He was deeply moved by her story.

"Why didn't you go to the papers with this? Or to a lawyer?" he asked.

She shrugged. "There were other things going on in my life at the time that sort of paralyzed me." She shuddered momentarily at the memory of David and the pregnancy. "By the time I was ready to deal with Nikki, she was in California and I didn't have the money to go out there and start a lawsuit."

"Couldn't you have borrowed it from your family?"

Reggie laughed joylessly. "Hardly. Once I decided to leave home and go to school in New York, they sort of disowned me. I have an aunt who I might have turned to for help, but she was traveling around the world and was unreachable until the whole thing was over." She took her hand from Cole's. "Do you mind if we change the subject? It's still very painful to speak about."

Deep within him, Cole felt a stirring, an instinct to walk over to Nikki and bawl the hell out of her for hurting Reggie. The unfamilar urge to protect someone startled him, making him more than a little uncomfortable. "Now I can understand your drive to succeed. You're going to show them all, aren't you?"

She sat up straight in her chair. "Don't patronize me, Mr. Weston," she said in a flat, unemotional voice. "And don't pretend to understand how I felt back then. You can't know, you've never been there."

He thought back to his years in college and graduate school and the way he had been cold-shouldered by his fancy classmates. He attempted to talk to her about it, but she clearly showed him that she was not interested. The spell of the evening had been broken by calling forth too many painful memories. After coffee, he motioned for the bill, signed it and escorted her to the waiting car. "Reggie, I think it's important to finish this conversation."

"For what possible reason?" she asked as she stepped into the limousine.

He didn't know. But there was a depth to Reggie Gates that he suddenly wanted to probe, and it didn't have anything to do with the loan or the patent. "You still have demons to exorcise," he said. "Perhaps I can help."

She thought about it for a moment. The only thing he could help her with was her loan, and they hadn't spoken about that at all. That had been the one purpose for the dinner date. "Perhaps," she said in a noncommittal voice.

"Would tomorrow evening be convenient?" he asked with a roguish smile.

After dropping Reggie at her Broome Street loft, Cole gave momentary consideration to stopping at Evyan's apartment for a nightcap. It was still early and he felt restless and oddly out of sorts, as if he had left something unfinished and couldn't quite remember what it was. He had an intense desire to talk to someone—not about business or his latest acquisition, nor did he feel up to the tired gossip of his glittering social circle. What he did want—and he smiled ironically in the dark at the very idea—was to sit companionably with someone he liked, with soft music playing in the background, a glass of good brandy in his hand . . . and . . . relax, unwind. Something had happened in Lutèce that night as he had listened to Reggie's story about her past. He had been genuinely interested, so interested that he hadn't wanted the evening to end. Now that it had, he felt as if someone had torn the last twenty-five pages out of a book he was enjoying, leaving him dangling. He didn't understand the feeling at all.

He reached forward to the highly polished walnut bar and poured himself a generous glass of cognac, inhaling the bouquet of the smooth liquor as he wrestled with the idea about seeing Evyan tonight. If companionship and conversation was what he wanted, Evyan was the wrong choice. She made love like a trained concubine, knew the juiciest *on-dits* about society and decorated his arm like an expensive piece of jewelry. But talk? Evyan couldn't string together an intelligible sentence without the words Gucci, Hermes or Vuitton. Strangely, until this moment, it hadn't mattered to him.

Reggie Gates. He closed his eyes and thought about her. Glittering green eyes that flashed fire when she was angry, which seemed to be most of the time, or that could enflame a man's soul when, for a moment, she let down her guard and smiled. And clever, he reminded himself, opening his eyes again. Not to be underestimated. Determined to get what she wanted without giving anything away. The loan and the patent. She wanted them both. She'd made that clear. He chuckled at her nerve. Did she really think she was dealing with an idiot? He knew the value of that patent . . . probably better than she. It would be worth millions, far more than her clothing company. Compared to the prospective worth of the computer loom, her little business was a mere hobby. No, he thought, Burlington and DuPont *wouldn't* get their hands on it. It would become part of WestCo, and he was prepared to do anything he had to in order to get it. And then there was the lady. What did he want of her? She was amusing, flirtatious, quite beautiful . . . but there were hundreds like her. Why did she stick in his mind? Because, Cole Weston, she doesn't give two hoots in hell about you—except for your money. His brow furrowed at the memory of how she had dressed that evening and what her motive had been in choosing a dress that left nothing to his imagination. But it was never Cole Weston, the man, she had been trying to seduce—it had been Cole Weston, the checkbook. And yet, as much as she wanted his money, she hadn't been brazen enough to carry through her plan . . . not yet, anyway.

He picked up the car phone, dialed information and asked for Regina Gates. Rapidly, he punched in the numbers and listened as the phone rang. She picked up on the third ring.

"Hello?" she said in a breathless voice.

"Hello." His voice had a smooth, mellow, husky quality. "Just wanted to make sure you got in all right. Your neighborhood was so dark and deserted that I was concerned."

"Mr. Weston?" she asked in surprise.

"Don't you think you could bend a little and call me Cole?"

She laughed. "Would you like me to?" She sat down on the edge of her bed and kicked off her pumps. When the phone rang she had been in the bathroom about to run a bubble bath. But this was much more interesting. She looked at her watch and noted that fifteen minutes hadn't passed since he'd dropped her off. A good sign!

"I would like very much for you to call me Cole."

"Then I will," she said. "And I appreciate the concern, but I'm fine. As dark as it is here, it's really a very safe neighborhood," she assured him.

"That's not the only reason I called." He waited for her to respond, to question him, but he heard nothing. "Reggie?"

"I'm still here."

"I called to tell you that I had a wonderful time tonight and that I'm looking forward to tomorrow evening." That was an understatement. In the cat-and-mouse game they were playing, he was delightfully anticipating her next move. Would she or wouldn't she continue her naive plans for his seduction? And if she did, would she see it through this time or back down the way she had tonight, pulling the opera cloak protectively around her body after she had given him a brief glimpse?

"I had a lovely time, too, Mr. Wes—Cole. I'm just sorry that we didn't get to discuss business."

"I'm not," he stated. "We'll have plenty of time for that tomorrow night, don't you think?"

I hope not, thought Reggie. "I certainly hope so. I would like there to be some sort of understanding between us."

There will, there will. "After spending an evening with you, I'm certain we will be able to accommodate each other. After all, I think you'll agree it is in both of our best interests to do so."

Reggie looked at the phone. I don't know what we're talking about, she said to herself. What did his "accommodate" mean? Was he trying to tell her that he would give her the loan without the patent as collateral?

He stopped her thoughts in midstream. "You're a very beautiful woman, Miss Gates."

"Does that have anything to do with my loan?" she asked boldly.

"It might," he answered with a low laugh. "It depends, doesn't it?"

She had her answer. She knew exactly what Cole Weston wanted. Fee for services. She shivered in distaste. She was going to go through with it. She had no choice.

"I'm glad you called, Cole, and I'm looking forward to doing business with you, but it's late now. I have to be up very early tomorrow morning, so you'll have to excuse me if I cut this a little short." Tomorrow evening loomed like an execution, and the idea that she was selling herself was so repugnant that she couldn't bear to continue the conversation. But the ends would justify whatever she had to do. It would be over quickly, maybe it would even be fun, and she'd get her loan and keep her patent. She wasn't ever going backward again!

"I understand completely. Go get your beauty rest and I'll see you tomorrow. Pleasant dreams."

"Thanks. Good night." Reggie put down the phone with trembling hands. This was going to be much, much harder than she had thought. "Coward," she said out loud. "Cole Weston's right. You are a coward!"

Like taking candy from a baby, Cole thought as he replaced the receiver. By tomorrow night, the signed contract would be in his hand—with the patent clause intact. Of course having the patent as collateral wasn't the same thing as actually owning the patent. That would be the next step, and the seeds of an idea were germinating about how he was going to accomplish that. It would all hinge on making absolutely certain that it would be impossible for her to repay the loan, and thus the patent would belong to WestCo.

It was nasty . . . and unfair. But most big financial deals were and any way you sliced it, Reggie Gates's patent meant big, big money. He would have gladly paid two million dollars for it outright had it been offered that way. But since it hadn't been, this would be the next best way of securing it for WestCo, but only if she defaulted. Which she would, of course, once he made a couple of phone calls.

A momentary twinge of regret pricked him. He was no saint, but he had never deliberately lured a woman to bed for any purpose other than mutual pleasure. This plan, which included letting Reggie think she had seduced him into insensibility, went against everything he believed in. But he would salve his guilty conscience with the reminder that she had been cautioned, first in his office, then later in the limousine on the way to the restaurant. But she had chosen to believe that she could outwit him.

He set the glass down in the holder next to him and closed his eyes. Ah, well, he thought with a deep sigh . . . so much for intelligence.

Reggie admired the delicate white tea roses that had been waiting for her at the door when she had returned home. The enclosed note read: "Wear something casual and be prepared for a long drive. See you at 7:30. Cole." She had little over an hour to get ready. His mention of the word *casual* threw her into a panic. The saucy, backless dress she had just bought at Henri Bendel could never be mistaken for casual. She wished she knew where they were going. After reviewing everything in her wardrobe and discarding most, she settled on a pair of midnight-blue suede jeans, black silk blouse and black suede pumps. Showering quickly, she dressed, applied her makeup and twisted her hair high on top of her head in an old-fashioned Gibson girl coiffure.

By 7:20, she was pacing the living room, having nervously checked and rechecked her appearance. She picked up her leather jacket and left the apartment.

Cole had just stepped into the lobby as the elevator doors opened. He whistled appreciatively as Reggie approached. There was a disturbing aura of sensuality about her, a casual artlessness that contradicted everything he knew about her. Her manner as she walked toward him was natural, unaffected. Yet, beneath it all, there was a singleminded purpose to tonight's date, and Cole knew precisely what it was. He had to hand it to her . . . her performance was brilliant, Oscar material. Casually, he reached up and placed a hand over the left breast of his jacket. A ghost of a smile hovered on his lips as he felt the papers. The contract was exactly where he had placed it before leaving home.

Reggie's anxiety increased when she saw his peculiar smile. For a wild moment she was reminded of Coco's face last summer when the cat was silently stalking a cicada. I wonder if I look like the cicada? she wondered.

"Is there something amusing you, Mr. Weston?" she asked.

"I thought we had decided that you were going to call me Cole," he remarked.

I can think of any number of names that would be more appropriate, she thought. Lucifer was the one that came to mind first. She shook her head and smiled slightly. "Forgive me. I forgot. Cole." Her voice seemed a little higher than usual. She blamed it on the accoustics of the lobby.

Cole's eyes were riveted to the deep V of her blouse. He noted with mixed feelings that she had left enough buttons open that the soft swell of her full breasts was obvious. That, her high-heeled pumps and the tight fit of her suede jeans told him all he needed to know. She was still very much a player in their game.

"To the victor go the spoils," he murmured.

"I beg your pardon?"

Cole cleared his throat. "I said Victor wanted to know if dinner was spoiled."

"Dinner? You mean last night?"

Cole nodded.

"What would have given him that idea?" she asked.

"I . . . uh . . . I suppose he came to that conclusion when you left the table so abruptly," he explained lamely.

"No, dinner was fine." She was anxious to get started, to get the evening over with. She would do what she would have to do . . . she just wanted to *do* it already. Her nerves wouldn't hold out much longer. "Don't you think we'd better get started?" she suggested and began to walk toward him.

At the same time, he began to walk to her. He smiled. "I did tell you that you look magnificent tonight, didn't I?" For a moment he stared into her eyes, and only their breathing could be heard.

She would have drawn away, but somehow, with his eyes locked on hers, she couldn't move. His hand moved to push a loose tendril of hair from her forehead and she held her breath, her heart hammering uncomfortably.

"Your eyes," he began in a soft, caressing voice, "are the most improbable color." In the dim light of the lobby they had changed from sparkling emerald to smoky jade. He'd never seen eyes that could change with a mood. What are you thinking, Reggie Gates? He let his hand slide down the soft plane of her cheek, then to the curve of her chin, and still her eyes never left his face. Her hands were held rigidly to her sides, pinioned there by nerves as she waited for his next move. "You're trembling," he noted.

"I am not," she denied hotly, trying to still the involuntary shivering that had started when he had touched her face. Calm down! she told herself sternly. You're supposed to be aloof, sophisticated and immune to Cole Weston's charm. Make *him* want *you!* Make him desperate for you!

The lobby dissolved as he placed his arms around her waist and slowly drew her closer to him. Cole's piercing black eyes were fixed on her full, sensual mouth and, with infinite care, he brought his head down so that his lips brushed hers. The contact jolted them both, and she sprang away, startled. With an enormous effort, she raised her eyes to meet his and saw the same surprise and shock. Confused, she tried to find something light to say but before she could speak, Cole stepped back two paces. "Sooner or later we had to get that out of the way," he said, but the curious expression on his face contradicted the flippant comment. He was as affected by their brief contact as she . . . and she knew it. "Come," he said, "lobbies are a little too public for my taste." He draped Reggie's jacket around her shoulders as they walked through the door to his car. A curtain had descended over his eyes and she could no longer decipher his mood. Had kissing him been a mistake? Was he angry?

She studied him thoughtfully for a long moment as he slid behind the wheel of the sleek red Ferrari. If there had been tension in the air when they had met in the lobby, now it hung between them like an impenetrable fog. She tried to lighten the mood. "Is this the way you always begin business meetings?" she asked coquettishly.

"Hardly," he answered brusquely.

What the hell was he angry at? *He* had kissed *her* . . . not the other way around. And if he hadn't wanted to . . . well, no one was holding a gun to his head.

Reggie had no way of knowing that Cole *was* angry—furious, in fact. This wasn't the way he had planned the evening. It had been his intention to be cool and to allow her the pleasure of making all the moves. If he hadn't been so taken by her aura of naive sensuality, everything would have proceeded according to plan. Now he had to rethink his strategy. He had shown his hand a little too early. Backtrack, he told himself sternly. Remember—this is business . . . big business. No matter that the client is the most bewitching woman he'd met. She was still a client and Cole Weston didn't generally go around acting like an adolescent with his business associates.

"Well, you should," she spoke, breaking the tension.

"Should what?" he asked, having lost sight of the previous question.

She giggled. "You should always soundly kiss your business associates. It definitely throws them off guard and you gain the advantage."

"Have I?"

She nodded. "Most assuredly, and I think it would be a good idea if we were both on even footing. Evened the score, so to speak."

He couldn't help himself from laughing at the comment he knew would follow. "How could we do that, Reggie?"

"By allowing *me* to kiss *you*. I always begin my meetings with a kiss." Good girl, Gates. Keep it up! Now you've got him interested. Blatant sexuality wouldn't move him but the combination of wit, humor and the unexpected, might. "So? What do you say."

"I never say no to a pretty lady." He leaned forward and pursed his lips.

"Come on, Cole. Even I can do better than that!"

"I'm all yours. Just tell me what to do."

She reached up and snaked her arms around his neck,

drawing him closer. She heard his sharp intake of breath as she placed her lips on his, opening hers slightly so that he could taste the sweetness of her mouth. Without warning, he drew her into his arms, capturing her mouth with his in a deep, searching kiss. There was a loud rushing in her ears, a pounding in her chest as his lips slanted against hers, and she felt his tongue probing. She moaned softly, melting in his embrace. Then suddenly, as quickly as it had begun, it was over, leaving her breathless. They stared at each other. Both knew a challenge had been issued. For some moments the only sound in the car was the purring of the motor and the beating of their hearts.

I want him, she realized with a mixture of surprise and dismay. I actually *want* to go to bed with him. The thought terrified her. It had been so long, so many lonely years since she had felt this way toward a man, any man. And now it had to be Cole Weston! Not since David had she felt this longing to be embraced and made love to. This wasn't part of the plan. The aching desire she felt would only hinder her, make her lose control of the situation and she couldn't do that. When they made love, and now she knew with certainty that they would, she would have to be very, very careful not to show him how much she wanted him. Giving Cole Weston that kind of advantage would be the death knell for her company and her future. Too many years and too much pain had elapsed for her to fall victim to the longings of her body. She'd done without love for so long, she would be able to go on for a while longer. Their coupling would be for only one reason . . . to get his money. That's it, Reggie! That's the only way to play this. Somewhere, there would be someone else who would awaken these feelings again. It would not be the man sitting beside her. Never!

Chapter 13

They drove for over an hour into the Long Island countryside, their conversation light and flirtatious, filled with tentative innuendos that successfully camouflaged the uneasiness they both felt. Every so often, Cole turned to Reggie and leveled a speculative glance at her face, as if he were searching for something. But Reggie's constant chatter and breezy manner put him off. No one looking at her now would have believed that beneath the beautiful face and genial personality lay a mind and heart as devious as Mata Hari's. Remember that, he warned himself as the memory of their kiss filled his mind. It meant nothing to her . . . merely a prelude to the completion of her scheme. For a moment, he loathed her for her deception. Why pretend? he thought. Even Evyan, with all her faults, was completely honest in stating what she wanted. Why couldn't Reggie? Because, he reminded himself sternly, women for the most part were cunning, dishonest, sly and manipulative. Stop trying to find something in her that's not there. She is what you think she is—nothing more. No morals, no scruples and no principles. What a pretty pair we make, thought Cole. Cold, calculating and conniving. Who could ask for anything more?

They drove for another five minutes, and then Cole turned the car into the driveway of a weathered, white clapboard house. A hand-carved sign to the right of the oak door was illuminated by a flickering gaslight. It read, "The Chipping Swallow Inn." As they walked side by side into the pre-Revolutionary farmhouse, Cole explained that he had discovered the little known inn during a summer's drive while he was trying to escape the crowds of the Hamptons.

The crisp crackle of a roaring fire and the tantalizing aroma of freshly baked apple pie enhanced the charm of the inn. Reggie followed the maître d' past tables set with plaid cloths, mini-printed floral napkins and tiny bayberry candles flickering softly in pewter holders. No sooner did they take their seats, when Cole stood up again.

"Excuse me for a moment, Reggie. I didn't see James Brighton when I walked in. He's the owner of the inn and an old friend. I'd like to go over and tell him we're here. Then I'll bring him back to the table for introductions."

Reggie's eyes followed Cole as he made his way back to the entrance and tapped a burly, bearded man on the shoulder. They embraced in a bear hug, and Reggie heard the innkeeper's raucous laugh. Cole drew Brighton off into a corner, turned to smile at Reggie and spoke quietly to his friend who alternately chuckled or nodded. They slapped each other on the back in some sort of mutual agreement, and then Cole walked back to the table. As she watched him approach, Reggie could almost feel the aggressive virility that emanated from him. Her mouth went dry, remembering the pressure of his lips on hers. This man was extremely dangerous. Who was she kidding? There was no way she could carry this whole thing off without his being aware of what she was doing. He'd see through her in a minute! And even if he didn't . . . when he eventually found out that she had slept with him with no particular regard for him other than his money, he'd very likely want to kill her. Cole Weston wasn't the kind of man who would take kindly to being duped. She bit her lip nervously.

"Sorry I was gone so long. We had some catching up to do," he said, slipping into his seat. "I've ordered dinner for us. The inn is famous for duck, which can be prepared twenty-four ways. I've chosen calvados and apples for me and green peppercorn sauce for you."

Reggie flashed her most dazzling smile, but in her attempt to hide her trepidation, it came off as a lopsided grin. "What if I told you I positively detested green peppercorns?" she asked.

He shrugged. "I probably would have gone ahead and ordered it anyway because, in this case, you would have been wrong," he said, teasingly.

"That's what I thought." She placed her elbows on the table, resting her chin in her hands, and looked at him thoughtfully. "Tell me, are you *always* right?"

He stretched his long legs in front of him and, after giving the question careful consideration, answered with a twinkle in his eyes. "Yes. Does it offend you?" When she said that it did, Cole's mouth twitched. "It shouldn't since I expect that you think you're always right, too."

"I do," she agreed, but there was no answering laughter in her voice. "And," she continued, "that doesn't bode too well for a relationship between us. If *I'm* always right and so are *you* . . . we'll always be at an impasse. Won't we?"

He let his gaze wander boldly over her body, his smoldering eyes lingering meaningfully on the rounded fullness of her breasts, where they pressed provocatively against the thin silk of her blouse. Something devilish flickered in his eyes, but his face remained impassive. Reggie lifted her head and returned his scorching gaze. He threw back his head and laughed at her defiance. "You're very much mistaken if that's what you honestly believe."

"I—"

She was about to retort when they were interrupted by James Brighton, who approached the table with a carafe of deep garnet wine and two sparkling goblets.

"Mademoiselle, Mr. Weston especially requested the house wine, which we make on the premises. I know you'll enjoy it." He poured a sample into Reggie's glass, which she picked up and brought to her lips, taking a tentative sip.

"It's lovely. Thank you."

"Cole," warned Brighton, "you'd better caution your lovely lady friend about my wine."

"James doesn't believe in low alcoholic content. His wine has been known to knock you for a loop if you're not careful," explained Cole.

"As long as you're warned," said Brighton, "I wouldn't want to spoil your evening by getting you drunk."

"Rest assured, James," answered Cole, "I'll go to *great* lengths to see that the lady enjoys the rest of the evening."

The line was delivered with such emphasis that Reggie swallowed convulsively. But when she looked at Cole for an explanation, his face revealed nothing behind his maddeningly cryptic smile.

By the time dinner arrived, Reggie had consumed three glasses of the potent wine in a vain attempt to calm her frazzled nerves. She was beginning to find it very difficult to concentrate, and through a lovely haze she decided to focus her attention on Cole's face instead of his conversation. She admired the strong planes of his face as the candles flickered, casting mysterious shadows on the curve of his cheek. He watched her carefully as she repeatedly blinked to clear her vision. Suddenly, Reggie had an overwhelming desire to reach out to his clean-shaven face and trace her fingers along the firm line of his jaw. She giggled. "You know," she said in a confidential whisper, "you are probably the most handsome man I've ever seen."

His lips twitched in amusement. "And you, Reggie dear, are by far the most sensual woman."

Coffee was served. The candles had burned down until they were mere pools of burning wax, and Reggie was desperately afraid that she had drunk too much of Mr. Brighton's homemade wine. It had to be the wine, she thought foggily, that was causing the room to spin so crazily every time Cole looked at her. And hearts weren't supposed to beat so erratically at the brush of a hand . . . not like this . . . where each ragged breath was a struggle because Cole Weston's eyes bored into her, setting her hands trembling.

His smoldering gaze came to rest again on the perfect ivory skin that swelled so invitingly above the last button of her blouse. Reddening under his blatant stare, she raised a shaking hand to cover herself. His hand shot out and held her wrist.

"Don't!" he commanded. "We both know why you left that button open," he said, pulling her hand away and holding it in a secure grip. "It's a little too late to play innocent maiden, Reggie. You've gone out of your way to beguile and entice me. Now that you've succeeded, don't disappoint me by chickening out."

His hand was biting into the soft skin of her wrist. "Let go of me this minute, Cole Weston! I never meant for you—"

"Oh, yes, you did. You meant every batting eyelash, every coy remark, every innuendo," he said flatly. He leaned over the table, still grasping her hand. "Where's your spirit now, Reggie? What's become of the courageous spitfire?" he taunted. The smile was gone from his face. "The farce is about over," he said, glaring into her green eyes. "Let's go."

She held back. "Where the hell do you think you're taking me?"

"Exactly where you've wanted to go since you got into the

car this evening." With one hand still securely around her wrist, he pulled her from her chair. "I'd hate to pick you up and carry you upstairs, but I will if I have to."

"Don't be absurd!" she whispered harshly as several people at the next table turned to stare. She gasped as he began to pull her away from the table. "You're making a spectacle out of us. Will you stop this!"

He dropped her hand, turned and glowered at her. "The check is in my pocket, Reggie. Two million dollars. And all you have to do is come upstairs." She watched, mesmerized, as he withdrew a key from his pocket and began flipping it nonchalantly in his hand.

Somewhere, a distant warning bell dimly went off in her head. She could still leave . . . she knew he wouldn't stop her. But if she left, she could kiss her future good-bye. The choice was hers. "All right," she said, all attempts at pretense gone. "All right, you bastard! Let's get this over with!"

A wicked smile broke out across his face. "Look who's calling whom names." Without another word, he put his arm around her shoulders and led her from the dining room, through the lobby and up the one flight of stairs. "This way," he said as they reached the landing.

"You've been here before, I see."

He shrugged. "Does it matter?"

She didn't answer as she watched him fit the key in the lock and swing open the door. Reggie could actually see the tension in his body. The things she had planned, the lovely words of seduction and cajolery died in her throat as she turned to see the naked hunger in his intense eyes. He closed the door with a resounding thud. "I'm not sure that I . . ." she whispered, voice quivering.

"But I am," he said with absolute certainty. "I've never been so sure about anything." There was a cynical light shining in his dark eyes as he searched her face. "You were sure last night when you chose that particular dress, you were sure when you 'forgot' to button the top four buttons of your blouse, and you're still as sure. Nervous, possibly, but you want this money so badly, you can taste it. Can't you?" he mocked. When she didn't answer, he narrowed his eyes. "It's too late to tell me this isn't what you've been planning all along."

"Damn you," she hissed.

He ignored her. In a deep husky voice he said, "Shall we see what two million dollars buys in today's market?" As casually as if he were in his own bedroom, he began to unbutton his shirt.

She whirled around to face his taunting words, unleashed fury finally breaking through her fear. Her heart was banging so loudly she could hear it. "You're wrong," she said coldly, "I never had any intention of—"

"You had every intention," he contradicted. "You haven't made one move that wasn't calculated to insure this seduction." He reached into his jacket pocket and threw a folded piece of paper on the bed.

"What's that?"

"Payment. Up front. I don't know if that's the correct protocol, but I'm sure you'll correct me if I've made an error. It's a hell of a lot of money for one night with you. I hope to hell you're worth it." He stepped back a pace, studying her expression. The fear in her eyes was gone and dark anger had replaced it.

"Just like that? Two million dollars?" she said, picking up the check.

"No, not quite. There's still the matter of the contract."

"Where is it?"

"Right here," he said, removing it from his pocket and handing it to her. "I've already signed it," he told her in a matter of fact voice. "All that's required now is your signature."

She took the heavy contract from his hand and sat down on the edge of the four-poster bed. "You wouldn't expect me to sign this without reading it, would you?" she challenged.

"Be my guest," he said, sitting down on a chair to wait.

"It may take me awhile," she said, thumbing through it and remembering the fine print and difficult phrasing.

"I'm not going anywhere, Reggie. We have *all* night." He watched her through lazy, half-closed eyes. "In fact, while you do your reading, I'll call down for some champagne. I'm in the mood for celebrating."

She heard him speaking softly into the phone while she began to read. Five minutes passed and, in the hushed room, it felt like eternity. Cole picked up a magazine and began leafing through it. "How are you doing?" he asked in an offhand manner.

"Just fine," she answered as she turned another page. She still had fifteen more pages to go.

"Interesting?" he asked conversationally.

"I've read it before. I'm just waiting to get to the good part," she said. When she heard Cole's laugh she wanted to smack him.

"We will," he said, still chortling. "If you don't back down again, that is."

She couldn't stand his smug, self-satisfaction. "If you've kept your part of the bargain, so will I," she said, angrily. "Believe me, Cole, I'm positively chafing to get tonight over with."

Page twenty dealt with the rate of interest she would pay Cole during the course of the loan. Page twenty-one described the manner in which she would pay—dates, amounts, penalties. By page twenty-two, she was completely bogged down in legalese and realized that rereading the entire thing was a waste of time. The only thing she was interested in was the last paragraph of the contract . . . right before the signatures. She flipped to the last page and studied it carefully. The final paragraph had been deleted. There was no mention of the patent at all. Her heart flipped over. She'd won! She'd beaten Cole out of her patent rights and nothing else mattered. Sometime today, he had had the contract amended.

"I'll take that pen now," she said and furiously scribbled her name beneath his. "There," she said, sparks of emerald fire shooting from her eyes. "I only hope you get your goddamned money's worth."

He chuckled mirthlessly. "So do I." He handed her another copy of the contract. "You wouldn't mind signing my copy, would you?"

She took the papers and turned to the last page to make sure this wasn't some sort of trick. There was no mention of the patent in his copy, either. She signed it and handed it back to him. He put it in his pocket. "You surprise me, Cole. I didn't expect you to give in so easily."

"I couldn't resist your persuasive techniques. I'm satisfied with what I'm getting for my money."

There was a knock on the door. "The champagne," said Cole, opening the door.

James Brighton walked into the room carrying a tray with a chilled bottle of champagne, an ice bucket and two glasses. He set it down on the table and turned to Cole with a grin. "The best in the house. Exactly what you wanted."

Cole returned the smile and strolled over to check the bottle. He picked it up to study the label. James grabbed it away. "I told you—only the best. Don't you trust me?" asked the innkeeper. "Now allow me . . ."

Cole took it back. "No, thanks. I want this pleasure all for myself." With great ceremony he wrapped a white linen napkin around the bottle and popped the cork with a flourish. Champagne exploded all over Cole's jacket. James reached for a napkin, but Cole was already wiping his soaked clothing. "Forget it," Cole said. "I can kiss this jacket good-bye."

"Don't be ridiculous," said James. "Give it to me, and I'll have it cleaned in a minute. Mary's a wizard at this sort of thing." Cole started to protest, then reconsidered at the thought of what the jacket would smell like in the morning.

"Here," Cole said, taking off the jacket and handing it to James. "But leave it outside the door in the morning." He turned to Reggie, who had been watching the incident with an expression of boredom. "We're not going anywhere tonight, are we, darling?"

She threw him a menacing glare. I'd love to cut your heart out, Cole Weston, she thought. "No, of course not, 'sweetheart.'"

An odd look passed momentarily between Brighton and Cole, and then the innkeeper left with the tray and Cole's jacket. With the closing of the door, Reggie's heart began to thud. Here it comes, she thought with a horrible sense of foreboding. Cole poured out two glasses of champagne and walked toward her.

"The next move is yours, Reggie. How shall we play it?"

When she stood there mutely, riveted to the spot, he blithely continued. "Shall I seduce you, or do you prefer to be the aggressor?" He sipped thoughtfully on his wine, waiting. He set her glass on the nightstand.

Panic ripped through her. I can't! she thought wildly. Silently, she prayed for a miracle, a reprieve, anything to get her out of the room, but as he started to advance toward her with a determined smile tugging at the corners of his lips, she knew there would be no last-minute pardon. In that moment, every last ounce of courage deserted her. Her heart was pounding so loudly in her chest that it hurt.

It happened so quickly that Reggie had no time to react. His hand shot out, grasping her wrist in a painful vicelike hold and pulling her toward him in a crushing embrace. She struggled fiercely, trying to break free. The more she twisted in his arms, the closer he held her. To her horror, she felt him hardening against her.

"Pay up, Reggie," he whispered hoarsely into her hair, one hand holding the nape of her neck against his body.

Her head was buried in his chest, and she was finding it increasingly difficult to get air. "I can't breathe," she finally gasped.

He loosened his hold slightly, but as she raised her head and opened her mouth for air, his lips came down on hers in a blistering, possessive kiss. "I own you tonight," he reminded her huskily, and then his mouth captured hers again with such yearning greed that she felt the breath was being stolen from her body.

"Cole . . . don't . . . please . . ." She managed to get out the strangled words, but only barely as his mouth slid demandingly over hers, parting her lips hungrily in an endless kiss that left her weak-kneed and breathless.

This isn't the way it's supposed to be! she screamed silently. She felt betrayed by her body, by the way her heart pounded at the touch of his mouth. It had been so long for her . . . so many years of denial that a long-forgotten need to be held and touched and caressed seized her in a vicious, traitorous grip. God help me, she thought as the pressure of Cole's mouth increased and her starved body began to respond. With a low moan, she gave in, wrapping her slender arms around his strong neck, feeling the muscles tighten at her touch and pulling his hard, lean, aroused body against the full length of hers.

She was falling through a bottomless tunnel, past time and space, lost forever in the exquisite sensations that were shooting through her as again and again, Cole's lips sought hers. Helpless, she clung to him, past caring who won in their battle of wits, everything forgotten but the rough texture of his skin touching her cheek and the rush of blood to her head that left her dizzy, gasping. Heart thudding, she heard him whisper her name as his lips trailed fire along the side of her face, around her ear and deep into her hair, which had come loose and now cascaded down her shoulders in wild abandon. Over and over, he called her name, like a litany to a goddess.

Driven by a nameless need to possess him, she dug her hands into his thick, black hair until she heard him groan. Suddenly, he drew away, scorching black eyes searching her face, and she gazed at him with such intense desire that a triumphant laugh ripped from his throat. With one sweep, he lifted her effortlessly into his arms, cradling her head against his massive chest, and carried her to the bed.

"No more games?" he whispered huskily as he gently put her down.

She only nodded, no longer trusting her voice. Her breathing was shaky and ragged as he lay down next to her, scooping her into his arms and once more taking her mouth prisoner. I'll drown, she thought, clinging fiercely to the back of his neck. Then there was no more time for thought as Cole gently slipped his hand inside her blouse and cupped her soft, rounded breast, lightly thumbing her peach-tinted nipple into arousal with such infinite tenderness that she shivered uncontrollably. A tear of pure pleasure gathered in the corners of her eyes and rolled down her silken cheek.

Cole tasted the salt and suddenly pulled away from her in dismay. Games, yes, but the idea that his touch was so hateful that it would make her cry tore at his heart. He had been so certain she was willing when he had seen the blaze of light in her eyes . . . a light that had shone with such brilliance that it had taken his breath away. He had been so damned sure she wanted him with the same intensity that he wanted her. "Reggie?" he said, softly. "What is it? Please tell me."

Her green eyes sparkled with the light of a thousand stars as she raised a shaking hand to his cheek. Tremulously, lest she break the spell, she whispered, "No, Cole. I'm not crying," she tried to explain. "It's been so long . . . I haven't allowed . . . I . . ." She bit her lip, searching for the right words.

"Tell me," he urged quietly, stroking her hand while she

struggled to explain away her tears. In that moment, he saw a side of Reggie Gates that was new to him . . . the lost little girl, frightened of her emotions, scared to death of letting anyone in . . . anyone who might hurt her. He pulled her into his arms and placed his hands on both sides of her small, perfect face so that her eyes were locked to his. "We'll stop if you want. I can't bear to see you cry."

She leaned forward slightly and placed her lips on his, kissing him softly, then she extricated herself from his arms and stood up beside the bed. She very slowly began to unbutton her blouse. He stared at her in shock but she shook her head and smiled. "It's not what you think, Cole. It's just been a long, long time since I've felt this way about anyone. I was crying because it felt so . . . so . . . good. I didn't think I'd ever feel this way again." She slipped the blouse from her shoulders and stepped out of her jeans while Cole simply lay there mesmerized. She stood proudly before him in glorious splendor, opening her arms to him in total honesty.

He thought he had never seen a more beautiful woman, and he was awed by the way she offered herself. Not in surrender but with pride that it was right and natural that they come together. "I don't think I've ever wanted to make love to a woman the way I want to make love to you right now," he said in a voice that was achingly tender. He reached out his hand for her, and he pulled her back to the bed, gently pushing her down into the pillows. He bent his head to touch her lips. "Wait," he whispered, slipping off the bed quickly and shedding his clothes while she watched, her eyes never leaving him.

In the dim light of the room, she studied his body, profoundly pleased at the stark masculinity she found in the breadth of his shoulders, the expanse of his chest and the way his dark hair curled down the entire length of his body. When he saw her smiling, he couldn't help but laugh. "Do I meet your approval?"

She blushed but didn't avert her eyes as she nodded. "Make love to me, Cole. Please, please, make love to me."

Those were the last words she spoke before Cole came to her, lying down beside her on the hand-stitched quilt, his dark, desire-filled eyes fastened on hers. She felt the mattress shift as he moved toward her, gathering her in his arms and raining thousands of tiny kisses on her hair, her eyes, her nose and finally holding her in a fierce, possessive, all-consuming kiss that shot liquid fire through her veins. With poignant sensitivity, Cole's hands moved intimately along her body, familiarizing himself with each swell, curve and indentation . . . the way a master sculptor might reverently touch the most priceless piece of unmarred alabaster. "How perfect you are," he marveled and then lost himself in the magic of her mouth as she slanted her lips against his in a rising tide of heated passion.

She closed her eyes, a sensual haze enveloping her as his mouth slowly followed the path of his hands. He traced his tongue along the column of her neck, down the hollow of shoulder and then teasingly flicked at her nipple, causing a moan of ecstasy to escape from her mouth. He wanted to make tonight perfect for her . . . to make up to her for all the years she'd thought were lost to her. And strangely, it was important for her to call out *his* name as he rekindled fires that had been smoldering too long beneath the facade of confident, competent, aloof businesswoman. She was so much more than that . . . sensitive and sensual . . . excitingly naive yet curiously knowledgeable. The intoxicating dichotomies could drive a man wild with longing to be the one to unearth the quintessential woman.

His mouth fastened on her breast, pulling the nipple between his lips, tightening then releasing it until her back arched with the incredible dizzying sensation that was rapidly spreading throughout her entire body. His hands moved with deliberate, delicious languor down her flat stomach, past the reddish triangle between her legs, to skim along the creamy, soft skin of her inner thigh. Momentarily, she stiffened then shuddered as Cole raked his nails gently upward again, just barely touching the soft mat of hair. Her breathing was ragged, rapid, anticipating instinctively where his hand would next travel.

With the utmost care, he parted her legs just enough to graze against the moist velvet that throbbed beneath his gently probing hand. It was all he could do to maintain his control when Reggie arched her slim hips to ease his way. He heard her cry out with urgency as he stroked her with patient, unerring skill. He allowed her to set her own pace, moving his hand inside her, letting her muscles contract around him, then withdrawing when he felt she was on the verge of exploding. Expertly, he teased and tormented her, driving her frantic with exquisite, pulsing pleasure until she began to increase the tempo of her wildly gyrating hips.

"Don't stop! Don't stop! Don't stop!" She panted over and over again as bolt after bolt of electricity passed through her. She finally erupted in a violent explosion, grabbing Cole's shoulders and calling out his name in wild abandon.

While the shuddering still shook her, Cole shifted position, lifted her hips and placed his rigid manhood against her. Digging her fingers into his back, she pulled him into her. A groan tore from his lips as she encircled his shaft, pulling him farther and farther into her, pressing her hips to him in a rhythm that moved them to the edge of ecstasy. Back and forth, she tossed her head as he thrust his full length into her, quickening his tempo as her body demanded more. "Now. Now, Cole. Oh, please!" With one final stroke, he plunged into her, shuddering convulsively as the frantic explosion tore at them. They melted together in one last desperate kiss.

For a long time after, neither moved, their breathing harsh and labored. A last delicious shiver passed through her body. Cole lay his head gently into the curve of her delicate shoulder, toying unconsciously with strands of the fiery mane that fanned out on the pillow, creating a crimson frame for her luminous face. Drawing deep breaths while his heartbeat slowed, he tenderly nuzzled her neck, inhaling the musky scent of their lovemaking. He let out a sigh of absolute contentment.

After a while, Reggie moved, looking into his half-closed eyes with a winsome expression. "Cole?"

"Hmm?"

"Two million dollars worth?"

He pulled her into his arms, cradling her as if she were the most precious piece of porcelain. "Easily," he murmured and touched the top of her head with his lips.

Twice during the night they reached for each other, and each time they made love it was a stunning revelation. Cole was all of the things that David had never been . . . tender, caring and a skilled, patient lover.

Reggie was an unexpected source of surprise to Cole; naive in some ways, wise beyond her years in others. Her natural ardor and unconcealed passion fired his blood. And the feelings that she stirred in him, when she looked up at him with her wide, trusting eyes, were unfamiliar and vaguely disconcerting.

At well past three in the morning, Cole whispered into her wildly tangled hair that it was time for both of them to sleep. Laughingly, she accused him of being far too old for her. He cupped her magnificent face in his hands and stared into the bottomless green eyes for so long and with such intensity, that Reggie finally asked him if anything was wrong. Something flickered in his eyes . . . confusion or uncertainty, perhaps. But then, as suddenly as it had appeared, it was gone and he merely wrapped his arms protectively around her body and drew her to him. "Shh," he said, quietly. "Go to sleep."

In the early hours of the dawn, with the gray light of morning beginning to illuminate their room, Reggie awoke. Longingly, she moved her hand and gently caressed Cole's shoulder. She was startled at how much she wanted him again. The familiar sensation of awakening desire curled in the pit of her stomach, and she closed her eyes, reliving every touch, every embrace. Even now her body ached for him, but she was still too unsure of their relationship to wake him. She lay quietly, listening to his even breathing until she realized with a sigh that she couldn't will him to waken, and sleep wasn't going to come to her restless body. Quietly, she eased herself from under the blanket. Cole stirred slightly then, with a sigh, turned over and slept. She tiptoed around the room, searching for her handbag, intent on brushing out her tangled hair before Cole woke. On the table with the champagne bottle and glasses, Reggie found her bag, the check and the contract. She scooped them all up together and headed for the bathroom.

Once inside, she felt around for the light switch, found it and turned on the tiny light over the sink. She gasped in horror at her reflection—wild hair, bright eyes and faint, reddish bruises on her lips. Blushing, she thought of the intimate places on which Cole had placed his searing lips and wondered if those parts of her body wore the same embarrassing marks of their lovemaking. Then she realized she didn't care. Happiness filled her, remembering the way he had held her, whispering endearments while raising her to heights she never knew existed. Just thinking about it brought another rosy glow of desire to her cheeks.

Eager to get back to Cole, Reggie half closed the door, washed her face and made use of the cellophane-wrapped toothbrush that the inn had thoughtfully provided. Then she took her brush from her handbag and went to work on her tangled hair, brushing it till it lay in soft curls around her face and naked shoulders. With one last look at herself, she replaced her brush in her bag, reached for the check and contract and was about to place them in her purse for safekeeping when curiosity got the better of her. She'd never actually *seen* a two million dollar check. Last night, she had hastily scribbled her name on the contract but had simply taken the check without so much as a glance. Now she opened the folded rectangle and stared. In plain English, in computer print . . . $2,000,000 payable to Regina Gates. Her future, she thought with a smile. Still grinning, she sat down on the edge of the bathtub and opened up the contract, turning to the last page where they both had signed. Her signature was barely legible; his boldly printed. Yes, she thought with little surprise, his signature was exactly as she imagined it would be—strong, sure, certain. Reggie began to refold the contract when it slipped from her hand, falling on the bathroom floor. She bent to retrieve it, noticing that it lay open to page twenty-four.

Then she saw it! 489-30001-48. Her patent number. The number she knew as well as she knew her name. Bewildered, she forced herself to read the paragraph that contained the number. Her mind registered disbelief as every fiber of her being shouted denial at the words that were so clearly written. Positive that her eyes were deceiving her, she read and reread the paragraph. There was no mistake. She had unknowingly signed away her patent rights! Included in the collateral for the two million dollar loan, hidden in an insignificant paragraph that she had neglected to read, was the patent for her computerized loom.

It had all been a lie. A vile, contemptible lie! Everything that he had said to her last night, all his soft, eloquent endearments had meant nothing to him. He had been playing a role—and brilliantly, she had to add—the entire time he had been making love to her. No, she mentally corrected, as rage overcame reason, Cole Weston had never made love to her. He had *screwed* her! Plain and simple. And all to achieve *his* goal!

Her well-thought-out plan had backfired in her face. He had made a complete fool of her, teasing and arousing her physically, taunting her into submission, and like the biggest kind of fool, she had been had! What would it take before she learned? First Nikki then David and now Cole. There must be something wrong with her that, over and over again, she let herself be taken in by sweet talk and empty promises. And, she remembered, with piercing clarity and overwhelming embarrassment, she had actually reached out to him during the night to plead for more. How he must have laughed at her. Close to tears now, Reggie tried to convince herself that the aching void she felt was merely the result of her stupidity and foolishness. But she knew it wasn't. The despair came from a far deeper source. Once again, after so many years of carefully erecting a protective wall that no one could break through, she had let down her guard and had allowed Cole to shatter her utterly. The painful truth came down on her like a thousand-pound weight as she was forced to face the truth. It had all been a monstrous charade!

Not once during all her silent soul-searching did she stop to think or to consider the original purpose of accepting Cole's invitations to dinner. In her misery, she conveniently forgot her vicious plan to seduce him in order to get his money. She couldn't admit that she would readily have slept with Cole, prostituted herself, if necessary, to get that contract.

The contract! She could still get it—destroy it! Then he would have nothing, and she still would have his certified check for two million dollars.

Stealthily, she left the bathroom. Cole was still sleeping soundly as Reggie searched the room for his copy. Then it hit her! The champagne! James Brighton! The fight over the bottle to insure that when Cole popped the cork, it would explode all over his jacket . . . and in the jacket pocket—the contract. James Brighton had the contract securely in his possession, and Reggie Gates would never get her hands on it.

A deadly calm settled over her. Her blood felt like ice water and, with quiet determination, she walked back to the bathroom with her clothing and dressed quickly and quietly. As a last gesture, she re-entered the bedroom, took a lipstick from her bag and printed three words on the mirror above the dresser. She then picked up Cole's car keys and, without a backward glance, left the room.

Within moments, Reggie was behind the wheel of the sleek Ferrari, heading back to Manhattan.

As the sun rose, she clenched her teeth and said a silent prayer that she would never see Cole Weston again.

Chapter 14

Cole's wristwatch went off at 7:00. The tiny beep raised him from a pleasant, erotic dream. With a chuckle at the lewd thoughts that were spinning in his head, thoughts that he hadn't awakened with since he was a teenager, he reached over for Reggie. What an enchantress she was, he thought. Part innocent schoolgirl, part sophisticate. She aroused passions in him that he hadn't known existed. He couldn't remember the last time he had made love three times in the space of a night, and now he wanted her again.

His hand sought the warm contours of her slender body and, startled, he suddenly realized that she wasn't there. He rested his head on the headboard, waiting for her to return to bed. Memories of her aroused body beneath his and her proud breasts arching against his mouth brought a familiar tightening between his legs. What magic did she have, he wondered, that the mere thought of her could stir his body? He was so consumed by his plans for the next half hour that several minutes ticked by before Cole's eyes came to rest on the huge red message on the mirror. From his angle in bed, he couldn't make out the words. He pushed off the blanket, stood up and walked curiously to the dresser. He stared uncomprehendingly at the words. TAKE A TAXI! What the hell did that mean?

He called out to Reggie for an explanation. There was no answer. Puzzled, he walked to the bathroom and knocked on the door. Still no answer. He turned the knob and pushed open the door. The room was empty. There were no signs of Reggie, her clothes or any of her belongings. Once again, he studied the words on the mirror, perplexed. His eyes flew to the dresser top in a sudden flash of comprehension. His keys and his check for two million dollars were gone.

His body went rigid and a tiny pulse began to beat in his temple as Cole realized with blinding clarity that he'd been had. For a split second, he thought he would send his fist crashing through that mirror with its mocking words. The conniving bitch had taken his check, his keys and his car and left him stranded in the middle of nowhere. All his warm thoughts of her were replaced in the space of a minute by a cold savage fury, the strength of which he had never felt before. He strove to keep his raging temper under control while he dressed.

When he saw her again, he would break her deceitful neck!

By the time he had finished dressing, his rage had abated somewhat and grudgingly, he admitted that Reggie had bested him. No matter whatever else he felt about her at the moment, he was forced to give her credit for the way she'd achieved *her* ends.

He slipped his wallet into his pocket and headed for the stairs. Once in the lobby, he explained to James that Reggie had been called away during the night. Cole winced inwardly at the skeptical look on the innkeeper's face as he phoned two car services in an effort to hire transportation for Cole's trip back to the city.

As his rage subsided to a slow simmer, he began to plan how he would approach Reggie. He imagined by the time he spoke to her again her anger at his ploy would have cooled, and he would somehow make everything right between them again.

He could not have been more mistaken.

She refused to speak to him. On four different occasions she hung up before he could begin a conversation. By the end of the third day, she told him in a clipped, businesslike tone of voice to stop harassing her. She also threatened to change her phone number if his calls didn't stop. He couldn't reason with her; she wouldn't even stay on the phone long enough for him to complete a sentence.

What the hell right did she have, he wondered, to be so furious at him? They were both guilty of the same thing, and he knew damn well that she would have done just what he had done, given the opportunity. She'd underestimated him when she had incorrectly assumed that he had amended the contract.

He waited two more days for her to cool off, then called her again, this time at her factory. As soon as Alison Granger had put through the call, Reggie, hearing his voice, hung up.

Still, he persisted. He let another week go by and called, only to find out that she was out at a fabric and textile seminar and wasn't expected home until well after five that night. Hoping to catch her off guard, he grabbed a cab, sped down to Broome Street and stood in a leaky doorway across the street from four o'clock on. As the freezing rain slashed through his thin raincoat, he cursed himself for behaving like a lovesick schoolboy. But still he waited.

She saw him before he saw her. At first she feared the tall man lurking in the doorway was a mugger waiting for a helpless victim, so before she let the cab drop her off, she made him drive slowly past the doorway. With the brim of his hat pulled over his eyes and his coat collar turned up to ward off the rain, she almost didn't recognize him. Then Cole turned slightly and the lamplight hit his face, causing her heart to lurch wretchedly in her chest.

"Quick!" she directed. "Drive around the corner! Don't stop!"

The cab took off and Reggie gave a last, lingering look at Cole. The ice in her heart didn't melt. It would take more than a few flowers, some phone calls and a half hour's wait in a doorway to ever forgive him for what he had done to her. In fact, she thought as she directed the cab to leave her in front of a coffee shop ten blocks from home, she couldn't think of *any* way for Cole to ever redeem himself. And she told herself that she didn't care.

Two hours later, when she was certain he had given up, Reggie trudged through the icy rain for home. She was drenched by the time she reached her loft. It was well after seven and she knew Lee would be waiting inside for the dinner she had promised him. She'd just have to tell him that her meeting had run late.

Cole saw her enter the building and, with the determination of a bulldog, followed her. As she entered the lobby and rang for the decrepit elevator, he tapped her on the shoulder.

She nearly jumped out of her skin. "Jesus Christ!" she screamed as she turned and saw him.

"Hello, Reggie," he said softly, as if he had just left her that morning.

She stared at him for several long moments in the silent lobby, torn between the violent desire to throw herself in his arms and beg him to tell her that it had all been some sort of hideous mistake, and an equal and opposite inclination to slap him hard across the face. Instead, she simply looked up into his questioning eyes and said, as softly as he had, "Drop dead, Cole." Then she stepped into the waiting elevator and closed the steel grating in his face. Her heart was pounding as the elevator started to rise.

Dumbstruck, he stood there like an idiot. Of all the stupid, moronic things he had ever done . . . this had to top the list. Short of flagellating himself, he had tried everything he could think of to make her understand that things weren't the way they seemed. Now it was his turn for anger; at her obstinancy, her refusal to listen to reason and for turning the whole thing around to make it look like only he was to blame.

Well, it was over! He was finished with her! He stormed angrily through the door and, with the driving rain slanting painfully across his face, every coarse, vulgar degrading epithet he could think of spewed out into the winter night. He was sick to death of chasing her. Fed up with her childish games. In that moment, his tender thoughts of Reggie Gates turned to annoyed distaste, then to icy contempt and finally, as Cole retreated into his familiar, comfortable cocoon, cool indifference. He strode down Broome Street looking for a cab, and reminded himself that there were other women with magic green eyes, women who would offer themselves to him willingly, even ardently.

With that comforting thought, he put Reggie Gates firmly from his mind.

* * *

"What the hell is eating you?" asked Lee after Reggie stomped into the loft, slammed the door and headed straight for the bar, where she poured herself a stiff scotch. Lee was sitting comfortably in front of the fireplace reviewing some briefs, waiting for what he thought would be a nice, relaxing dinner. Now, seeing the scowl on Reggie's face, he doubted he would have dinner at all.

She turned on him, eyes sparkling, but he wasn't sure if he saw anger or tears. "Nothing!" she replied. "Absolutely nothing!"

"My, my. Aren't we ill-tempered this evening," he commented.

"Don't!" she warned, making no attempt to hide her mood. "If you start with me, I can guarantee we're going to have a fight and I don't want that. I just had a tough, lousy day, and I'm tired." She looked at him with a plea for understanding. "Do you mind if we go out for a bite? My heart isn't in cooking."

He shook his head. It was on the tip of his tongue to ask her exactly where her heart was, but he demurred. And she was lying, he realized as he watched her drain her glass. In fact, she had done a lot of prevaricating in the last two or three weeks. Ever since her meeting with Cole, she had been remote, removed. Lee hadn't been able to find out anything about that meeting other than the information that she had signed the contract and received the money she needed. But he knew both of them too well not to notice that something was askew. Neither Cole nor Reggie would discuss it. Furthermore, whatever had transpired was still bothering Reggie. She was distracted, unable to concentrate and quick to anger. Cole was also tense and jumpy. His reknowned temper, which he prided on being able to keep in check, now flared at the slightest provocation.

Reggie was absently straightening the perfectly tidy loft in a vain attempt to take her mind off Cole's appearance at her door.

"Problems?" asked Lee, after she had dusted the same spot three times.

She whipped around. "No, why do you ask?"

"Come on, Reg. This is me you're talking to. I know you better than that. Something happened between you and Cole, something besides the simple signing of a contract, and it's time to talk about it."

She looked around the room, searching for something to do, anything that would keep her from answering Lee's questions. How could she hope to explain to Lee the turmoil within her? Not once in the past weeks had she allowed herself to think about Cole, and she knew that once she started, all the pain would come flooding back. Why did it still hurt? There was an ache in the back of her throat that would not go away.

Despite her protestations, he sensed her unhappiness. But she didn't want to share it with him, not yet. So instead of telling him the truth, she dissembled, blithely telling him that she hadn't liked Cole Weston very much and that the meeting, although successful, had been uncomfortable. Beyond that she wouldn't say.

Lee's eyes narrowed into a frown, a thoughtful expression on his face. He hadn't seen Reggie so unnerved in a long, long time, or Cole so strangely furious. Lee suspected that neither one of his two best friends realized yet where their relationship was headed.

He decided to drop the subject and asked, "Now, what about dinner?"

Chapter 15

David Astin sat in the breakfast room of his Lake Shore Drive apartment waiting impatiently for Lucilla, his Jamaican housekeeper, to finish preparing his fried eggs and toast. Looking around the room with a satisfied smile, he marveled at how well life had turned out. This renovated duplex apartment had been a wedding present from his father-in-law, and David had left the decorating to Patrice and her gaggle of gay interior designers. The results had far surpassed his wildest dreams. Their home had recently been featured on the cover of *Architectural Digest*.

The lower level of the duplex had been done entirely in black and white, a combination of European contemporary and art deco. Huge black and white marble squares began at the entry foyer and ran through the kitchen, hallways and dining room. The walls were highly lacquered in black, and gleaming chrome and mirror accessories reflected the view of the lake from the huge picture windows.

It was not a house for children, and since David had no desire to see grubby fingerprints or hear whining, sniveling voices, he had made absolutely certain that that possibility never arose. In the second year of his marriage, on the pretext of attending a tax seminar in Manhattan, he had checked himself into a small, private hospital in downtown Chicago for a vasectomy. Three days later, he had returned home, swollen, uncomfortable but satisfied. No one ever discovered the true reason why Patrice couldn't conceive the grandchildren Francis Munsey so desperately wanted. All of the tests that Patrice underwent came back negative, and David's results were conveniently falsified by a doctor who owed him a huge favor.

All in all, David thought smugly, life wasn't half bad. Except for his father-in-law's constant nagging about children, Francis had fulfilled his promises . . . the house, the law practice and an almost unlimited amount of cash. The only catch was Patrice. David turned at the sound of her footsteps as she entered the breakfast room. At thirty, her promise of beauty hadn't been realized. She was paler, thinner than she had been when he first met her, and the weight loss was unattractive on her, leaving dark rings around her eyes and a sunken, half-starved look. The sight of her so early in the morning nauseated him.

"David," she ventured timidly, having learned over the years that a wrong word or expression could suddenly send him into a towering rage. "Could you meet me for lunch at the club today?"

"For what possible reason?" The thought of spending the afternoon with her revolted him. He deliberately looked her up and down, knowing how nervous it made her, then sat back with his hands behind his head and watched critically while she struggled to answer.

She fidgeted with her wedding ring, and David had to suppress the overwhelming desire to slap her. Everything she did irritated him. "I . . . uh . . . we . . . we hardly spend any time together and I . . ." She pulled nervously on her sweater. "I thought it would be nice if we had lunch together," she finally said.

He turned back to his newspaper. "I can't."

"But, why?"

He turned to her with such burning hatred in his eyes, that Patrice actually flinched. "Since when do I have to answer to you?" he asked, scathingly. When she didn't answer, he said, "I'm meeting with Sprutt and Stewart about the renovation of the stockyards. You know damned well how important this deal is going to be for Chicago. Bigger than Quincy Market, Ghiradelli Square or the Meadowlands. And get your goddamned fingers out of your mouth!" he said, noticing that repulsive habit she reverted to whenever she was upset.

"One hour?" she said, then was immediately sorry as David stood up, pushed the chair angrily away from her and swept by her as if she were invisible.

At the doorway, he turned. "I said I can't! Don't you understand simple English?" he snapped while she stood there focusing on a chip in her nail polish. He stormed out of the room, and she heard the front door slam. She stood where she was, shaking.

"Pain in the goddamned ass!" he cursed as he drove the silver 560SL Mercedes convertible onto the open road, heading for his office. Even work was preferable to spending time with Patrice.

His thoughts abruptly left Patrice as he ran through a red light on the corner of Lake Shore Drive, missing a young mother pushing a carriage by inches. The car swerved dangerously out of control for several mind-shattering seconds, careening this way and that as David attempted to regain control of the powerful machine on the ice-slicked street. Blurred images of trees and pedestrians flew by.

He braked sharply, a bad mistake, sending the automobile into a skid. His hands flew over the leather steering wheel, twisting and turning, vainly trying to make some contact with the street which was no longer under him. His pulse raced, speeding adrenaline to his brain. The solid concrete retaining wall was there before his befogged brain registered its presence. A screech of burning rubber on a tiny piece of pavement, which had somehow escaped the ice, caught the tires, finally bringing the careening vehicle to a screeching halt.

Sweat poured out of David's pores. His breath was shallow and rapid. His body was flung over the steering wheel, staring straight ahead at the cement wall that had almost caused his death. He was suddenly conscious of a tingling in his groin. When he looked down he saw that he had a tremendous erection.

In the grim silence of the automobile that had almost become his coffin, David wondered wryly if it now took a brush with death to achieve what Patrice and a string of professionals found nearly impossible to accomplish. With a huge grin on his face, David placed his hand on his rigid member and within moments brought himself to the edge of orgasm. Had it not been for the appearance of curious pedestrians rushing toward the scene of the near accident, David Astin would have exploded in his pin-striped trousers.

Danger and death. He would have to explore the possibilities.

Chapter 16

Cole sat up lazily in the king-size bed, his arms folded comfortably behind his head, a cool smile of contentment on his handsome face as he watched Evyan brushing her black shoulder-length hair. There was no denying that she was beautiful. Taller than most women, five-foot-ten in her stocking feet, she wore her height aristocratically, proud of the way she towered over most men. She inherited her rich caramel skin tone from her Spanish and Indian ancestors. Her almond-shaped ebony eyes, full sensual lips and insatiable sexual appetite had held Cole's interest for more than a year. They were attuned to each other's physical needs, each knowing which touch, which caress would please the other most.

At fifteen, when her father was appointed United States Ambassador from Peru, Evyan discovered that New York was very different from Lima. With a ripe, fully developed body and sexual curiosity to match, her well-publicized romantic escapades caused rampant gossip throughout the diplomatic community within months of her arrival in Manhattan. It was with great relief that the Ambassador walked her down the aisle when she turned seventeen, only to have her back at eighteen when, upon finding her in bed with her chauffeur, Nikos Kariokis threw her out.

Cole met her at a cocktail party, ten years and three husbands later and the mere fact that her latest husband, Luis Bolivar, wouldn't grant her a divorce even though they had been separated for over a year, only drew Cole closer to the sloe-eyed Peruvian beauty; it relieved him completely of the tedious necessity of explaining why marriage was something he would not attempt. Their arrangement suited him totally and if he suspected that Evyan wasn't entirely faithful to him, he gave it little thought. She was there when he wanted her and little else mattered.

Lately though, Cole found Evyan too available, too predictable, too eager to please him. There was something intangible missing from their relationship. Despite her beauty, Evyan was no longer fresh or vital; the ravages of her pursuit of pleasure had taken its toll. The little that they might have said to each other had been said long ago. Their relationship had always been physical and, in recent weeks, Cole had grown restless and bored.

It was a pity, he thought with a resigned sigh, that it was just about over between them. He hadn't told her yet, as if he were gathering the strength for the scene he knew would follow. But each time she whispered *cara* or *mi amor* in his ear, she unwittingly drew that inevitable day closer. His body enjoyed the release she provided, and he still liked to have a beautiful woman on his arm at the many public functions he was forced to attend. Tonight was one of them; a charity fund-raiser at the Metropolitan Opera. Five hundred of New York's most influential patrons of the arts had gladly paid their thousand dollars for a chance to be photographed for the next issue of *Women's Wear*.

Cole smacked her botton as Evyan strolled past him, naked. "Hurry up. It's late and I don't want to miss the curtain."

With a petulant frown, she sat down next to him, raking her long fingernails through the darkly matted hair of his chest. "Do we have to attend, *cara*? I could order dinner from Pietro's and we could spend the rest of the evening in bed. That would be much more *simpatico* than the opera." Her hands began a slow, sensual descent.

Deliberately, Cole removed her hands and placed them above the satin comforter. "Tomorrow night," he lied. "Tonight is *La Bohème*, my dear, and five hundred people are waiting for us to put in an appearance. Be a good girl and get dressed."

He started to get out of bed, but Evyan pushed him down. "Tomorrow night is impossible. Luis is coming to New York in the morning. I cannot see you."

Cole shrugged indifferently. It made no difference. "Then it will wait until after Luis leaves." This time he was successful in extricating himself from her hands. She sat on the edge of the bed, watching as he headed for the bathroom, making no effort to get up to dress. He turned back to her. "I am leaving this apartment in a half hour, with you or without you."

"*Cara*, wait! I have something to tell you."

Cole stood facing her, impatiently tapping his foot. "What is it, Evyan?"

"Luis is flying into New York to see his attorney," she explained.

"And?"

She drew in a deep breath. "I think he is going to agree to a divorce." She offered the words to Cole as if they were a gift of extreme value. To her horrified amazement, he showed no reaction. Nothing, not even the merest flicker of an eyelash. She felt a red-hot current of anger surge through her body. "You have nothing to say? I am doing this for you—for us!" she said furiously.

He laughed, a cold, hard sound. "Don't," he advised. "Our relationship has lasted this long because of your ties to Luis, not in spite of them. If you are hoping that I will marry you once you are free, please dismiss that thought from your mind. I have no intention of marrying anyone." His voice was uncompromising. "Have I made myself clear?"

"How dare you?" she hissed, lunging for his face with her nails.

Cole's hand shot up, grabbing her in a painful grip. Enunciating clearly, he said, "You know as well as I do, Evyan, that we both entered into this affair with our eyes open. You were still married at the time, remember?"

Numbly, she nodded her head. "But I want to change that now," she whispered.

With a voice like steel, Cole answered, "You may do exactly as you please. However, your divorce had better not have anything to do with me. Do you understand?"

"But you love me!"

A rueful smile flickered over his eyes as he released her hand. "Whatever gave you that idea?" he asked. "As I recall, love is a word that has never been spoken between us. Am I wrong?"

Evyan's shoulders sagged. "No."

"That's what I thought. Evyan, don't do this," he warned. She began to press her heated body against his in a familiar gesture, rubbing her brown-tipped breasts against his chest, grinding into him.

She whispered into his neck, "Of course, you are right. What I do with Luis is my own business." She reached her hand between his legs, caressing him the way she knew always aroused him. This time it failed to elicit any response and she shrugged her expressive shoulders resignedly.

Cole relaxed. The subject was closed for a moment, but he knew he had wounded her pride, and Evyan Bolivar would not forget in a hurry. He patted her cheek and headed for the bathroom.

The steady buzz of conversation died down as the house lights dimmed and the orchestra struck the first chords of the overture. Cole and Evyan slipped into their seats quietly. Cole was still annoyed at Evyan, who had purposely dawdled for over an hour, changing gowns four times before she was satisfied with her appearance. In defiance of Cole's preference for understated elegance, she had chosen a blood-red, sequinned, floor-length sheath, slit up one side to her hip. The bodice of the gown plunged into a deep V to her waist. She had added a single ruby and diamond pendant that fell, invitingly, into the crevice of her breasts.

Cole leaned his head back with half-closed eyes, listening to the hightly emotional, moving strains of *La Bohème*. Within moments, he was lost in the reveries of student life in the Bohemian Latin Quarter of Paris in the late nineteenth century and, though he had seen the opera many times before, he had to admit that the new Franco Zefferelli production promised to be exceptional. Yet, even as he listened to the hopeful Rodolfo and his three friends in their cold, sparsely furnished garret, dreaming their great dreams, an odd melancholy came over Cole. What had become of his dreams, he wondered? Were WestCo and Evyan Bolivar enough for him? And after Evyan—what then? Other Evyans?

Next to him, oblivious to the magnificent music and not privy to Cole's thoughts, Evyan cracked a piece of gum and fidgeted with her handbag, unclasping it several times until Cole, in desperation, reached over and grasped her hand, securing it in his. Evyan smiled in the darkness, her hand delving into his lap and fondling him in an intimate, demanding fashion, intent on finding a more interesting way to pass the long, boring hours of the opera.

"For Christ's sake!" Cole whispered, trying to remove her hand. It was impossible. Her hand searched still deeper between his legs. Cursing under his breath, he dug his nails deeply into the soft fleshy underside of her wrist. She cursed in fluent Spanish, a long string of epithets that Cole was intimately familiar with.

The couple in front of him had had enough. The woman turned angrily in her seat to demand silence. In a paralyzing moment, Cole found himself staring into Reggie's penetrating green eyes. Every muscle in his body tensed as he watched with increasing embarrassment as her eyes flew to his face, then in a dawning of understanding, to his lap. His eyes stared into hers for an endless moment until, with a contemptuous glance, she tore her gaze from his, staring blindly at the stage.

A thousand emotions tore through her, an aching lump

building in the back of her throat as she tried to concentrate on the performance, but all that her glazed eyes could see was that woman's hand. In the space of a few tortured seconds, Reggie's eyes had forever imprinted that image in her mind. Now, as she tried to swallow, the one thing that kept her in her seat was her pride, stubborn and outraged. Her neck felt as if it would snap in two from the effort it took for her not to turn around. Valiantly, she suppressed the urge. Stupid, pathetic Mimi, she thought to herself as Puccini's heroine encountered Rodolfo for the first time. Don't you know your love affair will end in misery? Run! Run . . . before you can't!

Cole's eyes bored into the back of her head with such a powerful intensity that he was certain she would feel it. He saw the rigid arch of her back and knew instinctively the effort it cost her to remain in her seat. For a fleeting moment he wondered what her reaction would be if he asked to speak with her in the lobby. There were words that needed to be said between them, explanations, apologies. The demeaning scene she had just witnessed was so damning, and Cole was seized by a sudden overwhelming need to explain. His impatience increased as the music built to a powerful crescendo, signalling the end of the first act. The moment the house lights were turned on, he would speak to her.

Evyan was still smarting from the wounds on her wrist. She left her seat during the curtain call, ignoring Cole. With an insolent swagger of her hips, she went to look for the bar. Cole remained seated, applauding mindlessly, waiting for Reggie to turn around. When she did, he was struck by the cold control on her face. Whatever she had felt during the first act was now successfully buried. She stared through him as if he were a stranger, and blithely walked past him, leaving him to stare after her in amazement. Her escort, an exceptionally handsome man with blond hair and piercing blue eyes, looked at Cole with barely concealed curiosity. Then he too left.

Cole jumped from his seat. Fuming that she would actually ignore him, he headed for the lobby, determined to set things right between them once and for all. As he scanned the crowds he thought about what he would say to her. He had no intention of apologizing for his behavior with Evyan; that wasn't Reggie's business. Yet, he did feel a need to . . . to . . .

dammit! He didn't know what he wanted. The more he thought, the more convinced he became that perhaps it was she who owed him an explanation. Hadn't she walked out on him? Stolen his car? Refused his phone calls?

He continued to search for her, but by the time the house bells began to sound, announcing the beginning of the second act, he hadn't caught sight of her in the mad crush of people surging about the lobby. Several important people stopped to talk to him, but Cole brushed them off. The bells rang for the third time, the final warning, and Cole reluctantly made his way back.

He would speak to her after the opera.

Chapter 17

Reggie's head ached with the effort necessary to hide the agonizing feelings that had torn at her when she had recognized Cole. At the sight of Evyan Bolivar's hand caressing him, she had found it almost impossible to breathe. She had forced herself to turn her attention to the stage, drawing deep, unsteady breaths as she held in all the raging emotions that smoldered. The image of Cole and his mistress flashed repeatedly before her eyes. In a daze, she had calmly walked past him, down the stairs and into the fresh air, where she had pleaded a migraine and gratefully accepted her brother Robert's silence when he placed her in a taxi.

All the way home, Reggie silently cursed Lee for offering her the two tickets for tonight's performance. She had accepted them only because Robert was in town and, when he had called to say hello, he had mentioned the difficulty he was having trying to get good tickets to this very performance. In an effort at family reconciliation, Reggie had invited him. Now, as the cab turned into Broome Street, Reggie began to wonder if Lee had orchestrated the entire night in order to bring her together with Cole. He never could have foretold the distasteful scene of Cole and Evyan virtually making love at the opera.

But Reggie had seen them, and it had been unbearably painful. She spared herself further agony by leaving. Now they would have their privacy, she thought bitterly.

An hour later, dressed in an old, faded football jersey, Coco purring at her side, Reggie sat gazing blankly into the crackling fire. Her legs were tucked under her as she absently sipped a cup of herbal tea. An open book lay next to her, but she was far too distracted to read. She drank the tea like medicine, hoping it would relax her, allowing her to finally fall asleep. When the buzzer sounded, she was not surprised. Robert had mentioned he would try to stop by after the opera to see how she felt. She returned the buzz on the intercom, allowing him to enter the vestibule, and waited for her doorbell to ring.

When Reggie opened the door, her throat constricted at the sight of Cole leaning casually against the doorjamb, his darkly handsome profile accentuated by the hallway light. There was a peculiar look on his face as his eyes appraised her. Reggie was instantly self-conscious about her appearance. Clad in a large T-shirt that reached to her thighs, with her wild mane of hair tumbling in disarray around her shoulders, Reggie felt she looked dreadful.

On the other hand, Cole thought he had never seen her look more magnificent as the suffused firelight played off her brilliant hair and hinted at the voluptuous curves partially hidden beneath the translucent shirt; familiar curves that he could almost feel beneath his hands.

For several seconds neither spoke. Cole studied her face thoughtfully, searching for words to explain his presence at her door. A thousand questions raced through Reggie's head. She was conscious of the quickening of her pulse as Cole stared intently into her surprised eyes.

"You're cold," he stated, mistaking her trembling for a shiver. His dark brows drew together in a slight frown. "Don't you know better than to open the door to strangers?"

"You're not a stranger, Cole," she said, softly. Why was her heart beating so erratically? Why couldn't she catch her breath? Her head pounded as she tried to sort out the wild swings of her emotions. One minute she hated him, the next moment her legs grew weak at the sight of him.

"Reggie," he said, interrupting her thoughts, "you can't stand in the doorway like that." Gently he pushed her back into the living room. With a swift glance around the room, he observed the well-worn furniture, the glowing brass lamps, the many objets d'art that cluttered the room and stamped it undeniably hers. It was so different from the formal decor of his own townhouse, yet he immediately felt at home.

An eternity passed before Reggie spoke, and when she did, it was in a whisper. "Why are you here?" She looked up at his face and, as she saw the intensity in his eyes, the look of tenderness and confusion, her heart gave an erratic leap, hammering in unsteady beats.

Cole gave her a long, penetrating look, his eyes glinting with the hint of an embarrassed smile. "Would you believe me if I told you that I honestly don't know? When you didn't come back to your seat after intermission, I no longer wanted to stay. Before I knew what had happened, I was standing in front of your building." His smile faded slightly to be replaced by a questioning look. "Do you want me to leave?" he asked her softly.

Part of her screamed silently for him to go, but she knew that she desperately wanted him to stay. Her eyes rose to meet and hold his. "Would you leave if I asked you to?" she inquired.

"If I thought you really meant it. Do you?" he asked, already knowing the answer. When she shook her head silently, he continued. "There are things that need to be discussed between us. I've been trying to speak to you for weeks, but you haven't given me a chance. Now that I'm finally here, I'm not leaving until we talk." He sat down on the edge of the sofa, motioning for her to sit next to him. "Will you listen?"

Reggie sat down next to him and nodded her head. She had regained some of her composure but was still nervous and unsettled. Trying to hide those feelings, she said tonelessly, "I'm listening."

At the tenor of her voice, Cole's mouth twisted in a grimace. Damn! She wasn't making this any easier. Driven by some inexplicable need, he had raced here, leaving Evyan with friends, and now Reggie was acting as if it didn't matter whether he had come or not.

She infuriated him with her aloofness, yet he still held the memory of how she could amuse, delight . . . and ignite him. Those memories were the very things that had driven him here tonight. He chuckled to himself at the bizarre effect she had on him. While she waited for him to begin speaking, she inadvertently extended her long, sleek legs. He was struck sharply with the remembrance of her slender, sensual body beneath his, and it took every ounce of discipline he possessed to keep his mind on what he had to say. He tried to ignore the blood rushing to his head, but as she leaned back, his eyes fastened on the sharp outline of her rounded breasts against the thin fabric of her T-shirt. He was finding it increasingly difficult to concentrate, and his hands longed to slip beneath the jersey.

Reggie noticed the hardening of his jaw, the sudden tension in him, and lifted her startled eyes to his face. She saw the naked hunger, the desire in his dark eyes. Her body, too, was beginning to respond to his nearness, the memory of his betrayal fading in the close, charged atmosphere of the room. She held her breath, waiting for him to break the tense silence between them, but he didn't move. Tentatively, as if she were afraid of being burned, she reached over and laid a hand on his leg.

Their eyes locked and, in a low, warning voice, Cole asked, "Are you sure?"

She made no pretense of misunderstanding. Slowly, deliberately, she nodded, not trusting her voice. In that single moment, Reggie brushed aside every other thought except for the overwhelming need to feel the hard strength of him deep inside her.

Her hand was like a searing flame as desire ripped through him. He leaned back his head, groaning as her silken fingers raked lightly over him, sending sparks throughout his body. He reached out to trace the full curve of her breast and teased the tips with his fingers. Beneath his hand, he could feel the quickening of her heartbeat in response. Every movement of her wakening body increased his need for her. Reggie moaned as his mouth came down on hers in a consuming kiss. Suddenly, Cole stopped, wrenching her hands from his body and holding them in his, his searing black eyes searching her face.

With a voice thick with passion, he said, "Do you know what you're doing to me?" He drew in a ragged breath.

Reggie smiled, her voice low and seductive. "About the same thing you're doing to me, Cole."

A dam burst within him at the caressing sound of his name on her lips. For weeks she wouldn't even speak to him, and now she was warm, vital, ready for his touch, eager for him. Once more he tried to warn her.

"I can get up and leave now, or I can stay for the night," he said meaningfully. "The choice is yours, Reggie. But if this is some sort of game you're playing—end it now. If we continue, I won't give you another chance."

For long moments, Cole waited as Reggie struggled with some inner conflicts that she wouldn't share with him. Only the hissing of the logs in the grate disturbed the silence. She wanted him so desperately, caring about nothing except the demands of her body. If there was a price to be paid tomorrow, she would gladly pay it. But tonight belonged to them. "Don't go," she whispered.

A building, gathering force consumed them both and Cole's need was so intense that with a violent shudder, he reached for her, pulling her roughly against him, his lips devouring her eyes, her hair, her cheeks, her neck. His burning mouth trailed over her shirt until he grasped her aching nipple between his lips, drawing it into his mouth. Reggie's whole body writhed under the exquisite sensation. Cole's demanding hands ran up the inner curve of her thigh, seeking the moistness between her legs. An intense cry of pleasure escaped her lips as his searching fingers entered her, filling her with liquid fire, stroking her most sensitive spot with unerring skill until she was beyond thought.

Cole's body could wait no longer and, with a single motion, he swiftly undressed and entered her quickly. It was not a tender coupling, but then, neither of them wanted tenderness. Tonight, there was only the screaming need of two people to quench fires that raged within them at the sight and feel of each other. Raw, unleashed passion overcame them as, time after time, Cole thrust into her. She threw back her wild hair, grasping frantically, matching his increasing tempo with her hips as the ecstatic need drove them nearly insane.

"Now, darling," he cried. "Now!" And one last demanding time he drive his manhood into her, rending a cry of pure joy from her throat as wave after wave of exquisite heat shuddered through her body to join him in an explosion that threatened to devour them both.

While they were still intimately entangled and Reggie's breathing was still ragged, Cole held her to him in a possessive embrace. She reached up and ran her fingers through his thick, dark hair. Smiling, she whispered, "You need a haircut."

The non sequitur tickled him, and he laughed softly, running his fingers along her high cheekbones and tracing the slightly swollen outline of her lips. Her slender hand held his fingers to her mouth and very tenderly, she kissed each one.

I love this man, she thought with grim resignation. After all the deceptions, all the pain and all the running away to deny her feelings, the truth finally had to be faced . . . she loved him, and she knew, as surely as she knew her name, that it would eventually destroy her, exactly the way loving always had. Her only hope lay in keeping it from him, because once he knew and he was armed with that knowledge, she would become one more conquest in Cole Weston's legendary list of women. She would rather give him up now than have that happen.

She eased herself from him and stood up, pulling the T-shirt down around her thighs.

"Where do you think you're going?" he demanded, reaching up to recapture her hand.

"I thought you said you came here to talk," she said, silently warning herself to keep everything between them light and uncomplicated. Once Cole knew he had touched her heart, she would be lost. This time, if there was to be anything between them, it would be only on her terms. "Give me a moment, and I'll be ready for heavy conversation." She flashed him her brightest smile, pulled her hand from his and walked into the bedroom, where she sat on the bed, trying to still the rapid beating of her heart.

For an insane moment, Cole thought about following her, desire beginning to stir anew. No sensible, mentally sound man should want a woman with the intensity that he wanted Reggie Gates. He couldn't get enough of her. Yes, he admitted wryly, she was a very, very desirable woman . . . and a dangerous one. He didn't completely trust her, the memory of how she had left him in the inn was still too fresh. If he weren't careful, he could get very badly burned playing with such an unpredictable woman . . . but, he reminded himself with a predatory grin, if he could handle Evyan Bolivar, Reggie Gates shouldn't pose too much of a problem . . . once they set down the ground rules.

When she returned to the living room several minutes later, she was dressed in a long, monklike terry-cloth robe. She had brushed her hair until it crackled like summer lightning. Cole shook his head and laughed at how very young she looked at that moment. Was she really the same woman who had moved with such abandon, returning his passion with an ardor that more than matched his?

"Would you like a drink?" she asked as politely as if they were at a garden party.

"Brandy, if you have."

She walked into the kitchen and returned a few seconds later, bearing a tray of cheese and crackers and two Ronald McDonald glasses half filled with brandy. She handed one of them to him, then set the tray on the coffee table. "What would you like to talk to me about?" she asked, as if they had just met.

"Our relationship," he answered, sipping the fine brandy from the silly glass.

"Okay," she said agreeably, tucking her feet under the voluminous folds of the robe as she sat down next to him. "What is there about our relationship that you want to discuss?"

His eyes searched her face with such intensity that she felt she was melting. "Do you regret what happened between us tonight?" he asked.

Silently she challenged him. "Should I? We're both adults, Cole. We made love tonight because we both wanted to. I wanted it as much as you. I don't regret it at all. Do you?"

"Me? Of course not!"

"Then why should I?" she asked with a casual shrug of her shoulders. "Please don't make more of this than it is."

"I just don't want to hurt you," Cole said, suddenly realizing that that was true.

"You can't," she lied, her voice calm, factual. "Cole, I am not a lovesick girl. I accept the physical attraction between us. If you're nervous that I expect more from you, don't be." Reggie waved her hand in the air. "What's one night between friends?"

Suddenly his eyes grew cold. "The one thing we have never been is friends. We have been business associates, adversaries and lovers. But friends?" He stared into her eyes but they revealed nothing. "Are you willing to continue our relationship the way it is now? No strings? No commitments?"

His words stabbed her like thousands of tiny glass shards but she kept the pain from her face. "Are you asking me to become your mistress?" she asked when she finally found her voice.

He nodded thoughtfully. "I suppose I am."

Reggie stood up with a forced smile on her face. "You already have one too many. Besides, if I were to accept your proposition"—she paused—"that is what it's called, right?"

He nodded again, smiling ruefully.

"If I agree to become your mistress then I would have the right to make certain demands on you, and you would have the same rights. Correct?"

Cole remained still, his smile growing broader.

"That's what I thought," Reggie stated. "In that case, dear Cole, I refuse your offer."

A perplexed look passed over his strong features. "Isn't that a little illogical after tonight?" he asked dryly.

Reggie pursed her lips in deep concentration as if she were giving great thought to his question. Finally she answered. "I really don't think so. I've come to cherish my feedom and have no desire, at this time, to give it up. When we want to be together, we will. If you care to become involved with someone else, or I do, neither one of us will feel any guilt," she finished, grateful that he wasn't standing near enough to hear her pounding heart.

"You're actually standing there asking me to believe that you could accept that kind of casual relationship?" he asked incredulously.

"Certainly," she lied. "Couldn't you?"

He threw back his head and laughed at the unexpected turn of events. "It would be ungracious of me to refuse." Cole reached for her hand and pulled her down on his lap. His lips began nuzzling the creamy skin above her breast. His mouth felt the tiny flutter of her quickening heartbeat in response to his touch. When she suddenly pushed herself from his lap, he stared at her in surprise. "What's the matter?"

"Not a thing, darling," she responded with a twinkle in her eye.

"Then why are you getting up?"

"Because," she began, "it's late and you're going home."

"Am I?" he asked, and when she didn't answer, he continued in a teasing note. "I could make you beg me to stay," he stated. The lazy smile that she was beginning to know so well was working on the corners of his mouth, but she steeled herself against it. Although there was nothing she wanted more than to surrender to him again and lose herself to his lovemaking, it was important that he believe her. More than that, it was vital that he leave before her shaky resolve crumbled.

"Undoubtedly you could convince me," Reggie said, "but you will honor our agreement." She handed Cole his clothes and pointed down the hallway. "There's the bathroom. I'm going to bed. Would you mind letting yourself out?"

He grabbed her around her waist, pulling her against him and inhaling the fresh scent of her skin. "One of these days," he warned, "I'm going to call your bluff." He kissed the top of her head and walked toward the bathroom.

With shaking knees, Reggie entered her bedroom, sat down on the bed and waited until she heard Cole leave. Then she lay down and spent the better part of the night staring at the ceiling, wondering if she was capable of playing out this charade. There was a magnetism about Cole Weston that threatened to breach the wall she had so carefully erected after David Astin. She was determined not to let that happen, whatever the cost.

Chapter 18

"Th-th-this is yo—your idea of a g-g-good t-time?" Reggie finally managed to say through chattering teeth as she and Cole sat huddled together under a ratty blanket in the buggy he had rented for the afternoon.

He pulled her closer, trying to keep warm, but the biting wind had them both shivering. Even the hack driver, a toothless native of the Bronx, thought the two lovers were slightly crazy to subject themselves to the open-air carriage when the wind-chill factor was minus two degrees. But, two hundred dollars was two hundred dollars, and who was he to argue?

"If you had let me buy you that silver fox coat yesterday, you'd be warm now," Cole reminded her.

She buried herself in her ski hat, scarf and down parka. "Hey, darling." She looked up at him with laughter in her eyes. "I'm a wealthy woman now. If I wanted that coat, I would buy it for myself."

He looked at her in surprise as the horse clip-clopped past Fifty-ninth Street, and they caught a glimpse of F.A.O. Schwarz. It was the first time either one of them had made any reference to the two million dollars since the night at the inn. "Stop!" he yelled at the driver through the roaring wind. The carriage came to an abrupt halt, and Cole jumped down. "Stay there," he directed and made a mad dash through the throngs of early Christmas shoppers on Fifth Avenue. to the doors of the world's most exciting toy store. Reggie watched him disappear.

Ten minutes later, he returned carrying the largest stuffed camel she had ever seen. Cole hoisted himself into the buggy and presented the animal to Reggie with a huge grin. "Since you wouldn't accept a fox," he stated, "I bought you a camel!" He looked like a little boy who had diligently saved all his pennies to buy his favorite teacher an apple. He positively beamed.

A surge of overwhelming love rose in her, but she kept it hidden as she placed the camel between them. "Coco's going to be very jealous," she murmured, hiding her face in the camel's neck.

By the time they reached Fifty-fourth Street, the tip of Reggie's nose had lost all feeling. Even the driver was ready to give back Cole's money when big, fat, wet snowflakes began to fall. She turned wishfully to Cole. "Does this mean skating is out?"

The brim of his furry shearling hat was covered in a blanket of white. "Are you chickening out?" he challenged.

"Not me!" she denied, shaking her head. "It's the camel." When he started to laugh, she turned a very serious face to him. "Have you no compassion for a desert animal?"

Finally, Cole relented and stopped the carriage. He helped Reggie down and, dragging the camel with them, they walked four blocks to the Plaza, where, camel and all, they entered the Palm Court and sat down to hot chocolate. "I want you to understand," Reggie began, "that it's not necessary to show me *all* of your New York in two weeks." Since the night of the opera, they had been on a whirlwind tour of the island, freezing on the Staten Island ferry, shivering as they stood in line to see the Christmas windows of Saks, Tiffany and Lord & Taylor, and fighting the crowds at Rockefeller Center to catch a glimpse of the famous tree.

On Christmas Eve, Reggie prepared a traditional dinner of baked ham, glazed sweet potatoes, peas and pearl onions, and pumpkin pie. Cole sat back after they had eaten, stuffed but more contented than he could ever remember. "You spoil me, you know," he commented as Reggie began to clear the table.

She smiled. "I like to. It keeps me busy."

He frowned at her like a petulant child. "Is that all I am? Busy work?" Their arrangement was beginning to bother him more than he was willing to admit. At first, when she had agreed to his edict of "no strings," he had thought that no one could ask for more. He never tired of her beauty, her irreverant sense of humor or the fiery rebellious spirit that stubbornly refused him the comfort of her bed for an entire night. In fact, it had amused him that she was so independent. When they parted after a long day together and an evening of glorious lovemaking, his thoughts constantly returned to her warm embrace, the way her sparkling eyes melted whenever he touched the body he was beginning to know so well. Her incredible capacity for passion awoke emotions in him that he found hard to identify, and he knew beyond a doubt that she had never shared this with anyone else. It was revealed by the incredible look of surprise in her eyes and, for some reason, it pleased him beyond words. "Well? Is that all I am?" he repeated when she hadn't answered.

She came back from the kitchen and sat down on his lap, snuggling deep into his arms. "Fishing, Cole?" she asked, reaching up and running her fingers through his thick hair. "Hmm?"

He cupped her face in his palms and gazed into her amused eyes. "You're a bit of a bitch, aren't you?" he commented, but there was no anger in his voice, only gentle teasing.

"Most assuredly," she answered, "but . . . I suspect that's why you like me. Would you be happier with a cloying, simpering, grasping woman?"

He uncrossed his legs, and she fell off his lap onto the floor. "No," he answered, "just a more compassionate one."

Reggie rubbed her bruised bottom and stood up, laughing. "Compassionate? When have I not been compassionate?"

"Every goddamned night when you throw me out in the cold!"

"Bothers you, does it?" She was enjoying herself immensely, delighting in the heady feeling of having the upper hand in their relationship, and she knew with certainty that the moment she lost it, the instant that Cole suspected that she cared more than he, he would lose interest in her. So she kept up the lively banter, a facade to hide her true feelings. "Poor Cole," she sympathized. "But this is the way you wanted things, isn't it?"

"Oh, be quiet!" he demanded and pulled her into his arms. "Tomorrow night we have tickets to the *Nutcracker*, and afterwards you are coming home with me and *staying* for the entire night. Then we'll have breakfast together and—"

She pulled out of his arms. "Oh, Cole, I can't, I've already made plans for tomorrow night. I'm so sorry. I wish you had told me earlier about the tickets."

A frown marred his forehead. "What do you mean you've made plans? What kind of plans?" For two solid weeks, day and night, they had been together and now suddenly, out of nowhere, she made plans? Without telling him? What the hell was this?

"I'm staying home tomorrow night," she said firmly. "Alone. I need some time for myself . . . to sort of catch up on things. We've been so busy lately that I've neglected everything else." She batted her long eyelashes. "I really am sorry. I had no idea you thought we were spending the evening together."

"Reggie," he said, anger flashing, "I have tickets that are impossible to get and you can 'catch up' another night." What the hell kind of game was she playing?

"Uh-uh, Cole. I can't. I *need* this time for *me*. Please try to understand."

"I don't want to understand! This is ridiculous—*you're* ridiculous!"

She shrugged her shoulders indifferently. "I'm sorry that you feel that way."

"That's it?" he asked, drawing his eyebrows together in a deep scowl. "That's all you're going to say? No explanations?"

"Do I owe you any?"

"No. You don't owe me a damned thing. I just thought . . . I guess I was wrong."

"Who was the one who wanted it this way?" she reminded him sweetly. "Who was the one who wanted to know if *I* could handle *this* kind of relationship? It was you, wasn't it?" She knew she was pushing things, but she wanted to make her point. "Look, Cole . . . I'm going to be home. I'm not going out anywhere with anyone else, I simply need some time alone. Is that so difficult to understand?"

A veil of ice descended over Cole's face and he looked into Reggie's eyes with the merest hint of warning. "You, my dear one, are playing a very dangerous game and, if I'm not mistaken, the last time you tried this . . . you were less than successful. Take that in the spirit in which it's intended."

"And that is?" she asked, her heartbeat speeding up at the cold tone of his voice.

"Don't play with me, Reggie. I'm much better at playing than you. I've done it for much longer . . . and with greater finesse." He wanted to explain that, for the first time in his life, he was letting someone in . . . someone that he cared for. She had hurt him when she left the inn that night and, in the days and weeks that followed, he had slowly come to the realization that Reggie Gates meant more to him than a few nights in bed, a multi-million dollar patent or a pretty accessory for his male ego. But the words were lodged in his throat and the fear of making himself that vulnerable to another person kept him silent. He sighed in quiet resignation when she didn't answer. "All right. Have your little evening by yourself, but I'm still going to see the *Nutcracker*. I'm sorry you've decided not to go. I think you would have enjoyed it." He turned and walked out of the kitchen area into the living room, where he picked up his coat. "Please call me when you've finished 'catchng up.' I'll be home."

"You're leaving now?" she asked in astonishment. "It's only nine thirty."

He leveled a speculative glance at her. "I need some time alone, too. It has suddenly occurred to me that I have some rethinking to do," he said in a stone-cold voice. He was furious . . . at her because she insisted on playing infantile games, and with himself because he was powerless to stop her. He felt like shaking her!

"Cole, I—"

"What?" he asked brusquely.

She shook her head. "Nothing."

"Good night, Reggie." And he opened the door and left, closing it softly behind him.

For a very long time, Reggie just stood there, looking at the closed door. She felt foolish. She no more wanted to stay home alone on Christmas night than she wanted to grow another nose. Why in the world had she said that she did? Because, you idiot, she berated herself, *you* had to show him that he wasn't *that* important to you, didn't you? Well? she asked herself. Did you do it? Did you accomplish anything? She turned away from the door. Sure you did. You made yourself very, very unhappy.

Cole never went to see the *Nutcracker* the next night. He sat alone in his darkened study, polishing off a half bottle of Napoleon brandy and wondering what had ever possessed him to become involved with Reggie Gates again. More than once he reached for the phone but replaced it, knowing full well that it would be playing into her hands to admit he missed her and wanted to see her. The familiar words *no strings* and *no commitments* ran through his mind over and over again, and he scowled at the bitter irony of having his own words flung back in his face.

The problem, he reflected morosely, was with both of them. He was still unwilling to give up his freedom . . . yet, he desperately wanted Reggie to give up hers; to be there when he wanted her. Tonight was her way of telling him that she wouldn't do it. She was showing him that she could come and go as she pleased—and it was driving him crazy. After more women than he could count, more romances than he could remember, this one stubborn, infuriating girl had managed to pierce his veneer. He was absolutely determined to keep that knowledge to himself. Here we go again, he thought . . .

Reggie waited for Cole to phone but three days went by without hearing from him. On December 27, she finally broke down and called him, only to be told by his secretary that he was out for the day and she would see that he received her message. By three thirty, Reggie began to pace. She checked her daily agenda book to make certain that she hadn't made a mistake. No, it was clearly entered. She and Cole had theater tickets for an off-Broadway show. At four thirty, the phone finally rang. It was Marjory King, Cole's secretary, with the news that Cole had been called away unexpectedly and would be unable to attend the evening's performance. Did Miss Gates still want the tickets? She said no and hung up the phone, fighting the rising tide of confusion and uncertainty. That night, she stayed home trying to concentrate on an afghan she had started to knit, but the yarn kept tangling in her fingers, and finally she threw the whole thing across the room in frustration.

At eleven thirty, she couldn't stand it anymore. *Okay! Okay! I'm wrong. I deserve this! I acted like an idiot and he's giving it back. And you don't like it, do you! No, dammit, I don't! So call him. I will not! Don't, then, but stop this infernal pacing!*

She called Cole's number. Sleepily, he answered. "Hi, Reggie," he said when he recognized her voice. "I'm sorry about tonight."

"That's okay," she lied. "What's new?"

For several minutes they maintained a light conversation, but then Cole told her he was very tired and would call her in the morning. She distinctly heard a new reserve, a guarded reticence in his voice. She sensed his withdrawal and for a split second she wondered if she had pushed him too far. With an attempt at nonchalance, she said a breezy good-night, all the while feeling a cloud of dread descending over her.

Still pondering the disturbing phone call, Reggie absently leafed through the evening newspaper. Her eyes froze when she saw the picture of Evyan and Luis Bolivar kissing each other good-bye at the airport the afternoon before. Quickly, she scanned the caption. "After a two-week Christmas sojourn in Manhattan, Venezuelan oil baron Luis Bolivar returns to Caracas to negotiate new oil leases. International jet-set wife, Evyan Bolivar, bids her husband a tearful good-bye and wishes him a safe trip."

A tremendous weight settled on Reggie's chest and, for a moment, she thought she could actually feel her heart shattering. The picture in the newspaper explained everything. It was abundantly clear to Reggie that the two weeks that Cole had been dancing attendance on her, Evyan had been dutifully entertaining her husband. Now that Luis was leaving the country, Cole and Evyan could safely resume their affair. Reggie had been nothing more than a convenient time-filler. Her shaking hands clutched the newspaper as desperately she tried to maintain her equilibrium. Her emotions veered back and forth between hatred and despair and finally to bleak acceptance. After all, she tried to reason, *she* had turned down his offer to become his mistress. Obviously, he needed something more permanent than she was willing to give. A crushing sorrow enveloped her as the truth struck with brutal clarity. Their two weeks together had only been a foolish diversion to him, and now it was over. It had to be, she realized as tears began to slip down her cheeks, because she could never share Cole Weston with another woman. She loved him too much.

From that moment on, Reggie threw herself into her work with a singlemindedness that her employees had never seen. She turned down date after date with Cole, pleading the pressures of getting her summer line ready. She refused to offer any explanations to him, refused to answer his probing questions. Two weeks later, Reggie left unannounced for the Milan and Paris "Ready-to-Wear" shows. She never informed Cole of her sudden decision to go to Europe. But just as the newspapers had informed Reggie of Cole's perfidy, he happened upon her picture at Harry's American Bar in Paris, tête-à-tête with an influential European manufacturer.

There was no name to the emotion Cole felt as he stared at the damning photograph with a look of complete disbelief. What a consummate actress she was! What a lying, contemptible . . . then he stopped. No, he admitted grudgingly, she had never, never lied. She had told him the truth from the very beginning. Reggie had wanted no commitments and had demanded the freedom to do exactly as she pleased. It had been his mistake to believe she was different.

An ugly little laugh escaped Cole's compressed lips. The little game that she had begun was far from finished. There would come a time when he would exact his revenge . . . all he needed was time.

He reached for the phone to call Evyan.

Chapter 19

The four months following her brief romance with Cole were exceptionally successful for Rag's Raggs, but unhappy ones for Reggie. Suddenly, Galaxy was paying promptly for their orders, and reorders were pouring in at an alarming rate. Reggie had to hire three more seamstresses, two cutters and a permanent bookkeeper. With the money borrowed from Cole, she leased a small factory on Thirty-eighth Street, filling it with sewing machines, clickers and cutting tables. It wasn't very glamorous, but it was all hers, and it kept her mind off Cole.

Stores from all over the country were begging for her line, but Reggie decided to maintain her exclusive arrangement with the Galaxy chain. Invitations flooded her mailbox asking her to attend gala openings, charity functions and speaking engagements at design schools. She had neither the time nor the inclination to accept any of them.

The one exception Reggie made was, by invitation of the Commerce Department, to attend a forum of textile manufacturers who were trying to regulate the Untied States' import of foreign textiles. When the decision was made to tighten the "rules of origin," it effectively barred the importation of tens of millions of dollars of foreign textiles to the American market. It was a decision that immediately changed the nature of the domestic textile industry, increasing the value of Reggie's domestic computer loom.

Lee spoke to her about taking Rag's Raggs public, but Reggie turned down the idea, explaining that until she had repaid her loan to Cole she couldn't contemplate any major changes.

When Reggie was informed that the "rules of origin" decision had in fact been approved, she understood Cole's insistence on the inclusion of her patent in their original contract. Because of his connections in the Commerce Department, he would have know exactly what that piece of machinery would be worth. She cursed her naivité and vowed that he would never get his hands on that extremely valuable patent. More than ever, she was determined to pay off that loan.

Sales at Rag's accelerated at a dazzling speed. Reggie listened carefully to Lee's advice about overproduction and overdistribution. It would be a major error, he explained, to produce in anticipation of orders. Cut only what has actually been ordered, he advised. Don't let the merchandise find its way into off-priced outlets. She did exactly as he told her, creating an impatient demand for her goods.

Her time was no longer her own. With the incredible growth of Rag's came the inevitable demands for personal appearances at each Galaxy boutique. She could no longer refuse to appear. Reggie flew around the country in the lavishly appointed private jet supplied by Simon Hastings, whom she had yet to meet. Suffering from jet lag became a permanent condition, and she snatched precious hours of sleep whenever she could. Sandwiches and endless cups of coffee became the staples of her diet. Another woman might have complained, but Reggie needed the hard work, the insane hours. At last she had achieved the kind of professional success she had dreamed of when she left Boston so many years ago.

During the long, lonely evenings in strange hotel rooms, Reggie's thoughts returned to Cole. She no longer lived with the violent anguish of his deceit, but neither had she forgotten the feel of his body nor the way he could make her laugh. And when she allowed her mind to wander too long, a stabbing emptiness grew inside of her. It was her pride that always came to her aid; that and the knowledge that one day she would repay him . . . in spades!

In New Orleans, as she prepared to attend a party being held in her honor in the multi-million dollar Galaxy Promenade, Reggie noticed with horror that a piece of her luggage was missing. That suitcase contained her clothing for the evening's festivities. Frantically, she left her hotel room in search of an open dress shop. She didn't dare enter the mall, fearful that someone from the press might see her buying another designer's outfit. She made it a practice, indeed an obsession, never to be seen at a public function in anything but her own designs. The only store that was still open was a sorry-looking variety store. Though her choices were limited, she zipped through the aisles in a trance of creative fever, making a dozen rapid purchases: a package of men's extra large T-shirts, a half-slip, two yards of white grosgrain ribbon, a length of jet beads, rubber bands, needles, thread and a bottle of blank India ink.

Back in her hotel room, Reggie dumped the contents of the bags on her bed. Quickly, she stripped off her clothes, ran to the bathroom, where she filled the tub, pouring India ink like bubble bath under the scalding water. Rolling the slip and T-shirts into a ball, she tied them securely with a dozen rubber bands. When the bath was a quarter filled, she submerged the garments. After ten minutes of soaking, she removed and unrolled the dripping mess, hanging everything to dry on hangers. She then blew them dry with her hair dryer. It had worked! The slip and the cotton T-shirt had absorbed the ink in certain places, missing it in others. Where the rubber bands had been, beautiful designs of grays and blacks whimsically floated over the fabric, suggesting butterflies at play over a field of flowers.

Reggie pulled the slip over her head, allowing the elastic waist band to settle just above her rounded breasts, creating a short, strapless dress. Then, working swiftly with her manicuring scissors, she snipped away the collar and sleeves of one of the T-shirts. She took what was now a cotton vest and cut a straight line from neckline to hem. When she had finished, she put the jacket over her dress. The length of jet beads were twisted tightly around the white ribbon and tied with old-fashioned macrame knots, a technique she had learned in Girl Scout camp. This accessory was used to tie up her heavy auburn hair, allowing a few maverick curls to escape down her creamy naked shoulder. The effect was enchanting, elegant and totally novel.

Thousands of tiny light bulbs had been strung on the dozens of white birch trees that surrounded the promenade. It seemed to Reggie, as she stepped onto the escalator, that the mall had been transformed into a star-filled evening. The promotion was planned in Reggie's honor, but as she nervously studied the elegantly clad, bejeweled and sequinned women who eagerly awaited an introduction to the famous designer, Reggie had to fight back the overwhelming desire to flee to the safety of her hotel room. Instead, she momentarily closed her eyes, straightened her back and whispered, "Courage!"

The moment that Reggie's foot left the escalator, Claire Connors, Galaxy's star buyer, approached her in an obviously expensive black beaded evening gown. Reggie had only a second to catch her breath before Claire took her by the elbow and maneuvered her through the crowd.

"Simon Hastings is waiting to meet you," she whispered, pointing vaguely in the direction of the bar, where a dozen men were standing.

Although Reggie had been employed by Galaxy for many years, she had never met the store's president. She knew very little about him other than that he and Claire had been involved in an affair for years.

Possessively, Claire slipped her hand through the arm of a tall, handsome, silver-haired man who was leaning nonchalantly against the bar. His piercing gray eyes beneath pitch-black eyebrows shone like beacons in his richly tanned face. Reggie knew that Simon was in his early fifties, but he had the athletic body of a man in his thirties and a look of authority and arrogance that Reggie found disconcerting.

"Simon, darling," Claire said with an emphasis that left no question about her status in his life, "this is our famous little designer, Reggie Gates."

Simon turned toward Reggie, his eyes boring into hers. Reggie returned his look, unflinching. Was it her outfit, she, wondered, that shocked him? She couldn't afford to offend this man who was so very important to her business. Claire watched the surprised look on Simon's face with satisfaction. Her eyes roamed contemptuously over Reggie's clothes, mentally relegating the youthful designer to obscurity. Reggie's nails bit savagely into her palms, but she refused to tear her eyes from Simon's face.

But Simon was not feeling displeasure or shock at Reggie's outfit but rather interest in the alluring woman who recently had been the subject of Claire's acrimonious tongue.

Claire, observing Simon's stare, mistook it for a sign of disapproval.

"Amusing," she commented dryly. "Simon, this must be Reggie's new underwear collection." She gave Reggie a malicious grin. "How very clever of you, my dear, to introduce this tonight when you knew everyone would be simply dying to see what our creative genius was wearing." She turned to Simon for confirmation. "What do you think, Simon? Is she as elegant as you anticipated?" She didn't wait for an answer but plunged headlong into another stinging diatribe. "One is always a wee bit apprehensive when Reggie arrives at an affair. There is a certain—what should I say—foreboding? Or perhaps—"

"Claire," he interrupted quietly, "I think you've said enough."

Claire misunderstood the unstated warning. "I suppose you're right," she sighed. "What can one expect, after all?" she said and looped her arm within his once more. "But, Reggie, you never answered my question. Is this a new underwear collection?"

Simon's lips turned up mischievously and he winked at Reggie, telling her that he was on her side.

Filled with a new confidence, she answered calmly, "Why no, Claire, it's my new spring line. Do you like it?" She looked up at Simon, who was smiling broadly now.

Blindly, Claire continued to dig at Reggie. "I think it's a delightful premise—and how bold! How many of us can wear our underwear to a formal affair? And the rest of the collection," she asked with biting sarcasm, "is it as inspired? Do we wear our panties and bras, too?" The vicious words spat from her crimson lips. "Tell me, Reggie. Have you given any thought to jockey shorts, boxers, garter belts? Oh, and there's always athletic supporters. Are they included in the line?"

Simon edged carefully away from the two women. He watched the familiar, jealous curl of Claire's lip. Had he cared to, he could have ended the venomous attack right then by the merest warning pressure on Claire's arm, but he was too curious to see how Reggie would handle the confrontation. Very few women could stand up to Claire once she'd started.

Reggie knew exactly what Claire was doing. By making Reggie look small, Claire thought she was elevating herself in Simon's eyes. Reggie countered, "Claire Connors! You've done it again! Did the press leak this to you? How could you possibly know all the details of this collection!" She sighed exaggeratedly. "I never could put anything over on you, could I?" Reggie watched as Claire's eyes turned from glee to confusion and then to anxiety as she noted Simon's approval of Reggie. "Yes," Reggie continued, "the entire line is based on underwear. It's going to start a revolution in women's undergarments. Imagine, women wearing boxer shorts and muscle shirts!" she continued cheerfully. "But, Claire, I have to admit that I didn't include athletic supporters in the line because, until this very moment, I couldn't think of a single woman who might need one."

Bravo, Reggie Gates! Simon said silently. In the space of five minutes, Reggie had been awed, uncertain, frightened, and then, calling upon some inner spirit, had shown a bold streak of courage in the face of fierce antagonism. Simon found her delightful and intriguing. Claire did not. Flushing scarlet from the inescapable feeling that she had been not only bested but deserted by her lover, her face registered all the enmity she felt toward Reggie. She was so enraged that she couldn't trust herself to speak. Instead, she turned abruptly on her heel and strode angrily toward a group of New Orleans businessmen and their wives.

Reggie was left alone with Simon, who signaled to a passing waiter and handed her a glass of champagne. "You've earned this, my dear. Claire can be difficult." He raised his glass to her, waiting for her to respond. Reggie quickly downed the sparkling liquid. "May I suggest that you sip the next glass?" he said with a touch of amusement. "Champagne," he continued, "is like a beautiful woman. It should be savored."

For the first time, Reggie became aware of Simon as a man, not as her employer, and she blushed hotly. Simon found that it only added to her beauty. He took pains to assure her that standing up to Claire was to her credit. "To be a success in this business," he told her while he casually slipped an arm around her waist, "we all have to bare our teeth now and then. Don't concern yourself, she'll recover." He led her toward the bar. "Shall we have another glass of champagne now?"

Reggie spent the remainder of the evening at Simon's side, suffering Claire's angry glances. Simon seemed totally oblivious to the antagonistic looks, and he ignored Claire's ill humor. In fact, he ignored Claire altogether, finding Reggie's outspoken charm and originality more than adequate replacement for Claire's fury. Reggie was thrilled at having been singled out as Simon's partner for the evening and shed her nervousness, impudently flirting with the man at her side.

By the end of the evening, Reggie, more than a little tipsy, was finding Simon more and more attentive and attractive. She studied him thoughtfully while he spoke to a Texas oilman, beginning to fantasize about what it would be like to go to bed with him. She would have been thoroughly flustered had she realized that Simon was wondering the very same thing, and he was determined to find out. More than a little experienced, he knew beyond a doubt that, with the amount of champagne she had consumed, he would have no trouble seducing her that night. That wasn't what he had in mind. When he took her to bed, as he knew he would, he wanted her totally sober. For the present, he was content to banter, flirt and dance with this fresh and lovely woman. His parting thought, as he led her to the escalator at the end of the evening, was that someone ought to warn Claire Connors that Reggie Gates was more than her match.

By morning, *Women's Wear* had photographs and descriptions of Raggs' newest line, lauding it as yet another triumph for Reggie Gates. "An innovation in women's casual wear, lighthearted, totally original and eminently wearable" were the phrases used to describe her outfit at the promenade opening. And the underwear concept? The phones from Fruit of the Loom, Hanes and Jockey were busy all day trying to secure the licensing agreement that would allow them to produce a women's underwear line bearing the name Rag's Raggs.

While Claire Connors spent the morning planning her revenge, Reggie, a little hung over, spent it in the bathroom, scrubbing India ink stains from her body. My chemists will have to work on this, she thought.

The excitement that was generated by Reggie's underwear line was unheralded in the history of the lingerie market. Reggie researched fabrics and dyes with her textile experts until they finally developed a fabric which, when immersed in water, exploded with color and design. It was an idea that came to her suddenly when she remembered the coloring books her mother used to buy her as a child. Tiny dots of black were printed all over the pages of the books. It wasn't until one touched the dots with water and brush that colors began to appear. Once again, Reggie patented her invention and, in so doing, raised herself up another rung on her ladder to financial security.

Thus, from a malevolent remark made by a jealous Claire Connors at the New Orleans reception, a totally new industry was born.

Simon was kept aware of the phenomenon from his office high atop a skyscraper in Dallas. He demanded that Claire buy the entire line despite her insistence that it was a seven-day wonder and totally inappropriate for the Galaxy image. Sales from the Rag's Raggs boutiques climbed steadily as the line was delivered. Simon, according to Cole Weston's peculiar demand, made certain that Claire continue to reorder the underwear clothes. He took unexpected pleasure in Clair's grumblings as UnderRaggs became a household word. Simon's interest in the piquant designer increased with each ring of the cash register. Soon he would be ready to make his move. But first, he wanted to know what Cole Weston's interest was in her.

Chapter 20

"We're ready whenever you are," said Alison Granger as she breezed into Reggie's office, clipboard and pencil in hand. "Everything's perfect. The models are fabulous, the clothes are divine, and you're a genius!" Seeing the panic in Reggie's eyes, she spoke soothingly. "Come on, Reg. You're going to knock 'em dead!"

"I'd better," warned Reggie, laughing nervously, "or you're out of a job." She slipped out from behind her desk and smoothed her sharkskin skirt. "Who's here? What about the press? Is Lee here? Why didn't he come back?" She spit the questions out like bullets from a submachine gun. "I'm babbling, aren't I?"

Alison nodded. "Uh-huh, and you'd better stop or you're going to make a fool out of yourself." She squeezed Reggie's shoulders for luck. "Honey, this is the best line you've ever done. Everyone who saw the preview agrees so why are you so frightened?"

Reggie twisted her hands. "Because this is the first time I've ever done an actual show. Do you have any idea what we spent on scenery, music, flowers? Who convinced me to hire a theatrical designer to do the backdrop?" she asked. "A curtain would have sufficed." The entire show was to be staged in a 1920s speakeasy that had actually been built within the loft in the past week. When Reggie had reviewed the bills, she had shuddered. If the line of beaded evening clothes with their two and three thousand dollar price tags didn't do what she anticipated, she might as well close up shop. Every penny she had was invested in this unexpected holiday line. No one had ever shown holiday in May. It was unheard of—and very chancy. But because of the tremendous amount of time it would take for delivery, she'd had no choice. Now, she was terrified. She looked at her watch. Eleven forty-five. The show was due to begin at noon. "Give me five minutes alone then knock. Okay?"

She walked to the huge floor-to-ceiling windows and stood looking out at the glorious spring day. "Holiday in May," she'd called it. What if it didn't work? What if none of the department stores would commit their money this early in the season? Hell—it wasn't even the season yet! It was too late now. She'd gambled everything she had on this show. She took a deep breath, squared her shoulders and was just about to walk to the door when she heard Alison's knock.

"Let's go, boss!" called Alison through the door and Reggie heard the first chords of the musicians.

"Please," she whispered out loud and opened the door.

"A million two!" screamed Alison, running into Reggie's office two hours after the show had ended. "Reggie, they were scribbling numbers so fast they couldn't keep up. Galaxy's order alone would keep you in business for the rest of the year. And note takers . . . sheaths and sheaths of paper. They'll be sending in written orders by the end of the week. You're going to do over three million in initial orders." She slapped the thick stack of papers on Reggie's desk. "Now, where's the champagne?"

"Alison, I can't." Reggie's expression of utter exhaustion was overwhelming, begging for sympathy. "I've been up for seventy-two hours without a wink of sleep. All I want to do is put my head down right here on this desk and sleep for about a week. Then we can celebrate." It had taken every ounce of courage and strength for her to get through this afternoon without collapsing.

The phone rang and Reggie shook her head. "You get it. I'm too tired to speak to anyone else."

Alison picked up the phone and brought it to her ear, taking the ever-present pencil away first. "Yes," she said. "That's right. No, I'm sorry she's not taking any calls today. Would you like to leave a message?" Alison picked up a notepad and scribbled a name and number. "What is this in reference to?" she asked then paused and frowned. "Yes. I'll see that she gets the message." She hung up and looked at Reggie, who actually had taken her own advice and was resting her head on her desk. "Reg?"

"Mmm?"

"Reg, the phone call."

"Important?" she asked with a yawn. Nothing was as important as sleep right now.

"I think so. A Miss Marjory King calling for Mr. Cole Weston." She sat down on the other side of Reggie's desk at the same time that Reggie lifted her head in surprise. They stared at each other. "It seems," Alison said slowly, "that you owe Mr. Weston some money . . . and the note is due Monday."

There was a deadly silence in the room as the two women let the words sink in. Finally, Reggie said, "It can't be six months already. Can it?"

Alison calculated on her fingers. "May, April, March, February, January, December. Did you borrow the money in December, Reg?"

Reggie thought about the night at the inn several weeks before Christmas. "Yes! Oh god, it's six months. It is." She looked at the stack of papers on her desk, orders for over a million dollars worth of clothing and more still to come. She ran her fingers through her hair in panic. There was no way—no way she could come up with two million dollars by Monday. Not if she wanted to have a business on Tuesday. Everything she had, all her capital, was tied up in "Underrags" and this new line. Everything she had! She'd be bankrupt. "That son-of-a-bitch," she sputtered. "Not a word, no warning, nothing."

"But you owe it, don't you?"

"Yes. But I'm not paying it. Not now! I'll do something. Go to him. Ask for an extension. That's what I'll do. I'll show him the books, the orders and tell him I need another six months. That should put us in the black. We're a healthy, growing company . . . how can he refuse? I'll even offer him an extra point in interest as incentive." With that thought in mind, she relaxed. She knew exactly how to play Cole Weston.

Cole wasn't interested in another point of interest, or another fifteen points, for that matter. He had waited patiently for this meeting with one single purpose in mind. And now, seeing Reggie walk through the door to his office, he knew with certainty that he would carry through his plan; a plan that had been set in motion the day they had first met, a plan she knew nothing about.

"Good morning, Reggie," he said casually as if they had seen each other the night before instead of over four, angry, confusing months ago. She looked radiant in a two-piece white cabled knit sweater and skirt that heightened her green eyes and ivory skin. Under other circumstances he would have . . . But these weren't other circumstances. She was only here in his office for one purpose, and he had allowed this meeting to take place for as selfish a reason as she. Cold-heartedly, impersonally, he would now inform her of the price she would pay for trying to play a game with his money, his time, his mind and, most importantly, his heart. No one had ever dared that before. No one, including Reggie Gates, would ever get that close to him to try it again.

She slipped into the leather chair that faced his desk and busied herself with her briefcase and papers before she even acknowledged his greeting. Her heart was pounding so furiously that she knew if she tried to speak, nothing would come out. Keep it professional, she warned herself silently. Just deal with the loan and the extension and forget the past, forget the past, forget the past! "Good morning, Cole. I assume that you've looked over all the papers?"

With very little expression on his face, he nodded. "Are those the latest figures?" he asked, pointing to the sheath of papers in her hands. He noticed her hands were trembling slightly but chose to ignore it. Pity or sympathy had no place at this meeting. Everything that was about to occur had been brought upon Reggie by no one but herself.

"Yes, would you like to see them?"

He reached over the desk for the papers. "Thank you. I only need a moment." Quickly, he scanned the thirty-odd pages of her latest financial statement and finally lifted his head. "Is there anything you'd like to add? Anything that isn't included in this statement?" he asked coolly.

"You understand the reason that I'm asking for this extension?" she asked. "I mean you can see that Raggs isn't in financial difficulty. . . . I just need a little more time."

He looked up at her with a peculiar smile that caused her heart to beat uncomfortably. Unconsciously, she gripped the arms of the chair as she waited for him to speak. For a long time he simply stared at her.

"Well?" she asked, finally breaking the unbearable silence. "Will you agree to an extension?"

He had clasped his hands together on his desk, his brow furrowed in deep thought. Slowly, he shook his head. "I'm afraid not, Reggie. Either you come up with the money by tomorrow morning or I'll foreclose."

"You wouldn't!" she hissed.

He arched his eyebrows in mock surprise. "Oh, really?" he asked. "What possible reason would I have not to foreclose? We happen to be dealing with an enormous amount of money."

Her eyes blazed. "You wouldn't take advantage—"

He smiled. "Of course I would, and so would you if you were given the opportunity. For whatever it's worth, we're very much alike in that respect."

"No we're not, Cole. I would never—"

His expression remained impassive as he spoke. "Yes you would, and you have in the past. You may have temporarily forgotten, but I haven't. You have gone to extraordinary lengths to achieve what you want. You are as unscrupulous as you believe me to be. You've played up to me, flirted, lied . . . in short, did everything you could to get me to lend you two million dollars. And you succeeded brilliantly. Then, you unceremoniously spit in my face!"

"I never—"

A harsh, bitter laugh escaped his tightly compressed lips. "Oh, indeed, you did. Flying off to Europe without a word." He leaned forward slightly. "Did you really think I wouldn't care? Or that I would forget what we had so easily?" His eyes narrowed imperceptively. "I didn't give you half the credit you deserved. Hell, Reggie, you were positively brilliant!"

"Never mind, you bastard! I'll find the money elsewhere."

"If you think you can find two million dollars by tomorrow morning, then I underestimated your resourcefulness. I rarely make that mistake." With an unconcerned shrug of his shoulders, he collected his papers and headed for the door. "Good luck, Reggie. I have always admired your confidence. Oh, you can leave a cashier's check with my secretary in the morning. She usually gets in by nine." He strolled past her, stopped and said, "Should you run into a problem, she knows where I can be reached."

"What happens if I can't repay you?" she asked quietly.

He sighed. "I told you. I'll be forced to foreclose on your business, your co-op, your car, your factory and whatever assets you have—*including your patent*. Either way, you can be assured that I will recoup my money." He stared meaningfully at her apprehensive face. "Have I made my position absolutely clear?"

Her anger and frustration were beginning to consume her, but with great difficulty, she managed to contain them. Coolly, she replied, "I would like to continue this conversation. Surely there must be another way to resolve this without your losing your entire investment or having me declare bankruptcy."

Cole barely lifted his head.

"Don't you care if you lose two million dollars?" she asked in desperation.

"Of course I care, but it won't be the first time I've made a bad investment. At the time, the rewards seemed worth the risk."

"What rewards?" she asked impatiently. "Everyone told me they couldn't understand why you agreed . . ." She stopped short. Slowly, a light was beginning to dawn. "Cole, why did you agree to lend me so much money? It was never just the patent, was it?"

For a fleeting moment, Cole thought about abandoning his wild scheme, but as he studied the woman in front of him, he knew beyond a doubt that he still wanted her. He was as certain today as he had been from the moment she had first entered his office. More so. He felt a tiny flicker of guilt for knowingly backing her into this untenable position. It was the first time in his life that he had deliberately duped anyone. "No," he admitted finally. "It was never just the patent."

"Then, why?" she asked, genuinely confused. "What did you want?"

He stared into her eyes, looking for something that he had once seen but now was gone. "You," he answered simply.

"I don't understand."

He nodded knowingly. No, he thought, I don't suppose you do . . . but, then, neither do I, not completely. Over the last four months, ever since he had seen her picture in the newspaper, he had wrestled with his emotions about what he felt for Reggie—yet, still, he couldn't define it. Nor could he come to grips with the almost obsessive need he had to bend her to his will. At times, the need to possess her was consuming, shattering his normal complacency and driving him to the edge of distraction. Then, at other, saner moments, he could almost laugh at the way she had unknowingly breached his cool, unemotional facade.

"I have a proposition to put to you," he began. "When I've finished explaining it, you'll understand exactly where we both stand."

Icy tentacles closed around Reggie's heart. This was it, then, she thought. He's going to force me to become his mistress or else he'll foreclose. As unlikely and as archaic as it appeared, she knew what his next words would be. This can't really be happening to me. No one, not even Cole Weston, could force a woman to do that against her will anymore. But then she recalled his warnings, especially on Christmas Eve, *Don't play with me, Reggie. I'm much better at playing than you. . . .*" A chill ran through her body. I'm Alice in Wonderland and he's the Mad Hatter. I've finally fallen through the rabbit hole! That's the only way any of this makes sense.

He sat down at his desk and leaned back with a calm, dispassionate expression on his face. "As you already know," he began in a slightly mocking tone, "I'm forty-two, reasonably attractive, exceedingly wealthy and considered, by the general public, to be an exceptional catch." He didn't miss her derisive sneer—he just chose to ignore it for the moment. "However," he continued, "over the years, I've decided to remain a bachelor. I've never had the least inclination to marry. My consuming interest is WestCo. You might say," he added with a half smile," that, if anything, I'm married to my business. From all accounts, it's proven to be the only lasting relationship I've heard about." He got up and walked to the back of the room where a serving table was laid out with coffee and cups. He turned to her and smiled genially. "Coffee?" he asked as he poured himself a cup.

She shook her head impatiently. "No, thank you. Could you just please finish your explanation!"

He leaned against the server, balancing the cup and saucer

in his hand. "Recently," he began again, "I've had reason to change my mind about matrimony."

Reggie's heart jumped into her throat and her hands trembled. A muscle worked in her cheek as she clenched her teeth. "What do you mean?" she asked, trying to sound as calm and detached as Cole, while actually her heart was thudding wildly. Marriage? Does he mean me?

He took a sip from his cup. "Coffee's good. Sure you don't want any?"

She shook her head and he came back to his desk and sat down. He was deliberately tormenting her. She could tell by the twinkle in his eye.

He cleared his throat dramatically. "I've been giving this a great deal of thought," he said with great seriousness, "and although our relationship has been stormy, I think that after we work out the particulars, a marriage between us might not be a bad idea."

She was quiet for a long moment, and then laughed nervously. "You sound like you're discussing a business deal," she said shakily.

His face was implacable, unmoved by her light laughter. "I am."

A wave of confusion washed over her and a horrible sense of foreboding began to swell in the pit of her stomach. "I—I don't know what you mean."

"It's quite simple, really. I've decided to get married and, since neither one of us has had much luck with *affaires de coeurs*, I think this can be a mutually beneficial arrangement." His eyes hardened imperceptibly when he saw the look of horrified disbelief on her face. "Come on, Reggie," he chided, "we'll both get what we want. You'll get your patent back and—"

"And what will you get? What's in it for you?" she burst out, quaking with fury at his audacity. "You don't need a wife or love or—"

"Whoever mentioned the word love?" he asked caustically. "Love's for other things . . . it's fleeting, it makes people act peculiarly, irrationally. And if it exists at all," he added harshly, "it's a damned poor reason for marriage."

"You're insane!"

"Hardly," he contradicted and, seeing her bolt from her seat, raised his voice a notch. "Sit down!"

"Don't you dare tell me what to do!" But she sat down, legs quivering. What a fool she had been to think that Cole Weston had wanted her for love. Her first instinct about hiding her feelings from him were right, after all. He was cold and would always remain cold. Nothing she could do or say would ever touch him.

"If you don't love me, why do you want to marry me?" she asked in a small voice.

"Convenience," he stated simply. "Keeps me from having to answer to everyone about why I haven't called their recently widowed or divorced friends. It's great press, makes me look good. And, it will give me a certain freedom to do what I please." And, he added silently, it will keep you near me at least until I figure out why you disturb me so. "I don't like to put it this way, Reggie, but my position on this issue is not negotiable. I really do think I'd like a wife."

"So go buy one."

"Actually, I have," he stated matter-of-factly, "unless, of course, you want everything you've built to fall in on you."

"You actually expect me to marry you for those reasons?" she asked incredulously. "Because it will be 'convenient' for you?"

He shrugged imperceptibly. "I don't see that you have any other options . . . short of losing your company and your patent. Besides," he added in an affable manner, "except for attending a few public functions together, you can pretty much go your own way. Don't worry, Reggie. The marriage will be in name only."

"You're the lowest, vilest excuse for a man I've ever met," she said, her eyes blazing contemptuously. Cole inclined his head slightly, as if in agreement with her estimation of his character. How had she ever thought she loved him? She didn't even like him! Now, as never before, she was seeing him as he *really* was and she hated what she saw. Like a slithering serpent, using fear to paralyze its victim, Cole Weston had managed to back her against a wall. This time he had her. But only this time. Oh, she'd marry him all right, but she would make sure it would be the biggest error he'd ever made. She still had a few aces up her sleeve. She was playing against a strong hand, but with a little luck and good timing, she'd see him pay for this.

"Name the date," she demanded.

He looked at her curiously. It had been too easy. "Then you agree?"

She saw the look of shock on his face. Good! she thought. Let him worry a little. She shrugged her slender shoulders and laughed devilishly. "You'll live to regret this, you know," she said in an offhand manner. "But, yes, I agree. I assume that means I get the extension?"

His shoulders sagged ever so slightly. So, she didn't at all care. She would sell her soul for money. "Yes, you get the extension."

"Fine. Then I agree to your 'arrangement,' but, so help me God, you'll be sorry you ever offered it to me."

He sat back wondering what he'd done. "Time will tell."

In the month that followed that extraordinary meeting, Cole met with Reggie and her attorney three times. Carefully, they worked on a contract which spelled out in explicit detail the conditions under which the marriage would take place.

A prenuptial agreement was prepared whereby the two parties agreed that if the marriage lasted more than three years, all prior debts, obligations and liabilities between the parties would be considered to be discharged, even if one of the parties were to seek a divorce on any grounds. The agreement also provided that if the marriage were terminated before the expiration of the three-year period, the outstanding debt, with interest, would still be owed.

The other stipulations, which Reggie insisted be written into the agreement, were separate and totally private living quarters, the unquestionable right of either party to seek his or her own social life, provided it didn't interfere with the public events planned as a couple, and provided that said social life be conducted with discretion. Cole, for his part, insisted that if the contract was nullified in any way, Reggie's debt became payable immediately. If he defaulted, Reggie would receive an amount far exceeding the loan he had made to her.

Each time they met to amend the agreement, the air

crackled due, in large measure, to the undisguised enmity that flew from Reggie's icy emerald eyes. No matter how many times Cole tried to engage her in conversation, Reggie spoke only through her attorney. She pretended Cole wasn't in the room. In the beginning, he found her stubbornness and perversity amusing. By the third meeting, he had given up any attempt at conviviality and sat in bored ambivalence as the final draft was signed and notarized.

As they rose to leave the room, Reggie nodded perfunctorily to Cole. Exasperated by her deliberate indifference to him, he purposely grasped her hand and brought it to his lips. "I breathlessly await our wedding night," he mocked. "I'll see you in three weeks in the judge's chambers."

Reggie angrily pulled her hand from his firm grasp and spun on her heel. "And I'll see you in hell!" she promised with equal ardor as she left the room.

She was a little bit of a thing, a piece of fluff, cornflower-blue eyes, curly blond hair and painted cheeks. David Astin picked her up at the bus station, fed her a hamburger and french fries, then promised her a job. But first he wanted to get her settled in a room so she could get a good night's rest. She was a runaway, sixteen years old, from a small town in Iowa. More than anything else, Maggie wanted to escape her background of hand-me-down clothes and creamed chipped beef on toast. David nodded sympathetically. He understood her.

Three hours after they registered in the run-down hotel, Maggie's face was unrecognizable. Huge black and blue bruises ran from her cheeks to her jawbones. Her eyes were swollen slits, and she was bleeding from her mouth. Her breasts and inner thighs bore the marks of David's teeth. As he dressed with meticulous care, Maggie cringed, wide-eyed with terror, in the corner of the room. Her voice, barely coherent, droned a steady, unrelenting moan. For a moment, David thought he should call an ambulance but changed his mind. The wounds were superficial; they would heal within a week and the two hundred dollars he left on the dresser would take care of her needs until she was presentable again.

For the first time in years David felt alive. His body, which should have been exhausted from the afternoon's pleasure, was relaxed, sated. He had finally found what he had been searching for. There were many, so many bus depots. . . .

Chapter 21

Reggie sat at her mirrored dressing table, retouching her makeup for the tenth time that morning. In two hours she would be meeting Cole at the Justice of the Peace. Two more hours of freedom. All around her were cartons, barrels and boxes, labeled and taped, ready for the moving van that would be arriving at any moment. Her home, from now on, would be Cole's townhouse on Sixty-eighth Street, which she had refused to see before their marriage. He had told her that he would refurnish an entire floor of the townhouse to her specifications. Dispassionately, she had chosen a few fabrics and a color scheme. She left the rest of the decorating to Cole's interior designers. She had refused to participate in anything that had to do with their marriage—except allow a reluctant Coco to be brought by liveried servant to her new home.

Reggie checked the jeweled Piaget that Lee had given her as a wedding gift. At first, Reggie had refused it, finding the idea of gift-giving ridiculous under the circumstances of the wedding. But Lee, who was aware of each detail, had insisted she accept his small token and good wishes. He was now waiting to attend the wedding, at which he would be the only guest.

As the minutes ticked by, Reggie realized there would be no last-minute reprieve. Cole was obstinately determined to carry this through and, no matter how hard she had tried in these past three weeks to reason with him, she had not swayed him. Still, the whole thing made no sense. He was not the kind of man who needed a wife so desperately that he had to coerce someone to marry him.

With drooping spirits, Reggie went to the closet to get her wedding dress. She had made it a year ago as the final piece of one of her collections and, as the model had waltzed down the runway to the strains of "The Wedding March," the entire audience had stood and applauded. It was made entirely of snow-white suede, heavily appliquéd with antique Valenciennes lace and encrusted with thousands of caviar-sized seed pearls, which Reggie had sewn on by hand herself. The neckline of the gown was high, grazing the underside of the model's chin, emphasizing the long, swanlike neck, then, as it reached the back, it flared upward slightly, creating a lace frame for her face. Suede leg-of-mutton sleeves reached to elbow length, then embraced the arm in pearl and antique illusion, ending in an elegant point at the hand. The hem of the gown whispered down the aisle, lightly kissing the ankle.

Now, holding the opulent dress, Reggie knew she wouldn't wear it today. It would be a travesty, a mockery to pretend there was anything resembling romance attached to this wedding. Instead, she reached deep into the back of her closet for a simple unadorned black silk suit, better suited for a funeral. She laughed ironically. The outfit was perfect.

A half hour later, she had finished dressing. She wore no jewelry, refusing to add even the tiniest hint of sparkle to her otherwise somber outfit. What Reggie didn't realize was that the simple black suit set off her radiant beauty, enhancing her ivory complexion and wide green eyes. Had she tried, she could not have chosen a more intoxicating outfit.

Cole saw it at once. As Reggie entered the judge's chambers, Cole was struck by her breathtaking beauty. He had imagined what she would look like this morning, but never had he expected to see her like this, calm, serene, ice cold. She barely acknowledged him as she took her place by his side. She stood silently through the short ceremony, and it was only when Cole reached for her hand to place the simple gold ring on her finger, that their eyes met. Her eyes, with their bitter, contemptuous stare, told him everything. There was no mistaking the frozen anger. For not the first time in these last few weeks, Cole wondered if he had made a mistake. When their vows were spoken and the judge instructed the groom to kiss the bride, Mrs. Cole Weston turned on her heel and walked out of the room, leaving her new husband and the judge to stare after her in open-mouthed disbelief. Cole recovered first, looking at the judge and shaking his head. "Nerves," he explained awkwardly. Then, his back rigid with embarrassment, he followed Reggie and left the office.

Bright sunshine blinded her as Reggie walked down the granite steps that led from the courthouse. Automatically, she reached into her handbag for her large black enameled sunglasses. Cole stood several steps behind her, and beyond them, waiting at the curb, was the long, black limousine. Without speaking to her, Cole placed his hand under her elbow. Angrily, she shook it off, stepping into the limousine unaided. The chauffeur stood at the curb, confused, turning his questioning eyes to his employer. Cole motioned for Timothy to get back into the car, then he slid in next to Reggie. Silently, the car slipped away from the curb.

Neither Cole nor Reggie had uttered a single word to each other since the obligatory "I do's." Reggie now sat in stony silence, her head turned away from Cole. He paid little attention to her mood; there would be time enough for conversation when she recovered from her anger. For the time being, he was content having achieved the first of his goals. She was Mrs. Cole Weston. She was his.

The limousine had left the busy Wall Street area and was making its way uptown when Reggie turned to Cole and asked where they were going.

"Le Cirque," he replied. "I planned a wedding brunch for us."

"Funny, I don't recall your mentioning it to me," she said politely. "Under different circumstances I would love to join you, but I've already made plans." She smiled brightly at him. "I know you will have a lovely brunch without me." Then she tapped the driver's shoulder and asked him to drop her on Fifty-seventh Street.

Cole compressed his lips; she was doing this purposely to irritate him, and she was succeeding. He turned to face her, his dark brows drawing together in a frown. "You may find your antics amusing, Reggie, but I don't. Whatever you are trying to accomplish by deliberately opposing me will only prolong this difficult period of adjustment." Suddenly, he changed his tone. "Things haven't always been this way between us. In fact," he said softly, "there were times when you enjoyed being held in my arms." Reaching out, he traced his finger along the line of her lips. "There were quite a few times, my dear wife, when you were the one who reached for me first. What happened to change that?"

She shivered at his touch, frantic in the knowledge that he remembered how her body had responded to his warm caresses. Steeling herself against his hands, which now cupped her face, she replied, "Any man can make a woman respond to his touch if he is accomplished. Whatever else you may be, Cole, you are an exceptionally skillful lover. That was all there ever was to our relationship."

Grinning, he took his hands from her face. "Really?" he asked. "You never felt anything other than physical release?"

There was no way she could respond without revealing her true feelings.

Cole was waiting patiently, his jaw set with determination. "Are you going to answer my question?"

She lifted her head, her sparkling emerald eyes glaring defiantly. "No," she said, "I am not."

The exasperation showed in his eyes. "It doesn't have to be this way between us. You know that, don't you?" he asked, his voice low.

Green eyes flared. "There isn't going to be anything at all between us."

"I'm beginning to get that message," he stated finally.

"Do you know," she continued, "that from the day we first met, I found you pompous, smug and self-centered. Nothing has happened since that day to change my opinion of you."

Cole watched her face. "Nothing?" he asked with a slight challenge in his deep voice. "Can you honestly tell me that those nights we spent together meant nothing to you? Can you?" he demanded.

She raised her eyebrows. "My dear Cole, I hardly remember them."

In an ice-cold voice he said, "You are either deluding yourself or you are a consummate actress."

With a short, bitter laugh, Reggie spoke. "I am a little of both." The car was making the turn onto Fifty-seventh Street. "Now, if you don't mind, I have a lot of things to take care of this morning. In all the excitement of the wedding," she added sarcastically, "I forgot to buy a trousseau." As the car eased over to the curb, Reggie inclined her head slightly to Cole. "I suppose I have to join you for dinner tonight?"

"And every night thereafter, according to our contract." Her annoyance was obvious as Reggie opened the door and stepped out. He began to speak, then thought better of it. What he had to say to her could wait until tonight. In fact, he thought with smile, they had always dealt better with each other after the sun had gone down. He stretched his long legs out in the limousine, smiling his lazy smile and contemplating the evening ahead.

Chapter 22

Bergdorf Goodman had always been Reggie's favorite store. The landmark department store on the corner of Fifth Avenue and Fifty-seventh Street represented wealth, success and the epitome of high fashion. It had never bastardized its quiet aura of elegance and opulence for the kitchy eye-catching cuteness of Henri Bendel or the trendy frenzy of Bloomingdale's with its unending, mazelike counters and crowded aisles. There was a serenity about Bergdorf's, a hushed sophistication that whispered . . . money. In seasons past, whenever she'd been blocked and needed inspiration, she had found it within these well-known fashion halls. Until today, she had never had the courage to actually make a purchase, knowing full well that a good copy could be found on Orchard Street. Today was different. Today she was going to buy . . . to give in to the hedonistic desire to feel a part of the moneyed patrons who meandered nonchalantly through the store in their crisp linen summer dresses, gold Rolex watches, Cartier "love" bracelets and exorbitantly expensive leather Hermès "Grace Kelly" handbags. And she was doing it for one reason and one reason only . . . to prove to her newly acquired and most unwelcome spouse, that he was going to pay through the nose for forcing her into marriage.

Since she was now married to one of the wealthiest men in Manhattan, Reggie *Weston* could shop herself silly in Bergdorf's. Before she was finished, the immaculate, white-jacketed cosmetician at the Clinique counter would greet her by name, remembering that she only wore rose-beige foundation and ginger-peach lipstick. By demanding that she become his wife, Cole had unwittingly given her the gilded key of entrée into a very elite circle of women whose uniformed chauffeurs waited patiently in the blistering heat while their perfectly coiffed, unrumpled employers clickety-clacked about the travertine lobby in white kid and black patent leather Chanel pumps, making purchases to stuff in their already overflowing closets.

Because it was summer and most of the habitual Bergdorf shoppers had already departed for the Hamptons or other equally fashionable resorts, Reggie had no difficulty finding a seat in the lush, beige-carpeted shoe salon.

All around her, delectably displayed, were shoes and boots—lizard, suede, alligator and python—poking out of brightly colored tissue-filled boxes. The display was dazzling. Reggie delicately extended her foot to a waiting salesman. "I'd like to try those, those and the ones over there," she said, pointing decisively at the varied selection.

Jacques Lyon had worked at Bergdorf Goodman for fifteen years; he didn't raise an eyebrow at her request. Moments later, he returned, carefully balancing eleven boxes. As Reggie rapidly tried on and either approved or discarded one after another, she gave him alternate styles to bring. By the time she had finished, she had tried on more than forty-five pairs of shoes and boots. Jacques sat back on a tiny maroon chair, completely exhausted.

Other salesmen and a handful of shoppers were openly gaping as Reggie stood over the weary salesman to wrap up the black alligator pumps, the forest-green suede boots, the gold kid sandals with jeweled buckles, the bone lizard boots trimmed with intricately braided python in shades of soft taupes and brown. She pointed to garnet calfskin pumps, five pairs of flat walking shoes, an eight hundred dollar pair of mauve crocodile cowboy boots and, as an afterthought, added winter white ones as well. She couldn't remember a time when she had had so much fun. Strangers were beginning to stroll past her, straining to recognize the young woman who most assuredly was a celebrity. Reggie gave them all a charming smile. When she had finished, Jacques had twenty-two boxes set aside. He had never made such a large sale.

"I'd like to send these, today, if possible," Reggie instructed.

"Your name and charge card, please."

"Mrs. Cole Weston," she replied, trying out her new name. "I don't have my new charge card yet."

Jacques flushed crimson. "I'm sorry, madam, but I can't charge these without a card," he told her, crestfallen that he was going to lose the sale.

"I believe that if you call my husband's office, they will authorize all my purchases. Have you a piece of paper and a pen?" Rapidly, Reggie scribbled Cole's private office number on the paper and handed it back to the nervous salesman.

He held the paper in his hand carefully. "Let me have the manager call your husband's office for verification. I'll be right back," he added hastily.

Reggie relaxed. "Certainly." Cole would have to okay her purchases, it was part of the agreement. What she didn't know was how far she could go. But, she thought with a smirk, she was about to find out.

Cole's phone was ringing as he stepped into his office. Who would be calling him on this line, today of all days? Making a lunge for it on the fifth ring, he tripped over the wastebasket, cursing at the pain. "Hello?" he barked.

"Mr. Weston? Mr. Cole Weston?" asked an unfamiliar, British-accented voice. Cole struggled to his feet, trying to recognize the speaker. He couldn't place it, which was unusual; only a handful of people had access to this number.

"Hello, Mr. Weston?"

"Yes, yes, this is Weston. Who is this?" he asked, untangling the phone cord, which was wrapped around his arm and chest.

"This is the manager of the shoe salon at Bergdorf Goodman."

"How did you get this number?" he asked angrily.

"Your wife, sir. She gave it to me. That is why I am calling. She is purchasing some shoes and does not have a credit card.

As the amount is rather substantial, I had to call for verification. Can she charge to your name?"

"Reddish hair, green eyes?" Cole asked.

"Yes, sir."

"How much do her purchases come to?" Cole asked thoughtfully.

Cole heard papers rustling in the background. "About four thousand, nine hundred dollars."

Cole expelled a deep breath. "For shoes?"

"And boots, sir," added the manager, quickly.

"Of course, and boots." That was Reggie's new game, he thought, repressing a smile. "By all means. Give her unlimited credit and have the bills sent to my office, care of Cole Weston, personally."

Moments later, the smiling Jacques returned to Reggie, who had been impatiently drumming her fingernails on the counter. "Well?" she asked. She could picture Cole's face when he heard the news that she was at Bergdorf's trading on the new name she had insisted she despised.

"No problem, Mrs. Weston. Your husband has authorized your purchases. A charge card in your name will be ready at customer service in a few minutes. I'm so very sorry if this has caused you any inconvenience."

Speechless, Reggie stood up. "You spoke to Mr. Weston?"

"Yes, ma'am."

"Did you mention the amount that I wanted to charge?"

"Yes, ma'am, I did," answered the salesman.

Reggie exploded inwardly. Cole had taken the initiative once again. By authorizing her charges without a word with her first, he had taken the perverse pleasure out of her shopping spree. What did five thousand dollars mean to him? It was a pittance, a paltry sum; he undoubtedly spent that much on two suits. No, Reggie realized, five thousand was simply not enough money to irritate him. But ten thousand? Forty thousand? Those were numbers so far out of her ken that even Cole would know she was deliberately, wantonly throwing away his money. For a reason that Reggie didn't understand, it was imperative that she take an action that would unsettle his complacency. She was just beginning. By the time she finished her trousseau today, even Cole would be appalled at what his new wife was going to cost him.

With that delicious thought in mind, Reggie's next stop was the handbag department, where she chose a red Fendi clutch; two Judith Leiber evening bags, one in gold lizard to match her new sandals, the other a small black alligator envelope with an onyx, pearl and marcasite clasp; a huge caramel cabretta carry-all; a hunter-green shoulderbag trimmed in python; and three woven leather clutch bags completed her purchases in that department. As she stepped up to the cash register, Reggie's eyes lit on a metal evening bag in the shape of a duck, completely encrusted with tiny, nine-millimeter rhinestones. The minaudiere's price was astronomical and she bought it, only for that reason. She couldn't imagine anyplace where she would need such an extravagant accessory.

And she was far from finished. A charge of electricity surged through her as the cash registers rang up purchase after purchase. The entire lower level of Bergdorf's was whispering about her and she loved it. For the first time in her life, Reggie was experiencing the seductive spell of money. Saleswomen virtually groveled in an effort to accommodate her. With single-minded determination, Reggie moved to the lingerie department, trying on peignoir sets trimmed with maribou, nightgowns imported from Paris, whose prices started at nine hundred dollars. In the cosmetic department, Reggie had a complete makeup demonstration, after which she bought six hundred dollars worth of beauty aids. The tab mounted steadily as she bought and bought useless items, obscenely overpriced, for which she would never have a need.

It was only when she stood in the doorway of Van Cleef & Arpels, contemplating her next audacious move, that Reggie experienced her first moment of misgiving. The famous jewelry store was small and intimate, with several glass desks, flanked by Louis XVI chairs, lining the walls. Discreet display cases with dark velvet interiors twinkled seductively, beckoning at Reggie to peek at the extravagant diamond, emerald and sapphire offerings. Off in the corner, seated at one of the glass tables sat a middle-aged, silver-haired man and a young, blond beauty who, Reggie decided after a moment's glance, could not possibly be a day over twenty. Spread out before them was a black velvet cloth on which rested ten loose diamonds. The smallest stone was at least twelve carats. The couple held hands under the table, smiling into each other's eyes as they fingered the fiery gems. Reggie looked at the slim gold band on the girl's hand then at her ring finger. They weren't married. She shrugged her shoulders. It figured.

An exceptionally well-dressed salesman in his mid thirties approached her. "May I help you?" he inquired politely while, unbeknownst to Reggie, he scanned her clothes, shoes, handbag and accessories in order to gauge the type of jewelry to show her. His experienced eye very rarely failed him. He was shaken badly when Reggie casually pointed to a diamond and emerald necklace. The primary stone of the necklace was a faceted emerald of about fifteen carats, surrounded by half-carat diamonds set in platinum. Connected to the center stone were six smaller replicas, each attached by platinum links.

"Madam, are you quite sure that this," he said, pointing to the fabulous necklace, "is what you had in mind?"

Reggie gave him a scathing look. "Is it sold?" she asked.

He hesitated, perspiration breaking out on his forehead. "No, but the necklace sells for over ninety thousand dollars."

Reggie swallowed convulsively. "And?"

"I just wanted to make sure you were aware of it. Is that within your price range?" he ventured nervously.

"My dear sir, I have no price range," she answered imperiously. "Is that necklace for sale? I don't have all day to stand here while you decide."

"Certainly, it's for sale." He almost tripped over his feet as he rushed to take the necklace from the case. Who was she? he wondered as he unlocked the glass display case. He racked his brain for any sign of recognition, but he could find none. He prided himself on his ability to recognize women who could afford to shop at Van Cleef. He should know who she was. She certainly is beautiful, he thought, pausing to stare at her before he brought her the necklace. But when he inquired whether she wanted to try it on, she told him in a bored voice that she was very tired from shopping all day. He insisted, lifting the heavy necklace toward her neck.

Looking at it out of the case, Reggie decided that she didn't even like it. It was vulgar, showy, not at all the kind of jewelry she would have chosen if she were actually buying something to give herself pleasure. She had chosen it simply because it looked like the most expensive item in the store. "I don't need to try it on. I know I look wonderful in emeralds, redheads always do. Don't you think so?" She fluttered her heavy eyelashes.

"Certainly, madam," he concurred, willing to agree to anything she said.

"Wonderful," she said. "Now please wrap it up."

"Uh," he sputtered, "how would you like to pay for this? Do you have an account?"

Bored, Reggie looked away, staring into space. "So they tell me."

"Could I see your card?" he said.

"I don't have one. Call customer service; I'm sure they will okay the purchase," she answered.

Reggie gave the salesman her name and watched as he made his way back to the office to make his phone calls. She must be mad! she thought. Ninety thousand dollars for a necklace she didn't even like? Suddenly she began to wonder whether this last step had been wise. Suppose Cole refused to pay the bills. Or suppose he added the amount she had spent today to the already staggering sum she owed him? For a moment, her heart constricted at the imagined look on his face when he discovered what she had done today. Then she recalled his stubbornness, his cold intractability and the fear left her. He would have to pay for her luxuries. That, too, was in their contract. Too bad if he had not anticipated the recklessness of his new wife.

"Mrs. Weston," drooled the returned salesman, "I am positively mortified that I didn't realize who you were. Everything will be sent to your home. We're even sending a special security man for the delivery." Reggie shrugged her shoulders. She really didn't care if the things got there by carrier pigeon. She probably would never wear most of her purchases anyway. But the salesman had no way of knowing what Reggie was thinking. His only concern was to please this obviously wealthy customer. "What else may I show you?"

She couldn't resist. "There wouldn't happen to be a pair of earrings to match my new necklace?"

"My dear Mrs. Weston, I was about to suggest that very thing."

Reggie laughed at his obsequiousness. "Don't bother. I find matched sets vulgar."

He bobbed his head up and down. "You're right, absolutely

right. I should have known that you were a woman of more refined tastes. Now I do have . . ."

Reggie just picked up her purse and sailed out of Van Cleef, leaving the salesman gaping after her.

Chapter 23

By five thirty Reggie was exhausted from her efforts to deplete Cole's bank account. She'd managed to shop at every store on Fifty-seventh Street, and if her computations were correct, she'd spent $158,000. In a mixed state of nervous anxiety and self-satisfaction at her audacity, she stood in front of Cole's newly painted townhouse, summoning the courage to ring the bell.

Charcoal-gray, with black shutters and shiny wrought-iron grillwork, the jewellike building nestled splendidly between two taller structures. Imposing bronze lanterns set on each side of a carved, maroon door, flickered in the dusk. The house, a rare find amid the huge, impersonal multi-dwellings that characterized Manhattan, even sported a two-car garage. It was a ridiculous contrast to the loft she was used to.

Hesitantly, Reggie lifted the horseshoe-shaped knocker. Though she had been given her own set of keys to the impressive brownstone, she felt ill at ease using them, as if by using her own key she would admit to herself that this was actually her new home. She knew she wasn't ready to do that. An elderly, uniformed butler answered her knock. "Good evening," she said nervously. Joseph? James? John! That was his name. "Good evening, John."

"Good evening, Mrs. Weston," he said graciously. He stepped aside, allowing her to enter. "May I offer you congratulations on behalf of the entire staff?" he asked as he took some packages from her arms, leading her through the huge entry foyer.

"Thank you," she replied as she looked around for any sign of Cole. Breathing a sigh of relief when she didn't see him, she assumed that she arrived before him. "Have you any idea when my husband will be home?"

"Mr. Weston has been home for an hour. He's dressing for dinner and has requested that you join him in the study at seven."

"I see," Reggie said civilly, realizing that there was no point involving this innocent gentleman in her private war with Cole. The servants would know soon enough that this wasn't a conventional marriage. Reggie glanced quickly at the stately Tiffany grandfather clock that stood in the corner of the foyer. She had a little over an hour to bathe and dress before she had to face Cole. In a perverse way, she was looking forward to the confrontation.

She walked toward the staircase, then remembered her agreement with Cole. To avoid the necessity of explaining their comings and goings, Cole had suggested that Reggie use the elevator, while he would use the staircase. As she stepped into the tiny suede-lined cage and pushed the button to the third floor, she wondered idly whether he intended to bring his mistress to his rooms. Was that the reason he wanted her to use the elevator? She shook herself at the ridiculous thought. Even Cole wouldn't openly flaunt his love affairs in her face. It would be a breach of their contract.

Reggie entered her newly decorated suite, gasping in surprise at its magnificence. It was far more beautiful than she had ever expected. She was happy to see Coco sleeping, curled up on an armchair. With a weary sigh, she dragged her tired body toward the plum velvet chaise that hid in the corner of the massive room. Lowering herself into the feather-filled cushions, she leaned her head against the antique lace backrest. Waves of melancholy washed over her as if a window had been left open and an unwelcome fog had drifted into the room. Fighting the loneliness that seized her, a loneliness that she hadn't felt since David had left her so long ago, she urged her aching body and spirit to struggle against the overwhelming fatigue that seized her. She had to bathe and dress. . . .

The insistent buzzing of an intercom awakened her. Disoriented, she searched for the source of the annoying noise. Slowly, as the cobwebs cleared, she remembered where she was. She picked up the phone.

"Mrs. Weston, I'm sorry to disturb you, but Mr. Weston said to tell you that he would be in the library in fifteen minutes."

He'll just have to wait, she thought, realizing that she would never be ready on time. It would do Cole no harm to wait for her anyway. He might as well get used to the idea that she wouldn't be at his beck and call. Reggie hung up the phone and entered the lavender marble bathroom, turning on the bath water and choosing a delicate sandalwood from the many fragrances of bath oil. Slowly, she slid her suit off, dropping it to the floor, and stepped into the half-filled tub. As the water reached the level of her calves, she slid under the soothing, scented water. She stayed, submerged up to her chin until the water began to cool. Only then did she step from the tub. She was already ten minutes late.

She sat at her dressing table, arranging and rearranging her hair until she was satisfied with the look she had achieved. With heavy silver combs, she had twisted her gleaming hair into an elaborate coiffure that accentuated her sculpted features and almond-shaped eyes. For a fleeting second, Reggie caught a glimpse of her own beauty, then cast the image aside as if her eyes had deceived her.

A half hour later, her chin held high, Reggie strode to the elevator. For her first dinner with her husband, she had chosen bone linen trousers, a simple cream silk shirt that did nothing to hide the jaunty sway of her breasts, and high-heeled almond suede sandals. Even in the extravagantly high heels, she would still only reach the top of his chin. Still, she felt the added inches gave her courage.

The door to the library was ajar. Softly she knocked, then entered. The room was empty. Obviously, promptness was not one of Cole's virtues either. Now it was she who was annoyed. Alone in the library, she studied the handsome room. The walls were of solid walnut, purchased at a Parke Bernet auction when the Fifth Avenue mansion of a former New York State governor had been demolished. Priceless Kirman rugs in muted shades of cocoa and cream covered the elaborate parquet floor. Rich medieval tapestries, depicting unicorns and other mythical creatures hung from heavy brass rods. The room had the aura of another place, another time. Though there was no fire in the huge stone hearth, it added to the feeling that this room belonged in an English manor house. The room captivated her.

"Surprised?"

Reggie jumped at the unexpected voice, her heart thudding. Cole was seated in the shadowed corner of the room in an oversized Queen Anne wing chair.

He smiled at her with indulgent amusement. "I've been watching you admire the room. I hated to disturb you." He stood up and walked toward her. "It is a remarkable room; it enchants people." He looked at her for a reaction. "Feel free to use it anytime you wish."

"Frankly, I find the room stifling and pretentious," she said derisively. "Rather than admiring it, I was wondering how anyone would have the nerve to create a room that looks as if it were taken, plank for plank, from the pages of *Country Homes I Have Known and Loved.*"

"Do you know, Reggie," he drawled, "you are rather like a spoiled child. You cannot even conceive of our being friends, can you?" he added in a low voice, coming to stand directly in front of her. She could feel his breath on her hair, smell the cologne that she remembered so well. She stepped back several paces, furious that Cole was smiling.

"I prefer to choose my own friends," she said coldly. "In this instance, my preferences were not considered."

"I have told you before that it doesn't have to be this way between us," he replied impatiently.

For one wild moment, Reggie wondered what would happen if she walked into his arms, let him hold her the way he had done so many times before. She swallowed hard, pushing those dangerous thoughts from her mind. "As far as I am concerned," she lied, "I will continue to play out this charade as long as I have to. But don't expect me to pretend that I enjoy it." She started to say more, but an unexpected lump had settled in her throat as his black eyes burned into hers. She felt treacherous tears begin to fill her eyes. Confused at the swing in her emotions, she turned her back to him.

He shrugged his shoulders. "Dinner is ready. Oh, in the future, I don't like to be kept waiting." He left her standing alone in the middle of the room, his footsteps echoing in the hall.

Angrily, she followed him into the dining room. He was standing in front of a chair, which he eased out from under the table as she approached. Deliberately, she ignored him, settling herself into another chair.

"Is there something wrong with this chair?" he asked affably.

Their eyes locked and she couldn't look away. She was glued to the spot. His eyes searched her face, and time stood still. Every detail of his face, the line of his jaw, the angle of his chin, the soft thick hair that waved over one eye . . . and his lips, his full sensual lips. She couldn't take her eyes from those lips. She felt small and helpless and she knew instinctively that if he had moved toward her at that moment, all her resolve would have melted away. Her heart raced as his eyes bored into hers. When he finally spoke, his voice held a hint of menace.

"You play a very dangerous game, Reggie. You can push me only so far." There was a palpable undercurrent of tension in the room. "One day even you will exceed the limits of my endurance." With a superhuman effort, he regained his composure and took his seat. "Now again, I asked you if there was something wrong with the other chair?"

She flinched under his steely gaze. "I don't care to sit there," she answered in a small voice.

He stood up, walked over to the offending chair and studied it thoughtfully. He turned inquiring eyes to her. "Are the other chairs distasteful, as well?" he asked.

"I prefer this one."

In two strides he was at her side. "Get up!" he ordered gruffly, pulling the chair out from under her.

"What is the matter with—"

"John!" he barked. "John, get in here, this instant!" Reggie tried to fight Cole for the chair.

"John," he said to the butler, "remove all these chairs from the dining room at once. Mrs. Weston doesn't care for them."

The elderly retainer threw his employer a bewildered look.

"You heard me. Remove them immediately!" instructed Cole.

"What shall I do with them, sir?"

Cole turned to his wife. "Reggie, what would you like done with the chairs that you dislike so much?"

Under his angry stare, Reggie couldn't answer. She felt small and childish, exactly the way he had described her. Oblivious to her discomfort, he directed John to take the chairs out to the garage and to replace them with two bridge chairs. Cole shifted his gaze to Reggie as the butler struggled with the heavy Hepplewhite chairs. Scathingly, Cole asked, "Is that better, Reggie?"

"I never meant . . ." she whispered as John huffed with the effort of carrying the chairs.

Cole's eyebrows turned down, and he said contemptuously, "Then, in the future, stop these silly games."

Reggie sat in the bridge chair in silent mortification as the exhausted butler returned to serve. He spooned a ladle of creamed asparagus soup into her gilt-edged bowl. Cole turned to John with a kind look in his eyes. "John, you must be exhausted. Is William still here?"

The butler nodded tiredly.

"Good. Ask him to finish serving dinner." John started to protest, but Cole insisted. When they were once again alone, Cole raised his eyes and gave Reggie a meaningful stare. "I'm glad you were successful with your trousseau shopping today."

She barely swallowed her soup before she began to choke. Quickly, she covered her mouth with the heavy linen napkin.

"Are you all right?" Cole inquired solicitously, his eyes never leaving her face.

She nodded.

"Good. Your packages arrived late this afternoon before you came home. I took the liberty of helping Elsa unpack for you. You don't mind, do you?"

She threw him a withering glance. "I prefer to do my own unpacking."

"In the future, I will make sure that you do," he assured her, unruffled. Finished with his soup, he pushed it away. "I must say, your taste in clothing is exceptional."

She was caught off balance by the compliment.

His eyes narrowed imperceptively. "I especially liked the crocodile boots. Such a steal at eight hundred dollars. I'm surprised you only bought them in two colors."

Her eyes widened in surprise, then sensing the sarcasm in his voice, she replied coolly, "I have a penchant for shoes and boots. I never told you, but I can't resist them. I hope I haven't overstepped myself."

"On the contrary, Reggie," his face an unreadable mask, "my money, indeed everything I possess, is as much yours now as it is mine." He looked so unshakable that Reggie itched to throw something in his face. A slow, lazy grin swept across his handsome face. "I was, however, very disappointed in your choice of a wedding present."

"What are you talking about?" she snapped angrily.

"Your little trinket from Van Cleef. Really, Reggie, I'm surprised at you." He shook his head in disappointment. "Don't you think it's a trifle vulgar? For a woman with such outstanding taste, your choice of jewels shocked me." He paused, his face a study of weary patience. "I can see that we have to cultivate that area of your education. We can't have a woman in your position wearing anything so blatantly obvious, can we?"

"May I ask what you would have thought more appropriate?"

"Certainly," he replied, smiling. He stood up and withdrew a small velvet box from his pocket. Without a word, he handed it to Reggie. Reluctantly, she lifted the lid and gasped in disbelief at the enormous emerald-cut diamond.

"My God, Cole!" she said. "This must be twenty carats."

"Close," he conceded politely, taking the ring from her hand, "give or take a few carats." He walked back to his seat. "What's the difference? You've already chosen your gift."

She stared at him with undisguised malice.

"I'll just put this away for another happy occasion," he added sarcastically, fueling her mounting rage. "Perhaps our fifth anniversary," he suggested innocently.

She jerked her head around. "That day will never happen, Cole. Trust me," she answered savagely.

"You are absolutely certain?"

"About as certain as I've ever been about anything in my life."

Cole slipped the ring back into his pocket. "I think you are mistaken, but we will have to wait and see, won't we?"

The remainder of the meal was eaten in strained silence. Reggie fumed, while Cole dined with apparent relish on a delicately prepared rack of lamb. "I strongly suggest that you eat something. The lamb happens to be delicious." He attacked his dinner with gusto while she, unable to swallow, merely pushed hers around on her plate.

After dinner, Cole asked Reggie to join him for a drink in the library. She refused. "I'm going to bed," she replied, then could have bitten off her tongue at Cole's rejoinder.

"Your room or mine?" he asked, smiling broadly.

"That's not what I meant, and you know it!"

"Isn't it?" he asked, a sharp edge to his smile.

"Go to hell, Cole."

"Your vocabulary is singularly uninspired, Reg. Is that the only expletive you know?" he asked dryly. "I would be happy to teach you some more colorful profanity. I've learned them from an expert," Cole said, thinking of Evyan's store of vulgarities.

"That's very kind of you to take an interest in my education. However, it won't be necessary. I'm going to bed—alone!"

"How dull!" he observed, beginning to enjoy himself. "And on your wedding night, too."

"Cole, I'm warning you . . . just drop it. It's been a long, trying day," she told him, gritting her teeth. The sparring chatter was beginning to wear on her nerves.

"Your 'long trying day' brings me to the subject I wanted to discuss with you before you almost invited me to your bed."

"I did no such thing!" she denied hotly.

He ignored her, handing her a glass of scotch, and sipping on his own drink. "You said you're tired so I'll make this short. In the future, if you need money, if you feel you must add to your trousseau, or wish to irritate me by spending my money extravagantly, you needn't bother. I've instructed Lee to open a checking account in your name. The initial deposit will be fifty thousand dollars. When you go through that, another fifty thousand will be deposited. I trust that will keep you in shoes and boots. It also will eliminate at least one area of friction." With deadly calm, he continued, "I've tried to explain to you before, money means very little to me. I have more than we will ever spend, even if you feel you have to have crocodile boots for every day of the year. It is only the pursuit of money that intrigues me."

He lifted a dark brow letting the words sink in. Carefully, he enunciated so there would be no misunderstanding. "I like the chase. When things are too easily accessible, I become bored. If you are hoping to be released from our contract by annoying me, think again. Your antics amuse me. When they stop amusing me, it will be obvious to you."

Reggie slammed her glass down on the table. "Amuse you?" she repeated furiously. "You find me *amusing?*"

"Infantile might be a more appropriate word for your behavior," he conceded. Then thoughtfully, he added, "Yet I seem to recall a sensual, exciting woman. I fully expect to find her again," he concluded with certainty.

"Don't bet on it!" she hissed, walking to the door.

"I never bet on a sure thing," he said as the library door slammed with a resounding thud.

Chapter 24

Early the next morning, Reggie was awakened by the sounds of sanitation trucks grinding their way through the Upper East Side. The sun shone brightly through the sheer mauve drapes. Lazily, she lay snuggled in her bed, watching dust motes dance in the rays of the early morning light.

Her bedside clock read 7:00, but she was wide awake, eager to get to her office. She pushed the blankets off, stretched and stepped onto the deep cream carpet. She shivered in the unexpected cold of the air-conditioned room as she slipped her arms through her thin, silk dressing gown. For a moment she was tempted to crawl back under the satin comforter but thought better of it. There was a tremendous amount of work to be completed before her fall line would be ready, and she barely had two weeks in which to do it. Though Reggie had already done the initial sketches, picked the fabrics and sewn the first rough samples, it was imperative that she oversee the completion of the collection. Even with detailed instructions, Alison was not experienced enough to do it alone. The burden still rested solely on Reggie's shoulders.

It was odd, she mused, how life goes on. Despite her hideous, enforced marriage to Cole, she had a business to run, bills to pay and salaries to meet. Her personal problems couldn't be allowed to interfere with the running of Rag's Raggs. Quickly, she scanned her appointment book for the day. As she began jotting down notes and ideas in the margins of the diary, she was so absorbed that she barely heard the knock on the door. Absently, she said, "Come in."

Cole stood at the entrance of her bedroom dressed immaculately in a gray pin-striped suit. He carried a heavy Georgian silver tray laden with a coffee pot, milk pitcher and basket of hot croissants. In the center of the tray stood a small, crystal bud vase containing one white rosebud. By the time his presence registered, he was inside the room, casually studying her barely concealed body. With a crooked smile, he nodded appreciatively.

"Very, very nice," he commented as his gaze wandered blatantly over her body. His eyes paused insolently to admire her full breasts, her long, long legs. "Part of your trousseau, I assume?" he asked, gesturing to the peignoir.

Reggie clutched at her robe, blushing furiously as she realized the negligee left her completely exposed. "What do you want?" she snapped.

Benignly, he answered, "Breakfast. I'd have thought the coffee and croissants would have given it away." Inwardly he smiled at her obvious displeasure. If she had any idea how magnificent she looked with that auburn-red hair falling riotously around her nearly naked body, she gave no indication. All he detected was discomfort and anger. He paid little attention to it. "Breakfast in bed or out?" he asked.

"Put the tray on the table and leave!"

Cole put down the heavy tray while Reggie sat on the edge of the bed, waiting for him to leave.

"Join me?" he asked as he drew a chair up to the table.

"Aren't you making a mistake? This is *my* room. If I wanted company for breakfast, I would have extended an invitation. Would you get the hell out of here so I can dress?" She sat perfectly still, waiting for him to get up.

Her request brought a warm gleam to his eye. "Don't let me stop you," he commented. "As much as you might like to pretend otherwise, I am intimately familiar with what you are trying to hide," he added as Reggie pulled the comforter up to cover herself. "Your memory may be temporarily deficient, but I can assure you that mine is not."

Her color deepened. Every feminine instinct warned her to get him out of her room as fast as possible before she lost control entirely. "There is nothing wrong with my memory," she told him as she watched his mouth curve into one of his devastating smiles. "However, there are events one chooses to forget. Our past is one of them. Now please leave!"

His jaw tightened. "Are you afraid of what might happen if I stayed? Frightened of how you really feel?"

"Don't flatter yourself," she told him coldly.

"I rarely have to." His smile faded and he stared hard into her eyes. "Reggie, stop acting like a child. Haven't these games gone on long enough? Come have breakfast with me."

"Is that a command? Part of the contract?"

"No, it is simply a request." He pulled out the other chair and waited for her to join him.

With a resigned sigh, Reggie stood up and walked toward him, conscious of the intimate way he was watching her. As she eased herself into a chair, their eyes met and held. Slowly, Cole lowered his gaze, mesmerized by the way her silken robe molded itself to her curves, accentuating the fullness of her breasts, the narrow waist and the faint shadow where her legs met. Uncomfortably aware of the increased pressure between his legs, he shifted in his seat.

This time it was Reggie's turn to smile wickedly. "Problems, darling?"

"Shh," he whispered and leaned over to trace the line of her cheek with a tenderness she had nearly forgotten. Her chest constricted at his touch.

"Please stop," she asked, but Cole ignored her as his fingers trailed down the long column of her neck to the hollow of her shoulder. He slipped his hand inside her robe and cupped her breast. She sat perfectly still, knowing he could feel the pounding of her heart beneath his palm.

"Do you really want me to stop?" he asked in a ragged voice.

She opened her mouth to speak, but no sound came out. Her will to fight and her anger had suddenly dissipated. Gently, Cole pushed the flimsy gown away from her body, exposing her shoulders and breasts. Reggie's hands were trembling as Cole stood and walked over to her side of the table. Boldly, he cupped her breasts in his hands and leaned over to place his lips on one rosy crest. A moan of pure pleasure escaped her as he took the nipple into his mouth and when, half-heartedly, she tried to push him away, he ignored her as his tongue increased its circling, drawing on the sensitive bud with his lips until he felt it grow hard and erect in his mouth.

He caught her arms, lifting her from the chair, and pulled her to him, pressing her body against his. Hungrily, his mouth came down on hers, and she instinctively reached around his neck to draw him still closer. An exquisite shudder passed through her as his tongue probed her mouth.

Then suddenly, as abruptly as he had caught her to him, he pushed her away. She opened her eyes with tremendous effort, looking up at him in surprise and confusion.

"If you will take some advice," he began softly, visibly striving to contain the demands of his own body, "you will admit the truth for once. You want me as much as I want you and there is no reason in the world for us to deny ourselves that pleasure."

Something snapped inside her. With a strength she didn't know she had, Reggie pushed him away from her. "Get out! Get out of my room," she ordered. "And if you ever come in here again, I swear on everything holy that I will cry breach of contract the moment you set one foot inside the door. Do you understand? It's over between us. Absolutely, irrevocably over! Leave me alone!" Cold anger strangled her voice, and tears of rage slipped unnoticed from under her eyelids. "The truth? You want the truth?" she spat while Cole stood with his arms at his sides, waiting. "Yes! I lied to you! I wanted every touch, every caress with a need I didn't even understand. But I don't want it anymore, Cole. I don't ever want you to touch me again. Do you understand?"

Before he had a chance to respond, Reggie ran to the bathroom and slammed the door, leaving Cole stunned. Without so much as another word, he turned on his heel and left her room, vowing silently that he would never, never enter it again.

Chapter 25

"Screw her!" he exclaimed aloud, banging the banister with his fist as he descended the staircase two steps at a time. When he reached his own suite, he kicked open the door, slamming it behind him with a vicious curse. He was furious with himself. He knew full well that according to the stipulations of their contract he had absolutely no right to enter her suite. Why, he wondered, had he deliberately set a course that might well have given her the very excuse she needed to break their agreement? Why was it so damned important for him to gain mastery over her? He tried to convince himself that it was simply the obsession to control that drove him to quell her spirit, to break down her defenses to subordinate her will. But he knew it was more than that.

Her very presence in a room disturbed him. Her artless movements, her scent, the way she tossed her hair when she was angry made him forget everything but the overwhelming need to possess her, to own her. It was a need he couldn't explain. Even her constant defiance and rebellious obstinancy, which ordinarily would have irritated and annoyed him, only increased his inexplicable compulsion to pursue her. Cole's brow furrowed in concentration as he sat down on the edge of his bed, faced with the knowledge that he still couldn't define Reggie's place in his life.

In the past, he had avoided emotional entanglements with remarkable ease, setting down ground rules from the beginning. But with Reggie there were no rules, no guidelines, no parameters. The wild swings of their relationship confused and unsettled him. Was she simply the beautiful accessory that he had bought, or was she more?

He didn't want to think about their relationship anymore. What he wanted more than anything, at that particular moment, was to get rid of whatever spell Reggie had cast over him. He had been infatuated before and knew the perfect antidote for this most unpleasant ailment . . . another woman . . . Evyan. With his former mistress's skillful ministrations, his ridiculous obsession with Reggie would fade and he would be able to stick to the letter of their contract. In fact, he thought, strengthening his determination to purge Reggie from his mind, he would leave New York for a while. By the time he returned, this morning's unpleasant encounter would have been forgotten, and he and his wife could begin their contractual marriage on a new foot. Satisfied that he had made a sound decision, he picked up the phone and called down for his luggage.

Reggie knew she'd won nothing in her encounter with Cole. If anything, she was disgusted with herself and the way her body had responded to him. But now, after the callous way he'd toyed with her, she would be damned in hell before she'd allow him to use her for his convenience. Instead, she had called upon the only defense she could think of—their contract. Her message to him had been brutally clear. If he ever attempted to touch her again, she would leave. Reggie realized what an empty victory it would be. More than anything, she longed to be held in his arms—but not on those terms. Now more than ever, she was determined to extricate herself from this ridiculous contract. The only way to accomplish that would be to throw herself into her work and quickly accumulate the money she owed Cole. Resolved to set her life back in order, she showered and dressed.

Half an hour later, dressed in doeskin jodhpurs, kelly-green blouse, heavily sculpted silver belt and her new white cowboy boots, she was ready for the office. Her new resolve—and her new clothes—had bolstered her smarting ego a bit, enough for her to face Cole with icy reserve if they happened to meet downstairs. Work was the best medicine for her. Already there were several half-formed ideas for the upcoming fall collection percolating in her mind. She picked up her portfolio and appointment book, cast a quick glance in the mirror and noted with pleasure that she looked unperturbed by the morning's experience. In fact, she observed with a wry smile, she had rarely looked better.

But when she reached the foyer she found herself looking for

Cole. She half wanted to slip unnoticed from the house while the other half of her yearned for him to see her proud, resplendent, confident. No one was about. She headed for the door when she heard a voice behind her.

"Good morning, ma'am." She turned, startled. John was walking toward the staircase, his arms laden with luggage. The elderly butler was having difficulty negotiating the slippery marble floor while trying to juggle two large valises, an overnighter, two attaché cases and a zippered garment bag. He paused to rest, huffing. "Are you going out, ma'am?" he wheezed, making a desperate lunge for the smallest case that was slipping from under his arm. As he reached for it, the other suitcases scattered, landing all over the foyer. Suffused with embarrassment, he hurried to retrieve them.

Once they were back in his arms, she responded, "I'm going back to work today. I took a two-day vacation before the wedding, but I do have a business to run."

He frowned in disapproval. "Does Mr. Weston know that you're going out?" he asked suspiciously.

Surprised, Reggie asked, "Do you think I ought to get permission?"

John's face flushed. He hadn't meant any intentional disrespect. He stammered an apology. "Sorry, ma'am, I just assumed . . ."

Reggie felt awful. "Don't apologize. I'm the one who should be sorry." There was no need to berate the hapless butler. Her argument was not with him. "Mr. Weston knows that I go to business everyday. It's perfectly all right with him."

Still trying to balance the luggage, John raised his craggy eyebrows. The wife of Cole Weston didn't have to earn a living. It seemed not only silly, but downright wrong for this pretty little thing to go to work everyday when Mr. Weston had all that money. "Ma'am?"

"Yes, John?"

"Ma'am, it's not my place to interfere . . . but if you spoke to Mr. Weston . . ."

Reggie smiled indulgently at John's attempt to protect her. "It is okay, John. Really. I love my career. It's the most important thing in my life. Mr. Weston knows that. He expects me to work."

John shook his head in bewilderment. Why would his

overly generous employer insist that his new bride go to work? It didn't make sense. Everyone knew that Mr. Weston had enough money to support a wife. It was shameful to allow Mrs. Weston, alone and unescorted, into those terrible areas of the city, where all sorts of horrible things could happen to her. John would never let a wife of *his* go out there. Fortunately, he didn't have to worry about that. When his wife of thirty years had passed on, he could say proudly, with his head held high, that she hadn't worked a day in her life. The idea that a woman, any woman, might actually choose to work was quite beyond his comprehension.

"John," Reggie asked gently, "would you like some help with those bags?"

"No, ma'am!" he hurriedly assured her. "I can manage fine. But I must hurry now so Mr. Weston can tell me what he wishes me to pack."

"Is he going somewhere?" Reggie asked, taken aback.

"Yes, ma'am. He called down a moment ago for his bags. He's leaving town for a few days."

"Is that so? He didn't happen to mention where he was going, did he?" she asked, absurdly irritated that Cole was leaving town without informing her. Wasn't there something in the contract . . . ? She searched her mind, trying to remember all the clauses, but she couldn't recall anything that prohibited unannounced trips.

John stared at her in disbelief. "Me?" he asked incredulously. "Do you mean did he tell me?"

"Yes, did he tell you where he was going?" she asked, a note of impatience creeping into her voice.

"No, ma'am, he never tells me where he's going. He's always on his way somewhere, either to some big conference or up to that cabin of his. Have you seen the cabin yet?" he asked, trying to change the subject.

"No." Reggie tried again. "Did Mr. Weston happen to mention for how long he would be gone?"

"No, ma'am," he said, then added hastily, "but that's not unusual either. He never exactly tells us when he's returning. Usually calls ahead to tell us to get things ready. And there's no use in asking; he simply won't answer. Doesn't like anyone questioning him, especially when he takes Miss Evyan—oh, Lord! Excuse me, ma'am . . . I didn't mean he was going with . . . I don't think he means to see . . . well, he actually—"

"Never mind!" she snapped. Her head twisted in the direction of the staircase. Evyan? Was Cole actually going away with his mistress the day after his wedding? Jealousy and pure hatred raced through her. Was she supposed to fill the role of wife according to their contract while he gallivanted around with his South American whore? Reggie thought angrily that Cole Weston wanted it all, his mistress and his wife, both neatly packaged. With a careful rein on the temper that was rising within her, she fumed in silence. Images of Cole's body entwined with Evyan's seared her heart. How casually he slipped from one woman to another, all in the space of a morning. To think that she had almost given herself to him, had just barely managed to escape from his arms before her own aroused body betrayed her. Damn him! Damn!

John cleared his throat. "Mrs. Weston, I'm terribly sorry if I—"

"Don't worry, John. You haven't given away any state secrets." She nodded to the perturbed servant and walked angrily through the foyer. Seething, she opened the front door, stepped outside into the bright sunshine and slammed the door. "Good riddance to bad rubbish!" she said aloud, echoing one of her mother's favorite sayings. She so startled the mailman who had just approached the mail slot beside her that he dropped his envelopes.

"I beg your pardon, ma'am?" asked the postman.

"None of your business!" she snapped and quickly marched toward the corner in search of a taxi.

Reggie never noticed Cole standing at his bedroom window, watching his wife stride down the street. He rubbed his jaw, abstractly wondering what she would think when she arrived home tonight and found him gone. After the fiasco of the morning, he had decided to leave her alone for a while, to ignore her until she accepted the inevitability of their situation. Today's trip would be his first step.

Cole's trip was legitimate enough. He was deeply engrossed in a huge business venture in Chicago, involving a sports complex, apartment developments, shopping malls and single-unit housing. It was a deal that he had been working on for the last five years, and although this particular trip could certainly have been postponed had he desired, Cole now felt it gave him a good excuse to leave town.

This was as good a time as any, Cole thought, to pay a visit to his old friend and business associate, Francis Munsey. Theirs was an old friendship, originating at the 1968 Democratic Convention. Cole had been invited as a financial advisor to one of the candidates and had inadvertently become involved in a peace rally. In the midst of the demonstration that was taking place outside the Cow Palace that night, a young, overzealous policeman had mistaken Cole for one of the peace rioters and had gone after him with a raised billy club. Francis Munsey had just pulled up to the building in a long, black limousine and the Chicago attorney recognized Cole from a recent *Time* magazine article. In an uncharacteristic move, one that Francis would never be able to explain in the years to come, he had shown his official shield to the cop and pulled Cole into the safety of his car.

In the long drive from the Cow Palace to Francis's home, Munsey and Cole began a friendship that would span more than a decade. Francis became Cole's liaison and attorney in all Midwestern WestCo ventures. On his many trips to the West Coast, Cole made it a practice to stop off for at least one evening with Francis, often staying the night in the huge Lake Shore Drive mansion. To his great surprise and delight, Cole grew to love the long nights of drinking and arguing with the brilliant attorney. Francis was the only person besides Lee to whom Cole would turn for advice.

The only regret both men shared was that nothing romantic ever developed between Cole and Francis's daughter, Patrice. As much as he liked Patrice, Cole never thought of her as anything other than a pretty child. When she finally became engaged, Cole was delighted for Francis as well as Patrice. He could never come to admire the man she married, finding David Astin parasitic and predatory. But he never voiced his opinion to Francis, who for reasons unknown to Cole, accepted his son-in-law with equanimity. If Astin was acceptable to Francis and made Patrice happy, Cole was satisfied.

John knocked lightly on the bedroom door. He stood in the doorway, his arms loaded with baggage. "Sir?"

Cole turned. "Come in."

Momentarily, John considered discussing Mrs. Weston's need to work, but when he saw the familiar furrowing of his employer's forehead, he thought better of it. "Where would you like these, sir?"

Cole pointed to the floor next to the massive king-size bed. "You can pack after I leave for the office. "I'll take out whatever I need and leave it on the bed. See that these bags are delivered to my office by three." He walked toward an eighteenth-century armoire that completely flanked one wall of the huge room. He casually turned back to the butler. "By the way, did you happen to see my wife this morning?"

"Yes, sir. She was on her way out—to *work*," he answered, accusingly.

Cole frowned. "And . . . ?"

John's gaze shifted uncomfortably back to the suitcases, and he mumbled something under his breath.

"Speak up! Is there something else?" Cole asked, irritably.

"No, sir," John answered quickly.

"Did she happen to notice the luggage?" asked Cole.

"Yes, sir. First she asked where you were going, then she asked if I needed help."

"Did you tell her?"

John looked at Cole dumbly. "How could I tell her, sir? I don't know," he answered honestly.

"How did she act?" Then he could have kicked himself for asking the butler such a stupid question. He rephrased it. "What did she say?"

John shrugged. "She didn't say anything."

"Nothing? She said absolutely nothing?" Cole queried.

Without blinking, John answered. "I'm sorry, sir, she didn't say . . . oh, yes, she did. I didn't hear her, but the mailman told me that she said something about rubbish."

"What do you mean, 'rubbish'?" asked Cole. Why would Reggie care about rubbish? He ran his fingers through his hair in exasperation. "John, do you mean 'garbage'?"

"I couldn't honestly say, Mr. Weston. She didn't say 'garbage,' she said 'rubbish.'" John thought this was one of the most peculiar conversations he had ever had with his employer.

"I see," Cole said finally, although he really didn't have any idea what John was talking about. He nodded curtly to the butler, walked back to the armoire and rummaged in one of the many deep drawers. He turned to face John, handing him a fat manila envelope. "Give this to Mrs. Weston when she comes home tonight." The envelope was filled with hundred dollar bills. "This ought to tide her over until I get back, unless of course she goes on one of her trousseau sprees again," he said, under his breath.

"I beg your pardon, sir?" John asked. I must be getting old, he thought sadly. I've never had any difficulty understanding Mr. Weston before. Suddenly, nothing in the house was making any sense. He scratched his balding head in bewilderment. "Is this money for Mrs. Weston to go shopping?"

Cole realized that John couldn't possibly comprehend what was going on. How could he, Cole thought dryly, when he was having trouble himself. "I know I don't seem to be making much sense this morning, John, and I apologize. Perhaps living with a woman is more unsettling than I anticipated.

John understood that. "I could have told you, sir."

"Yes, I'm sure you could." Cole smiled, knowing that if he didn't stop John right there and then, he was going to get a lecture. "But please just take care of the packing and have Timothy deliver everything on time." Cole finished pulling the clothes out of the armoire and closets and grabbed a lightweight herringbone jacket from the bed.

"Sir?"

"What is it, John?" Cole asked impatiently.

"Timothy is off today."

"Is William still here?"

"Yes, sir."

"Then have him bring the luggage to the office," he instructed.

"Fine, sir, and one more thing, Mr. Weston."

Cole tapped his fingers against the door post. "Yes?" he said with a long sigh.

"The herringbone jacket, sir. I don't think you need it."

Cole looked at the jacket in his hand. "And why is that?" he asked.

"Because, sir, you are already wearing a suit."

Cole gritted his teeth. "Thank you, John. That was very perceptive." He flung the jacket on the bed and stalked from the room.

John sat down on the edge of the bed. Things were not running smoothly in this house and he wasn't used to that. Since Mrs. Weston had arrived yesterday, Mr. Weston was not himself. Just looking at the mess of clothing on the bed, anyone could tell. Mr. Weston was usually meticulous about packing. But the disarray in front of him had him completely baffled. John counted twenty-two pairs of black socks, fifteen ties, a single change of underwear, one short-sleeve polo shirt, a set of thermal underwear, and the tie and cummerbund to Mr. Weston's tuxedo. Something was definitely wrong.

Although John's days of courting were long over, he still could recognize a man who was distracted by a woman. And a beautiful one at that. But the fact that Mr. Weston was leaving his bride after one day of marriage, the separate beds, indeed, the separate apartments, puzzled and upset him. What was the matter with the two of them? As John began to arrange the odd assortment of clothing, he knew there wouldn't be any more peaceful days until the Westons' straightened out their affairs and started living like a normal married couple. Unfortunately, he would have to keep his mouth shut and his thoughts to himself.

In the days and weeks to come, John would be the only person living in that house able to exercise such control.

Chapter 26

If Reggie thought "breakfast" with Cole had been unpleasant, it was only a brief glimpse of what the rest of the day would bring. She arrived at her office an hour late after looking in vain for a taxi or bus and ultimately settling for the subway which sat in a dark tunnel for twenty minutes. The stifling underground heat left her hair stuck to her face and her makeup dripping down her neck. As she rode the elevator to her office, Manhattan suffered a summer brown-out, leaving her to walk up the remaining flights in her high-heeled cowboy boots.

Alison frowned as Reggie dragged herself through the office door. "Where on earth have you been?" she asked, puzzled by the state of Reggie's clothing and makeup.

Reggie flopped into a canvas swayback chair, panting. She held up her hand, indicating that she needed a minute to catch her breath.

Alison looked worried. "Are you okay?" she asked her boss.

Reggie shook her head. "Coffee," she said weakly.

Alison returned a moment later with a steaming cup. "Here," she said, handing the coffee to Reggie, who was beginning to feel better. As she sipped the coffee, Reggie described her trip downtown. Like any true New Yorker, Alison nodded knowingly. "I'm glad you're feeling better because you have to leave now."

"What are you talking about?" Reggie asked.

"I came in early because I didn't know if you were still on your mysterious vacation," Alison began, "and the phone rang at eight o'clock. It was Simon Hastings."

Reggie's heart gave an unexpected lurch. "What did he want?"

"I tried to reach you at home but . . . did you know your phone has been disconnected? Did you forget to pay your bill?"

"I'll explain that in a minute. What did Simon want?" Reggie asked anxiously. She hadn't thought about Simon in a long time, but she had never forgotten the one special night in New Orleans. "You have to leave for Dallas this morning," Alison told her, waiting to see Reggie's response.

"I have to leave for Dallas? This morning?" she jumped out of her seat. "Are you sure?"

"The message was quite specific. Mr. Hastings said, and I quote, "Please tell Miss Gates that it is imperative that she leave for Dallas immediately. I must meet with her."

"Doesn't he believe in telephones?" Reggie asked.

Alison shrugged. "I'm just repeating the message."

"Do you happen to have any idea how I am supposed to accomplish this feat when I have a line to show in two weeks?" she asked.

"All I know is what he told me," Alison continued. "There's a Galaxy jet waiting at La Guardia for you. You're not even supposed to go home to pack. He said you can pick up anything you need for the next three or four days at Galaxy."

"Three or four days!" Reggie gasped, incredulously. "I can't go to Dallas for three or four days."

"Why not?" Alison asked, already picking up Reggie's handbag and portfolio. "I can manage the office," she assured her.

"It has nothing to do with the office," she said.

"What is it, Reg?" Alison waited for Reggie to offer an explanation, but Reggie was standing, coffee cup in hand, with a pained expression on her face.

"I can't discuss it." Reggie had decided that the fewer people who knew about her marriage, the better. Now she realized that she was going to have to tell her friend. A fabrication would never hold up to Alison's direct questions.

"Well? I'm still waiting," Alison said, thinking back to Reggie's two-day absence from the office and then the disconnection of her telephone. Suddenly, she knew the answer. "It's money, isn't it? You're in trouble."

A ghost of a smile flickered across Reggie's face. To say that she was in trouble would be putting it mildly. And money? That, too. But it wasn't the kind of trouble that Alison was thinking about, and as Reggie watched the concern on her friend's face, she knew she would have to tell her the truth. "Sit down," she requested. "I'm going to tell you quite a story and, when I've finished, you'll understand everything . . . or as much as I do, anyway."

Surprisingly, the story took less than fifteen minutes to tell. During its recounting, Reggie toyed with her hair, twisted the long strands around and around her finger until she had a mass of ringlets surrounding her face. Her eyes were huge green orbs, her color pale. Far from being a glowing bride, marriage to Cole Weston had rocketed Reggie back to a past when she had been shy, uncertain and totally lacking in self-confidence. It was a past that Alison had shared with her. Now, sitting and listening to the unbelievable story, Alison once again saw the girl Reggie had been.

"Do you understand now why I can't just fly off to Dallas?" Reggie asked. "I don't know whether that's violating the contract or not. Do I have to give him notice? A valid reason?

The whole thing is so ambiguous. The only thing I'm concerned with is keeping the patent out of his hands." She wrung her hands in her lap. "I hate this! I hate having to answer to anyone. I've been on my own for too long," Reggie complained. "I don't know what the rules are; he keeps changing them on me."

"Isn't everything spelled out in this contract of yours," Alison asked, "legally?"

Reggie nodded. "You've read contracts, do you always understand them?"

"Me?" Alison inquired. "I don't even understand the terms of my apartment lease." An idea struck her. "Why don't you call Lee? He's a lawyer."

"Brilliant!" Reggie answered with a small sound that fell somewhere between a laugh and a sob. "Who do you think got me into this whole thing in the first place?"

"Lee would never do anything to hurt you, never," Alison insisted.

"Not intentionally," Reggie agreed, "but this time, even he had no idea what would happen after I borrowed the money from Cole. I know he thought he was doing me a favor, hell—I was the one who asked him to find someone to lend me the money in the first place."

"You have to call him," Alison still insisted. "Whatever he tells you to do will be far better advice than I could give you. If he tells you not to go to Dallas, I'll call Simon's office and make up something." She wished there was more she could do.

Reggie finally agreed. "Call Lee's office and when you get him on the line, buzz me. I'll be in my office."

"Thatta girl," Alison said. "Grab another cup of coffee. I'll place the call right away."

Ten minutes later, angry and frustrated, Alison stalked through the door of Reggie's cluttered office. Reggie picked up her head from a stack of mail. When she saw Alison, she reached for the phone. Alison clamped her own hand over Reggie's. "Don't bother. No one is on the line." There was a peculiar expression on Alison's face, one that Reggie didn't recognize.

"What happened?" she asked. "Is he in the office yet?"

Alison expelled a long breath. "He's there, all right, but he's not taking any calls."

"Call again, this time use my name." Reggie suggested. No matter how busy Lee was, he would always take her call, even if it was for a moment to tell her he would get back to her. Unless, of course, Cole had given instructions . . . no, Reggie thought, shaking her head. Lee would never take that from Cole. No matter what ever happened between Cole and her, Lee could be depended on.

"Reggie, I already used your name. I said I was calling for Reggie Gates. The receptionist told me that Mr. Taggett was in a conference and had left instructions not to be disturbed by anyone." Alison spread her hands in front of her, palms up. "Now what?"

Reggie chewed her lower lip. Why did she have the uneasy feeling that somehow Cole was responsible for this? He was arrogant enough to do something to prove his control over her. She slammed her fist down on her desk. Who did he think he was? Alison's eyes glowed when she saw spark come back into Reggie's. "Alison, I'm going to try to place that call. In the meantime, you can call Simon Hastings's office and tell them I'm on my way."

Alison consulted her watch. "It's still too early to call Dallas. I'll place the call in an hour. Simon must have called you from home." Alison noted the two high spots of color on Reggie's cheeks, signs of suppressed fury. Good, she thought. Better angry than unsure; it was far more becoming. "You're absolutely certain that you're doing the right thing?" she asked. The last thing she wanted was to be responsible for getting Reggie into more trouble.

Once again, Reggie remembered Simon Hastings's delicious smile. There had been a promise in his eyes, a hint of unfinished business. Certainly, if her own husband could go off with his mistress, he could find no fault with her for going on an extremely important business meeting. Reggie reached for the phone and punched in Lee's number. As the phone began to ring, she looked up at Alison with a brilliant smile. "I've never been so certain of anything in my whole life," she assured her nervous friend.

* * *

When he reached his office, Cole's mood had not improved. He snapped at Marjory, who had brewed a bitter pot of coffee, and then slammed the door to his office when she suggested that he might prefer to prepare his own. Twice, Cole reached for the phone to call Reggie then changed his mind, remembering his resolve to give her no details about his sudden trip. There was, however, one phone call he was determined to make, but as he checked the time, he realized that 9:30 was much too early to call Evyan. He would have to wait at least another two hours.

There was a light tap on the door. "Come in," Cole said.

Lee stood in the doorway, a grim expression on his face. "Good morning."

"Good morning," Cole said unenthusiastically.

"Sit down. I have some bad news for you," Lee said as he entered the office and took a seat.

Cole arched his eyebrows. "I suppose she called you already?" he asked, knowing that Reggie would probably run to Lee with the story. He could see by the disconcerted look on his friend's face that he was about to get a lecture. "Get it over with."

"How did you know she called?" asked Lee, genuinely surprised.

Cole shrugged his shoulders. "She always tells you everything, doesn't she? Why should this time be different?" He didn't notice a growing look of confusion on Lee's face. "Let's get on with it, man. Give me the lecture already!" he said impatiently.

"About what? You didn't have anything to do with it."

"Is that what she told you?" Cole asked, surprised.

"Cole," Lee said, trying to reassure his friend, who was taking this whole thing personally, "whatever you did, or think you did, had nothing to do with the stroke."

For a split second Cole thought he would pass out. His knees buckled and he made a grab for the edge of the desk to keep from falling. "Stroke?" he whispered. "I just left her, she was angry but she was fine."

Lee's face registered shock. "You were in Chicago last night?" he asked incredulously.

"Chicago?"

The phone intercom buzzed. Cole spun around, grabbed the receiver and pressed it to his ear. "Take a message. Mr. Taggett is in conference," he said angrily and hung up. Turning back to Lee, he asked, "Who said anything about Chicago? What the hell are you talking about?" He grabbed Lee's lapel and stared into his eyes. *"Where is she?"*

"At Michael Reese Hospital in Chicago. She tried calling here twice, but you weren't in yet, so she called me," Lee explained, hoping that would soothe Cole's distress. "Don't worry, she's not angry that you weren't home—"

"What the hell is she doing in a hospital in Chicago?" Now *he* was beginning to get angry. He glared at Lee with thinly disguised hostility. If Lee was playing some sort of game with him . . . He spoke in a murderously low voice. "If you value our friendship, you will tell me exactly where my wife is and why you are doing this." His eyes were like icicles as he struggled to contain his concern and his fury.

"Reggie?" Lee asked in surprise. "How would I know where Reggie is?"

Through clenched teeth, Cole spat out the words, one at a time. "You-just-told-me-she-had-a-stroke!"

As Cole watched in dumfounded amazement, Lee's shoulders began to shake uncontrollably, then his whole body, until finally he threw back his head, laughing until tears were rolling down his cheeks. "Not Reggie, you idiot!" he gasped. "Francis. Francis Munsey. Patrice called me, not your wife. Francis had a stroke during the night."

Cole collapsed in his chair. Wave after wave of relief swept over him as his mind registered that Reggie was fine. Slowly, his pulse returned to normal. He began to see himself as Lee must have seen him, and a sheepish grin started at the corners of his mouth. "I'm sorry. I don't mean to sound unconcerned, but I thought . . . I was certain you were talking about Reggie," he apologized.

A slow, knowing look crossed Lee's face. So, strong, invincible Cole Weston was vulnerable, after all, and he didn't even know it. Somehow, Reggie had crept under Cole's skin, as Lee had hoped she would, and poor Cole was still denying it. Lee's lips twitched in amusement as he imagined what life at the Westons' would be like until each of them realized they were perfect for each other. Lee wondered how long it would take.

Cole had recovered from his confusion and was fussing with some papers on his desk in an uncharacteristic attempt to hide his embarrassment. "Let's begin this conversation again, shall we?" he suggested.

Lee discreetly coughed into his hand, sublimating the urge to laugh again. "Certainly," he agreed, more serious now. "Patrice Munsey called twice this morning to speak to you. Francis Munsey suffered a stroke late last night and is in Michael Reese Hospital in Chicago."

"Do you know his condition, did Patrice tell you?" Cole asked, concern evident on his face.

"The doctors haven't determined the severity of the stroke yet. Patrice said that there is some weakening on his left side, but he is able to speak."

"Thank God for that," breathed Cole, knowing that Francis would prefer death to the life of an invalid. "I'd better call Patrice."

"She's in ICU with him. I don't think you'll be able to reach her. She asked if you could fly out there today. Apparently Francis requested it."

Cole nodded, thinking how ironic it was that long before he knew about Francis he had planned on leaving for Chicago today. Now he had a plausible excuse for the trip, but what an excuse! He was frightened for Francis. He picked up the phone and gave Marjory instructions to book him on a flight as soon as possible, after which she should call his home and have William meet him at La Guardia with his luggage. Cole then turned to Lee. "While I'm out of town, I want you to do something for me."

"Sure. What is it?" Lee asked.

"Find out everything you can about David Astin. With Francis in the hospital, I have a feeling that Astin is going to be in charge of the Stockyard deal. Investigate him. Find out his business record, his friends, his hobbies, habits, anything that will give us insight into his personality."

"Everything is in that preliminary report I did for you six months ago. It's still in the files. Do you want me to start all over again?"

Cole nodded. "Get me the file to read on the plane then call Hugh Coffin and have him begin a new in-depth investigation on Astin."

"What are you looking for?" Lee asked curiously.

Cole stood up and began pacing the room. "I don't know. You know I never liked him, but it's more than that. It's a feeling, a gut instinct that I have about him. Maybe Hugh will find something to support that instinct."

Lee understood completely. Both men had always gone with first impressions and had very rarely been wrong. If Cole didn't like something about Astin, the chances were very good that he was right. "I'm just curious about one thing," Lee said cautiously. "If Francis trusts him, why don't you?"

Cole thought about the question for a moment. "I'm not a hundred percent sure that Francis does trust him. He covered up one sloppy job that Astin did already. I think Francis watches him very closely now. But if Francis is going to be incapacitated for any length of time, he won't be able to keep an eye on him. Let's see what Hugh comes up with before we blow this out of proportion."

"I think you're right. Let's go ahead with this investigation, but keep it quiet. Don't even mention it to Francis," Lee advised, wondering if he should mention that he, too, felt a vague uneasiness every time the name David Astin was spoken.

Cole must have noticed something because he searched Lee's face for a moment before asking, "What is it? Something bothering you, too?"

"I know Astin's name from somewhere, and it's driving me crazy because I can't place it. Every time we discuss him, a warning bell goes off in my head," Lee explained.

"You have no idea?"

Lee shook his head. "Absolutely none."

"For Christ's sake! We have three hundred million dollars riding on Astin and you can't remember why you don't like him?"

"Cole, don't bark at me," Lee warned. "Whatever's eating at you, take it out on someone else."

Cole was instantly apologetic. "Look, I have too much on my mind today."

I know, thought Lee with a smile. But now was not the time to remind Cole that, even more than worry for a dear friend, it was a certain green-eyed redhead who was the cause of Cole's short temper. Sooner or later, he would discover that himself.

But Cole could reach that conclusion by himself. He looked at Lee, whose head was bent to hide his knowing smile. Cole suddenly felt the need to open up to his old college buddy. "Lee," he began, his face clouding up, "believe me, my mood has nothing to do with you. I had a—a slight altercation with your dear friend this morning."

"That bad?" Lee asked.

"She's impossible, absolutely impossible. The moment that I try to be nice, she sees it as her advantage and turns my words around to suit her meaning. We're deadly together. She won't bend and I won't either. She's like a wild, unbroken horse!"

Lee looked Cole straight in the eye. "Why must you break her?"

Cole sat down at his desk. "I haven't the slightest idea," he admitted. "But we are like opponents in the ring: first we circle, then we attack." He shook his head to emphasize his point. "It's a mess! Not at all the way I planned it."

Lee laughed. "Life rarely is," he said, thinking about the way his own marriage had turned out. "Unfortunately, you can't plan your life the way you would plan a deal for WestCo. The cards don't always fall the way you want." Lee pointed a finger at his chest. "Look at me," he said, noticing a flicker of pain in Cole's eyes. "I accept my life," he said, quietly. "Don't you think it's time that you did too? You've always known about me. . . ."

Cole was quick to come to his own defense. "You're wrong. I didn't know. I only found out during your divorce when Liza came to me for advice."

"You never told me."

"Liza asked me not to," Cole explained, knowing that reason would suffice. Neither man would betray a confidence. "I think I can tell you now, though. She loved you very much, Lee. She could have fought another woman, but she didn't know how to fight homosexuality." Cole stated it in a matter-of-fact voice, and Lee was relieved the subject was finally out in the open.

"I think we could have worked it out. I swore I would go for help." Lee stood up and walked to the window, staring out into space. "Cole," he said, turning around, "I would have done anything to save that marriage. Maybe I still would," he said with a harsh laugh. "Why didn't you tell me she wanted help?"

"Wait a minute!" Cole said suddenly, stupefied by the accusing tone in Lee's voice. "First of all, it wasn't for me to tell you. It was up to Liza. Secondly, am I mistaken, or do I still detect a note of regret in your voice after all these years?" he said.

"I haven't stopped loving her if that's what you mean, and I probably never will," he admitted unashamedly. "I lavished all my time and attention on Reggie because Liza wouldn't let me give it to her anymore. Why do you think there is such a bond between your wife and me? I helped her over a difficult healing period and she did the same for me."

Cole's curiosity was aroused. "What was Reggie recuperating from? A love affair?"

"You'll have to ask her," Lee said. "As far as I'm concerned, what went on between Reggie and me during those years is none of your business. Sorry, old pal, but that's the way it is."

A muscle began to twitch near Cole's eye while he fought for control of his vivid imagination. He drew a deep breath, knowing that he had to ask Lee a question and hating himself for doing it. "Back then, were you and Reggie . . . lovers?"

There was an uncomfortable silence in the office as Cole waited for Lee to answer. Cole watched with crushing disbelief as Lee's head dropped to his hands, his shoulders shaking. He cursed himself for asking. Slowly, Lee raised his head, his features distorted by laughter. "Lovers?" Unable to control himself, Lee once again doubled over in amusement.

Cole looked on sheepishly. "I had to ask," he explained lamely.

When Lee recovered, he turned his piercing blue eyes on his friend. "Why?" he queried. "Why did you have to ask? What if the answer had been yes. Would it have changed anything between us or between you and Reggie?"

Before he would answer, Cole wanted to give the question some thought. After considering, Cole admitted to himself that, yes, it would have changed something. He just didn't know what or why. To Lee, who was sitting there waiting, arms folded, Cole said, "It shouldn't have made a difference, but I'm glad there was nothing between you."

"Why?" Lee shot back.

"Because now she belongs to me."

"Belongs? What kind of word is that? No one belongs to anyone! Certainly not in a marriage, especially not in your kind of marriage. I think you're confusing two different ideas—ownership and commitment. I also detect a note of jealousy. . . ."

Cole sprang from his seat. "Enough! Can we drop the whole subject? I'm sorry I asked." He grabbed the phone, ending further discussion, and called Marjory to check on his plane reservations.

Lee picked up the morning copy of *The Wall Street Journal* and casually leafed through it. The plan that he had set in motion when he had encouraged Reggie to borrow money from Cole was beginning to take on a life of its own. Where it went from here, though, would be anyone's guess. He had always assumed that there were only two players in the comedy-drama that had begun to unfold the day he introduced his two dearest friends. He had discounted the Fates, who were determined to play a major role in the production.

No sooner had Cole left his office, promising Lee that he would call Reggie from the airport to explain the reason for his hasty trip, than Reggie phoned Cole. She was told by a receptionist that Mr. Weston had just left for Chicago. By the time Cole reached La Guardia and placed his call to Reggie, Alison had the unpleasant job of informing him that his wife was on her way to Dallas.

They missed each other at the airport by minutes. Fuming, both Mr. and Mrs. Weston boarded their respective planes, alone.

Chapter 27

At even the best of times, Reggie was a bad flyer. But the flight to Dallas was a white-knuckle flight from beginning to end. The small jet was buffeted by strong headwinds, updrafts and a sudden electrical storm. The plane dove, rolled and gyrated until the insane acrobatics drove Reggie to grab for the white airbag. Thanking God for its presence, she willingly gave up the contents of her stomach.

By the time she heard the landing gear being lowered, her body was shiny with nervous perspiration. From the depths of her misery came the silent prayer that Simon would not be at the airport to greet her. When the steward bent toward her and pointed out of the window to the waiting limousine, she had the sinking feeling that her prayers had not been heard.

Deplaning in the midst of the torrential downpour was a nightmare. Reggie made a wild dash toward the waiting automobile, slipping on the wet tarmac and landing with a resounding thwack in an oil-slick puddle. The solid sheet of rain made it impossible for her to see, so it was difficult to cast blame when no one came to her aid. Soaking wet, she finally got up and ran to the car. The heavily tinted windows prevented her from seeing inside, and the rain kept the waiting chauffeur from noticing her approach. By the time she banged on the car's window, she was soaked to the skin.

The window slid down and Reggie heard a man's voice yelling over the noise of the storm and shrieking winds. "You can't come into the car like that!"

"Like hell, I can't!" she yelled back, grabbing the handle of the door and ripping it open. She fell into the freezing interior, surprised that, except for the chauffeur, the car was empty. She shivered, as much from the chauffeur's disapproving glance as from the air-conditioning. At least Simon wasn't there, she thought gratefully as she watched the toes of her eight-hundred dollar boots begin to curl up. Miserably, she searched for a way to turn down the air-conditioning. Finding none, she huddled into the velour seat, vainly seeking some kind of warmth.

How was it possible for so many things to go wrong in one day? She longed to place all the blame on Cole, but even he couldn't be held responsible for the terrible flight or the weather. The window that separated Reggie from the driver rolled down silently. "Mr. Hastings is on the phone, miss. He would like to speak to you." The window began to rise again.

Reggie reached forward to pick up the phone. "Hello?"

"Hi," said a deep male voice. "I heard about your flight. I feel terrible. Are you all right?"

"You may feel terrible, Simon, but it can't compare with the way I feel—or look, for that matter. I can't wait until I get to a hotel, a bath and some clean clothes."

He laughed richly. "I know. Worthington told me what you look like."

"Worthington?" she repeated.

"Don't laugh! He'll hear you. Ridiculous name, isn't it? Even for a chauffeur. I once tried to have him shorten it to Worth but he wouldn't hear of it. In any case," Simon continued, "he did give me a brief description of your appearance. He's going to take you over to Galaxy, where you'll ask for Gary Colby. He'll see that you get everything you need for a few days. Then, Worthington will take you to your hotel. I'll be in touch with you later this afternoon and we'll set up our meeting. You must be eager to find out what was important enough to drag you down here on such short notice."

She admitted that she was more than a little curious. He promised to tell her as soon as he saw her, perhaps for dinner if he could swing it. Then he apologized again for the short notice. "I have a tendency to be very impatient and more than a little overbearing when I want something."

"You must know Cole Weston," she muttered under her breath.

"As a matter of fact, I do. Why?" asked Simon. "Do you?"

Had she spoken out loud?

"Reggie, are you still there?"

"Yes, I'm here." Then, in answer to his question, she said, "I've met Mr. Weston."

A silence followed and then Simon said, "I'll call you at the hotel later."

Reggie replaced the receiver, wondering how Simon knew Cole. She hoped it was only casually, through business.

The streets of Dallas were completely empty. Reggie didn't see people walking dogs, children playing or men watering lawns. As soon as they reached the front entrance of Galaxy's flagship store in downtown Dallas and Worthington opened the door, she suddenly understood why. The skies were still leaden and, though the rain had stopped, the humidity hung in the air, making it impossible to breathe.

Reggie walked toward the crisp green and white awning that stood sentinel over the glass and bronze revolving door of the famous department store. Once inside its cool interior, she was amazed at the hubbub of activity. Beautiful women buzzed around, giving it the appearance of an active beehive. Compared to the drab silence outside, the lobby of the department store looked like a movie set.

Reggie began to fidget with the clasp on her handbag as trendy, well-dressed women suddenly took notice of the bedraggled redhead who was dripping puddles on the polished granite floor. Then, from the corner of her eye, she spotted Worthington speaking on the house phone. Within moments, a tall, blond man, who looked as if he might have stepped from the pages of *GQ*, approached her with a dazzling smile.

"Welcome to Galaxy, Miss Gates," he said.

"Shh," Reggie said in a conspiratorial whisper. "Don't let anyone know who I am." She pointed to her sodden clothing. At that moment, she would have admitted to being Genghis Khan before she would tell anyone she was Reggie Gates. She prayed that this young man had enough perception to sense her discomfiture.

Gary took her by the hand and unceremoniously led her to a rear elevator. Then, turning a bright smile on Reggie, he laughed, saying, "You really do look positively dreadful." As Reggie passed by a glass column, she stole a look at herself. It was worse than she had imagined. Her mascara, the one that was supposed to be waterproof, was running down her cheeks in rivulets. Her long hair hung limply on her neck like the sodden back end of a dirty mop, and her clothes were absolutely unsalvageable. Gary tried to keep her mind off her appearance by chattering amicably about her boutiques while they rode up the elevator. Despite her disheveled appearance, Gary's gifted eye saw the promise of great beauty, Claire Connors's nasty description to the contrary.

Gary reminded Reggie a little of Lee: slim, boyish, deeply tanned, with navy-blue eyes and an innate kindness that she felt immediately. Reggie found herself relaxing. Gary was fashionably dressed in khaki trousers, pale blue and white striped shirt, navy cashmere cable-knit vest and tassled loafers.

As he hurried her into a private suite on Galaxy's eighth floor, he turned to her, glowing. "Well, we did it! We got you here without a single person recognizing you. I call that quite an accomplishment, don't you?" He laughed. "It would have been unforgivable for you to make your first appearance in Dallas like this."

Reggie grimaced. "That bad?"

"Worse." Gary nodded. "Let's see what we can do about getting you back in shape to meet your public." He motioned for her to sit down on a chaise longue in the corner. The room was furnished to resemble an old-fashioned French boudoir. It was the type of room, Reggie thought with a smile, that would have made Marie Antoinette feel right at home. On the other hand, in her present state, Reggie felt gauche and ill at ease.

The walls of the room were richly upholstered in the most subtle shades of watered silk moiré. Pale pinks, muted blues and lavenders set off the priceless aubusson rugs on the bleached hardwood floors. Small couches, loveseats and chaise longues, all dressed in antique French fabric, were nestled in the many nooks beneath the windows, which were covered in fine Valenciennes lace. In one corner of the room, a skirted table tiered with row upon row of ruffles was surrounded by four delicate Louis XIV gilt chairs. On the table stood a fine set of Sevres china. The room was a bit of European fantasy spirited away from the eighteenth century. Suddenly it struck Reggie how much Cole would have appreciated it. He would have the eye and the knowledge to understand the love of detail that went into creating such an atmosphere. It was peculiar, she thought. She had spitefully derided his magnificent study, and now she wanted to share every detail of this salon with him.

While Gary watched her admire the room, he busily

arranged the delicate chairs around the table. "I've ordered hot mint tea for us. You might prefer something else, which you certainly can have, but we natives have found that hot drinks are more refreshing in this kind of weather. Before they bring it, why don't you go into the dressing room and get out of your wet clothes. There's a robe hanging on a hook." As she started for the dressing room, he added, "Let's relax a bit before we get started."

Grateful to get out of her wretched clothing, Reggie stepped into the mirrored dressing room and gasped in horror at her reflection. Quickly, she shed her clothes and boots and kicked the whole mess into the corner. She slipped her hands through the satin robe, zipped it closed and, unable to find any slippers, re-entered the room barefoot. A uniformed maid was carefully pouring fragrant tea into the cups. "We created this brew here at Galaxy," Gary explained. "It's stronger than conventional tea, almost like coffee. Try it."

Reggie wriggled her nose. Her only experience with tea was as a child when it was considered a cure-all, like chicken soup. Taking a first tentative sip, she was pleasantly surprised at the light, crisp taste. They fell easily into pleasant chatter while Reggie began to unwind, and they were utterly startled moments later when Claire Connors burst into the room unannounced.

She stood directly in front of Reggie. "Simon just told me that he invited you to Dallas. I had no idea that you could simply drop everything and run here like that. Is business so slow?" she asked maliciously.

"On the contrary, Claire. And it's lovely to see you again, too. I'm positively astounded by your Texan courtesy. You are such a wonderful example of that 'down home' charm."

Gary averted his head so Claire wouldn't see him smile.

"Gary, be a dear and go downstairs," Claire requested. "I'm sure I can help Reggie finish up with anything she needs here."

Gary shook his head. "Can't do that, Claire. Simon's orders. I'm supposed to stay with her and see that she has everything she needs. So why don't you scurry along? We'll be fine. I know exactly what Reggie needs, but if we have any questions, we'll call you."

"Your type would know exactly what she would need,"

Claire said vindictively. As she turned to leave the room, she called over her shoulder, "I bow to Simon's judgment." And then to make certain that she had not been misunderstood, she added masterly, "You needn't worry that he'll make a pass."

Gary smiled. "Who? Simon or me?" he asked with mock innocence.

Claire took a long look at Reggie's straggly hair and runny makeup. "Frankly, I don't think I have to worry about either one of you."

"Things aren't always the way they seem," Gary said cryptically. "You should know that. Look what happened with Olympus Center."

"What happened?" Claire asked, suddenly frightened. Olympus was a huge mall being completed five miles from Galaxy. It represented the only real threat to Galaxy in the greater Dallas-Fort Worth area. Since Claire had introduced the mini-designer boutiques, rumors had been flying that Olympus would do something equally innovative. Everyone in the market had been waiting to see what that something would be, Claire with fear.

Gary poured himself another cup of tea. "Rumor has it that Olympus signed contracts with Gucci, Vuitton, Charles Jourdan and Fendi this week. Right this minute, the contractors are meeting with the architects to plan the boutiques. I heard that each designer has been given a hundred thousand dollars just to decorate their own departments. Now, of course, they will never be as successful as Galaxy, but—"

"You said that they already signed contracts?" Claire interrupted.

Gary nodded. "But I told you it could be a rumor."

"I have declarations of intent from every one of them. I'm waiting to get the contracts back from their lawyers. I signed them up!" she exclaimed angrily. "Do you understand what this means? They can't be in Olympus; it isn't possible. I'll have every one of them in court tomorrow morning. You handle Reggie, I've got more important things to do. Does Simon—" She stared hard at Reggie. Was this the reason that Reggie had been summoned to Dallas without Simon even consulting her? Something was going on behind her back, and Claire was going to find out. She ran out of the room without even a backward glance.

"That's terrible," Reggie said to Gary after Claire's abrupt departure. "Are you sure they're all signed up?"

Gary shrugged his shoulders. "Maybe I exaggerated a little, but the rumor is that they are pouring millions into that mall. Each designer that I spoke of has been offered his own boutique, designed to his own specs. It's a hell of an offer to turn down."

"But what about Claire's contracts?"

"You heard her. She has no contracts, yet. She's got declarations of intent. I don't even think that's a legal term. I think it's something that some sharp attorneys thought up to keep Claire on the hook while they negotiated with Olympus. Once they've committed themselves to Olympus, I suppose they don't feel threatened by a lawsuit. I don't know, that's just the gossip around Dallas."

Reggie shook her head in amazement. "Do you have any idea what this could do to Claire?"

"It could very well be the end of Claire," Gary said. "I thought that was the reason you were here. If I knew you didn't know about it, I wouldn't have brought it up."

Reggie thought for a moment. "I have no idea why I'm here. I know that sounds ridiculous, but when I arrived at my office this morning, there was a message from Simon to come right down to Dallas. I came but I still don't know the reason."

Gazing appreciatively at the woman next to him, Gary could understand why Simon might want Reggie in Dallas, and if he had a free reign, he would show her how to set not only Simon, but all of Texas, on its ear. The possibility of throwing any obstacle in Claire's path always brought a shiver of delight to Gary. And what an obstacle he'd make out of this warm, magnificent woman. He broached the subject to Reggie, very carefully. "We have to get you ready to meet Simon. I can hardly wait to find out what this is all about." Gary studied Reggie's face carefully. "I don't know you at all. Why don't you tell me what kind of woman you think you are?"

"I don't understand."

"When you think about yourself, do you think you're beautiful?" Gary asked.

Reggie laughed. "Hardly."

"Cute? Glamorous? Sexy, sensuous?"

"I don't know." Reggie answered uncomfortably. "I never thought about it before. What kind of woman do you think I am?"

"It depends on what you want to be," Gary responded. "Since we are starting at zero, you can be anything you want."

Reggie rested her chin in her palm, thinking. "I want to be the most magnificent, dramatic woman around, the kind that men turn around to look at twice. More than twice! Can you do that?" she asked.

"That's exactly what I was hoping you would say. Yes, I can do it, but you have to listen to everything I say, do anything that I tell you to. Will you trust me?"

Reggie smiled. "If you can fulfill a promise like that, I would have to be a fool not to. Go ahead."

Gary jumped out of his chair. He took a large tooth comb from his pocket and, working rapidly, combed out all her tangles and then pulled her hair high onto the top of her head, securing it with a large clip. With a black grease pencil, he made bold strokes under her cheekbones, along her jaw and brow. "Those are your prominent bones. That's what we emphasize. You actually have the bone structure to be a photographer's model, you just lack the height. I can't make you taller, but I can do magic with everything else. Ready?"

Reggie nodded. "Go ahead. I'm all yours."

In less than two minutes, Gary had Reggie behind a dressing screen. Normally, she would have been appalled at her total lack of modesty in front of a stranger. But Gary had no interest in her sexually; he appraised her the way she would touch or study a bolt of fabric, the way an artist would stand in front of an empty canvas or a sculptor admiring a block of granite. He sat in the chair by the bay window and asked Reggie to walk toward him in her bra and panties. She peeked her head out to make sure they were alone. When she was certain, she stepped out. Gary let out a low, appreciative whistle. Reggie turned scarlet. "I thought you said you weren't interested!"

"I didn't say I was dead." He laughed. "Even a die-hard anorexic can appreciate the way a hot fudge sundae looks. Stop walking like that!" he said suddenly. "Stand up straight! That's better. Aerobics? Jazzercise?" he asked.

"No, I was just born this way." Reggie grinned.

"Lucky girl," he commented. "Now I have to call Vittorio."

He picked up the phone, punched some numbers and spoke into the receiver. "Yes, now please. Also, call Abby, extension 117, and have her up here in half an hour."

"Who's Vittorio?" Reggie asked.

"Your new hairstylist."

"What's the matter with my hair?" Reggie asked, annoyed. Of all her features, she had always considered her hair her best asset.

"How long have you been wearing it like that?" Gary asked.

"Since I was about seventeen," she answered.

"Exactly! That's what's wrong with your hair. Don't you think it's time for a change?"

"I never thought about it," she answered truthfully.

"Obviously. Go into the bathroom and wash all the black pencil from your face. Vittorio should be here any minute."

"You can be a little dictator, you know," she said with a smile on her face.

When Reggie returned, a small, dark man was waiting for her with scissors and comb. He settled her in a gilt chair, then stood back, staring at her seriously. Reggie began to feel uncomfortable, but Gary explained, as Vittorio turned this way and that, that it was necessary to study her bone structure, the natural wave of her hair, the shape of her face and her eyes in order to get the complete picture.

When Vittorio was satisfied with his examination, he led her to the small sink in the bathroom, where he washed and conditioned her hair, then he returned her to her seat. Reggie watched aghast, as Vittorio took her heavy hair in his hands and, with a few deft clips, left most of it shimmering in thick heaps on the carpet. He then took a razor from his back pocket and Reggie listened to the rasping sound of her hair being shorn. With an abrupt motion, he took her face between his hands, gave her head a few good shakes, turned her head upside down, tousled her hair with his fingers and returned her to an upright position.

"So much better," he said, satisfied. The whole thing had taken less than ten minutes. Her hair was still long but shaped closer to her face, highlighting her cheekbones and nose. It was natural, yet elegant. Her splendid green eyes, as yet unmade up, now became the focal point of her face. Her heavy hair no longer hid her exceptional features. "Where is

Abby?" Vittorio wanted to know. "I want to explain what kind of makeup she should use."

"Vittorio, you can't tell Abby what to do. She'll see the same thing that you saw, that I saw, as soon as she meets Reggie. But you have made Abby's job much easier." Gary knew exactly how to placate Vittorio.

Reggie couldn't stand it anymore. She jumped from the seat and raced to the mirror. But before she reached it, Gary caught her and whirled her around. "Oh, no, you don't. This artist won't let anyone see an unfinished canvas. Sit down, look—here's Abby."

A young girl, scarcely out of her teens, with long blond hair and a smattering of freckles across the bridge of her tiny nose skipped into the room. Reggie felt like a specimen as Gary, Vittorio and Abby studied her face. Finally, Vittorio left and Abby set to work. She played up Reggie's white skin, remarking on the unblemished perfection of her complexion.

"You're one of the few lucky redheads without freckles. Don't ever go into the sun without a hat." She applied contour cream under Reggie's exceptionally high cheekbones, then pale peach blush over them. "Don't use pinks, they clash with your hair. Your eyes are superb, only mascara, maybe a touch of lavender shadow, brings out the green, but only at night. Lipstick?" She studied Reggie's face again. "Absolutely. Always."

Reggie smiled at Abby's one-word sentences.

"Liner, too. First cinnamon lipliner, then peach lipstick and a clear gloss over it. Always reapply the gloss during the day. Your lips are beautiful, but they are pale and tend to fade into your face if you don't play them up. Stay away from anything that has a matte finish. Your skin is too dry." She took a can of spring water and sprayed Reggie's whole face. "This sets your makeup for the day. If you feel tired, spray it again during the day, as many times as you want. It's marvelous for your skin—hydrates it. Okay, that's it. Oh, one more thing. Always use sunscreen under your makeup, even when you think there is no sun out. Take a lesson from our ancestors who never went without hats or parasols. The sun will kill your complexion, actually anyone's, but yours especially because you're so fair."

Reggie was exhausted when Abby was finished speaking.

She felt like she had just sat through a lecture, but when Abby handed her the mirror and Reggie saw the change, she was flabbergasted. It could have been the haircut or the makeup or the combination of both, but whatever it was, the woman who stared back at Reggie was a stranger. "This can't be me!" she gasped in surprised delight.

Abby laughed. "It most certainly is. You are positively magnificent. Now let Gary finish you up." She waved cheerily as she left the room.

From that moment on, Gary was all work. Time was running short; he knew that Reggie had a tentative dinner date with Simon and, even though he had other appointments, Gary wanted to complete Reggie's renovation. There was a tremendous amount to do in very little time. While Reggie was being waxed, manicured and pedicured, they talked at length about her wardrobe. Though she had a flair with clothes, her wardrobe tended to accentuate her sauciness, not her elegance. Gary wanted to change that. He felt strongly that memorable women tended to have signatures. He tried to explain to Reggie that all of his memories of beautiful women were triggered by a hint of perfume. When he smelled Shalimar, he was reminded of his tenth grade girlfriend; a hint of Ambush and he was back in seventh grade. If Bal à Versailles was Reggie's fragrance, she had to wear it at all times, so the faintest whiff of the flowery perfume would remind people that she was in the room.

So it should be with clothing. White was her best color. It played off the clarity of her skin, the vivid contrast of her hair and eyes. It would be her signature, they both decided. He chose frothy bits of lace for her underthings, crisp white cotton, linen, sharkskin and raw nubby silk for day, voluptuous white cashmere coats, white snake boots, skinny white jeans, huge men's white batiste tuxedo shirts, white sweaters, white skirts, white, white, white!

"Enough!" argued Reggie. "People are going to think I'm a nurse."

"No, no. They might if we left you only in white, but not after we add the accessories. For these, we forget that white even exists. With every outfit you wear, you must employ the use of a totally unexpected splash of color." Like a magician, pulling rabbits out of a silk hat, Gary presented Reggie with vivid violet scarves, turquoise vests, a pair of fire-engine red pumps with a matching blazer, cobalt-blue beads, strands and strands of square-cut emerald, ruby, sapphire and amethyst faux jewels set in highly polished silver, and a shocking-pink wide-brimmed straw hat.

"Do you understand how it works?" Gary asked. "It's not enough to simply wear color, you have to explode with it. Think about an empty white canvas with one splash of crimson. It makes you turn around, look again."

Reggie marveled at Gary's concept. When he had finished dressing her in a pencil-thin white knit skirt to her ankles, white knit sweater with an over-the-shoulder cardigan, hunter-green alligator pumps and belt, emerald earrings and silver and emerald necklace, he led her to the mirror. What she felt in that one moment would change her whole life. Standing in front of her was one of the most arresting women Reggie had ever seen. It was more than beauty, more than chic. It was a combination of everything together. She turned to Gary and kissed him gently on the cheek. "You'll never understand what you've done for me, but I'll never forget this." Her voice was choked up as she tried to explain that what she had been trying to achieve her entire life he had accomplished in a few short hours.

"Sometimes it takes someone else, a stranger, to see the potential and know what to do with it," Gary said, truly touched. "Your beauty was always there; it was simply hidden."

Reggie continued to stare at the stranger in the mirror. Suddenly, she turned to Gary. "Have you ever thought about leaving Galaxy?"

"What for?"

"Designing. I think you are wasting your time here. There's a place for you at Rag's Raggs if you're interested," she offered.

"Doing what?"

Reggie thought about it. "I'm not sure yet, a little designing for openers, administrative work. Stuff like that."

"Have you ever considered taking in a partner?" Gary asked.

"God, no," she answered quickly. "Are you thinking that you might be interested in that?"

Gary shook his head. "Truthfully, the idea just struck me.

Why don't you give it some thought, and we'll talk about it. Frankly, that's the only way I would leave my position here."

"What is your position?"

"It doesn't have a name or title other than chief troubleshooter, I guess. Simon pays me very well to take care of special customers, like you. He says I have a knack for making the most obnoxious customers happy." He smiled while he said it, thinking about some of the more difficult Dallas-Fort Worth women.

"Are you suggesting that Simon considers me difficult?" Reggie asked, insulted.

"No. You fall into the category of VIPs."

"Thank goodness." Reggie sighed in relief. "I will think about a partner, after I find out what Simon wants. Will you be around for the next few days?"

Gary assured her that he was always available to talk, then hurried her back to Worthington, who was sitting in the air-conditioned car, waiting to take her to her hotel. "I wonder what Simon will say when he sees you," Gary mused. If Simon's reaction was anything like the shocked look on Worthington's face, Gary would be satisfied. The little bit of magic that Gary had performed had changed Reggie's looks from merely attractive to extraordinary. He could hardly wait to see Claire's face when she saw Reggie.

Reggie, on the other hand, was thinking that she couldn't wait for Cole's reaction.

Chapter 28

While Cole's plane was taxiing down the runway in New York, David Astin was trying to convince his father-in-law that the Stockyard deal could proceed in spite of Francis's illness. The old man looked terrible, David thought, silently cursing the way Francis had managed to pull through the stroke with only minor damage. Only because Francis's doctor had severely curtailed his immediate return to business had he grudgingly allowed David near the Stockyard deal.

Because of his love for Patrice, Francis had pushed David to the top, only to discover too late that David had neither the integrity nor the brains for the job. Now Francis was stuck with him. David had the plum in his hands, the Stockyard. From his bed at the Michael Reese Hospital, there was little Francis could do to stop him without letting his legal associates know how many times he had been forced to bail David out of messy situations. The last time that David had fouled up, it had taken a tremendous amount of fancy footwork and double talk to keep the news quiet. Without doing the required research, David had sold a large parcel of land to a developer of a shopping center. Only at closing had everyone found out that there were liens on the land in excess of two hundred and fifty thousand dollars. Francis managed to get David off the hook, but ever since that incident, his relationship with his son-in-law had deteriorated rapidly.

Neither one spoke about it, but underneath, they both remembered the calamity. Now, as he lay in his hospital bed, Francis wondered how Cole Weston would handle David. No amount of finagling would save David if he messed up this time. "Are you sure you're prepared to go ahead with the Stockyard?" Francis asked for the third time that morning.

"I told you I had everything under control. Why must you keep asking?" Old man, David thought, why didn't you die?

"I won't allow a repetition of the shopping center, David."

"There won't be," David said sullenly.

"See that there isn't," he commanded. "And make sure that you do your homework this time."

"For Christ's sake!" David mumbled under his breath.

"What did you say?" Francis asked in a low, warning voice. He might be in the hospital but he would be damned if he would let this incompetent upstart treat him as if he were no longer in charge. "What was it you said, David?" he repeated.

"Nothing."

"That's what I thought." Suddenly tired, Francis leaned back on his pillows. "Where's Patrice?"

"She went home about an hour ago. She's exhausted, and I think she was starting to get a migraine."

"Call her for me, please," Francis asked.

"Francis, leave her alone for a little while. She was up all night."

"I didn't ask you for your opinion. Please call her. She'll rest much easier if she knows I'm feeling better." Although he had been told by his physician to slow down and rest for the next few months, he had been assured that there had been no permanent damage. Francis wanted to give his daughter the good news.

Reluctantly, David dialed the number and handed Francis the phone. Lucilla answered on the third ring.

"Lucilla, may I speak to my daughter, please?"

"I'm sorry, Mr. Munsey, she's sleeping."

"How does she feel? Does she have a headache?" he asked, more concerned about Patrice's health than his own.

"Yes, sir. She took a sleeping pill a little while ago."

"In the middle of the morning?" Francis covered the phone with his hand and turned inquisitive eyes on David. "Does she always take sleeping pills when she has a headache?"

David nodded. Sleeping pills and anything else she can get her hands on, he thought.

When Francis hung up, he looked at David curiously. "Has she had migraines for a long time?"

A vague uneasiness stirred in David's stomach. Not now, he thought. Now wasn't the time for Francis to start poking around in his daughter's life. The last thing David wanted was to answer his father-in-law's questions about Patrice. He tried to make light of it. "She's had headaches for years," David said. "We never wanted to worry you about them. I assure you they're harmless, more annoying than anything else. And she's had all the tests," he continued in a reassuring voice, "CT scan, EEG, brain scans, the whole works. In fact, she's starting biofeedback therapy now, trying to learn how to control them before they get too bad."

"But why sleeping pills?" Francis asked, still not convinced.

"When they become especially severe, she pops a few Valium and sleeps through them. Honestly, Francis, she's not seriously ill, if that's what you're worried about," David said firmly.

"You're absolutely certain?"

"I wouldn't lie to you about something like this."

"Okay, David." Francis yawned. "As long as she's under a doctor's care."

David heaved a sigh of relief. "She is," he said, noticing the fluttering of Francis's eyes. Good, he thought. Francis believed him and was letting the subject drop. As David watched Francis drift off to sleep, he made a mental note to tell Patrice to back up his story. If she didn't, she knew what the consequences would be.

In her pink lace and organdy bedroom, with the heavy satin drapes drawn tightly against the late morning sunshine, Patrice lay with ice packs over her eyes. For a fleeting moment, when she had heard Lucilla speaking to her father, she had dared to hope that some miracle would send Daddy crashing through the door of her room to rescue her from the nightmare that had been occurring with increasing frequency over the past two years. But even in her semisomnolent state, she had heard the housekeeper repeat the well-rehearsed story she had been instructed to tell. Her father had believed it.

Why shouldn't he? Patrice thought. How could he possibly suspect that his daughter was lying in bed, pumped full of Demerol, courtesy of her husband. There was no migraine, there never had been. Headaches, yes, and aches everywhere else on her body. Huge welts on her back and thighs, bruises that were now turning pale violet and sickly yellow. There were no broken bones this time. David had become careful, inflicting excruciating pain without leaving any permanent evidence. He couldn't afford to bring her to the hospital again, couldn't risk the chance of someone asking too many questions about old fractures. He had to content himself with bruises that left no evidence.

Tears slipped from her half-closed eyes as she remembered how it had all begun. It seemed ages ago. A game, David had suggested, as he sat down on the edge of her bed, petting her and whispering in his mellifluous voice, "So beautiful . . . so lovely." His fingers had trailed down her neck to her breasts, her stomach, lingering at her tightly curled blond pubis. Her pulse had quickened under the hands that hadn't touched her for so many, many months. His fingers grazed the inside of her thigh, while his voice, husky with desire, droned on. "Lovely, white, virginal body. No one else has ever touched you, have they?" he asked.

"Of course not, David!" she answered, insulted.

"Shh! Lie there and don't talk!" he insisted and she complied willingly. If he had wanted, she would have stood on her head just to have him continue touching her this way, in those spots that he had never bothered with.

"Let's play a game," he suggested, as his hands moved lightly over her breasts again, sending shivers of delight through her body. "Let's pretend that I own you for the night, that you must do anything I say."

Her breathing was harsh as she responded to this idea. "Yes," she agreed, feeling an unfamiliar dampness between her legs. "Yes, David, anything."

"Good, good," he whispered. "You lie still and obey everything I tell you."

She nodded, waiting breathlessly for him to continue, her heart beating frantically.

"Do you know how to please me? Really satisfy a man?" he asked.

She shook her head.

"You're right, you don't. But tonight I'm going to teach you. By the time this night is over, you'll know everything I need you to know. I won't have to go anywhere else." With one vicious stroke, he ripped her nightgown from neck to hem, leaving her lying naked before him.

"David, my new—"

"Shut up!" he said savagely.

She lay silently. It was only a nightgown, after all, she thought. A small payment to have him back in her bed. Wide-eyed, even a little thrilled that he had done something so totally unexpected, she waited for his next move. He left the room suddenly, returning a moment later with a small pipe. "This is hash. We're going to smoke it together so you can relax." He placed the pipe in his mouth and took several deep drags.

"David, I am not smoking drugs!" she said.

He slapped her hard. "You'll do whatever I tell you." Quickly, before she had recovered fully from the stinging smack, he took four ties from somewhere near the edge of the bed and tied her wrists and ankles to the bedstands. "Now, you'll smoke whatever I want." He began to stroke her breasts again. "Right?"

She fought against the bonds that tied her to the bed. Once again, he slapped her face and she cried out in pain. "You don't leave me any choice, Patrice." He held her head securely and stuck the pipe between her lips. "Smoke it, bitch!" he commanded.

Vainly, she struggled, trying to twist away from him, but his elbows had locked her head into position. He pinched her nostrils, until with a gasp, she inhaled through her mouth, taking in a lungful of the sweet, pungent smoke. He watched her inhale, the pipe pressed against her lips until she had taken enough of the drug. She felt the effects of the smoke come over her as her arms and legs grew heavy.

David smiled. "Don't fight me again," he warned. "I have other drugs, Patti, more potent ones. But let's save them for another night." His pupils grew smaller as he continued to draw on the pipe. Patrice stared at him with frightened eyes. "You're so lovely," he began again, his hand stroking her neck gently, trailing to her breast, which despite her fear, quivered with an odd sense of excitement. He cupped one breast. "Small," he commented, "but firm, lovely, lovely, pink nipples." He circled the areola, lightly grazing the tip until it began to grow taut. "You like that, don't you?"

Surprised, she nodded.

"More?" he asked in a husky voice. "You want more?"

Once again Patrice nodded, transfixed.

"We have all night, Patti," he said, "all night to do anything we want. Do you want to experience the ultimate pleasure? Yes? But first, you have to have a little pain. First pain, then pleasure." He loved the look of fear in her eyes.

Slowly, he lowered his head to her breast, teasing her nipple with his tongue. He sucked gently, then with increasing urgency, almost as if he were nursing. The feeling was like nothing Patrice had ever felt, causing strange contractions between her legs. Her body began to move, arching toward his mouth. He sucked hard on her erect nipple. She flinched. "No, that's not pain. That's pleasure." Suddenly David bit down on her engorged nipple and Patrice screamed in agony.

He raised his arm high above her head and slapped her

cheeks. Both sides of her face stung as her head snapped from side to side by the force of the powerful backhand. "That's pain, Patti," he yelled joyously, over her screams. When she didn't stop, David reached into his pocket for a linen handkerchief, which he bound tightly around her mouth. The sounds that came from her were now merely pitiful moans. "Trust me, Patti. Pain only makes pleasure more intense."

He continued concentrating on her breasts, gently sucking then nibbling until she forgot the exquisite pain he had inflicted moments before. As he lightly twirled his tongue around the bruised nipple, Patrice experienced a sensation she had never imagined.

"You see?" he said, moving his head down her body, which had started to move rhythmically with his caresses. Drooling and licking her from her breasts to her navel, then downward until he reached her pubis, David continued to arouse his wife. As his mouth reached her most private part, David parted those lips with his hands, gazing into the moist, swollen pinkness. Patrice flushed scarlet. Never before, even in their most intimate moments, had David actually looked "there." Mortified, she struggled to close her legs and was rewarded for her attempt with a vicious backhand that sent stars careening wildly through her head. "Try that again and you'll wish you hadn't!" David warned, once more spreading her legs.

He was in command. For once, Patrice had no one to turn to for help, and the glazed look of terror in her eyes sent blood rushing to David's head. He wanted her to beg him, plead with him to give her the gift of release. His tongue worked on her enflamed center of pleasure until he began to hear the moans of passion rising from her throat. When the sounds reached a fevered wail, he stopped. She looked up at him in confusion. She had been so close, on the very edge.

David smiled wickedly, knowing exactly what she wanted. Now, now that he had her where he had always wanted her, he would make her do the one thing she would never consent to. Climbing on top of her until he was actually astride her body, with his knees locking her head in place, he unzipped his fly. With a single motion he removed her gag and guided himself into her mouth. He moved slowly at first, then with increasing speed, thrusting deeper and deeper into her throat, moving with a tempo only he could hear. Each time he pounded into her, he smacked her breasts until Patrice could no longer tell where the pain was coming from. Suddenly, through a haze of pain, Patrice saw him reach over and take something from the night table drawer. He held it to her nose. When she inhaled the fine white powder, he took more. Satisfied, he thrust deeply into her mouth again until, with a triumphant roar, he exploded.

Minutes passed and Patrice waited until David got up and stood over her, releasing her bonds. "Very well done, Patti." She turned her head away, but he grabbed her wet, slippery chin and yanked her around to face him. "By the way," he said casually, "anytime you want to watch that little performance, you can. I have the whole thing on video." He smiled at the look of horror on her face. "Should we show it to your father the next time he comes over?" When she didn't answer, he shrugged and left the room.

That was the threat that kept her his prisoner, that and the drugs. The perversion of his "games" and the potency of the drugs he administered to his wife increased. She lost the ability to fight him as she became more and more dependent on the cocaine, amphetamines, tranquilizers and finally Demerol. If she refused to participate, he invented scenarios to torture her. Threats of all the videotapes arriving at her father's office were the nightmares that kept her docile. That, the drugs, the beatings . . .

Now, in the loneliness of her bedroom, Patrice broke down. With her father's illness, the last vestige of hope left her. There would be no one to rescue her now. She fumbled in her drawer and placed two more tablets on her tongue before burying her face in her pillow to muffle her sobs.

Chapter 29

There was the possibility, Cole thought, that if he had to spend five more minutes in David Astin's company, he would wring his neck. Astin was one of the most irritating men Cole could ever remember meeting. During the two hours that Cole spent visiting with Francis, Astin hovered over them like a vulture. He required constant reassurances, both from Cole and Francis, that the Stockyard deal would proceed even with Francis in the hospital. Everytime Cole tried to direct a question at Francis, David would butt in. It was only for Francis's sake that Cole didn't demand that David leave the room.

Sensing Cole's exasperation, Francis finally asked David to return to the office for some totally unnecessary information that he wanted to show Cole. David was annoyed at the request but, not wanting to show his displeasure in front of Cole, left, disgruntled.

As soon as Cole was certain that David was no longer on the floor, he turned to Francis. "Thank you," Cole said.

"Don't thank me. I've been trying to get rid of him all day. He seems to think that I am on my way out and wants to secure his future. Unfortunately for my illustrious son-in-law, however, I'm fine."

"Francis," Cole said gently, "you're not fine. You have got to slow down whether you want to or not—and sooner or later you're going to have to deal with your son-in-law. Do you or don't you want him involved in the Stockyard deal?"

Francis studied Cole's face. "Would you go ahead with it if David were involved?"

"Only for your sake. You know how I feel about him," he said bluntly. "I do have another idea, though."

"Yes?" Francis asked.

"Patrice," Cole said. "I think we ought to get her involved in this deal. In fact, to be frank, I think she should have been groomed from the time she was young to step into your shoes. You always treated her as if she didn't have a brain in her head. I think she does. I know she does. Given half a chance, she could take an active part in your business."

Francis looked at Cole in shock. "You must be kidding!" he said. "She's never expressed the least bit of interest in anything that dealt with business."

"Did you ever give her the opportunity?"

"No," Francis said thoughtfully. "I just assumed she would be like her mother, content to let me take care of her . . . wanting me to—"

"I think it's time that Patrice learned to take care of herself, Francis. I'm going to try to have dinner with her tonight, feel her out, see how she feels about her husband."

"She's madly in love with him, Cole," Francis answered.

"We'll see," Cole said coolly. "Your job is simply to keep David occupied tonight so I can meet with Patrice. Will you do that?"

"No problem," Francis said. "How are you planning to approach my daughter?"

"I have no idea, yet. I'll have to play it by ear," Cole stated. "I'll speak to you tonight or tomorrow morning and let you know how it goes, okay?"

Francis nodded. As Cole got up to leave, he noticed that the older man's eyes were beginning to close. As mild a stroke as it had been, it had taken its toll. The future, and Francis's health, were still very much in question. Cole wanted to make certain that David Astin would create no problems for Patrice if anything happened to her father.

True to his word, Francis found some busy work for his son-in-law that evening. It was not David, however, but Patrice who proved to be the problem. When Cole first called her, he was told that she was asleep. He left a message. After three hours had gone by without a return call, he called again. This time Patrice did come to the phone but pleaded a splitting headache when Cole suggested that they dine together. It was only the threat that he would stop by to see her at home that finally convinced Patrice to accept his invitation.

When he saw her enter the tiny French restaurant, he was aghast. She looked horrible. Thin, pale and drawn with huge circles under her eyes, Patrice looked ill, even weaker than her father that afternoon at the hospital. She was silent during most of the meal, unresponsive to Cole's attempts to engage her in conversation. Finally, as they sipped tiny cups of espresso, Cole looked deep into her eyes and, as gently as possible, asked her if there was anything bothering her, besides her father's health. For a moment, as tears gathered in the corners of her eyes, he thought she would open up to him. But just as suddenly as they appeared, she blinked them away and a curtain of silence was drawn across her face once more.

Cole realized that questioning her further was useless. After dinner, he took her home, kissed her tenderly on the forehead and promised to see her the next day before he left Chicago. Once again, he thought he saw the glimmer of tears, and a mute plea of some kind, but when he went to lift up her chin, she turned away abruptly and entered the house, closing the door behind her.

The next morning, Francis's condition had markedly improved. He was angry at the doctors who insisted he remain in the hospital when he felt fully recovered. Yet, there must have been a small part of him that was not certain that he was well because, as much as he protested, he didn't sign himself out.

He sat comfortably propped up on two pillows as Cole described the previous evening to him. "I didn't have the kind of success I anticipated," Cole said apologetically. "Obviously you were right and she is either very much in love with David—or protecting him."

"Why do you say that?"

Cole sighed. "Francis, I couldn't get her to answer one question about her husband. Every time I brought up his name, she changed the subject. And as far as getting involved in business . . . I didn't even mention it to her."

"I told you she wouldn't be interested."

"I think you're wrong. I think she's hiding something, and I intend to find out what it is." Cole felt that he owed that much to Francis and Patrice. "It's going to be difficult to accomplish this long-distance, but I may have a way." He was thinking about the investigative report he was waiting for from Hugh Coffin. If David was involved in anything shady, and perhaps that was what was disturbing Patrice, surely Hugh would be able to pick it up. "You rest up," he advised Francis. "I'll call you in a few days and let you know if I've been able to find out anything. In the meantime, try to keep David busy with other matters."

On his way to the airport, he stopped at Patrice's house, where he was informed that Mrs. Astin was out and wasn't expected home until five or six that evening. Puzzled that Patrice hadn't let him know she would be gone all day, he walked back to the cab and sat back, reflecting on her odd behavior. There was a great deal that Cole didn't understand and before too much time elapsed, he was determined to find the answers. Lost in thought, he rode back to the airport.

As he waited impatiently at O'Hare Airport for his plane to be announced, he thought about the last time he had spoken to Reggie. Their marriage had begun on such a bad note. He'd been so absorbed in the business and personal worries of this trip that he suddenly realized just how exhausted he was. He saw her green eyes and a flash of her hair in his mind. He decided to call her. He called her New York office only to be informed that she was still in Dallas on business. He was so infuriated that he couldn't get any more information from Reggie's close-mouthed secretary that he didn't bother to leave his name. He rattled the whole bank of phone booths when he slammed his receiver down.

He drove around downtown Chicago for about an hour before he spotted her. Shoulder-length soft brown hair, wide frightened eyes, high-heeled boots, gold lurex halter top that accentuated her youthful breasts, and tight, thigh-high kelly-green skirt. She wasn't a pro . . . he could tell by the tentative way she hung back in the doorway of the sleazy hotel, trying to get the nerve to approach a car in the way of her cronies. She was different. A novice. He pulled over to the curb and stepped out of the car. She instinctively drew deeper into the doorway.

"First night?" he asked. He saw fear in her eyes. The ache between his legs increased.

She nodded.

"Scared, huh?"

She nodded again.

"What's your name?" he asked.

"Sarah."

"Sarah, I'm not going to hurt you. I just want to talk to you.

I'm from Lights, the organization for runaways." He saw the stark terror in her eyes and knew he had hit pay dirt. "Don't be afraid," he urged. "We just talk to kids like you . . . no police, no parents, nothing like that. Sometimes we can help get you off the street." She relaxed imperceptibly. "What do you say we go somewhere to talk. Maybe grab a hamburger?"

"Just to talk? You're not going to turn me in or anything?"

God, she was young . . . and so frightened. He liked that. His erection grew as he imagined her on her knees, begging him not to bring her to the police. He reached out and gently patted her head. "No, honey. We're going to hop into the car, go somewhere to talk. That's all."

She sat huddled against the car door while he drove fifteen minutes into the suburbs then pulled into the parking lot of the Travelbest Motel. She eyed him suspiciously. "We keep a room here just for this very purpose," he explained. "Keeps the police off our trail. They watch our offices downtown and we've been burned a few times."

He didn't need to register. He had taken care of all that beforehand. He took the key out of his pocket along with a five-by-seven index card. "I'll just need some information for our files," he said by way of explanation. It sounded logical to Sarah. David put his arm around her in a fatherly fashion, his hand accidentally grazing her breast. He thought he'd explode with anticipation, right there in the parking field. "Come on, darling," he drawled. "Let's get this over with, and if you don't want to go home after we talk, I'll drop you back where I found you. Promise."

They walked up the outside staircase to the room, and David fit the key into the lock. Sarah followed. The hardest part was over. He sat down on the edge of the bed and motioned for her to sit down next to him. Out of his breast pocket he pulled a pen and a small notebook. He asked her name, age, present address and some other impersonal questions. Sarah leaned back, no longer frightened. When he started to ask her why she had left home—had she ever been beaten, molested, abused—she hesitated. He urged her to trust him and, seeing the kindness in his eyes, she poured out the story of her father's brutality.

She never noticed David's hand unzipping his fly . . . or the knife that suddenly appeared. He never touched her with the knife; it hadn't been necessary once he told her what would happen to her pretty little face if she didn't do exactly what he wanted. Terrified, she'd taken off her clothes and called him Daddy; she lay passively on the bed while he stroked her soft, white breasts and bare thighs. It was when he ordered her to turn over that terror finally took hold of her and she began to cry.

"Bad baby, bad baby!" he cried through clenched teeth. He removed his belt.

She never knew what was coming. A half hour later, he left the motel room with a smile of deep contentment. It was so very easy . . . so good.

Sarah's was a more brutal initiation into prostitution than most kids got, but perhaps more profitable, too. There were horrible welts all over her thighs and buttocks, and a hundred dollar bill on the dresser.

Reggie's suite at the Parkland Plaza was permanently reserved for preferred Galaxy clients, and it came as a surprise that it had been given to her at Simon's personal request. Complimentary cheese and crackers, accompanied by a bottle of champagne, had been sent to her room, and she languidly sipped on the dry wine, nibbling on a Carr's biscuit as she waited for Simon's arrival. When she heard the light tap on the door, she was well into her third glass of champagne. Swaying slightly, she managed to navigate her way to the door. A bluish-gray dusk had settled outside, bathing the room in a soft glow, which was echoed by two flickering candles on the coffee table. As she opened the door, the ethereal light formed a halo behind her and Simon's eyes widened in shock at the dazzling woman before him. Dressed blindingly in an ankle-length stark-white cashmere dress, with her deep scarlet hair falling in gentle waves around her shoulders and her heavily fringed, impossibly, incredibly green eyes smiling at him with undisguised delight, Reggie Gates caught him completely off guard. He stood, mouth open—mesmerized.

"Reggie?" he asked when he had finally found his voice. He remembered an extraordinarily attractive, bright-eyed kid from the New Orleans opening. But here was no child—standing before him was one of the most hypnotic women he had ever seen.

"Hello, Simon," she said softly. "Thank you for the lovely room and the royal treatment today. I must owe Galaxy a fortune."

Simon continued to stare. "What have you done to yourself?" he asked as she backed away from the door and motioned for him to enter. "I'm sorry for staring so," he apologized. "It's just that there's been such a change in you since we last met."

"Oh, dear," she said, "and I thought Gary had fixed up everything. Judging from your expression, I think I had better go back tomorrow for phase two."

"On the contrary! I think I may have to give Gary a raise. You look magnificent! What happened?"

"Frankly," she said with a decided lilt in her voice, "I can't take any credit for this. Gary did it all." Her laugh was so different from the artificial sounds that passed for amusement in his circles. He thought of Claire, always snickering or bitching behind someone's back . . . never this genuine sound of mirth.

Reggie interrupted his thoughts. "There's still more than half a bottle of champagne left, and if you don't help me, I'll be too drunk to go out for dinner." She poured some of the bubbling liquid into a tulip-shaped goblet and handed it to him. "To Galaxy," she said as she lifted her glass in a toast.

"To you, my dear," Simon responded, lightly touching his glass to hers.

They both took a sip. "I don't think anyone ever toasted me before. Thank you."

"Don't thank me, Reggie. I should be the one to thank you for coming to Dallas on such short notice. It was a ghastly request for me to make."

Reggie nodded. "It *was* rather presumptuous of you," she agreed, "but on the other hand, I do work for you, and when the boss whistles—"

"I never could whistle," Simon said in mock seriousness. "It was the bane of my childhood. Do you have any idea how embarrassing it is to grow up being unable to whistle? Everyone was always making fun of me because, when I pursed my lips, the only thing that came out was bubbles."

Reggie smiled at the silliness. She was having a marvelous time. She realized that she hadn't had this kind of light playfulness with a man in a long time. Certainly, she had never had it with Cole. She understood the difference immediately. She and Simon were cautiously flirting with each other, shyly testing, circling, trying to determine what their relationship was, what it would be. Neither one was certain yet what to expect. Of one thing Reggie was certain, there was still chemistry between them, that very same charged reaction she'd felt when she had first met him in New Orleans. She leaned over to refill his glass, coyly looking into his eyes and then dropping hers.

"Do you think it would help if I got a little drunk before you tell me why I'm in Dallas?" Reggie asked.

"If you're asking me if you'll need courage for this, no. In fact, I hope you'll be pleased and flattered when you find out."

"In that case," Reggie replied, "I'll pour myself another glass of champagne just for the fun of it."

Somehow, they found themselves on the terrace leaning on the railing. A light breeze blew Reggie's hair around her face. Simon unconsciously leaned forward to push it away. For a moment Reggie held her breath as Simon stared into her wide, curious eyes. Instinctively, she knew that he was going to kiss her and suddenly she knew she didn't want him to. Not now, not yet! Casually, she slipped away from Simon and re-entered the suite. Obligingly, he followed.

Reggie moved quickly around the room, straightening pillows, emptying glasses and studiously avoiding Simon's eyes. The moment outside had unsettled her, thrown her off balance. Under any other circumstances she would have responded to his advances, but tonight something held her back; and that something was Cole Weston!

Simon took his cue from Reggie. Wondering what had changed her mood, he simply sat back on the sofa and watched her as she tried to regain her composure. He smiled to himself at her efforts to conceal her discomfort. Finally, he realized that unless he said something, she wasn't going to relax. Casually, he began to speak about the store, retailing in general and Rag's Raggs specifically. Within ten minutes he noticed that Reggie had relaxed considerably and was actively taking part in the safe conversation. She came over to the sofa and sat down next to him. She's like a soft young bird, he thought with a smile. One moment she's certain she's ready to fly, the next, she doesn't trust her wings. The odd combination of innocence and sophistication served only to heighten his interest. Ultimately, he knew they would go to bed, maybe even have a relationship. All the signs were there. But the time hadn't arrived yet, it wouldn't be that evening. All right . . . he could wait.

"Where would you like to have dinner?" he asked as he watched her nibbling delicately on a cracker.

"Anywhere!" Reggie laughed.

Simon looked at her thoughtfully. "Would you take it the wrong way if I suggested that we order room service? I promise to behave like a gentleman."

It was on the tip of her tongue to tell him that she wished he wouldn't, but, remembering the confusion of his nearness outside, she said, "Room service would be lovely and," she continued with a laugh, "I trust your behavior."

"Tonight, you may trust it," he answered.

Once they had established the ground rules for the evening, both Simon and Reggie relaxed. Dinner was a delightful affair, casual, informal and comfortable. They chatted through the meal about their pasts, his divorce and her struggle to achieve success as a designer. She never brought up Cole's name, although she still wondered what their connection was. Then he surprised her by asking for her opinion of Claire Connors.

She slowly shook her head. "Simon, I can't answer that."

"Why not?"

"Because the answer would be influenced by my knowledge of what your relationship is with her," she answered diplomatically.

"How would that affect your judgment?" he asked.

"Because if I told you the truth it would be tantamount to my telling you that I think your taste in women is atrocious!" Oh, dear—she was a little tipsy.

Simon burst out laughing. "I'm not sure, but I think that is exactly what you just did."

Reggie shrugged her shoulders. "You see what I mean?" she said, embarrassed. "Blame it on the champagne."

"My dear Reggie," Simon said gently. "Those were your emotions, not the champagne, speaking."

They had left the dinner table and were now relaxing on the sofa. Simon's arm was resting on the back of the couch, his fingers lightly toying with her hair as she leaned back. Once again, she averted her eyes, frightened that this time, if she looked into his face, she would be helpless to avoid physical contact. Oddly, she now wanted to kiss him very much. She started to toy with his other hand.

His voice was slightly husky when he spoke. "I want you to understand that this is not why I asked you to fly to Dallas."

"I know," she said in a whisper.

"If we stay here on the couch," he continued in a low voice, "I won't guarantee my behavior anymore. You're so very beautiful by candlelight." When she didn't respond, he leaned his face toward hers and very lightly placed his lips on hers. Gently, he parted her lips with his tongue. She offered no resistance. Time and place disappeared as Simon lowered his mouth to Reggie's neck, placing soft, gentle kisses along her silken skin. His lips tasted her perfume, felt the rapid pulse beat in her neck.

They both jumped at the unexpected sound of the phone. Reggie looked around the room, perplexed. "It must be for you," she said as she walked over to answer it. "No one knows that I'm in Dallas."

Simon said nothing. No one knew he was sitting in Reggie's suite either. The phone rang again. "I think you had better get it," he said.

She picked it up and said hello. Silently she listened for a few moments and Simon could see bright spots of color appear on her cheeks as impatiently or angrily—he wasn't sure which—she began to drum her fingernails on the table. "Who gave you the number here?" he heard her ask. "Look, Lee, I have every right to be here, or anywhere I damn well please, for that matter. Don't bother explaining the details of the contract to me . . . I don't give a damn what Cole thinks or says for that matter . . . yes, you can tell him I said so!" She listened for a moment. "I have no idea when I'll be home, mm-hmm, yes . . . you can tell him—never mind! I'll tell him myself when I see him. Is there anything else? . . . Good!" She slammed the phone down and turned to face Simon.

"Trouble?" he asked curiously.

"Not really trouble," Reggie answered. "Annoyance."

Simon stood up, smoothed the creases out of his trousers

and walked toward her. "Reggie, is the Cole you were referring to on the phone Cole Weston?"

Reggie hesitated, then answered, "Yes, why do you ask?"

"How are you involved with him?" Simon asked. "I'm not asking out of idle curiosity or jealousy," he asked. "I'm asking for a perfectly legitimate reason, which I will tell you in a moment."

"We're involved in a business deal," she said. It was true, she tried to tell herself. Certainly not the complete truth, but it wasn't exactly a lie either. "Now will you tell me why you want to know?"

"Sit down," Simon requested. When Reggie had resumed her seat on the couch, he continued. "I asked you, demanded really," he corrected when he saw the slight arch of her eyebrows, "that you come down to Dallas on such short notice because I'm about to fire Claire Connors."

"What?" Reggie asked, open-mouthed.

"You heard correctly. Claire has made enormous errors in judgment over the past six months. I ignored the first few mistakes because I chose to. They weren't terribly important, and I was able to correct them without too much difficulty. However," Simon continued, "the errors have escalated in importance to the point that they threaten Galaxy's future. I can't make excuses for her anymore. She has to go."

"What has all this got to do with me?" Reggie asked. "Does this involve my boutiques, as well?"

"No. It has nothing to do with that. Claire was in line for a very big promotion at Galaxy. Due to certain changes, changes no one knows anything about yet, we've created a new position that I thought Claire would hold. Obviously I've changed my opinion. I asked you to Dallas to discuss that position with you," he concluded.

Reggie looked puzzled. "What kind of position are you talking about?"

"Galaxy is about to expand. We're opening four new stores in this country and three in Europe in the next two to five years. I want you to be in charge of the entire expansion," Simon explained.

"Me?" Reggie asked, surprised. "What about my own business? What about Rag's Raggs?"

"You can still continue to operate your business," Simon

said. "Reggie, I need new talent—innovative . . . creative. I've watched what you've done with your own company, and I've been very impressed. You are absolutely the right person for this position. I'm sure of that. Are you interested?"

Reggie shook her head. "I don't know," she answered honestly. "I don't see how I could do both things at once. Raggs takes up an enormous amount of time." She sat silently, mulling over the proposal. "I assume this would mean a lot of travel?"

Simon agreed. "Yes, a tremendous amount of travel, but the compensation would make it very worthwhile."

"You mean salary?" she asked.

"The starting salary is over two hundred thousand a year, plus stock options and the usual perks—an apartment in each city you'd be staying in, cars, an expense account. Those, plus whatever you net from Raggs, should make you a wealthy woman."

Reggie sat back on the sofa to think about Simon's proposal. If what he was offering was legitimate, if she could find a way to continue to operate her own company and put her salary from this new job toward her debt to Cole—she did some quick mental arithmetic—she could pay Cole back within a year, two at most. Once her debt was repaid, she could leave Cole. It was a very attractive proposition.

"Simon," she began, "on the face of it, it seems too good to be true. Are you just in the thinking stages of this or are you actually making me a job offer now?"

"This is a certified job offer. Are you interested?"

"I think I might be," she answered. "I would have to go back to New York and speak to my financial advisor first. When do you need an answer?"

"As soon as possible. We're supposed to break ground in Los Angeles in three months. You would be in charge of the whole thing—right down to color of the carpet. It's a major undertaking," he warned.

"I can see that," she said seriously. "I'm not sure that the salary is even adequate." She couldn't believe she was aiming even higher, but perhaps . . . ?

"We can negotiate a salary when you tell me that you want the job." Then he picked up her hand. "I want you, Reggie," he said.

The double entendre wasn't lost on her but she chose to ignore it. Dollar signs were spinning through her head as she tried to compute the amount of the time it would take her to repay her husband. "I like the sound of the job, Simon. I like it very much." She didn't add that it would give her the perfect excuse to move out of Cole's townhouse and, for all intents and purposes, out of his life.

Simon stood up, pulling Reggie with him. He placed his hand on her cheek. "Think about it for a while, but try to make a quick decision. As you can see, we're running out of time." He drew a line with his forefinger from her cheekbone to her lips. "Let's put everything else on hold until you make this decision. Okay?"

She nodded and followed him as he walked toward the door. He turned to her as he opened the door. "I hope you make the right choice. Call me when you've decided." He bent down and lightly placed a kiss on her lips. "Have a good trip back to New York," he said, closing the door behind him just as her telephone began to ring. He yearned to stay, if only to find out who else would be calling her at this hour of the night.

Reggie picked up the phone on the fourth ring, fully expecting to receive another lecture from Lee. "What is it now?" she asked, the weariness and annoyance easily discernible in her voice.

"That's hardly the kind of hello I expected to receive from my wife after an entire day of not speaking to her."

"Cole?"

"Yes?"

"What do you want? And how did you find me?" Reggie asked angrily.

"Find you?" he chuckled. "I didn't know you were hiding."

"You know damn well what I mean. Who told you where I was? Oh never mind! I know. How long did it take for Lee to call you once he tracked me down?" Reggie demanded.

There was the sound of rich laughter from the other end of the line. "I called him and asked him if he knew where you were. It was as simple as that," he answered. "Would you mind telling me what you are doing in Dallas?"

"Yes, as a matter of fact I would mind, very much."

"I see," Cole mused. "I could find out very easily, you know."

"Well, why don't you do just that!" she said, her green eyes glinting furiously.

"I would much prefer to hear it from you," Cole said softly.

There was little point in continuing the argument, Reggie decided. By tomorrow morning, or afternoon at the latest, she would have to tell Cole that she was accepting Simon's offer. She might as well tell him now.

"Simon Hastings asked me to come to Texas this morning. I met with him, and he offered me a very important job with the Galaxy chain. I have to let him know if I'm interested," Reggie said.

"And are you?"

"Yes, I think I am," she answered, a hint of defiance in her voice.

"I suppose Simon asked you to head up the expansion?"

"Yes . . . as a matter of fact he did," Reggie responded, surprised that Cole knew.

"I should have told him," he said.

"Told him what?"

"That you and I are married. It would have saved Simon a great deal of money and energy."

"Dammit, Cole. What are you talking about?" Reggie asked, her fingers gripping the phone in a viselike grasp. "What possible difference do you think it would make to Simon that we are married?"

"Amalgamated Stores owns the majority of shares in Galaxy," Cole explained patiently. "Guess who owns Amalgamated Stores?"

"Oh, no!"

"Oh, yes!" Cole answered, and she could hear the satisfaction in his voice. "The board would hardly approve the wife of the chairman for the position Simon offered you. Legal dilemma. I'm terribly sorry, Reg, but you can see that it would be an impossibility, can't you?"

"No one knows that we're married, Cole. If you don't tell Simon, I could take the position."

"I don't want you to take the position. Besides, within a week everyone in the country will know about our marriage. I just called in the announcement to the *Times*," Cole said.

"You did what?"

"Our wedding announcement will be large but tasteful in this Sunday's paper. I didn't think you would object. I have the feeling I was wrong."

"You pompous . . . self-centered . . . egotistical . . . how could you do that without consulting me?"

"It was quite simple actually. I placed a call to the social editor—"

"Cole?" Reggie said, as calmly as possible.

"Yes, my dear?"

"Go to hell!" she said and slammed down the receiver.

Chapter 30

Reggie returned to New York the following day. Cole's assessment had been correct; Simon's offer was no longer even a remote possibility. In the wee hours of the morning, Cole had placed a phone call to Simon, who had coldly explained to Reggie over breakfast that morning why he had to withdraw his offer. Reggie saw barely suppressed fury in Simon's eyes when he asked her point-blank why she had never mentioned her marriage to Cole. As much as she tried to explain the peculiarities of her contractual marriage agreement, Simon did not understand. It was obvious, by the grim set of his mouth as he listened to her bizarre explanation, that he felt used and foolish.

As he was finishing his coffee, he told her that it was probably all for the best. "If you and I were thrown together too much," he said, "you know damn well what the end result would be. Circumstances are far, far different this morning than what they were last night."

"You're referring to my marriage, I assume?" Reggie asked.

"Yes, of course."

Reggie shook her head in frustration. "You haven't listened to one word I've said, Simon. It just *isn't* that kind of marriage." But Reggie saw in his eyes that her words were accomplishing little. As far as he was now concerned, Reggie was married to Cole Weston. Whatever their relationship was, that was the bottom line. It was a closed subject.

The trip to Dallas had been a fiasco. Not only had Reggie lost the means to escape from Cole, but grim reality of her indenture had been brought home to her with brutal clarity. Theirs was a double-edged agreement. Although she was allowed to have a private life, the contract, by its very nature, negated the possibility of any kind of meaningful relationship with a man. For Cole, the agreement couldn't be more ideal. He could carry on a romance with a woman and then tell her that he was married. Reggie was livid as she realized how she had been duped again. With icy resolve, she silently swore to have her revenge.

Cole, Lee and Hugh Coffin were reviewing the private investigator's report on David Astin. "Give me a quick rundown. Your own private assessment," asked Cole.

"Difficult to do, Mr. Weston," answered Hugh with a frown.

"Why?"

Hugh tapped the report thoughtfully. "There's not much here. Nothing specific, if you know what I mean. A few affairs, harmless . . . kept a mistress for a while, hangs out around the porno district . . . likes dirty movies, I guess. I just can't get anything concrete on him yet. Oh, there is one important thing I *did* find out. He spends money like crazy on drugs. My bet would be cocaine. He can well afford it and, since no one has ever seen him stoned, cocaine would be the obvious choice."

Cole grimaced. The more he heard, the more certain he was about his instincts. "What else?"

"Not much." He thumbed through the report then picked up his head. "But did you ever just have a gut feeling?" Cole and Lee looked at each other. They had both experienced the same sensation about Astin for their separate reasons. "I'm going to come up with something more tangible. I just need some time. But I can tell you from the gut that I don't like the little I see."

"Look, Hugh. Astin's father-in-law and I go back a long

time. If there's something rotten about Astin, I want to know it so I can protect that family. Got it?"

"I'll do my best, Mr. Weston."

"I know you will. Try to be quick. I need information soon," Cole said then turned to Lee. "Set up a meeting in Chicago . . . no, better yet, I'll plan a little dinner party or wedding reception to get him in New York. I'll speak to Reggie."

"She's coming home?" Lee asked.

Cole threw him an icy look. He had no intention of discussing his marital affairs in front of Hugh. Lee got the message and, gathering the investigator's papers, helped him return them to his briefcase. "Thanks, Hugh. And please keep in touch with any new information," Lee said.

Hugh practically saluted. "Will do," he said and walked out of the office.

Lee strolled back to Cole's desk, sat down and put his feet up. "Is Reggie coming home tonight?" he asked again.

Cole yawned. "I assume so."

"Oh, come on, Cole—enough already. Can't you and Reggie find some middle ground on which to meet? Does it always have to be the same battles over and over again? Doesn't it wear you out?"

"I have no idea what you're talking about," Cole said in a bored tone.

Lee was beginning to get angry. It was one thing for the two of them to joke around about the marriage, it was quite another for Cole to tell him an out-and-out lie. "I think," Lee said slowly, "that you are being absolutely impossible where she is concerned. You won't even give her a chance."

Cole sprung to his feet. "Me? I won't give *her* a chance? My good friend, you've got it all mixed up. She is by far the most obstinate, impossible woman I've ever met. Her pigheaded obstinacy, which she calls her *independence*, or quest for it, gets in the way of everything she does. She can't carry on a civil conversation without whining about how I stole her goddamned *independence* from her." Cole raked his fingers through his black hair in frustration. "Let her have it. Oh, let her have all the damn independence she wants. In fact, I wish I'd never gotten into this mess in the first place. Do you know that she actually flew to Dallas without telling me where she was going or for how long she'd be gone?" He looked at Lee for a response and, getting none, continued his diatribe. "Did you also know that she met with Simon Hastings while she was there? Do you believe, knowing Simon's reputation, that they were just talking business? Do you?"

"Yes." Lee nodded. "Quite honestly I do. Furthermore, if they weren't, it doesn't happen to be any of *your* business. You were the one that insisted on that idiotic clause about discreet whatever it is you called them."

"I would hardly call what she just did as being discreet!"

"Tell me something," Lee asked. "Do you have any reason to suspect that they are romantically interested in each other? She's met Simon before and she's never indicated to me, at least, that there was anything between them. Do you have information indicating otherwise?"

Cole had to admit that he didn't.

"Then for Christ's sake, leave it alone. Give your wife the benefit of the doubt. It wouldn't hurt if you tried to be just a little more realistic. Think of it as a business trip. That's all it was. You're beginning to sound like a jealous husband."

Cole sat silently for a few seconds. "How awful," he mused.

"Don't get too concerned, Cole." Lee laughed. "Reggie does that to men. She just doesn't buckle under. It's very important to her that she and men meet on equal terms. She'll never submit to you, mentally or otherwise, if that's what you're waiting for. On the other hand, if you can learn to accept her as a dynamic, captivating woman, you may be able to form a friendship with your wife. If you don't . . . you'll be the loser, not she."

"What do you mean?" Cole asked.

"She may very well turn out to be the best friend you ever had if she learns she can trust you not to hurt her."

"Why should she think I would want to hurt her? I only wanted friendship from her in the first place."

Lee raised his eyebrows. "Oh, really?"

"Let's just leave it as that's what I would like from the relationship now," Cole said firmly. "I don't know how this whole thing got turned around."

"I do," Lee said with certainty. "Both of you are so determined to master the other that neither one of you will take the time to see what you really have. Let me give you a little advice; go home, be there when she arrives. For my sake, try again. Start over and, for the love of God, give a little."

Cole shook his head. "Lee, you know me well enough to know that I don't give in easily. I very rarely back down when I take a position. Both your friend Reggie and I know that this marriage is a contest of wills. I doubt either one of us can change."

"Try. Maybe you'll discover that there is a middle ground where neither one of you has to give in completely. You might even plan a discreet whatever it is with your own wife."

Cole chuckled. "There was a moment yesterday morning when the idea did enter my mind."

"And . . ."

"She almost dumped a pot of hot coffee in my lap."

"Yeah," Lee said, nodding, "that's Reggie."

"Yeah," agreed Cole, "it certainly is!"

Chapter 31

Both the limousine and the taxi pulled up to the front of the brownstone at the same time. Reggie grimaced as she saw Cole's long legs slide out of the sleek automobile. Cole didn't notice the cab's passenger until the taxi pulled sharply away from the curb, narrowly missing the limousine and causing Timothy to swear loudly. At the sound of the screeching tires, Cole turned to stare at a striking redhead who was stopping traffic in her sparkling white cotton tube pants, off-the-shoulder top and wide brimmed white straw hat. It was several moments before Cole realized that this startling vision in white was his wife.

"Hello, Cole," Reggie said as she reached for her new suitcases filled with her new wardrobe.

He walked over to the curb. "Can I help you with those?" he asked, trying to hide his astonishment. What had she done to herself? he wondered.

"That would be a new twist," she responded with barely concealed sarcasm.

He ignored the comment and effortlessly tucked the two large valises under his arm and walked to the door. Reggie took out her key and opened the door before Cole had the chance. He turned to her in surprise. "I forgot you had a key."

"I live here, remember?" she answered.

Cole could feel the anger beginning to churn inside. Still, he was determined to take Lee's advice and begin again despite how difficult Reggie was making it. "Where would you like these?" he asked.

"Can you manage to bring them upstairs or would you like me to call John?"

"I think I can manage. Are you coming up?"

Reggie shook her head. "Not right now. I would like a drink before we have dinner, and if it isn't inconvenient, I'd like a word with you. Do you think you could join me in the study after you bring the luggage up?"

"I'll ring for John to take the luggage and I'll join you for that drink right now. Besides, it will spare me the possibility of embarrassing myself if I can't make it upstairs with these," he finished with an attempt at a smile. He was still trying; Lee would have to give him that much.

"Fine." She led the way through the foyer into the study without a backward glance.

As pleasantly as he could, he invited her to sit down then offered her a drink. "Sherry or wine?"

"Sherry will do," she answered, "on ice."

Cole turned to the bar, busying himself with the crystal decanters and ice trays. "How was Dallas?" he asked casually, never turning to face her.

Reggie cleared her throat. "That's what I wanted to discuss with you."

He poured himself a snifter of Rémy Martin and turned to hand her the sherry, then he sat down opposite her in the leather loveseat. Slowly, he sipped his drink. "I'm all ears."

Reggie kicked off her white snakeskin sandals and tucked her feet beneath her. She still hadn't touched her drink. "I would like to talk about us . . . and our arrangement."

"All right," he nodded agreeably.

"There are some side effects to this marriage that I never

envisioned when I agreed to it. It was bad enough," she began, "that I had to leave my own apartment and move in here . . . I could have learned to live with that. I could also have learned how to deal with you on a day-to-day basis if I had to . . . but some things have now occurred that make it impossible for me to continue this farce. I have to get out and want to know what it will cost me. I want to make a deal. Will you go along?"

"No," he stated simply.

Angrily, Reggie jumped from her seat then, seeing the smile on Cole's face, casually smoothed her clothes and sat down again. "Why not?" she asked as calmly as possible.

Cole swirled his brandy around in the glass. "Why the sudden need to get out?" he countered.

"Sudden? This is hardly sudden! I never wanted any of this—"

"This is all related to Simon Hastings and Dallas, isn't it?"

"Yes," she admitted, "but it's not what you're thinking."

Cole stared directly into her flashing eyes. "How could you possibly know what I'm thinking?" He was trying hard to contain his temper, but the anger was obvious in his voice. The thought of Reggie and that old man together . . . the picture playing in his mind drove reason away. "Don't make the mistake of thinking I'm a fool, Reggie. I know where you were and what probably happened while you were there. It has no bearing on our agreement."

"You don't know anything!" she said angrily. "You're assuming that I—" She stopped and tried a new tack. "Look, we're a lot alike in some ways. If you suddenly disappeared on an unannounced business trip, stayed overnight and came back asking me for a divorce or an annulment, I would also assume that you were having an affair and that's why you wanted out."

She set her glass on the table and leaned toward Cole. "But I am *not* having an affair with Simon. Oh, I'm not going to lie and tell you that if circumstances were different I wouldn't have slept with him. I might have, but I haven't yet." Reggie noticed a tightening around Cole's eyes and mouth. "Cole, I met Simon long before you ever conceived this marriage idea. We were attracted to each other back then, but I wouldn't go to bed with him then and won't now. I have to feel something for the person I'm involved with. I have to care! Can't you understand?"

"Of course," Cole whispered.

Reggie leaned forward. "I'm sorry, I didn't hear what you said."

"I said, go on."

"This is very hard for me." Cole sat perfectly still, waiting. "Under the terms of our agreement I'm free to have a relationship with another man if I'm 'discreet,' right?"

Cole nodded.

"Well, dammit, I can't! I can't even get to know anyone in any real sense of the word under these rules. Don't you understand? Men are different—they don't care who they sleep with."

Oh, my darling, this one does, thought Cole.

"Women want more than just sex. How can I spend time with someone I care about, get to know him and still be 'discreet'? Don't you know me well enough by now to know that sneaking around isn't for me? If you care at all about my feelings, let me out of this arrangement," she pleaded.

"Are you in love with Simon Hastings?" Cole asked very quietly.

Reggie leaned back and closed her eyes. Cole thought that she had never looked lovelier as he waited for her response. "It's funny," she finally said, "that you should ask me that. Simon wanted to know if I was in love with you. He doesn't understand anything I tried to explain to him about our marriage. I couldn't make him understand because . . . because . . . it's unexplainable!"

"Look, let's get some things straight," Cole said in a voice that surprised him. He had meant to sound understanding and compassionate; instead he sounded angry. He softened his tone. "I want to remain married. For a while I thought I had made a horrible error by pushing you into this. I still think there are problems that have to be ironed out, but, Reggie, I want this to work."

"It can't," Reggie stated simply.

"Let me finish what I have to say and then you can have your turn." He noticed the dead look in his wife's eyes. "Dammit! I can't stop you from falling in love with another man. Even if we had a real marriage, that possibility would always exist—just look at the divorce statistics. It is also conceivable," he continued softly, "that I might fall in love with someone. If that situation ever arose, I don't know what I would do. Fortunately, it hasn't and I rather doubt that it will. As you know, it's not in my nature to be that giving to another person . . . that's why I prefer our kind of marriage."

She waited in the silent room for a moment. "Have you finished?" she asked.

"Not quite. I know you're furious because you wanted that position and couldn't have it—right?"

"Cole, that's only a small part of the problem."

"But you blame that on me, too, on our relationship."

"Yes, I do."

"I'm sorry, Reggie. Whether you choose to believe me or not, my hands are tied on this issue. There is nothing that I can do to change the fact that my wife simply can't hold that position in my company. I have too many stockholders and board members to contend with. But," he said sincerely, "I would like you to know that I never dreamed anything like this would come up." He walked over to her and placed his knuckle under her chin, forcing her to look into his eyes. "I know how you must feel about me right now. I'm genuinely sorry that this happened when it obviously meant so much to you."

Reggie stared into his eyes, trying to decipher the peculiar look she saw. For a wild moment, she thought she detected something close to tenderness, then it was gone. "I can't stand that you hold so much control over my life. I've lived on my own for so many years, answerable to no one. I'll never get used to having to answer to someone. Can't you understand that?"

"Yes, I can," Cole responded as he returned to his seat. "I don't think I could do it either," he admitted. "But, for the most part, you don't really have to answer to me, you know."

She shook her head, sadly. "You really believe that?" When Cole nodded, she said, "It's not so. True, I don't have to ask you every time I buy a pair of pantyhose, but I can't run my own life any longer. That's what I can't bear!"

"What is it that you want to do that this marriage makes impossible?"

Reggie shrugged her shoulders in frustration. It wasn't any

one thing . . . it was a state of mind . . . a lifestyle. She couldn't explain what it felt like to suddenly lose the ability to make choices, plan a future. "I feel . . ." She stumbled over her own thoughts. "I feel like a child again, a prisoner, an indentured servant."

"I think that is the first thing you've said that makes sense," Cole said. "Let's begin with that comparison, it's a very good one. Let's pretend that you are indentured. It's worked in the past. One serves a period of indenture to pay back a debt. That seems to be the case here."

"Yes," Reggie agreed, "but I can't live the next three years of my life like this. It's making me crazy!"

"Would it help if we adjusted the time period, say to one year? Could you do it for a year, Reggie?" Cole asked.

Reggie couldn't believe her ears. Was Cole actually offering her a deal? A way out? "Yes," she answered without hesitation. "If I knew it was only a year, I could make it work. I think," she added.

Could he prove to her in twelve short months their arrangement would work? That it would be beneficial to her as well? He thought so. If she would stop struggling against him, learn that he had no intention of hurting her, perhaps they could learn to be friends instead of adversaries. Maybe, just maybe, Lee was right. He had little choice. A year of her life would be all Reggie would forfeit.

"Suppose," Cole bargained, "we give it a year. After that, if you still believe it won't work, you can get out." He saw the immediate effect his words had on her. Her smile, in fact her whole face, lit up. "But there are stipulations," he cautioned.

"Aren't there always?" she said, the smile fading slightly.

"Stop frowning, you'll wrinkle," he said, smiling. "The stipulations are very minor. We'll agree to really give this marriage a chance, for a year—no more, no less. But you have to cooperate. You have to make a genuine effort to make this work. Can you do that? Can you stop fighting me at every turn?"

Reggie's smile returned. "I don't know," she answered honestly. "I have a volatile personality. I could try, though. I could try to cooperate. I can't promise you that it will always be easy. By its very nature, this whole thing is repugnant to me. On the other hand, I've held other jobs that I couldn't stand and I've managed to survive." This time she laughed at the expression on Cole's face. "Oh, stop being so sensitive, Cole. Face it—it *is* a job of sorts. I've been hired to be your wife for a year, and frankly, the salary and the living conditions are great. . . . Yes, I think if I look at it like that, I can do it. But what about you? Will you really let me go at the end of a year? Will your ego allow it?" She was treading on dangerous ground, but the questions had to be asked.

"Yes," Cole said, his eyes twinkling from a private joke. "If you want out at the end of the year, you've got it."

"And all the money?"

"We'll forget about the loan," he answered.

She leaned back in her seat, closed her eyes for a moment, then said, "Well then, for a couple of million dollars a year, I'd be Jack the Ripper's wife."

Cole flinched at the comparison. And Lee honestly thought they'd be friends one day? "Okay, Reg. We have a deal and, since we've agreed to begin again, I would like to suggest that we have dinner. Would you like to eat home or would you prefer to go out?"

Reggie relaxed imperceptibly. She had gained more than she had hoped when she first suggested they speak. For a man like Cole to give up any point to an adversary—and Reggie had no illusions that she was exactly that—was a victory. Accordingly, she decided to try it his way. As pleasantly as possible she told him that she was tired and preferred to eat dinner at home. As Cole watched, she got up and started for the door.

"Where are you going?" he asked.

"To ask Elsa to prepare a light dinner for us," she answered.

He walked over to her and took her arm. "There's no need. I asked her to make dinner at the same time John took the luggage upstairs," he said with a slightly wicked grin.

"How could you possibly know what the outcome of this conversation would be before we even sat down to talk? Didn't you consider the possibility that I wouldn't want to have dinner with you at all?"

"That was most definitely a possibility," he agreed, "but unlikely."

"Why?"

"Because I was ready to give in to almost any demand you

might make in order to give this marriage a chance of working."

Reggie eyed her husband suspiciously. "Why would you do something like that?" she asked. "It's so out of character for you."

"Damned if I know," Cole said honestly as he led his wife toward the dining room.

Part Two

Chapter 32

Life in the brownstone began to run more smoothly. Reggie had agreed to Cole's proposition and felt that one year out of her life could be tolerated, especially when she considered the amount of money involved. For the most part, she hardly saw Cole anyway. Her time was spent concentrating on Raggs' latest line, while Cole was involved with his real estate deal in the Midwest. Occasionally, when they did find themselves at home together, Reggie began to enjoy their private dinners. She found that Cole was interested and helpful in her business and she didn't hesitate to ask his opinion about problems that she found insoluble. His expertise in business matters was invaluable.

Several times during the next month, Reggie spoke to Simon, and though he was friendly enough, she detected a strain in his voice when he told her that he was interviewing several people for the key European division. It was obvious that he hadn't forgiven her for keeping her marriage a secret. He did tell her that Claire was no longer associated with Galaxy; her failure to obtain legal contracts from top designers was too serious an error to keep her with the company. It was also obvious, although Simon never said anything, that he was no longer personally involved with Claire. Reggie wondered how that would affect her once her year with Cole was over. She never explained the new arrangement to Simon, knowing he wouldn't understand it. But the possibility of beginning a relationship with Simon always lingered in the back of her mind.

Cole spent a great deal of the month of September trying to complete the Stockyard deal. Flying back and forth to Chicago was exhausting, yet he felt that with Francis still recuperating, it was vital that he keep an eye on David Astin. He still couldn't pin anything definite on David, but Cole's second sense was working overtime and it kept cautioning him to watch for something more sinister than what an obnoxious, irritating or even incompetent young attorney might do. He spoke about his suspicions to Reggie while they were having dinner.

"I know you're not going to like this, but I think it's time we announce to the world that we're married. After you raised your objections, I withdrew the notice from the *Times*, as you already know. I'd like to hold a reception for friends and business associates."

"Is it really necessary?" Reggie asked.

"I think so," Cole answered. "There are a few men I have to get to know better, business associates. A splashy party will give me a perfect excuse."

Reggie looked at Cole quizzically. "Is it something serious, someone particularly worrisome?"

Cole set down his fork and knife. "You're quite astute. You are somewhat familiar with the Stockyard deal that I've been working on, I assume?"

Reggie nodded.

"There is an attorney involved in the operation that I don't care for. I've done some research on him but still haven't been able to come up with anything concrete. If we throw a big party and invite him with his wife for the weekend, perhaps I'll be able to figure out what it is that's making me so uncomfortable."

Reggie wriggled her nose in disgust. "I'm going to hate this, you know. I don't think I'm very good at it."

"Don't worry," Cole said, "whatever help you need, you can hire. There is also another reason for the party."

"Oh?"

"I've been receiving a lot of . . . invitations again, none of which I care to accept. It's time to take my name off the single-man list."

"You're one of the few men that wouldn't be flattered to be on that list," Reggie observed.

"How is it that you were never part of the swinging set?" Cole asked.

"I've always kept a relatively low profile," Reggie answered. "For a long time, I was too poor and too busy to go anywhere at night. I could hardly afford busfare to work, much less fancy clothes and the accoutrements that went with that kind of life. When I could finally afford them, I found that I didn't have the interest."

He agreed. "It's a lousy life and I want no part of it, either. I have to let everyone see that I am no longer available as an escort, and I think the best way to display it is to hold a large reception in our honor. When people see what a happily married man I am, the invitations should cease."

Reggie winced. "Happily married?" she repeated.

"Yes, my love. As far as the public is concerned that is exactly what I am." Cole leaned back in his chair. "Do you think you could help plan a party for three or four hundred people by the end of October?"

"I hope that at least three hundred and eighty-five are friends of yours because I don't know more than ten people that I would care to invite," she answered.

"I'll give you the guest list this week. Whoever you want to add, you can. If you don't want to invite anyone, that's all right, too."

Three days later, Cole handed Reggie a typewritten page with three hundred and forty-five names and addresses. To her surprise, he had even included his mother, who lived quietly in Maine in an updated Victorian home, which she'd bought with the profits she had made from investing in Polaroid, Xerox and Chrysler at the right time. She had made her fortune quietly and now lived a very pleasant life, playing bingo with her friends four nights a week. The other three nights she entertained a certain Dr. Robert Chapping, who, at seventy, thought Ardith Weston was the most captivating sixty-four-year-old woman he had ever met.

"Are you inviting your parents?" Cole asked as Reggie looked over the list.

She lifted her head. "Must I?" she asked.

Cole shrugged his shoulders. "Certainly not for my sake. I just thought you might want to."

Reggie laughed bitterly. "They wrote me off years ago. Maybe I'll just drop them a note to let them know I'm married." Suddenly, as her eyes scanned the list of names, Reggie found a name that sent the room spinning. She looked up at Cole with such a look of horror that he jumped out of his seat.

"Are you all right?" he asked.

"Cole, who are Mr. and Mrs. David Astin?" she whispered. It couldn't be, she thought wildly. It wasn't possible for David's name to appear in her life after all this time. "Who are they?"

Cole looked at Reggie's face with a mixture of concern and curiosity. "That's the Midwestern attorney I was speaking of. The one I want to invite for the weekend before I consummate this deal. Does the name mean anything to you?"

"No!" she replied with a great deal more force than necessary. "For a moment I thought it was . . ." She searched her mind for something to tell Cole. "I thought he was someone I had done business with a few years ago. But now, I think the name was Astrow, not Astin."

Reggie's heart was beating furiously. The last person she wanted to see again was David Astin. Just his name conjured up visions of herself in those hellish months when she had struggled to survive Nikki Broad, pregnancy, David's desertion and, finally, abortion. No one but Alison and Lee knew what those events had done to her. Did Lee remember the name of the man responsible? Had she ever told him? She couldn't remember. She had to find out. Cole was still searching her face. She had to reassure him.

"This guy, this David Astrow, was a sales rep who gave me a lot of trouble once. He phonied up some invoices, sent me a ridiculous commission bill . . . made a real mess of things. It took months for me to straighten it all out." Reggie looked up at Cole. "You know how bad I am at bookkeeping. . . . I had no records."

Cole nodded his head. He didn't believe one word his wife had just told him. Reggie might be many things, but she was scarcely a liar. It didn't sit well with her. There was more to the story, and if she chose not to discuss it with him, he would find out another way.

Regaining her composure, Reggie asked, "Where do you want to hold this extravaganza?"

He noted that the Astin-Astrow subject was closed. She wasn't going to elaborate. For the time being, he let it lie. "Originally," he said, "I thought we would have it here at home, but I don't think we can accommodate so many people. Have you any suggestions?"

Reggie thought for a moment. "I like the Regency. It's very elegant without being flashy. I think it fits your image."

He laughed, a strong, exuberant, masculine sound that delighted her. "I'm elegant but not flashy?" he asked. "For a second that almost sounded complimentary, but I know I must have been mistaken."

"Yes, you were," Reggie responded lightly. "I was merely talking about the image you like to project as a Renaissance man: knowledgeable, polished, so wealthy that you needn't show it off. The money lies quietly under the surface, but one knows without voicing it that it's there."

"How does one know it's there?" Cole queried.

"I don't know exactly. It's little things. The Saville Row suits, the cuff links when everyone else is wearing buttons, the tiniest monograms on your shirts that no one can see but you. That kind of stuff."

Cole's eyes twinkled. "Don't you think that as my wife you ought to project the same kind of image?" he asked.

"Is it very important to you?" Reggie asked. It was Saturday, and Reggie was sitting cross-legged on the floor of the study in white sweat pants and sweat shirt. Her hair was pulled off her face in a ponytail. Cole thought she looked eighteen. "I'm happy with my own image. I don't need to impress anyone."

"The man who washed the windows yesterday told me that my daughter had paid him," observed Cole.

"And that bothered you?" Reggie asked, surprised.

"I suppose if I mentioned it, it must have," Cole admitted. "And frankly, I can't imagine why it should. I've dated younger women."

"But you have never been married to one before. Maybe that's the difference."

"Perhaps," Cole said and then changed the subject back to plans for the reception. Still, he mused silently, there was something about being married to this woman that worried him every time he noticed the beginnings of gray at his temples. Would Reggie have been attracted to him without the allure of his money? The question nagged him for the rest of the day.

* * *

Cole watched Reggie blossom as she began to take on more responsibility for the running of their home. He was astounded at the difference their new agreement seemed to make. She attacked her marriage with the same enthusiasm that she would any new job. She took an active part in planning their meals, consulting with the household staff on their duties, and even went so far as to hire a new handyman, feeling that John's age prohibited him from doing the more arduous physical tasks around the house. The elderly retainer couldn't hide his gratitude, especially when she saved his pride by creating a new position for him; that of personal valet to Mr. Weston. He gladly relinquished the carrying, polishing, and odd jobs to settle gracefully into a state of semiretirement. Cole noted how artfully she had handled the whole affair.

Even their time alone was, if not wonderful, certainly not unpleasant. Reggie became a combination secretary, chatelaine, and sidekick to Cole when he was home. Since the inception of their new arrangement, Reggie had been giving Alison more and more responsibility at Raggs. She went to the office each day, sorted her mail, met with buyers, cutters and salesmen and found that she could be home by three or four o'clock. To her surprise, she discovered that she enjoyed the time she spent at home. Never having had the time or interest in homemaking before, she now indulged in a flurry of cooking, baking and gardening. The only black cloud on an otherwise perfect horizon was the daily reminder that sooner or later she would come face to face with David Astin and, still, she hadn't mentioned to Cole that she knew him. The longer she kept her silence, the more difficult it became to find a way to admit that she had lied.

In mid-September, Cole asked her how the plans for the reception were coming. She had pleaded with him to let her organize the event by herself and, touched, he'd agreed. "Things are moving swiftly on the Chicago deal," he said. "I have to be out there in November to finalize. Have you set a date yet?" he asked.

Reggie nodded. "Not only have I set a date, I have already finished the invitations and should be mailing them this week."

Cole looked surprised. "I didn't even realize you were that far along!"

"The party is set for the night of October thirty-first," she began, "and it has a theme."

"What has a theme? The party?" Cole asked.

"Yes. Since it's Halloween night—"

"Reggie—" Cole began to protest.

"You didn't even let me finish," Reggie argued.

"I don't have to. You want to make it a Halloween party and all of my friends and business associates are supposed to come to the Regency Hotel on Park Avenue dressed up like pumpkins. How the hell does that jibe with your projected image of elegance?"

Reggie glared at him. "You didn't even give me a chance to explain it to you."

"You don't have to. I hate the whole idea."

"For your information, I have been doing research on this idea for the past two weeks. I am not, repeat, not holding a children's Halloween party. Part of the round of balls and parties that were given for the debutantes during their first season of the nineteenth century was a masked ball. The most beautiful masks, known as dominos, were worn by everyone—both men and women. And, if you don't believe me, I'll show you the literature," she concluded angrily.

"Reggie, this is not the nineteenth century!"

She gave him her coolest smile. "So I tried to explain to you when you insisted I marry you. Now, when it is inconvenient for you, we are back in the twentieth century. No sir! This time we'll do it my way or not at all," she told him.

"Is that your final say in the matter?" he asked.

"As a matter of fact, it is!"

"Then do whatever the hell you want, only don't expect me to dress up and make a fool of myself. I will not do that, Reggie," Cole warned and stormed out of the room.

She sat on the floor after he left, her hands trembling. It had taken some doing, but she had won. She would have her masked ball. Hopefully, if her disguise was good enough, and if she were introduced simply as Cole's wife, David would never know who she was.

Chapter 33

Mr. and Mrs. David Astin received their invitation to the reception honoring Mr. and Mrs. Cole Weston the morning after Patrice tried to commit suicide. David had rushed her to a small private hospital, outside of the city, where the emergency room staff pumped her stomach, then kept her overnight to be certain that the effects of alcohol and Valium were out of her body. Patrice denied taking the pills and drinking the half quart of vodka that Lucilla had found on her bedside table. Enough money was passed around to assure that her real name never appeared on any hospital records.

For the first few hours after the hospital admittance, David had paced the corridors while his wife was being treated. His nerves were frayed. The fear that someone would discover who he was kept him on edge. A young doctor finally came out to speak to him.

"Mr. Green?"

"Yes, yes," David responded, quickly, "I'm Green. How's my wife?" He knew the agitation showed in his voice and he hoped it would be mistaken for concern over Patrice's condition.

The physician pulled him into the waiting room. "If you're asking whether or not she'll survive, the answer is yes. But, Mr. Green, your wife is in very serious trouble. The contents of her stomach revealed enough drugs to stock a pharmacy. I think that she should stay here or be admitted to one of the private clinics that deal with this kind of problem. Certainly, she needs psychiatric care—and soon. This can't wait, sir. We have no way of knowing when she'll try to do this again."

David shook his head sadly. "She's been under psychiatric care for a year," he lied. "We lost our only child and she's been unable to come to terms with it yet. Somehow, she feels responsible." Falsehoods had always rolled smoothly off

David's tongue. "I'm going to put in a call to her psychiatrist. Would you speak with him, please?"

"Of course."

"Doctor, I can't tell you how grateful I am for your help and understanding." David noted the name Pascal on the plastic ID the young physician wore. "I'll have him call you today, as soon as I can reach him. Will you be here all day?"

"I'll be here for most of the day. If you can't find me, my service will know where I can be reached. You are aware that I should report this."

"I know, I know," David said, clasping and unclasping his hands. "Could you put it off until you've spoken to her doctor? Perhaps there is some way to avoid that. You see, if this leaks out"—David ran his fingers through his hair—"I think it would kill her." His voice cracked with emotion. "I think the idea of a private sanatorium is the answer. Please, please take care of her—she's all I have left."

Carl Pascal was a young resident with much to learn. He was no match for David Astin. In another two years in medicine, given the same set of circumstances, he would have called the police immediately. But today, he bought David's whole story, sympathizing with the anxious husband. He would wait to speak to the psychiatrist.

David hurried from the hospital to the public library, where he found the name of a psychiatrist in an obscure Chicago suburb. Noting the doctor's name and address in the phone book, he jotted the information in his memo pad, then left the library and returned to his office. He placed a call to Dr. Pascal using the name Dr. Graham Wyent and a voice more gravelly than his own. He kept his conversation with Pascal short. Yes, he agreed with everything Dr. Pascal said. Yes, he would certainly see that Mrs. Green was admitted to a clinic immediately. He had been gently suggesting it to her for a few weeks, hoping that she would admit herself voluntarily. Now he agreed that the matter could no longer be left up to his patient. He would arrange to have Mr. Green pick his wife up that evening after he had made the necessary arrangements with a clinic. Thanking the young doctor for all his help and the judicious way he had handled the situation, David hung up the phone.

He picked Patrice up from the hospital on his way home from work. During the ride home, she wept silently, huddled in the corner of the car. David was burning. I'll make her pay for this, he thought with disgust. Whimpering, sniveling little . . . yes, you'll pay for this one, my dear Patrice. As they pulled into the garage, he was lost in thought, dreaming of the punishment he would inflict on his wife. He had to help her from the car; her legs would not support her.

All the recipients of the antique fans, hand-painted with the party information, had mixed reactions. Lee was simply pleased that Reggie and Cole were getting along better. Lately he had noted a change in Cole, but when he tried to question him, his old friend was secretive, telling him only that the arrangement was working better. Cole neglected to tell Lee the new terms he and Reggie had worked out. It was enough for Lee to know they were surviving together.

Simon opened his invitation on the morning he planned to decide on the new head of the European division of Galaxy Stores. He felt a wrenching pain as he looked at the beautiful fans. Over the last six weeks he had kept his conversations with Reggie clipped and businesslike, dealing only with the Raggs boutiques. Neither one of them had mentioned the interlude in Dallas. To Simon, the chapter had closed once he knew about Reggie's marriage to Cole. As he stared at the names on the creative invitation, marveling at her ingenuity, Simon knew he would attend their party, torn between the unspoken need to see her again and the certain knowledge that it would do neither one of them any good.

Ardith Weston had to call Dr. Chapping for something for her nerves. Cole, married? Inconceivable! Who had finally caught her elusive son? Was this a prank for Halloween? How silly. No, it looked real enough, all right. She would have to call Cole immediately.

But as she reached for the receiver, she stopped. She would wait until the party to meet her long awaited daughter-in-law. She whispered a silent prayer that her daughter-in-law wouldn't be one of the many women whose names had been paired with Cole's through the years. Ardith sat outside on the wide wraparound porch, holding the fan in her hand.

Long ago, she had given up the hope of seeing Cole married. And grandchildren? A long forgotten dream. Now, she thought about the possibility. Young dark-haired children playing in her garden, sailing on the small pond behind the Victorian house.

It was too bad that Cole's father hadn't lived to see this day. He had sworn it would come sooner or later. *When the time is right, when Cole meets the woman whose very presence, whose nearness causes him to feel complete, he will marry as if nothing else matters.* Ardith remembered the conversation as if it had taken place that morning. Her husband had gazed lovingly into her eyes. . . .

But Cole always gets what he wants without marriage, she had argued later. Her husband had thrown back his head and laughed at her naiveté. You're talking about sex, he had explained patiently, while I am speaking of love. Once you've found the latter you want to capture it, hold it close to you, make it yours forever.

Was there a woman, Ardith wondered, who could have made her son as romantic as his father had been?

Others opened the invitations with mixed reactions.

Evyan Bolivar sniffed in disgust. Cole? Married? For heaven's sake, why? She hadn't seen him for two months but she had attributed that to her fling with a French count. So foolish, she thought, for Cole to run off and marry just to spite her. Who would have imagined that he cared that much? Certainly, they had never pledged any kind of faithfulness to each other. She knew that he fooled around when she was away. It was a mutual agreement, unspoken, surely, but a fact nonetheless. Now this! She would have to speak to him before this party. She was annoyed. It would make things so untidy. She laid open the fan and watched the air current blow the papers off her breakfast table.

When Norma and Ned Gates opened the pale pink box that held the decorative fan, they read it, looked at each other and resolutely dropped the offensive article into the harvest-gold trash compactor.

Reggie had included Gary Colby on her guest list. When Cole questioned the name, she simply answered, "He's the man who made me what I am today," and refused to elaborate. She did, however, call Gary in Dallas and asked for his help in planning the party. Gary was flattered. They agreed to meet in New York the following weekend when Gary would be able to see the room where the party was to be held. Reggie payed all his travel expenses. She thought briefly about flying to Dallas to discuss the party plans then discarded the idea. It would be foolish, even dangerous, for her to be so close to Simon. She had shelved that affair for now. . . .

She and Gary discussed a few ideas, tossing around some thoughts on menu and decorations. After ten minutes of disagreement, they decided to discuss it in person.

When the subject of costumes came up, Gary was adamant. "Don't do anything about them until I see you. I already know exactly how you should look. Just make sure that your factory will be available to make your gown."

"What about Cole's costume?" Reggie asked, remembering her husband's warning about being made to look foolish. She explained her predicament to Gary.

"Don't worry. Just bring me a good picture of him, then I'll know what kind of costume will be appropriate."

"You're a darling, Gary," Reggie said.

"So I've been told. If there are—"

"Hold on a minute, I have to answer the other phone."

She came back moments later. "Gary, I'll speak to you this weekend. That's my brother on the other line."

"Okay, I'll call you with the hotel information during the week."

"Don't bother, I've already made reservations for you at the Park Lane. Bye."

Matthew extended his congratulations to Reggie but told her that he wouldn't be able to attend the reception. She hadn't heard from him in so long that it made very little difference. When he promised to call her the next time he was in New York, she expected that it would be another six or seven years till she spoke to him.

* * *

Lee called the next morning. "You must be kidding!" he said.

"About what?" she asked innocently.

"You think I will come in costume?"

She laughed. "I don't think you will come in costume, you *have* to or you can't come at all."

"And Cole is getting dressed up, too?"

"Yes," she answered with a small grin that Lee could almost see. "Don't you love it?"

"Reg, I've seen you do some miraculous things over the years, but I don't believe you can get Cole Weston to wear a Regency costume. Did he know his wedding reception was going to be a costume party?"

"You're rather gauche, my bright friend. If you had read the invitation, you would have seen that this isn't a costume party. This, my dear, is a *bal de masque*."

"You can call it whatever you want, in whatever language sounds most *élégante*, but it is still a costume party and I'll bet no one is going to show up in costume!" Lee finished.

"On the contrary," Reggie assured him, "everyone will because I just slipped a little note to the press announcing this highly original wedding reception for Mr. and Mrs. Cole Weston. You can bet it will appear in the columns tomorrow, and there won't be a person in New York who won't be waiting to see what everyone else will be wearing."

"You didn't!"

"I most certainly did!" Reggie countered.

"He'll kill you."

"I doubt it," she said with more certainty than she actually felt. "He was the one who wanted to announce to the world that he was married. I simply helped spread the word."

Lee couldn't help but laugh. "By the way, how are things working out with the two of you?"

"Beautifully. We were made for each other," Reggie answered sardonically.

"Seriously, Reg," Lee asked.

"Seriously?" she repeated. "How can you possibly be serious about something like this? The whole thing, the agreement, the contract, everything is absurd. It went out of fashion centuries ago."

"But you *are* handling it much better than you were in the beginning, aren't you?" Lee asked hopefully.

"What do you think?"

Lee laughed. "I think I'd better hang up now."

"Good idea, Lee. Love you." She hung up the phone. She never asked him if the name David Astin meant anything to him.

As September slipped into October, Reggie worked feverishly on the wedding reception. She began to think it was more work than anything she had ever attempted in the garment industry. A great deal of work would be done by Gary Colby, who, after seeing the ballroom at the Regency, declared it too mundane for words. He then decided to decorate the room in the style of the famed seaside resort of Brighton, England, which had been made famous by the extravagant prince regent in the early eighteen hundreds. He chose as his model the outrageous Brighton Pavilion, a building so ornate, so expensive that its very creation almost bankrupted England. Although Cole had given Reggie carte blanche for this party, the bills began to worry her as she threw herself into the project. Gary flew back and forth from Dallas to New York in the early part of October, the way men commute from Long Island to Manhattan. He found theatrical set designers who recreated the feeling of the grand ballroom at the Pavilion. Four hundred gold-leafed chairs were rented from an English firm and flown to New York along with a complete dinner service of hand-painted twenty-four carat gold leaf. The dishes had to be insured for the evening by Lloyds of London, who insisted that special security officers be hired to watch over their investment.

The entire ballroom was tented with yards of white moiré shot through with silver threads. The maître d' of the dining room stood with his mouth agape as truck after truck backed up to the building to unload their precious cargo. It was by far the most opulent party that had ever been planned in the long, illustrious history of the hotel. Reggie stood back to admire their joint efforts with Gary standing next to her. Although the room didn't exactly duplicate the picture she held in her hand, its beauty was just as staggering. Cole had insisted that the room be rented for the entire month of October so no one would see what they had created until Halloween night.

Things were moving along so smoothly, and time was passing with such speed, that Reggie thought she might actually survive her year of indenture to Cole. Besides, for one of the first times in her life, she was having fun as she and Gary set out to design the men's costumes. He explained to her that there were two different routes they could take; the first idea that he had was to dress Cole in the formal attire of the early nineteenth century. The outfit would consist of a formal shirt, an elaborate tie, a brightly colored brocade waistcoat with jeweled buttons, satin knee breeches, stockings and pumps. Gary explained that the dandies of that period adored jewels, bright colors and outlandish fabrics.

"I can't." Reggie giggled when she saw the feminine-looking costumes, complete with lace handkerchiefs tucked into the cuffs of the jackets. "You have to know Cole," she tried to explain, "to understand that he would never, never set one foot out of the house in something like this. We'll have to do better . . . even if it's not absolutely, authentically from that period. I wouldn't even have the nerve to show him this picture."

Gary stared hard at the photograph of Cole that Reggie had brought him. He studied the tall, well-built man dressed in a fisherman's sweater and a pair of jeans, his dark hair dipping carelessly over one eye. The muscles in the man's thighs bulged through the well-worn denim of the jeans. "You're right," Gary said with a resigned sigh, "he would never have been a dandy. Too bad. We could have had a lot of fun with the idea."

"Couldn't he just wear a tuxedo?" Reggie asked wishfully. She knew that getting Cole into any kind of costume was going to be difficult. If she made it embarrassing for him, he wouldn't get dressed up at all.

"There is the other alternative. It isn't formal, but I think it fits your husband much better. The period placed tremendous importance on horsemanship."

"Horsemanship?"

"Drivers of the lightweight carriages of the era were as

famous as football players are today. You have no idea how much money was wagered on their performances."

"What does that have to do with Cole?" Reggie asked.

"There was a very exclusive club . . . The Four-in-Hand, I think it was called, very difficult to become a member of. There was a costume of sorts, almost a uniform. It was every bit as important that the members dressed correctly as it was that they drove well."

"What was the costume like?" Reggie asked.

"White starched batiste shirts, less ruffled than the ones we talked about before, tight buckskin breeches, highly polished Hessian boots, riding gloves, subdued, well-fitting jackets—a very masculine look. I think"—Gary glanced at Cole's photo —"that it would be perfect for your husband."

"Can we make it without having him see it?"

"If you have his measurements—"

"I can bring you one of his suits," interrupted Reggie.

"That's fine. We'll baste the costume together first, but eventually you will have to fit it on Cole. If it's not a perfect fit, the whole thing will look dreadful."

"No problem. I'll get him to try it on at home and I'll pin it. We can do the tailoring here at the factory."

They agreed and spent the rest of the day working on Cole's costume. At four thirty, Reggie realized that they still had hours of work to do and, since Gary was leaving early the next morning, she called Cole to tell him that she would be working late and would not be home for dinner. She suggested that he might want to take the opportunity to work out at his club, perhaps even take a massage. He agreed, telling her that he would see her at home later.

As Cole placed the receiver on the hook, he felt a peculiar sense of disappointment. He looked forward to dining with Reggie, enjoying her vibrant laughter as she recounted some of the more amusing anecdotes of her day. They had begun to settle into a comfortable pattern as the October nights grew chilly, moving into the study for after-dinner drinks, lighting a fire in the huge stone hearth and sipping cognac while they read quietly and the hours slipped by.

Yet, as comfortable as they had become with each other, he still couldn't break through the fence that separated her from him, the shell that she crawled back into whenever he got too close. What had hurt her so badly in the past to force her to protect herself so fiercely? Long before they were married, in those few evenings he could not put from his mind, he had seen her let her guard down, had felt the depth of her passion, had known he had touched her heart.

But that was before. The most she would give him now was to inadvertently rest her head against his knee as she sat gazing into the fire while he read. Once, a week before, he had gently rubbed the back of her neck as she assumed her favorite position on the floor by his chair. She had lifted her head to stare into his eyes, then, sensing what might happen, had torn her gaze from his, unfolded her long legs, stood and stretched before she told him she was retiring. He had pulled her to him, taking her face between his strong hands, and had gently deposited a kiss on her nose. It had taken all of his willpower not to pull her into his arms, to once again feel the arch of her body against his, and she had clearly seen the longing in his eyes. With aching tenderness he laid his palm against her cheek but she had pulled away, a look of distress on her face.

"Don't, Cole," she had whispered. "Don't confuse me."

He knew she was right. She had begun to trust him again, begun to allow him to get a step or two closer to her. If he rushed her, she would bolt. For now he would have to accept what they had and settle for being with her on her terms. He accepted her conditions. He had little choice for the time being.

Chapter 34

Reggie and Gary worked well past nine o'clock that night, stopping only to wolf down the pastrami sandwiches Gary bought at the deli across the street. Cole's costume gave them more trouble than they had anticipated. Working with leather and suede, Reggie had to adjust her new machines to take the thicker material and dozens of broken needles lay scattered on the floor, having refused to punch their way through the chamois cloth.

Finally, at nine thirty, they were satisfied with the jacket and breeches. Reggie was exhausted, but because he was leaving in the morning, Gary prevailed upon her to work a little longer. He wanted to leave New York with her correct measurements and an okay for the dress he was certain would make her the star of the evening. Reluctantly, she agreed and headed toward the tiny dressing room tucked in the corner of the room. Moments later she re-entered wearing bra and panties and an old wrapper that her showroom model used between changes.

Cole stayed at the health club for a few hours, worked out and had a massage. At nine fifteen he left the club and began to walk home, then changed his mind. He hailed a passing cab and gave the cabbie the address of Reggie's factory. He sat back smiling, anticipating her face when he surprised her. He knew she appreciated things like that and, more and more, he found pleasure in pleasing his wife.

The taxi let him off in front of Reggie's factory. The building was dark except for the light coming from her loft. This was, he decided as he entered the dark, desolate building, the last time he would allow her to work alone at night. It was then that he heard the screams. He had no time for thought as he raced for the narrow, dark staircase, taking the steps two and three at a time. The blood was pounding in his ears as he reached her floor. The screams increased in intensity and then suddenly there was deadly silence. In the few seconds that it took Cole to bolt from the staircase to the door of the loft, a sense of terror, unlike anything he had ever felt, clutched him. He wrenched open the door, shouting her name. As his terrified eyes scanned the room quickly, looking for signs of struggle, a sound halfway between a whimper and a strangled hiccup came from the corner. There was his wife, dressed only in her underwear, locked in the arms of a stranger, a look of panic on her face. It occurred to Cole, in the minute it took him to assess the scene before him, by the way Reggie's arms were locked around the man's neck, that this was no attack by a stranger. Plain and simple . . . he was witnessing a lovers' tryst, had heard lovers' ecstasy. He almost doubled over with the pain he felt.

Wide-eyed, Reggie mouthed Cole's name and ran toward him. He brushed her aside as if she were insignificant and strode in cold fury toward the man who had just released his wife.

There was a black rage inside Cole as he approached Reggie's lover. It wrenched and twisted his gut with such ferocity that it threatened to strangle him. His icy voice was like a razor, cutting wrathfully through the silence of the room. "Is she any good?" he asked scornfully. "Is my wife a good lay?"

Gary's face turned bright red and twisted in disgust. "What? I didn't touch—"

"How dare you!" screamed Reggie at the same time.

"Shut up!" demanded Cole, unclenching his fists and pulling Reggie behind him as she made a move to go to Gary's side. He took a menacing step toward Gary. "I don't need your explanations. There's nothing wrong with my eyes. I'm giving you until the count of three to get the hell out of here, and if you haven't gone, I'm going to jam my fist down your fucking throat!"

"Don't be an ass!" she snapped angrily. "He's—"

"I told you to stay out of this!" he warned in a murderously low voice. "One . . . two . . ." His features were contorted in a mask of savage contempt.

Gary shook his head, not quite believing this Gothic scene. To stand there and try to explain that it was the sight of a huge rat running across the room that had sent Reggie screaming into his arms, seemed, at the moment—imprudent. On the other hand, to leave Reggie alone with this madman was unthinkable. "Reg, I—"

She held up her hand to stop him. "Just go, Gary. I'll explain," said Reggie, her voice flat.

Cole advanced, but Gary had already made his decision. "Don't waste your time on three, Mr. Weston," said Gary as he picked up his portfolio and walked to the door. "I'll speak to you tomorrow, Reg, when you've straightened this out with your husband."

He waited until he heard Gary's footsteps on the stairs. "We're going home now," Cole stated, his mouth a thin, bitter line.

Enraged, Reggie answered, "You can go to hell if you like. I have no intention of going anywhere with you—now or ever again!"

Cole lifted his eyebrows. "Oh, really? Let me give you a bit of friendly advice, my love: either you leave with me now, or I will pick you up and carry you home. Whatever has to be discussed, will be, once we get home. Understand?"

Reggie looked at him incredulously. "You're the one who doesn't seem to understand. I'm staying here. Your display tonight was embarrassing and totally inappropriate. I've had enough, Cole."

"Enough of what? Your boyfriend? Me? Other men?" He spat out the words as Reggie stood facing him, her green eyes flashing. "How many others are there?"

"Are you crazy?"

"I asked you a question. How many other men are there?"

She looked up at the ceiling in deep concentration. She began to say something then shook her head. Cole waited as she tapped her bare foot on the floor.

"Fourteen," she answered finally, the merest hint of a smile on her face. "Actually," she continued in a light tone of voice, "there were eighteen when I married you but having to spend so much of my time with you hindered by sex life so I had—"

"Don't you *dare* joke with me now!" Cole could never remember being as angry at a woman as he was at that moment.

Reggie opened her eyes in innocence. "Oh my! I am *so* sorry—"

He grasped her then by her shoulders, his fingers digging into her bare flesh, and for a second he wanted to hurt her the way she was hurting him. "You're not even particular, are you?"

Reggie shrugged her shoulders as much as was possible within the confines of Cole's hold on her. "Not especially. Why? Are you?" She was goading him, taking delight now in fueling his rage. At any other time, under any other set of circumstances, Cole would have seen what she was doing but the white blaze of jealousy and pain blinded him to anything other than the picture of his nearly naked wife in another man's arms. It drove all reason from his mind.

Suddenly, he pulled her close to him. Their faces were mere millimeters apart. Reggie could feel his breath on her cheek. "Yes," he answered, unsmiling. "I happen to be very particular."

Without warning, his mouth came down on hers in a crushing, punishing kiss that didn't offer; it took. His tongue forced its way past her lips, deep into the soft recesses of her mouth. At first she struggled against him, twisting and turning to get out of his arms. But the more she writhed, the more persistent he became. His fingers entangled themselves in her hair, pulling her head back until she thought her neck would snap. Suddenly, she went limp in his arms and he had to hold her to keep her from falling. Cole looked at her in surprise.

Reggie's eyes were wide open. "I'm not going to fight you, Cole. If this is what you want, take it, then leave."

"Do you want me to make love to you?" he asked.

"No."

"But you won't fight me if I do?"

"That's right. You're stronger than I am. I can't stop you if that's what you intend to do. But I won't help you either by struggling or encouraging you."

Cole nodded his head in acceptance, then swept Reggie into his arms and carried her to a sofa that flanked one of the walls. Gently, he set her down, his eyes never leaving her face. "I would have preferred you to participate," he said mildly, "but if you don't care to, that's your prerogative." He stood back, admiring her slender body. "Take off your bra and panties," he requested with the same lack of emotion in his voice as if he were asking a stranger to pass the salt at dinner.

Incredulous, Reggie started to get up. "I will not!"

A lazy grin began to tug at the corners of Cole's mouth. "I thought you were going to be cooperative."

"I didn't say that! I just said I wouldn't fight you. You want my clothes off, do it yourself!"

He shrugged his massive shoulders. "If you insist." He leaned over and, with one deft motion, reached behind her, unsnapped her bra and flung it to the floor. "The rest?" he asked.

Reggie didn't answer.

"Have it your own way," Cole said and slid the tiny bit of nylon and lace down her legs. She lay there naked, goose bumps covering her flesh. "Cold or nervous?" Cole inquired.

"Bored," Reggie said.

Cole arched his eyebrows. "Pity, but it will be over soon and you can return to whatever it was you were doing before I walked in."

"Are you really going to go through with this?"

"As a matter of fact, I am. I haven't had an offer this enticing in a long time." Cole's eyes glimmered. "Did you, for one moment, doubt that I would accept your challenge? Reggie, I thought we knew each other better than that."

She turned her eyes up, concentrating on the cracks in the ceiling, willing herself not to respond to Cole's innuendoes. Casually, Cole sat down on the edge of the sofa near her feet. He picked up one of her feet by the ankle and gazed at it as if seeing it for the first time. He brought her foot up toward his mouth, caressing it gently. Slowly, he began to trace his finger up her calf, toward the satiny smoothness of her inner thigh. Inadvertently, Reggie shivered, remembering in that moment what Cole's touch could do to her. The memory sent her head spinning.

Treacherously, her hands reached out, grasped his neck and pulled his head toward hers. Their mouths met tentatively at first, then, as the warmth flowed within them and she could feel his heart keeping pace with hers, all boundaries disappeared and his mouth, his touch was the only reality. What was happening to her? Where had her resolve gone? Suddenly, Reggie realized that it didn't matter anymore. What mattered was Cole's arms around her, the irresistible tide that was pulling them together again after so long.

He lifted his head with a tremendous effort and searched her eyes for answers to questions he had yet to pose. She tried to speak, but her voice no longer belonged to her; it refused to respond to her command. With a superhuman effort Reggie tried once more to speak, but her mouth felt swollen, her lips paralyzed. Cole didn't need to hear her voice, everything she was trying to say was in her eyes, in the fact that she couldn't look away anymore. He wanted to devour her, to absorb her into himself and, as he saw one tear roll down her cheek, the expression on her face took his breath away and he had his answer. He could no sooner do this abominable thing to her than he could plunge a knife into his own heart. Gently he sat up and looked around the room for something to cover her nakedness.

Reggie held out her arms. "Please," she whispered. He didn't move. She closed her eyes and waited, praying silently that more words would not be necessary, that he would read her thoughts. The next thing she knew she was in his arms, and his mouth and body molded itself to her, reshaping her. When he entered her endless moments later, she actually felt that he was touching her heart. She had come home again. As he moved inside her, as her body rose to meet his every thrust, Reggie gloried in the knowledge that she loved this man, had loved him from the first moment she had seen him. Her plan to hold back had backfired, ensnaring her as she had hoped to ensnare him, and it didn't matter anymore. Nothing mattered except the man beside her—her love, her life. Cole Weston had reached deep into her soul, locked the door behind him and pocketed the key forever.

When it was over, when they both lay sated in each other's arms and their breathing had finally returned to normal, Reggie's eyes searched his face. "Is this another ploy, another trick, Cole?"

As gently as possible, he brushed her damp hair from her face. With a smile that lit the room, he spoke quietly. "If it is, my love, then this time the joke's on me." He sat up, drawing her into his arms, holding her, reassuring her and wanting to give her everything that her question had asked. He clung to her, his face buried in her glorious hair. "I wanted to hurt you," he admitted. "I wanted to strike out at you."

"Shh, darling. I know. I know."

"I can't hurt you because it hurts me, too. When I push you away from me a piece of me dies." He looked into her eyes in surprise. "I've never felt that way about anyone before."

"Nor have I," she whispered. "I've never allowed myself to feel before."

"And now? Will you?"

"Oh, Cole"—her voice was ragged—"I'm so frightened.

Terrified of letting anyone so close. Don't you see how vulnerable you are when you love someone? Why does it hurt so?" She looked at him for an answer.

He kissed her eyelids, her cheeks, the tip of her nose . . . tiny little kisses. "Tell me what you're afraid of. Tell me exactly what it is that frightens you so much."

"I . . . the . . . what if . . ." The words stumbled off her tongue.

"You don't have to say any more. 'What if' says it all." He held her tightly in his arms. "I don't know the answer to 'what if,'" he admitted. "I doubt there is an answer. I do know that this is too precious, too rare a feeling to let go. I want to keep it, to hold on to it. I'm terrified, too," he told her, "if that's any consolation. I've never even known I was capable of feeling this. Now that I know, I never want to be without it . . . without you."

Tiny tears had gathered in the corners of her eyes. He wiped them away with his fingertip. "It's very special, isn't it?" she asked in a small voice, not yet fully trusting him.

"Yes, my love. It's very special. Very, very special. Let's keep it, shall we?" A smile broke out on his face as he saw her eyes answer.

"Cole?" she asked.

"Hmm?"

"Could we please go home now? Really and truly home?"

He nodded.

Chapter 35

But still, Reggie remained adamant about maintaining her separate quarters in the house. She couldn't explain why she needed to keep her own room, but somehow Cole understood. Keeping her suite of rooms was her security blanket . . . an unspoken way of saying "if this doesn't work out, I can always go back." He truly believed that she loved him. But complete trust? That was something entirely different, something that he had to earn with time. When she finally convinced herself of their love for each other, he was certain she would change her living arrangements.

"You're not fooling anyone in this house, you know," he told her as she slid from his bed one morning.

She hadn't even known he was awake. "What do you mean?"

He laughed. "Everyone in the house knows that you're not sleeping in your own bed anymore, Goldilocks."

"No, they don't!" she insisted. "I rumple up my sheets and comforter every morning so Elsa will think I slept there."

"Of course. How clever of you." He nodded sagely, thinking how the scent of her permeated his room and his bed for hours after she had slipped away. "You may think that you're fooling Elsa, but John has known we've been sleeping together since the very first night."

"How could he? Did you tell him?"

"Me? I didn't have to tell him. He has a second sense where I'm concerned. When you've looked after someone for as long as he's looked after me, you become attuned to them. He notices that my habits have changed."

Reggie looked genuinely confused. "How?" she asked.

"How is it that I used to sleep like a corpse, never disturbing the other side of the bed, but now the bed suddenly looks like fourteen people have played hide-'n'-seek under the covers. And my shirts keep disappearing because you wear one of them back to your room each night."

"But I always drop them in the laundry chute before I go to work."

He smiled. "But I never did. And it confuses him that I've begun to smell like Bal à Versailles instead of Paco Rabanne."

Reggie chuckled. "So he knows. Big deal!"

"He wonders what we're trying to hide and, much as I hate to admit it, so do I." He pulled her close to him, nuzzling the soft hollow of her shoulder.

Gently, she disengaged. "I'm not hiding from anyone. At least I don't think I am. I just like my own . . . no, that's not true. I suppose that as much as I love you, there's still a tiny part of me that doesn't believe this will last."

“Don’t you think I know that?” he asked softly. “Do you still believe I could hurt you?”

Reggie hesitated before answering. “Yes, my darling,” she began. “You could destroy me if you chose to.”

Cole sat up. “How could I?”

“Shh. Let me finish, please. I’ve fallen in love with you—completely, irrevocably. And, you know it. I am totally vulnerable, something that I swore would never happen to me again.” Reggie stared into his smoky eyes. “Can you promise me that you will always be here to love me?” she challenged.

“With the same certainty that you can swear that, when you leave for work, a bus won’t hit you and take you away from me forever. No, my dearest, no one can give either one of those kinds of guarantees. We have to learn to live without them.”

“I do understand,” Reggie responded, “but I still don’t believe it’s true.”

If Cole knew of some magical answer that would have convinced her to trust his love, he would have told her. But he knew only that time and caring would prove that he would always be there for her. “Reggie, listen to me for one more moment. What we have is precious and very, very rare. People spend a lifetime searching for it. To keep it alive takes nurturing and hard work and trust. With time, I won’t have to reassure you or convince you. You’ll know it. A long, long time ago, I told you that I was a patient man, and I am. You take all the time you need to believe in us. But, darling, for now just let yourself enjoy letting me love you.” He pulled her into his arms once more. “Can you do that?”

She nodded. “Yes.”

“That’s all the reassurance I need. Now go be a good girl and pack a suitcase.”

She laughed. “It’s over, already?”

“No, it’s just beginning. We’re going to the cabin. I want to show it to you in the fall before the snows come. I also want to make love to you on the floor, in front of the fireplace, in the woods, on a blanket of leaves and in my canoe.”

“Canoe? Oh, dear Lord.” Reggie giggled. “We hardly manage to stay in a king-size bed and you want to make love in a canoe.”

“Mm-hmm,” answered Cole, diving into her hair.

* * *

They drove straight through the Adirondacks without stopping until they reached the Eighth Lake region. Cole pulled the car off the road to savor the beauty of the sun's reflection on his favorite glacial reservoir. He helped Reggie out of the Ferrari. Both of them rolled up their jeans and kicked off their sneakers as they walked hand in hand toward the beach. A vacationing family, their Winnebago parked near the highway, watched as they approached. Two children, a boy and a girl, were wrestling with the sails of *The Lightning*, an old wood-hulled sailboat whose sails were hopelessly flapping high atop the mast.

"Need some help?" Cole asked the father as he and Reggie walked toward the shore.

"Damn sails got caught up there on the mast. I can't get them to go up or down," answered the full-bearded man. "I told them"—he pointed to the teen-aged boy and his younger sister—"they could take it out alone today, but on the way in they tried to take down the sails. Made a real mess out of it." He looked at Cole skeptically. "You know anything about boats?"

"A little," admitted Cole. He walked over to the little boat to inspect the damage. The children stepped back as he neared, awed by Cole's size.

Cole fussed with the sheet and the halyard for a few minutes while Reggie watched, fascinated. Like a magician with a rope trick, Cole worked the ropes, yanked twice and suddenly the lines fell free.

"Well, I'll be damned! How'd you do that so fast?" asked the man.

"Nothing to it," laughed Cole, then, seeing the children's faces as they stared disappointedly at their father, corrected himself. "Actually, I owned, or rather my family owned a boat like *The Lightning* when I was a kid. Used to sail it every day during the summers. You think your kids make a mess out of the sails?" Cole asked, looking toward the children. "You would congratulate them on a job well done if you had seen what I used to do with sails."

"Do you still sail?" asked the father.

"Occasionally, not nearly as much as I'd like to."

"Hey, my name's Joe, Joe Wychek. This is Michael and Rya. We really appreciate your helping us out."

Cole stuck out his hand. "Cole Weston, my wife, Reggie," he answered, taking the man's hand. "You certainly had a magnificent day for a sail."

"Still plenty of it left. Why don't you and your wife take her out?"

Cole looked longingly at the lake shimmering like glass in front of him. There was the merest whisper of a breeze, more than enough to send a small boat like *The Lightning* skipping through the water.

"You wouldn't mind?" Cole asked.

"Not at all. In fact, I'd be grateful. Then it would be your responsibility to bring her in and get her set for the night, right?"

Cole nodded. "I suppose you're right."

"Besides, my wife's in the camper waiting for us to eat, and she hates it when we're late," Joe said.

"Reg, would you mind?" Cole asked.

She saw the light in his eyes, the need to recapture some part of his youth, and she couldn't refuse. "I'd love it, but I hope you're not depending on me to help. I've never set foot in a sailboat before."

"Okay," Cole said, already heading for the boat. "Thanks a million, Mr. Wychek."

"Joe."

"Thanks, Joe. Here, Reg, put this on." Cole flung an orange life jacket from the well of the boat. "We'll take good care of her."

"Have fun!" Joe said, then spent a moment telling Cole how to attach the boat to the small trailer. They agreed that Joe would come back later to pick up the boat. Cole and Reggie pushed the blue and white boat into the water.

Once they were afloat, Cole raised the sails. As he worked, he explained each step to her, as if he expected her to be able to do it the next time. She tuned out his words, preferring to concentrate on Cole's muscles and the way the slanting rays of sun played on the planes of his face as he worked. He started to perspire from the heat and the exertion. Soon, he removed his cotton sweater, tying it to the mast with its sleeves. The black hair on his body curled on his massive chest, trailing down to the top of his jeans. Wickedly, Reggie's eyes followed the line far below the waistband. Cole caught her gaze and held it with a steady, knowing look.

"Here?" she asked innocently, the bulge in his pants quite noticeable. Her eyes scanned the tiny confines of the boat.

Cole shrugged. "Why not?" He tied the sheet to a metal cleat, set the tiller in its holder and climbed out to Reggie, who was resting against one of the seats. Lowering himself next to her, he quickly slipped out of his clothes, watching intently as she followed suit. The quarters were tight but magically, in the cool beauty of the late afternoon, as *The Lightning* sailed itself toward the other end of the lake, they made love. Their bodies blended, flowing to the sounds of the wind in the sails, the water skimming past the hull of the boat.

When they lay sated, full of each other, he stroked his wife's magnificent hair until she purred contentedly. They lay quietly wrapped in each other's arms.

Unexpectedly, Reggie began to recite a poem from her childhood: " 'The owl and the pussycat went to sea in a beautiful pea-green boat.' "

Cole continued. " 'They took some money and lots of honey wrapped up in a five pound note . . .' "

Reggie stared, surprised. "Do you know the rest of it?"

Cole thought hard. "I used to," he said. "Something about sailing away to the land where the jujubes grow."

"Do you know where that is?" she asked, laughing softly.

"Wherever we are," he answered.

The sun was just beginning to set when they brought the tiny boat in. Flames of crimson streaked the sky as, side by side, Cole and Reggie worked at furling the sails by the water's edge. Cole walked up the beach, pulled the trailer to the shore and attached the boat. Arm in arm, shivering in the chill autumn dusk, they walked back toward the car.

It had been a perfect afternoon, Cole thought, as he pulled Reggie deep into the warmth of his arms. Still, he marveled at the complete turn of events that had brought this unexpected joy to his life. Had anyone ever told him that he would revel in the absolute pleasure of caring for another human being, he would have doubted their sanity. Yet, at that moment, the most important task of his was to envelop Reggie in the security of his love. Lee had once told him what a relationship with her could mean, but Cole hadn't the slightest idea how loving Reggie and being loved by her could change his life.

He leaned down and pressed his lips to hers.

"I love you," he murmured.

"I know." She turned her face to look at him. "Is it as incredible to you as it is to me?"

"More so," he smiled. "I've had many more years of waiting for you." He pulled her close and held her tightly, until he could feel the beating of her heart against his chest. They remained locked in an embrace until Cole broke the spell. "We'd better return the boat, my love."

"Mm-hmm," Reggie agreed, shivering in the rapidly approaching mountain evening.

"Cold?" he asked.

"Frr-eezing," she replied through chattering teeth.

Cole wrapped her in his cotton sweater and grabbed her hand. "Hurry up. I think there are some heavy sweat shirts in the trunk."

"Hey! Hey, down there!"

Cole and Reggie jumped. They watched as two men in dark hooded sweat shirts lumbered down the sandy hill toward them. Cole couldn't tell in the shadowy dusk whether they were kids looking for trouble or grown men. He pushed Reggie behind him as the figures drew near.

Joe Wychek saw Cole move to protect his wife from unrecognizable figures and called out, "Hey, Mr. and Mrs. Weston—it's just me, Joe. We were starting to worry about you so we came to check." He walked over to Cole until his face was visible in the rapidly diminishing light. Reggie stepped out from behind Cole.

"Mr. Wychek, we're terribly sorry if we worried you. It's been the most beautiful afternoon. Thank you so much," Reggie said.

Joe's face lit up. It wasn't every day that he was able to share something of his. "You liked her? The boat, I mean?" Joe blushed as he saw the look of embarrassment on Reggie's face.

"So much that I may try to buy her from you. Would you consider selling her?" Cole asked.

"Ah, she's not worth very much. She's probably older than any of us. You could buy a new sailboat, fiberglass, slim, fast and easier to handle."

Cole shook his head. "She's something special to us. We're very sentimental, and since this is our honeymoon—"

"Your honeymoon? You didn't tell me that this afternoon. That changes everything. You come back to the camper with me and Michael, and we'll talk to Rya and Roberta. I already told her about you."

Cole hesitated, but Reggie nudged him in the ribs. "We would love to. Wouldn't we, Cole?"

Fifteen minutes later, the boat was attached to the Wycheks' car, and the Westons were following their new friends to the camper.

"Michael Wychek's a nice kid," Cole mused. "All arms and legs right now but in a few years he'll fill out. He reminds me of myself at that age."

Reggie detected an odd note in Cole's voice. "Are you jealous of Joe Wychek? Of the fact that he has a son?" The car was silent. "Cole?" Reggie said.

"I never thought about it before," Cole admitted. "Never even considered the possibility of having children some day."

"Do you want them?" she persisted, not certain how she wanted him to respond.

It was so long before he did speak that Reggie wasn't sure he heard her question. "I don't think so, Reg," he said thoughtfully. "I love children but only when they belong to someone else. I'm not sure that I have the time or energy anymore to devote to raising children." He tried to search her face but the car was too dark to catch her expression. "How do you feel about it?"

She was sorry she had brought up the subject at all. Having children was almost an impossibility for her. She had been told after the abortion and the subsequent pelvic infection that the chances of her ever conceiving were so minuscule that she had given up using any sort of contraception since then. Now that she knew that children were not a priority with Cole, did it make any sense to bring up the past and tell him the whole sordid story about the abortion?

"Reggie?" Cole interrupted her thoughts.

"I'm sorry, I was just thinking about what it would mean to have children at this stage of our lives."

"And? Have you reached any conclusions?" he asked.

"Once I was so certain I wanted them. I thought I'd make a terrific mother. . . . Now, I'm not so certain."

"What's changed?"

This time Reggie was especially careful to appear casual. "Oh, I don't know . . . working, age . . . becoming more selfish as I grow older."

"You're hardly ancient," observed Cole. He reached out and placed a hand over her stomach, patting it. "You'd look cute with a belly, and I could hold your head every day when you throw up. . . . Maybe we should reconsider. What if we had just one? For our old age."

A stab of grief hit her as she thought of what she had lost. All because of David, she and Cole would never share the joy of creating and raising a child. Her past had seen to that. But it was her burden, not Cole's. It was better letting him think that she just didn't want children.

"You're all the responsibility that I can handle at this time, Cole Weston. You're too stubborn, too jealous and much too overbearing to share with a child. So, my darling husband . . . it's just you and me." The car had slowed and stopped as they were speaking. Reggie stepped out into the starry night, carefully wiping the tears from her eyes before Cole could see them.

But Cole had seen them. What he didn't understand, but was now determined to discover, was their cause. But, he decided as he stepped from the car and saw the Wychek women approaching them, now was not the time to probe.

Roberta Wychek was startled by the beauty of her guests. The man, tall, muscular, ruggedly handsome with the hint of a sunburn on his cheeks could easily have passed for a movie star. He had his arm lazily slung around the shoulders of a woman whose beauty might have graced the covers of any one of the many fashion magazines Roberta subscribed to. Wistfully, she looked down at her cord trousers and sneakers and fidgeted with her long brown ponytail. It wasn't that the strangers were dressed so differently than she, but rather the aura they projected, the glow of self-assurance, confidence and money. Roberta could tell with a woman's second sense, that Mrs. Weston was different from the girls she associated with in Farmington, Connecticut. Little things gave her away: the perfectly manicured nails, the cut of her hair, the slim body inside the faded jeans, and the tiny emerald stud earrings that matched her eyes. No, this girl didn't go to Sears or J.C. Penney to have her hair body-waved. And she certainly didn't cook and clean or look after two busy children all day. From Joe's naive description alone, Roberta was prepared to dislike both of them on sight. She had only agreed to meet them because Joe and the kids had insisted they had been so helpful with the sailboat. Now she felt awkward, ungainly and ugly.

Reggie sensed Roberta's discomfort immediately. She disentangled herself from Cole's arms. Oh yes, she thought to herself, she'd felt that way on more than one occasion in her life. She was determined to put Roberta at ease. "You haven't any idea how grateful my husband and I are that you invited us here. Cole, come and meet Mrs. Wychek. Roberta, may I call you Roberta? This is my husband Cole and I'm Reggie Weston."

"How do you do?" Roberta asked stiffly. "I'm glad you could come," she added with a decided lack of enthusiasm.

But Reggie still remembered all her years of growing up in her sister's shadow and she wouldn't be put off. "Your hair!" she exclaimed.

Roberta's hand flew to her long ponytail. "What's the matter with it?" she challenged.

"The matter? Nothing's the matter with it. I'm just jealous. I just had my own cut recently, and am I ever sorry. I'll never let anyone talk me into doing something like that again. Don't you ever let anyone convince you to cut yours."

It was the opening that Roberta needed. "You know, it's so funny that you should say that. I'm having a running feud with the beauty parlor I go to. They think I should cut it, but Joe and I like it like this."

After that Roberta relaxed. She accepted Reggie and, when she saw the way the children chattered happily around the beautiful redhead, Roberta began to make a new friend.

"Did you go near the waterfall?" asked Rya.

"Near it? We almost went over it!" Reggie winked at Cole.

"What happened?"

"We got distracted, weren't paying attention to where we were going. Luckily, my husband is a master seaman and brought us out of it safely."

Michael looked at Reggie then at Rya. Rya shook her head, but Michael proceeded anyway. "You wouldn't happen to know how to play Monopoly, would you?" he asked.

"Michael!" warned Roberta.

"Are you kidding? I'm a world-class Monopoly player. Someone must have told you, right?" Reggie played along.

Michael laughed. "Naw, it's just that it's boring playing with only two people, and Rya isn't much competition. You wanna play?"

"Michael, I'm sure that Mrs. Weston doesn't want—"

"No, I really do. I haven't played in years and I happen to love it."

"Great! Move over Rya and let Reggie sit here between us." Rya moved over and Reggie, a smile on her face at the comfortable way Michael had used her first name, squeezed in between the children, who started to divide the money.

"Cole?" Reggie asked invitingly.

"If I play . . . and win—"

"You won't. But if I win . . . will you take my winnings as partial repayment of the loan?" Reggie asked with a grin.

Her husband responded in kind. "You don't give up, do you?"

"Do you?" she countered.

"Check!" Cole answered. "Roll those dice, lady."

Cole picked up the beer that Roberta offered him and sat down to wait for his turn. They played for well over an hour. By the time they had finished, Roberta had dinner on the table. Reggie started to protest, but neither Joe nor Roberta would let them leave. After dinner everyone joined in another game of Monopoly. This time Cole won everyone's money. Reggie was beginning to yawn. It was after eleven o'clock. Cole drew her to his side, thanked the Wycheks for the dinner, their hospitality and especially for the small sailboat that he had bought from Joe. Michael and Joe were going to deliver it to Cole's cabin in the morning.

The next two days were idyllic. They fished, hunted, sailed and made love everywhere that Cole had promised. Neither of them had ever experienced such total contentment in the company of another human being. On their last night, as they lay together in the antique four-poster bed, Cole turned to Reggie, who had just finished brushing her hair with an old silver-handled brush, long forgotten in one of the bureau drawers.

"Happy?" he asked.

She reached for his hand, holding it gently between hers. "Yes. Are you?"

"I am totally, completely, unalterably, ecstatically happy. I could quite possibly get used to this kind of life. Give up business altogether and become a bum."

She shook her head. "No, darling. You'd last a month, maybe two, but the lure of money and power would pull you back to Manhattan."

"One day I'll surprise you and give it all up, Reg. It's not nearly as important to me as you think. There are so many things I'd like to do now, things that seemed ridiculous before."

"What kind of things?"

"Travel . . . perhaps a family . . ."

Reggie flinched.

"Are you definitely opposed to that idea?" Cole asked, a note of disappointment in his voice.

"N-no," she stammered. "Maybe in the future sometime. Now let's just concentrate on you and me. Okay?" Her hand crept under the blanket and rested lightly between his legs. Smiling, she looked into his eyes. "I'm all for practicing, though."

Moments later they were lost in each other's bodies, but in the back of his mind, Cole couldn't quite forget the way Reggie had reacted at the mention of children. It didn't make sense to him, and he intended, now more than ever, to find out what was behind her fear. He loved her far too much to allow her to suffer alone. Wherever the fear came from, Cole was certain that by working together, they would conquer it.

Chapter 36

Saturday morning, October 31, was so unusual a day that even the morning newscaster commented on it. Reggie was watching the small-screen TV in her dressing room as she applied a little mascara to her eyelashes.

". . . and at eight A.M. the temperature at Kennedy Airport is seventy-two degrees. Looks like Indian summer is back for one last go-round. The forecast is for more of the same throughout the day, high in the mid-seventies, low humidity and plenty of sunshine."

Reggie switched off the television as she pulled on a pair of white jeans, ivory cowboy boots and a light white cotton turtleneck sweater. She had an appointment to meet Gary at Lee's apartment at 9:30 for the final fitting of his costume. Hastily, she looked at her watch, a new gold Cartier that Cole had left on her pillow that morning. She realized she had better hurry if she were going to have time to join Cole for breakfast. Besides, she was dying to know the reason for the watch.

She tucked her handbag under her arm and ran down the stairs to the breakfast room, nearly colliding head-on with John as she pushed open the swinging doors. "John, I'm so sorry."

"No need to hurry, Miss Reggie," he said. "Mr. Weston's gone out already. He said that he would speak to you later."

Disappointed, she turned to the buffet table where an array of breakfast foods were beautifully laid out. But Reggie lost her desire for the meal now that Cole had already left.

"Did he say where he was going?" she asked John. She had so much to discuss with him before that night. She had finally decided that sometime today she had to tell Cole the entire story about David Astin. She had hoped it would be at breakfast. She tried to remember if Cole had told her he was leaving early, but all that she could recall was a light kiss and a grunt from him as she tiptoed from his room that morning.

"Are you okay, Miss Reggie?" John asked.

"What? Oh, yes, I'm fine. Why?"

"Because I answered you twice and then asked you if you wanted coffee, but you didn't even blink."

Reggie apologized and answered yes to coffee. "John, if Mr. Weston calls or comes back before I do, tell him that he can reach me at Mr. Taggett's until about ten thirty. After that, I'll be at the Regency for a while. Will you remember that or should I write it down?"

John arched his eyebrows in disdain. He never forgot anything. "Yes, ma'am. I'll tell him if I hear from him."

Reggie searched his face. "Are you sure he didn't mention where he was going?"

"No," he said as patiently as he could. "If he had told me, I most certainly would tell you."

"All right. Oh, and, John, one more thing. I'll see you and Elsa at the party tonight, right? You both have your costumes?"

A momentary shudder passed through the elderly retainer. "Yes, Miss Reggie."

"Good. I'll see you later. Please don't forget—"

"To tell Mr. Weston. No, I won't."

Reggie arrived at Lee's apartment a half hour early. He answered the door barefoot, still in his pajamas. In his half-asleep state, he looked young and vulnerable. With an aching heart, she wished that somehow he would find some happiness. The lonely life that he lived couldn't make him happy.

"Who needs your smiling face at this hour? Aren't you early?"

"Never mind. You should be grateful I'm here at all. Have you any idea what I have to do today? Go take a shower, and I'll make a pot of coffee. We'll get started on the costume as soon as Gary gets here." She walked past him into the startling white industrially inspired kitchen. "It looks like a hospital in here," she shouted over her shoulder. "Why did you make it so sterile?"

He peeked his head into the austere kitchen. "Two eggs, scrambled easy, a side of bacon, lightly toasted rye and coffee."

"I never said I'd make you breakfast."

He blew her a kiss. "You didn't think I'd let an opportunity like this go by, did you? Besides, why should Cole have the benefit of your culinary expertise and not me?" Lee asked.

Reggie looked aghast. "*I* do not cook for Mr. Weston. That is the job of our chef."

"Well, I beg your pardon, Mrs. Weston. Had I known that—"

"Oh, all right. But don't tell anyone or it will ruin my image," Reggie consented.

"Which image are we trying to preserve? Mrs. Cole Weston or the famous designer Reggie Gates?" Lee asked.

Reggie thought for a second. "It's interesting that you should ask that," she mused. "Since my marriage, I find that I've let Alison take much more responsibility for Raggs than I ever thought I would. Oh, I still go into work three or four days a week, but everything is so organized and running so smoothly that they hardly need me. And the most peculiar part of it is that I find I don't even miss it. Isn't that odd?"

"Not especially. You've been using that business as a substitute for everything you lacked in your life for years. Now that you've found something else to care about, Raggs has lost its importance for you." He noticed the quiet smile on her face and added, "Obviously you've already come to the same conclusion."

Reggie considered Lee's evaluation as she took two eggs and cracked them into a stainless steel bowl. Picking up a wire whisk, she began beating the eggs. "But Raggs has always been my life, my baby. I should have more than a passing interest in it now."

"No, darling," Lee corrected. "No business, no matter how much love you've poured into it, can give you the caring and nurturing that you get from another human being. When you and Cole discovered each other, you found the other half of yourself, that part of you that you've been searching for for so many years. Everything else pales in comparison. Don't you understand that yet?"

"Yes," she whispered. "I simply never put it into words before." Then she blurted out words that she was instantly sorry she had spoken. "Is that the way you feel—felt—about Liza?"

He was silent.

"Lee, I'm so terribly sorry. I shouldn't have asked. It's none of my business. I don't know how—"

"Stop berating yourself," Lee said gently. "And, yes, that is exactly the way I *feel* about Liza. I have always felt that way about her and I always will. All the years haven't dulled the memories of what we shared. But in one respect I'm far more fortunate than most gay men. I have Melissa. She is something that was created by the two of us, and if Liza and I were never to see each other again, I still have a part of her to love in Melissa," Lee explained. "You will understand better when and if you and Cole have a child."

The bowl containing the beaten eggs slipped from Reggie's hands and crashed to the floor. The yellow froth spread slowly on the immaculate white ceramic floor. Reggie stared, open-mouthed, at Lee. Her heart was beating furiously. Had Cole said something? Had he questioned Lee? What did Lee actually remember about that day in the hallway so many years ago? How much did he remember about the ensuing days? Had she ever told him the abysmal results of her abortion? She just couldn't remember.

She needn't have worried. Lee wasn't even aware that his statement had caused her clumsiness. He grabbed a roll of paper towels and was trying to blot up the elusive eggs. Without raising his head he said, "Marriage has certainly changed you. There was a time when you were terrific in the kitchen. Now you're all thumbs!"

Grateful for the misunderstanding, Reggie took the toweling from Lee's hands, making the mess infinitely worse. "Go take a shower. Men in my kitchen always make me nervous. By the time you've finished, I'll have your breakfast on the table." She hoped he hadn't noticed that her hands were trembling.

He left the cleaning up to her and padded into the bedroom. In fifteen minutes, she cleaned the floor, set the table and prepared his meal exactly as he had ordered. She was glad to have something to do. When he re-entered the kitchen, Lee was met by the smell of brewing coffee.

"Much better," he stated. "I hope you change the rules and begin cooking for your husband."

"I don't think Cole would permit it. He would think it was an insult to his chef. Besides, if I ever made a mess in our kitchen like I did here, I could never face our chef again. Let's leave it that I only cook for you. Okay?"

Lightly, Lee kissed the back of her neck. "That's fine with me. I'm beginning to think that the most self-destructive thing I've ever done was to introduce you to Cole in the first place. I should have saved you for myself."

Reggie laughed. "You were glad to be rid of me. I've been a noose around your neck since the day you first met me." She paused and then said, "I always knew you still loved Liza, you know. You have hidden it very well for many years but the pain is in your face whenever you talk about her."

"Well, it's been over between us for years and you know exactly why. It's hardly as if I ran off with another woman," he said bitterly.

"It has never been over between you two. You speak to her all the time. I know you do. Every time there's a problem with Melissa, she calls you. She doesn't discuss things with the guy she's been seeing, does she? Of course not! And it has nothing to do with the fact that he isn't Melissa's father. It deals with bonds that she hasn't been able to break, either. Don't you see that no matter what happened between you, she still cares?"

He smiled at her. "You think you're so clever, but there are things that you still don't understand. Whenever two people have a child together, there are strings. They never break, Reg. They're attached to your heart. Liza is a wonderful mother, but there are some situations that she can't handle by herself. I try to be there for her as much as I'm able. It's not Melissa's fault that I am not there all the time to be her daddy. It's not Liza's, either," he added. "I want to make life as easy and comfortable for both of them as I possibly can. Do you understand that?"

She looked at him with anger. "You're the one who's not so smart. How come she hasn't married that guy out there in all these years?" Then she answered her own question. "Because she still loves you, you idiot!"

"And I'm telling you that it has nothing to do with loving me. It all revolves around Melissa. Wait till you have a child, you'll understand," Lee said.

Again! Every conversation seemed to revert to the same subject. She stared hard into Lee's eyes, trying to decide whether he was deliberately bringing it up.

"What is it?" he asked, noticing the look on Reggie's face.

"Why do you constantly talk about my having children?"

"Do I? I hadn't noticed."

"Yes, you do. This is the second time today that you've brought it up. Cole and I would make rotten parents. We're too busy and too selfish. We've discussed it already. Even you have to admit that Cole wouldn't have time for a baby. It wouldn't be fair to the child."

Lee shook his head in disagreement. "I didn't think that Cole would have time for a wife, either, and I was wrong. Who knows? Maybe that's exactly what the two of you need."

"Stop trying to play God!" she snapped, and Lee was shocked at the tone in her voice. "The very last thing I need in my life is a baby. First of all, I couldn't very well continue with my career—"

"You just got finished telling me that you were losing interest in it anyway."

Reggie faltered. "No . . . I didn't say that. I meant that it was a temporary thing. You don't throw away something that you've spent your entire life building. Would you give up WestCo?" she challenged.

"Depends for what," he answered.

"If Liza called you right now and asked you to start all over again, to move out West, would you give up everything that you have here to do it?"

"Loving isn't demanding that someone give up everything for the other person. It isn't necessary for someone to prove their love for you that way. If Liza ever demanded that I move out there simply to prove that I loved her, I would know that she didn't love me. Am I making sense?" he asked, noticing her confusion.

"No . . . yes . . . I don't know. I guess I do understand what you're saying, and maybe I'm asking the wrong questions. I'm so mixed up about this baby issue. All of a sudden that's all anyone is talking about."

"As far as I can tell, *you're* the only one who keeps bringing it up. Have you and Cole discussed it much? Has he brought up the subject?"

"I can't remember exactly who brought it up. I think I once asked him if he wanted children," she confessed.

"So you're the one who is obsessed with the concept, not Cole or me. Do you want a baby, Reg?" Lee asked with great tenderness.

Tears filled her eyes and spilled over onto her cheeks. She buried her face in her hands and her body began to shake with silent sobs.

Lee walked around to her side of the table and gathered her slim body in his arms. "Shh, shh. Whatever it is, it can't be this bad." He patted her head, trying to comfort her the way he had done so many, many times through the years. "Tell me. Trust me, Reg. Trust someone," he urged. "Whatever burden you're carrying can be lightened if you share it with someone who loves you. Believe me, I know." He lifted her chin so he could look into her eyes. "Do you think you can trust me with whatever is torturing you?"

She extricated herself from his grasp and blew her nose in the beautiful linen napkin. "I've ruined your napkin."

"Yes," he agreed. "You have. Now do you want to talk to me or should we forget it?"

She took his clean napkin from him and dried her eyes. "Yes, I think I do want to talk about it. But you have to swear to me that it stays here. It's never to be discussed with anyone else, including Cole . . . especially Cole. Will you give me your word?"

"Of course. I'll go to my grave with the secret unless you give me permission to tell anyone. But what could be so terrible that you can't tell Cole?"

"I'm getting to that." Reggie took a few deep breaths before she began. "I think Cole will want children. Maybe not this year, but eventually. We spoke about it casually the other night, and I was able to make him drop the subject by mentioning our ages and how busy we were. But you know as well as I that if he really wants children, there's going to be more discussion."

"And you are definitely against the idea?" Lee asked.

"No. I've always wanted children. . . ."

"But?"

"I can't have them. I'm sterile," she admitted finally.

"There was never any need for Cole to know before because under the original terms of our contract that issue would never come up. Now everything has changed. Don't you see? I can't tell him now. He'll feel like he was cheated."

For a moment Lee digested what she was saying. It didn't make sense. "Reg, I know you couldn't have forgotten, and I don't think that you blocked it out, but you are not sterile. You conceived at least once that I know about. I was the one who held your hand while you recovered from the abortion, remember? I'm sure that if you were pregnant once, you can conceive again."

She laughed at the irony. "You're wrong. That's exactly why I can't conceive. The infection that I developed after the abortion wasn't caught in time. It screwed up my Fallopian tubes. End result: no kids!"

"But that was years ago. There are new methods to treat sterility, methods that weren't available then. Have you spoken to a doctor recently?" Lee asked.

"I don't have to. I've already been told that there would be only a ten percent chance of my conceiving even if I underwent major surgery. If I were lucky enough to get pregnant after that, the possibility is strong that I would have a tubal pregnancy."

Lee studied his old friend for several minutes before he spoke. When he did, it was quietly. "You made a mistake a long time ago. You were very young then and now that mistake is costing you far more than you thought possible. But there isn't one of us who is innocent. We've all made errors in our youth and there isn't an error made that isn't forgiveable if someone loves you enough. Do you love your husband?"

Reggie nodded.

"And do you believe that he loves you?" Lee asked.

Again she nodded.

"Then you must tell him before he finds out some other way. I would want to know. Don't you think that he deserves the right to discuss it with you before you go ahead and make a decision alone that there will never be children between you? What about the other options that are available—test tube babies, adoption? You owe Cole that discussion, Reg," Lee said.

"There's more," Reggie said. "That's not the end of the story. Do you remember the apartment that you moved into when we met?"

"Of course. What does that have to do with this?"

"Do you happen to remember the name of the former tenant?"

"No," Lee answered, puzzled.

"The man who lived there before you . . . he, uh, the father of the baby that I—"

The doorbell rang. Both of them ignored it.

"Go on, Reg. Tell me the rest," Lee pleaded, ignoring the insistent tattooing on the front door.

"I can't now. That's Gary, and I can't speak in front of him. But I will tell you the rest of the story later. I promise," she added, noting the skeptical look on his face.

Of all the rotten timing, he thought. She was about to confide in him and now he wasn't at all certain that the rest of her story would ever be forthcoming. She might reconsider.

Within moments Gary bustled into the apartment, his arms filled with parcels, bags, boxes and suitcases. Between fitting the peacock-blue waistcoat, carmine paisley vest and black satin knee breeches and listening to the incessant chatter about the ball, Lee began to wonder how he was going to survive the rest of the morning let alone the party that night. Fortunately, just as his patience was at an end, Gary announced that the fitting was over.

By 10:30, Gary and Reggie left for the Regency to oversee all last-minute preparations. Lee relaxed with another cup of coffee. He still had an hour to waste before he was to meet Cole for a game of squash at the health club. He didn't feel much like playing since Reggie's conversation about Liza. He picked up the phone and rapidly dialed. After two rings, Liza picked up the phone.

"Hello? . . . Hello?"

For a moment Lee said nothing. Why had he called? "Good morning," he said, finally.

"Lee?"

"Did I wake you?"

He could picture her lying in bed, her dark hair spread out over the pillows.

"Of course you woke me," Liza answered sleepily. "What time is it here? Good God, Lee—it's only seven thirty!"

"Don't you have to get up with Melissa for school?" he asked defensively.

Liza laughed. "Not on Saturdays."

"Oh," Lee said, sheepishly. "Then I did wake you. I'm sorry."

"What's the matter?" She couldn't keep the concern out of her voice. "Are you sick? Where are you?"

"No. I mean I'm fine. I'm here in my home. I just called because I'm going to be out in California next week and I would like to see you and Melissa. Could you arrange it?" Why the hell had he said that? He wasn't planning on being anywhere near California.

There was silence at the other end of the line. Finally Liza spoke. "I'm taking Melissa to Tahoe next week for some skiing. We're just going alone, she and I. I don't know how healthy it would be for me and you to spend that much time together. I don't want to confuse her."

"If I stayed somewhere else and met you two accidentally on the slopes . . . do you think that would confuse her? I mean it is conceivable that the three of us were in the same place at the same time." He looked up at the ceiling. Even to him, the story sounded thin.

"I wouldn't do anything underhanded," Liza said. "If you really want to come out, spend some time with us—I guess we could all handle it, but only on the up and up. Let me talk it over with Melissa first. If she says it's okay, then it's fine with me."

"Then you'll call me and let me know what you've decided?"

"Of course," she said, "but you *are* okay? You're not sick?"

"No. In fact, I've never felt better. I just missed you guys and wanted to see you."

"I'll call you tomorrow morning. You'll be home?"

"Yes, Liza. I'll be here waiting for your call."

Chapter 37

David stood at the window of his room in the Regency and watched the light morning traffic on Park Avenue. Patrice was still sleeping, her breathing light and shallow. Dark shadows under her eyes gave her the appearance of a sleeping ghoul. How ugly she is, thought David. He'd dump her the minute this deal with WestCo was consummated. Then it would be all his. His name would be on the contracts and he wouldn't need the Munseys anymore. In the meantime, he spoke to her as little as possible and tried to ignore her as best he could. Even in bed she had ceased to amuse him. Her only use to him now was her influence and her relationship with her father. He still needed Francis to get the Stockyard deal going. When he had accomplished that . . . out she'd go. He hoped it would be soon. Maybe even this weekend.

He glanced at the pathetic creature in the bed. Though she was totally dependent on him for her daily morphine shot, she hated him with the same intensity that he despised her. Only she couldn't afford to leave him. The price for her leaving was too steep. There was no one that she could turn to for help.

She watched him at the window for a moment through slitted eyes. He didn't know she was awake yet. In the years that they had been married, he hadn't grown older. He had simply aged beautifully like a good wine, getting better and better with time. His dark hair, slightly sprinkled with silver, complemented his perpetually tanned face. The pipe he now sported added to his image of distinguished respectability. Oh, if only they all knew what he really was. She turned over. It was far too late for her. She could do nothing to bring about his demise. He would unearth any secret plot, withhold her medicine, show her father those hideous tapes that he always threatened her with. No, for her there would be no future without David. Her only escape from him would be in death, and he denied her even that.

He wondered idly how they were going to get through this party tonight. He never would have brought Patrice to New York, but Francis had insisted that he was strong enough to make the trip and requested—no, demanded—that Patrice come as well.

Tonight he had to make damn sure that she was able to stand up and look, if not breathtaking, then at least presentable. It would be a mammoth undertaking. He would start soon with a morning injection to get her through the day at Elizabeth Arden. He heard her stir and turned to face his wife. God, she was ghastly! Her hair alone would take hours.

Ardith Weston's tiny gold travel clock buzzed at seven thirty. A little disoriented, it took her several seconds to shake the sleep from her head and to remember that she was in the Park Lane hotel in Manhattan, that tonight she was attending her son's long-awaited wedding reception . . . and meeting her new daughter-in-law.

She reached for her silver glasses on the night table and pulled herself into a sitting position before rereading the lovely little note that Regina had mailed her. A nice touch, and totally unnecessary . . . but Ardith had been oddly touched by the way Regina had taken the time to introduce herself. Now, she thought as she reached for the telephone to call down for coffee, if only she's as pleasant in person. There was reason for doubt, however, if one judged by the two other women Cole had brought to Maine in the last five years; the "blond bombshell" who spent the greater part of the weekend in the bathroom and the "Peruvian princess" who sat sunning herself in the microscopic bikini.

Later, Ardith was finishing her third cup of coffee, secretly smirking at her indulgence now that Robert wasn't around to chastise her about the evils of caffeine, when the phone rang. She picked it up in surprise.

"Mrs. Weston? Ardith, I mean," asked a pleasant female voice.

"Yes. This is Ardith Weston. May I help you?"

"Welcome to New York. This is Reggie. Cole's wife. I hope I didn't wake you."

"Not at all. Not at all. What a delightful surprise. How do you do?"

"I'm fine," said Reggie. She sounded a little nervous. "I was wondering if you might be able to spare an hour or so today, any time would do, so we could meet before the reception tonight."

Ardith thought about her full schedule. Saks for a manicure, Arden for hair.

"I'm free all day, my dear, and I would love to meet you. Name the time and place." Hell, she'd been doing her own hair and nails for ten years.

Reggie described a tiny French restaurant hidden in the back of a vintage clothing store down in SoHo. "Would one o'clock be convenient?" she asked.

"Perfect!" Wasn't SoHo where beatniks hung out? Or was that Greenwich Village? It had been so long since Ardith had been in New York that she was sadly out of step with the times. "How will I know you?" she asked.

"I'll be wearing a white sweater, white jeans, white cowboy boots and a ponytail. I have red hair."

A hippie, Ardith decided sadly, having no idea that the Henry Lehr jeans, Thiery Mugler cashmere sweater and crocodile boots would have kept a beatnik in batik muumuus and leather thongs for five years. "Yes, well, dear, I'll see you at one in SoHo. I'm looking forward to meeting you." As soon as she hung up the phone, Ardith called the concierge for directions to SoHo then thought about her navy Chanel suit. . . . It was perfect for Saks and Arden, but did one wear that to SoHo? A ponytail . . . oh my!

At precisely 12:50, Ardith entered the charming clothing store on Prince Street and was pleasantly surprised to note that the patrons did in fact wear shoes and there wasn't a marijuana cigarette in sight. She relaxed as she strolled through the store admiring the antiques that were displayed in cut-glass vitrines dating from Victorian times.

"Mrs. Weston?"

Ardith turned at the sound of her name to face a petite Oriental girl with a face painted like a geisha. "Regina?"

"She's waiting for you in the garden. She sent me to find you." The girl led Ardith through the store to the back room, which led out to a small patio with six tables set for lunch. Only three were occupied. At one, Ardith saw a beautiful, wholesome redhead and immediately knew she would like her daughter-in-law. Reggie's face lit up with the brightest smile Ardith could ever remember.

From the moment they met, they never stopped talking. About Cole, his childhood, Reggie's history, Ardith's life in Maine, Cole's old girlfriends, Reggie's business and everything else that the two women could think about. They totally ignored the crabmeat-stuffed avocados they had ordered and, by three o'clock, were madly in love with each other.

"And don't let him bully you," Ardith cautioned. "He can do that. I've seen him. He can be selfish and overbearing and if he ever tries it, you come right to me. *I* can handle him."

Reggie laughed gleefully. "I know exactly what you mean." It was then that she told Ardith the whole story of how she and Cole had come to be married.

"But you love him?" Ardith asked with her heart in her mouth.

"Absolutely. More than I ever thought possible."

"And he? Does he love you?"

Reggie nodded shyly. "I think so."

Of course he does. How could he not love this lively, striking, warm-hearted girl? They were perfect for each other. "Just keep him on his toes, darling. Keep him slightly off balance. It'll be good for him. I promise." Ardith wasn't a fool and, though she dearly loved her son, she also knew him very, very well. He needed an independent, tough woman . . . a warm, loving one, but one who wouldn't pamper his streak of arrogance.

When they parted fifteen minutes later, Reggie leaned toward her mother-in-law and kissed her smooth cheek. "I think we're going to be great friends, and nothing could make me happier."

Ardith took something from her handbag and pressed it into Reggie's hand. "This is a small gift for you. Open it when you're alone. I'll see you tonight." All thoughts of Saks and Arden had long been forgotten in the delight of meeting this exceptional girl. Her son was a fortunate man.

Chapter 38

"Good night, sir," said John, standing just outside the door of Cole's study in his blue satin and gold-braided livery costume. "Elsa and I are leaving now. Are you quite sure you wouldn't want us to wait?" John would have done anything to postpone being seen in public in his costume.

Cole shook his head. "Yes, I'm sure. You go on ahead and pick up my mother. Mrs. Weston and I will be along shortly. It's still only seven thirty." He wished it were tomorrow. How had he ever consented to this masquerade business? He must have been out of his mind! It made no difference that the fawn-colored suede breeches, formal pleated shirt, mahogany lambskin jacket and mirrorlike Hessian boots set off every muscle and tendon in his body to perfection. Nor did it matter that his outfit flattered him in a way that his tuxedo did not. He still felt like a jackass, dressed up like this. It wasn't Reggie's fault; she had made every effort to see that his costume didn't embarrass him. It was that little twerp from Dallas. Even after Cole had been forced to listen to Reggie's explanation of that night in the factory and, at her insistence, had apologized to Gary Colby, there would never be any love lost between the two men. It would be a fitting revenge for Gary if Cole came off like a buffoon tonight.

He sat down in his leather wing chair to wait for Reggie and let out a surprised curse as Coco jumped into his lap from thin air. "You!" Cole exclaimed as the feline chatelaine of the townhouse made herself comfortable. "And how she ever convinced me to let you come, too, is beyond me!" But even as he berated the cat, he absently stroked her soft fur. "The two of you!" he said with a half laugh. "Incredible that at my age I'm gallivanting around in pantaloons, living with a woman who plays hopscotch from bed to bed every night and have to contend with a cat who thinks I'm her father!" Coco stretched and snuggled deeper into Cole's lap, enjoying the touch of the soft suede against her body. "And," Cole added as an after-thought, "I like it!"

Bored with the conversation, Coco jumped from Cole's lap and strolled from the room as the phone intercom buzzed.

"Hello?"

"Hi, darling," said Reggie. "Are you all ready?"

"Unfortunately, yes. And you?"

"Any minute now."

"Hurry up," he said. "I'm lonely." He was, he ruefully admitted to himself, anxious to be with her, to touch her, to hold her. The last few weeks had been pure hell. He'd been tied up with the Chicago deal and his investigation of David Astin, trying to find answers where there were none. She had been so wrapped up in the final preparations for the gala, that he had seen little of her. When she did creep into his bed, she snuggled into his arms and fell into an exhausted, dreamless slumber, while he, awake and aroused by her nearness, let his hands roam over her body, willing her to waken. If she did, she was confused and disoriented. So, he let her drift back to sleep while he tossed and turned in frustration. In the mornings, he would rise to find the lingering scent of her perfume on his pillow, the only evidence that she had been there at all.

He would never smell Bal à Versailles without remembering those tortuous nights. He made a mental note to buy her a new perfume—tomorrow!

"And don't wear that perfume tonight!" he said out loud.

"I beg your pardon? What perfume?"

"Never mind!" he muttered, embarrassed that he had spoken his thoughts. But she did that to him . . . shook his implacable composure and constantly kept him ever so slightly off balance. It irked the hell out of him.

She hung up the phone with just the tiniest smile on her face and returned to her dressing table to administer the final touches to her face: a light dusting of shimmering, translucent powder and a heart-shaped black patch at the corner of her full lips—an affectation she was borrowing from the early nineteenth century. That patch and the three-quarter white feathered and sequined mask that would hide most of her face were the only things besides steel nerves that were going to get her through tonight and seeing David Astin.

God, she wished she had told Cole everything! After all

these years, her past would mean nothing to him. She simply should have recognized David's name and told Cole about her brief romance. It would have been so simple—then. There would have been no need for lies or to even mention the pregnancy. No one except Lee and Alison knew; and her secret was safe with them. Now it was too late. Long ago she had decided to bury that ugly, unhappy time in her life, and now she was stuck with her decision. She'd have to brazen it out tonight, sustain the deception.

Her gown, a floor-length, silver wisp of fabric, hung on the back of her closet door. Thinner than tissue paper, the semitransparent cloth would fly away from her body at the merest whisper of wind . . . left alone, it molded itself to her and slid down her body at the same time. Her own creation, not yet on the market, it was almost like liquid. She had named it mercury.

Cole sat in the study, savoring his second glass of cognac. At eight o'clock, he thought he heard her footsteps. He set the glass down on the inlaid marble table and rested his hands behind his head. Slowly, the door swung open. He turned in his chair and let out a long sigh of appreciation. She was, at once, icicle then flame. The gown floated about her like waves of crystal-clear water. For a moment he swore he could see through it. It was an illusion, tall, like a column of ice capped by fire. Diamonds shimmered in her upswept, scarlet hair. Her magnificent breasts were outlined, separated by diamond-like strands that fell to the floor. He was totally mesmerized. As if in a trance, he rose and walked toward her. She stood perfectly still, waiting and watching. He placed his hand under her chin, gazing questioningly into her eyes. "Would I spoil you if I kissed you?" he whispered, awed by her quiet sensuality.

She didn't speak as she reached up, wrapped her arms around his neck and pulled his head to her lips. He tasted the familiar sweetness of her mouth, inhaled the scent that wafted from her hair. Suddenly, he wanted her with a desperation he couldn't control. With one deft motion, he reached behind her neck and released the one snap that held the enticing gown in place. She gasped in surprise as it slid, soundlessly, down her body, leaving her in only a shimmering slip that was far, far more provocative than nakedness.

"You astound me," he murmured into her hair, then corrected himself as she pulled the pins from her thick, lustrous tresses. It fell around her shoulders like a cape of living fire. "We astound me!"

She threw back her head, intent on demanding that he let her dress, but the raw hunger that burned in his smoldering eyes stopped her short. "We'll be late," she warned.

"Then we'll be late," he answered, overcome by an impatient urgency to feel her lithe, supple body surrender to him. It had been so long. . . .

Her green eyes twinkled with naughty amusement as she felt the full thrust of his arousal pressing against her stomach. "But," she continued devilishly, "four hundred guests are waiting for us." She was baiting him, deliberately, and it gave her an accustomed feeling of power to know that she could do this to him.

With a low growl, he swept her into his arms. "Let them wait!" he said. "I can't!" He lowered his head and a breathless moan escaped her lips as his mouth devoured hers in a hungry kiss. She could feel him shudder, and her lips opened to his demanding tongue, welcoming the warmth that spread through her at his touch. Her heart thudded joyfully as he picked her up and carried her to the sofa, gently laying her down while he shed his clothes, his burning eyes never leaving her face.

All the hectic weeks of preparation that had kept them apart disappeared and were forgotten as, frantic with repressed need, they came together. "You torture me," he sighed raggedly against her neck, pushing aside the heavy mane of her hair so that he could place his trembling lips to her skin. "You can't know—"

"Oh, but darling I do, I do." And as he kissed first one breast then the other, she felt the familiar tightening in the pit of her stomach and gloried in the unexpected spasms that ripped through her.

Her fevered response, so well remembered and so welcome, broke his restraint and ignited fires that had to be quenched. He lowered himself between her thighs, entering her boldly and finding to his surprise that she was wet and warm, ready for his hard, throbbing shaft, arching against him, driving her slim hips into him and welcoming him home. Groaning with the exquisite warmth that wrapped itself around his manhood, he drove into her, giving up himself to become part of her and, with a last violent shudder, he poured himself into her, answering her quest for sweet release.

With the fine sheen of perspiration shimmering on their bodies, they lay wrapped together, savoring the last twinges of their quick explosive union. Absently, he stroked her breasts, her stomach, her thighs as their breathing slowly returned to normal. Nothing he had ever experienced had prepared him for the aching love he felt for his wife and, in that moment, he knew that he could never, never be without her again.

A chime rang softly in the foyer, and Cole suddenly looked at his watch. "Uh-oh!" he laughed, disengaging himself from the long, graceful legs that were wrapped around him, "I think we're in deep trouble."

Reggie's eyes were closed in blissful relaxation. "We're late, aren't we?" she said, but there was no concern in her voice. If four hundred people were waiting for them and Cole didn't care, she certainly didn't, either. There was no place on earth where she wanted to be except here in her husband's arms.

He kissed her eyelids. "Very. It's almost eight thirty and, I believe," he said with a chuckle, "that we have a party to attend."

She snuggled into his arms. "Don't want to. Tell them we couldn't make it." She sighed contentedly. "So sorry . . . the Westons have other plans . . . something like that."

"What a commotion that would start. No, my love. I think this is one party we have to attend. Get up!" He rose from the sofa and began collecting his clothes. "Can you put yourself back together?"

With a weary sigh, Reggie stood up. "If I absolutely must."

He smacked her behind playfully. "You absolutely must."

"Okay, okay." She scooped up her gown and the brilliant diamond hairpins and hurried from the room, up the stairs and into her room. Quickly, she washed, brushed her hair off her face with the pins and redressed. She reapplied her makeup, but the patch was forever lost. Within fifteen minutes, she walked into the study where Cole stood, dressed and waiting.

"What took you so long?" he asked in mock anger.

"I couldn't find my shoes," she said, her stockinged feet

Lee returned to her side. "I can't locate Cole. You said he was with the Espinozas?"

She nodded.

"Then I'm sure he'll turn up any second. He's involved in some tin and silver mines in Argentina. I suppose they stepped out to discuss business somewhere."

The captain appeared at Reggie's side with a steaming plate of hors d'oeuvres. She felt a wave of nausea as she looked at the food. "I'm not sure this is such a good idea," she said, her face turning slightly ashen. "I think I'd much prefer some crackers and cheese. Lee, would you mind terribly . . ."

He swept the plate off her lap. "Sit here, I'll be right back. Do you think you'll be all right?"

"I'm feeling better already." She looked up at him. "Wouldn't this be a hell of a time to get sick? After all this planning."

He patted her head. "You're not getting sick. I won't let you. Oh, by the way, when I saw Ardith tonight she told me how pleased she was about your afternoon together. She thinks very highly of you."

"I think she's pretty special, too. How come I never had a mother like that? Do you know what I would have given . . . ?"

"Don't look back. Look to what you now have—a husband who adores you and a mother-in-law who can't believe her good fortune."

"Where is Ardith? I haven't seen her yet," Reggie asked.

"In the powder room. Look, let me get you some food and try to find your husband."

"No, don't bother Cole. I'm feeling so much better. Just bring me something to eat."

"Okay." He disappeared into the crowd of gaily costumed guests. While he was gone, Reggie's eyes scanned the room for Cole. It was then that she saw David. Her heart jumped. Suddenly, she found it difficult to breathe. He was standing at the entrance to the ballroom, a frail but beautiful blond on his arm. Reggie's stomach lurched. Trying to steady herself, she grabbed on to the edges of the chair. Cole! Where was Cole? Suddenly she realized with a terrible force what a horrendous error she had made in not telling her husband the truth. She needed him desperately to stand beside her and give her moral support to face David—and all the ugly memories of those months in New York so many years ago that now came flooding back to her.

Slowly, David and his wife were making their way toward her. She knew he hadn't recognized her yet, but she also knew it was only a question of time.

She watched as David took a glass of champagne from one of the waiters then shook his head when his wife reached out to accept a drink. What was that all about? she wondered. Maybe his wife was an alcoholic. Who cared? What mattered now was David and how she was going to avoid meeting him.

She couldn't wait anymore. The room had become suffocating. She had to get out of there. Without another thought, she jumped from the chair and fled, past David and his wife, through the door.

At that moment, he saw her.

It was impossible . . . it couldn't be. Yet the resemblance to a girl he had known many years ago was uncanny. The hair color, the body, the way she moved. He had barely seen her face, but the profile? Jesus! He shook Patrice off like an annoying bug and extricated himself from her cloying grasp. He had to go after the girl. Had to find out. A hand tapped him on the shoulder.

"David?" Cole asked.

David turned around, obviously annoyed at the intrusion. Then he saw Cole's face and his expression changed somewhat. "Cole, how are you?" He couldn't have cared less at the moment, and he let it show. His eyes searched for the girl, but she was gone. Damn! And it was all Weston's fault.

"David, are you looking for someone?" Cole asked pleasantly.

Like a chameleon changing his colors, David changed personalities, quickly regaining his composure. He took Cole's outstretched hand and, at the same time, pulled Patrice protectively toward him, drawing her into the conversation. David noticed the way Patrice avoided meeting Cole's eyes, and he dug his nails into her arm, warning her silently to be on her best behavior.

"Is Francis here yet?" asked Cole.

Patrice turned to David as if she expected him to answer all the questions addressed to either one of them.

"Francis stayed upstairs, Cole. He thought he could make the party, but when it came time to get dressed, he found it too tiring. He asked me to extend his congratulations and suggested that you meet him for brunch tomorrow."

Patrice nodded her head in affirmation when Cole turned to her. She acts like a marionette, he thought. Her husband pulls the strings and she moves. He tried a different approach. "Patrice, does your dad want to see a doctor tonight? I would be happy to send up my personal physician if you think it's necessary."

"No, it is really not necessary," David answered again. "He simply needs to rest and I'm sure he'll be fine. By the way, how are the plans for the Stockyard coming along?" As he asked, he put his arm around Cole's shoulders. Cole didn't like the obvious attempt at familiarity and shrugged off the gesture.

"Excuse me, David, this isn't the time for that conversation. I have to get back to my wife and guests." He addressed his next comment to Patrice. "I seem to have misplaced my bride, but as soon as I find her I'd like the two of you to meet. I think you'll like each other." He nodded his head and turned toward the crowded dance floor.

"Cocky son-of-a-bitch!" David said as soon as Cole was out of earshot. He looked at Patrice, who was smiling slightly. "What the hell are you grinning at?" he asked angrily.

The smile vanished. "I . . . uh . . . I don't know, David. It was just nice to see Cole again."

"Oh, really?" David asked with a nasty grimace. "He's an arrogant, pompous ass. And don't you start believing everything he tells you. He's very adept at compliments. I understand that he has mistresses all over the country. He keeps them in fabulous apartments and drops in on them whenever he gets bored. So don't get any ideas about him. Your father warned me to watch over you whenever Cole Weston was around. Said he couldn't be trusted."

David walked away from her, leaving her alone to make her way through the crowd. He had to find that girl in the silver gown. Like a mongrel with his nose to the ground, he was sniffing around. He had asked a few of the guests if they had seen a redheaded woman in a silver dress but no one seemed to know who he was talking about. The smile that he had fixed to his face turned to a malignant scowl.

Unbeknownst to David, Cole noticed the change. He had been watching Astin very carefully, studying the man, unable to rid himself of his intense mistrust for his friend's son-in-law, though he had nothing but a personal, almost visceral dislike for the man. Cole sensed David would eventually be trouble tonight more than ever, but he felt powerless to stop it. He couldn't identify exactly why he felt the way he did but as Cole strode through the crowd, nodding to acquaintances and making small talk with friends, he watched David out of the corner of one eye and looked for Reggie with the other. Where *was* she? One moment she was speaking with Lee and the next minute she had disappeared. He had exhausted every possibility, even asking his mother to check the ladies' room. He was beginning to feel totally uneasy, and he didn't like it at all. He started at the light touch on his shoulder.

"Hi, stranger," a warm, sensual voice whispered in his ear. Evyan Bolivar stood on tiptoe next to him, dressed in a clinging black gown with two enormous diamond teardrops dripping from her ears.

He whipped around angrily. "Will you stop it!"

"*Chéri*, why? You used to like it so much. Men don't change that easily. Believe me, I know. I'm bored, darling. Luis and I are finished. I'm all yours again."

"Evyan, I'm married, *darling*," he whispered sarcastically.

She pouted. "You needn't be so mean, *chéri*. I know *all about* marriage. Marriages of convenience. In my country they are the most successful kind. But they shouldn't interfere with . . . pleasure." She smiled languidly.

"Evyan, I'm sorry," he replied soberly. "I should have called you first. I owe that much to you after all this time." She looked at him expectantly, but his next words were not what she wanted to hear. "What we had was lovely, my dear. It satisfied both of us at the time. Things have changed."

Her eyes glinted dangerously. "How have they changed, Cole?"

"I happen to love my wife very much," he stated.

She laughed bitterly. "You must be making a joke. You? In love? The very thought of it is ridiculous. It's a contradiction in terms. You don't have the capacity for love any more than I do. We've discussed it many times. Haven't we?"

He sighed. "Yes, I suppose we have."

"So? How could you possibly say that you love her?"

He smiled and shrugged his shoulders. "How? Like this . . . I love my wife. It's quite easy to say it when you mean it."

Evyan stamped her foot. "That is not what I mean and you know it. I can mouth words, too. You will not do this to me, Cole. I will not allow you to leave me for that little—"

Cole placed a warning hand on her shoulder. "I would be very careful of your next sentence. That is my wife you're speaking of."

"Don't you dare tell me what to do! She's nobody! Nothing! I spit on better than her."

In a voice that was so low that Evyan had to strain to hear, Cole answered his former mistress. "That is precisely why I married her. Reggie doesn't spit. While you will always be an alley cat, she will always be a lady." He turned on his heel, leaving her alone in the middle of the room.

All the years of Peruvian aristocracy that ran through her blood rose to her aid. Her ancestors would have been proud of the way she held herself together as Cole strode away. But they also would have been the first to understand the burning jealousy she felt. He would be back, she decided, when he tired of his little bitch. They always come back. . . .

Reggie sat on the mezzanine level of the hotel, one floor above the grand ballroom. She had made her escape through the crowded dance floor into an elevator and had gotten off at the first stop. Sitting alone in the elegant hallway, she wondered dismally how she had ever thought she could pull off seeing David again, how she could have been naive enough to believe that, without Cole's support, she could face the man who had almost ruined her life. Perhaps, if she had told her husband the truth from the beginning, perhaps if he had been standing by her side . . . but that wasn't the case at all. She closed her eyes, letting her head fall back on the headrest of the chair. She was drained, both emotionally and physically. When she opened her eyes, she jumped. Lee was standing in front of her.

He kneeled down so that he was at eye level with her. "Okay, what is it?" he asked gently.

She stared through him, her face a tortured mask.

"Reggie, tell me. Let me help."

She picked a piece of imaginary lint from his shoulder, flicking it away with a long fingernail. "I can't. I've made a mess out of this and I can't get out."

"Yes, you can. Whatever it is, I'll help you. Cole will help you. Won't you let me go find him?"

"No!" She grabbed his shoulder. "Don't get Cole. Just stay here with me. I'll be all right in a minute. Please don't leave me."

"Reggie, stop this! I won't get Cole, but you have to tell me what's bothering you. I can't help you if I don't know." He looked at her curiously. "Is it Cole? Are there problems again?"

"No. But there will be. Oh, Lee, please stop badgering me. I can't tell you. You'll never understand."

He wanted to shake her. "What are you talking about? This is me, remember?" He picked up her hand and held it gently. "Haven't I always understood?"

She nodded.

"Then don't you think I will this time?"

"No," she said.

"Reggie, we never had secrets between us. Don't you remember the vow we made that first day on the stairwell? Never to hurt the other. I still believe it. I think you do, too."

She sat thinking. She had a desperate need to share her fear with someone. She couldn't bear the weight of her knowledge of David Astin alone anymore. She needed someone beside her when she finally met him again. More than that, she needed Lee's sound advice on how to tell Cole about her former lover, now that she had kept it a secret for so long.

"Well?" he interrupted her thoughts. "Are we going to spend the rest of the evening up here? Because until you get this off your chest I'm not leaving you."

Reggie moistened her lips and leaned toward him. "I know David Astin."

"You knew him before tonight?"

She nodded.

"For Christ's sake, Reggie, talk!"

"Don't yell at me!"

"Okay, okay. I'm sorry. Let's start again." He pulled a nearby chair close to her and sat down. "You knew David Astin before tonight and you never mentioned it to Cole or me, even when you knew how much importance we placed on finding out all about him? Why not?"

"I was afraid."

"Of what?" he asked, raising his voice again.

"If you don't stop shouting at me, I'm leaving."

Lee gritted his teeth. "Do you know how damned frustrating it is, trying to get a story out of you?"

"This is the same story I tried to tell you this morning. Do you remember when you moved into the building on Twelfth Street?"

"Yes. You asked me already. Then you wanted to know if I remembered the name—"

The elevator opened with a ring of a bell, and they turned to see Cole walking toward them. "There you are! I've been looking all over the place for you. Are you okay?"

Reggie looked at Lee in desperation, pleading silently with her eyes. Lee stood up and walked over to Cole.

"She's okay now. She felt faint in the ballroom so I took her up here to get some fresh air. It seems that she had lunch with your mother today, but somehow both of them forgot to eat."

Cole was standing by Reggie's chair, listening to Lee's explanation. Reggie still hadn't said anything.

"She didn't want to frighten you so she thought if she just sat here for a while, she'd feel better. I was keeping her company." Lee turned to Reggie. "Do you feel better now?"

Cole looked skeptically, first at his wife, then at his friend. He didn't believe one word of the story. "Interesting," he mused out loud, "that neither one of you thought to tell me that Reggie wasn't feeling well. I'm sorry that you're ill, Reggie. However," he added caustically, "there are three hundred guests downstairs who would like to know where their hostess is. I couldn't tell them because I hadn't any idea. If you're feeling better, I'd like to return to our party." He grasped Reggie's wrist and pulled her from the chair.

"Cole, you're hurting me."

"Am I? Sorry." But he continued to hold her hand in a tight

grasp. He turned back to Lee. "I assume that you will rejoin the party, too, or shall I have someone send your dinner up here?"

"I'll be down shortly," Lee replied, ignoring the sarcasm in Cole's voice. His main concern was Reggie. He could explain to Cole later.

Cole was impatiently pressing the elevator button again and again. Reggie wriggled her hand, trying to loosen it from his grip. "I see that your 'illness' had no effect on your strength." He dropped her hand as the bronze doors to the elevator opened at last. He stepped back politely, allowing her to enter first. When they reached the ballroom floor, he turned to her. "I have no idea what is going on. Nor for one moment do I believe the story that Lee just told me. However, if you don't see fit to confide in me, then at least act like my wife and be a hostess in front of our guests. Now, if you'll excuse me, there are several people who have been waiting eagerly to meet you." He left her standing alone in the middle of the room.

The joy had gone out of the evening for Reggie. The hours spent planning the gala, the painstaking preparations and excitement all faded. Reggie knew in her heart that Cole would never understand what she was going through. Now she could never tell him about David. It was too late.

Cole was seething. He had been made to look like a fool in front of his friends and business associates. What the hell was going on between Reggie and Lee? And one thing was certain: whatever was going on, Lee would never tell him if Reggie had asked him not to.

As he turned, Cole bumped into David Astin. There was a peculiar twisted smile on Astin's face, as if he had overheard Cole's argument with his wife and was taking pleasure in it. Always go with your first instincts, Cole thought. He'd never liked this bastard. Now, more than ever, as he saw the snide grin on Astin's face, Cole berated himself silently for ever getting involved with him in a business deal.

"Weston, I've been searching all over for you. Francis managed to come downstairs for a while and we are all looking forward to meeting your beautiful bride. What did you say her name was?" asked David as he slipped his arm through Cole's.

Cole shook David from him. "Her name is Regina. Bring Francis and Patrice to the bar in five minutes and I'll introduce you. Oh, and do me a big favor, Astin. Keep your hands off my clothes." He stalked off to find Reggie.

David's smile widened in spite of Cole's rebuff. It was Reggie, just as he had thought. Somehow, and he didn't know how just yet, he was going to use that knowledge to his advantage. He went to find his father-in-law and his wife. He was looking forward to renewing his acquaintance with Reggie. That alone would make the trip to New York worthwhile.

Cole found Reggie talking to Simon Hastings and a blond woman whose back was to him. They were deeply engrossed in conversation when Cole joined them. Reggie turned nervously to her husband.

"Cole, you know Simon," she said lamely.

Cole nodded curtly.

"And this is Nikki Broad," Simon said as the handsome blond woman in her forties turned around. "Nikki is heading up our European division. She just returned to New York from Rome."

"Congratulations, Nikki," Cole said. "You had some stiff competition, but I think Simon made a wise choice. Best of luck with your new job. I'm sure we'll all be seeing a great deal of each other in the future." He turned to Reggie and said deliberately, "I see you've met Nikki. What do you think of Simon's choice?"

Simon stared first at Cole, then at Reggie. What was he doing? Simon knew how hurt and disappointed Reggie had been when she was turned down for this position. Even Nikki was surprised at the iciness in Cole's voice as he spoke.

"Well, Reggie, where's your drink?" Cole continued. "We have to propose a toast to Nikki and her new job, don't we?"

Quietly, Reggie spoke. "I already have. Nikki and I go back a long time, as I told you once before. I'm sure she doesn't remember." She let Nikki have the time to examine her. For the first time in their relationship, Reggie felt that she had a slight advantage. Whereas Reggie was in the prime of her life, young, beautiful and married to one of the wealthiest men in New York, Nikki's artfully made-up face did little to hide the age lines that radiated from the corners of her eyes. Her strong jawline that had once added beauty to her face, now hung with extra flesh. Nikki Broad needed a face lift. "Well, Nikki? Do you remember me?" asked Reggie.

Try as she might, Nikki couldn't place the face or the name. Both were vaguely familiar, but she couldn't trigger her memory. "I give up," she laughed. "Give me a hint."

Reggie bit her lip. She closed her eyes momentarily in thought. "Okay, here's your hint. I was eighteen, just starting out as a designer, and you bought my entire first line. Then, you copied every piece and passed it off as your own. Does that jog your memory?" Nikki and Simon gasped in unison, and Cole raised his eyebrows in disapproval. Reggie smiled. "So much for your brilliant choice, gentlemen." She slipped away and left the three of them staring after her. Simon was the first to break away, going after her. Cole put out his hand to stop him, but Simon ignored him. He caught up with Reggie as the band was beginning the opening strains of "What Kind of Fool Am I?"

"Dance?" he asked. "The melody is apropos."

She didn't answer as she slipped into his arms and they danced in silence. The floor was rapidly filling around them. Simon held her closely, feeling the outline of her body through the flimsy fabric of her gown. It made everything that much more difficult. He knew he was in love with Reggie but tried to push it from his mind. She belonged to someone else, and he had never broken up a marriage. He would not start now, regardless of what that marriage was. He had told her that much in Dallas when they had parted. Since that time, he had tried to keep their relationship on a business level. But she was the most beautiful woman he had ever met and the most outrageous.

"Reggie, why do you always have to upset the applecart?" he asked.

Never losing a step, she pulled away from him slightly. "Would you have preferred that I hadn't told you what I knew about her? Would you have preferred to go ahead without knowing the kind of woman you were involved with?" She sighed. "Do all men want to keep their heads buried in the sand? Is your ego damaged because I knew something that your investigations failed to pick up?"

"It has nothing to do with my ego. Why didn't you let me know about this before? Before I offered her the position, signed the contracts?" he demanded.

"Because neither you nor Cole asked me for my opinion before you filled the position."

Simon said nothing. Around and around the dance floor they twirled. Simon noticed Cole watching them carefully. If Reggie realized it, she gave no sign as she deliberately put her head on Simon's shoulder. She pressed her body closer to his. Simon saw Cole turn on his heel and walk to the bar.

"You can stop now. He saw," said Simon.

Reggie picked up her head. "What are you talking about?"

"Your husband, Reggie. He saw you trying to make him jealous."

"I don't know what you mean, Simon. I told you in Dallas what our marriage was all about. He means nothing to me." She suddenly felt like weeping.

"Perhaps that was true then," he mused. "But I think things have changed between you. Reggie, we had more than a casual evening together in Dallas. You never tried to pursue it. That tells me something. I don't know where it would have led," he continued, "but now that things have changed, don't you think you owe me some sort of an explanation?"

"I know what we experienced in Dallas," Reggie admitted. "I wasn't pretending with you. I thought . . . I wanted . . ." She tried to go on but couldn't find the words.

"Don't bother. It's written all over your face. I was there, I was available. It happens." Simon sighed. "Don't look so miserable. Go find your husband; tell him what you feel for him and stop playing games. If you love him and want him, go after him," Simon advised. "Do you know how few of us find what you've found? Don't play games and risk throwing it away."

"Thank you, Simon. It's just as rare to find a friend, you know." She squeezed his hand. His gold signet ring cut into his hand just as her words had pierced his heart.

I can't be just your friend, Reggie darling, he said to himself. But to her, he said, "I'll always be here for you. You know that."

Silently, she slipped from his arms and from his life. He had never told her that he hadn't even consulted with Cole on his choice for the European position. And that thought brought him back to the present and the problem of disposing of Nikki Broad. He straightened his cuffs, smoothed the creases from his burgundy velvet breeches and walked off to get a drink. He had earned one.

Chapter 40

Cole watched Simon and Reggie with mixed feelings. The rage that had threatened to erupt had finally been extinguished by the one emotion that had always come to his aid in the past—icy indifference. He felt as if his body had been drained of blood and replaced instead with pure ice water. Those who knew him well would have seen the transformation in his eyes. Those who didn't, would not have noticed anything.

Two people in the ballroom watched the change with dismay. One was his best friend, Lee, the other was someone who had seen it happen many, many times before. Ardith Weston's eyes hardened as she watched the glacial curtain descend over her son's face. Her eyes searched the room for Reggie. Would her daughter-in-law know how to handle Cole? Ardith had never been able to discover how to bring Cole back when he crossed over to that other world where no one was allowed to enter. Time was the only key that unlocked his heart. For Ardith, the evening was over. She wanted to go home. She made her way to the cloakroom, got her coat and walked to the door, where the doorman hailed a taxi for her. No one noticed her leave.

"There you are, Weston. We've been looking all over for you," David said. He went to place his arm around Cole's shoulders, remembered the prior warning, and quickly removed it.

Cole barely acknowledged David. He bypassed him and

walked over to Francis, giving him a bear hug. "It's good to see you, Francis. How are you feeling?"

"Lousy, thanks. But enough about me. Where's the magician who finally got you to the altar?"

Where, indeed! thought Cole as his eyes searched the room. The last time he had seen Reggie, she had been hanging all over Simon. Now he noticed that Simon was sitting at a small cocktail table with Nikki. Then he saw Reggie. She was standing in the corner of the room, deep in conversation with Gary Colby. The man was dressed as a troubador. His gaily colored costume was a perfect guise for him, thought Cole. He motioned to them but they paid no attention.

"Excuse me, Francis. I see my wife. Let me bring her over to meet you. We've hardly been able to spend a moment together all evening." He didn't tell his guests that she had been so busy with other men that she hadn't had time for him. He stormed over to her. She looked up in surprise.

"Cole, I was just complimenting Gary on the wonderful job he did tonight." She waited for Cole to agree, but he said nothing. Gary, who would never forgive Cole's behavior that night in Reggie's office, became angrier at Cole's indifference to Reggie.

"If you can tear yourself away," Cole said disdainfully, "the Astins are waiting to meet you. Would you mind coming with me?" He strode back to the bar, leaving Reggie to follow alone.

She steeled herself for the inevitable meeting. Her only hope was that in the years that had passed she had changed so much that David wouldn't remember her. She stole a glance at herself in one of the mirrored columns. Older, more sophisticated perhaps, but the changes in her appearance were less than she would have liked. David would recognize her. She thought fleetingly about Nikki. They had both known her at the same time and Nikki hadn't had any idea who Reggie was. But, of course, Reggie thought ruefully, Nikki had only met her twice.

She approached the bar. David's eyes widened slightly as Cole introduced Reggie as his wife.

"Mrs. Weston," David repeated. "How do you do?"

Did he recognize her? Surely if he had, he would have given some indication. She searched his eyes as they shook hands.

No, she was sure there was nothing there. Cole made the other introductions. She acknowledged Francis and Patrice, yet stealthily watched David's face. Still there was no sign that he recognized her. Reggie let out a silent sigh of relief. All her worrying had obviously been needless.

Their voices were lost as the band started another set. David watched Reggie. Very cool, Mrs. Weston. But why the charade? he wondered. Where's the recognition, the surprise? Not for a moment did David doubt that Reggie remembered him. What was the purpose of keeping it a secret? Until he understood her motive and decided if it could be used to his advantage, he would play her game.

"Patrice," suggested David, "why don't you dance with Cole. I'd love the chance to talk to Mrs. Weston."

Reggie was about to refuse when Cole took Patrice by the hand and led her out to the floor.

"Shall we?" asked David, politely.

Reggie followed silently. The tempo changed from contemporary to a classic from the early seventies. David put his arms around Reggie and said, "How nice of them to play this just for us. Just like old times?"

She pulled away from him. "You knew all along?"

He drew her quickly back into his arms. "Didn't you think I'd recognize you? I saw you as soon as I walked in, but then you disappeared."

Reggie said nothing.

David waited. He was very good at waiting. Sooner or later Reggie would slip, explain why she hadn't acknowledged their past.

"What have you been doing all these years, David?" she asked finally. Her tone was light, casual. "I understand you've made quite a name for yourself in the Midwest."

"Where did you hear that?"

"From Cole, I guess, or possibly Lee Taggett. Have you known my husband long?" She was trying to stay on safe topics. Had she any children, she would have spoken about nursery schools and diapers.

"Yes, I've known him almost as long as I've known Patrice."

"And how long is that?"

"Patrice and I have known each other since I was about

eighteen. We were engaged before I came to New York to go to law school."

"You were engaged when we were—the whole time in New York you had a fiancée in Chicago?" She pulled away so she could see the expression on his face.

He drew her back closer into his arms. "Reggie, how could I have ever known that I would meet someone like you? Do you have any idea how painful it was for me? To be torn like that?"

"Like what?" she asked innocently. He had no right to talk about pain! She was the one who had been left, abandoned while he'd gone home to his nice, safe, comfortable life.

"To be torn between staying in New York with the one woman I truly loved, yet knowing that Patrice and the whole future we'd planned was waiting for me back in Chicago?" The words rolled off his tongue like greased ball bearings. "My God! For months after I left New York, I wanted to die!"

I wish you had, you bastard! she thought to herself. If the room wasn't filled with people, if she wasn't a lady and if Cole wasn't involved in a multi-billion dollar deal with him, Reggie would have liked nothing better than to have slapped David's face. Instead, she gave him her brightest smile. "All's well that ends well, I suppose. And it does seem like we've both survived. You know, I never could figure out where you disappeared to or why I never heard from you again."

"Does it matter now? Now that we're together again?" he asked in a smooth, oily voice that made Reggie want to retch.

You just bet it does, you bastard, she thought. I can still remember what it felt like . . . the pain, the betrayal. What a complete ass I was. "We're hardly together again, David. You're very much married and so am I."

He shrugged. "So? There are ways of getting around that. . . . Neither one of us was born yesterday. By the way," he asked in an offhand manner, "have you ever told Cole about us?"

Her head jerked up in surprise. "Have you ever mentioned our little affair to Patrice?" she countered, trying to figure out what David was up to. If there was such a thing as a sixth sense, Reggie's was working overtime. She could almost hear the wheels turning in David's head.

"Are you nuts?" he asked, genuinely shocked. "Why would

I ever risk something like that?" He pulled her very close and she felt his rigid erection against her stomach. She tried to draw away, but the pressure of his hand against the small of her back made it impossible. "Now see what you do to me?" he whispered, grinding his hips into her. "What you've always done to me? We can have this again . . . only better now. Reggie, Reggie. I've missed you so!"

"So this would be our little secret, right?" she asked, her head pounding in anger.

He moved his hand around her back so that his fingers were touching the edge of her breast. It was an unmistakable gesture. The pressure increased as he tried to insinuate his thigh between her legs. "You know the expression, 'you scratch my back and I'll scratch yours'? You just see to it that your husband goes ahead with the Stockyard deal and I'll be in New York every weekend."

So, that was the deal. David was frightened that Cole would pull out of David's big venture. Sure, she thought, with me in his pocket, I'd be able to influence Cole in his favor. Like hell, I will!

"David, darling," she began, placing her mouth seductively against his ear.

"Hmm?"

"I think you're the lowest scum that crawls on this earth. Not only am I uninterested in starting anything with you, I'm going to do everything I can to see that my husband doesn't do business with you. I wouldn't trust you in a business deal any more than I would trust a snake. Go slither back to whatever hole you escaped from." With that she pulled herself out of his arms and walked off the dance floor, leaving him standing by himself.

How dare she, he thought, as he wiped the moisture from his upper lip. Just who the hell did she think she was? No one, no one would destroy everything he had so carefully constructed. He would stop her. As he walked off the floor in search of a sorely needed drink, David was shaking with rage. He'd fix her . . . just the way he always fixed anyone that got in his way.

At 2:30 A.M. Cole and Reggie began saying good night to their guests. Neither had spoken more than a few necessary words to the other. Reggie cringed as she saw David, Patrice and Francis heading in their direction.

Francis shook hands with Cole, thanking him for the lovely evening and making arrangements for future meetings. Patrice smiled and said nothing, waiting for David to speak for her.

"It's been a long night, Cole," David said. "I'm going to hustle Francis and Patrice upstairs. Thank you both for a wonderful party and congratulations on your marriage. Cole, you've made a fine choice, believe me, a fine choice." He leaned over to kiss Reggie's cheek. She recoiled in disgust. "I'm sorry, did I startle you?"

"A little," she said. Cole gave her an odd look.

"I was simply saying good night, my dear," said David with a glint in his eye. "Next time I will be very careful." He took Patrice's arm and led her and Francis from the room.

Cole and Reggie were left standing alone. He glanced at her and opened his mouth as if to say something, then changed his mind and left the room.

Reggie felt as if her life were collapsing. The only one left she could depend on was Lee. She went in search of him. He would make everything all right.

I'm a successful young businesswoman, married to one of the most sought-after men in the world, and yet, here I am alone, in the center of the Grand Ballroom of the Regency Hotel, as afraid for my future as I was back on West Fourth Street. It was Lee who had saved her then. It would be Lee who would save her now. But as her eyes scanned the nearly empty room, she saw no sign of him. He had already gone.

The ride home was unnaturally quiet. Cole sat on his side of the limousine deep in thought. Reggie tried to engage him in conversation several times, but to no avail. Finally, she gave up, joining him in stony silence. They parted company in the entryway of the townhouse. Cole nodded a curt good-night, taking the stairs two at a time. Reggie put her silver and diamond minaudiere on the marble sideboard, shrugged off her sable coat and headed to the study.

She was far too agitated to find solace in the loneliness of her bedroom, and she didn't think she would find a welcome in her husband's bed tonight. Even at this late hour, there was a small fire glowing in the fireplace. Kicking off her sandals, she walked to the bar, poured herself a small snifter of cognac and slipped to the floor, tucking her feet under her. Thoughtfully, she sipped the smooth liquor. Logic and reason escaped her as she tried to retrace the events that had led to the evening's disaster. She stared into the dying embers.

She couldn't blame Cole. With three hundred people waiting to congratulate them on what should have been the brightest night of their lives, she had disappeared. She couldn't blame him for being annoyed when she wouldn't tell him what was upsetting her. And, she rationalized silently, he had every right to be angrier still when he knew that she had confided in Lee, not him. She shivered as she remembered the look on his face.

She took another sip of her drink. The door to the study opened slowly. Cole stood there, his face impassive. She looked up at him in surprise.

"Did you forget something?" she asked.

He ignored her as he walked to the bar, uncapped a cut-crystal decanter and poured himself a generous helping of brandy. His back was to her so she couldn't see his face. She repeated the question.

Slowly, swirling the amber liquid in the goblet, he turned to face her. "I just got an interesting phone call," he said. The expression on his face was unchanged.

She glanced at the clock on the mantel. "At almost four o'clock in the morning?"

He nodded his head. "I thought it was odd, myself."

"Who was it, Cole?" Her heart began to beat faster.

He stared down into her eyes. "I was hoping you might be able to tell me."

"Me?" Her voice was much too high. She cleared her throat. "How would I know? You took the call. What did the caller say?"

"She told me that the mole on the inside of your left buttock should be removed."

"What?!"

Cole let out a long sigh. "Mmm, she said it might become malignant someday."

Viselike bands constricted her heart. She tried to rise but her legs wouldn't obey her command. She sank down into the rug.

With great precision of movement, Cole stepped over her, moving to the wing chair. He sat down, putting his feet up on the ottoman. He stared long and hard at his wife. "Would you happen to have any idea why someone would be so concerned with your health at four A.M. in the morning?"

"Cole, this must be a joke. Why would anyone do that?"

He shrugged. "I couldn't tell you. By the way," he said conversationally, "do you have a mole there?"

"Yes, as a matter of fact, I do. So what?" she asked, angrily.

"That's what I would like to know. Incidentally, I never knew about the mole. This night is filled with surprises," he reflected.

A log fell in the grate, disturbing the silence that had fallen over the room. Reggie made a move to readjust it. She picked up the poker and tried to reposition the remaining logs. She concentrated on the task as if it were the single most important thing she had ever had to do.

Cole watched silently. He knew his wife well . . . very, very well. He knew she was stalling for time, thinking, searching for a way to answer him. What's the mystery, Reg? he thought. What's so earth-shatteringly distressing that you can't tell me? What is it that I can't know but Lee can? Patiently, he waited as she played with the burning cinders. Finally, she resumed her position on the rug, cross-legged, her gown hiked up above her knees. He studied her long graceful legs; from his chair, he could see part of her thigh.

"Where's the mole, Reg?" he asked quietly.

"Oh, Christ, Cole! What the hell difference does it make?"

He jumped from his chair, and in two steps he was standing over her, pulling her to her feet. "Where's the fucking mole!" he shouted.

She wrenched her arm from his grasp, pulled her gown down to her ankles and stood facing him defiantly. "It's on my left buttock where it's always been. I told you that and if that answer doesn't satisfy you, it's too damned bad! I've had enough of this interrogation. If it's so all-fired offensive to everyone, I'll have the goddamned thing removed. Have you finished?"

"Not quite."

"Oh, there's more?"

"Who called me?"

"How am I supposed to know?"

"Who knows about the mole?"

"Cole, do you have any idea what you sound like? Do you realize how insane this conversation is?" she asked.

"You're stalling, Reg. You haven't answered the question, and don't try to turn this around and put me on the defensive. I asked you a simple question. A simple answer will do."

For a fleeting second she was tempted to tell him her suspicions. She knew very well who had called Cole. Or if she didn't know exactly who had placed the actual phone call, she was fairly certain she knew who had instigated it. But at that moment, after the ugly way he had been interrogating her, she felt she didn't owe him an explanation. Instead, she smiled sweetly and said, "Very well. My parents know. My family doctor knows, and I expect the obstetrician who delivered me must have noticed it, too. Then there are my sisters and brothers . . ."

"Good night, Reggie," he said and walked out of the room. He closed the door quietly behind him. The courage that had held her up fled the moment he left the room, and she crumpled to the floor. She remained there until the first rays of sun peeked through the drapes. Wearily, she made her way through the silent house to her room and collapsed on the bed.

Patrice sat in the corner of the king-size bed holding a wet towel to her face. The phone lay off the hook next to her. Her body was shaking, perspiration glistened on her white skin. She looked fearfully at her husband, who was pacing back and forth in the confines of their bedroom. She had seen it all before, had felt the stinging blows from the back of his hand when first she had refused to cooperate with him. The pain didn't bother her much anymore. It was the threat of no more medicine. When he wouldn't give her the medicine she always gave in, consented to anything he wanted.

"David, please!" she pleaded. He didn't pay any attention to her. "David, I did it. I called. You said I could have a shot if I called. You promised."

Mechanically, he walked to the dresser, opened the drawer and withdrew his shaving kit. With his back to her, he fingered the hypodermic wrapped neatly in cellophane. He picked up the vial that contained the liquid which kept Patrice his slave. He turned to face her. Her sleeve was pushed up.

"The next time I won't ask you twice," he said. "Do you understand?"

She lay back on the pillows, the towel dropping from her cheek revealing a purplish bruise. "I understand, David. I didn't know how important it was."

"You don't have to know. You just have to do what I tell you."

As he inserted the needle in her arm, she closed her eyes, wishing she could blot out his voice forever.

When he left the study, Cole returned to his bedroom, but sleep eluded him. A restlessness invaded him and, by five A.M., when New York is the color of day-old snow, he dressed quickly in an old gray hooded sweat shirt, sweat pants and sneakers. He tied an old towel around his neck and headed for the street.

Starting slowly, at an easy stride, he soon worked himself into a rapid run. His long, muscular legs ate up the pavement as block after city block sped by. He lost all awareness of time and place. Sunday morning pedestrians, walking their dogs or heading for the newsstands nodded as he ran past. He took no notice, his mind and body on another plane. His only conscious thought was to keep moving. One more block, one more mile. By six thirty, his muscles were starting to protest. Sweat poured from his body as he ripped off his sweat shirt in the chill, early morning. He slowed his place, allowing his body to recover slowly from the punishing abuse. Soon he was trotting again, still refusing to stop, afraid to allow his mind to dwell on the previous evening.

By seven, he was walking. The sweat shirt was on again. He checked a street sign—Wall Street and Broadway. He had run from Sixty-eighth Street, crosstown to Fifth Avenue, entered Central Park on Seventy-second Street, looped the park twice and exited on Fifty-ninth Street. Without stopping to think, he had continued down Broadway, past Canal Street, Little Italy and Chinatown, into the financial district. Finally, exhausted, he came to stop in front of Trinity Church. He stood with his hands on his hips, drawing irregular breaths, as he wondered how he was going to get home. He had run out without so much as a quarter for a phone call. He had to find a no-coin phone booth where he could call Lee. He had no desire to go home and face his wife's lies again.

Chapter 41

Cole walked four blocks and found every corner phone either out of order or with its receiver missing. Slowly he began the long walk north toward Lee's SoHo address. He cursed his stupidity as the perspiration began to evaporate and the cold morning air seeped into his body. He shivered, swearing silently at the lunacy that had driven him from the warmth of his home into the icy dampness of the November morning. Ten more minutes of walking and, finally, Cole's aching knees made him surrender. He flagged a passing taxi, gave the Filipino driver Lee's address and prayed that his friend would be home with the needed fare.

The cab pulled up in front of an old factory building. The sign BUCK'S TOOL AND DIE was barely legible on the facade. The driver turned to Cole.

"You sure this is the right address, mister? This place isn't open anymore."

Cole nodded. "I know. A friend of mine bought the building and is renovating it. Wait here a minute, I have to go get some money."

"What the hell do you mean you have to get some money? How do I know you'll come back? This city isn't famous for honest people."

"Here." Cole took a gold watch from his wrist. "If I'm not back in five minutes, it's yours." He checked the taxi meter.

"It's worth a helluva lot more than three dollars." He opened the door.

"Wait a minute," said the driver. "How do you know that I won't pull away with this?"

"I don't, but you have to trust someone, don't you?"

The Filipino shook his head. "Not in this city, you don't."

Cole thought about Reggie. "You're right. Not in this city."

He rang the buzzer more than a dozen times before he was able to rouse Lee. Unable to explain his situation quickly, Cole simply rushed past him into the apartment and pulled a twenty dollar bill from Lee's trousers.

"I owe you," Cole said over his shoulder. "Put up some coffee, I'll be right back."

The taxi was gone. Cole couldn't believe his eyes as he searched the empty street. He crumbled the twenty into a ball in his fist. Cursing, he re-entered Lee's building, where Lee was measuring coffee.

"What happened?" Lee asked as Cole threw the twenty dollar bill on the counter.

"I took the world's first seven thousand dollar cab ride."

As Cole explained about the watch, Lee had to turn his back to hide his smile. He busied himself with separating bacon slices. "So you were taken. It happens every day in Manhattan. Besides, the watch wasn't so great."

"You actually find this amusing, don't you?"

Lee turned. "Come on, Cole. If I had burst into your house at this hour and told you this story, wouldn't you find it funny?"

"No, I wouldn't!"

Lee smiled. "Yeah, you would. You didn't happen to get his ID number or his name?"

"No, I didn't!"

"Weston, you're getting careless," observed Lee.

"You don't know the half of it," admitted Cole.

"Then there *is* more to this story. I thought it was unusually friendly of you to pop in on me this way, especially after last night. When do I get to hear the rest?"

"After my shower," he said and headed for the bathroom.

The steaming water felt wonderful on Cole's chilled, exhausted body. He let the powerful spray beat down on him while he stood still inside the enclosure. Finally, he picked up the soap and began to lather himself. The sleepless night was beginning to catch up with him. He sat down on the marble ledge, letting his head rest on the smooth wall. If and when he decided to leave the shower, and he wasn't one hundred percent sure that he ever wanted to, he would have to sort out what was happening to Reggie and him. He didn't want to.

He closed his eyes, picturing her lying in his arms, her breath sweet on his face. Images of their weekend in the Adirondacks flashed through his mind, the fireplace, the rug where they had made love for hours, the tiny sailboat. Unconsciously, he reached out as if he could summon her presence. Was he ready to give her up? he wondered. His first thought was no, until he remembered the middle-of-the-night phone call and her refusal to answer his questions. How was it possible to love and hate someone with the same intensity?

"Are you coming out?" called Lee. "Breakfast is ready."

"Yeah," he shouted. "I'll be right there." He rinsed off the soap, shook himself and stepped into the heated room. An orange glow from the infrared lamp cast an eerie light against the black marble. Cole shivered in distaste. He slipped into a terry-cloth robe he found hanging on the back of the door. Casting a final look at himself in the too-small robe, he noticed he needed a shave. His body instantly rejected the thought. Too tired.

"I made screwdrivers," Lee said as Cole reached for the juice glass. "You looked like you could use something stronger than orange juice."

Silently, Cole ate breakfast. Lee waited for him to explain the reason for the unexpected visit. As the last bits of egg and bacon went into his mouth, Cole finally spoke. "I want to know what you and Reggie were discussing last night when I found you two on the mezzanine."

"Have you asked your wife?"

"Not in so many words, but she knew damn well that I wanted to know, and she wouldn't offer any explanation. I expect that you will enlighten me."

"I'm sorry, Cole. I know she's your wife and you're due some sort of explanation, but not from me. Whatever Reggie told me was said in confidence. I can't betray that," Lee explained.

"So you would betray me instead?" Cole asked angrily.

"I'm doing no such thing! You haven't told me anything confidentially—she has."

"What was it?" Cole demanded.

"What the hell is the matter with you?" His voice rose. "I just finished telling you that I wouldn't reveal anything about that conversation. I am no more or less a friend to her than I am to you. Stop trying to make me take sides in this. I won't do it!"

Cole pushed his chair slowly away from the table, folded his napkin at his place and stood up. "I am not making you take sides; it appears that you already have." He shrugged out of the robe, donning his damp sweat suit once more. A shiver ran through him as the clammy clothing touched his skin. "Lee, there is something unpleasant going on and you know what it is. For some reason, I'm to be kept in the dark. That is neither a position I care for nor one in which I intend to remain for long. Therefore, I would advise you to tell your little friend that I will undoubtedly find out what the mystery is sooner or later. If the two of you don't choose to tell me, I will find out elsewhere. But, rest assured, I will find out!"

He picked up the crumpled twenty dollar bill from the table and put it in his sock. "I'm borrowing this until tomorrow. I'll see you in the office in the morning." He walked toward the door, stopped and turned. "Thanks for the shower and the breakfast." He closed the door.

As soon as Cole left, Lee slammed his fist down on the table. Why in God's name had he ever gotten involved between the two of them? He cursed the day he had suggested that Cole might be able to lend Reggie the money to save her business. It would have been better for everyone concerned if the goddamned business had folded.

Most people who live in Manhattan have a Sunday routine, especially in the fall and winter months, and Reggie's hadn't changed since the first weekend she'd arrived in New York. She would wake up late, wrap herself in a voluptuous robe—years ago it had been chenille, now it was velour—wash her face, brush her teeth, run a comb through her hair and settle down to brunch with the Sunday *Times*. With her first cup of coffee, she perused Sections A and B, examining the fashions and checking both the advertisements and the editorials on women's apparel. Occasionally, she would pick up a trend or an idea that she would incorporate into a line.

With cup number two, it was the Magazine section. First, she would flip through the ads, the glossy pictures that tempted womankind to buy. More often than not, one of her own designs would grace these pages. Finally, she would skim the magazine's editorials on fashion and accessories. She hardly ever gleaned new information from this source since the fashion editors only raped the trade papers or the European fashion shows for their information. Reggie knew far before they did what was news and what wasn't.

With breakfast, she would finally settle down to read the news stories and feature articles, saving the crossword puzzle, which she did in ballpoint pen, for the remainder of the day. She very rarely left the house on Sunday. It was her only day of rest, and generally she felt she had earned it.

But this particular Sunday, Reggie didn't want to stay home. Though she had had barely four hours of sleep, she was awake, showered and dressed by nine thirty. At nine forty-five, she called Alison and asked her if she would mind working for a while. Alison was reluctant but finally agreed. They arranged to meet at eleven with Reggie promising to provide coffee and danish.

As she walked into the dining room, hoping for a croissant and coffee before she left, she was assaulted by the odor of frying sausage. Her stomach turned. Too little sleep, she thought. Then she remembered the light-headedness of the night before. I must be getting sick, she thought. Alison had been out most of the week before with the flu and perhaps she had given it to Reggie. It would certainly account for the lousy way she felt this morning. She didn't have time to get sick now. She had let business slide while she'd been preparing for the reception.

As her thoughts returned to the previous night's fiasco, she grimaced. What she needed now was to get back to work. Her holiday line had only been so-so, designed quickly on the backs of envelopes. The name Raggs had been enough to sell it, but Reggie knew that a name, even a good one, would only carry an indifferent line so far. She would have to come up with a hot idea for spring.

Faced with the challenge of designing a new line, she was

able to push all thoughts of her marriage, Cole and David to the back of her mind. As she closed the front door behind her, she marveled at the capacity of the human mind to repress.

She and Alison worked diligently throughout the morning and well into the afternoon. Alison filled her in on all that had happened in the last few weeks, and Reggie was amazed at her assistant's complete grasp of the business. Reggie complimented her.

"Someone had to do it, Reg," Alison said, somewhat apologetically. "Your mind was a million miles away. I wasn't sure you'd ever come back. I mean really come back. I haven't seen you work this hard since you got married."

"Well, I am back. Marriage was nice—" She paused, realizing that she had inadvertently used the past tense. Then she pointed to the sketches she had made, the scraps of fabric pinned to each one and the color chips. "This is what makes me breathe. I think we have the beginnings of something spectacular here. Don't you?"

It was an inspired collection. Reggie had reached deep into her vast knowledge of fashion, from the schoolgirl uniforms of *Parisiennes* to the military of the Eisenhower era to come up with a cruise-spring line that featured cropped jackets, new sleek, slim skirts and crisply tailored trousers. Jackets were the predominant theme of the line. Graphic red and black short jackets for luncheon suits, double-breasted schoolgirl blazers paired with short saucy skirts and walking shorts, one button spencers and full back-buttoned blouson jackets highlighted the collection. The clothes were angular, the colors fragile. Reggie had mixed white with tremendous amounts of mauve, mint, lilac, daffodil and powder blue. She tried to explain the concept to Alison.

"The cuts are all masculine, the colors and fabrics are feminine. That's what makes it interesting. It's like opening a new book. You think you know what it's going to be about by the cover, but when you read it, you're surprised. Understand?"

Alison laughed. "It's wonderful."

"Oh, I want to use pearls," Reggie continued. "Strands and strands of them. Use seed pearls for the lapels of the ivory dinner suit and accessorize the white wool sailor suit with at least six different lengths and sizes of them. Also," she said as she made some notes on her sketch pad, "the band on the white straw boater—forget the grosgrain ribbon and do it in pearls."

Alison finished taking notes and checked her watch. "Reg, it's after four. Don't you have to get home?"

"Not really. But I don't want to keep you here. You can leave. I still want to work on the active-wear collection. I'm going down for something to eat, then I'll come back here to work. I want Inez to start the first samples tomorrow morning."

"I don't have to rush home. If you're staying, I'll keep you company. Let me go down and get us something to eat," Alison suggested.

Reggie had a pencil in her mouth and was chewing thoughtfully on the eraser. She took it out and stared at it. "I guess you'd better. This is my sixth eraser today. Do you feel like Chinese food?"

"Fine." Alison picked up her battered trenchcoat and handbag. All the way to Chun Fu, she thought about Reggie. She was more than a little puzzled by the zeal Reggie was showing. She hadn't seen her boss work with so much intensity in months. It was getting dark as Alison hurried through the streets, bucking the rising winds. Leaves swirled around her legs and a small branch whipped her calf, causing her to wince. The sky looked ominous and Alison was thinking that perhaps they ought to call it a day. She walked into the restaurant and made her way to the phone. She dialed the factory number. Reggie picked up on the second ring.

"Reg, I'm in Chun Fu but there's a terrible storm blowing up outside. Maybe you should close up and meet me here for a quick bite and we'll head home."

"No," Reggie said. "You go ahead. I really want to finish up. I have some marvelous sketches. I'll see you in the morning."

"Nothing doing," Alison said. "I'll be back soon. If you're staying, so am I. Do you want egg rolls?"

"Whatever you want is fine with me. Just get me a pint of hot and sour soup."

Reggie felt much better than she had that morning. Whatever bug she thought she was getting seemed to have passed.

Now she was looking forward to Szechuan specialties. The room had grown considerably darker since Alison had left. Reggie walked around the loft, turning on all the overhead lights. There, she thought. That was much better. She sat down to look over her drawings.

Yet as she flipped through her sketchpad, the images blurred, her eyes filling with tears. . . . She was so very, very alone. What was happening to her marriage? Was it her fault or Cole's or were they both to blame? She tried to study the problem as she would attack an unacceptable line of clothing. Start with the premise. What was it they were trying to accomplish? In the beginning, the working hypothesis of their commitment to each other had been a marriage of convenience, set forth by Cole, under his conditions, with Reggie complying only under extreme duress. She had hated him then. And he? How had he really felt about her? She shook off the question. It was irrelevant whether he had admired her or had been ambivalent. The premise had remained the same. Neither one of them was supposed to be in love with each other.

Somewhere along the way, though, their feelings for each other had warmed. They had believed the marriage could function if she accepted it as she would a job: services rendered, fee paid. Then suddenly, all bets were off. Love entered; nowhere had there been a proviso for that contingency in the contract she had signed. Yet, in declaring his love for her, Cole had never given back her complete control of her patent. He hadn't even made the suggestion that they return to the lawyers to nullify the premarital agreement. Did he still hope to hold her to her side of their bargain with it? Was he that skeptical and doubtful of her that he still needed the edge? Did he still consider her an adversary?

She tried to examine her motives for marrying Cole. Yes, she had married him to save her company. Yes, she had resented him, hated him for having the power to force her into marriage. Did she still feel that resentment? Was that the real reason she was keeping her relationship with David a secret? Not because she was afraid that Cole wouldn't love her anymore, but that he would call in his debt, stripping her of all her possessions if he found out. If that was the case, and the more she thought about it, the more she thought it might be, then the spiral would continue forever. Unless they changed the original premise under which they had married, the hidden resentments would always remain. Until their positions were redefined, a real relationship was impossible. She would go on trying to prove to him that she was a model wife so he wouldn't have cause to revert to the clause in their contract that allowed either party the right to huge reparations if misconduct occurred. She was in no better position than she had been before they had fallen in love. If anything, her present position was much worse. Now she desperately wanted the marriage to last.

Suddenly, Reggie wanted to go home. She needed to speak to Cole, to explain what she had just discovered. If they truly loved each other, then he would see why it was imperative to destroy the contract and the premarital agreement before it destroyed them. She would wait for Alison to return with dinner, apologize and send her home. She hoped Alison would understand.

Twenty minutes later Reggie heard the creaking elevator making its laborious trip to the fourth floor. Thank God, Reggie thought. She was so anxious to speak to Cole that butterflies were skipping around her stomach. Alison pushed open the steel door to the loft, and the sight of her made Reggie gasp.

"What happened to you?" she asked as she took the water-logged cardboard box from Alison's arms. Alison's hair streamed around her face. Her eyeliner and mascara ran down her cheeks; her battered trenchcoat was plastered to her body.

"The storm. I told you there was a storm coming." She shivered. Her shoes, jeans, shirt and underwear were soaking wet.

Reggie couldn't bear to send Alison back into the rain. She helped her undress, placing the dripping clothes over the huge steam radiators that surrounded the loft. She handed her a model's robe.

"It's not that warm," Reggie said apologetically, "but at least it's dry." Alison's teeth had finally stopped chattering as she hunched over one of the radiators trying to absorb some heat. "Stay there until you thaw out. I'll set dinner up in my office and we can eat in there. Maybe the weather will let up a little and we can get out of here."

Alison looked up as Reggie retreated to the back of the room. "I thought you were staying late to do the active-wear line. Don't tell me I made this trip for nothing," she moaned.

"I'm sorry, Alison. I thought I would stay but I changed my mind."

"Just like that?"

"It's a long story. I would explain but you'd never understand. You see, I have something else on my mind besides the line, and you know I can't do two things at once," Reggie said, trying to lighten the mood. Alison had every right to be furious, but Reggie couldn't discuss her marital problems with her just now. It was bad enough that she had involved Lee. That was another piece of unfinished business. She had to explain her little tête-à-tête with Lee to Cole.

All she wanted to do was to eat, clean up and go home. Hurriedly, she opened the sodden carton. Spicy, greasy scents smacked her in the face. She felt the familiar upheaval in her stomach, and she began to gag. Holding her hand in front of her mouth, she ran for the bathroom, hoping to get there before she heaved onto the floor. She ripped open the bathroom door, taking deep gulps of air, valiantly trying to fight the rising tide of nausea. She fell to her knees in front of the bowl as she began tasting the contents of her stomach. Perspiration covered her face as she continued to wretch, long after her stomach was empty. Reggie looked up. Alison was standing behind her, a worried look on her face. Reggie attempted to make some sort of explanation but her throat was raw. With trembling hands, Reggie tried to flush the toilet, but her hands were shaking too badly. Alison reached over to help. Then she took a handful of towels from the dispenser, wet them with cold water and, helping Reggie to her feet, led her back to her office.

"I can't go back in there," Reggie pleaded in a tiny voice.

Alison peeked through the door noting the open carton of Chinese food. She turned Reggie around and helped her walk back into the main area of the loft. She pushed her gently into a chair, placing a cool towel on her forehead with one hand and wiping her mouth with another.

"Sit here," she ordered. "I'm going to clean up and then we'll talk." She left, and Reggie leaned her head against the chair's backrest. She had felt it coming all weekend. Now, she knew for certain that she was sick. She placed her hand on her forehead. Although it was clammy, she didn't have a fever yet. She wanted to go home, crawl into her bed and be miserable alone. Even the thought of her impending conversation with Cole lost its importance. She simply didn't have the strength for it tonight. A wave of pure exhaustion swept over her and she felt herself drifting off.

"Here." Alison was standing over her. "Drink this." She handed Reggie a mug of hot, sweet tea. "Don't gulp it, just sip it. If nothing else, it will take the lousy taste out of your mouth." She pulled over a stool and settled next to Reggie. Like a mother hen, she watched carefully as Reggie nursed the soothing drink. Neither one spoke until Reggie had managed to empty the mug to the halfway mark.

Like a sick child, Reggie handed the mug back. "Did I drink enough?" she asked.

Alison laughed. "How should I know? I only gave it to you because I didn't know what else to do. How do you feel?"

"A little better," admitted Reggie. She tried to stand, but Alison pushed her gently back into the chair.

"Stay there for a little while. Do you want me to call Cole to send a car or to come get you?"

"No!" Reggie answered.

"Okay, Okay. I'm sorry I even suggested it. I just thought it would be easier than trying to find a cab in this rain."

"You can't call him because he's—he's in a very important meeting right now," she stammered.

Alison checked her watch and eyed Reggie suspiciously. "At five thirty on Sunday night? Who's kidding whom, Reg?"

"No, really. It's with those Chicago people. I told you they were coming in for the reception. Besides, I don't want him to know I'm sick."

"Why not? Does he dock you?"

In spite of herself, Reggie smiled. "Of course not! It's just that I wasn't feeling great last night, either, and I know he'll give me a hard time about coming in to work today, and I'm just not up to arguing."

Alison wondered why Reggie was lying. She didn't have to be a brain surgeon to figure out what sickness Reggie had. Sure, a stomach virus or a bout of the flu was a possibility, but

Alison would have bet a month's salary that there was nothing wrong with Reggie that wouldn't be cured in about eight more months.

"Have you . . . ?" Alison began.

"Have I what?"

She decided against speaking her mind. "Have you had a physical lately?" she asked. "You push yourself too hard. I'm sure you haven't any idea the toll this reception and running a business has taken on you. Why don't you see your doctor? Maybe you need B-12 shots or iron. Then, if I were you, I'd take a long vacation."

Reggie shook her head. "I'm fine. I swear. I feel much better already. I just don't think I ought to eat Chinese food tonight."

"I agree," Alison said. "But what about a little broth from the won ton soup?" She went back to the office for the container and stood like a sentinel while Reggie sipped the broth.

"Alison, I can't drink any more. I'm floating."

"I don't care if you float as long as you don't throw up again. And promise me that you'll see your doctor."

Reggie sighed. "If I still feel lousy, I will. I promise."

"Okay. Let's get the hell out of here."

Chapter 42

Reggie was surprised to find the house dark when her cab pulled up to the front of the brownstone. She had fully expected to find Cole waiting for her. He was not. Nor were there any signs of John or Elsa. She roamed through the empty house turning on lights. Quickly, she entered the kitchen, pulled out a mug from the cabinet and prepared another cup of tea. She was eager to get upstairs to her own room.

Then she saw the florist's box propped up on the kitchen table. Tucked carefully into the bright red ribbon was a piece of her own stationery: cream-colored Crane paper with three pale taupe initials written on it . . . RAW. How she and Cole had laughed at her new monogram when they had chosen the note paper at Cartier. She unfolded the stationery. "These were delivered while you were out. I opened them accidentally. Sorry. Cole."

She stared at the long, glossy, white box with a mixture of curiosity and foreboding. Chiding herself for being ridiculous, she reluctantly drew the top off and cast it aside. Carefully, she separated the layers of green tissue to reveal two roses just beginning to bloom. One rose had been sprayed silver, the other gold. How odd, she thought as she searched the tissue for a card. She found it under the flowers. In small, cramped handwriting, the message read: "Make new friends, but keep the old; one is silver, the other's gold." She dropped the card to the floor as if she had been burned. David!

Had Cole read the note? Of course. How else would he know that the flowers were not meant for him? Suddenly, in an action born as much from fear as disgust, she picked up the floral box, ran to the back door, threw it wide open and, with as much strength as she possessed, flung it into the teaming rain. She slammed the door, leaning on it to make sure they remained outside. Slowly the fear turned to rage. How dare he! No, David, I won't allow this! I will not see my whole life go up in smoke while you play your sick, twisted games. The time had come to tell Cole everything she knew about David Astin. In fact, she thought with a heavy heart, the time was long past.

The phone rang and she jumped to answer it, hoping it was Cole. She picked it up breathlessly.

"Hello?"

There was no response from the other end of the line.

"Hello?" she said again. "Hello?"

"Are you home alone?" whispered a female voice.

Reggie's hand began to shake. "Who is this?"

"Are you alone? I have to speak to you," whispered the caller again. "Please don't hang up."

"Yes, I'm alone," Reggie admitted finally. "Who is this?"

There was a long silence. "I have to hang up. Someone is coming. Stay off the phone, please," pleaded the voice. "I'll call you back." Reggie heard the click of a receiver.

The hair on the back of Reggie's neck stood up. She was terrified. The phone rang again. This time Reggie simply stared at it, lacking the courage to pick it up. It continued to ring incessantly as she grabbed her handbag and fled from the kitchen to the safety of her bedroom. She slammed the door and locked it, but the phone still rang. Whoever was calling wasn't going to stop until she answered. Her hand reached for the phone, knocking over her handbag as she did.

She held the phone in her hand, saying nothing, waiting for the caller to speak. Again the whispered voice: "Are you still alone?"

"Who is this!" Reggie demanded in a voice that sounded foreign to her ears.

"I have to speak to you. It's urgent! Please tell me if you're alone."

"No, I'm not alone. My husband is in the next room and if you don't stop calling, I'm phoning the police. Now, who the hell is this?"

"Mrs. Weston, I don't have time for games. I'm as scared as you are. Please, I'm not going to hurt you. I only want to help. I can—" Abruptly, the conversation ended with a strangled gasp and the click of the phone.

With surprising calm Reggie hung up. Somehow the phone calls were related to David. She didn't know how she knew, but she was as certain of it as she had been of anything in her life. And this time he wasn't going to get away with whatever he was trying to pull. She was no longer eighteen and he couldn't manipulate her anymore. This time she wasn't waiting to see what he had up his sleeve. She was going to confront him. She reached for the phone. Damn! She didn't have any idea where the Astins were staying in New York or even if they were still in the city. The story she had told Alison about Cole meeting with David had been a lie. Yes, she vaguely remembered something being said about a meeting, but she couldn't remember when it was supposed to take place.

Lee would know. Quickly she dialed his number. After the eighth ring, she hung up. It didn't matter. She would call every hotel in the city until she found them.

Reaching into the night table by the side of her bed, Reggie withdrew the immense Manhattan Yellow Pages. As she lifted it to her bed, she noticed the contents of her handbag still lying scattered on the carpet. She bent to retrieve them. Replacing her lipstick, wallet, credit card case and sunglasses, she paused to stare curiously at a small gift box which was carefully wrapped in dove-gray paper. Then she remembered that Ardith had handed it to her the day before at lunch with the admonition that it wasn't to be opened until she got home. But in the mad rush to prepare for the reception, Reggie had forgotten all about it.

Without hesitating, Reggie ripped off the paper, opened the white carton and stared at the blue velvet jewelry case. As she lifted the cover from the box, Reggie gasped in delight as she touched the perfectly crafted antique pocket watch. The entire face and back of the gold case was studded with old miner's diamonds, rose quartz and tiny pearls the size of imported caviar beads. On the side of the watch were three gold knobs with a single sapphire set in each. She pushed down on one stone. The case sprung open to reveal the timepiece's face: ecru ivory with old English numerals. The hands of the watch were filigreed gold. She depressed the second knob and listened carefully as "Drink to Me Only with Thine Eyes" tinkled in the silence of her bedroom.

Delighted, she tried the last knob. Nothing happened. Disappointed, she tried again. This time she heard a noise like a spring being released. Nothing opened and she turned the watch over in her hand. There, on the gold back, Reggie saw a tiny depression, large enough for a fingernail. Gently, she pried it open. Inside, she found a folded piece of blue paper. She wondered how old it was. Carefully, she withdrew the paper which had been folded several times to fit into the tiny space. As she unfolded it, she saw that it was not old. What she held in her hand was a check made out to Regina Weston in the amount of twenty-five thousand dollars, signed by Ardith Weston. She looked again. It was not made out to Cole and Regina Weston, simply to Regina Weston. She picked up the carton, looking for a card. She found it tucked carefully in the lid of the blue velvet box.

Dear Regina,

The news of Cole's marriage delighted me. I never

thought that I would live to see such a thing come to pass. You must be a very special person to have captivated such an elusive man. As soon as I heard the wonderful news, I began searching my mind for a gift for both of you. Then it struck me. My son needs nothing more than you can give him. Any gift from me would be superfluous.

But I wanted *you* to have something, some part of me. I am giving you one of my most valued treasures. It was given to me by my mother-in-law when I became engaged to Cole's father. It has always been lucky for me. I hope it will be for you.

The other part of my gift, the check, is not nearly as dear. Nor is it meant to be as meaningful. When I received this watch, it came with love and a thousand dollars. My mother-in-law always felt that no matter how happily married a woman is, she should always have a little money of her own. Of course, I realize that, being married to my son, you will lack for nothing. Still, this check is for you only. Use it all in an hour—or keep it for an emergency. All I ask is that you keep the watch. Perhaps some day you will pass it on to your own son or daughter.

I look forward to meeting the woman who succeeded where so many others have failed. May you know only happiness in the years to come.

Fondly,
Ardith Weston

Reggie read and reread the note, tears continually springing to her eyes, all the while clutching the antique timepiece in her hand as if it were a talisman . . . something tangible that should remind her of what she and Cole had. Or, what they could have if only she'd confided her secrets to him. They were stupid, meaningless fears, and somehow Reggie had almost let them ruin her life. But, oh, what a special, wonderful woman Ardith was! She had given freely, privately, a dear, delightful treasure to a young woman she didn't even know . . . but whom she trusted with this gift—and with her only son.

"May you know only happiness in the years to come . . ." her mother-in-law had written. Reggie gave a wistful laugh. If

I can straighten out the mess I've made of things, then maybe I'll have a shot at happiness. And with that thought in mind, she tucked the note and check in her wallet, determined that once she had set things to rights, she'd buy Cole the most extravagant present she could find. And something for Ardith, too. Something unexpectedly sentimental because, she was coming to realize slowly, money alone meant nothing.

She thought about her crazy shopping spree the day they had gotten married. How naive she had been to think she could anger Cole by spending money. He had foreseen every silly move she had ever made. His insight into her psyche amazed her. She had never met a man who was as perceptive to her moods as Cole. She wasn't going to throw away what they had and she wasn't going to let David Astin destroy it, either. More determined than ever to find David and to let him know, without question, that he couldn't manipulate her or Cole, she started dialing hotels.

Within an hour, Reggie had called the Plaza, the Hampshire House, the Essex House, the Palace, the Park Lane, the Waldorf and the Pierre. No one had a listing for Astin. Then she began calling second-rate hotels. Not only were there no Astins presently registered at any of the hotels, but there hadn't been anyone by that name in the previous week.

Reggie lay back on her bed, staring at the ceiling. What had she missed? Of course, they could have returned to Chicago, but she doubted it. Or they could have been staying with friends. She was determined to find them. Something within her told her that David was still in New York trying desperately to find some hold on her, some kind of advantage. Once more she tried Lee's number. Still no answer. Where the hell was everyone tonight? Cole, Lee, David?

Suddenly, a thought occurred to her. It was a long-shot but anything was better than the dead ends she was reaching with the hotel operators. She dialed Information in Chicago and, when the Midwestern operator answered, asked for the number of David Astin on Lake Shore Drive. She had remembered their address from when she had done the invitations.

"The number is 312-555-0684."

Quickly, Reggie jotted it down on her bedside memo pad, then dialed the number. On the second ring, the Chicago number was answered by a housekeeper with a heavy Jamaican accent.

"Astin residence."

"Hi. Is Patrice home?" Reggie asked, casually hoping that she sounded like one of Patrice's friends. It was the only way the maid might slip and give out some information.

"I'm sorry, Mrs. Astin is not at home. May I ask who's calling?"

"This is her old friend Lynn, you know—from New York. We have a date for lunch tomorrow, but I seem to have misplaced the piece of paper with her New York number. Would you happen to know the name of the hotel where they're staying? I'm afraid I'm going to have to cancel, and I wouldn't want Mrs. Astin sitting in a restaurant all afternoon waiting for me."

"Mr. and Mrs. Astin will be at the Regency Hotel on Park Avenue until Tuesday. Do you want the number?"

"No, thanks. I'll look it up and give her a call now. You've been so helpful. Thank you."

Of course! They had stayed in the same hotel in which the reception had been held. With Francis ill, it made sense to make it as convenient for him as possible. Reggie cursed silently at her stupidity. She looked up the number in the phone book and placed the call, but when the hotel operator rang the room, there was no answer. She checked her watch. They might have gone out for dinner. She would try again later. Now that she knew where to reach David, she wouldn't give up.

Somehow those odd phone calls were supposed to frighten her, but she'd be damned if she'd let him do that to her. Besides, she thought as she rechecked her watch, it would be only a matter of time before Cole came home and, as much as she hated for him to hear the story, it would be much easier for her to confront David with Cole's support. In the meantime, she wanted to do nothing more than take a hot bath while she waited. After her bath, she would put on fresh makeup and a pretty negligee and greet Cole looking her best. She turned the tap on full force and stepped into the tub. She never heard the insistent ringing of the telephone through the closed bathroom door.

* * *

Cole slammed down his end of the phone. Reggie still wasn't home. He had been calling her intermittently all day. Now, as he stood in the men's locker room of the health club, he was ready to give up. He had had about as much annoyance and mystery as he felt he could handle. Cole shrugged angrily, retrieved his quarter and followed the burly masseur who was waiting patiently for him to finish with his phone calls.

As Lars began to work on the wide expanse of Cole's back, Cole's mind drifted. His body was finally resting, gradually recovering from the arduous punishment it had sustained. After his run down to Wall Street and his hasty visit to Lee's, he had stopped off, still in the early morning hours, at the townhouse before going to the club. He worked out on the Nautilus machines, then did thirty laps in the Olympic size pool, all in an effort to burn away the raging anger and sense of impotence he felt. Love! He'd always said it was nonsense. Why hadn't he listened to his own sage advice? He tried to recall his conversation with Reggie when he had first proposed. Hadn't he said that love was nothing more than civilized man's explanation for the need to reproduce? If you let yourself really fall in love, you were doomed to drown in it. If he and Reggie hadn't strayed from their original contract, if he hadn't mistaken intense physical desire for another emotion, he wouldn't be here now. He wouldn't be trying to avoid a confrontation with a woman who . . . who . . . He was furious that he couldn't even put into words what she had done to him. She was nothing more than a conniving liar, keeping secrets from him, involving his best friend in her intrigues—the phone calls . . . the disappearing acts . . . the flowers. . . .

And Lee. He would have to deal with that betrayal also. Where did Lee's loyalties lie? Didn't he owe anything to Cole after twenty years of friendship? "Find out from your wife," he'd said. Oh, he would find out, all right, but it wouldn't be by asking his wife. Never again.

Until she came to him with the answers, he would simply resume his posture of cool indifference. He had already asked her to confide in him, questioned her twice, in fact. It would not happen again. It would be a stand-off, at least for a while.

But he could wait. He turned over at the masseur's gentle prodding. As he gave in to the relaxing hands on his body, he felt himself drift off to sleep.

By eleven o'clock, Reggie couldn't keep her eyes open. Several times during the evening she had lowered the television, positive that she had heard Cole's footsteps, but she had been mistaken. She tried the Regency again but there was still no answer in the Astins' room. The strange telephone calls had ceased. After trying Lee a few more times to no avail, she gave up. Exhausted, Reggie turned off her bedside lamp, found a comfortable position and within minutes was asleep.

When Cole awoke, the health club was quiet. He was disoriented. It took him a few seconds to remember that he had fallen asleep during his massage. A quick glance at his empty wrist reminded him of his frustrating morning. He sat up, wrapped himself in a towel and went to find the masseur.

He located the young Swede in the locker room. "Lars," Cole asked, "what time is it?"

"Close to twelve."

"Do you know if there are any available beds?" The health club maintained several small rooms for out-of-town guests, businessmen or club members who simply didn't feel like spending the night at home.

"I'll go check, sir. You want to stay here tonight?"

Cole raised his eyebrows. "You didn't think I wanted to take one of the beds home, did you?"

"No, sir. I was surprised, that's all. You never stayed over before."

Cole didn't have any desire to explain. "Tonight, I do. Please find out. I'll take a quick shower." For a moment he thought about letting Reggie know where he was then changed his mind. Screw it, he thought. Let her worry a little.

By the time Lars came back, Cole had showered, dried off and was dressed in a clean set of underwear from his locker. "Do I get a bed?"

"Of course, sir. There are two empty rooms."

Cole picked up his terry robe and followed Lars through the maze of dark hallways toward the guest rooms. "What time do you come in tomorrow?" Cole asked as he sat on the edge of the bed testing the mattress.

"Not until noon."

"Too late. Leave a message at the desk for someone to wake me at six. I assume there will be someone in by that time?"

"Sure, Mr. Weston. People start coming in to exercise as early as five. We open up the doors by four thirty. I'll leave a wake-up call for you," Lars promised. "By the way, if you want breakfast we always have coffee and danish."

"That's fine." Cole took a ten dollar bill from the pocket of his robe. Handing it to Lars, he asked, "Do you think you could lend me your watch for the night? I seem to have misplaced mine. I'll leave it at the desk in the morning."

Lars looked at the bill and smiled. "Of course, Mr. Weston." He removed his watch and placed it on the bedside table. "Well, I guess I'll be going home. Sleep well. Is there anything else I can do for you?"

"No, thanks. Good night, Lars." In the morning, Cole would call John to bring him a business suit. He made a mental list of all the things he had to do the next day. It would be a busy day. The last thing he thought of as he drifted off to sleep was what Reggie would make of his absence. According to the original terms of their contract, there wasn't much she could actually do to him. He intended to return to living under the original tenets of the agreement until she explained her actions to his satisfaction.

A little after three thirty A.M. Reggie's phone rang. She jumped up to grab the receiver. Her heart was beating furiously.

"Hello?" she rasped.

Silence.

"Hello? Hello?" she repeated.

Heavy breathing.

"Who is this? Who's there?"

No one answered.

Summoning her courage, Reggie turned on the small light over her bed. "I know who this is. If you're trying to frighten me, you're wasting your energy."

"Mrs. Weston," whispered a female voice, "your husband—!"

There was a click on the other end of the line, then a dial tone. Quickly Reggie grabbed her memo pad, flipped through the pages and found the number for the Regency Hotel. After five rings the hotel operator answered.

"Excuse me," Reggie said, "I was just disconnected from the Astins' room. Would you please reconnect me."

"One moment, please."

Reggie tapped her fingernails on the phone as she waited. She could still feel the rapid beat of her heart.

The operator came back on the line. "I'm sorry to have kept you waiting," she said apologetically, "but I've been ringing their room and there is no answer. Are you certain they called from the hotel?"

"No . . . I'm really not," Reggie admitted. "I just assumed . . ."

"Would you like to try again later?"

"No, thank you. I must have made an error. Sorry to have bothered you."

"No bother at all. Good night."

Deep down, Reggie knew that that call had come from the hotel and that something had happened to cause the caller to hang up. She knew it with the same certainty that she knew it had been David who had instigated the call to Cole about the mole, who had sent the flowers and who was now trying to terrify her with these phone calls. What she didn't know was why. But Cole might know, she realized with a start. When she told him everything, he just might be able to put all the pieces together until what seemed like an insane jumble to her would make sense.

Though it was almost four A.M. Reggie pushed back the lilac comforter and slipped her feet into slippers. She was going to see Cole. The house was quiet as she made her way toward Cole's room. The sound of her slippers echoed on the parquet floors of the corridors. When she reached the door to his room, she paused, took a deep breath and turned the knob. The room was dark. She listened for the sound of his breathing. She peered into the inky blackness, trying to make out his shape in the huge bed. She could do neither.

Slowly, she tiptoed toward the bed, her hands feeling the darkness in front of her. Her knee touched the edge of the bed and she placed her hands on the blankets, feeling for his body.

The bed was empty. The bedspread was in place, the pillows smooth. She reached over to his nighttable, felt for the lamp and switched it on. Soft pink light illuminated the room, and Reggie realized that his bed had not been slept in at all.

"Cole?" she called quietly into the empty room. "Cole?" she repeated. There was no sound in the room except the ticking of his bedside clock. She glanced at it—four A.M. Where the hell was he?

Unconsciously, she wrapped her arms around her body protectively. She realized she was shivering. The room was cold and, in her haste, she hadn't bothered to put on a robe. Almost without thought, she pulled down the neat covers of Cole's bed and slipped between the cold sheets, drawing both the blanket and the bedspread up around her shoulders.

A nameless fear paralyzed her. Wide-eyed, she sat staring into space. She waited for something to happen. The clock moved with agonizing slowness, and still she sat, huddled in the huge bed waiting, as if at any moment she expected Cole to walk through the door with an explanation. Hideous images of car accidents, muggings and murder flew through her exhausted head. She made a valiant effort to chide herself for being overly dramatic, but she failed. By four thirty her body was shaking badly. Perhaps she had misinterpreted the phone calls. Now she began to wonder if someone had been trying to tell her that something had happened to her husband. A hit and run? Had the caller been a witness to a horrible crime in which Cole had been injured?

By four forty-five, she couldn't wait anymore. She picked up the phone and dialed 911. "I'd like to report a missing person," she told the police operator.

"I'm sorry, miss. This is the police emergency number. To report a missing person you have to call your local precinct."

"I don't know what it is. Could you help me?" she pleaded.

"I'm sorry, I can't tie up this line. Call Information and the operator will tell you what you want to know." She hung up the phone.

Reggie's trembling hands had trouble dialing, but she reached the Information operator, who gave her the name and number of the local police station. She placed the call.

"Sergeant Kelly, Eighth Precinct. Can I help you?"

"I want to report a missing person."

"One minute. I'll connect you with Detective Burnam." Reggie held on as the police switchboard transferred the call.

"Detective Burnam."

"I want to report a missing person."

"How long has the person been missing?"

"I don't know."

"When did you see this person last?"

"It's my husband. I saw him about five o'clock yesterday morning."

"Yesterday? At five A.M.?"

"Yes."

"When did you realize that he was missing?"

"I came into his room at about four A.M. this morning. He wasn't here. I mean he wasn't in his bed." Even to Reggie the recounting of the story sounded ridiculous.

"Did you say that you went into *his* room?"

"Yes," Reggie answered quietly.

"I see. Has anyone seen him since five this morning?"

"I don't know. I was gone all day and when I got home, he wasn't. I fell asleep and something woke me. I went to check to see if he was home and found that his bed hadn't been slept in."

"Ma'am?"

"Yes?"

"Has this sort of thing happened before?" asked the detective.

"No, never!" she replied quickly. It was obvious from the tone of his voice that the detective thought this was a routine domestic problem. "My husband just doesn't disappear, Detective. I'm very concerned that something has happened to him."

"I'm sure you are, but we can't start any kind of investigation until the person has been missing for at least forty-eight hours. I suggest that you call his friends. Most often, in domestic situations like this, the person is staying with friends."

"That's all you can do?"

"If he doesn't show up by this afternoon give us a call and we'll send someone over. But I really think you ought to try his friends," repeated the detective.

Reggie hung up the phone. Lee! They must be together, she thought. She hadn't been able to reach Lee all day, either.

Quickly, she dialed his number. On the second ring, he answered.

"Hello?" he said, the sleep still in his voice.

"Lee, it's Reggie. I'm sorry I woke you, but I have to speak to Cole."

"Cole?" Lee repeated, confused. "Honey, Cole's not here. Isn't he home?"

Under the blankets Reggie could see her foot shaking. "No, he's not home. Are you sure he's not . . . he has to be there!"

"Reggie, quiet down. He was here early this morning but he left by ten. Did you see him at all today?"

"No." She was beginning to cry.

"Stop it!" he commanded. Fully awake now, Lee sat up and looked at the time. He hadn't spoken to Cole since that morning. He'd gone to a museum and then to the movies, not returning until well after eleven o'clock. "Reggie, look around. Maybe he left you a note."

"He didn't leave me anything, no note . . . yes! Yes, he did leave me a note."

"Well? What did it say? Did he tell you where he was going, what time he'd be back?" Lee probed.

"It wasn't that kind of note. The note was . . . the flowers . . ."

"What flowers?" asked Lee.

"There was a box of flowers on the kitchen table when I got home from work. Cole had been here and accidentally opened them."

"Then they weren't from him?"

"No, they weren't. But that's not important. I don't know who they were from. He saw the box, opened the flowers and then left me a note apologizing for opening the box."

"Reggie, I don't understand what you're telling me. I'm coming over. By the time I get there, I'm sure Cole will be home. Will you be okay until I get there?" Lee asked.

"Yes, but please hurry. I've already called the police."

"What?" he roared.

In a hushed voice, she repeated her last statement. "He's missing, isn't he?" she asked. "I wanted to report it to the police. I got a weird phone call before I even knew he was missing. Do you understand now?"

He didn't, but he told her that he did. Hurriedly, he assured her that everything would be all right. He explained he had seen Cole very early that morning, asked her to stay where she was until he got there and pleaded with her not to call anyone else, especially the police. He didn't want her to tie up the phone in case Cole was trying to reach her.

Chapter 43

Reggie was still sitting in Cole's bed, the blankets pulled up to her shoulders when, half an hour later, she heard the doorbell ring. She swung her body out of bed and catapulted down the stairs toward the front door.

"Who's there?" she asked, forgetting to use the peephole. "Who's there?" she repeated nervously, her voice barely audible through the heavy oak door.

"It's me, Reg. Open up."

The red light on the metal box near the door flashed a warning. The alarm was on. Had she set it before she'd gone up? She couldn't remember. "Wait. I have to shut off the alarm." It was a simple set of numbers that had to be pushed in sequence. If the buttons were pressed wrong, the entire system would go off. She had done it every day for months. Suddenly she couldn't remember the numbers. Like a safecracker preparing for a big job, she clenched and unclenched her hands. Everytime she thought she knew the combination, she changed her mind. She kept pulling her hands away from the panel, terrified that she would set off the alarm.

"Reggie, dammit! Open the door!" roared Lee, knocking violently.

"I'm trying!" she screamed back. She finally remembered the right combination and the red flashing ceased. A green light appeared. She opened the door, falling into Lee's arms, sobbing.

Gently, he pushed her inside, closing the door behind him.

He soothed her, stroking her hair and murmuring words, nonsense syllables, actually, in an attempt to quiet her. All the while, he was carefully leading her to a chair. He was horrified at the sight of her. Her eyes were sunken in her face, red-ringed from crying. Her skin was the color of pale green chalk. "My God! What happened to you?"

"I . . . I . . ."

"Never mind." He walked over to the stove and put the kettle on to boil. Neither one of them was going back to bed. He'd even brought over a duffel bag with clothes for work, anticipating that he wouldn't get back home. He sat down at the kitchen table, indicating the chair opposite him. Gently, he placed his hand over hers. "Can you tell me, quietly, rationally, what the hell is going on around here?" He tried a small smile, but she didn't pick up her head.

"I don't know where to start. Cole is missing, he didn't sleep in his bed last night. I went into his room and . . ."

"His room?"

She looked up, surprised. "Yes, his room."

"I'm sorry," he shrugged. "I didn't realize you slept in different rooms."

"I got a phone call at three thirty, or was it four? I don't remember."

"It's not important," he assured her.

She pulled her hand through her tangled hair. "Everything is important. That isn't even the beginning. It started after the party. Cole got a phone call in the middle of the night."

"I'm sorry, I lost you. Who got the phone?" He was trying very hard to concentrate on her story, but it was difficult. "Stay here a minute. I'll be right back." He went into the study, poured two fingers of scotch into a glass and returned, handing it to her. "Before we go any further, drink this." He watched as she gratefully accepted the drink and swallowed the fiery liquid in three gulps. She gasped as it burned its way down, spreading warmth throughout her body. She began to feel better. "Ready to begin again?" Lee asked.

She nodded. It took her the better part of a half hour and three cups of tea for her to pour out the whole story. She began with her affair with David, the pregnancy, his abrupt disappearance, the abortion and sterility, her marriage to Cole, the Stockyard deal, her knowledge that David's name was on the guest list and her stupidity in keeping everything a secret from Cole.

Lee took a deep breath and stared at Reggie. "Of course," he said as if that explained everything. "I knew I knew that name. I just couldn't place it. Astin's name was on the mailbox when I moved in. I kept getting his junk mail for months. I also knew you had dated the man who had lived in my apartment, but I never put two and two together." Then he got angry. "For God's sake, why didn't you tell *me?* Even if you wanted to keep it from Cole, you could have trusted me."

She smiled a slow, sad smile. "I tried to tell you. Twice. The last time was at the reception. I told you that I knew David Astin."

Lee shook his head in frustration. "Yes, you did," he admitted. "And I stupidly wasn't paying attention. I heard you say that you knew him before that night, but I wasn't concentrating. We were interrupted by Cole, weren't we?" All the time Lee had thought the big secret Reggie was trying to hide was only her sterility. It hadn't been that at all.

"I wanted to warn both of you. I didn't want you to do business with him, but there was no way I could tell Cole why. What could I say to him?" she asked. " 'Don't do business with the guy who made it impossible for you to have children with me?' I couldn't do it. I chickened out. I told him I didn't want children, I was too old, he was too old. I told you the same thing, didn't I?"

Lee nodded.

"But when I saw David at the party," she continued, "I knew I couldn't keep it a secret anymore. He's looking for an angle, any edge he can grab to get this Stockyard deal tied up. He'd use anyone—me or Cole or—you should have seen his face. I think he's capable of almost anything."

"Are you trying to imply that he might have done something to Cole?"

This time it was Reggie who nodded.

"That's absurd!"

"No, it's not." She explained the phone calls. The first one to Cole about her mole, the next ones to her. She got up and walked to the back door, opened it and stepped into the courtyard. She came back with the now-damp box of flowers.

"I know that none of these things makes sense alone," she said as Lee read the card, "but don't you understand that someone is warning me or trying to frighten me? Lee, listen to me. I know how David's mind works. He wants that deal so badly he'll do anything. Now Cole's missing and I can't stop thinking that—"

"That's enough!" Lee got up from the table. "I'm calling the Astins' room. Where did you say he was staying?" Reggie told him and gave him the number. She watched as he placed the call. After speaking to the operator and waiting awhile, he replaced the phone on the cradle. "No one answered."

"I know. Now what?" she asked.

"We wait."

"Just wait? Cole could be hurt, even dead. I can't just sit here and wait."

"Okay. Tell me what you want to do. I'll do whatever you say."

She slammed her fist down on the table. "I don't know!"

"Neither do I, darling. That's why we'll wait. It will be dawn soon. I can start calling around at about seven."

She looked at him quizzically. "Calling whom?"

Lee had been thinking about Evyan, but he didn't need to tell that to Reggie. If Cole was indeed at Evyan's, Lee intended keeping it from Reggie. He couldn't bear to see any more unhappiness in her face. In so little time she had gone from bliss to misery, and Lee felt it was all Cole's fault.

"Get up, Reg. I'll stand watch while you go shower and fix up. When you're finished, I'll shower and shave. I'll get dressed for work here. I'm sure Cole will be back long before that."

Reggie stood up. "Thank you. Since you've come here I feel much better."

As she left the kitchen, he called after her. "Things always seem more frightening when you're alone in the dark." He wished he felt as secure and confident as he sounded. Whether it was David Astin or anybody else who was responsible for Cole's absence, there would be hell to pay when Cole finally returned.

By seven, Lee and Reggie were showered, dressed and still waiting. John had come in, murmured something about a bag and had gone out again. Lee continued calling the Astins' room. Still there was no answer.

"I'm calling the police," Reggie stated at seven thirty.

"Look, I know you're worried—"

"Worried? I'm not worried! I'm terrified. No matter how angry he is, he wouldn't do this to me. He wouldn't stay out all night without calling. Something has to have happened to him."

The concern for her husband was etched into her face. Her enormous green eyes, now ringed with sooty shadows, looked too large for her face and her complexion was sickly. The long night of waiting and knowing nothing had taken its toll. Lee had to look away from the pain and worry on her face. He fiddled around with the coffeemaker, having convinced her earlier that they would both feel better if they ate something. As he waited for the coffee to finish dripping, he took a frying pan out of the cabinet, then turned to her.

"If he's not back after we have breakfast, I'll call the police myself. Just wait another half hour," he conceded as he flicked a drop of water into the pan. He peeled off several slices of bacon and dropped them into the searing skillet. It didn't take more than two minutes for the odor of the frying bacon to hit her. She blanched as the nausea rose from her stomach and, with her hand covering her mouth, she ran from the room. Lee turned at the sound of the scraping chair in time to see her face. He mistook her flight, thinking she was fleeing the room before she began to cry.

Quickly, he removed the pan from the stove, turned off the burner and ran after her. He heard her in the foyer bathroom. What he thought were the sounds of uncontrollable sobbing were actually wretching and heaving. He pounded on the door.

"Reggie, let me in!"

She couldn't answer. Her head hung limply over the toilet. For a moment she forgot Cole. What the hell was the matter with her? For three days she had been sick. It wasn't the intense sort of illness that forced her to stay in bed. She had no aches or pain. No fever. This was an intermittent illness, striking at odd hours, and she was terrified because she couldn't explain it. She wasn't the sickly type, didn't catch colds or stay in bed when she had a headache.

Suddenly she was afraid for herself instead of Cole. She didn't need anyone to remind her that any change in digestion and sudden weight loss were one of the signs of cancer. She had both signs. In the space of three days her life was collapsing around her.

She heard Lee's continued banging on the door. "I'm okay," she said. Getting up from her knees, she wiped her face with a wet guest towel. When she looked in the mirror, she gasped and turned away. No one could look that awful without being seriously ill. She saw the concern in Lee's eyes as she opened the door.

"What happened?" he asked. When she didn't answer, he said, "I want you to lie down. I don't care whether you do it in the study or in your room, but you have to rest. Do you have any sleeping pills in the house?"

She shook her head violently. "I'm not taking anything, and I'm not going to sleep until I find out what happened to my husband. Just give me a minute. I'll be fine," she said, as much to reassure herself as Lee.

He settled her on the couch in the study then went back to clean up the kitchen and prepare a cup of tea. When he came back with the tea, she was dozing. Good, he thought as he covered her with a light afghan. He walked back to the kitchen and quietly dialed Evyan's number. It wasn't a number one could forget easily. Cole had once told him that if one substituted the letters for the numbers on the receiver, it spelled out "I am sexy."

Evyan answered sleepily. He glanced at his watch. It was not yet eight o'clock. He hoped he wouldn't find Cole there.

"Evyan, this is Lee Taggett. I hope I didn't wake you," he said. "Have you heard from Cole this morning?"

She yawned. "No, should I have? Is he back?"

"Back from where? Did he tell you he was going away?"

"No. I meant from his silly attempt at marriage. Why don't you call his wife. She should have a better idea than I. Good-bye." She hung up.

He was immensely relieved that Cole wasn't there. As much as he wanted to locate Cole, he hadn't wanted to find him with Evyan. It would have been more than Reggie could have taken. Now he had to try the cabin, but, because Cole always disconnected the phone when he knew he would be away for a long time, he wouldn't have had time to have it reconnected. Lee tried anyway and got a recording.

"Who were you talking to?" Reggie asked as she walked into the kitchen.

"Me? No one." It was almost the truth.

"Who were you talking to, Lee?" she repeated.

"I was trying to reach Cole at the cabin," he admitted. "I wasn't able to get through. The line's been disconnected."

"Give me the phone." He handed the phone to her. "What's the name of the town where the cabin's located?" she asked.

"Eagle Bay."

She busily punched some digits and waited. "Is there a state troopers' station located in Eagle Bay?" she asked the operator. "Thank you," she said and hung up. She looked at Lee. "I thought I could get someone to go over and check the cabin, but I just thought of a better idea. I have to go get my phone book. I'll be right back."

She came back and dialed another number. "Roberta? Hi. This is Reggie Weston. . . . I'm fine, thanks. How are you?. . . Mm-hmm, and the kids? . . . Great. Would you or Joe do me a favor?" She quickly explained that Cole had gone to the cabin to check it over for the winter, and she hadn't heard from him. Since the phone was still disconnected, she had no way to reach him and she was beginning to get concerned. Roberta assured her that she would send Joe out to the cabin to check. She would call back within the hour with whatever news she had.

"I'm impressed," Lee said. "Who are Roberta and Joe?" Reggie told him about the family and the little boat. "They take their kids up there every weekend, and they have a phone in their camper."

"Nice people," observed Lee. He noticed Reggie's eyes were starting to close again. "Reg, will you be okay for a few hours? I have to get down to the office to meet with Francis Munsey. It's just possible that Cole will show up for this meeting. Do you want to come?"

"No, I'm staying here. I'll be fine for a while. If Roberta calls, I want to be here. Or if Cole . . ." She couldn't finish.

"He's fine, Reg. I know it. But you're not. Get into bed and wait for him there. I'll have John bring you breakfast on a tray."

The thought of food made her stomach turn over again. After all this is over and Cole comes back, I'm going to the doctor, she thought sleepily. "No breakfast, please. I'm going to take your advice and lie down, but you'd better call me as soon as you get to the office. Promise?"

He patted her head. Once in a great while he wondered what life with Reggie would have been like. Now, as he watched the grave concern on her face as she worried about the man she loved, his mind flashed back to the first time they had met on the stairwell. She had been grieving for a lost love then also. Dammit! David hadn't deserved to be loved that way, and neither did Cole. Lee didn't doubt for one moment that Cole was doing no more than just playing games with Reggie. What a fool!

He watched sorrowfully as Reggie dragged her weary body to the doorway. She paused and turned. "Find him for me, Lee. Please find him." She turned and left the room.

Chapter 44

The November air smelled like snow as Cole stepped from the cab onto the sidewalk in front of his office. He paused to check the clock atop the adjacent highrise—8:45 A.M. Handsomely dressed in a navy-blue pinstriped suit, crisp white dress shirt, deep maroon and white pin-dot tie and dark gray belted trenchcoat, he felt as well rested as he looked. His night at the spa, although unplanned, had been exactly what he had needed, a welcome respite from the confusion and deterioration of his relationship with Reggie.

He stepped from the elevator into the plushly decorated reception area of WestCo. Four desks, each occupied by four of New York's highest paid secretaries, flanked the perimeters of the room. The walls were rounded, padded then upholstered in pale beige linen. The floors, in the same color Berber carpet, cushioned all noise. He nodded to his employees as he strode through the reception area to his own office. As he approached his outer office where his secretary had her desk and stood sentry for all those wishing to see him, he heard voices. Someone was arguing with Marjory. He couldn't decipher the words but the decibel level warned him against entering, at least not until he knew what was going on.

He bypassed the door to the outer office and headed for the private entrance to his inner office, an entrance that only he, Lee and Marjory knew existed. The door looked like the others, highly polished oak, brass doorknob and small bronze plaque. Instead of presenting a name on the plaque, the words ELECTRICAL STORAGE CLOSET. HIGH VOLTAGE. KEEP OUT were etched into the metal. As he opened the door and entered his office, a tiny red light lit up on Marjory's desk. Immediately, she knew someone was in the inner office. She excused herself from the conversation and entered the room. Cole immediately questioned her.

"It's Mr. David Astin. He's been waiting to see you since eight o'clock. I told him that his appointment wasn't until nine thirty, but he insisted on waiting. What should I tell him?"

"Did he happen to mention why he was here so early?"

"Yes. They took Mr. Munsey to the hospital some time in the middle of the night—another stroke. The daughter is with him now, waiting for the results of some tests. In the meantime, he's in ICU. Mr. Astin is anxious to get back to the hospital. He said he doesn't like leaving his wife there alone. He hoped he could see you earlier than the scheduled appointment.

Cole scowled. "He wasn't even supposed to be involved in this conference."

"Should I make some excuse to get him to leave?" asked Marjory.

Cole hung up his coat, using the time to think. If Francis had suffered another stroke, he might be completely incapacitated this time, unable to participate in the Stockyard deal. That left Cole with Astin. Or, Cole thought, he could simply reneg on the whole deal. Before he made any decisions, Cole wanted to check with the hospital on Francis's condition. He did not trust Astin to give him a true picture.

"Go back to your desk," he told Marjory, "and I'll call you in ten minutes. Tell Astin that I'm on my way in. Tell him you think I will be here within a half hour or so. Make up something about a delay. I'm going to try to reach Lee and have him call Lionel Dern at Columbia Presbyterian. He's an old friend of ours and I think he can get me the information I need. Do you understand what to do?"

Marjory flushed indignantly. "Mr. Weston," she said icily, "I am not an idiot." She turned on her heel and left the office.

Cole smiled at the way she had taken offense. She was the most competent secretary he had ever had. She would know just how to handle Astin. He withdrew a private phone from his desk drawer. He dialed Lee's home. After letting the phone ring six times, he replaced the receiver and returned the phone to the drawer. Lee was obviously on his way to the office. Cole glanced at his wrist. He cursed out loud as he pulled his cuff back over his naked wrist. A small digital clock on his desk read 9:05. Lee should be arriving at any moment. Cole placed a surreptitious call to Marjory.

"Good morning, Mr. Weston's office," she answered, brightly.

"Is Astin still there?"

"Yes, I'm expecting Mr. Weston shortly. He has a meeting at nine thirty. If you'd care to leave a message, I'll have him return your call as soon as possible."

"Listen, when Lee comes in, tell him to use the private door. Also, see if you can sneak in here with a cup of coffee for me. If not, I'll have to—"

"No, I'm terribly sorry. That would be quite impossible. Mr. Weston's nine-thirty appointment is already here and waiting for him. You'll simply have to wait for Mr. Weston's associate. Perhaps he can get you that item."

Cole laughed. "Marjory, you're the greatest. I assume by your conversation that Mr. Astin isn't leaving?"

"Yes, sir. That information is correct. Is there anything else I can do for you?"

"Yes. Get Lee in here with coffee as soon as possible and stall Astin until I speak to Lee. Okay?"

"Certainly, sir. Oh, here's Mr. Taggett now. Would you like

to speak with him?" Marjory nodded to Lee as he entered the office.

"No. Step into the hallway and tell him what's going on. Then get him in here with that coffee."

"Thank you, sir. I'll see that either Mr. Taggett or Mr. Weston gets back to you immediately. Good morning." Marjory hung up and motioned to Lee, who was staring at David Astin with such a look of surprise on his face that Marjory did a double take.

"Marjory, please step outside for a moment, I would like to have a word with you."

Marjory followed Lee into the hallway. "What is it, Mr. Taggett?"

"How long has he been here?" he asked impatiently, wanting to find out and then call Reggie to tell her that at least he had located Astin.

"He's been here for an hour or so." She filled him in on Francis Munsey's stroke. "Mr. Weston wants you to bring him a cup of coffee and join him in his office. Oh, and use the private entrance. He doesn't want Mr. Astin to know he's in."

"Cole is in his office?" asked Lee, now totally confused. "How long has he been in?"

"Just a short while. Mr. Taggett, are you all right?" A furrow of concern deepened in Marjory's forehead.

"I'm fine. I'm going in to see him now."

"Don't forget the coffee."

"Coffee?" Lee repeated. "I'll give that son of a—sorry. You get him the damned coffee!" He headed down the hall to the private entrance.

When he entered the room without knocking, he found Cole leaning comfortably back in his desk chair with his feet up on his desk. For a moment, Lee had an uncontrollable urge to throw him through the picture window. "Where the hell have you been all night?" he demanded.

Cole sat up. "Why?" he asked curiously. "Were you looking for me?"

"Everyone in the whole goddamned city of New York was up looking for you last night," he answered angrily. "Now where the hell were you?"

Cole eyed him coolly. "Since when do I answer to you?"

"Since I spent most of the night at your house—with your

wife, I might add—while she went crazy worrying about you. Couldn't you at least have had the decency to call someone to let them know where the hell you were?"

"I really don't think it's anyone's business, frankly."

Steam exploded behind Lee's eyes. "Oh, you don't? You really don't give a good goddamn about anyone but yourself, do you?"

The pulse near Cole's eye began to throb dangerously. He looked at Lee strangely. "Should I? Should I really care?" he asked. "When I came to you yesterday for some answers, you as much as told me to go fly a kite. Now you want answers? Well, I owe you as much as you owed me yesterday. Nothing." He fingered some loose papers on his desk. "Now if you could bring yourself to concentrate on the business at hand, Astin is waiting outside and I—"

"I know Astin's waiting. He'll have to wait a little longer. I am going to call your wife right now. I would like her to know that you've been found. You'll have to excuse me." Lee strode angrily from the room, slamming the door behind him. He could never remember being angrier at Cole than he was at that moment. He was seething at Cole's indifference, his utter lack of feeling. How could he possibly do this to Reggie? And that Lee, himself, was indirectly responsible for her unhappiness made it that much worse. Oh, yes, he had seen this uncaring side of Cole before, but never on a personal level. They had had minor disagreements in the past, but this refusal to communicate, the curtness, the inaccessibility was new. Where he once might have tried to talk about it with Cole, today he was just too angry. As he stormed toward his own office he wondered what kind of explanation he was going to offer Reggie. What could he possibly say? "I found your husband, he's safe and sound in his office; he just wasn't in the mood to talk to you?"

He dialed Reggie's number. When John answered, he asked to speak to Mrs. Weston but was told that she had fallen asleep in the study. John explained that when he returned this morning he found Mrs. Weston asleep on the couch.

"What time was that?" asked Lee.

"Well," John thought out loud. "I got back from the health club—"

"I beg your pardon?" Lee interrupted. The idea that John was exercising at a health club was ridiculous.

"I had to bring Mr. Weston some clothes this morning at his club. I told Mrs. Weston I had to deliver a bag. You heard me, too."

Lee vaguely remembered the comment about a bag. "You mean that you knew where Mr. Weston was this morning?"

"Yes, sir. He called me early this morning at home. Said he spent the night in the club."

"Well, why didn't you tell anyone?" Lee said, his voice rising.

"Because, sir, nobody asked me."

"John," Lee said, trying to maintain some semblance of patience, "didn't you think it was the least bit peculiar that Mrs. Weston and I were up at that hour of the morning, or even that I was there in the first place?"

"Frankly, Mr. Taggett, there are lots of things that are peculiar in this house. However, it is not my place to question them. I just do my job and mind my own business." When he heard no response from Lee, John asked, "Do you want me to wake Mrs. Weston?"

"Yes."

With no attempt at softening the blow he knew she would feel, Lee began. "Hi. I'm at the office and I found Cole here. He's fine. Apparently, he spent the night at the health club and had John bring him his business clothes early this morning."

He waited for the inevitable questions. They came at him like staccato bursts from a submachine gun. He fielded them as best as he could and, even as he answered, knew that the words he was speaking were hollow. They didn't answer the one question that he knew Reggie was silently asking: Why hadn't Cole called?

"By the way," he continued, "Astin is here, too. The reason we couldn't find him last night was because the father-in-law had another stroke during the night. They spent the better part of the night at the hospital."

Reggie held the phone in her hand as if it were an object she had never seen before. She stared at it, barely hearing the words Lee was speaking. Cole was fine . . . he simply hadn't called . . . hadn't called . . . hadn't called. Over and over the words repeated themselves in her brain until she was too numb to think anymore.

"I see," she said finally. But she didn't, not really. She didn't see at all. All that she saw was the charade that her life had become. Now you love me, now you don't. David didn't even matter anymore. Nothing did. Like an automaton, Reggie hung up the phone and headed for the stairs. Now I love you, now . . . the daisy game didn't work. She was always left holding the petal that said, "I love you still."

Chapter 45

Lee walked toward Cole's office slowly. He opened the door to the outer office, saw David Astin, nodded briefly, and entered the inner sanctum. Cole was on the phone, his back to Lee. Calmly, Lee sat down. Cole must have heard his entrance but chose to ignore it as he continued his conversation in a clipped, businesslike tone of voice.

"I see. And could you explain the prognosis to me? . . . I see." Cole jotted down a few notes. "That's wonderful news. I really appreciate the information, Lionel. . . . Same here. Give my best to Edith and the kids. Oh, if there are any changes in his condition you'll let me know? . . . Great." He hung up the phone and turned to Lee with a huge grin on his face. "Did you get that? Francis had another minor stroke, no permanent damage. I think we can go ahead with the Stockyard deal as planned—without Astin. We may have to stall awhile, until Francis is on his feet again, but if everything goes smoothly, there's no reason not to expect ground breaking in two or three months. What do you think?"

"I'm delighted to hear that Francis isn't as sick as you thought. I'm also delighted that the deal can proceed without Astin. After that"—Lee shrugged—"I don't give a hoot in hell!"

"What exactly does that mean?" Cole shot back.

Lee stood up, stretched lazily and ran his fingers through his thick blond hair. "I'm no longer interested in the Stockyard deal."

"Are you crazy? We've got millions riding on this!" Suddenly, Cole changed his attitude. "Are you all right? I mean, do you feel well? Is there something that you're not telling me?" Cole asked more gently.

"I'm in perfect health. Why?"

"You may be in perfect health, but you're behaving like an irresponsible kid. I want to know why!"

Lee ignored him. "I'm flying out to California tonight, then on to Tahoe, if I can make arrangements. I'll leave all the information with my secretary. I should be back in two or three weeks."

"What the hell are you talking about? You can't leave New York now. There's a mountain of work to be done now that Francis is in the hospital. Especially since we've decided not to let Astin in—"

"Cole," Lee said, quietly, "*we* haven't decided anything . . . never have actually. It's always been you who has done the deciding, exactly like you've done this time. I've always gone along with your decisions because they've been in my best interest to do so. Now they aren't. Right now, the most important thing for me is to be in California. You can handle everything in my absence. If it's a legal question, ask one of the fellows in the legal department. As far as giving you any explanations . . . you have made it clear that we don't answer to each other. In this instance, I choose to agree." Lee started for the door.

Cole walked over and grabbed his shoulder. "Just wait a minute."

"One minute."

"Is this an ego thing with you?"

"Do you really believe that?" Lee asked incredulously.

"It's the only thing that makes sense."

"I could sit down and talk to you for the next two hours but what I had to say would mean nothing to you because it's about feelings. Just let me give you one piece of advice, my friend: one by one you are going to lose all the things, no, all the people who mean anything to you. They are simply going to decide that it isn't worth the pain to try to reach inside you and find anything. I'm leaving because I want a vacation and have some personal business to take care of. I also need a break from you. Don't worry, I'll be back when I'm ready to go another ten rounds with you. But there are others who aren't that strong. You'll wake up one day and find that you're all alone again."

Cole let out a harsh laugh. "Is that really what this whole thing is about? Your *feelings* are hurt?" But Lee never heard him; he had already left the room, telling David Astin that Cole was waiting for him, as he passed through the outer office.

David stood by the door to the office waiting for Cole to invite him in. When he didn't, David cleared his throat. Cole regained his composure quickly, stepping aside to let David enter.

"Mr. Astin. Sorry to have kept you waiting so long, but there were some details I had to straighten out on another deal. How's Francis this morning? Have you spoken to the hospital?" Cole sat down behind his desk, leaving David to stand awkwardly in the middle of the room.

David felt his palms beginning to perspire. He wiped them on his trouser leg. This was his moment. . . . Everything he had worked for for so long was riding on how he handled the next ten minutes. He had to convince Weston that Francis was too old, too infirm to be entrusted with as large an enterprise as the Stockyards. Not knowing what else to do, David leaned on Cole's desk. "I called the hospital about fifteen minutes ago. It doesn't look good. He's in a coma and even if he comes out of it, they have no idea about the extent of the damage. They won't even let my wife in to see him."

"I see," murmured Cole, pausing to jot something down on his agenda. *The lying son-of-a-bitch.* "If that's the case, then we have to do some rethinking on this deal, don't you agree?"

Careful, David cautioned himself. Feel Weston out . . . see where his head is. "As far as I'm concerned, I would feel much more comfortable with Francis at the helm."

"I couldn't agree more," stated Cole.

"However . . ."

Here it comes, thought Cole. Now Astin is going to make his big pitch. Cole leaned forward, letting Astin think he was amenable to whatever ideas David might have. "Yes?" prodded Cole.

"However," David repeated, "I don't honestly think Francis is up to it. His mind isn't on this deal—it's on his health. Even if he pulls through this stroke and, dear Lord, I hope he does, what kind of condition is he going to be in? He's weak . . . tired. . . . I'd like to make a proposal if I might."

"By all means," encouraged Cole. "That is why you're here, isn't it?"

David relaxed and sat down. Everything was going smoothly. "I believe that I can step in, take over the deal. Of course, as soon as Frank is back on his feet, he'll be right there beside me. But for now, with the deal so close . . . well, you can't really depend on him. If I took over, got his power of attorney . . . that's where you would come in . . . have to convince him, you know . . . give him a sense that you were behind me . . ." He let the sentence hang, giving Cole time to see the light.

Cole looked faintly skeptical. "I don't know, David. He's so stubborn. How are we going to get him to agree to let go of the reins?"

"He won't have any choice."

"Why do you say that?" Cole asked, a hint of a smile in his eyes. "Even in poor health I would suspect that no one could pull the wool over Francis's eyes. How do you propose to accomplish such an enormous feat?" Cole asked because he wanted to know exactly what David had in mind and knew instinctively that David was going to voluntarily give him all the information he needed.

David was like a lamb being led to the slaughter. "Francis had me do all the negotiations for the Stockyard property. A great deal of it he already owned, but there were odd parcels that had to be purchased before we could go ahead and convert the land to our goals. Because he was aware of his age and his health, he's been making gifts to Patrice for the last six or seven years—large parcels of land. He also bought up those few remaining parcels in her name. I don't have to explain the tax advantages to you in case he should die. As it stands right now, Patrice owns almost all of the land outright." He paused to make sure Cole understood the implications.

Gently Cole prodded him, telling him how clever that bit of foresight was in the light of the present situation.

David, puffed up by Cole's acknowledgment of the brilliant scheme, continued. "Of course, I was the one who suggested the whole thing to Francis."

"Of course."

"Well, I don't have to tell you about wives and business. They don't take an interest. They are so busy decorating or lunching or playing cards that the last thing they want to know about is the nitty-gritty details of business. Patrice is no different."

Ah, thought Cole, Reggie is different. They had spent hours together in front of the fireplace, arguing on the way to get an edge over a client.

"So he doesn't really have any control over the situation anymore. It's all in my wife's hands. Knowing Patrice, you understand that she'll agree to almost anything I suggest. In this case, Francis will have to take a backseat—until Patrice and I think he's strong enough, of course." He pulled on his cuffs proudly.

Cole was stunned. Francis really wasn't in control of the land. David Astin had the Stockyard tied up through Patrice. Now Cole had to stall. To tell David now that he wasn't going through with the deal without Francis would be tantamount to throwing it down the drain, and Cole wasn't ready to do that. The key was Patrice. Unless Cole could prove that David wasn't acting in her best interest . . . but he needed time. With a false conviviality that was as foreign to his nature as honesty was to David's, Cole walked around to the other side of the desk and put his arm on David's shoulder.

"Well, David. It looks like you've figured out all the angles. I take off my hat to you."

David positively beamed. "Sometimes it's necessary to take matters into your own hands. I felt this was one of those times."

"I couldn't agree with you more." Cole practically lifted David from the chair and led him from the room. "Now you run along to the hospital. I know your wife must be waiting. Let's keep this under wraps for now." When David nodded agreement, Cole continued, "Call me later—say, four or five o'clock this afternoon? We'll go further at that time. Give my best regards to Francis and your wife. Oh—and David, congratulations. You must be very pleased with what you've accomplished."

"I'd be a lot happier if Francis were in perfect health. . . ."

I'll just bet you would, thought Cole.

"But," continued David, "since he isn't, just knowing that we can go ahead because of Francis's foresight, makes me realize again what a genius he is. I'm sure that he did this all just in the event that something like this could happen."

I doubt it, thought Cole. He was now more certain than ever that Francis had no idea the depths to which David's morals would plunge to get his way. If he had had an inkling, Cole knew that Francis would have thrown him out on his ass. Now it had become Cole's job. He smiled slightly and looked forward to that event. First he had to get Patrice alone, sound her out, find out exactly how deep her involvement was and what she was willing or unwilling to do for her husband, against her father. She might be a willing accomplice to the whole scheme. Cole had heard of stranger stories—infighting among families, brother against brother, father against son. Yes, it was possible.

"David, a thought just occurred to me. You wouldn't happen to have the Stockyard papers with you in New York?"

"Right here." He patted the briefcase on his lap. "Deeds, architectural plans, even the proposals from the firms interested in buying or renting space."

Cole slapped him on the back. "That is phenomenal. You are on top of everything. Now listen very carefully. I'm going to send you over to the legal department. You'll meet with Lee . . . no, make that Joel Geyter. Between the two of you, let's just make one hundred percent certain that everything you said is so. If we're going to go ahead without Francis . . . well, better safe than sorry."

David checked his watch. "I should be getting back to the hospital." He thought about Patrice. Leaving her alone for that length of time worried him. She was going to need a shot soon. He saw Cole's frown. Screw it! he thought. She'll suffer a little longer. "You're right. Of course, I've already been over these papers with a fine-toothed comb, but to satisfy you, I'll be glad to do it again."

Cole pushed the intercom on his desk phone. "Marjory,

would you please come in and escort Mr. Astin over to legal now? Thank you." He stood up. "It looks like we're well on our way. I'll check back with you in an hour or so." He walked David to the door, where Marjory was waiting.

"This way, Mr. Astin," she directed.

David stuck out his hand. "It's a pleasure doing business with you. I've heard you were sharp, Mr. Weston. Now I'm certain of it."

You haven't seen anything yet, thought Cole as he took the man's hand and gave it a hearty shake. When David and Marjory disappeared around the corner, Cole left the office. He had roughly an hour or so to make the trip to the hospital, speak to Patrice and get back before David finished the busy work Cole had mapped out.

He found her immediately sitting in the lounge reserved for the families of ICU patients. He walked over to her and sat down. She was surprisingly friendly, acting almost glad to see him. He couldn't remember her behaving this way toward him in a long, long time. She went over everything the doctors had told her about her father's condition, reassuring Cole that there had not been any permanent damage from this stroke.

"But, God, Cole, he's getting old. It's terrifying to watch."

"I'm sure it must be," he agreed. They spoke about Francis and the times they had spent together when Cole used to come out to Chicago regularly. Then Cole suggested they get something to eat in the hospital cafeteria. He didn't have much time to find out his information and return to WestCo.

In the cafeteria, he began, "Patrice, you know that your father and I are supposed to be completing a very important business deal. Your husband is involved, too."

She looked up from her coffee quizzically. "Cole, why are you speaking to me like I was a child? I'm perfectly aware of the Stockyard operation. My father filled me in on all the details after his last stroke. Are you concerned about it because he's had another stroke?"

"He told you everything?"

"Since I don't know what you mean by 'everything' that's a hard question to answer." She began to play with a packet of Sweet 'n Low. Several times Cole thought she was about to open up, but then she stopped. Finally, she drew in a deep breath. "Cole, you know that Dad and I used to be very close. Since my marriage, especially in the last five years or so, we've drifted apart. But when he realized that he wasn't in good health he began divesting some of his holdings. The land that's involved in the Stockyard deal belongs to me." She sipped her coffee. "He wanted me to understand all the legal ramifications in the event that anything happened to him."

"What about your husband, Patrice?" Cole asked. "How does he feel about the transfer of title?"

"Cole, I'm not particularly brilliant, nor am I a moron. I know you love Daddy, but I also know that this visit isn't merely social. Please level with me. What is it that you want to know?"

"I have reason to believe that your husband is trying to force your father out of the whole deal. He is going to use you and your name on the deeds to that land in order to pull it off. I'm trying to find out how much you know and if you plan to go along with this scheme. If not, I thought it might interest you. I didn't want to tell you today, though. I was trying to be subtle."

"I see," she said thoughtfully. They sat in silence while Patrice digested the information Cole had just given her. It didn't surprise her at all. She noticed her hands were beginning to shake, the first sign that she was due for a shot soon. She'd have to hurry this conversation along before she fell apart. Briefly, she thought about confessing to Cole her role in David's nefarious scheme to frighten Reggie into exerting pressure on Cole. Was this the time to tell him about the middle-of-the-night phone calls, the silver and gold flowers? Her whole lurid life with her husband? She thought not. It wouldn't make any difference anymore. She was finished with David, and when she told Cole all she knew, he would write David Astin off, as well.

"Cole, I'm divorcing David. He doesn't know it yet, and I would appreciate it if you didn't tell him. I'm not going back to Chicago with him. I'm staying in New York with Daddy. I hope to see an attorney about both my marital situation and my financial affairs." She paused having surprised herself. Because of David's damning tapes, the actual possibility that she could divorce him had never been an option. In the years following their marriage, she had been enslaved to him. But now she didn't care about his threats. If she could get her father's help, she saw a way out. It wouldn't be easy. She needed more than emotional support. It was imperative that she get medical help immediately. She didn't know the extent of her drug addiction, but she did suspect that it was deadly serious.

"Patrice, I have to ask you one more question," Cole said.

"Yes?"

"Are you prepared to go forward with the Stockyard deal without your husband?"

She chewed on her lower lip thoughtfully. Could she handle it? "I don't know, Cole. I don't know if I'm qualified." Or strong enough, she thought.

"Look, there's nothing wrong with your father's brains. It's his body that's impaired. He functions better in the condition he's in than most other men. I'd be willing to take the chance and go ahead with you and your father, but I won't continue at all if David is involved. What do you think?"

"Why would you take the chance on an inexperienced woman and a sick old man?" she queried.

"Because Francis has done more for me than my own father. He is the one who is responsible for my being where I am today. His trust in me, when I was just as inexperienced as you, deserves repayment. This is my way of doing it. I think the Stockyard deal was conceived by him when he saw an end to his days as an active attorney. Everything that he has is tied up in that land. He's spent the last five years of his life working on it. It's not only for him, Patrice. It secures your future as well. Maybe he knew all along what kind of man you had married. I don't know, I'm only speculating." Cole reached across the table and held her hand. "Go talk to him. Ask him if this is what he wants. If it is, I will do anything I can to see that we accomplish it. I'll be standing right beside you if you need me." He looked into her eyes. "Can you do it?"

"Everything has always been done *for* me. I don't know if I can."

Cole stood up, smiling broadly. "I say you can. I say that you have your father's genes and his brains. Patrice, you can do any damn thing you want! Now you go talk to him. I've got to go back to the office. Call me at this number after you've made a decision." He scribbled the number on a napkin and tucked it into her hand. "Come on—get up. We have a hell of a lot to do in the next few months." He walked her to the elevator. "I have a feeling you're going to make one hell of a businesswoman!"

Patrice smiled for the first time that day. "I think I'd like to try. I really think I would," she said as the elevator doors closed.

Cole walked confidently toward the hospital exit.

Chapter 46

"Your husband thinks it will be better if you don't go into the ICU until he gets back, Mrs. Astin. He feels it's too much strain on you," the sympathetic intensive care nurse told Patrice as she sought admittance to her father's curtained-off cubicle.

"Miss . . ." Patrice searched the white uniform for a name plate. "Miss Avery," she pleaded. "Please, I've been waiting all night and morning to see him alone. I just want to go in and tell him I'm here. I'll only be a moment. I don't have to wait for my husband. I'm fine, really I am."

Donna Avery looked at the haggard young woman. True, there were rings under her eyes, but why not? She had been there for hours, sitting patiently for news of her father's condition. It didn't seem fair to keep her from seeing him. She decided to act against the husband's wishes. Sometimes it wasn't fair to protect the family from news they would eventually hear anyway. She decided to let Patrice into the unit.

"Just a few minutes. He's dozing. He's comfortable and stable now. Don't agitate him; just let him know you're there." Donna Avery opened the glass doors and led Patrice to the bed where Francis lay hooked up to bottles and machines. He was snoring lightly, a sound Patrice could barely make out against the whirring and bubbling of the medical paraphernalia in the room. She sat down on the straight chair by his bed and placed her damp hand in his cool, dry one. He didn't move.

The nurse nodded. "Just like that. If he wakes up, he'll find you holding his hand, and he'll know that you're okay. Sometimes, that's as important as anything we can do for him. I'll be back for you in a few minutes." She closed the curtains a bit so Patrice could have some privacy with her father.

Patrice sat there silently, waiting. Francis stirred. She leaned forward. "Daddy?" she whispered to the sleeping figure. There was no response. She held Francis's hand against her cheek so he could feel the tears that streamed down her face. She spoke to him quietly, hoping he would hear, doubting that in his state he could. Still, she tried. "Daddy, you have to get better. All of my life you've been there to hold my hand, to help me. I've never taken a step without your being by my side." She paused, searching for any sign that would tell her he had heard. There was none but still she continued. "Daddy, I've never needed you more than I need you now. There are things that you don't know . . . about me . . . about David . . . things you have to know! I don't know what to do if something happens to you. Daddy, if you die . . . I have to say this . . . if you die I think David will kill me."

As soon as the words were out of her mouth, she gasped in horror. She hadn't meant to tell him that. Not when she didn't even know if he would be alive by nightfall. She glanced at the monitors. They hadn't fluctuated. Suddenly, she made up her mind and plunged ahead. It was the only hope she had—an act born of desperation. "David's been poisoning me with drugs. I'm addicted . . . have been for years. That's why I do whatever he says. He threatens to keep them from me. I've always been terrified that I couldn't live without my 'medicine.' Do you hear me, Daddy? Do you?" There was no sign that Francis heard. "He's got films. Films of things we did together when he had me doped up. Horrible, disgusting things. He's threatened to send them to you, to the magazines. Daddy, I can't fight him alone!" She was gasping for breath. "I can fight him with you, but you have to get better for me. Please, Daddy . . . please . . ." She was sobbing uncontrollably.

Francis struggled to open his eyes. Suddenly, Patrice felt the pressure on her hand as Francis pressed his thumb into her palm. He was trying to speak. She leaned closer until she could feel his breath on her ear. "Kitten," he whispered softly.

"Yes, Daddy. I'm here."

"Kitten," Francis struggled, "I heard . . . shh . . . we'll fight him." The effort was exhausting him, but still he continued. "I never knew, never suspected . . . how could I be so blind?"

"Don't, Daddy." She was weeping now, but behind the tears there was a strength of purpose Patrice had never felt before. "Just rest now and get better. When you're out of here, we'll fight."

"I'll be fine, darling." His voice had picked up in strength as he learned of the battle he would have to face. "I promise."

He watched as the nurse came and parted the curtains, leading Patrice from the room. Now he knew he would recover. He'd always paid his debts. He also always collected them.

Chapter 47

Reggie sat in Dr. Seidman's office. After Lee's phone call she had remained in bed most of the morning, alternately crying and cursing. At one o'clock she couldn't stand being in the house anymore. She had pulled herself from the bed, showered, dressed and decided to go to work. She hadn't made it. Like an enemy in ambush, the nausea struck again sending her running for the bathroom. Scared to death, she knew she couldn't wait anymore. She called her internist and pleaded for an appointment.

Now, two hours later, she waited for the consultation. Eric Seidman had listened to her complaints and had given her the most thorough examination she had ever had. The door opened. A smiling, rotund, slightly balding man bustled in. He squeezed his portly body between the chair and his desk, huffing as he sat down. His head all but disappeared behind the stack of mail and journals that littered the desktop. Reggie waited with her hand clasped tightly in her lap.

"Stop looking like I'm going to hand you the death sentence," he admonished. He took off his glasses and scratched his nose. "I'm delighted to tell you that although you look perfectly dreadful, I can't find a thing wrong with you."

She shook her head vigorously. "Then you missed something. No one can feel this lousy and be healthy. I'm exhausted, nauseous, weak, lightheaded and vomiting all the time. That hardly sounds healthy to me."

"If you would let me finish, Reggie, I could give you a diagnosis that fits your complaints. I'm not sure how you'll feel about my opinion, but I can tell you exactly why you feel the way you do."

Reggie looked up, frightened. "I thought you said I wasn't sick."

"I don't consider pregnancy an illness."

"Pregnant? Me? You know that's impossible!"

Dr. Seidman smiled. "The only way that a pregnancy would be impossible is if you haven't had intercourse. I assume that is not the case here."

"Yes. I mean no. I mean you told me that I couldn't ever have a baby."

"No, Reggie. After reading your GYN report, I said the chances were very, very slim that you would ever be able to conceive because you had so much scar tissue matting down your tubes. I also told you that if you ever did get pregnant, there was a strong likelihood that you would have an ectopic. Neither of my predictions has occurred. Not only are you eight weeks pregnant, but the uterus is soft and the tubes aren't tender. I'd say you'll give birth in mid-June."

"I don't believe this. I just don't believe it!"

"I also think it's time for you to see an obstetrician. Do you have the name of anyone you would like to use?" He didn't bring up the subject of her marital status. Since the name on her chart still read Reggie Gates, he assumed she was unmarried.

"Use for what?"

"For prenatal care, for one thing, and for the delivery of this baby. I don't do obstetrics, Reggie."

A giggle escaped. "I never thought about it. I suppose sooner or later I'll have to see someone." She stood up, shaking her head in wonder. "Dr. Seidman, you'll have to forgive me. I had absolutely no idea that I was pregnant. I didn't even think it was possible. I have . . . there are . . . things . . ." she stammered.

"Nothing has to be done today. Go home and think it over." He took out a prescription pad. "Here's the names of two fine obstetricians. You should try to see one of them this month."

Dazed, she put the paper in her handbag. "Thank you. I don't know if I'm relieved to hear the diagnosis or more concerned than when I walked in," Reggie said honestly.

He walked her to the door. "I've done routine blood work just to be certain that my diagnosis is correct. If anything shows up, the office will call. If you don't hear from us within a week, you can assume that nothing is wrong with you. Okay?"

"Uh-huh," she answered and headed for the exit. Pregnant? Holy shit!

She arrived at her loft at two thirty. Alison was out to lunch, but Inez and the rest of the pattern and sample makers were busily executing the new designs that had been left for them. It seemed like weeks ago that she and Alison had worked on them; yet it had only been yesterday. She negotiated her way to her private office, where she placed a call to Lee. She still wasn't ready to talk to Cole. She hadn't seen or spoken to him since he had walked out on her Saturday night. He hadn't slept home the next night, offering no explanations, no excuses, nor had he made any attempt to reach her in two days. No, she certainly wasn't ready to speak with him. Lee's secretary came back on the line with the news that Lee had left for the day and wasn't expected back. She dialed his home number. He picked up on the second ring.

"Why are you home?" Reggie asked.

"I was just going to call the house again. How do you feel?"

"Fine, and I'm not at home, I'm in the office. But you still didn't answer me. Why are you home?"

"Because I'm leaving in an hour for California and I had to come home to pack," he explained.

"Business?"

"Nope. I'm going to spend a week or two with Liza and Melissa in Tahoe. Didn't I mention it to you?" he asked innocently.

She laughed. "You're such a lousy poker player. No," she said sarcastically, "you never mentioned it to me. How come?"

"Afraid that you would tell me not to go or maybe afraid that I'd chicken out."

"You should have gone a long time ago. Maybe this time you can reach some sort of conclusion that will make you both happy." She paused for a moment. "Lee?"

"Yes?"

"Where's Cole? I mean right now."

He wanted to lie to her . . . tell her that there had been a blackout . . . an emergency meeting with the President . . . a bad fall from a horse . . . anything but the truth: Cole simply hadn't wanted to call his wife. But he couldn't lie to her, not to protect Cole and not to shield Reggie from learning something about her husband that might be better if learned sooner. "He's in the office meeting with Astin. I suppose the meeting is still in progress."

"Why aren't you there? Isn't this meeting about the Stockyard?"

"I walked out on him when I found out where he spent the night. When he told me that he hadn't called you, I exploded. I told him exactly what I thought of him. It wasn't pretty. He told me to butt out," he laughed, "so, I did."

"And he let you walk out?" Reggie asked incredulously.

"He didn't have much choice."

"I see. Well, I'm sorry to have to say this, but I guess we both know where we fit in his life."

"Don't make generalizations. He'll come around. Right now, he's stewing over something, probably having nothing to do with either one of us. I simply wasn't letting him take it out on me. But you're a different story. I'm sure he'll call you today to make up."

"Are you?" she asked skeptically. "I'm not." Perhaps it was her secret knowledge of the pregnancy or maybe she simply didn't care anymore. "I'm tired of his foul moods, his demands, his needs. Dammit! I have needs, too." And suddenly she realized that she really did. She needed to be loved the way she was capable of loving. She had never had that kind of love from her parents or David. She had hoped, even believed briefly that she had found it with Cole. Now, she knew better. No one, no matter what the cause, could intentionally inflict this much pain and anguish on someone he loved. "When I entered into this arrangement with Cole, I thought I would die if I lost my business. You know what?" she asked with a bitter laugh. "I don't give a damn anymore. If I have to start over, I will, but this time it won't be with someone holding an ax over my head." She realized that there was really nothing standing in her way anymore except her huge debt to Cole. And now she knew how she was going to rid herself of that monkey on her back. "Lee, would you do something for me before you leave?"

"Honey, I would, but I only have a few minutes before I leave for Kennedy. I'm not even booked on the flight . . . never mind. What do you want me to do?"

"I just need some legal advice. You don't even have to handle it, in fact—you shouldn't. Meet me at the airport. I'll leave the city now. What terminal are you going to?"

"United. Are you sure you want to meet at the airport? I can spare a few more minutes."

"No, I don't want to discuss this over the phone. I want to speak to you in person."

They agreed to meet at the United terminal in an hour. Reggie arrived just as Lee was pulling up to the curb in a taxi. She ran over and gave him a bear hug, then waited as the cabbie unloaded his three large valises. They walked to the ticket counter, where Lee was able to secure a seat on the next plane to L.A. He suggested a drink in the cocktail lounge. When they sat down, Lee ordered a scotch, and Reggie, thinking about the baby, ordered a club soda. As they waited, Reggie began her story. Lee listened quietly until Reggie finished.

"Can I do that?" she asked.

"Yes. You can sell off everything. Burlington has left the offer for the patent open. You can probably find a buyer for Raggs and you know the loft won't be a problem."

"Will I get enough from those sales to pay back the debt to Cole?" she asked.

He shrugged. "I guess so. A lot depends on Cole's willingness to let you sell the patent—he does hold it as collateral. But why bother? He won't demand the money from you anymore, you're married."

"Because I want out of the marriage. Now. At any price. It's given me nothing but unhappiness and it isn't worth it to me anymore." She thought about Ardith's check. "I have a little money of my own, enough to keep me going for a while."

"Keep you going?" he repeated. "What are you talking about?"

"I'm leaving Cole and New York," she said quietly.

"Slow down," he said, "you're angry and hurt right now, but as soon as you straighten this out . . . You love him, Reg, and he loves you," he finished lamely. He knew he should say more but he couldn't think of anything else to say in defense of Cole.

"It doesn't appear to be enough to make the marriage work," explained Reggie. "I guess there has to be more than simple chemistry. Cole mouthed a lot of words to me, Lee . . . but the commitment wasn't there. One peculiar set of circumstances occurred and it was as if nothing we had ever said to each other or felt toward each other mattered." She sighed heavily. "Maybe what I'm looking for doesn't exist . . . maybe it's only a fairy tale . . . you know . . . happily ever after . . . ?"

"You're wrong, you know. It does exist and you and Cole have it. He'll come to his senses and come after you. He won't let you run away from him." He took her hands in his. "He'd be a fool if he did."

She smiled. "Thank you."

"Don't thank me, everything I've said is true." Lee looked up at the clock. "I've got to get going soon. Is there anything else you want to ask me?"

"Yes. Will the sale of everything be enough to cover the monetary penalties that are in the contract?"

Lee reached into his breast pocket and withdrew a memo pad and pen. Quickly, he jotted down some figures. "You'll probably just about break even after legal fees."

"You're going to charge me?"

"I'm not going to do anything. I think what you're doing is wrong, and I think that you're doing it for all the wrong reasons. You're running as hard and as fast as you can so you won't be hurt anymore. That's right—you can look at me any way you want, but it's the truth and you know it! Sure, run away, don't try to resolve it. God, Reggie! I'm so damned angry at you!"

"Me? Why?"

"Because you're a coward."

"Don't you dare call me that, Lee Taggett! You don't know what it's been like being married to him. It's been like slavery, and I'm just not for sale anymore." People were beginning to turn around and stare at them so she lowered her voice. "He would never end this marriage. He has everything and I have nothing." Then she remembered the baby. "No, that's not true anymore, but what I have isn't for sale. Not at any price."

He couldn't persuade her to change her mind. "Would you consider postponing any action until I get back from California?"

"No. I'm going home now to pack."

"And where are you planning to go?"

"I'll let you know when I know. Don't worry, I'll be fine." She couldn't give him any more information because she didn't have any idea where she was heading. All she knew was that she was leaving New York.

"There are things that you will have to do in New York, papers to sign, closings to go to. You have to be available."

"You take care of it—I'll give you power of attorney or whatever it is you need. Just see that Cole gets his money and I get out. Can you do that?"

"I suppose so. What am I supposed to tell Cole?"

"Whatever comes to mind. No, on second thought, tell him the truth. I gave you those instructions and you don't know anything else."

"Reggie, be serious. You don't expect him to believe that? He knows you tell me everything. You're putting me in a very uncomfortable position. You know that, don't you?"

"I'm sorry," she told her dearest friend. "If there was any other way of doing this, I wouldn't ask you. Please don't be angry with me. I have to do this my way."

"Why?"

"Because for the first time in my life, I'm trying to grow up and I want to do it all by myself."

They spoke briefly about the prices she could expect to realize from the various sales of her properties. He explained about the tax consequences as best as he could in the short period of time they had left before he boarded his plane. Once or twice he tried to pump her about where she was going, but she steadfastly refused to divulge anymore information. She simply insisted that she was tired of city life and wanted peace and quiet. He was torn between betraying her, running to phone Cole, and the promise he had made to Reggie to keep silent. Why was he forever in the middle? he wondered.

As they walked toward his gate, she turned and hugged him, tears in her eyes. "Stop worrying about me. Get on with your life. Try to see if you can make it work for you and Liza. That is why you're going out there, isn't it?"

He nodded. "But you won't try to work your life out with Cole?"

"With you and Liza there was love from the beginning—then other things got in the way. With Cole and me, it was all business. Do you understand the difference? Why it can't work for us?"

"Frankly, no. Love is love. What the hell difference does it make if it came before, during or after your marriage?" he asked angrily. He couldn't make sense out of the small distinction that seemed to be so important to her.

"In this case, I think it makes all the difference in the world. That's all I can explain. Trust me on this, Lee. I do know what I'm doing. Sometimes you have to walk away in order to see things better."

As he ambled toward the waiting plane, he tried to convince himself that she did know what was best for her. But as he turned, one more time, and saw her standing all alone in the terminal, he doubted her wisdom. No, this time he didn't believe she knew what she was doing.

Reggie returned to the house in time to receive the phone call from Roberta Wychek. She and Joe had been up to the cabin and, though the electricity was working, the phone was not. There was no evidence that anyone had been there for some time. The thermostat was set at fifty. There was no food in the refrigerator. The new dusting of snow over the weekend showed no footprints leading to or from the cabin.

Reggie thanked her for her help. She suddenly knew where

she was going. She would use the cabin until she decided where else to go. Cole wouldn't be using the cabin until late Friday night. She would have four days alone. By the time the weekend arrived, she would be gone.

She began to pack.

Chapter 48

Monday night when Cole called home and found Reggie out, he was mildly annoyed. Their little game had been played out as far as he was concerned. She'd punished him by not answering his questions; he had reciprocated by staying away from the house. He had meant to call her during the day but had become so immersed in trying to restructure the Stockyard deal, that he simply had not had time. By seven P.M., when he did call, he assumed she was working late, no doubt to punish him still further.

David's papers were in order; the land belonged to Patrice, just as he had said. However, David had no idea that both Patrice and Francis were finished with him. Cole had returned to the hospital to check on Francis at five o'clock, leaving David still tied up in the legal department. Cole, Francis and Patrice had sat in the private room that Francis now occupied, discussing their future plans. Cole patiently explained his ideas to Francis, who readily agreed with everything Cole had thought through. Patrice was sitting on a chair by the side of the bed when she suddenly leaned over and whispered something in Francis's ear. He put his arm around his daughter.

"Cole, we're both ready to go forward, but both Patrice and I have something to tell you that may affect your decision."

"What is that?" he asked. He thought he'd gone over everything.

Francis cleared his throat with great difficulty. "In the years that Patrice has been married to David"—a look of pain passed over the old man's face—"while I was busy with business and my own social life, that little . . . prick kept Patrice his prisoner by feeding her . . . drugs. Demerol is his latest goodie."

Cole's face registered shock and disgust. He turned to Patrice for some kind of denial but there was none. "Why didn't you tell anyone? For God's sake, why didn't you come to us for help?"

Patrice lowered her eyes in shame. "I couldn't," she whispered. "You see, there's even more." Now that it was out in the open, she was going to tell everything, make a clean breast of it. "It's dirty and ugly and shameful . . . there are movies, horrible pictures . . . things he made me do." She covered her face with shaking hands and Cole heard her soft moans. "I couldn't tell you," she charged. "Don't you see how impossible it would have been?" She looked up at Cole with red-ringed eyes. "It would have killed my father."

Disbelief was etched in Cole's eyes, disbelief and a slow, burning rage. "So you suffered alone? All these years? Ah, Patrice—anyone who loved you would have helped. Me. Your father . . . How the hell did you continue to live with that . . . that . . ." His voice faded. He just couldn't think of a word to describe what he felt for David Astin. Or himself. He should have known. All the signs were there, the veiled eyes, the suspicious reticence. He'd been blind, for God's sake. And he'd had those gut feelings all along about Astin . . . Somehow, he felt that he had let this family down.

Obtuse, blind, self-absorbed. Cole berated himself for his inability to see what was clearly right under his nose. What else had he missed? he wondered as he held Patrice's hand in a belated effort to comfort the broken woman.

In that moment, he thought about Lee walking out on him this morning. What was it he had said? "You'll wake up and find that you're all alone." Was that really what was happening? Patrice hadn't come to him for help . . . she didn't think he'd be interested enough, and now Lee had voiced the same feelings. Cole's shoulders sagged under the immense realization that he had turned his back on two people who thought they could depend on him.

And Reggie. She was by far the most important. To her, he had been the cruelest. A viselike cramp bit into his abdomen as he remembered the accusations he had hurled at her only two nights ago. Accusations that were unfounded . . . undeserved. He'd never even given her a reasonable chance to explain or share in his confusion of the bizarre flowers and phone call. He'd just pronounced her guilty of some vague heinous crime and sentenced her. God, how he'd betrayed the trust she'd finally given to him!

"Cole?" Francis spoke weakly. "Cole, what now?" Everything that Francis Munsey had so carefully built for Patrice's future now lay in Cole Weston's hands. Without Cole, the Stockyard deal wouldn't go forward. Now, faced with David's depravity, Patrice's weakness and his own impotence in dealing with any of it, Francis had his serious doubts whether Cole would want anything to do with the Munseys again. Francis closed his eyes. He was so very tired.

Cole reached over and covered Francis's hand with his. "I've got a lot of making up to do, it seems. I had David investigated awhile back and everything you're telling me was there in the report. Oh sure, they were only hints . . . but I'm smart enough to have picked them up. And I didn't. It's inexcusable!"

"You couldn't have known!" argued Francis, unwilling to let Cole take the blame for any of this.

"Yes." Cole shook his head in disagreement. "I could have. I should have." Then, quietly, as if there was no one else in the room, he said, "There's a lot I should have known and didn't." Like the fact that Reggie would never, never have betrayed him. And that his best friend had been trying to tell him that for months. Suddenly, he straightened his shoulders. He knew what had to be done. "First, we'll get Patrice better. There's a private clinic, South Gables, out in Suffolk County. It's small and discreet and has a wonderful reputation for treating alcoholism and drug addiction. We're getting Patrice in there immediately. Next, we make sure that Mr. David Astin never, never gets the chance to do this to anyone again. Finally, we go ahead with the Stockyards." And I try to straighten out the mess I've made of my own life, he said silently.

Francis's eyes open incredulously. "You'll go ahead?"

"Absolutely!" assured Cole. "But only under those conditions. Patrice, once you're in treatment, I'll need your help in going after David."

Patrice winced. She wasn't very brave. It had taken every ounce of courage she had to simply tell her story. Now, she wanted it out of her hands. She was terrified of David's wrath once he knew what she had done. She looked to Cole for help and understanding. "I can't help you. He'll know that I told you and he'll . . . he'll . . ." She started to tremble violently. "He'll kill me!"

"No. You don't understand. I'm not sending you back to that monster. I'm going to need you for information. Where he goes. Who he sees. His habits . . . Can you do that?"

Hesitantly, she nodded. "Yes. I don't know how that will help, but as long as I don't have to go back to him . . . I'll do anything. Where is he now?"

"I sent him on a wild-goose chase. Right now, he's with a friend of mine, a private investigator, searching for a man who died two years ago. I told him that one of the deeds wasn't in order. He tried to disagree, but I told him that I had to be one hundred percent sure that the deed was free of liens. Most of it was mumbo jumbo," admitted Cole, "but Hugh Coffin knows all about what's going on. He'll keep him busy all night on my say-so."

The three of them stayed in the hospital until well after ten o'clock that night. Because Patrice was genuinely terrified to go back to David, Cole arranged for her to enter South Gables that night. While she was in treatment, her divorce proceedings would begin. After she had left the private room, Cole assured Francis that he knew the proper attorneys to speak to and that Astin would never bother Patrice again. Francis sank back into his pillows, a tired, sick old man . . . but hopeful now that he had entrusted his daughter to Cole's care.

"I've bungled this badly, Cole," Francis said in a low voice. "She was the only thing in my life that ever mattered and I let that monster do this to her. Where was I? How could I have been so blind?" Tears gathered in the corners of the old man's eyes. "You don't know the excuses, the lies that I chose to believe because it was easier than confronting him. He's the worst kind of evil that walks on two legs because he takes advantage of those who are weaker than he is." He heaved a heavy sigh. "She never had a chance against him, and I led her right into it." He pounded his mattress. "I've been rescuing him from disasters for years. And this scum is what I chose for my daughter?"

He reached over and placed his hand over Cole's. "Listen to an old man, my friend. When you have children, look and listen all the time. Don't assume that they can grow up all by themselves. You never stop being a parent. You never outgrow the responsibility." He shook his head in sorrow. "Somewhere I lost sight of everything that was important. I was so delighted to see her married and living in the lifestyle I envisioned that I never took notice that things weren't right. Don't ever let yourself become so involved in business that it rules your life." He settled back, exhausted. "You have a lovely wife, Cole. Take care of her, cherish her. Oh, God, here I am lecturing you about your family and you should be with your wife right now. Where is she tonight?"

Cole shrugged. "Home, I guess. She has quite a business of her own, you know. It keeps her pretty busy," he answered lamely. Actually, he didn't have any idea where Reggie was. Sooner or later there would be a confrontation between them, one that wouldn't be pretty. He'd said some lousy things to her and she hadn't deserved that. He had a lot of explaining to do. "Okay, I think that about wraps it up for now. I'll be in touch with you tomorrow morning. Are you going to handle your son-in-law, or should I?"

"Oh, no! That's one pleasure you're not going to take away from me. It's the one thing that is going to get me through Patrice's treatment. We'll bury him." Francis smiled.

"Sleep well." He took his coat from behind the door. "I'd like to bring Reggie out to South Gables to see Patrice. I think they would like each other," he added, but Francis was already snoring gently. Cole closed the door. He was exhausted. It had been a grueling day and facing Reggie now to settle their differences would insure an even more exhausting night, but he wanted to do it as soon as possible. He had to. He hailed a cab and gave the driver his address.

When Cole put his key in the lock at ten thirty, John was waiting for him. The elderly servant was sitting in a straight-back chair in the foyer. He had been waiting for a long time. Slowly, he rose to his feet as his employer approached. He handed Cole a cream-colored envelope imprinted with the initials RAW.

"Mrs. Weston asked me to wait up to give this to you when she left."

Cole took the envelope, a puzzled look on his face. He slit it open, carefully extracting the single card with his wife's initials. In her precise script she had written:

> My friend and I have built a wall
> Between us thick and wide:
> The stones of it are laid in scorn
> And plastered high with pride.
> By Elizabeth Cutter
> (borrowed by Regina Gates)

Chapter 49

Once in a great while, a course of action that begins as an act of desperation evolves into something positive. Not often. Most of the time, the acts, by their very nature, lead to disaster. On the afternoon that Reggie met with Lee in the United Airlines terminal to give him her instructions, he foresaw nothing less than catastrophe. He was wrong.

Within three months, Reggie had sold her business to Alison and three other young designers who had given Reggie some up-front cash and a buy-out agreement. The patent rights were gobbled up by one of the biggest knitting mills in the country. Her condominium sold the first week it was on the market. Cole's money was repaid, along with the penalties, though he made it clear to Lee that he had no interest in the money. He angrily placed the entire amount in an interest-bearing escrow account in the name of Regina Weston. It wasn't long thereafter that Regina Weston ceased to exist. Once Cole learned of her plans, through Lee, he didn't contest the inevitable divorce. She resumed her maiden name. Hurt beyond words, he steadfastly made no attempt to locate her after Lee made it absolutely clear that she chose not to be found.

His brief attempt at matrimony a failure, Cole plunged all his energies into the Stockyards. He and Lee never discussed Reggie, although Cole was certain Lee was still in touch with her. Cole acted as if she had never existed. He briefly resumed his affair with Evyan, who was delighted to have him back. When once she chided him about the failure of his marriage, he had warned her in a bone-chilling voice never to mention the subject again. Wisely, she didn't.

Patrice was released from South Gables in February. She returned to Chicago, still under a psychiatrist's care, to begin her career as her father's full partner. Francis, though still weak, sat next to her in a wheelchair, smiling proudly at the ground-breaking ceremony. When Cole flew out for an extended visit, he was delighted to see how well she looked. She had gained weight, filling out the hollows in her face and body, and had regained much of her youthful beauty. The long, peaceful months in the clinic had also erased the constant look of fear on her face. She smiled now, something that she had rarely done in years. She even managed to talk about her former addiction. Cole found her charming, and Francis beamed when Cole complimented him on the fine job he had done for his daughter.

It was later that evening, while sipping brandy in the living room after Francis finally had bid them good-night, that Patrice decided to tell Cole what she knew about her former husband and his former wife. At first Cole insisted that he didn't want to discuss anything about Reggie, but Patrice would not be deterred. She told him everything she knew. The night of the reception David, drunk and out of control, had told her everything about his relationship with Reggie: how he had left Reggie alone in New York because he'd suspected that she might be pregnant and it would upset all his future plans; what happened to the pregnancy, David never knew. She admitted to Cole that David had then forced her to call him that night, giving her the script about the mole, and, after beating her up, had made her send the flowers. She had tried to call Reggie the next night to explain, to apologize in some way, but every time she was able to dial their home, David walked in, forcing her to hang up.

"I understand why *you* did what you did. But his motives? What were they?" The emotions that threatened to explode inside him were kept strictly under control. Until he understood all the pieces, he couldn't put the puzzle together. He wouldn't let himself feel anything. Not yet.

She shrugged. "I wish I could give you a black and white answer, but I can't. Perhaps he hoped to gain some advantage over you by terrorizing your wife. Maybe he simply couldn't stand to see anyone happy, and it was obvious that the two of you were happy together." Patrice took a small sip of brandy. "I'm still trying to understand what he did to me, Cole. I couldn't begin to understand what he was trying to do to Reggie."

In the months that Patrice was in South Gables, Cole had been a frequent visitor. Though his visits began as a favor to Francis, more and more, he found himself drawn to her. If there was a future for the two of them together, it was never discussed. He admired her courage, her commitment to rid herself of her addiction. They became friends. For the time being, both were content with their relationship as it stood.

"I'm going to look for my own apartment this week," she told him.

"That's wonderful. Have you told your father yet?"

"No. He's gotten so accustomed to having me around that I'm a little nervous about his reaction. My doctor thinks I'm using that as an excuse. He thinks I'm hiding."

"From David?" asked Cole.

Patrice nodded. "He's here in Chicago. He is violently contesting the divorce. He doesn't like the settlement. He thinks he should be getting alimony."

"He should be grateful that you didn't press criminal charges against him. Are you still afraid of him?"

"Yes and no," she admitted. "I have a restraining order against him. He can't come near me. Still, I can't help wishing he were in another state. It's so much easier living without the fear of bumping into him. Cole?" she asked quietly. "Have you ever heard from Reggie?"

"No."

She pressed. "Do you know where she is?"

"No. I never heard from her after the night she left. The divorce was handled through attorneys. She didn't want anything from me. I gather she had some money put away. She made it clear that she wanted no communication between us. I respected her wishes."

Patrice wondered what kind of woman would walk out on a man like Cole Weston. She tried hard not to dwell on what a life with Cole would be like. She knew instinctively that neither one of them was ready to begin again. "You have no interest in seeing her again?"

"Patrice, I don't want to talk about it. It's over. Please drop the subject." He stood up. "It's getting late, and I'm flying out in the morning. I'll be back next week to start negotiations for the mall. By that time, all the bids should be in. Can you handle everything here?" he asked.

"Uh-huh. Mr. Hastings called about the Galaxy bid. He wanted to meet with either one of us this week. What should I tell him?"

Simon. Another reminder of his foolish jealousy. "I won't be available this week at all. If he can accomplish whatever he wants by meeting with you—fine. If not, put him off until I come back to Chicago." Was Simon seeing Reggie? wondered Cole. He put the idea from his mind.

"I don't see any reason to put him off. As far as I'm concerned, I would like to see Galaxy in the mall. It will be a tremendous draw for the other kind of stores we want to attract. Let me see what he has to say. I can always set up a second meeting with you at a future date."

Cole agreed. He didn't want to meet with Simon. There must have been some communication between Reggie and Simon when she had sold Raggs. He didn't want to know, just as he hadn't tried to find her in the months since she had been gone. The less said, the sooner healed.

On the morning shuttle from Chicago to La Guardia, Cole battled it out with himself. He knew he could have traced her whereabouts at any time. But he hadn't. He had let her walk out and had resumed his life. He had thought it was the right thing for her at the time. He had buried that part of his life, he had thought, but now as he closed his eyes and leaned his head against the window of the plane, images of his wife drifted in and out of his consciousness. There was a moment when her image was so clear, he felt that he could almost reach out and touch her. Then the image faded, replaced by the mocking face of David Astin. He had won after all, thought Cole. No, they'd all lost—all except Patrice, who had managed to get her life back. But, my God, thought Cole, the price they had all paid!

Reggie . . . the long graceful legs and rich russet hair. The perfect lips that parted so sweetly under his, the slender, gentle fingers that played his body so well. Was that what he missed? Her passion? Her touch? Her scent? Was that love? And if it was, why couldn't he feel the same toward any other woman? Why only Reggie? "Because she reached inside you, you fool. She captured your soul. You opened a door and let her in, and when she had one foot in, you slammed the door in her face. She was as afraid of making a commitment as you," continued the voice in his head, "but she was honest; she told you how frightened she was. You mouthed empty reassurances. She had every right to leave you. You violated the trust she placed in you. The trust *you* begged *her* to give you. You were the betrayer, not the betrayed!" accused the voice.

"But," he argued silently, "I warned her. The contract . . . I told her I'd make a lousy husband . . . no love, no promises."

He opened his eyes as the plane touched ground. The interior lights went on as the plane stopped. Reggie's image faded. Thankfully, he reached under his seat for his briefcase. He felt the smooth leather, the embossed initials. A gift from Reggie, another reminder. He made a mental note to send Marjory shopping for a new briefcase.

"It's not that easy," chided the voice. "Send her shopping for new memories, too. Play your games. Sooner or later her image will fade, but for once in your life, admit you fouled up. You let the only woman you ever loved walk out of your life. Why didn't you go after her . . . ?"

Part Three

Chapter 50

The light gray Chevy station wagon skidded on the tightly packed snow that blanketed Clover Road. Reggie grabbed the wheel, trying to turn into the skid. Five feet ahead she saw a spot of asphalt that had miraculously escaped the snowstorm. The spinning tires touched the bald spot and held. She straightened the car, pulling it slowly over to the side of the road. Visibility was terrible. She'd had no business starting out in this weather, not up here where, within minutes, a few flakes of snow could become a blinding blizzard. She checked the gas gauge and saw that the needle was well into the red danger zone. If she had to stay on the side of the road for long, she'd have to turn the motor off or she'd run out of gas. Either way, she knew she was in trouble. At five thirty in the afternoon, with mounting snow beginning to obstruct the windshield, she could barely make out the front of the car, much less the distance to the town's only gas station.

Suddenly, the engine died. She tried to restart the car but knew that it was useless. She was out of gas. Clover Road wasn't too long, and normally Reggie would have no problem walking the few miles to the station. But in her eighth month, with the wind and snow blowing against her, she didn't know how far she could go. A blizzard in May? No matter how unlikely, she was right in the middle of it.

As she rolled down the window, a clump of snow landed in her lap. She brushed it off the fur-lined cape she now wore every day and quickly raised the frosted window. She would wait for a passing car. The car was still warm enough for her to be comfortable as she waited. Her mail lay in a stack next to her. That was the reason for this foolhardy trip. She hadn't picked up her mail for three days and she was eagerly awaiting a letter and a fat check from Alison. She sorted through the envelopes, finding the one she had waited for, and rapidly ripped it open. Twenty-eight thousand dollars. That and the balance of the money she had left from Ardith's check would be enough for the down payment on the house.

It was perfect. Large enough for her and the baby, with its three bedrooms, two bathrooms, country kitchen and sunny enclosed porch; yet small enough so that she could care for it by herself. And the best part of the house was that it was within walking distance of Ardith. Her mother-in-law could stroll over every day to play with her grandchild. She'd even agreed to stay with the baby if Reggie still wanted to open the clothing boutique once the baby arrived. She hadn't made her mind up yet. Decisions came slowly to her these days. Life was to be taken one step at a time. She preferred it that way. Ardith complained that she was getting too countrified, but Reggie simply laughed, explaining patiently that she used up her store of adventure when she had fled from New York.

On that day, she had rented a car, driven well into the night until she had reached Cole's cabin. There she had stayed until the weekend when, fearing Cole might decide to visit his retreat, she'd gotten back into the car and headed to Boston. It wasn't until she pulled off the Mass. Pike and onto Storrow Drive that she actually decided where she was going. She bypassed her parents' house and ended up at Amy's. She and her sister had done little over the years other than to exchange Christmas cards, but when she arrived, unannounced, Amy was surprisingly gracious. Reggie remained in Brookline until she thought that one more day with her sister's family would cause her to lose her mind.

The next week and a half were spent meandering through the tiny villages of New England, where Reggie carefully avoided the big cities. She slept in inexpensive inns and ate most of her meals in their dining rooms while she valiantly tried to sort out her past and make some sense of her future.

Ardith's money would not last forever and she needed a home soon. It was then that she thought about her mother-in-law. Yes, it was farfetched. She had no idea what kind of life Ardith led or how she would feel if her ex-daughter-in-law suddenly showed up on her doorstep. But Reggie was being backed into a corner. She had to land someplace. And she remembered how easily they had talked and laughed that afternoon in SoHo.

The arrangement suited both of them. Ardith asked surprisingly few questions. She remembered the look on Cole's face the night of the reception. Her daughter-in-law's unheralded arrival in Maine four weeks later was a surprise, but the breakup of their marriage was not. Ardith opened her arms, her house and her heart, and Reggie gratefully accepted. She moved into a sunny apartment over the garage, which had once housed the rambling Victorian home's servants. A good part of the house was closed off because Ardith didn't need the space. She offered to reopen it, but Reggie much preferred the privacy of the garage apartment.

At dinner, one week after her arrival, Reggie was introduced to Ardith's friend, Dr. Robert Chapping. In a conspiratorial whisper, Reggie asked him if he did obstetrics. Ardith whooped with glee. Having her grandchild near her was the price Ardith would charge for Reggie's stay. They never spoke about Cole. Reggie suspected that he spoke to his mother, but as far as she knew, Ardith somehow neglected to tell her son that Reggie was in Maine.

The snow was showing no signs of decreasing in intensity. Reggie wished she had left Ardith a note. She opened the door a crack and peered into the swirling snow. It was now or never, she decided, pushing hard on the door. The wind resistance made it difficult for her to open it. Finally she had it opened wide enough to squeeze her enormous bulk outside. With one hand grasping the door handle, her feet slipped out from under her and she went down with a resounding thud. Her cape and the snowy bunting cushioned her fall. Quickly, she tried to get up, out of the way of any traffic that might be coming. Sweating profusely under the woolen smock and fur cape, she struggled with her awkward body. Her equilibrium was off completely and, after her third attempt, she was ready to give up. Panting from exertion she lay in the snow. Perspiration that had gathered under her tight ski hat had started such itching that she ripped the cap from her head. Now the raw wind against her uncovered ears sent daggers through her skull.

She tried to get up one more time. This time, she used her knitted scarf under her boots in order to gain traction. It worked. She was huffing and puffing but she was upright.

The last vestiges of daylight soon departed, and Reggie was

left trudging through the raging snowstorm in the dark. In spite of the freezing temperature, rivulets of sweat formed under her arms and breasts. She felt the moisture collecting and running down her body in icy streams. Her teeth were chattering and she was shivering under the fur-lined cape. First she was flushed with heat then a blast of arctic wind would assault her and she would be freezing.

In the silent world of darkness and snow, her pulsebeat echoed in her ears. Thump! Thump! March to its rhythm. She felt a trickle between her legs. More than a few drops. She was horrified. Had she urinated from fear? She couldn't summon the muscles to make it stop.

Her body wobbled, then tottered, and she struggled to maintain her footing. Like a novice ice skater, she slipped this way and that, gyrating on the frozen street. Instinctively, her hand went to protect her middle as her reeling body finally lost its battle and she pitched forward. She hit the ground hard, barely managing to pivot slightly as she fell. The bottom half of her body became bathed in amniotic fluid.

Lying by the side of the road, soaking wet and covered by a blanket of still falling snow, Reggie's body trembled violently. Huge spasms of fear and cold wracked her already weakened body. She drew her legs up to her stomach in a long forgotten position of comfort and security. For a brief moment, she forgot where she was. She put her head down on the snow pillow. The quaking receded. She was warmer. As if it were a blanket, she drew her cape around her and yawned. "I'll just stay here for a moment," she murmured, "just enough time to rest, then I'll get up and have my baby."

She closed her eyes and listened to the slowed beating of her heart. The longer she remained curled up in a ball, the more comfortable she became. She drifted in and out of a trancelike state, half awake, half asleep. Someone was waving a wand over her, telling her in a soft whisper that it was okay to rest, okay to give up the fight to go on. She listened to the soothing voice. The snowflakes were so beautiful, she thought, as they filtered through the trees in the reflected light of a streetlamp. She watched as they danced. Her eyelids closed, opened, then closed again. The waltz of the falling snow had hypnotized her.

Somewhere in the distance, as though it were happening to someone else, a band tightened around her middle. Lazily it held her in an embrace, then released her. It was done so lovingly. She dozed as the snow continued to drop its blanket of warmth on her. She dreamed of Cole holding her, whispering to her, kissing her face, her eyes. She felt him lift her in his strong arms and carry her off. In her dream she put her head on his shoulder and he brushed the snowflakes from her face with his lips. She loved him so much. She struggled to tell him but the words that formed in her brain wouldn't make their way to her lips. She was much too tired to fight. She surrendered to a hypnotic somnolescence.

With a weary shrug she slept in his arms despite the tightening bands that constricted her abdomen. She wanted to tell him that he was holding her too tightly, but even that was beyond her. She finally lost consciousness.

She was found a half hour later. They missed her the first time they passed by, so covered was she by the snow. They mistook her curled up body for a snow mound. She had barely managed to walk thirty yards before falling into the drift of snow that threatened to hide her from the rescue squad. The seasoned volunteers retraced their steps from her car once more. With flashlights and walkie-talkies, they fanned out in a circle. The raging wind made their voices useless.

Ardith sat in the cab of an ambulette nervously biting her knuckle. Once the rescue party was five feet from the vehicle she lost sight of them. She tried to concentrate on the squeaking and squelching of the shortwave radio. She could barely decipher the words. There was no point in looking out the window; it was now totally covered by snow.

Suddenly she heard a commotion and the rear door of the ambulette was thrown open. Ardith gasped in horror as she recognized Reggie's hair. The body was still, the head thrown back over the arm of the rescuer who quickly placed Reggie on a waiting stretcher. The interior of the vehicle came alive like a disturbed hornets' nest. Lights were turned on and machines started buzzing. The driver jumped into the seat beside Ardith, and within seconds the siren was screaming.

They stripped Reggie of her wet clothes, exchanging them

for warm, dry blankets. Ardith heard words like hypothermia, frostbite, exposure. She sat and stared, horrified. A tall, thin paramedic was tucking towel-wrapped hot water bottles, over, under and around the unconscious patient's body. Another volunteer hooked Reggie up to an IV set so she could receive warm intravenous fluids. A third man connected her to monitors that measured her temperature, respiration, pulse and cardiac arrhythmia. Ardith watched nervously as the men checked Reggie's extremities for signs of frostbite. Fortunately, there were none; her skin was not whitened, mottled or swollen. Ardith breathed a sigh of relief that didn't last long as the monitors began to show the slowed respiration and pulse of the unconscious woman.

During the rewarming procedure, the technicians were constantly in touch with the Waterville Community Hospital, relaying Reggie's vital signs. By the time the ambulette pulled up to the hospital ramp, Reggie's core temperature had risen to ninety-eight. She was no longer hypothermic. During the short ride, she had regained consciousness once or twice but had then slipped back into a semiconscious state. Ardith ran after the stretcher into the emergency room where Bob Chapping waited.

The next twelve hours passed in a blur for Ardith. Bob examined Reggie in the emergency room and found that she was in active labor. He notified Ardith and then, after ascertaining that her vital signs were normal and stable, had her admitted to the obstetrical floor. Ardith sat on the edge of a vinyl chair in the waiting room for five hours. Bob ran out a few times during the night to reassure her that although Reggie was six weeks early, labor was progressing normally. Reggie was alert, despite her ordeal, and would be sedated only if absolutely necessary. At four forty-five A.M. Reggie delivered a five pound, four ounce baby boy.

He found Ardith stretched out on one of the waiting room's sofas. Gently, he tapped her on the shoulder. She woke with a start.

"Relax, Grandma," he reassured.

She jumped from the sofa. "Is it . . . Reggie, did she . . . ?" Her hands were shaking.

Bob put his arm around her shoulder. "She's wonderful.

You're a grandmother and the baby is perfect. He's beautiful." Bob answered all the unspoken questions.

Ardith began to giggle. "Oh my, oh my." Then she broke down and began to sob into Bob's shoulder. He held her tightly, stroking her hair and murmuring words of assurance. He'd known her for years, this diminutive, strong woman who had always been so capable. Now for the first time, he was seeing the vulnerable side of her character. The near tragedy had unraveled her. "Come on. You and I deserve a drink." He began to lead her down the corridor.

She shook her head. "I want to see my grandson first."

"Soon," he promised. "Let's skip the drink and get a quick cup of coffee in the lounge. Then you can see the baby."

She looked at him suspiciously. "What's the matter, Bob? Is there something wrong with him?" she asked as they entered the doctor's lounge. "And, please, don't keep anything from me."

He walked over to the coffee urn and handed her a plastic foam cup. "The baby is fine. His birth weight is appropriate for gestational age. His Apgar is good, too, but right now he's in a radiant heater to keep him warm. We've also put him in the suspect nursery.

Ardith's heart skipped a beat. "'Suspect?' What does that mean? Is he sick?"

"No. I told you that he's fine, but I'm not sure that Reggie is. She began to cough and had a low-grade fever about two hours ago. I have to assume that the baby is infected until proven otherwise. We've already done blood cultures, a spinal tap and taken cultures from the baby's ear, nose, throat and the chord. We're doing this sepsis work-up because there is a real possibility that he is infected." He pulled Ardith into his arms and held her close to him. "There's every reason to think he'll be fine, but as a precaution I'm also ordering that he be placed on triple antibiotics until I get the results of all the tests. Ardith, all this is routine."

"Don't give me that nonsense! What else?" she said angrily.

"Reggie won't be permitted to breast-feed."

"Why not?"

"She's febrile and also on antibiotics. I can't risk letting her feed or even touch the baby." The fear etched on Ardith's face made Bob go on. "Please trust me, Ardith. This is all precautionary. We'll watch her carefully. Later this morning we'll x-ray her. Until then, there's nothing to do. She's going to be fine, I promise," he assured her with more bravado than candor.

"I want to see him now. I have to!"

"Come on. I can see that, until you see him with your own eyes, you're not going to be satisfied."

"Do you know the baby's name? Did Reggie tell you?" asked Ardith.

"Yes."

"Well?" she asked impatiently.

"She told me what to put on his birth certificate."

"What is the matter with you? What is my grandson's name!"

"His name is Alex Jordan *Gates*."

"Damn!"

It was the first time that Dr. Robert Chapping had ever heard Ardith Weston use profanity.

Chapter 51

In the early predawn, Reggie spiked a temperature of 104.8. She had chills, a nonproductive cough and continued to moan when not in delirium. The floor nurse put Dr. Chapping on emergency page. He arrived within half an hour. He decided to examine Reggie before he alarmed Ardith. He heard her labored breathing as soon as he entered the room. On examination he found dullness to percussion and tubular breathing involving the lower two-thirds of her right chest. He ordered an immediate chest X ray and nasal oxygen prong. The films only confirmed what he already knew. She had a massive patch of pneumonia on the right side, involving both middle and lower lobes. He placed her on 4.8 million units of IV penicillin a day and went to call Ardith.

By six o'clock that night, her condition hadn't improved. Her temperature fluctuated between 103° and 104°. Ardith waited impatiently for Bob, who had promised to join her at the hospital after his afternoon hours. The hours had crawled by as she maintained her bedside vigil. Only once during the day had she left Reggie's side to peek at her grandson.

At six thirty, Bob walked into the hospital room. His face was deeply etched with lines of fatigue. There were bags under his bright blue eyes that were now dulled by the sleepless night and long office hours.

He opened Reggie's chart and flipped through the many multicolored papers. When he put it down on the nightstand, he asked Ardith to step into the corridor so he could examine Reggie. Ten minutes later, he joined her.

She stopped her nervous pacing. "Well?"

He shook his head and shrugged helplessly. "There's no change. Her fever is still hovering around 104. So far there's no response to the antibiotic." When he saw the panic in Ardith's eyes, he added, "But it's still early."

"What do you mean?"

"Right now it means what I said. She has not responded to the treatment, yet. But it's still too early to tell anything. Let's see how she's doing in the morning." He leaned against the wall, stifling a yawn. "You're going home with me right now. I'm going to feed you and see that you get some rest. Let's see who's available from the nursing registry for tonight."

"I'm sorry, Bob, but I'm not leaving her."

"Ardith," he said, sternly, "I am not suggesting that you go home. I am ordering you to leave her alone tonight. I already have two patients from your family to worry about. I will not add you to the list. There is absolutely nothing to be gained by your staying!" He virtually pulled her down the corridor.

Reluctantly, Ardith followed him down the two flights to the nurses' office where they made arrangements for private-duty nursing. With a heavy heart, she let Bob help her into her car and followed him to her house.

"I'll call the hospital before I go to bed. If there's been any change in her condition, I'll call you. If you don't hear from me within half an hour, you can assume her condition is the same." He waited until she was safely in the house and the living room lights were on. Then slowly, he trudged through the melting snow to his car.

The house was cold. Ardith pushed the thermostat over seventy degrees, something she rarely did. But tonight, alone for the first time in months, she wanted the warmth. The burden of Reggie's illness was beginning to wear her down. Tonight, she felt every bit an old woman. She brewed a cup of tea in the unusually quiet kitchen and brought it back to the living room, where she settled into her favorite armchair to await Bob's call.

Thoughtfully, she sipped her tea, wondering what would become of her grandson if Reggie didn't recover. From the moment Bob had told her of the failure of Reggie's body to respond to the antibiotic, the nagging question of the baby's welfare had plagued her. The very thought that Reggie might not survive was so unthinkable that she had tried to push it from her mind, but it kept resurfacing. Would Alex stay with her if something were to happen to his mother? Did Ardith have the right to keep him, to raise him? He did have a father. Did she have the right to notify Cole that he had a son now that Reggie was so sick? If she told him, she wondered if he would believe her. And how would she justify her decision to call him after the solemn oath she had made to Reggie that Cole not be informed of the pregnancy? She had given her word when she'd asked Reggie to stay with her. But this was something that neither one of them had anticipated. Didn't she owe something to her son and grandson?

She reached for the phone. Her hand rested there as she continued to argue with herself. I'm too old to make these kinds of decisions, she told herself wearily. Let Cole work it out. She picked up the phone and began dialing. "He has the right to know, he has to be told," she told herself as the phone began to ring in New York.

"John," she said to Cole's valet, "this is Mr. Weston's mother. Is my son at home?"

"No, ma'am. He was called to Chicago unexpectedly. But he did phone me awhile ago and said that he should be back in New York tomorrow or the next day. Would you like to leave a message?"

"I want him to call me as soon as he gets home. I'm fine,

but this is terribly important, so make sure he gets the message." She hung up, thinking about what she had just done. She wished she could call Bob to ask his opinion. He knew the whole story. Reggie had told both of them everything when she had decided to remain in Maine. It was why Reggie's naming the baby Alex Gates came as no surprise to the doctor.

Ardith checked the kitchen clock. Over half an hour elapsed since she had entered the house. Still Bob hadn't called. She found waiting impossible. She called him.

He had been sleeping. "Dr. Chapping," he answered.

"Bob, it's Ardith."

"Yes, I know," he replied, yawning.

"Well? Did you call?"

"Mm-hmm. I spoke to the night nurse. There's been very little change." He yawned again and apologized. "Get some rest, Ardith. It will be another long day of sitting and waiting tomorrow."

He was right. Tomorrow would indeed be a long day.

Chapping stopped at the hospital at six A.M. the next morning. He checked on the baby first. He was satisfied that the infant was doing well. He issued orders for Alex to be removed from the suspect nursery. He then handed the infant to a waiting nurse and headed for Reggie's room.

Things had not gone as well for Reggie during the night. She had required an oxygen tent. Her fever had risen to over 105° and restraints had been necessary to keep her from pulling the tubes and IV lines from her body. She alternately thrashed, rambled and slept fitfully. The antibiotics weren't working.

The private-duty nurse echoed his thoughts. "She is worse. Her breathing is more labored and her pulse has become much more rapid."

Chapping examined Reggie, and his observations corresponded to the nurse's. He thought he detected fluid in her left lung as well. Why was the pneumonia not responding to treatment? He signed the chart, continuing the medication as ordered, and strode to his office on the floor above. He slammed the door and began to scan the bookshelves for his texts on respiratory infections. Pending the culture, he had to assume that Reggie had pneumococcal pneumonia, but if that were the case, she should already have begun to respond to penicillin. He flipped through one of the books, checking and rechecking symptoms and treatment, hoping to find something he had missed.

But he knew the time had come to call in a specialist on infectious diseases. He leafed through the Maine Physician's Directory, noting that the nearest University Hospital was well over sixty miles away, but he felt strongly that Reggie should be seen by Syd Barron, Chief of Infectious Diseases. He found the number he was searching for.

Dr. Barron answered his own phone. Chapping quickly identified himself and gave the physician a brief summary of the case. The two physicians agreed to meet in Reggie's room at 2:30.

Chapter 52

On the morning of the fourth day, Ardith and Chapping were standing outside of Reggie's room, speaking softly. Ardith was leaning against the wall. "I told him the whole story," she said. "He's leaving now. If he can get a flight out, he should be here within five hours."

Chapping nodded grimly. "You didn't have any choice." He ran his fingers through his thick gray hair. "Did she recognize you at all this morning?"

Ardith compressed her lips. Her eyes were glazed from lack of sleep. "She never even opened her eyes. It's almost as if she's saving all her strength just to breathe. How much longer can she go on like this? I can't stand seeing her like this."

He shook his head. "I don't know, I just don't know. Barron is coming back this afternoon. We should know more then. There is nothing to do now but wait and pray."

In spite of Ardith's reservations about calling her son, Bob was relieved that Cole was on his way to Maine. Should the worst occur, it was important that Ardith have someone to lean on. She was balancing precariously on the edge of a precipice and Bob doubted whether she could hold up much longer.

Chapping and Ardith had pulled strings, and there was a waiting police escort for Cole when he landed in Maine. With siren and lights flashing, they sped from the airport to the hospital. Cole sat with his hands folded tightly in his lap, his face completely unreadable. He hadn't yet digested everything his mother had told him during the hurried phone call. All he had heard was that Reggie was desperately ill and had been placed on the critical list the night before. Words had been exchanged but he had heard nothing more than the name of the hospital. He didn't know how she had come to be in Maine or why it was his mother who was calling him. He didn't care. His one coherent thought was to be with his wife. The months that had passed since they had separated disappeared from his consciousness as if they had never been. He felt as if he had seen her yesterday, had held her in his arms and had promised to love her forever that morning. Now she needed him and he had to be there.

The car screeched into the hospital parking lot and Cole jumped from it before it came to a complete stop. There was so much to do, so much to say, he thought as he sprinted to the emergency room entrance. Wildly, he looked around for a familiar face. Where was his mother? He asked an orderly for directions to Reggie's room. He was given the room number and, declining to wait for the elevator, he turned toward the stairs. He reached her floor, looking right and left for some indication of room numbers. Then he saw his mother standing outside the last room in the corridor talking to a tall gray-haired man. He began to move in that direction. Ardith saw him and broke into a run, flinging herself into his arms. The dam burst and she sobbed into his shoulder. His heart stopped. Roughly, he pushed her away from him, staring into her eyes.

"Reggie?" he rasped.

Ardith pointed to the doorway that she had just left.

Cole hesitated momentarily in front of the door, afraid to enter. The gray-haired man stepped aside, allowing Cole his first glimpse of Reggie. But it couldn't possibly be his Reggie. This woman was dying. The noises coming from the bed were all the sounds that Cole would forever associate with hell. The stertorous breathing, the rattling respiration, and the rapid panting completely unraveled his blind belief that he could save her. Chapping drew him gently out of the doorway. Like a child, Cole let himself be led to the lounge, where Ardith, once again in control of herself, sat and waited. He sat down next to his mother, looking to her for answers that he hadn't sought in over thirty years.

She held her son's hand between hers. His was trembling, hers were not. She began to speak slowly, pouring out the whole story, beginning with Reggie's unannounced arrival in Maine. She made no apologies for harboring her daughter-in-law. She didn't feel that she owed any. Cole listened carefully, never breaking in to ask the hundreds of questions that whirled through his mind. Ardith told him about the snowstorm, the race to find Reggie and get her to the hospital after her exposure to the cold. She explained the subsequent pneumonia that appeared to be resistant to penicillin. As best as she could, she told him what was being done for Reggie.

Chapping had entered the lounge again after leaving the two of them alone for a while. Now he interrupted Ardith. "She's been seen by the best infectious disease expert in Maine. We're doing everything that's humanly possible. Your mother hasn't left Reggie's side for days, Cole. She's totally exhausted and in danger of collapsing. That's why I insisted you get up here." He paused and looked at Ardith. "There's also another matter."

Cole looked up.

"Quiet, Bob," insisted Ardith.

"No. Either you tell him about Alex or I will. There's no more time for games!"

Cole looked at his mother. "Alex?" he asked. "Who's Alex?"

Ardith expelled a long sigh and stood up, pulling on Cole's hand. "Bob, stay with Reggie for a while, won't you, dear?" She eyed Cole warily, searching for the right way to tell him that he was a father. "Cole," she began. "When Reggie . . . the reason . . ." She looked to Bob for help but he stood with his hands by his sides in silence.

"Spit it out, Mother!" snapped Cole, impatiently. He wanted to go back to Reggie. "Whatever it is—just tell me!"

Ardith tried again. "When Reggie came to Maine, she was pregnant." There! It was out!

"And?" asked Cole as if Ardith had just told him she had a run in her stocking. Then, ever so slowly, as he saw the peculiar glances that his mother and the doctor were giving each other, the words penetrated. He grabbed Ardith's shoulders as his knees sagged. "Pregnant? Reggie?" he gasped and a look of utter confusion passed over his face. He had to sit down.

Ardith took the seat next to him as Bob slipped unnoticed from the lounge. "Yes, dear. She gave birth to a beautiful little boy. His name is Alex."

"My God. My God," repeated Cole over and over again. It was too much to absorb at once. His head spun with the revelation that Reggie had had a child. His child. His son. No wonder she hadn't wanted anything from him when she'd fled New York. She'd already had the most important thing he could give her. No wonder she'd given up her business and sold her patent. Growing inside her was the one thing he didn't own, couldn't repossess. But to make positively certain that it wouldn't be taken from her . . . she'd left without telling him about the baby. It was a fitting revenge, the quintessential counterplay. A momentary bubble of laughter escaped his lips when he thought about the way in which his redheaded sorceress had outwitted him . . . almost.

He turned to his mother with a mischievous glint in his eye. "Where is he?" he asked and a prickling of uneasiness stirred in Ardith's body.

"Here. In the hospital nursery." Ardith's voice had a cautious edge to it. She didn't trust Cole's accepting response.

Cole stood. "Let's go. I'd like to meet this baby."

"You're not shocked?"

He shook his head. "Is that the reaction you expected?" He started for the door then turned to his mother. "There is nothing, absolutely nothing that Reggie could ever do to me again which would shock me. Other emotions, yes. But not shock! This, I assume, is the reason for Reggie's hasty departure from New York?"

Ardith misunderstood. "Yes. But Alex *is* your son," she said adamantly.

He stared at her in surprise. "Mother, of all the questions that need answering between Reggie and me, with all the explaining that we have to do to each other, that is not one of them. My paternity is not an issue. Now, are you coming along to introduce me to my son?"

"Uh-uh. This is a time for you and Alex to be alone. I'll be in Reggie's room waiting for you." She stood on tiptoe to kiss him. "Congratulations." She walked back to Reggie's room, smiling for the first time in five days.

An hour later Cole entered Reggie's room. He had held his son, undressed him and touched every part of him. He had even given Alex part of his feeding. Cole had remained hypnotized by this tiny human being that he and Reggie had created, until the nurse had gently suggested that it was time for him to leave. Reluctantly, he left the nursery, but his feelings were too unsettled for him to return to his mother, so he headed for the waiting room where he sat thinking.

In later years, Cole would remember that half hour he spent thinking, almost dreaming. It lasted for a thousand years and passed in a minute. The anger that had obscured his vision for so long lifted as he suddenly realized, with startling clarity, that he now stood to lose the most valuable possessions he owned.

Reggie's voice echoed in his ears. "You don't own people, Cole."

She had been right, of course. He had never owned her, nor would he ever own Alex. Oh, he had tried to possess her, to own her. Binding her to him by contracts, mortgages, leases and legal agreements. Would he try to do that to his son? Was he so insecure that he doubted his own capacity to keep someone by his side only because he or she wanted to be there?

He had been so certain that Reggie would never leave him if she owed him money. He had tried to secure her love for him with his demand that she mortgage her life. It hadn't worked. She had given up everything she loved, even him, he thought with a sad smile, in her effort to be free. And what had she really wanted that freedom for? To love him and be loved by him on equal terms, with neither having an unfair advantage over the other. How he wanted to show her . . . to prove to her that he had learned. When she got well, he would show her this time . . . if only she—and God—would give him a chance.

Waiting silently at Reggie's door, he watched a nurse readjust the oxygen tent that was easing her labored breathing. His mother was sitting on the far side of the bed, an open magazine in her lap. She looked up at him, curiously. He waited until the nurse left the room then walked over to Ardith. He kissed her gently on the cheek.

"Go home, Mother. I'm staying. It's my turn to take care of her. It seems everyone has been doing my job. I have a lot of making up to do. Thank you for everything you've done," he added. "You'll never know what it means to me." He helped her gather up her belongings. "Tell me something," he asked. "Do we sleep in this chair?"

"When we get tired," she said and left the room.

Chapter 53

From that moment on, Cole only left her bedside to snatch a few precious moments with Alex. He canceled the private-duty nurse, insisting that he would take far better care of Reggie. Yet, despite the constant vigil, her condition remained unchanged. For the first time in his life Cole prayed.

On the morning of the sixth day, Cole thought he detected a change in her breathing. Frightened, he ran for the floor nurse. Reggie's temperature still registered a dangerous 104.6°, but her rapid respiration was slowing. Even to Cole's untrained eye, she looked different, less labored—better. Chapping confirmed Cole's appraisal but cautioned him that the change could be temporary. She was far from out of danger, he told him, and the next twenty-four to thirty-six hours would be crucial. Cole waited as the hours ticked by. He lost all sense of time. The lights were always on in her room, always dim. If he didn't raise the shades, he had no conception of night or day. It didn't make any difference as he sat on the edge of her bed for hours on end, like a sentry, hoping to ward off that which he feared most.

And he spoke to her constantly; of love, of the future, of their son. He caressed her face tenderly under the oxygen mask, in need of constant reassurance that she still lived. At times he could have sworn that she was reaching, struggling to return from whatever place she now occupied. Once, her eyelids fluttered as if she were trying to lift an enormous weight that held them shut. In a moment of desperation he reached under the tent and shook her, trying to bring her back to the living. When nothing happened, he sat down again to wait.

Garbled words filtered into the deep cavern that kept her a prisoner. Suspended in a trancelike nightmare, unable to sleep, unable to wake, she was constantly running, constantly out of breath. And she was so tired, her body cried out for elusive rest. The voice continued to call to her. From outside of the dark cavern, from all sides, above and below, she heard the never-ending whispers. She thrashed against the bindings that held her hands to her sides. If only she could break free, reach the source of the voice that incessantly called her name. Butterflylike wings fluttered through her hair, caressing her face, kissing her eyelids. For one painful moment she managed to open her eyes. She imagined she saw the back of Cole's head but, as suddenly as it appeared, it vanished, and back she tumbled into the abyss.

He called out to her, urging her to waken, to leave the place she now inhabited, but she couldn't find the exit. He urged, demanded that she come to him until his voice was hoarse and his throat raspy. When he couldn't speak any longer, he whispered. Then he pleaded.

Chapping stopped into the room at dusk to check on Reggie's condition. He found that her fever had dipped slightly. He handed the thermometer to Cole so that the tortured man could read the digital printout himself. It registered 103.6°. For the first time in a week he was cautiously hopeful.

"Maybe, just maybe, the antibiotics are beginning to fight the infection. But," he said as he studied Cole's exhausted face, "don't for one minute think that the danger is passed. I won't lie to you, Cole. She's still critically ill."

Cole nodded. "I understand, and I know that as a physician you're going to have trouble believing this, but I think she hears me. Wherever she is, I think she knows I'm here."

"If you believe that, keep trying to reach her. Maybe you're right, maybe she does hear you or sense your presence." He stopped suddenly as Reggie began thrashing again, flinging her head from side to side. He hurried to her bedside. Again, her eyes flew open and she saw Chapping's face. Valiantly, she tried to open her mouth to tell him something, but the effort was too much, and her eyelids fluttered and closed again.

"There!" Cole said excitedly. "You see what I mean? She's aware. She knows something is going on. She tried to talk to you."

Chapping sighed. He didn't want to disappoint Cole, to dash his hopes. "I don't know, Cole," he said cautiously. "Perhaps she did recognize me. Granted it's the first time in days that she's opened her eyes . . . it's something to hope about."

"What can I do?" Cole whispered.

Chapping put his arm around Cole's shoulders. "Stay with her, keep trying. There's nothing else for you to do." He checked the tent and the monitors. "She's certainly no worse than she was this morning." He headed for the door. "I'm going home now, Cole. I'll call your mother when I get there. She'll probably want to come in tonight because, after this evening, she won't be able to."

"Why not?"

"Because Alex is being discharged tomorrow morning. Ardith is taking him home. Hasn't she discussed it with you?"

"No," Cole said, anger beginning to creep into his voice. "She's agreed to look after him?"

Chapping studied Cole curiously. "Of course. She'd never let Reggie down." The implication that Cole had already done that to Reggie was obvious. "If anything happens to Reggie, Alex legally goes to—"

"Oh, no!" stormed Cole. "Not a chance! If anything happens to my wife, I'll be responsible for my son." He glared at the physician. "Do you understand that? Me! No one else."

"Calm down, Cole! Up until the other day you didn't even know Alex existed. Reggie and Ardith made this arrangement many months ago," explained Chapping.

"Months ago? How many months ago?"

"I'll let your mother tell you, if she wants to," Chapping answered. "Please, Cole, I don't want to get involved in this."

"I have every right to know!" he continued. "I'm her husband and that baby's father."

"You may or may not be Alex's father, I never discussed that with Reggie. However, from what I have been told, you are definitely no longer her husband. Cole, I'm not sure that you have any rights, legal or otherwise, where this baby is concerned. Your mother becomes Alex's legal guardian if anything happens to Reggie." He was sorry he had to be so harsh with Cole when he knew how Cole was suffering. He tried to soften his words. "I'm sorry. That's the way Reggie wanted it. Until she's better, the baby goes with Ardith."

Cole's mouth was set in a grim line. "That's not possible. He is my son."

Chapping shrugged and left the room.

Cole sank down on the bedside chair, his face registering his anger and frustration. He stared at Reggie's face under the oxygen tent. "You really fixed me this time, Reg," he said out loud, knowing full well that she couldn't hear him. "Did you really think I wouldn't acknowledge him? Did you have so little faith in me? Or did you despise me so much that you would rather let his grandmother raise him than me?" Reggie slept on, apparently oblivious to Cole's questions. "What happened to us, darling? We could have had it all, everything. Why did we throw it away?" He placed his face in his hands to hide his anguish. The gesture was futile. The pain was still there, as raw and as angry as an open wound.

She moaned as she tried to free her arms from the restraining bonds. Cole once again reached under the tent to cover her hands with his, to soothe her. "I had it all reversed," he said. "I convinced you, who had always been so frightened, that you had finally met someone you could trust and then, like everyone else in your life, I betrayed you. I'm no better than your parents or David. I abandoned you, too. I told you that I was different, but I wasn't." As he spoke to her in the dim hospital room, tears ran down his cheeks. "No wonder you walked out on me," he said. "The phone calls, the flowers—all planted by a psychotic who I chose to believe rather than you . . . oh, my love, please . . . get well. Give us another chance . . . I can't—"

"Good evening, darling," Ardith said as she entered the room. Cole jumped away from the bed. How much had she heard? he wondered as he looked at her face. Judging by her knowing expression—it had been enough.

"I've been quite a fool, haven't I?" he asked bluntly.

"Why, yes, Cole. I believe you have," she answered. "What revelation finally made you reach that obvious conclusion?"

He sighed heavily. "I've been sitting here, thinking about what I did to her . . . how devastated she must have been to leave without even telling me that she was pregnant . . . how she made you Alex's guardian instead of me." He looked at his mother's expressionless face. "Mother, if Reggie doesn't . . . if anything happens to her, I'm going to have to fight you for custody of my son, you know," he stated simply.

Ardith shook her head. "No, darling. There won't be a fight. No legal proceedings. First of all, Reggie is going to recover. In the second place, there was never, ever any question about your being Alex's father. Reggie only arranged that I would be the baby's legal guardian if she were unable to care for him because she doubted that you would have any interest in him, even if you believed he was yours. I only have to look at his face to know who his father is." She sat down on the edge of the bed to be closer to her son. "Darling, Alex belongs with his parents. If it can't be both of them, than it certainly should be one or the other." She studied his face. "Do you honestly believe that I would try to keep your son from you?" When he didn't answer, she repeated the question. "Would I?"

He blinked away tears. "No."

"Cole, if I could, I would shake you until your teeth rattled! Why is it that you, who can build empires worth millions of dollars, who can rearrange corporations and business deals, can't do anything as simple as loving and allowing yourself to be loved?" She stopped to readjust a tube on Reggie's arm. "There always has to be a bail-out clause for you, doesn't there?"

"I don't understand what you mean."

"Oh, I think you do," she laughed. "A dissolution agreement . . . penalties . . . everything neatly packaged beforehand so that you'll land softly if the deal falls apart. Parachutes, darling. You have a whole carton of them. Just in case you have to jump. You demanded that Reggie love you and trust you, but when she wanted the same from you—out came your trusty parachute and you bailed out. She made an honest commitment to you and your marriage. What did you do?" she challenged.

"Nothing," he answered with a sad sigh, finally forced to admit his failure. "I was never her husband."

"I beg your pardon?"

"Oh, we were legally married, but I owned her . . . like a property. As long as I held paper on her, she was mine." He thought hard about what he was about to say. "Then an interesting thing happened."

"Which was?" Ardith asked.

"I fell in love with her. It was so much more than possession. More than I . . ." His words trailed off. Calming himself, he continued, "I convinced her that she could trust me, that I would always be there for her. But I was lying to both of us. At the first sign, I backed out."

"You *bailed* out," corrected his mother.

"I bailed out. Same thing, isn't it?"

"Yes."

"That's not a marriage," he conceded.

"And she tried to tell you that, didn't she?"

He nodded.

"And now?"

"Now I'd give everything to start over."

"So do it! Ditch your parachutes. Make a commitment to her, to yourself."

He got up and started pacing the tiny room. "Do it? Just like that? What makes you think that she would be the least bit interested? Has she spoken to you about me?" he asked.

"Me?" asked Ardith. "Hardly!"

"Will you speak to her when she gets better?"

"Certainly not! This isn't something Mother can fix, like a tricycle. Frankly, darling, in this case, I'm as helpless as you. And, my dearest son, as far as the immediate future is concerned, I'm far more concerned with Reggie's recovery and Alex's care than your reconciliation."

Something had disturbed Reggie. She began stirring and mumbling. Cole leaned over her, lifted the tent and pressed his ear close to her lips. He could barely make out her words.

"The baby . . . so cold . . . please . . . cold."

He didn't know if the last word she had said had been *cold* or *Cole*, but tears rushed to his eyes as he closed his hand over hers. "I'm here, my love. Shh. The baby is fine. He's perfect, a little boy, and I'm staying right by your side, darling. I'm not leaving you. You're going to be fine. We're all going to be fine." He looked at her face, but she was sleeping peacefully once more. Her rambling had ceased. He lowered the tent but continued to hold her hand.

That voice again. It was so far away. Why wouldn't it come closer? Everytime she thought she was approaching it, the voice faded. She drifted on a blue-gray cloud that enshrouded her one moment, than lifted her closer to the voice. She struggled against the weights that held her eyes closed. For a second, she succeeded and opened her eyes. It was Cole's face she saw . . . or was it? It looked so much like him, yet it was distorted . . . like looking through the wrong end of a telescope. She tried to conjure up his face again. He was walking toward her, his arms outstretched, tiny lights twinkling around him. The light was hurting her eyes. She drifted back to sleep.

The next time she opened her eyes, it was much later. It was just daybreak, still dim, but Reggie thought she recognized Robert Chapping standing near her bed. His image was distorted, too. She tried to speak through dry, cracked lips.

He placed his hand on hers. "Relax, Reggie. Can you hear me?"

She nodded weakly.

"Do you know who I am?"

"Bob," she croaked.

"Good girl!" he smiled.

She tried to move her hands. When she couldn't, a puzzled look came over her face, and she began to thrash, pulling at the restraints. Bob quickly squeezed her hand.

"Easy, Reg. Your hands are tied down to keep you from

injuring yourself. You're in the hospital. You've been here for over a week. Do you remember anything?"

She tried desperately to remember, but nothing came. She shook her head, frightened.

"Don't worry. Everything will come back slowly," he reassured her. "You've lost seven days from your life. . . . It takes time—"

"The baby!"

"He's fine, perfect. Ardith has taken him home and is caring for him until you're on your feet again. Do you understand?" He didn't mention Cole at all. Nor did she.

She nodded her head to show that she understood. "What's . . . erhimm . . . er . . . hmm?" She tried to clear her throat. It felt like razor blades everytime she tried to swallow.

"Let me get you some water. I think we can remove the restraints now, don't you?"

Chapter 54

Chapping ordered the oxygen tent removed and had nasal prongs inserted instead. He was satisfied that she finally was on the road to recovery. Though his patient still was somewhat disoriented and confused, the doctor was confident that it would only take a short time for her to clear the cobwebs from her head. Reggie repeatedly questioned him about the baby, and he spent a great deal of time reassuring her, trying to make her believe that Alex was fine and safely at home with Ardith.

When he finally left her room, he walked thoughtfully to the nurses' station, where he called Ardith to tell her the good news about Reggie's condition and ask her to bring Alex to the hospital that afternoon. From Reggie's room the parking field was clearly visible. If Ardith held the baby in her arms and Reggie could be helped to the window, she would be able to see her son.

After that . . . well, after that, Robert Chapping wished he could excuse himself from Reggie's private life. He knew there were plenty of problems she would face once she was out of the hospital, the most pressing, Chapping mused, was the real possibility that Cole would not relinquish Alex to Reggie. The thought of any ugly custody battle made him shiver. Poor Ardith, he thought. She was bound to be right in the middle of the fray.

Chapping didn't give Ardith enough credit, for she also anticipated a battle regardless of what she and Cole had discussed. When she saw her son's haggard face as he entered the house, she was prepared. She kissed him on the cheek, told him how delighted she was about Reggie's apparent recovery and sent him to bed, knowing he had been up for the better part of two days. Tonight, she intended to tell him that it was time for him to leave Maine. As much as she adored her son, she felt that Alex's welfare came first and she would not allow her home to become a battlefield on which Alex's custody would be fought. Cole and Reggie would have to resolve their problems elsewhere, if possible. Within her heart, she feared the worst when they finally did meet head-on. But she was going to make sure that it didn't happen under her roof.

Cole woke up at nine o'clock that night. He was hungry, moody and restless. He waited impatiently as Ardith warmed up the pot roast and potatoes she had made for dinner. As he ate, she told him all about her and Alex's visit to the hospital parking lot and Reggie's overwhelming relief when she first saw her son. Ardith went over Chapping's latest report. Reggie was doing as well as could be expected, still weak and running a fever, but the crisis was obviously over.

"When will she be coming home?" Cole asked as Ardith poured him a cup of coffee.

"Bob thought she would be strong enough in a week or so. That brings up another problem. Cole, when she gets home I want you to be gone."

"I understand why you're asking and I'll abide by your edict since you've asked me so nicely," he said, sarcastically, "but I'm more difficult than that to get rid of." He walked around to her side of the table, bent down and kissed her. "You are a very special lady, Ardith Weston. Someone must be watching over me because, even though I don't deserve them, I seem to have been blessed with two exceptional women."

"You no longer have Reggie," she reminded him.

"That remains to be seen, doesn't it?" he asked and winked. "By the way, has anyone told her that I was here?"

"No. We didn't think it was a good idea."

"Good. Do me one more favor and I'll get out of your hair. Don't mention it to her." He smiled like a small boy. "Will you do that little thing for me?"

"Will you go back to New York?"

"Mother, stop worrying. I promise to be out of your house in a few days. Before Reggie gets home. Is that good enough?"

"Yes. If you keep your promise to be out of here before she gets home, I'll see to it that Reggie never knows you were here. Is that what you want?"

"Exactly." He began to walk out of the room. "I'd love to continue our chat but my son is crying. I think I'll take a peek at him." He gave her a mock salute and went to tend to Alex.

A vague uneasiness settled over Ardith as she began to clear the table.

But Cole was as good as his word. On the morning of the day they had decided he would leave, his bags were packed. He sat in the kitchen with Alex in his arms. The baby had just finished a bottle and was sleeping peacefully in his father's arms.

"You're certain that you won't reconsider?" he asked, smoothing a curl from Alex's forehead.

Ardith laughed. "Reconsider? Are you crazy? I can't wait for you to get out of here. You've monopolized my grandson, had me on pins and needles that Reggie might phone and you would answer, and have generally made a nuisance out of yourself."

He laughed good-naturedly. "I apologize for everything except monopolizing Alex. You'll have plenty of time to care for him after I've gone."

"Cole, I'm certain that if you contact Reggie after a while, you will be able to work out some kind of visitation rights."

"I'll certainly keep that in mind." He stood up and handed his son to Ardith. "Here he is. He's all yours until his mother gets home. By the way, when do you expect her?"

"In two days. Bob wants her to take the entire summer to recuperate. I've hired a housekeeper—"

"You've hired a housekeeper?" Cole asked. "You?"

"I'm looking forward to a nice quiet summer of caring for Reggie and Alex. I can't do the house, too. What are your plans for the summer?"

"Oh, I don't know yet," he answered lazily. "Maybe I'll rent a place by the Jersey shore or up in Connecticut. Or spend lots of time in the cabin. Your idea of a summer of peace and quiet sounds very appealing. I might follow suit. It will be good for me to relax this summer, too. It's been an unbelievably hectic year for me."

"I would imagine," Ardith said, a sardonic bite in her voice. "Whatever happened with that woman in Chicago? The one you put in charge of the Stockyard?"

"Patrice? She's doing very nicely. She grasped the whole concept right away, and of course she has her father around if she runs into any snags. I think she'll be fine now."

"Now?"

"Oh, I guess you don't know the whole story. Remember when you called New York looking for me, and John told you that I had been called to Chicago?" Cole asked.

Ardith nodded.

"I was called because Patrice's ex-husband and some of his cronies were caught planting explosives in the foundation of the new mall and sports complex. They were caught red-handed. Patrice didn't know if she and her father should press charges."

"Did they?"

"You bet they did! He's finished. If ever he had a chance to make a new life for himself, it's all over now. He'll be disbarred and probably face a jail sentence, too. Frankly, it couldn't happen to a more deserving man," Cole finished.

"And the woman? How does she feel about it? After all, he was her husband once."

Cole laughed. "If they put him away for life that wouldn't be enough for her. She's delighted and so am I. Patrice deserves some happiness in her life. She's even seeing someone now."

"Well, if only you could straighten out your life so tidily," Ardith observed dryly.

"Give me some time." He walked into the hall and picked up one of his suitcases. "It's been a most edifying visit. I'll call you later this week to check on Alex."

"Fine, darling," Ardith said, kissing her son's cheek. "I'm

sorry, Cole, but this really is the only way. You do understand, don't you?"

"Absolutely!" he assured her, a hint of a smile playing at the corners of his lips. "Don't worry, Mother. I'll be fine. You just take care of all your charges. If you need anything, money—"

"Thank you. That's quite generous but completely unnecessary. I'm rather comfortable, you know." She put her arms around his massive shoulders. Though she knew what she was doing was the right thing, it still hurt her to see her son leaving his son. She hugged him, burying her face in his chest. "Go now. I'm going to start crying if you stay much longer." She tried to smile.

Cole squeezed her, a reassuring gesture. "You pushed me out and I'm leaving. Do you want me to stay, now?"

"No," she said, backing away from him. "I'll speak to you later this week."

"Let me call you," he suggested. "I really am going to look for a summer place and, until I find one, I don't know where I'll be."

She wiped her eyes with her handkerchief. "Please keep in touch."

"I will. I promise." He threw her another kiss and strode out the door to his car. As he pulled the rented car out of the driveway, he saw Ardith slip into the green wicker rocking chair on the porch. She rocked back and forth as she watched the car disappear around the corner.

Reggie came home three days later. Thin, pale, weak, with legs like a newborn colt, she was unsteady and unsure. The simplest tasks such as eating and walking to the bathroom, exhausted her. Unhappy with her enforced inactivity, Reggie was cranky and irritable. Ardith found that she had not one, but two babies to care for. Reggie's only interest was Alex, and even that frustrated her. She couldn't care for his daily needs, couldn't breast-feed him as she had planned and, though she was grateful for Ardith's help, she was also resentful that she couldn't take care of her own son. It was an impossible readjustment for the new mother.

Ardith made some swift changes in their arrangements to ease Reggie's discomfort. She moved all of Reggie's possessions from the garage apartment to the main house. She opened up two of the interconnected rooms, which were both bright and sunny. One room was Reggie's own, the other would be Alex's nursery when Reggie felt strong enough to take on the responsibility of his care. For the time being, Alex was settled comfortably in a bassinet in his grandmother's room.

"This is so unfair to you," complained Reggie the second day she was home. Both women were seated in rocking chairs on the big wrap-around porch. The May weather was warm, but the breeze off the lake insured that the days never became too uncomfortable. Reggie had borrowed a crocheted shawl from Ardith but had discarded it soon after coming outside.

"Nonsense!" Ardith protested. "If I didn't want to do this, I wouldn't. Being this close to Alex is the most important thing to me now."

"But it was so much easier for you when I had my own apartment in the garage. At least you had some privacy. That's why I was looking for the house."

"First, you'll recuperate," Ardith told her sternly. "Then you can worry about moving out."

"In any case," Reggie continued, "I must call Anne Kirk today. I was supposed to let her know what I was doing about the house before I went into the hospital. We'd even agreed on the price." She rocked back and forth thoughtfully. "Did you know that was what I was doing out in the snowstorm? I went to pick up a check from Alison." She laughed bitterly. "It was going to be the down payment on the house."

"I know. We found the check in the car. Go call her," Ardith suggested.

Reggie got up slowly, hesitating ever so slightly and hoping Ardith wouldn't notice how weak she still was.

Ardith was in her bedroom when Reggie burst in ten minutes later. She was redressing Alex and preparing him for a feeding. She looked up when she heard Reggie enter.

"Were you able to reach her?" Ardith asked.

"Yes. She's a complete bitch!"

"Reggie!"

"She is. She sold the damned house out from under me . . . didn't even bother to give me the courtesy of a phone call. She said that when she didn't hear from me, she assumed I was no longer interested." She sat down on the edge of Ardith's bed. "How could she do that to me? Ardith, I told her

I was just waiting for a check and then I could go to contract. She knew how I felt about that house." Reggie's face was pathetic. "How could she go ahead with the sale?"

Ardith came around to the other side of the bed and put her arms around her daughter-in-law's shoulders. Poor Reggie, she thought. It seemed that she just couldn't put her life together. "I know you're disappointed."

"No, you don't know!" she answered angrily. "No one knows. That house was perfect for the two of us. It was small enough for me to afford but sunny and bright and—" She threw back her head and stared at the ceiling. "Dammit all!" she cursed. "Maybe I'll just go back to the city after all. Or I could try Boston. I could probably get a job there and . . . and . . ." She looked at Ardith for help. "What am I going to do?"

"Nothing. Absolutely, positively nothing! And, Reggie, if you don't stop feeling sorry for yourself this instant, so help me, I'll throw you out of here!"

Reggie was so startled by the anger in Ardith's voice that she blanched. "I didn't mean to sound—"

"Ungrateful?" Ardith finished. "No, I'm sure you didn't. I don't expect gratitude from you. I expect you to pick up the pieces of your life, with time, mind you, and get on with it. You've had setbacks before, you'll have them again. We all do." She stroked Reggie's hair. "We'll find a better house, a bigger one. We'll start looking next week, if you feel up to it. Okay?" When Reggie didn't answer, she lifted her chin up so their eyes met. "Okay?"

Reggie had to smile at Ardith's ministrations. She giggled in spite of herself. "Okay," she said finally.

"Good. Now do you think you'd like to give Alex his bottle?" She didn't wait for an answer but handed the baby to Reggie and went to the kitchen.

"Well, little one," Reggie cooed to Alex, "it looks like it will be a little bit longer till I find us a home." Alex screwed up his face, preparing to cry. "No, no, please. Not you, too," she begged. "Don't cry, Alex. Please, don't. No, baby . . . there, there. Mommy will make everything okay. Shhh. That's a good boy." Gently, Reggie rocked him in her arms.

Ardith stood at the doorway with the bottle in her hands,

loath to interrupt. Wonderful, she thought as she watched them. Finally Reggie was strong enough to get to know her son. Did Reggie notice the startling resemblance to Cole? Ardith wondered. Did she ever think of Cole when she looked at Alex? Would she ever discuss what had happened? Ardith was sorely tempted to tell her about Cole's visit. The girl ought to know that her former husband had been to Maine, had stayed by her bedside night and day, and had cared for and held their son. But she had made a promise to Cole. She couldn't even tell Reggie that Cole now knew he was a father. Pigheaded fools, both of them!

"I'm going to the market while you finish up the feeding."

Reggie looked up, panic stricken. "You're leaving me alone with him?"

"I think it's time, dear. He'll drink his bottle, burp and fall asleep. You can handle that."

Reggie smiled. "Isn't it funny how competent I am with things that I'm familiar with, yet this whole baby thing scares the daylights out of me? I'm all thumbs. It's as if Alex was the only baby ever born. Does it ever come naturally?"

"Of course it does, but you're starting with a disadvantage. Most new mothers have the first few days in the hospital with their babies. With nurses and other mothers to ask questions of. You're just starting. You also have another disadvantage. You're a single parent." She couldn't help it, but it had to be spoken of. "You aren't going to be able to call Alex's father to gloat over every feeding or burp."

"Plenty of women raise children alone and quite successfully, too," Reggie argued defensively.

"I know they do. But they, like you, have a rougher time of it. Don't look so downtrodden. I'll be here to help, you know that. But darling, are you absolutely certain that you don't want to call Cole? He really does have a right to know."

"You really believe that? You've been wonderful to me. I'll never be able to repay what you've done for us, and I know this must be impossibly difficult for you, but I swear I know what I'm doing. I know Cole's indifference, his callousness. I can't do that to myself again. I just can't leave myself wide open again. Please, please try to understand," she begged.

"You're both foolish children. You're so sure that you know

him and he's certain that he knows you. Both of you don't know the first thing about either one of you! In your own way, you're as stubborn and idiotic as he is. But you're right about one thing," Ardith agreed, "it's none of my business. I'll let the two of you figure it out by yourselves."

She was so angry at both of them and, for the first time, she wasn't trying to hide it from Reggie. How in the world, she wondered, was she going to keep this whole thing a secret? Cole was bound to return for Alex sooner or later. She was certain. She should prepare Reggie, yet she had promised Cole. . . . The web of deception was tightening around Ardith's neck and, as Bob had forewarned, it was beginning to choke her.

"Do what you want, Reggie!" she said angrily. "But remember: eventually the piper gets paid." She stalked out of the room, leaving Reggie to wonder what in the world she meant.

By the time Ardith returned from the market, Reggie and Alex were sound asleep, Alex in his carriage and Reggie next to him in a rocking chair on the porch. Ardith covered her with the shawl, peeked into the carriage and, finding the baby sleeping peacefully, went into the kitchen to unload her groceries. She had met Bob in town and had invited him to dinner. As she started to season the roast, the phone rang. With her hands covered with paprika, she grabbed the receiver.

"Hello? Mother?" Cole asked.

"Don't 'hello, Mother' me! You and your ex-wife are idiots and I have no patience for either one of you! I'm so furious, Cole, I could—"

"Mother!"

"I don't want to talk to you now. I have to prepare dinner. Tell me where you are and I'll call you back when I calm down."

"I'll have to call you, I'm out looking at houses," he said. "Would you please tell me what you're so angry at? Is it Reggie?"

"Yes, and it's you, too!" she responded. "I suggested to her that she tell you about . . . never mind! I don't want to talk about this nonsense anymore. Go look at your houses and call me tomorrow or the next day. By that time, you had better figure out some way to resolve this because I'm getting tired of playing your silly games!" She hung up. Darn children! she thought.

Cole held the receiver in his hand, smiling at the dial tone. "It won't be too much longer, Mother. Just have a little patience," he said out loud. "Not too much longer."

Chapter 55

As May slipped into June and then July, life in Maine assumed a leisurely, bucolic pace. The long days were warm and sunny, perfect weather for lazing by the lake. Each morning, Reggie woke early, fed and bathed Alex and strapped him into a papooselike contraption that Chapping had given her. She spent her mornings at the lakefront, catching up on her reading as Alex slept peacefully on a blanket next to her. It was a time of peace and solitude, broken only by the elderly gentleman who now owned the house she had wanted and religiously walked the circumference of the lake each morning. He never failed to tip his large canvas hat as he passed them. Reggie could set her watch by his daily strolls.

Alex's afternoons belonged to his grandmother, an arrangement mutually acceptable to both women. While Reggie napped, Ardith tucked the baby into his carriage and set off for long walks, often lasting two or three hours. Reggie argued that Ardith was overdoing the walking, but Ardith explained that she often stopped to visit or lunch with an old friend. When Reggie suggested that Ardith's friend might prefer she come without the burden of an infant, Ardith assured her that, were it not for the pleasure they both took in the baby, she was not at all certain that her friend would even want her company.

After six weeks of inactivity, Reggie was becoming restless. She had put off decision-making about her future, at Ardith's insistence. Now with her strength almost back to normal, Reggie began to silently formulate plans for a life with Alex.

She had to have her own home. Though Ardith never complained, never would complain, Reggie was feeling as if her mother-in-law's patience was wearing thin. She could sympathize. Playpens, carriages, swings and toys were strewn in the kitchen, living room and den. It was time to move on.

She walked into the kitchen to call Anne Kirk when the phone rang. "Hello?" she answered.

There was a moment's silence then the slow inhalation of breath from the other end of the line. "Well, hello."

Reggie's heart flipped over and she dropped the phone. She stared at it, her pulse racing. Nervously, she bent to retrieve it, bringing it to her ear.

"Hello, Cole," she said carefully. It had to happen eventually, but she wasn't prepared. She wasn't ready to speak to him yet. It had been almost nine months. A lifetime. A moment. In a millisecond, a thousand emotions flooded her brain. Her legs were quivering. She pulled the kitchen chair closer to the phone so she could sit down.

"Hello, Reggie," he said coolly, nonchalantly, as if he had spoken to her only last week. "It's nice to hear your voice. It's been a long, long time."

"Has it, really?" she answered, wishing her heart would stop that awful pounding. "Why, yes," she conceded, "I guess it has. How have you been?" she tried to ask casually. This is ridiculous! she thought angrily. *Where* have you been? would have been a better response. Why haven't you been searching the country for me? I left a trail that a blindfolded beagle could follow, she added silently.

"Fine, just fine," he answered. "What are you doing in Maine?"

What do you think I'm doing in your mother's kitchen on a Thursday afternoon in the middle of July? Passing through on my way to Alaska? How about "I just happened to be in the neighborhood and I noticed your mother's car in the driveway so I decided to pop in and say hello?" She finally answered, "Visiting."

"How nice," Cole commented. "For how long?"

For nine months, for a year, forever. What difference would her answer make? "A week or two, I guess." Now it was her turn to be polite. "And what are you doing for the summer?"

"I'm also staying in the country. I guess we both had the same idea."

"Very few of us like the city in the summer," she commented. Of course he'd be spending the summer at the cabin. The cabin. Scenes from their weekend in the Adirondacks flashed through her mind and, before she could stop herself, the words were out of her mouth. "How's the sailboat?" She wanted to kick herself!

"The sailboat?"

"Never mind." How quickly he'd forgotten that golden afternoon of lovemaking.

He recovered. "Oh, *The Lightning*. It's fine, I guess. I haven't seen it recently." He paused. "What made you think about the boat?" he asked.

"A natural progression of thoughts . . . summer, the cabin, the lake, the boat. Simple, really. I think it's called association. You know, one word makes you think of another."

"Why are you so nervous?" he asked.

"Me? Nervous? Whatever makes you think I'm nervous?"

"Because you're rambling, and I know you well enough to remember that you are very economical with words. You always say what you mean and leave out unnecessary explanations. Don't you?"

"Do I?" she asked stupidly. Her pulse was racing again as she waited for him to answer.

Finally, he spoke, so softly that she had to strain to hear him. "Yes, I think you're rather sparing with your explanations. If I'm not mistaken, I'm still waiting for you to explain your unannounced flight from New York last November. Don't you think that called for some kind of explanation? Don't you think you owed me that much, Reg?"

He made her name sound like a caress. She closed her eyes, picturing him, his lean hard body in faded jeans and his favorite chambray shirt. In her mind, she saw his rugged face, tanned by the summer sun, and she ached for him. She felt a physical pain when, once again, he spoke her name. This time, before her precarious protective veneer crumbled completely, she hung up the phone, dissolving in tears that could no longer be held back. She cried until the tears were gone, and still she hugged the chair as if she were holding him once again.

It was only when she heard Ardith returning with Alex that she hurried to her own room, closed the door softly and lay down on the bed feigning sleep. When Ardith called to her, she didn't answer.

She spent a hideous night not sleeping—constantly checking the clock, hoping to move time forward by sheer force of will so the night would end. Her mind spun like a wildly careening top. One moment she hated Cole for what she had allowed herself to feel for him, and tears would run down her face. The next moment the loneliness she felt for him was overwhelming, and she would have given anything she had for one more night, one hour in his arms. Throughout the interminable night, she found no sanctuary, no respite from the haunting memories of her love. In the early hours of dawn, she finally dozed fitfully. Her last thought as she slipped into sleep was how naive she had been to believe that, because her body had convalesced from pneumonia, her heart had healed as well.

At seven fifteen, she heard Ardith stirring in the kitchen. Fighting the inertia that gripped her, Reggie struggled to get out of bed. The attempt was like manual labor, a strenuous, arduous task. A lassitude had enveloped her, and she moved in an apathetic, indifferent state, caring little whether she ever left the bedroom, but knowing she would face Ardith's questions if she stayed in bed. The morning was hot and muggy with the threat of rain hovering. Heavy, humid air sapped whatever little energy she managed to summon. Vaguely she wondered whether she was regressing, backsliding into a relapse. She didn't care.

She barely managed to drag herself to the kitchen table. Ardith was making breakfast but turned and blanched when she saw Reggie's splotchy face.

"My God!" she exclaimed. "What's the matter? Are you ill?" She walked over to her daughter-in-law and placed her hand on her forehead. "You're not warm," she murmured, "but I'm calling Bob."

"No. I'm fine," she insisted. "I just had a terrible night. So bad, in fact, that if you don't mind, I'd like to switch with you. Would you take Alex this morning and I'll take him this afternoon?"

Ardith assured her that since she had nothing special planned, she would be glad to change their schedules. "Let me make you a cup of herbal tea," she suggested, "then get right back in bed and see if you fall asleep."

Ardith straightened the house, looked after Alex's needs and, by eleven o'clock, had nothing to do. The sun had finally broken through the clouds. She peeked into Reggie's room and, finding her daughter-in-law fast asleep, decided to take Alex out for a walk. Though she tiptoed around the house trying not to waken Reggie, Alex was far less cooperative, crying lustily as Ardith tucked him into his carriage.

Slowly, Reggie came awake to the sounds of her son's wails. By the time she had washed her face and brushed her teeth, Ardith and Alex had gone. Guilty at leaving Ardith to care for Alex alone, she quickly showered and dressed. She left her hair to curl naturally around her face and down her back—how quickly it had grown out of Gary's glamorous cut!—while she donned an old pair of cut-off jeans and a bright cotton T-shirt. Barefoot, she left the house, hoping to catch up with her mother-in-law.

At the edge of the grassy area that abutted the beach, Reggie paused to search the strip of land that led to the lake. She saw neither Ardith nor any evidence that she or Alex had arrived yet. She continued to scan the property on either side of their house. As she turned to the left, she caught sight of Ardith and Alex out of the corner of her eye. They were heading away from the beach toward the house that now belonged to that elderly man. So that's where she goes every day, thought Reggie, with a smile. They both like to walk. . . . As she turned away, she saw something that caused her to stop and stare. Ardith was handing Alex into the man's open arms, nodding and turning to leave. As Reggie watched, perplexed, Ardith continued down the beach, away from the house, while the stranger, with Alex in his arms, closed the door.

More confused than annoyed by Ardith's odd behavior, Reggie headed in that direction, looking for an explanation. It was one thing for Ardith to take Alex visiting her boyfriend, it was quite another for her to leave her grandson with a stranger. The more she thought about it, the angrier she became. She didn't know the first thing about this man and doubted that, in six weeks, Ardith knew a great deal more. Purposefully, she started down the beach with the intention of retrieving her son even if she risked Ardith's displeasure. She would deal with that later.

She reached the spot on the beachfront where she had last seen Ardith. The back of the house was clearly visible with its new two-tiered redwood deck, but neither the man nor Alex were in sight. She had hoped that they would be near the deck so she could casually stroll up and introduce herself before reclaiming Alex under some pretext. Now she would either have to walk onto the deck and knock on the sliding glass doors or go around to the front door to ring the bell. Either way, she wasn't leaving without her son. How many days, Reggie wondered, had Ardith dropped Alex off? No wonder she didn't mind taking the baby every afternoon—she had had a built-in babysitter.

A crackle of summer lightning and the sudden appearance of dark storm clouds increased Reggie's anxiety. She didn't want to be caught in a summer storm as she carried Alex home. The skies blackened and heavy drops of rain began falling, stinging Reggie's barely clothed body. Within seconds she was drenched, and the decision of which entrance to take was decided. She bolted up the deck stairs, slipping on the wet wood and began pummeling the sliding glass doors with her fists.

Her wet clothes clung to her, emphasizing her slim figure and cupping her firm breasts. The rain, glistening on her bronzed skin, made her appear as if she had been oiled. She threw back her head trying to get the heavy, sodden hair off her face so she could see into the dark house. Suddenly, she was blinded as a cloudburst sent a solid sheet of water cascading down on her. She banged on the door with all her strength but nothing could be heard against the noise of the torrential rain and thunder. She ran from the deck, sliding down the last step, through the soaking grass until she reached the front door. She alternately banged on the door and pushed the bell as bolt after bolt of lightning lit up the dark summer sky.

She was screaming against the wind when suddenly the door opened and she fell into the house. From the floor, she looked up into the surprised eyes of the elderly man.

"Where's my son?" she demanded. "Where's Alex?"

He looked confused. "The baby?" he asked, his bright blue eyes staring at her wet, shivering body.

Unconsciously as she rose, she folded her arms across her breasts to shield her erect nipples from his sight. "Yes," she answered angrily. "The baby! Where is he?"

"I think he's napping upstairs," he answered, still confused. He tried to explain. "I was cleaning the kitchen, you see. I just gave him . . . I'm not sure where . . . "

"What do you mean 'you're not sure'?" she repeated furiously. "Is he upstairs or not?"

"Yes, he is, but you can't just—"

"Watch me!" she roared and raced for the steps.

"Please!" he yelled after her. She ignored him.

When she reached the head of the steps she paused, looking frantically down the hall. There were four doors, all closed. She turned the knob on the first door and hurriedly pushed the door open. The room contained a single bed, dresser and desk. Alex was not there. She ran for the second door. It was filled with half-packed cartons and odd bits of furniture. She sprinted to the third door, found it ajar, and walked in. In the corner of the room, beyond the king-size bed, Alex was sleeping peacefully in a port-a-crib. She strode over to him, reached into the crib and was about to pick him up when she heard the bathroom door open. She turned and jumped. Cole Weston, clad only in a bath towel, began to walk toward her.

"Well, well," he said, smiling broadly. "What a pleasant, unexpected surprise."

"You? Here? I . . ." The room spun crazily around her as her words dissolved in a haze of confusion. He was across the room in two strides to catch her as she fainted.

Slowly, she came awake. Her eyelids fluttered and for a moment she thought she was back in the hospital. Then she saw the crib and her memory returned. Cole, here! She jumped up and the covers on the king-size bed fell away, leaving her naked. She slithered back under the covers. The room was empty, Alex wasn't in the crib, and Cole was nowhere to be found. Instinctively she flushed, knowing who had removed her wet clothes and tucked her into bed. How long had she been out? The room was immaculate. Her wet clothes were nowhere in sight.

She pulled the blanket out from under the edge of the bed and carefully wrapped it around her body. She padded to the bathroom where one look at herself in the mirror made her gasp in horror. Her hair had dried in a mass of tangles. She opened a drawer, extracted a brush and attacked the mess with a vengeance. It was stupid and vain, but it gave her something to do while she tried to figure out what the hell was going on. What was Cole doing here? How had he gotten here? Who was the old man? And, finally, what was Ardith's role in this charade?

She finished with her hair. She had brushed it until it crackled then fanned out full around her face in a red-gold halo. Her tanned face, lightly scattered with summer freckles, stared back at her, anger and bewilderment obvious in her green eyes. Somebody had better explain some things to her very soon or there was going to be hell to pay!

She hiked the blanket around her breasts again and went to look for Cole. She found him in the kitchen. Alex was sitting on the table in an infant chair, finishing a bottle that Cole was holding. Reggie stared. What the hell is this? she wondered. He was feeding "her" son as if it were something he did every— She stopped.

"Of course!" she said out loud. "You do this every day, don't you?"

He turned at the sound of her voice and his face lit up with a smile. "Take care of 'my' son, you mean? Yes, I do. It seemed like a fair arrangement, don't you think? You get him all morning and I get him all afternoon. What could be more equitable than that?" He lifted Alex out of the seat, placed him gently over his shoulder and rubbed his back until the baby burped. Kissing the soft black curls, he returned Alex to the infant seat. Nonchalantly, he said, "By the way, William is washing and drying your clothes."

"William?" she whispered. "That's William? Oh, no wonder he looked so familiar whenever he walked by."

"Yes, well, it keeps him in shape, he claims."

"Why is William in Maine?" she asked, although she was beginning to think she already knew all the answers.

"To keep house for me," Cole stated simply. "Keep an eye on Alex, would you? I'm going to make some coffee."

She glared at him. "No," she said sarcastically, "I'm going to let him jump off the table."

"Very unbecoming," he admonished.

"What?"

"Sarcasm. It doesn't become you." He stared at her, wishing there was some way to tell her what he was feeling.

"I'm taking him home, Cole. Now! Could you please get my clothes?" she said as she stood up, the blanket slipping momentarily from her breasts. Flushed with embarrassment, she quickly hiked it up, hoping he hadn't noticed.

He had seen enough to send the blood racing to his head. It shocked him that she could still do that to him. He had convinced himself that all he wanted was his son, but her nearness, the sight of her naked breasts made his heart lodge in his throat. Good God! he thought, his eyes widening in astonishment. His breathing quickened as, slowly, he ambled over to her. He placed his hands on her shoulders and gazed questioningly into her eyes.

He was watching her changing expression carefully. The bravado that had carried her until now fell away, leaving her very soul exposed. Without a word he took her face in his hands. He saw suspicion, but he also saw desire in her eyes. She stood stock-still, anticipating.

"I want you," he stated simply.

A shudder ran through her. He stood looking at her, neither demanding nor questioning. He was giving her the choice to decide. And she understood. He waited. Everything in the room disappeared except his eyes, his lips, his scent, his presence. Like a melting candle, her resolve slipped away, and her shaking hand reached up to touch his cheek.

And then Alex cried. The magic of the moment was broken.

She jumped away from Cole, escaping to the safety of caring for Alex. She grabbed him from the infant seat, holding him so tightly in her arms that he cried louder.

Cole left the room. In a haze, she changed the baby and readied him for the walk home, all the while holding the blanket close to her body with numb hands. She forced herself not to think, to concentrate only on Alex, on getting home.

The rain had ended, and a brilliant rainbow was arching across the beach when, minutes later, Cole returned to the kitchen with William in tow. Gently, he took the baby from Reggie's arms and handed him to William.

"Take Alex back to my mother's and tell her that Mrs. Weston is with me. I'll see that she gets home," he instructed. When William left, Cole turned to her. "You and I have some important matters to discuss."

She crossed over to the sink and, with shaking hands, poured herself a cup of coffee. Cole watched and waited. Unable to bear the silence any longer, she finally spoke. "I don't want you anymore, Cole," she said against the backdrop of her pounding heart. "I want Alex. That's all I came here for. Please let me go," she pleaded.

He stepped aside. "You're free to go anytime you want."

Silence. She stood still, unable to move.

"You're free to go," he repeated.

She knew he would do nothing more to keep her there. She struggled to move, to ask for her clothes, to leave his house. Her feet were stuck to the floor, her reflexes useless.

"If you leave," he began, "and the decision is yours . . . at least tell yourself the truth, Reggie. Know that you're leaving because you're terrified that the wall you've erected so carefully will crumble and you might feel again." He watched the play of emotions on her face and knew that his words had hit home. It was a chance he had to take. He continued, "For God's sake, don't lie to yourself. I felt your heart. . . ." He wanted to take her, to demand, but more than that, he wanted her to be honest, to recognize her fear, face it and overcome it . . . as he had overcome his.

When she didn't answer, he sighed. "I'll get your clothes."

"No."

"Then tell me what you want," he demanded. "I won't do it for you."

She stalled, nervously fingering her coffee cup. Oh God, help me, she said silently. I can't do this myself. . . .

He waited patiently.

She put the cup on the counter. From somewhere deep within her, a moan escaped. "I want you. I've always wanted you."

Without another word, Cole crossed the kitchen to her and with a desperate need, clasped her to him. He kissed one eye, then the other, then the delicate curve of her cheek. His eyes closed as he began to refamiliarize himself with her face. She opened her mouth to accept his tongue, but he brushed by it, lightly planting kisses on her cheek, her chin, her neck.

He took her hand and silently led her upstairs to the bedroom, where gently he set her down, unwrapping the blanket until she lay gloriously naked before him. He kneeled on the floor, lightly running his hands over her. He remembered every line of her body, every curve. With a cry of impatience, Reggie reached for him, and he allowed her to wrap her arms around him. Now he moved, locked in her arms, onto the bed. They lay perfectly still.

"Ask me," Cole demanded.

This time there was no pretense of misunderstanding. "Make love to me, Cole," she said, shuddering breathlessly. "I want you to make love to me."

His mouth came down hard on hers and she offered herself to him, arching against his hard, tanned body. She felt his strength, his utter maleness, and without thinking, she undressed him, all the while raining tiny kisses on his face, his chest, the line of hair that curled downward until her lips reached the hard evidence of his arousal. She drew him deep into her mouth. A moan of raw desire tore from his throat. Both of them wanted to be tender. Both wanted to be greedy. They wanted to linger, they needed to hurry. His fingers reached down to touch her and felt her open for him. She was so soft, velvety wet with her desire.

He let her lead. Her urgency obvious. He could have lingered. She could not wait. When he knew she was frantic, her body damp and writhing, he unleashed his passion and moved over her. She pulled him toward her, wrapping her legs around him until he could hold back no more. He plunged into her and heard her cry out, not in pain but in the ultimate pleasure of having her life back. Deeper and deeper he drove, her body meeting his in a confusion of demand and surrender. They rose together until, with a final roar of exultation, they exploded.

She was laughing. He looked down at her in surprise. "I couldn't fight you any longer," she explained.

He shook his head as he rolled over to rest at her side. "Don't do that. Don't lie again." He looked deeply into her confused eyes. "You couldn't fight yourself anymore, darling. You may not love me, but you wanted me every bit as much as I ever wanted you. Will you at least admit that?"

"No, because that would be another lie. I have always loved you and I have always wanted you," she conceded finally. "I left you because I could no longer live with you. But there has never been a time that I haven't loved you."

"I once told you that I would never beg you to stay with me. I told you that I would never, never plead with you," he mused. "I lied to you. I need you. Please stay."

"Why?" she asked suspiciously.

"Because I love you. Because life without you is empty. Because you are my life."

She held him tightly and spoke into his shoulder, her words barely intelligible. "Oh, God! How we wasted time! I would have stayed with you forever if just once you had showed me that it meant this much to you."

"I don't understand you."

She laughed again. "Of course you do. You always have. You might not have wanted to admit it, but you always knew in your heart what I needed from you."

"Would you tell me?" he asked. "I seem to have lost it."

Reggie sat up and stared at the man she loved. "It's so very simple. Love has to be by choice. You never gave me one. There were always contracts, agreements between us, binding us to each other. That's why I had to leave you, to run away. I had to rid myself of everything that bound me to you and you to me. Love is the only thing that can bind two people together. If we stay together now . . ."

"What do you mean 'if'?"

"Just that. I love you. I always will. That doesn't mean we can live with each other. Some things have changed, others haven't. You were right, my love, when you tried to tell me that there were no guarantees in life. I understand that now. Can't we just be together for a while?" she asked.

"Do you mean you don't . . ."

"I want to have the freedom to choose to stay with you because it is what I want—not what I have to do. I want to stay with you because it makes us both happy to be together. Nothing more, nothing less." She saw that her words were making him unhappy. "Do you think you could do that? Live like that?"

"Do I have a choice?" he asked.

She shook her head. "No."

"Then compromise," he suggested with a hint of a smile. "Move in with me for the rest of the summer."

It was a far better, more honest proposal than he had made to her more than a year ago. "All right," she consented. "I'll live with you for now, but that's all I'll promise." She laughed to ease the tension. "Besides, it's really my house anyway. You stole it from me when I was sick." She stopped suddenly. "When I was sick . . . Cole? How did you get here? Find me? Find out about Alex?"

"Darling, I've been by your side since you were in the hospital. I stayed with you, spoke to you, nursed you. I couldn't let you slip away from me again. I still can't. You get under a man's skin, Reggie Weston."

She leaned back on the pillows, smiling contentedly. "Reggie Gates," she corrected.

Chapter 56

Two weeks after Reggie and Alex moved in, Cole woke Reggie at six A.M. with a silly grin on his face. "Get up!" he demanded.

"Go away!" she answered, pulling the covers over her head.

Cole tore the covers from the bed, leaving her completely naked. He slapped her behind. "Up! I have a surprise for you."

"You're nuts!"

"Absolutely!" he agreed with a disarming smile and pulled her to the window. "Look!" He was as pleased and proud as a little boy presenting his mother with his first Little League trophy. "Well?"

There, tied up to the little dock on the lake, floated *The Lightning*. Freshly painted and rigged out with new sails and a jaunty blue and white jib, the tiny boat swayed gently on the easy swells. Reggie had to strain her eyes to make out the newly painted name on the rear of the boat. *The Reggie?*

"How—when—"

"When you decide on your name . . . we'll change it." It was his way of telling her that he had accepted her terms. He pulled her into his arms and held her tightly. "I love you so. Whatever the hell your name is."

They played during the day, but it was the evenings that Reggie loved best. During the cool Maine nights, with a crisp fire burning in the living room of the house that she had come to think of as the only one she and Cole had ever shared, they talked. He admitted to her that he had been determined to have her from the first moment he had seen her, and it hadn't particularly mattered to him how he achieved that goal. He had wanted her physically, but had felt an urgent need to possess her spirit, the essence that was uniquely Reggie Gates. It wasn't until after she had left him that he came to learn that by the very nature in which he had captured her, he had forced her to lock away that spirit. He had purchased an empty shell.

For the first time in her life, Reggie spoke openly of her disappointments in life. She recounted the emptiness of her childhood, her crushed career at Nikki Broad's hands and her disastrous affair with David. When she started to speak of David, her mouth tightened in a thin line, and Cole touched a finger to her lips, hushing her. It was irrelevant, he told her. It simply didn't have any bearing on them or their life any longer.

"But I also involved Lee," she tried to explain. "I put him in an intolerable position. By making him promise not to tell you anything, I drove him out of your life."

"No, darling," Cole corrected. "I did that all by myself. Once again, I demanded something from someone. When he wouldn't do what I wanted, I was furious." He laughed. "You both walked out on me at the same time." He reached over to Reggie and pulled her into his arms. "However, if he hadn't stayed in California with Liza, he would have come back," Cole told her, "willingly."

She threw her arms around his neck and gazed lovingly into his eyes. "Do I look like I'm here unwillingly?"

"No. But I had to come after you. Would you ever have come to me?"

She was quiet as she mulled over his question.

He watched her face in the firelight. How lovely she is, he thought.

"Truthfully?" she asked.

"Yes, darling. Truthfully. You've cured me forever of refusing to hear because I may not like the answer."

"If you're certain . . ."

"I am."

"I don't think I would have come back. Not because I didn't love you," she said, "but because I loved you too much. If I had told you about Alex, if I had come back with him, I think we would have resumed our old relationship because you wouldn't have let your son go. As long as you didn't know about his existence, I was safe."

"Safe from what?"

"From being hurt again," she admitted. "I just couldn't risk it again. If you wanted Alex and rejected me, I don't think I could have borne that."

This time he stared hard at her. "What made you let down your defenses this time? Why did you agree to spend the summer living with me? I could still hurt you, could possibly leave you or Alex or both of you. What made you take a chance?"

"I wasn't 'living' without you," she sighed. "Whatever we have now, for however long it lasts, is better than what I had without you. I'll take what I can now. You needn't make me any promises about forever. I don't need them anymore. I'm satisfied with what we have."

"Well, I'm not!" he said with such force that it startled her. "I want you to believe that this is forever . . . that I won't hurt you or leave you. How can I make you believe that?"

She chewed on her lower lip thoughtfully. "I don't think you actually can because you don't know if it's true." Then she held him in her arms. "Darling, don't you see that it's not important? I'll be here for however long we're both happy. Only promise me that you'll be here for as long as you love me . . . not one minute longer. Will you make me that promise?"

"Will you marry me?" he countered.

"Perhaps . . . someday. For now the only vow I need is that you promise to stay for only as long as you love me," she repeated.

"What about me? My needs? I want to marry you again. I want to live with you and Alex and raise more children. I want Alex to have my name. I want you to have it, too."

"You're right. He should have your name. We can change that immediately. But me? No, thank you. I wore the Weston name once and had all the legal papers that went with that dubious distinction. It didn't do either one of us any good. Uh-uh. We did it before, your way, with a marriage certificate. I'd like to try it my way this time."

"You leave me little choice."

"Does it make so very much difference? Have you been unhappy this summer?"

Cole held her tightly in his arms as the last of the evening's embers faded. "I have never known such complete happiness. If this is what our life together will be like, I will readily accept any terms you offer. Just stay with me."

"I'm thinking about it. . . ." she said as his mouth came down and buried her lips in a kiss that obscured the rest of her sentence.

Chapter 57

"You'd better hurry, Reg," Cole urged. "Everyone will be here soon." He watched with undisguised admiration as Reggie applied the finishing touches to her makeup. After four years of living together, he hadn't tired of her beauty. If anything, she had become more magnificent with each year. It was happiness, peace, serenity and contentment, she told him. And if those were the ingredients necessary, he had been more than willing to supply them—in abundance.

"I'll be ready in a moment," she replied. "Is everything in order downstairs? Has the caterer arrived?" She turned away from her mirror to look at Cole. His presence still had the capacity to take her breath away and, as he bent down to touch his lips to hers, she felt her pulse quicken. He smiled, that little half grin she had come to know so well again.

"Should we cancel the whole thing? Keep the guests waiting?" With an irrepressible twinkle in his eye, he slipped his hand beneath the towel that was secured above her breasts. He toyed with her nipple until he felt it grow hard. "I can feel a difference already, you know," he told her.

"You're imagining it. You won't be able to notice anything for another month, at least."

"You're wrong, my love," he answered, now cupping her full breast. "I was the one who told you I sensed a change."

Reggie stood up, dropping the towel to her feet. She wrapped her arms lovingly around Cole's neck, staring into his smoky eyes. "It's not too late to back out, you know. It doesn't make any difference to me. I could go on like this forever, never changing a thing." With a sigh of contentment, she layed her head against his shoulders.

His hands played with her heavy, shining hair, which today hung in lustrous waves to her shoulders. He breathed in the heady, sensual scent that she wore like a halo. "Don't back out on me now, brat! You promised."

"You don't think it will change anything, do you?" she asked, the uncertainty obvious in her voice. Everything had been perfect for the past four years and she was terrified that something might spoil their happiness. They had been over it again and again, rehashing all the possibilities until she had finally relented. But, still, she had some doubts about the step they were about to take.

"Of course things will change. For one thing, this baby will be born with a name that won't require changing. For another, I finally will have the wife I've wanted for five years." He tipped her chin up so he could look into her eyes. "I swear to you, on everything that I hold sacred, that nothing else will change. If anything, things will get better." His hand gently rubbed her smooth stomach. "I want this marriage as much as I've ever wanted anything in my life," he told her tenderly. "But if you're still uncertain, I'll go downstairs right now and call it off. You're more important to me, you and your happiness. Just tell me, Reg. You know I'll do whatever you want."

She stood quietly for a moment, wondering if she was doing the right thing. The whole concept of marriage still frightened her. Cole was silent, neither trying to talk her out of it nor trying to convince her. This time, the decision was hers alone. Yesterday, it felt right to her, today—well, today the doubts were back again. Suddenly she looked up at the man she loved so much. "What would you feel if I backed out?" she whispered.

There was a long silence. The air in the large bedroom seemed charged as Reggie waited for Cole's answer. Finally he spoke. "I would feel disappointment, of course, but I'd honor your decision and continue the way we've been living." He smiled slightly. "We'd go downstairs and announce to all of our guests that we decided to have a birthday party instead of a wedding. In another year or so, I'd ask you to marry me again."

"You would really do that?"

"Yes. I would really do that. I told you, with a license or without one, you're still the woman I've chosen to live my life with. I think marriage will make things easier for Alex and the new baby . . . and in a sense, for us, too. But we've proven it's not mandatory for happiness." Playfully, he tapped her behind. "What's it to be, my love? Candles on your birthday cake or a five-tiered cake with a little man and woman on top?"

Gleefully, she threw her arms around him and hugged him with all her strength. "Both!" she said. "I want the little man and woman on top of my birthday cake."

"You're certain?"

"Absolutely!"

"Just don't ever tell me that I pushed you into this one," he warned her, but his voice was loving and tender.

"I won't," she promised as his lips buried themselves in her hair. "Now go make sure that Alex is ready and knows what he's supposed to do."

"I will in a minute, but first there's something I want to give you, something I've waited a long time for you to have."

She looked at him curiously. "What is it?"

Cole walked toward his closet, opened one of the drawers

and withdrew a small, velvet box. "Here, darling. I told you I'd save it for our fifth anniversary but this seems like a much more auspicious moment." He watched impatiently as she opened the box.

She stared in disbelief at the emerald-cut diamond ring that blazed with a life of its own within the jewelry box. "You saved this? For five years?"

"I told you I would, didn't I? You said we'd never see our fifth anniversary. I knew differently. Put it on, please. I'd like you to wear it today."

"After all these years, I think I'd prefer a simple gold band."

"You'll have that, too. But this ring has certain sentimental meaning to me."

"It proves that you won, after all," she challenged.

"No, darling. It proves that we both did." He slipped the ring onto her right hand. "There." He laughed. "Now we're officially engaged. Will you marry me, Miss Gates?" he asked with a straight face.

She giggled. "Yes, yes, you idiot. I'll marry you. Are you satisfied?"

"Who wouldn't be?" he asked. "Now, you'll have to excuse me because I have to let my pregnant fiancée get dressed and make sure that our son is ready to be the ring bearer at his parents' wedding." He blew her a kiss and strode out of the room, leaving Reggie smiling after him.

She stood poised at the top of the stairs, listening carefully for the opening strains of "The Wedding March." Below, gathered in the foyer, waited her son, her mother-in-law, Alison, and Lee, Liza and Melissa Taggett, who had flown in from California that morning. Reggie glanced quickly into the antique mirror. Yes, the white suede wedding dress with its thousands of seed pearls was still perfect. A little tight across the chest, but no one would notice. And frankly, she thought with a smile, she didn't care if they did. There wasn't one person in the room who didn't know the details of her life with Cole. They were all there to wish the Westons well.

There! She heard the first chords and, holding her head up proudly, she began her descent. As she reached the bottom three steps, Cole came forward, holding Alex by the hand.

They separated, each reaching for one of her hands. Slowly, the three of them walked toward the judge.

Five years to the day, in the sunny living room of the house they had lived in for four glorious years, Reggie Gates became Mrs. Cole Weston.

Again.